A SHADE OF MIND - COMPLETE SERIES

RANDOM PSYCHIC - FOREVER MORTAL -
ELUSIVE BEINGS - IMPERFECT DIVINE

D.N. LEO

RANDOM PSYCHIC

EXCLUSIVE OFFERS

THE MULTIVERSE COLLECTION

A SHADE OF MIND
by D.N Leo

RANDOM PSYCHIC
FOREVER MORTAL
ELUSIVE BEINGS
IMPERFECT DIVINE

SYNOPSIS

Technologically incompetent Madeline has to use her random psychic ability to track down a secret identity of an avatar from the most advanced game technology on Earth, or her best friend will be killed. During the process, she falls for Ciaran, a man who possesses more dangerous secrets than the kidnapping ordeal she has already tangled herself in.

This is the first instalment in an urban fantasy thriller series, filled with paranormal romance and science fiction twists and turns!

PART I

THE RESCUE

1

Hate leaves ugly scars, love leaves beautiful ones.
Mignon McLaughlin, The Second Neurotic's Notebook, 1966

She stared at the last three seconds of her life.

A red double-decker full of passengers was racing straight at her, and she couldn't do anything but stare at it.

Like the traffic and everything else surrounding it, the bus seemed to move in slow motion, but Madeline was more than certain that it was zooming in full speed in reality.

The bus was going to crush her the same way the kidnap and ransom ordeal had cut short Jo's life.

Jo was like her sister. They had grown up together, but they might not grow old together.

Madeline kept staring at the bus. It was real. It was enormous. And her psychic ability didn't seem to help at all—if she did have such ability.

Five seconds ago, Madeline had seen it—the haunting blue dot hovering in the air, giving her guidance. She couldn't believe her eyes. She was a psychic after all. The blue dot glared at her and blinked. *That's unusual,* she had thought. It had been three days that she'd stalked this place, and now her psychic ability had finally decided to kick in. *About damn time!*

She could save Jo now, and her life would be back to the way it was. Not that her life had been spectacular, but it was much better than her current situation.

The second blue dot appeared, blinking at her. She gazed at the dots, and then they were no longer blinking. They weren't blue, either, but a bright yellow.

And they came with sound.

Honking.

Shouting.

She blinked. They weren't her psychic blue dots but the headlights of a double-decker racing at her in full speed.

She glanced around. In a blur of motion, she realized she had just stepped out in front of ongoing traffic in the middle of a busy road in the center of London.

She now stood in her reality and froze.

2

Someone grabbed Madeline's arm and pulled her back onto the sidewalk. The double-decker zoomed past, and the other cars kept moving. If it had been New York, she would have stirred up a hideous bout of road rage. Madeline was still dazed. She turned around and looked at the man who had just saved her life.

"Are you okay?"

"Thank you," she automatically said and immediately realized that those words she kept in her vocabulary inventory didn't exactly answer the man's question.

Then Madeline shook her head. *Focus. Stay strong. You're Jo's only hope,* she scolded herself. She turned toward the man, who was still looking at her with concern.

"I'm fine. Thank you. I'm sorry. The jetlag is killing me. And apparently, I was looking the wrong way." She gestured toward the traffic and smiled. "Madeline. I'm from New York." She reached her hand out for a handshake.

"Peter. I'm from . . . here . . . apparently." He fumbled with his briefcase, swapping it to his left hand so that he could respond to Madeline's greeting.

Madeline pointed at the building across the road. "I'm looking for LeBlanc Pharmaceuticals. But I think I've got the wrong address. That building looks more like military barracks than business headquarters."

Peter arched an eyebrow, looking Madeline up and down.

"I'm a journalist. I'm writing a business column about one of their new products. Is there a problem?" Madeline asked.

"Oh, no. No problem at all. Nobody has any problem with the LeBlancs."

Madeline smiled and waited for the next part of Peter's speech, but it never came. Instead, he shrugged. "Well, to be honest, even the locals know almost nothing about them. I'm sorry I can't help you. But I can certainly show you around if it does any good. And the I around the corner is one of London's hot spots. I'm sure it will help cure your jet lag."

Madeline smiled but cursed on the inside. Peter was a decent-looking man. She hadn't been in a serious relationship for a while —not that no one was interested in her, but her situation was too complicated to let anyone into her life. Still, it was nice to be hit on occasionally.

She was tall, slim, and attractive enough, but Madeline didn't consider herself pretty. She had a slightly long, oval face, big brown eyes, a generous mouth with full lips, and a dimple on her left cheek. A sea of brunette curls wrapped around her shoulders.

A hot cup of coffee was tempting, but now was not a good time. "I'm sorry. I've got to get this done, or my boss will be very unhappy. Thanks for the offer, Peter. Maybe next time." Madeline waved her gloveless hand goodbye and scurried away, shivering in the winter chill.

She glanced at the reflection on the shop window and saw that the smile on Peter's face had been replaced by a strange look.

She wouldn't be mistaken. She had seen that look several times. It was the look of a predator who had just lost his prey.

Instead of going straight home, she turned to the opposite direction and headed toward a crowed shopping center.

*H*ours later, throwing her light backpack over her shoulders, Madeline headed toward a small apartment on a back street in Knightsbridge. Rows of terrace houses that curved along a tree-lined street looked invitingly at her. The black gothic-styled light poles and street fences accentuated the beautiful blend of modern and classic London.

She normally adored and admired the architecture. But right now, Madeline was cursing the amount of money she had to pay to stay in Knightsbridge on such short notice.

There—she saw those blue dots again.

It had been a secret she'd only told Jo, and Jo called it her psychic ability. After the incident in the bush that both Madeline and Jo didn't want to remember, Madeline had appeared to be able to see people's *minds*—or at least she thought that's what it was.

Sometimes it came from those she had been in contact with. That was how Jo speculated she was able to track down a missing person. Sometimes it randomly came from a stranger when they directed their thoughts at her. Other times, she had absolutely no explanation of where the dots came from. She wasn't a mind reader

—she didn't know what the thoughts were about. She just saw them as the blue dots.

Ironically, her randomly found ability only worked when she didn't need it, like when it had led her in front of a fast approaching bus.

The dots hovered in front of her and then moved toward the alley leading to Hyde Park. After the near-fatal encounter with the bus, Madeline didn't think it was wise to follow the psychic specks anymore. She ignored them and headed home.

HER CELL PHONE buzzed as soon as she entered her apartment. She picked up the phone and kicked the door closed.

"Madeline," she answered while searching for the light switch on the wall.

At the other end of the line, a male voice croaked, "I miss you. It's been a few days. What have you got for me?"

"Zen, I almost got hit by a bus trying to get to the door of LeBlanc Pharmaceuticals. Their premises are guarded like a military barracks. Seriously, I'd have a better chance of running through the gates of Buckingham Palace to the Queen's private chamber than breaking into the front yard of that building."

"That's why I sent you there, honey. We can't compete with the LeBlancs using weapons, money, or manpower. Your little gift is just what we need."

Madeline finally found the light switch. She flicked it on and strode toward the fireplace. Her teeth were never going to stop chattering if she didn't get a fire going.

"I don't have any gift, Zen. You know I can barely operate a computer let alone hunt down a computer geek and ask him questions about an avatar."

"I saw the games you played with Jo, Madeline. Don't bluff with me."

Madeline closed her eyes. *Damn.* Jo made her play guessing

games just to prove that Madeline's psychic ability was real. Jo believed in it more than she did. Since Jo was doing research on a new simulation game, Madeline thought it would be fun to help out. Now those games were biting her in the backside.

"Look, Zen, it's been days, and I haven't been able to get inside. You have to give me more information than just 'look for a White Knight.'"

"But that's all I have!" Zen screamed though the phone. She could hear his heavy breathing and his swallow to suppress his anger.

She lowered her voice. "If you let me talk to Jo, we could figure something out."

"You want to talk to her? Okay." Zen turned on the video phone. He grabbed Jo's hair and smashed her face onto the screen of the phone. "Do you see her now? Talk away. You girls can figure things out, right?"

Madeline caught a glimpse of Zen's face, which was burning red with fury. Jo's eyes were dazed, and her forehead was bruised. Jo bit her lips and looked into the screen. Madeline knew Jo wouldn't cry.

"You hurt her, you bastard. You told me you wouldn't hurt her if I found your stupid avatar!" Madeline roared.

"But you found *nothing*!" Zen screamed.

"*H*e didn't hurt me, Madeline. I tried to run and fell down the stairs. Should have taken my stupid heels off." Jo smiled weakly.

A tear rolled down Madeline's cheek. Jo was barely five foot two, and she always wore those impossibly high heels. Madeline couldn't understand why she was so conscious about her height. Jo was gorgeous. She was a brilliant computer game designer, but no one could peg her as a nerd. Madeline wiped her tear and smiled back.

"You sure you're okay?"

"I'm fine. You take care of yourself, Madeline."

"I can't get the blue dots to work, Jo. Can you tell me what the game is about? What am I looking for?"

Jo was about to say something, but Zen yanked her off the phone. "All you have to do is to find out who plays with Jo using the name White Knight. You've seen the game—and the player. You should be able to tell who the guy is in real life. I told you he works for the LeBlancs and has been playing from that building. You don't have to go in. Just wait him out."

"Do you understand that LeBlanc Pharmaceuticals is a global company that employs millions of people?"

"But I gave you the *precise* location!"

"I told you, it's like a military barrack. I used my journalist credentials to ask for an interview with their PR department . . ."

"And?"

"The waiting list is a month."

"I don't have a month. I give you three days."

"It's not possible . . ."

"I don't give a shit. If I don't get this done in time, I'll be dead. But I'm not going down alone. I can guarantee you that. I'll send you more info as soon as I have it. But three days is all the time you've got."

Zen hung up.

Madeline slid down to the floor and curled up next to the sofa. She let the tears fall freely. She could fall apart right here, right now. Nobody knew, and nobody cared. Jo was her family—the only family Madeline had ever known. She had taken her in and had shared her family with Madeline unconditionally. Jo's parents had never once asked Madeline about her own family—they knew she didn't have one. Otherwise, she would've had to tell them that she had come in a basket, abandoned on the front porch of some random house.

Her teeth chattered, and her body shook with the chill. She couldn't remember the last time she'd eaten or slept.

At the corner of the room, the fireplace stood cold and empty. She had forgotten to start the fire.

A shadow hovered at the window and tripped over the potted plant at the front door, but Madeline had drifted to sleep and heard nothing.

A piece of paper slid under her door.

A crash woke Madeline. She jumped up to her feet, panting.

Then she let out a sigh of relief. She had kicked the side table in her sleep, and the vase on top of the table had crashed to the floor.

Madeline checked the clock. She must have passed out for the night. It was just past five in the morning. She glanced out the window without any hope of seeing the winter sun at this hour. Madeline went to the kitchen to make herself a strong mug of coffee and to find something with which to clean up the broken vase.

A short moment later, she settled in front of her computer and stared at the mountain of documentation she had researched about LeBlanc Pharmaceuticals.

Secrets.

That was the conclusion she had drawn. Not that she couldn't find any information. On the contrary, there was too much information. Ten years of experience in journalism had taught her that the information about the LeBlancs was only a facade. Even the underground information revealed nothing about the company that they didn't want the public to know.

The LeBlanc family was filthy rich—and extremely private.

Madeline had to congratulate herself after hours of searching. She found one picture of the current head of the family, Ciaran LeBlanc. One lousy picture. The picture must have come from a very keen stalker. It was taken from a distance, and the scene it showed was reflected on a traffic monitoring mirror in a car park.

Judging by the proportion of the cars and guards around him, Madeline speculated that Ciaran was tall and well-built, but on the slender side.

Young, she mused, and maybe long hair. The picture was so distorted that Madeline wasn't sure she would have recognized Ciaran if she met him in the flesh.

She drew imaginary lines with her finger around Ciaran's face, trying to make out the part that the poor quality image didn't catch.

Then she glanced at the corner of the door, on the floor, and saw the note.

Madeline picked the note up.

It read, "Hyde Park."

*M*adeline stretched for her morning run and winced at how stiff her body felt after slacking off for a week. Hyde Park was just around the corner from her place. *Had Zen wanted to tip her off as to where the LeBlancs lived?* She doubted that.

There were residential areas in Hyde Park, but she couldn't imagine the LeBlancs in these apartments, regardless of how exclusive they were. Madeline speculated that members of the LeBlanc family lived in castles in secret highlands.

She jiggled a container of self-defense spray in her pocket to ensure it was secured and within easy reach, then headed to the park.

The fog was as thick as clouds. Madeline could hardly see more than ten feet in front of her. She kept to the left, but then by habit drifted over to the right. Suddenly right in front of her, a man emerged from the fog like a warrior. Late thirties. Tall. At least six foot three, she would guess, with a slender build and well-toned muscles covered attractively in fair English skin. His thick, black hair almost touched his shoulders. His strong face, the face of a dark angel, looked straight ahead before it registered the coming motion. His eyes . . . Madeline was sure that it was his eyes that caused such an electrifying reaction in her body. Dark, smoky gray eyes. Intense, captivating, and striking.

Because Madeline had spent so much time evaluating the beauty of the human being in front of her, she didn't have any time to adjust her speed or steer herself away from the imminent collision. She would have been knocked off her feet and landed on her backside if he hadn't grabbed her.

"Goddamn it, don't you look when you run, Ciaran?"

The words were out before she could edit them. She had called his name, which meant she had to think with lightning speed right now to explain herself—to explain that she was not a stalker. Her thoughts ran rampant. She could tell him it wasn't him she was after, she wanted his company. No. She didn't want his company, she needed the guy who worked in his company. Hmm . . . but that wouldn't explain how she knew his name. Maybe she should tell him she's a psychic? No again. That would be a lie, and it wouldn't go down well. Her thoughts tangled in a mushy mess, and she felt as if her face was on fire.

Ciaran released Madeline after a swivel to balance the running momentum so that they both regained their footing. "Excuse me!" he said.

"Sorry, it was my fault. I should have kept right—no, I mean left."

"Is that an offense to run on a wrong side of a pedestrian path in a public park in New York?"

She wanted to swoon with the sexy accent, but her suspicion had gotten a better judgment of her. Madeline narrowed her eyes. "How do you know I'm from New York?"

"Your accent gave it away. I have a lot of business dealings in New York. I can tell." Ciaran grinned.

Her heart skipped a beat when she saw that grin. *For pity's sake, you're thirty-three, not a teenager, Madeline. Focus.*

Ciaran drank from his bottle water and sat down on the bench. "I don't think my name is written on my forehead."

"Talk to your PR department. I'm the reporter who's been bugging them for the past few days to get an interview. Of course I know your name." That was lame, she thought. Ciaran didn't have a public profile, and she couldn't even get a decent picture of him. But she couldn't think of anything else, so she settled with the statement.

Ciaran nodded politely, and waited.

"Oh, I'm Madeline Roux, from *The Trumpet*." Madeline reached her hand out for a handshake.

"*The Trumpet?*"

She didn't need to look at Ciaran's face to see his expression. "Oh, we're certainly not the *New York Times* or anything . . ."

"I beg your pardon. I didn't mean to offend . . ." He stood up quickly from the bench to return the handshake before she withdrew her hand.

Madeline laughed. "You have to do a lot better than that to offend me. We're young, small, and not a mainstream magazine. Of course you've never heard of us."

Ciaran smiled. "How off-stream are you?"

"Well, let's say we're just a bit quirky in our approach to serious issues."

Ciaran murmured, "Ah, interesting! So you don't just blow the whistle, you blow the whole magnificent trumpet to the glory!"

Madeline laughed. "You've got it, Ciaran!"

She suddenly realized that she hadn't laughed for days. It felt good. But it was much too friendly. Madeline tilted her head to look behind Ciaran. He turned, looking in the same direction.

"What are you looking for?"

"Bodyguards."

Ciaran looked at Madeline blankly. Then he just laughed.

"You think I'd have bodyguards with me when I go running? Who do you think I am? A prince?"

"Practically," Madeline muttered.

"I beg your pardon?" His smile faded.

"What do you expect people to think? Your family isn't media friendly. Your company has more security than the military. Nobody knows anything about your family. It is more difficult to approach you than it is to make an appointment to see the Queen!"

"Well, that's because the Queen has to answer to her people. We don't have to answer to anyone."

"Or you'd have everyone answer to you?"

Ciaran lowered his voice. "We have money. But we don't bribe or bully anyone. I don't care for my family being judged because we want our privacy." Ciaran jammed his hands in his pockets, waiting for Madeline's response.

She cursed herself. "I'm sorry. It's just been very hard to get in touch with you. I mean with your PR department. It's almost impossible, and my boss isn't happy at all about my progress."

Ciaran nodded. "What did *The Trumpet* want to talk to our PR department about? You came all the way from New York—it couldn't be a minor issue."

"Nothing serious, really. I suggested the topic. LeBlanc Pharmaceuticals is a very successful business. I'm sure the media has made the most of what they could. But for me, behind that business success is always the people. I always find your family . . . intriguing."

Ciaran smiled. "You think we have something to hide?"

"No, I think you have a lot to show. I'd like to have a bit of what you're willing to show."

Ciaran paused for a brief moment then nodded. "So is it my family or my family's business that you're interested in?"

She looked into Ciaran's eyes. They were intense now, deep gray and mysteriously serious.

"Both."

He shook his head. "You have only one option."

"Your family."

A slight smile crossed Ciaran's face. "Then you can interview

me. I will represent my family. Would tomorrow night be convenient? Over dinner?"

"What? Of course! Dinner?"

"That's the only time I can manage."

Madeline nodded.

Ciaran smiled. "Seven p.m. at One Hyde Park. I'm looking
forward to it. Goodbye for now, Madeline." Ciaran nodded a
goodbye and turned to walk away.

"Why? Your family has never talked to the media before."

Ciaran turned around, sending Madeline a look that made her
stomach quiver. "Simply because I'd like to see more of you!"
he said.

Then he walked away and disappeared into the fog.

adeline's internal clock woke her in the morning—it seemed she had adjusted to the time difference. She didn't have many hours of sleep, but they were good and solid hours, enough to get her going and be prepared. Tonight was her chance to end this and put her life back to normal.

Was that all she wanted with the dinner? Had she thought about Ciaran at all?

She got off the bed, giving herself a mental slap whenever her brain wandered in Ciaran's direction. She needed to stay focused and plan for the night.

She should have chosen the business rather than the family when Ciaran gave her the options. But the man headed the family *and* ran the business. He could give her the exact information she needed. If she had gone with the business option, then she might have ended up with one of the minions whose job was to withhold information from her.

Madeline made herself a cup of coffee and stopped that stream of thought. There was no point rationalizing a past action that she couldn't reverse anyway.

Her response to Ciaran in the park hadn't been optimal. But she was a woman, and his physical attraction was undeniable. *Hell, he was like a magnet!* Mental slap.

Madeline tucked at her hair, pulling it back into a ponytail and putting herself into active working mode. Her phone rang. Paul's voice squeaked through from the other end of the line when Madeline picked up.

"Here you are, still on the planet. Thank God. You can't just go poof and let me handle everything, Maddie!"

Paul was co-editor with Madeline at *The Trumpet*. His task was to add a feminine touch to the magazine. Balance the scales, he always said, as Madeline had made the magazine quite 'boyish.' Paul was a decent writer and a good guy in the industry, as far as Madeline concerned.

"A girl is entitled to a vacation, Paul!"

"I'm so glad that you finally realize you're a girl! Yes, you can take a vacation. But you have to give me some notice in advance of more than, say, half an hour! Also, I can take care for your half-finished stories, but not your half-eaten slop, half-finished carrot rubber, and half-decent boyfriend."

"First, the slop is homemade lasagna, and you're lucky to have half of it. Second, the carrot cake is from Jo's brother's one-of-a-kind bakery, and he specifically baked it for me. So you're welcome to have it, and I'll thank them on your behalf. Third, Stephen is not a half-decent man. He's better than a lot of guys I know."

"Oh, so Stephen is your boyfriend now, is he?"

"Who were you talking about?"

"Not Stephen, apparently! A bold guy. Shuffling through your desk like a thief. Took off when I called out. Be careful, Maddie. I think you might have a stalker . . . and that's a best-case scenario."

Madeline felt a pinch of worry. A dozen what-if scenarios flew through her mind. "Are you okay?" she asked Paul. "I'm sorry if this worries you."

"No, I'm all right," Paul said.

"You want me to call Stephen? He's a cop. He could do something about this."

"No, no," Madeline assured him. "I can handle this. Give me a few days. I'll sort it out, I promise. Let me know if anything else happens. Hey . . . how about you work from home for a few days?"

Paul chuckled. "Really, Maddie?"

"Yeah, really," Madeline said. "Just do that for me, will you? I'll talk to you later. I'll explain more. Everything. Okay?"

Paul reluctantly agreed and hung up the phone.

Madeline called Zen. He switched on the video phone when he picked up the call. His sleazy smile flashed on the screen.

"Miss me?"

"You don't have to sniff around my workplace and freak out other people. I said I'd get the information for you, and I will." Madeline fumed.

The smile disappeared from Zen's face. "I didn't snoop around no place. Who else knows about this?"

A missed step, damn! Slow down, she warned herself.

"No, I'm just annoyed, that's all. I have a few unkind readers sending nasty notes to my paper, that's all."

"Your job sucks. Poking your nose into other people's business —you'll end up with something as big as a bomb or as little a bullet. They're both lethal, though! What have you got for me?"

"Ah . . . not much yet. Is White Knight a game or a character?"

"It's an avatar. Jesus Christ! Don't you know anything about games?"

"No, not really. I don't even know exactly how to get the information. Even if I should get inside the LeBlanc premises, you want me just to go around asking who plays White Knight?"

Madeline could picture Zen wanting to knock his head against the wall to quell his frustration. *Maybe it was her head that he wanted to whack.* She chuckled on the inside and kept a straight face. Playing dumb was working for her at this point, so she kept at it.

Zen calmly explained, "No, don't ask directly, and don't alarm any one. All you have to do is to tell them that one computer within their premises was used to play an interactive game. Make it up. Say the game was illegal or whatever. Don't say anything about White Knight at this stage. I need a list of the real names of those who played games from that building. If you can narrow it down to the one guy who plays as White Knight, that's ideal. But I understand it might be difficult. Got it?"

Madeline nodded.

"When can I expect some results?"

"Come on, you only gave me Hyde Park. That's a residential address, not the business headquarters. How am I supposed to . . ."

"What? I didn't give you the address. I didn't know the address. Who tipped you? Who else knows about this?" Zen's face started to burn with anger.

Fuck! This is a total fuck-up. Who wrote the note? She searched frantically in her mind for an answer but found nothing.

"What happened? You better fucking tell me!" Zen yelled into the phone.

"I . . . I was . . ."

"*Tell me!*" Zen's demonic voice threatened to rip open the phone.

7

The ceiling-high, double-steel door automatically slid open when Ciaran approached, revealing a vast lush office with glass windows opening to the endless horizon of the city. Before the door closed, Lindsay called from behind, "Ciaran!" and trailed into the office with a stack of paper in his hands.

Ciaran turned around. "Yes, Lindsay, did I forget to sign something?"

Lindsay Freeman was in his late thirties and had been Ciaran's right-hand man as long as Ciaran had been in business. As they were of similar age, Ciaran could talk to Lindsay almost about anything. They were good friends, and Ciaran trusted Lindsay to be the face of the business when it came to dealing with outsiders.

"You'll want to take a look at this," Lindsay said and put a computer disc on the desk.

Ciaran glanced at the disc. "Gate security? Shouldn't Robert be handling this?" He slid the disc into the computer.

"I just checked things over, and this caught my eye."

Ciaran shook his head. "You can't keep an eye on everything. Robert's a very capable man."

"No doubt about that. But I'll sleep better checking everything this week because you're here."

"I don't want to be the cause of your sleep deprivation. By the way, how are Liz and Anna?"

"Enjoying their vacation at a warm beach in Bali now." Lindsay grinned. "Anna finished her exams with good grades and wanted a vacation before entering high school."

Ciaran stopped looking at the computer monitor. "You're saying you let your wife and daughter go on a vacation by themselves because I'm here this week?"

Lindsay laughed. "Come on. I know your schedule, and work is important, Ciaran. They decided on the vacation on a whim. It's hardly my fault."

Ciaran shook his head. "When they kick you out of the house, you aren't going sleep on my couch."

The secretary knocked on the door and walked in with a tray. She put the coffee on the desk. "Double shot, no cream for you, Ciaran. Double cream for you, Lindsay." She put a plate of four small cookies on the desk. "Mom made these and insisted I take them to work for you, Ciaran. She does this every week. She thinks you're in the office nine to five, five days a week." She smiled. "I ate your cookies every other week. But today, they're all yours."

Ciaran grinned. "Butterscotch. My favorite. Thank you, Lily." He reached out for a cookie and his gaze lighted on Lily's hand. Ciaran dropped the cookies back to the plate. He stood up, walked around his desk, and kissed Lily on the cheek. "Congratulations, Sam is a very lucky guy."

Lily smiled and twirled her engagement ring around her finger. "Thank you. It was last week. We're very happy . . . Well, I'd better let you go back to work." She nodded a goodbye and exited the room. Ciaran grabbed the desk phone and ordered flowers to be sent to Lily's address. Then he looked up and saw Lindsay shaking his head.

"You haven't seen me doing this before?" Ciaran arched an eyebrow.

"I only say this as a friend. It's been such a long time since . . ."

"Don't start," Ciaran cut in with a voice so low that it almost sounded like a growl. Then he pointed at the computer monitor. "What did you want me to look at here?" As soon as Ciaran finished his question, he saw the answer. On the screen was Madeline in front of the LeBlanc Pharmaceuticals, walking right in front of a double-decker.

"You see that?" Lindsay asked.

Ciaran nodded. "Yes, I know her. That's Madeline Roux. She's a journalist from New York."

"I'm not talking about her. I'm talking about the guy."

Ciaran frowned, looking at the man dragging Madeline out of the way of the bus. "He's no random pedestrian. From this angle, he must have been stalking right at our door steps. We got the scanner data on that, right?"

"Yep, that's where the ass-kicker stuff is," Lindsay muttered.

Ciaran pulled out the keyboard and typed in the command and codes to pull up the scanner data. On the screen was the x-ray scanned data of a five hundred meter perimeter outside the gate. Ciaran was about to ask something, but Lindsay said in anticipation, "Robert kept a very tight lid on the scanner. We know it's not strictly legal. You don't have to be the only one to keep an eye on everything!" Lindsay smiled to himself as he had evened the scores with Ciaran.

Ciaran's smile faded as he stared at the monitor.

8

*T*he room got colder by the second. The screen of the phone in front of Madeline felt as if it was going to explode. Her head wanted to evaporate.

She knew Zen was going to do something bad. *Think fast!*

"I was doing some research . . ." she said.

"Don't you fucking lie to me again . . ." Zen grabbed the phone and walked toward a door.

"I've got it. I've got the access . . ." she spoke too fast and stuttered.

Zen walked into another room and tilted the phone so that Madeline could see that Jo was tied to a bed. "You know why she doesn't scream? Because nobody can hear her from down here. No one can save her but you."

Tears streamed down Jo's face. She looked so tired and dazed with drugs.

Madeline wiped at the tears streaming down on her face as well. "I'm sorry. I'm so sorry, Zen. I'm not lying to you about anything. Please don't hurt her. Yes, I've done some research, and I got some information about a possible place of residence for the

LeBlancs. I might be able to get an interview tonight with my journalist credentials. Please don't hurt her!"

Zen tore off Jo's shirt.

Jo cried. But she did not beg.

"Please don't hurt her. I'll do whatever I can tonight to get you the information. I'll get you the list. No one else knows about this, I swear . . ." Madeline cried.

Zen climbed onto the bed. He grabbed Jo and hitched up her hips.

Madeline screamed into the phone. "Please, don't! I'll get you the list."

Zen turned slowly to the phone. "Then you'd better keep your promise. I'll call you tomorrow morning."

Zen reached out and turned off the call.

As soon as the phone was off, Madeline slid down to the floor and wept. She had never felt that helpless in her life.

In Ciaran's office, Lindsay pointed at the computer monitor. The video showed an enlarged picture of the brief case the man was carrying.

"What's he doing carrying a silencer and hanging around our front gate. I've checked the surveillance data. He's only been there this week. I think he's waiting for you, Ciaran."

"Only you and Robert know my schedule. There are much more convenient ways to get to me than lurking at the gate. Plus, I don't use that gate. If he's waiting for me there, then he's an amateur. Not worth our trouble."

"More convenient ways? Like at home? Man, Robert'd be offended hearing that!"

Ciaran nodded. "Yes, at home, wherever it is," he muttered. "I'm having dinner with Madeline tonight at One Hyde Park."

"You what? Holy shit. She's a reporter. She must be a corporate spy. They're the same gang. The guy stalked the gate, and the girl stalked you at home."

"I don't think they're in the same group. He's her adversary."

Ciaran rewound the clip. "Pay attention to the handle of his briefcase. See that? He slid the knife out an inch. Probably tried to take her hostage or make her walk to a quiet corner and do whatever he intended to do to her."

Ciaran enhanced the image on his computer. "He didn't expect that Madeline would want to shake hands. That forced him change the briefcase to his left hand."

"But if he'd wanted to kill her, why didn't he just let her get run over by the bus?" Lindsay asked.

"Too many variables. The bus might brake in time, or she might have been able to get out of the way by herself. Or the accident might not have been fatal. If he wanted to kill her, then he would want to do it himself. Maybe he just wanted to capture her."

"But why didn't he follow her afterward?"

"He might have. Not right away because it would be too obvious."

"I'll send Robert to the apartment for your dinner tonight then."

"We're good friends, but I don't intend to have dinner with Robert tonight."

"Ciaran!"

Ciaran laughed. "Okay. I'll be careful. You can tell Robert, but I don't want him to hang too close. It's only a dinner. You think I can't handle a girl?"

"All right. I'll call him now," Lindsay said and exited the room. Ciaran rewound the footage and watched again.

*F*ive minutes to seven. Madeline approached the corner of a series of luxurious apartments. She had no idea which one was actually One Hyde Park, nor did she know the exact number of the apartment.

What an idiot! She turned around the corner to the street front, and there he was, standing next to a marble pole at the entrance to a building, smiling at her.

When they closed the distance, Ciaran frowned. Madeline winced. She must look like crap after her crying marathon. A concerned expression crossed Ciaran's face briefly and then disappeared.

"It was inconsiderate of me not giving you the exact address yesterday. So I thought I should wait for you at the entrance. You look beautiful."

She loved his accent, but she knew a dig when she heard it. She was in black jeans, a deep gray turtleneck, and a long red leather jacket. Yes, the red leather jacket was respectable, given what she could stuff in her emergency travel bag. But what she wore was in no way compatible with the ten-thousand-dollar-minimum outfit on him.

Jo's image was still fresh in her mind, and Zen's voice still echoed in her head. *Oh hell!* She just realized that she'd forgotten to put her makeup on, and she was still wearing her ponytail.

"Madeline?"

"Huh?"

"What's the matter?"

"What? Oh . . . I'm sorry. I'm just very tired. . ." Madeline rubbed at her eyes.

She hated herself at the moment. What happened earlier had knocked all the wits out of her.

Ciaran looked at her, his eyes pausing on her face for a second. He was skilled, she thought. Before the gaze became an awkward moment, he reached out, wrapping his arm around her shoulders, protectively and friendly.

"Come on, let's get some food into you. It always does the trick."

Ciaran led Madeline through the entrance of a gigantic door, via a long hallway that had thick carpets, marble floors, and several pieces of contemporary artwork and into a so-called 'apartment.' Apartment was too humble of a word to describe what she saw, but given her mental state right now, she had to settle for the term.

At the door, Ciaran took his coat off, hanging it in a small cloakroom snugged in the corner. Then he took Madeline's jacket. There was no sign of anyone else in the apartment. There was only his coat and her jacket, cozily hung on fancy hooks.

Madeline glanced at the living room as the grandeur swept over her. She was in no way dressed for such a place, but she kept her poker face. She had a job to do.

The room opened to the city view via glass walls. A dining table was located in the middle of the room. Leather sofas curved cozily in corner. A long glass cabinet containing expensive wine and spirits sat in another corner.

This isn't a home, she observed.

Ciaran shifted a chair out for Madeline to sit down. He walked quickly to the counter of the open kitchen. Noticing her gaze, Ciaran turned around, giving her a big grin.

"You needn't worry. I didn't cook. The food comes from the best kitchen, however. Delivered just ten minutes ago."

"This is how you live?" Madeline gestured widely at the apartment. "Eating takeout by yourself? You don't even have a TV in here. What do you do after work?"

"Pity me!" He smiled again.

The wonderful grin was still on his face when he opened a bottle of red wine. She didn't want to guess the price tag.

"I'll let it breathe a bit."

He turned to the covered plates on the counter and lifted the lids.

"I'm not by myself tonight, am I? You'd make a good companion. I think you'd approve of this excellent menu." Ciaran paused and pretended to scowl. "You didn't expect a full-on banquet, did you?"

Madeline laughed. "I'm not very selective when it comes to food, so you're doing just fine!" She left her chair and helped him to fetch the food and bring it to the table.

They set up the table and started their dinner. The interview began casually. Madeline asked questions that she hated herself for asking because they weren't good enough for even the weather channels or the morning talk shows.

They nearly finished the dinner. Ciaran sipped his wine and looked at Madeline over the rim of the glass. "So what is it about my family that you really want to know?"

Madeline gave a small pause, then pushed on. "Where do you *actually* live? And don't say it's classified. You're not an FBI agent."

Ciaran laughed. "I can see you've got your real reporter hat back. I thought you'd turned into a robot when I saw you early tonight."

Ciaran paused and focused on Madeline's eyes. "What happened?"

The smile had gone from Ciaran's face. "You have circles under your eyes, and you look as if you spent the entire day crying."

Madeline rubbed absently at her eyes. "I asked the question first." Madeline stared at Ciaran, saying nothing.

Ciaran gave in. "I don't live here. I don't live anywhere for a long time. I travel a lot for business."

Ciaran looked at Madeline for a long moment. This time, he let it grow into an uncomfortable moment. "Now it's my turn to ask a question. What happened to you today that made you cry?"

"I'm interviewing *you*—I get to ask the questions. You agreed to it."

Ciaran calmly stared. "My turf, my rules. I agreed to the interview. I didn't agree to not ask you questions."

"I don't like this. I don't like the setting. I don't like your tone. I don't like your questions. Hell, I don't even like *my* questions. Let's end the interview here. Thank you for your time." Madeline stood up, heading toward the cloakroom.

Ciaran grabbed her elbow. "Wait." When she shrugged him off, he immediately released her and raised up his arms apologetically. "I apologize. It was rude of me to ask you that question. It was inappropriate."

Madeline paused.

"Could we finish the dinner properly, please? I'll answer your questions in the meantime."

Madeline hesitated.

"We still have the dessert. Don't make me eat it by myself." He lowered his voice. "It's a cheesecake. Dark, rich Belgium chocolate with a hint of chili, topped with strawberries, and a touch of . . ."

"Okay, okay, we'll have it!" She swaggered back to her chair. When Ciaran sat down, she shifted, inhaled, exhaled, and started the rant.

"Okay, I'm not interested in your family, your private matters, or your business. A friend of mine developed a computer game with some very special technology. She believes that her program has been hacked by someone using a computer located in your London headquarters. She doesn't have the evidence. So that's why I'm here. To help a friend. I have no proof of the game stealing, nor do I have any authority in this matter. I just need the names of your employees who might have used your equipment to hack my friend's game."

Madeline breathed heavily after the long speech that she had given without even pausing for punctuation. Lying felt horrible. But she had a job to do. Jo's life was at stake.

Ciaran looked at Madeline blankly for a second and cocked an eyebrow. "Is that all?"

Madeline nodded.

Ciaran stood up, heading toward the cloakroom. "Then let's go."

"Go where? Why now?" Madeline followed obediently without even realizing it.

"I won't be here tomorrow, so we have to do this now. I can't reveal the names of my employees who play computer games. Privacy policies. I don't care if they play games. However, I don't like my employees using work equipment to play interactive games with outsiders. That could potentially weaken the system and risk us being hacked. I'd like to think that there's no one playing any games from our operating systems."

They exited the elevator and walked down a long, shiny hallway from the foyer to approach the parking lot. Large screens were mounted on the walls, the sound muted and subtitles scrolling across the bottoms. Out of the corner of her eye, Madeline saw a familiar image flash on a screen. She stopped and watched.

The breaking news was about the unidentified dead body of a man in his mid-thirties found floating in the river. The image of Peter stared back at Madeline. She stared at the photo of the man who had saved her life a day ago. She didn't realize it, but a tear rolled down her face.

"Do you know this man?" Ciaran asked.

She shook her head. "Do you?"

Ciaran gazed into Madeline's eyes. "No," he answered. Then he wrapped his arm around her waist and led her along the corridor toward the entrance to the lot.

He lied, she mused.

*H*alf an hour later, Ciaran parked his car at the side entrance of the headquarters. Madeline noticed he always had his arm around her back to support, lead, or guide her. A primal protective gesture, Madeline thought. She caught the scent of him—natural, spicy, and masculine.

She didn't know what the scent of masculinity was, but at the moment, that was the only word she could find that fit.

She noted the way his Adam's apple moved when he spoke and the exquisite sound produced by the throat that she could easily spend a lifetime exploring. She loved the way he loosened his tie and yanked it off his collar, the way the corner of his mouth quirked when he made a joke, and the way his eyes twinkled. The emotions she saw in those striking gray eyes were genuine.

She wasn't sure at all about her psychic ability, but she was damn sure that her years spent in a relationship drought had led her close to being a slut.

Close.

She had never acted on her need and desire, although she knew she was entitled to. But the masculinity in Ciaran brought the beast out of her and made every fiber of her being vibrate.

He quickly led Madeline through layers of doors. The place was like a maze. Ciaran opened a steel door, revealing a room that looked like an enormous security scanner. "Leave any electronic equipment out here, including your camera or recorder. This scanner will wipe and destroy everything and anything that has a memory capability."

"Thanks. Good to know. I can't afford to lose this." Madeline took her camera and recorder out. "They're my life, you know!"

Ciaran smiled. "I wager."

He led Madeline through the scanner and into the control room. Madeline had never seen anything like it. The room was packed with endless rows of computer mainframes and monitors. She didn't know what the ten people in the room were doing, but they stopped and greeted Ciaran as he walked in. Ciaran responded with a friendly but authoritative nod. Whatever they were doing, she was sure it wasn't medicine they were making.

"This is just the electronic security control of the headquarters," Ciaran explained. "We don't make medicine here. Would you like a tour of the labs?" Ciaran gestured toward a series of monitors which displayed multiple screens of pharmaceutical labs, where several people in white coats were working.

"They're working at this hour?"

Ciaran chuckled. "Yes, at this hour, precisely, but not London time. These are the Australian labs you're looking at. It's office hours over there. They focus on the Asian-Pacific range. These are the London labs, here, in this headquarters." Ciaran pointed toward a couple of screens in the corner. "We develop new and important products here. Our overseas labs are mainly for production, not development."

Madeline nodded. "I appreciate you showing me all this. The security and the operation are very impressive."

"We operate within legal boundaries. We have strict security to protect us against the competition. Also to protect the consumer from any imperfect practice. We are responsible for what we do. Nothing comes in or goes out without scanning and quarantine. We are not media friendly, as you have mentioned, but we have nothing to hide. We just protect our privacy."

Madeline gave Ciaran a moment after his eloquent speech. "You must be proud of your family."

"You can meet them, if you like. They don't bite." Ciaran smiled.

Befriend the LeBlancs? Not in this lifetime. She wasn't cut out for this social circus. She never forgot where she came from.

"Could we look at the computer usage, please? I don't want to know more than I need to."

"As you like." Ciaran smiled politely and gestured toward a small door.

They entered a smaller room. Ciaran rolled up his sleeves and manually operated the mainframe computer. Madeline looked at him. *What a scene!* She could not believe that he manned the computer himself like this. She thought he would summon one of his technicians to ask for a report.

Codes and commands flowed through the monitor, none of which she knew or even recognized.

A river of paper streamed out from a printer. Ciaran fetched the paper and brought it toward Madeline. He tore off the last couple of pages.

"This is the summary of the computer usage in all of our international headquarters." He gestured toward the river of paper. "I can't give you the detailed log, but you can have this report." He pointed to a table. "As you can see, no computer in any of our head-quarters was used for interactive game play in the last three months. Specifically, working computers have supremely advanced firewalls. No foreign programs could be installed. No one would be able to play any games from our headquarters, Madeline."

Madeline shook her head.

"I can extend the search window to six months if you like, but I doubt it would make a difference, as the incident with your friend's game sounded recent."

A pounding headache ripped through her head.

"I can't ban employees from game play during working hours. But as you have seen, no foreign electronic objects with any game-playing capacity can pass through the scanner. There's no reason—and no way—for an employee to smuggle a computer into the workplace just to play games."

"Are you sure?" Her brain had stopped working. *A dead end!* She thought.

"This is the bloodline of our entire organization. When it comes to security, yes, I am very sure about it. Whatever your friend is looking for, it's not here, Madeline."

He led her out of the room.

After they had gone back through the scanner, Madeline put her camera and recorder into her bag.

She felt the warmth of his hand when he lifted her chin up. "Are you okay?" Those intense gray eyes looked at her with genuine concern.

She nodded. "Oh God, oh no, my phone . . ." Madeline pulled out her prepaid phone from her pocket. She had totally forgotten about it and had taken it through the scanner.

"Don't worry, it happens all the time," he said quickly and opened a small cabinet containing lots of cell phones. He picked one up, activated it, and gave it to Madeline. "Take this. It's prepaid. You can throw it away when you no longer need it. You'll have to reload your address book. You can log in online to change your username and password and put more credit in if you want to use it longer. At the moment, the password is your name. The credit is enough for normal usage for about a week if you call internationally, and a month for domestic calls."

He was staring at her face again and she was doing her best to hold back her tears.

"Oh, for pity's sake, can you tell me what's going on? What is the bloody game? What exactly is your friend looking for?"

"Could you please take me home?" Madeline murmured weakly. She hated the sound of her voice at the moment. She just didn't know what to do next. She needed time to think. There was nothing Ciaran could do to help. Right now, she needed her space.

Ciaran said something else to her, but she couldn't register the information.

In front of her apartment, Ciaran kissed Madeline good night. "I guess I should say good morning. It's two a.m."

"Oh . . . I'm sorry. I shouldn't have kept you that long. Thanks for all your help."

"This is my direct number. I'll be in France for a couple of days, in and out of meetings. I'd appreciate it if you'd be discreet regarding to my whereabouts. But please call if you need anything."

She looked at him. The magnificent Ciaran LeBlanc from the most mysterious— and possibly the richest—family on the planet was giving her his phone number just like any guy looking for a second date.

And she had used him this evening. She'd just given him a load of big fat lies. She wouldn't even do that to a pseudo-acquaintance.

Tomorrow, she would be watching her friend die because she could not get the lousy names of some computer-game fanatics. Yet she was proud of herself for being a good journalist. This had to be fate's biggest joke on her yet.

"Is there anything you want to tell me? Anything that I can help with?"

She couldn't get a word past her lips. She seriously need her space right now, and she needed to crash.

"You're tired. Get some sleep," Ciaran said in response to Madeline's silence.

Madeline nodded slightly. "Thanks. Bye, Ciaran." As cliché as it sounded, that was all she could say.

11

The next morning, as expected, Zen called. Madeline let the phone ring ten times before she picked up.

"What's with the new phone number?" Zen asked.

"Dropped and broke the other one. Put the video on—I want to see Jo."

Zen obliged, tilting the phone so that Madeline could see her friend. She was so pale and still drugged. But she knew that the second Jo was able to get free of her shackles, Zen wouldn't stand a chance.

"I expect some good news, Maddie," Zen threatened.

Madeline grabbed her cup of coffee, glancing at a painting on the wall of her apartment. After a sip of coffee, she spoke calmly into the phone.

"Samuel Kandinsky, that's the name."

Zen's eyes widened.

Jo stared at Madeline. Even with all the physical restraints and the effects of the sedative, the half-conscious Jo knew that Madeline had lied. She looked at Madeline, questioning her with her eyes, but said nothing.

"Give me contact details so I can talk to him."

"That wasn't the deal, Zen. The name is all I've got. Getting that name out of the LeBlanc headquarters was hard enough. I have seen the guy, so I can draw him out as we agreed. But he didn't exactly hand me his CV and contact details."

"You were inside the LeBlanc headquarters?"

"Impressive, huh? I spoke to Ciaran LeBlanc myself. I'm sure Samuel is your dude. He's probably off work by now. Do you want me to talk to him, or do you want to do it yourself?"

"No, no, I'll do that myself." Zen's eyes sparked with anticipation.

"When will you let Jo go? You want to talk to the guy yourself, so as far as I'm concerned, my task is finished."

"No, no, there's a step two. We talked about this."

Madeline clenched her teeth. "The last one?"

"Yes, and this one's easy. There is an alchemist named John Dee. He died in the 1500s and is buried in Mortlake. You go there and get me an artifact that was buried with him. It's only an hour or so outside of London. Piece of cake. The guy died a long time ago. Nobody will pay any attention to what you're doing."

Madeline stared at Zen for a long moment and raised an eyebrow. "Say that again?"

Zen exhaled to calm himself. "John Dee was . . ."

"I heard that part—you don't have to repeat it. You really want me to dig up the grave of some dead alchemist?"

"Well, it's not exactly tomb raider. All you need is a shovel."

"Why don't you do it yourself?"

"I could, but it wouldn't be very efficient. I'll have to get Jo to London to negotiate with White Knight. Then once he agrees, the artifact has to be available for him to work on. I can't be in two places at the same time!"

"Alchemists are those who squeezed gold out of steel, right? If you're after gold, wouldn't it be easier just to rob banks or jewelry stores?"

"Just like most ordinary people, you're very short-sighted,

Maddie. Get me the artifact, then we'll talk. I might even give you some gold dust if you cooperate!"

Madeline rolled her eye exaggeratedly so that Zen could see it. "Yeah, right. So what's the 'artifact'? And when will you need it?"

"You'll know it when you see it. I don't know exactly what it is. It had to have been something of great importance to John Dee. I'll need it within twenty-four hours."

"You've—"

"No, I'm not kidding. I'll get the plane tickets now. We'll be there in twenty-four hours. I need you to have the artifact ready and locate the White Knight for me." He paused and stared at Madeline. "The timing here is very critical. If you mess me up, I'll have no mercy for you and your little friend here."

Madeline stared back at him sternly. "Jo can't travel long distances without her meds. If you paid any attention at all and stopped drugging her, she'd tell you that she's diabetic and is probably overdue for her doses right now."

Zen scratched his head in frustration. Madeline could hear him cursing to himself. "All right, I'll get her the meds she needs. Do you know where she gets them?"

"Ask her yourself. If I remember correctly, it's somewhere in Midtown—between Park and Madison."

Zen nodded and noted it down.

Madeline smiled. "I can dig up an old grave. I'm sure the dead people won't mind. And I can get one ready for you, too—and bury you with pleasure."

Zen grinned crookedly. "See you soon," he said and hung up abruptly.

As soon as the screen went black, a tear trickled down Madeline's face. She quickly brushed it away and found her hand shaking. She couldn't afford to be shaky right now. She needed to focus.

She had flirted with fire.

12

*M*adeline took a deep breath. She gazed at the phone for short moment and quickly sketched a plan in her head.

Then she dialed. At the other end, Stephen's sleepy voice came across the line.

"You're sleeping at this hour, Stephen?"

"Madeline? Where've you been? I stopped by your office, and Paul said you're on vacation! You? Taking a vacation? Sounded almost as unlikely as breaking news of an alien invasion."

"I'm in London."

"Wow. You're really on a vacation."

"Listen, I need your help."

"Sure."

Madeline pulled hard at her ponytail as a form of self-punishment. "Really, Stephen? You don't even need to know what I'm asking you to do?"

"No, really. Okay, yes, so tell me what you want me to do."

"You know Zen, Jo's boss, right?"

"Yes, I saw him once at Jo's office. What about him?"

"This is going to sound weird, but it's serious, so please bear with me. Zen kidnapped Jo because of some role-playing interactive game Jo developed. He wanted me to come to London to find the guy who played a character in Jo's game. Zen beat Jo, and he's threatened to rape her if I can't find this guy."

There was a long pause. "And you didn't think calling the cops should be your first course of action?"

"How fast do you think the cops can pull their acts together in this case? Zen didn't ask for money or anything that the cops can leverage on. He wanted me to get information about a computer geek. Getting information is what I do for a living, Stephen. He sent me Jo's necklace and said if I make one wrong move, he'll kill Jo."

"And you didn't even think of calling me? Not as a cop, but as a friend?"

Madeline had never heard Stephen raise his voice before. They had been friends for more than five years. He'd asked Madeline out once, and she hadn't budged, so they'd settled on being friends. There were countless times Madeline had asked herself why she'd rejected Stephen and couldn't find a good answer.

"Stephen, I'm telling you now."

"I'll have him in jail within an hour."

"Be careful, Stephen. He came close to raping Jo yesterday. He's going crazy. He'd cut her throat if I said one wrong thing. I gave him what he wanted to hear. I told him I got the guy, and now Zen's on his way to London."

Another long pause from Stephen's end. "You don't sound like you've got the guy."

"No, I don't."

"Right. . . Okay, I'll find an excuse to detain him, legally or not. How does that sound?"

"Uhhhmm . . ."

"I'll beat the shit out of him and get Jo back then. How does that sound?

"Be careful, Stephen. I don't want you to get hurt."

Stephen snorted.

"Zen would have made up an excuse to Jo's family about her disappearance. She took off to write her games all the time. He wouldn't be stupid enough to hide her at his place. I tricked him by saying that Jo needed diabetic meds. She was half unconscious, but I think she understood. If she can fool him, he'll be at a drugstore in Manhattan for the medicine."

Stephen said irritably, "I'm a cop, Madeline. I can track this guy down, all right? Plus, Zen's record isn't exactly spotless. I ran him once. But I can get Jo out, okay? Don't you worry."

Madeline felt a wave of relief. "I should have called you earlier."

"You're telling me now. That's good enough."

Madeline closed her eyes and still couldn't figure out why she hadn't given Stephen a chance before. Then she saw the blue dots hovering in the corner of her room. "You've got to be kidding me," she muttered.

"Huh?"

"No, not you. I've got to go now, Stephen. Would you call me back and let me know what happens?"

"I'll call you when I've got Zen."

Madeline hung up the phone.

She slowly approached the dots. They swiveled, did a little dance, and grew to the size of soccer balls. She had never seen them this close before—so close she could feel the vibration they emitted. She reached her hand out to touch them. The closer her hand came to them, the stronger the suction felt. It intensified until she felt nothing but an explosion of blue.

13

*C*iaran glanced around the boardroom at the twelve directors sitting at the long shiny table. While they were busy taking notes on what he just said, Ciaran scanned the agenda in front of him. He frowned at the last two items and looked up.

"It's too premature to discuss the last two points on this agenda. That means the meeting today is concluded. Any questions?"

There was a murmuring in the room, brief discussions here and there, and then everyone seemed to be eager to move on with the day. Ciaran dismissed the meeting. As soon as the last person left, he turned on the video call. An image of a man in his sixties flashed on the screen.

"Doctor Thomas, how's Mother?" Ciaran asked.

Doctor Thomas smiled. "Ciaran, your mother is fine. It was just a mild flu. She is as stubborn as you are. Didn't want to take any medicine..."

Ciaran raised an eyebrow, and the corner of his mouth quirked waiting for Doctor Thomas to finish.

"... She loves her organic vegetable garden and refuses to eat anything that's not from there. She's never questioned how those vegetables survive in the Dublin weather. You've done a good job, Ciaran."

Ciaran smiled. "Thanks for looking after my mother, Doctor Thomas. I don't know what I'd do without you."

"Don't exaggerate, Ciaran. You always know what to do. Are you well?"

"Yes. Why do you ask?"

Doctor Thomas sighed. "I was there when your mother introduced you to this world. You don't think I'd know how you look when you're well?"

Ciaran laughed. He liked Doctor Thomas's gentle voice, especially when he tried to put on that authoritative tone. Most of the time, it didn't work for Ciaran, but he loved to hear it anyway. Ciaran realized that he was squeezing the pen in his hand a bit too hard, and he put it down on a pile of papers. A long, long time ago, he would hear that same authoritative voice from his father, and it always worked on him.

Ciaran ignored his pounding migraine and smiled. "I'm fine. Really."

Doctor Thomas nodded. "Fine. Go take the painkillers. I'm sure they'll fix it. Would you like me to send your regards to your mother?"

Ciaran stared at the screen. Doctor Thomas sighed again. "I guess not. Goodbye for now, son." He smiled and turned off the call.

Ciaran grabbed the desk phone, and when his assistant's voice came across, he said, "Could you cancel my meeting this afternoon, please? I'll get Lily in the London office to notify you with the reschedule." He then grabbed his jacket and his coat, and headed out of the room.

∿

HALF AN HOUR LATER, Ciaran stood in front of a dusty steel door. He stared at it for a long moment, then punched in a code.

The door whined and squeaked as it opened. The lab light

automatically lit up, and the musty air greeted him. Ciaran threw this coat on a steel bench.

He entered a security code on a keypad beside a cabinet and opened it. Inside was a row of medicines in colorful jars. He took a small tube from the end of the row and placed it on the bench. He stared at the tube for a long moment as it glared back at him in challenge.

The migraine had come back in the last two weeks, and it was unbearable. It was pounding in his head right now.

A soothing female voice echoed in his head, "I made this for you. Why put up with the pain, Ciaran? Just take it."

His vision blurred with the pain, his body swayed, and he braced his hands on the bench top to keep his balance.

"You don't know how much pain I can endure. I deserve this," he muttered to himself.

He grunted as the pain intensified. Beads of sweat began to trickle slowly down his forehead. The sharp pain pierced through his brain and before he knew it, he passed out on the cold dusty floor.

14

*M*adeline scrambled up from the floor, the sensation of the blue suction still pounding in her head. "What the hell?" she muttered. Then she recalled the vision. "Okay, stupid blue dots," she muttered, "Guide me if you're any good."

An hour later, she followed the blue dots into the British museum where a gold plate that had once used by John Dee to communicate to spirits stared at her from a display cabinet. Madeline shook her head and rolled her eyes. Based on her research, John Dee had been an astrologist and advisor to Queen Elizabeth I. In some capacity, he was an alchemist, but it didn't seem as if alchemy was how he had gained fame.

She muttered to herself, "If you knew how to make gold, you wouldn't have died poor."

Her research suggested that John Dee had died in poverty. He couldn't possibly have made—or had known how to make—gold.

The blue dots disappeared. "Right, just reappear whenever you feel like it." Madeline cursed in frustration and noticed that the people standing next to her turned to look. She shrugged and scurried outside the museum.

She wasn't out of the woods yet—not until Stephen let her know he had gotten Zen, and Jo was safe. Just in case Zen turned up, she had to come up with some artifact. She figured she'd better go digging now. She shook her head, not sure what to feel. Next, she had to do something about the *fictional* character Samuel, who played the *fictional* character White Knight in some *fictional* computer game Jo had created!

Madeline hired a car and headed out of London. Hearing the shovel rattling in the trunk of the car, she shook her head in disbelief about what she was about to do.

The blue dots were no longer directing her, so she was going to have to rely on technology. The portable GPS, called Tom, that she had requested with the car was blurting out the instructions in a monotone female voice. She had to remember to drive on the left-hand side of the road. After a couple of wrong turns, she started to scold the machine, "You're female, why in world do they call you Tom? Is that why you don't understand that I have to not only get from A to B in one piece but also have to drive on the opposite side of the road?"

The machine didn't answer her.

While trying to dodge a black cab that was honking at her, Madeline heard the machine instruct, "In 200 yards, turn left."

"So much for English manners," Madeline muttered to herself, thinking of the black cab.

She glanced ahead and gestured to the machine. "Turn left into what?" Then she realized that she was talking to the machine again, and of course, there would not be a response. Madeline made a guess and turned left onto a smaller, paved road, only to discover that it was a dead end.

The machine calmly instructed, "Make a U-turn when possible."

"Of course," Madeline spoke to herself.

She turned into a private driveway and made a U-turn. She heard a dog barking at her from inside a peaceful cottage at the end of the driveway.

"Bark away, and bark real loud, 'cause you can't bite me!"

Madeline turned left on the next block and was relieved because there was no objection from Tom-the-guide.

"You have arrived at your destination," the machine cheerfully announced.

Madeline stared at the destination—it was a roundabout.

She didn't want to waste any more time arguing with the machine, so she parked on a small street and walked toward St Mary's Church.

It was a beautiful church. Based on Madeline's research this morning, this was where she might find some useful information. She stood at the entrance of the church, staring at the door as if admiring its magnificence. Instead, a stream of strategies flew through her head, none of them viable.

Going inside and asking for the grave of John Dee so that she could dig it up wouldn't go down well. The church did publicize that they had no information about the exact location of the tomb. Of course they had to say that they did not know where the tomb was, Madeline deduced. It would only take a few more scumbags like Zen, and the church would have a gold rush on its hands.

The door of the church slid open and a lady in a beige sweater and a light green coat walked out. Noticing Madeline, she approached. "May I help you?"

"Ah, my name is Madeline Roux. I'm working on a research project on theology. I'd like to see Doctor John Dee's plaque and some exhibits of his life and his work, if possible, but I notice that you don't have a service today and aren't open to public visits."

"Oh, I'm Maggie. I don't work here. I'm visiting my friends. But you've come to the right place for this. They've just obtained some funds from the government, along with generous public donations, to make the plaque. They've organized an association in the name of Doctor John Dee of Mortlake. Let me tell you, they're very proud of it. Or I should say, we are so proud of the doctor for his achievements. We appreciate the recognition he brought to Mortlake. Even Queen Elizabeth visited his house. Come on in." Maggie churned out a stream of information that Madeline had known from her research. But she politely followed Maggie inside the church.

"Waste of time!" said an old man sitting on the steps in front of the church.

"Excuse me?" Madeline stepped back outside.

Maggie interrupted. "Oh, Shaun, aren't you supposed to be at the library? Don't tell me you're drunk again at this hour?"

There were some movements from beneath a thick carpet of beard on Shaun's face. Madeline suspected it was a grin to Lady Maggie.

"It's winter, Maggie. There isn't much to do in the gardens. People go to a public library to read, not to look at flowers in the gardens. I'm waiting for you here, my lady! You're my flower." Shaun stood up and approached Maggie.

"Excuse me, I'm sorry to interrupt. You were saying something about me wasting time?" Aware of her time constraints, Madeline butted in.

"Ah, at least three times in the last month I saw people asking the same questions as you did, looking at the doctor's stuff as if they admired him. Then they ended up searching the graveyard for his tomb. Let me tell you now, it's a waste of time."

Maggie looked astonished. "Shaun, have you been stalking the church?"

"Oh no, I would never do such a thing!"

Feeling uneasy, Madeline shifted her shoulders. "What's wrong if people just want to show their respect at his tomb?"

Shaun laughed. "I don't think they wanted to show respect. They looked like they wanted to dig out the gold he buried with him!"

"Don't say such a thing, Shaun. It's not nice, and it's disrespectful to the doctor," Maggie protested.

Shaun looked at Madeline. "You see, now I've upset my lady. Look, I don't care if you want the gold in his coffin or not—he wasn't buried here."

"How do you know that?" Maggie's voice was high-pitched.

Shaun smiled secretly. "A man knows many secrets!"

Maggie put her hands on her hips, insistent.

"All right, all right. I helped Mrs. Hanson with her gardens many times. That's what I got as payment—stories. You know her. Full of mysterious stories."

"Mrs. Hanson in the Rose cottage?"

"Green Rose's cottage."

"There is no such thing as a green rose."

Madeline raised her hands apologetically as if she was intruding on their conversation once again. "I'm sorry. I've got to go. As I said, I just wanted to show some respect at the tomb. But if it's not here, then there's no point in me wasting your time. I'll make a donation to the church."

"Oh no, you should come in for a cup of tea," Maggie chirped.

"If you want the gold, talk to Mrs. Hanson. She knows the secrets! Her cottage is just at the next block." Shaun winked at Madeline. Then he turned to Maggie. "You see, I'm a good man. I don't have greed in me. I'm not digging graves for gold."

Madeline's phone rang. She grabbed at it like a drowning person grabbing at a life preserver and went to a quiet corner to talk.

At the other end of the line, Stephen's voice sounded scratchy. Madeline noted that it was the middle of the night in New York. "I'm sorry, Madeline!"

Madeline felt a chill run down her spine. Instead of asking nonsense questions, she waited.

"I messed everything up," Stephen continued. "I ran some information on Zen after I talked to you. I found out he owns a cabin in the hunting ground in the national park. I couldn't help it . . . I went there. It was in the middle of the night, you know, and I figured if he'd hidden Jo there, then I could wrap it up sweet."

"Bottom line, Stephen, is Jo okay?"

"Yeah. She is. She's valuable to Zen. He'd pull the trigger on me, not on her."

"What? A gunfight? He shot at you? Are you okay?"

"Just a scratch. I'm fine. But it was unfair to have five of them on one of me, and I couldn't fire the weapon without reciting the procedures—I wasn't there in an official capacity."

Madeline sat down on a bench.

Stephen continued, "He recognized me as Jo's friend. He knew I was a cop."

"But he still shot at you?"

"If I'd been in my official position, he wouldn't—"

"I know, Stephen. I understand, and I'm sorry I put you in danger."

"Danger is a package deal with my job. I can't believe a computer geek like Zen would run a full-on organized crime hub in the middle of a jungle. They were all armed."

Madeline muttered, "He wants a lot more than just winning a computer game."

"What do you mean?"

"Oh, nothing. So he knew I sent you, and now he's coming after me?"

"There wasn't any time to talk or ask any questions. All shooting and shouting. He fled, taking Jo with him. It sounded like he was heading straight to the airport. Even if I'd pulled in my buddies, it would—"

"I understand. You don't know which flight, which route, how long it would take him to get to me?"

"I'm coming over there, Madeline."

"No, please don't. I can take care of myself. I've asked enough of you."

Stephen lowered his voice, "And I'm not asking anything of you. I just want to you count on me. Just this time. Trust me. Let me help you."

"Stephen!"

"I'll get Zen, and I'll find you, Madeline."

Stephen hung up the phone. It was the first time Stephen had hung up on her. Most of the time, she was the one cutting off a conversation.

15

*C*iaran stopped and waited patiently. A couple more blocks to his London headquarters, and the traffic had been crawling for fifteen minutes. Lindsay called again, and Ciaran picked up on his car phone. "You go ahead with your meetings, Lindsay. I'm not scheduled to be in the office, so you don't have to wait for me there."

"Are you sure? Robert wants to talk to you beforehand, and he said you didn't pick up."

That must have been when he passed out, Ciaran thought. "Ask him to wait for me in the office. I'll be there as soon as this mess clears up."

"What happened?"

"Traffic jam, I think. A couple of blocks from our south gate."

Ciaran inched the car ahead as the traffic controller signaled.

"Do you want to leave the car there? I'll send someone to pick you up, going the other way to the north gate."

"It's okay. I'm nearly there. Don't worry. I'll see you soon." Ciaran hung up as the police signaled him to move forward, and he made significant progress. Ciaran drove ahead. It was actually good timing. He needed this time to settle his headache. He still felt a bit shaky from the effects of it. It had been bad before, but never that nasty. What he needed right now was a strong dose of painkillers.

An officer tapped on the windshield to signal Ciaran to move ahead. He pressed the button to lower the window. "What's happening, officer?"

"A homeless person died."

"Accident?"

"I don't know. He just lay there and died on the sidewalk. They've nearly cleaned up the scene. It won't take long."

"Thank you."

This was going to take forever, Ciaran thought. He reached his hand out toward the control panel to take Lindsay up on his offer, but before he dialed, he saw a puppy standing right in front of his car. If he had inched the car ahead without looking, he would have run over the dog.

It wasn't just any puppy—it was a small, shabby Alaskan malamute pup wearing a dark saddle and a sign around its neck saying, "I've lost my mommy, and I need to eat." It was obvious that this dog had belonged to the homeless person, whoever that might have been. Ciaran glanced to the side window, looking for the officer he'd just spoken to, but he didn't see him. He glanced in his rear view mirror and saw a line of cars.

The puppy shivered. Its eyes were teary, and its fur soaked with the moisture from the winter air. Ciaran looked for the officer again and found no one. The car in front of him had moved up. He cursed and sneaked open the passenger door. The puppy didn't wait for an invitation—he jumped right in. Ciaran drove the car forward and waited in the traffic again.

"Let me take that sign off your neck. It annoys the heck out of me." He pulled off the sign and could feel the puppy shaking. Ciaran cranked up the heat, and warm air pumped out of the floor unit. The puppy dove right in front of the heater and rubbed against it, rolling on the floor as if in ecstasy. When its fur dried out, it sat up straight on the floor, looking at Ciaran. Then it raised a front leg in a handshake position.

Ciaran laughed. "You're very welcome, smart dog. I'm sure he taught you how to pick pockets, too. That's a pity. I don't do dogs, let alone a puppy." Ciaran's car had crawled up alongside the sidewalk where the homeless person had died. The body had been taken away, but a pile of rags and a crooked shopping trolley full of junk were still on the sidewalk. Next to the trolley was a small carton wrapped with rags that Ciaran was sure the person had used as the dog's bed.

Some officers were still standing around clearing the scene. "There you go. No need to thank me for the ride," Ciaran said and opened the passenger door. The puppy tried its last trick, looking at Ciaran with watery eyes. He shook his head and gestured toward the door. The puppy looked down to the floor, grabbed the sign Ciaran had peeled off its neck, and jumped out of the car.

Ciaran glanced in the rear view mirror and saw the puppy sitting on the road, watching with the sign in its mouth. He drove a bit more and stopped again for traffic. The puppy still sat there. Then an officer approached, and the puppy stood up and withdrew from the officer's reach. By doing so, he stepped backward out to the road. Another officer approached to help, and the dog backed further out onto the road.

The traffic was finally clear, and cars started moving fast. Ciaran cursed. He reached over and opened the passenger door again. From the rear mirror, he could see the puppy racing toward his car. In seconds, it stood at the door.

"I don't like that sign," Ciaran said.

In a heartbeat, the dog dropped the sign onto the road and hopped into the car.

his was a total screw-up, Madeline thought. Stephen not only couldn't get Zen, but had alerted him that she had sent a cop in. Now she had to execute the plan B she didn't even have.

She had to find someone to play the Samuel she had created. That was her priority. But she had to find the artifact first. That was a priority, too. She could explain to Zen somehow that it had taken more time to find the artifact, but she could not make an excuse for not providing Samuel. Maybe she should find the artifact, and then come clean to Zen about Samuel, using the artifact to compensate him? No, that wouldn't work.

She was in Mortlake anyway, so she would see what she could do. If Zen couldn't speak to her directly, he couldn't jump to any conclusions about anything too soon. As long as he was unsure, Jo would be fine, Madeline contemplated.

Madeline drove around the block to the Green Rose cottage and approached the small gate on foot. The black Pomeranian who had been barking at Madeline that morning was now baring his teeth at her. *Not very friendly*, she thought and gave the dog a stern look.

A woman in her nineties—or at least looked that old—dressed in gypsy clothes appeared at the doorstep.

"I've convinced Woody to forgive your intrusion this morning, but he's still upset, you see!"

"Mrs. Hanson, I'm so sorry I was rude this morning, but I . . ."

"All your kind are the same. So don't even mention it."

"My kind? Mrs. Hanson . . ." Madeline raised her voice in defense, but Mrs. Hanson cut in.

"You want to find John Dee's grave, right?" Mrs. Hanson smiled.

"Yes, I do. But I wasn't . . ."

Mrs. Hanson raised a hand to cut Madeline off.

"What you want to find in the grave is not my problem. I knew you were coming. You're just like the others. Greed will not bring anyone any good."

"But I didn't . . ."

"You do not have greed in you. I can see that. But you have grief. The grief you are carrying is horrible—and it's contagious. So stay far from me. Greed is easy for me to handle. I can help with that. But you will have to sort out the grief yourself."

She had no idea what the old lady was prattling on about. But something weighed heavily in her chest. It hurt. But there was no time to think about it. She had a task at hand, and her friend's life depended on it.

"Where can I find the grave?"

"Fosse Way. It's guarded by Roman soldiers. But I have to warn you, young lady, these soldiers cannot tell the difference between greed and grief. They will judge you by your actions. So be careful."

Mrs. Hanson turned around and disappeared suddenly behind the door. Madeline looked down to the dog and found that it, too, had gone.

She walked away from the manicured garden.

Right, so plan C then.

17

*F*atigue dragged at Madeline. The fact the she'd only slept a couple of hours a day in the last week was one factor in her exhaustion, but hunger was gnawing at her as well.

She got into her car and programmed the GPS for Fosse Way. The machine couldn't locate it. *Was it a road, a district, or a city?* Madeline just wanted to see how far it was from her current location.

She didn't have her laptop with her, so she used the phone Ciaran gave her instead. It was a smart phone with some data capability for temporarily usage. Ciaran wouldn't settle for anything less, of course. Madeline smiled to herself, remembering the look on his face when he had programmed her phone.

Google maps suggested that Fosse Way was a highway which connected several different towns and ran for more than 350 km. There were smaller sections of the road that deviated from the main road, and part of it was called Roman Road. That had to be it. She didn't have much time to research, but Mrs. Hanson had mentioned Roman soldiers. That narrowed things down a lot for her.

She tapped her fingers on the steering wheel. "Just a quick search, and I'll be back in London in no time," she muttered to herself. At least if she had to encounter Zen sometime tomorrow, she would have something to show him so she could stall for more time.

As the GPS had become useless at this point, Madeline used Google Maps and hit the road. By her gauge, it would take a couple of hours to get to Roman Road.

"I could use a blue dot right about now," she said out loud. Nothing. She shook her head. She'd thought the psychic dots weren't random, but they were really playing tricks on her.

After a couple of hours, she could see signs pointing to her destination. She veered off the highway, bearing in mind that she could come back to it at any time.

The smaller roads were a bit bumpy, but she figured as long as there were signs of civilization, she would be fine. It was going to be getting dark, so she knew she'd better find Roman Road soon, wherever it was. She was about to give up and turn around when she finally saw it—a small, narrow country road with stone walls running along it.

Wow. That was the only word Madeline could think of. The walls must have been more than a thousand years old. They were only knee-high, a meter at most. But they went on and on, black stones stacked together, forming what seemed to be the walls of time. If they could talk, Madeline bet they could tell stories. They had witnessed the history of a thousand years or more. Many people had lived and died here. Behind the stone walls were endless green fields, ditches, and marshes. Madeline was amazed. She was just a few hours outside vibrant London—and this!

The walls were mysterious, but there was no sign of a graveyard or even a single tomb. She didn't see how John Dee could be buried here.

The air seemed to have grown thicker, and the wind had stopped blowing. It was eerily quiet. Something kept urging her to go ahead. An ancient voice. A haunting chant.

Something was watching her.

Urging

Pushing.

Clouding her judgment.

It turned dark quickly. She wanted to turn around, but she couldn't seem to sync her mind and her actions. It wasn't possible to turn the car around on this narrow one-lane road. It was so narrow that two cars couldn't pass at the same time.

Madeline checked Google Maps to see how close she was to the main road and discovered the phone was totally dead—the battery was drained.

No worries, she thought as she turned on her GPS and programmed in her address in London as the destination. The machine flashed once, twice, and then it went blank.

Madeline glanced out the windows. It was completely dark now. The chanting still hovered in the air, and the wind started to weave through the stones and trees, making eerie flute-like sounds. She needed her blue dots, but she knew very well from experience that they wouldn't come to her when she needed them most.

She had to turn the car around somehow.

Madeline saw a broken part of the wall and veered toward it. In the beam of the car headlights, it appeared to be a grass field on the other side of the wall, not a swamp or a river. She was close to the gap in the wall when the car was suddenly pushed forward. A loud bang echoed in the interior of the car when it hit the stone wall, making her head ring. Still having momentum, she managed to steer back to the road, scraping the side of the car along the stone wall. It sloped down a bit. Maybe it was her imagination, but the car seemed to keep speeding forward. She hit the brakes.

It didn't work.

She kept hitting loose stones and tree logs, and the car swung from one side to another, but it kept moving forward.

For a very brief moment, Madeline thought she saw a line of Roman soldiers marching along the wall. She shook her head. She knew fatigue was dragging at her now. Her head seemed to weigh a ton, and her mind was drifting, unfocused.

She hit the brakes again. It didn't work.

She saw the Roman soldiers once more. One soldier turned around and looked straight at her. His eyes were evil and red. She pressed the accelerator.

It worked.

As she zoomed past, the soldier raised his body-length sword and his metal shield and threw his weight at the side of the car.

The car hit another log, jumped in the air, and almost flipped over.

Madeline drove faster. She didn't realize that she was crying. Her headlights shone on armory, weapons, and marching soldiers.

There was lightning sparking from the sky and flashing on the road right in front of her car. Madeline veered off the road.

But then she saw her blue dot. And another one. Many of them, flying over the sky in a flock. But it was too late now. The car flew over a wall, landing on a slope and rolling until it hit a large rock and lay motionless.

Am I dead? She couldn't move for long time as she was pinned between the seat and the airbag.

Then she heard footsteps. Madeline kicked hard and wriggled to free herself. She stumbled out of the car and looked up to the top of the ditch. Lightning cast light into the darkness of stone and trees. She saw the soldiers and their shadows. She heard them murmur in their search for her.

Which way is London? She scanned the vicinity aimlessly. The lightning created a spotlight right where she was standing. Thunder roamed across the sky. Madeline yelped and jumped aside to hide.

Too late. They had seen her.

The shadows moved toward her. They called her name. She ran. They chased. She kept running.

Madeline fell, rolling on rocks and tree branches. She scrambled up and kept moving.

She heard her name again. But this time, the voice sounded familiar. She knew that voice.

Lightning again, and in the brightness of the flashing light, she saw Ciaran running toward her. It was him. She couldn't be mistaken. She recognized the shape of him, and the sound of his voice.

"Madeline!" Ciaran shouted.

He rushed forward and grabbed her to stop her from running. They both tumbled and rolled on the hard rocks.

Ciaran helped her up. Madeline grabbed on to him. She felt like weeping. In fact, she *was*. Ciaran held her tight for a very brief second and pushed her to continue running.

Madeline was dazed. "Why are we running? You're here. We're safe."

Ciaran pulled at her. "Run!" he said.

Madeline didn't quite get it, but she went with him.

Lightning, thunder, and now pouring rain made it impossible to tell what they were running toward. Madeline guessed he was trying to get her to run toward the light. It felt right, running to the light.

She still heard footsteps and saw shadows. It was not clear to her who they were running toward and who they were running from.

A barrage of large stones flew toward them.

It had to be from the Roman soldiers, Madeline thought. She could see the holes the stones made in the mud, the walls, and tree trunks around them.

Ciaran grabbed Madeline and pushed her down to avoid the raining stones. He was covering her, Madeline knew.

And then silence, as if the sound had been suddenly vacuumed out of the sphere.

They stood up. She heard a whooshing noise, and then the stones commenced again. Both Ciaran and Madeline fell, rolling down a slope. Then she felt cold water. They might be in a pool, a pond, a lake—but it was cold.

That was the last thing she remembered before the world went black.

18

Thick embroidered curtains dripping with ropes and ribbons in royal colors hung around the bed and from the ceiling, looking down at Madeline.

Have I time-traveled? Madeline blinked and glanced around.

She was lying on a four-poster bed in the middle of a spacious room surrounded by walls covered in deep-colored patterned wallpaper and tapestries. Paintings in fancy frames were arranged on the walls at every corner of the room. Even the bedside lamps were ornate.

Had it not been for the sight of Ciaran standing at the window in his modern clothing, talking on his cell phone, Madeline would have argued that this was a castle straight out of the fifteenth century.

Ciaran murmured something in French. The language sounded like music to Madeline. Then, sensing Madeline's gaze, he finished the conversation and turned around.

He completes the scene, Madeline thought. Complementing the setting of the room, he looked like a king. His long hair was swept back, revealing a broad forehead and sculptured face—the face of a dark angel. He was too young to be a king, but she couldn't settle for a lesser description.

Within seconds, as quick and gentle as a cat, he was at her bedside.

"How are you feeling?" Ciaran slid the phone into his pocket.

Madeline moved her shoulders a bit. She ached everywhere. "I've been better . . . Are we in a castle? Is this your house?"

Ciaran grinned. "Yes, we are indeed in a castle. But this is not my house. It's Lumley Castle, converted into a hotel. It's the closest place I could find where the helicopter could drop us as you didn't want to go to the hospital, nor did you want me to contact the authorities regarding the incident last night. So the Queen Suite is what you have here."

"The haunted Lumley Castle?" Madeline's eyes widened.

Ciaran winked at her. "A commercial myth! Don't disappoint me by buying into it."

Madeline was puzzled and about to ask more questions, but Ciaran raised a finger, gesturing her to hold on. He picked up the handset of the phone at the desk.

"Yes, this is Ciaran. Yes, could you please bring it up here? Also, there should be a fax waiting for me. My assistant Lindsay would have gotten it by now. He's in the Courtyard room. Could you bring me the document as well? Thank you. In the Queen Suite. Yes. Thanks."

Ciaran turned around, smiling at Madeline.

"I didn't know what you like for breakfast, so I ordered the whole lot. The doctor said you can have solid food when you wake. Also . . ."

"Hold on a sec. What's going on here? What happened last night?" Madeline gestured widely. Everything was confusing to her at the moment.

"I should ask these questions, Madeline. What in God's name were you doing in Fosse Way at that time of night? Your phone sent out a distress signal to me."

"How? It was dead when I was desperate to use it."

"There's a chip in your phone. You're using my company's phone, remember? And don't stress, I wasn't monitoring your whereabouts. It's a standard function in all company phones. Based on changing operating conditions and a lot of other variables, if the phone detects that the user is in possible danger, it will send distress signals to the central operator. I coded your signals to be sent to my phone instead of our operator."

"Got it! And thank you for coming after me."

"You didn't exactly give me any other options," Ciaran murmured. "You know what your logs looked like? Again, it's standard data, I'm not spying on you. You went from London to Mortlake, then straight to the Roman Road during the severe storm warning hours. Then you circled on and off the ancient path, and on and off the road for hours. When I located you, you flew off a wall. Were you practicing for the Grand Prix?"

Ciaran looked at Madeline gently, but there was no amusement in his eyes.

"The Roman soldiers chased me," Madeline explained. She might have hallucinated it, but that was the only piece of information she had and could give at the moment. *I sound like a lunatic*, she thought.

Ciaran gave Madeline a blank stare. He jammed his hands in his pockets and rolled up slightly onto the balls of his feet. Madeline knew that signaled a sarcastic remark was coming. But somehow, he swallowed it before it came out.

Someone knocked on the door. Ciaran opened it to allow the staff to push in a breakfast tray—or a breakfast feast, by Madeline's gauge.

"I'll take this. Thanks." Ciaran took a piece of paper with one hand and grabbed a parcel that looked like clean clothes on coat hangers, wrapped in plastic, with the other. He walked to a wall cabinet to hang up the clothes, as if this was his room.

Madeline stared. Those were her clothes he was handling. She looked down. She was wearing a comfortable white robe. And she was pretty sure by now that underneath the robe was nothing but her skin.

Ciaran glanced quickly at the fax he held in his hand. Looking as if he had seen what he wanted to see, he put the piece of paper on the desk. Then he turned toward Madeline. "The bathroom is there." He pointed to a door in the corner of the room. Then he reached out his hand. "Would you like a hand to get up? Although you had no internal injuries, you had a minor concussion last night. The doctor said you might feel a bit queasy this morning."

Madeline narrowed her eyes, looking down at her robe and then up at Ciaran. "The doctor?"

"Doctor Thomas is our family doctor. He'll follow up this morning to make sure everything is okay."

Madeline looked down again to her robe and back up at Ciaran. She was in a hotel, a private doctor had examined her last night, and in her delirium, she had objected to going to the hospital.

Who exactly had put her in this robe?

Madeline remembered her situation. "I've got to go. I need to be back in London." Zen was coming at any time, and she'd found nothing to show him.

"You're not leaving until you tell me just what happened yesterday. I need answers, Madeline. You can't just brush this off and leave." Ciaran's tone was firm and authoritative.

"I've told you all I know. Look, Ciaran, I appreciate you rescuing me last night, but I really have to go. Right now."

Ciaran stared into her eyes. "You said Roman soldiers chased you. Just so you know, they didn't use guns in that era." His eyes were intense now with a hint of anger.

"Guns? What guns?"

There was a knock on the door.

"That must be Doctor Thomas." Ciaran strode to the door and opened it to let the doctor in.

The man entering the room looked more like a kind grandfather than a doctor. Ciaran fetched a chair and put it next to Madeline's bed so that Doctor Thomas could sit down. Then he went to a corner of the room to answer an incoming call on his cell phone.

"How are you feeling this morning, Madeline?" asked the doctor.

"Just aching a bit. But I feel fine. Thanks for checking on me last night."

"Based on my visual examination, there are no internal injuries. However, I'd like to run a scanner through your body to confirm. Ideally, we should do a head scan as well. But that has to be done at the hospital or at our private lab."

Embarrassment rushed through her. Her entire body had been examined last night, and she didn't even remember it.

"Madeline?"

"Huh?"

"The scan will be quick and gentle. It's better to be safe than sorry." Doctor Thomas looked at her calmly, like a father. Something tugged at her heart. Yes, he was like the father she thought she should have.

"Who was here last night when you examined me?"

Doctor Thomas smiled. "Only Ciaran and myself. There wasn't an army of people in this room if that's what you're worried about." Madeline caught a flash of sorrow in the doctor's eyes.

"I'm feeling fine right now. I'm pretty sure of it." Madeline wiggled her toes underneath the blanket and did a quick mental scan of herself. She did feel fine.

Ciaran finished his phone call and came to the bed.

"No scanning?" Ciaran asked.

"No, she won't agree to it." Doctor Thomas shook his head with fatherly disapproval. Then he turned to Ciaran. "Lindsay was kind enough to deliver my medical bag this morning. So it's time to take your bullet out."

"Bullet? You were shot?" Madeline sat upright in the bed.

19

"*J*ust a scratch." Ciaran smiled.

"No, it's not. The LeBlanc's painkiller is top of the line, but you can't rely on it any longer. And you can't carry a bullet in your shoulder for more than twelve hours —even one hour is too long for my liking," Doctor Thomas said.

"The Roman soldiers shot at you?" Madeline's voice was shaky.

Ciaran looked at her without a response. Madeline looked at Doctor Thomas, knowing how weird she sounded.

"Don't worry, Madeline. I've worked for the LeBlancs for more than thirty years, and I've heard some very unusual things," Doctor Thomas commented.

"All right," Ciaran compromised, "how long do you need?"

"Three hours."

"I don't have three hours. I have to be in France for an important meeting this afternoon."

"Two hours then."

"Twenty minutes is all I can give you."

"It's surgery, Ciaran. The bullet is in your shoulder, and the wound is deep. Without the scanner, I don't even know exactly where the bullet is. It might not be just a flesh wound, as you seem to think. The strong painkiller would numb your senses."

"Half an hour. You're a good doctor. I trust you can do it." Ciaran grabbed his jacket that was resting on the reading chair. "Let's go."

"Go where?" Madeline asked.

"My room, of course!" Ciaran answered, cocking an eyebrow.

"No, no, oh no! Do it right here!"

Ciaran looked at the doctor, puzzled, then looked at Madeline. "I beg your pardon?"

"We can talk after Doctor Thomas has scooped the bullet out of you. It'll save time, you'll see. It's just minor surgery. I'll explain to you all about last night. You should be fine talking while he's working." Madeline raised an eyebrow in challenge.

You got to see me naked, and you got the doctor to work on me? Well, it's time for payback. Madeline knew it was mean of her, but she couldn't help it.

"When you're finished with your surgery, I'll be gone. I have to be back in London. Right now," Madeline added.

"If you need things done within half an hour, I could use some help," Doctor Thomas said in support of Madeline's suggestion.

Ciaran was reluctant for a second, then nodded. "All right, no anesthesia, Doctor Thomas. Just numb it."

Madeline got up from the bed quickly, prepared for her role as nurse. Ciaran took his shirt off. In front of her was an exquisite, well-toned, and sculptured set of muscles on a slender body that God must have created when he was in a very, very good mood. Madeline pretended to cinch her robe.

Drooling in front of a guy is not attractive, Madeline. Preserve some of your dignity, she told herself.

Doctor Thomas removed the bandage from Ciaran's wound. Madeline gasped when she saw it. A slash of guilt cut into her. That could have been *her* bullet.

"Lie down in the bed for me, will you, Ciaran?"

Ciaran kicked his shoes off and obeyed Doctor Thomas without hesitation, showing that he just wanted to get his procedure over

with as soon as possible. Madeline had expected that the humiliation of being handled in front of her would be so enormous that
Ciaran would forget to ask her any questions. But apparently, he
didn't miss a trick.

He lay on his side, his back facing outward so that Doctor
Thomas could work on him. Ciaran looked at Madeline, who was
standing on the opposite side of the bed, her hands in the pockets
of her hotel robe.

"There were no Roman soldiers, Madeline. But you were
running from *someone*. When I found you and managed to land the
rescue helicopter, you were running away from me. You wouldn't
stop. Then after I'd gotten to you, bullets rained down on us. I
couldn't see anyone, but I'm sure it was more than one person.
When my rescue team approached us, they found no one, but they
did discover several bullet casings by the ditch."

Ciaran winced as he felt a prick from the needle.

"I can see the bullet," Doctor Thomas informed him. "I'm
numbing you now."

Ciaran nodded slightly in acknowledgement.

Madeline cleared her throat. "I was looking for John Dee's
tomb, but I'm not after gold if that's what you're thinking . . ."

"I'm not drawing any conclusions yet."

"An old woman at Mortlake . . ."

"Mrs. Hanson?"

"Yes, you know her?"

"Yes, but we no longer have any association. I sought her
consultation on natural medicine. I was told that people were
looking for John Dee's grave, and Mrs. Hanson claimed she knew
where it is. But people came to ask for her advice, and they were
never seen again."

"Well, obviously she sent the Roman soldiers after them!"
Madeline exclaimed.

"If you're not after the gold like the others, why do you need to
find John Dee's grave? Does it have anything to do with your
friend's computer game?"

"Look Ciaran, it could have been worse than a bullet in your shoulder. I . . ."

"This bullet is nothing. I need the truth, Madeline."

"Stay still, Ciaran," Doctor Thomas warned.

"Sorry," Ciaran muttered, his eyes flashing with anger but calming quickly.

First, Stephen took a bullet. Now Ciaran. Who will be next? Madeline bit her lips, unsure what to say.

"Madeline, I need answers."

She nodded, those deep gray eyes telling her he was not going to let this slide. "Yes, this has to do with the computer game my friend, Jo, developed. She was kidnapped. If I can't find out who is playing as an avatar in her game, they're going to kill Jo." A tear ran down Madeline's face.

Ciaran shook his head, trying to stay alert. "Who are *they*?"

"Jo's boss. The guy owns a game development company. I don't know why he wanted me to find John Dee's grave."

"What's the avatar?" Madeline flickered in front of Ciaran, starting to fade. Her voice seemed to echo in his head. "Damn it. God damn it, Doctor Thomas." Ciaran sat up, but then flopped face down back on to the bed.

Doctor Thomas looked at Madeline and shrugged. "I'm going to need more than half an hour. Please help me straighten him up."

Madeline climbed onto the bed and turned Ciaran so he lay on his side. His face had gone lax, and his skin burned. "He has a fever," she said.

Doctor Thomas nodded. "Yes, without the painkiller, he'd be in very poor shape. You may want to call his assistant, Lindsay, and tell him that Ciaran won't make it to the meeting this afternoon."

Madeline followed his instructions. She skimmed through Ciaran's address book and called.

"This is Madeline. Doctor Thomas asked me to let you know that Ciaran won't make it to the meeting this afternoon . . . Inform his family? . . ." Madeline saw Doctor Thomas shook his head. "No, no need to . . . He'd need . . . ah . . ." Madeline saw Doctor Thomas mime the time He'd need until tomorrow. So no more work today. Okay?"

Madeline hung up the phone. "Lindsay said to tell you he'd take care of Robert's family."

Doctor Thomas nodded. Noticing the flash of pain that came across Doctor Thomas's face, Madeline caught him giving her another unusual glance. She pressed, "Who's Robert, Doctor Thomas?"

Doctor Thomas was reluctant, but not for long. "Ciaran's head of security. He wasn't as lucky last night. He was shot in the head and died instantly. No pain. But he just had a daughter born last month. There will be a lot of pain for the living."

Madeline felt a heavy weight on her chest. It was hard to breathe. It was exactly the same heavy weight she felt when Mrs. Hanson mentioned her grief. How could she have been grieving *before* this happened? If that was her psychic ability, it certainly wasn't an ability she wanted to have.

She opened the window for some air, but when the cold wind rushed into the room, she closed it quickly. Someone died in an attempt to rescue her last night. What if the bullet hadn't just been in Ciaran's shoulder but somewhere fatal? Would there be more killing when Zen figured out she had lied to him?

Doctor Thomas looked at Ciaran, who was sleeping like a baby. "Robert and Ciaran were like brothers. Ciaran was really angry at himself last night..."

"At himself? Why not at me? Wasn't it my fault?"

Doctor Thomas stared at Madeline. "Your fault? No! Ciaran was angry at the cowardice, at the actions of those who shot at you from the dark. Robert was his people, his family. I know Ciaran. He'll never let this go. But before he does something about it, he'll need proper rest."

Doctor Thomas packed up his medical bag and shook his head. "I have a feeling that this one is going to be a long haul."

"I was blackmailed for information. They shot at my friend in New York. Now, they're shooting at me, and they ended up killing an innocent man, and almost killed Ciaran. Now I don't have what they want. They might kill my friend tomorrow. It's all my fault," Madeline cried. "It's what I did. It's my bad karma." Her suppressed emotions came out in a storm of tears.

Doctor Thomas held her and stroked her back like a father until the weeping subsided. "I don't know you, Madeline," he said. "But I have a feeling that you're much like Ciaran. So I'll say to you what I've always said to him. You can't take responsibility for other people's actions. You might have done something in the past that you're not proud of. But that does not translate into what happens to others. Robert's death cannot be because of Ciaran's bad karma. Your friend's fate cannot be your fault. Ciaran never listens to me. He's been stubborn since he was a kid. But I hope you'll give my advice some consideration."

Doctor Thomas headed toward the door while Madeline wiped the tears from her face.

"Robert's death came down really hard on Ciaran last night. I didn't need three hours to operate. I just wanted him to rest. I put him on some sleep-inducing drugs. In his normal condition, it would only give him a couple of hours sleep. But given what happened last night, I don't know how long the drug will knock him out. When he comes to, he would have any negative reactions to the anaesthetic. He's allergic to some of the ingredients in the sedative. Because of that, he might throw a tantrum. I'll leave that for you to handle."

"What? Me? No—"

"Yes, you can. No one has ever made him do what he didn't want to do. But you did it today. I am sure one of his little tantrums will be no big deal to you." The doctor smiled and left the room.

20

*M*adeline used Ciaran's phone to ask Lindsay to arrange a new cell phone for her. Within fifteen minutes, the phone was delivered to her door.

She used the new phone to access her email. As predicted, there was a message from Zen. The message read, "We had a date and you stood me up. I'm with Jo now in London. Looking forward to seeing you again. Jo says hi, by the way. She misses you. Also, thanks for sending your friend to pay me a visit. Please send him my regards. Hope to catch up soon. Love from Zen."

He didn't know what she was up to. As long as she didn't talk to him, he wouldn't do anything drastic and wouldn't hurt Jo. She was his only bargaining power.

Madeline sent Stephen an email asking his whereabouts and got an instant message back from his email saying he was still in transit.

She made herself a cup of coffee. The caffeine jolted her system and made her feel a lot better.

The longer she could keep Zen in the dark, the better it would be.

The current issue for her right now was the man lying on her bed. He had taken a bullet for her and had lost a friend for her. Yet they were total strangers.

Madeline went over to the bed, laying her hand on Ciaran's forehead to check his temperature. She was pleased to find that it had gone down. She tucked away a strand of stray hair on his forehead.

She couldn't help it but trace her finger over his lips. He looked so peaceful when he slept. *How many women have kissed those lips?* she wondered and shook her head. *Mental slap.*

She glanced at the clock. It had been four hours since he had fallen asleep—double the amount the doctor expected. "You're not invincible, after all," she said quietly and went back to the desk, using the internet from the phone to do more work.

When she next looked up, it had become dark, and she was famished.

On the bed, Ciaran stirred.

Madeline picked up the hotel phone and ordered dinner. Shortly afterward, Ciaran opened his eyes. She sat at his bedside and smiled. He didn't smile back.

He tried to sit up and was successful on his second attempt.

Ciaran stood from the bed. He swayed with dizziness and leaned against the wall to get his balance. Madeline watched and said nothing. Ciaran grabbed his shirt and walked toward the door.

She stopped him on his way and handed him a couple of pills and a glass of water. "Painkillers. You'll need them."

Ciaran grunted out a thank you and downed the pills. As soon as the water hit his throat, he had only enough time to put down the glass of water before he ran to the bathroom to vomit. When he emerged, he looked pale as a ghost. Doctor Thomas was right, Ciaran hadn't handled the anesthesia well. He put on his shirt and walked toward the door of the room. Remembering his shoes, he walked toward the bed where he had kicked them off earlier.

Dinner arrived just in time to break the awkward silence.

Damn it, she thought. She was usually a lot better at handling situations like this.

"Hungry?" she asked with a smile.

Ciaran shook his head. "I should go back to my room."

"Why don't you have something to eat? Doctor Thomas warned me the anesthesia wouldn't agree with you, but you needed it. He needed to do a proper surgery, and you needed to rest."

Ciaran gave Madeline a blank stare then smiled. "You think I'm grumpy because of that? What else did Doctor Thomas tell you?"

"I'm sorry." She couldn't find more words so she settled with those. "I'm sorry about Robert. I'm very sorry you've lost your friend because of me, Ciaran."

His eyes darkened. "It's not your fault." His voice was so low it was almost a growl. He backed out, nodded a goodbye to Madeline, and strode toward the door.

She grabbed him from behind and held him.

Ciaran paused.

She kissed his shoulder. Jo always said Madeline's sultry voice was her best asset. She might as well utilize it now. She murmured, "I'm so sorry, Ciaran, I truly am."

She felt his body tense up and turned him around. She wasn't sure whether it was what she said or her voice that captured him. She swiped a strand of hair out of his face. Black hair framing the face of a dark angel that was looking down at her. "I think it was my fault," she said.

He reacted, but before he could say anything, her mouth was on his.

Her kiss was persuasive. She could feel his muscles relax a bit. Madeline stopped the kiss. "Somehow you think you're responsible for what happened. You could have ignored the distress signal from my phone. But you didn't. And your friend died because of that."

Ciaran said nothing.

She kissed him again. This time, the kiss was deeper.

"If you don't accept that it was my fault, then you can't say it's your fault either." She looked into his intense gray eyes which were full of inexplicable emotions.

Ciaran slid one hand around her neck and the other at her lower back, almost lifting her off the ground, and kissed her. Strong and hard. Every muscle in her body quivered. Then he released her. "It wasn't your fault. And thank you for the sympathy kiss. I appreciate it." He nodded a goodbye and walked straight out the door.

She paused and stared at the wall.

"What did he just say?" she thought and cursed once she'd realized he had left the room. She stormed out after him. She had to let him know that she would follow him all the way to hell and back. It was her genuine intention, she was . . .

Madeline looked around the long, dark corridor of the fifteenth century castle. She had no idea where Ciaran's room was.

She heard a thud and realized that the door of her room had slammed behind her. Here she was, standing in a castle, wearing a hotel robe and nothing else—and without a key to get back into the room.

21

*S*he tiptoed across the cold tiled floor of the foyer, through a dark, cobblestoned courtyard to the reception desk and asked for a key to get back into her room.

"I'll be fine getting back by myself. Thank you," she said to the concierge who offered to escort her back to her room.

"Very well ma'am. And the King's suite is on the top floor, at the end of the East Wing."

"I'm in the Queen's suite."

"I know, ma'am. But I thought you . . . Oh, I beg your pardon . . ." The concierge nodded a goodbye and scurried out of the reception room as fast as he could while Madeline glared at him.

In his room, Ciaran yanked off his shirt and tossed it onto the bed. He went into the bathroom to try to get a look at his back in the mirror. He peeled the bandage off so hard that the new wound started to bleed again.

He could feel the warm blood trickling down his back. He braced his hands on the basin and closed his eyes to absorb the sensation of it.

Blood had been spilled, and he had to remember that. He'd never forgive those who harmed the people he loved and protected.

He turned on the tap to let the cold water run and then dipped his head in the running water. It didn't stop his blood from boiling with fury. Rage.

There were two people in his life who had seen and condemned his demon. One was his father, and the other one was, ironically, Robert.

He looked at himself in the mirror and could see the fury burning in his eyes, in his soul.

He made medicine, and he was one of the best. Yet his father died with illness before he could say a parting word to him. And Robert? What could he have done to save him from a bullet in the head?

Through his haze of anger, Ciaran heard a knock on the door. He ignored it.

Then came a bang.

He brushed his hair back with his fingers, mumbled some profanity, and, leaving the water and blood to drip down his body, yanked open the door.

In front of him was Madeline in her hotel robe and bare feet—and if he was not mistaken, she was angry. Ciaran braced his arm on the door frame, more to maintain his balance than to appear intimidating.

Madeline had her hands on her hips, and he knew from the set of that beautiful mouth that venom was coming his way.

She looked him up and down, and then her arms flopped down to her sides, and her big brown eyes watered.

Ciaran cursed on the inside. "You're here to give me another round of sympathy kisses? Or did you want to upgrade it to charity sex?" he asked.

Madeline snarled and flew at him. He caught her hand in the air before it hit his face. He could have let it slip and taken the slap. He certainly needed it.

"Leave me alone, Madeline," Ciaran said and retreated inside.

"Oh for pity's sake . . ." Madeline said and shoved him from behind so hard that he almost fell on his face. "You want to bleed to death, go ahead. I'll stand here and watch. But I'm going nowhere." She kicked the door closed.

That was it. His rage was coming on full-force. Ciaran stood up. "Get away from me. I don't want to hurt you."

Madeline kept her stance, blocking the door. Ciaran tried to yank it open to shove her out, but she was a lot stronger than he thought. Or maybe he was a lot weaker. He snarled and walked back into the room. The next thing he knew, a tray of crystal and a decanter flew across the room.

"*Keep your distance from Madeline, or you'll hurt her*" was the only thought in his mind at the moment. His father had been the only person who could help him control his rage. But his father wasn't here.

Now, he had to destroy.

Had to burn.

Had to ruin.

The fury clawed at him. It was a battle between Ciaran and the inanimate objects in the room, with the objects at a distinct disadvantage in the fight. He flew at a cabinet. The cabinet doors cracked and crumbled, one after the other. He crushed the bedside table. He destroyed everything and anything within those four walls. Then he stared at the mirror in the bathroom.

He felt her hands pulling him back from behind. He heard her beg, "Please stop, Ciaran. That's enough."

He fell to the floor, exhausted, and Madeline grabbed a towel to stanch the bleeding from his wound. He got up, staggered to the bed, and dropped face down onto a pillow, letting the fury wash over him.

It was strong and irresistible, and there was nothing he could do about it. Then he felt the warmth of her hands, wiping the blood from his back.

In his near delirium, he reached out and grabbed her hand. "Please stay."

PART II

THE LIES

22

A few hours passed. Madeline still stared at the broken cabinet doors. Lying in the bed in Ciaran's arms, she felt every movement of his body, his energy. Their bodies fit like two pieces of a jigsaw puzzle that were meant to be next to each other.

What would the big picture be like? Her life? His life? And everyone else around them? Would they make a complete picture? Would the other pieces fit to one another?

His heart rate had slowed, the pain that was seeping out of his pores had subdued, and he was once again peacefully asleep. Then he stirred. Madeline propped up on her elbow and rolled away from Ciaran. He opened his eyes, then sprung to his feet.

He looked her up and down. "Madeline, did I ..."

"No. I didn't offer anything, and you didn't take anything."

He let out a sign of relief, and looked around the room, or what was left of it. "Did I hurt you?"

"No. But the furniture wouldn't say the same."

"I asked you to leave. Why didn't you?"

"I thought you were going to turn into a werewolf, so I was curious," she joked. "But I didn't see any paws or fur. Plus, you needed a hugging pillow." She shrugged.

Ciaran stared at her. He shook his head and smiled, but his eyes suggested a laugh on the inside. He tilted her chin up and gazed into her big brown eyes. He rubbed the dimple on her left cheek with his thumb. "I'm sorry for what I said before."

"What did you say? I can't remember."

"I have issues with my anger, Madeline. When the rage comes, I know I'll say and do things I'll regret. It rarely comes but when it does, I don't have any control over it."

"What about an anger management program?"

Ciaran laughed and shook his head. Once the laughter had died, his eyes were once again intense. "The problem isn't psychological."

She should have known. The energy of his fury was strong and primal. It came in waves, and it was so catastrophic that she saw it in her psychic mind. The weight of his grief blasted at her like an explosion. This was what Mrs. Hanson had talked about. It wasn't Robert's death but what came afterward. It wasn't what the death had taken away but what the living carried with them. His grief was contagious, and now she was carrying the same baggage because of her psychic ability.

"Are you hungry?" she asked.

"Starving."

"Well, there's an absolute feast in my room that used to be dinner. But given that it's now three in the morning, I'd call it breakfast. Interested?"

Ciaran tucked a strand of hair behind her ear and kissed her forehead. "I'd love to."

LATER ON, after Madeline told Ciaran everything, he looked at her over the rim of the glass of red wine, contemplating, and smiled to himself.

"What?" Madeline asked.

"Regarding this Stephen character, have you ever considered giving him a chance?"

"To what?"

Ciaran chuckled. "He likes you."

Madeline laughed. "Stephen is harmless!"

"Uhmm!" Ciaran smiled and said nothing, but made some kind of sound that Madeline was pretty sure meant he didn't believe her.

"Don't call Stephen a character—he's a real cop!"

"I see! On that note, would you bring him into this later on?"

"Not if I could help it."

"You meant if '*I*' could help?"

Right. Madeline rolled her eyes. *Egotistical clash of the male species.* She said nothing, just smiled. She thought that would be best.

"Why don't you tell Zen that I'm the White Knight? I can talk to him and make him believe me. Then we can arrange a fake John Dee's tomb for him to dig up. When we've got him snug in our trap, we can politely hand him over to Stephen-the-cop and get Jo out of trouble."

Ciaran plainly played out the strategy out loud while leaning back in his chair, swirling the wine in his glass, and looking as if he was playing a harmless game of Monopoly.

Madeline said nothing. He made it sound so easy. *Jo wasn't the only one good at games*, Madeline thought.

"Don't like the plan?"

"Oh, yes, of course. It's perfect . . . So you don't think there's a real John Dee's tomb?"

"There must be one somewhere, but I'm not interested in his gold, nor do I have any desire to dig up a grave."

"Zen is a computer game fanatic. You think you can make him believe you?"

Ciaran smiled. "I'm an excellent player."

"Have you ever gotten into trouble with the police?"

Ciaran kept sipping this wine.

"Just a rhetorical question," Madeline muttered and smiled, looking at Ciaran. Her prince had returned to his full, magnificent form, post-surgery. "What . . . what are you going to do about Robert?"

His face was unfathomable. "We'll pay his family a visit." He stood up to leave the room.

"I don't think your room is inhabitable at the moment."

"You slept on my bed before!"

"I didn't. But you did."

He nodded. "I'll arrange another room."

She arched an eyebrow. "Another hotel room?"

"We can come back to One Hyde Park. I've got it reserved for a couple of days."

"A couple of days! Don't you have a home? A permanent address?"

He gazed into her eyes. She couldn't read his emotion. Whatever skills she'd obtained in her day job didn't work on him. Her psychic ability gave her nothing but his contagious grief.

"I have a number of addresses. They're permanent because they are mine. But none of them truly qualifies as a home. The apartment at One Hyde Park will do for a week,"

"Then what?"

He shoved his hands into his pockets. "Then we'll see." Then he turned around and walked back to the mess he called his room.

23

The lush carpeted corridor of LeBlanc Pharmaceuticals unfolded before Madeline as she walked alongside Ciaran to his corporate wing. People greeted him, some with a smile, some with words, and some with a courteous nod. But they all had one thing in common—respect. But it wasn't respect based on the power and intimidation that money could buy. Madeline didn't need her psychic ability to be aware of the aura around Ciaran. Something about him was insanely humane but yet distant and powerful at the same time.

She would be scared if she got on his bad side. None of the people here had seen his rage—she was sure of it.

The corridor opened to a reception area at the entrance where a large secretary's desk was located. The secretary was busy on the phone when Ciaran and Madeline entered. At the corner of the room, Madeline saw the most gorgeous dog ever, fast asleep on the carpet on his back with four legs in the air. A bowl of dog food was tucked in the corner, and the most of the food had been spilled all over the carpet. Bags of extra food and toys were scattered all over the floor of the 'dog quarters'.

"What we have here?" Madeline asked.

The puppy woke instantly as Ciaran approached. "He jumped into my car when I was stuck in a traffic jam," Ciaran said as he crouched and reached his hand out to the dog. The puppy dove into Ciaran, wagging his tail in excitement and licking Ciaran's hand. Ciaran frowned at the sign the puppy wore around his neck, which stated: "I am Ciaran's dog. Please treat me nicely."

That would explain all the food and toys the dog had. The smile faded from Ciaran's face. He put the dog down and approached the secretary, who had finished on the phone.

"Ciaran," she greeted.

Ciaran smiled. "Good morning, Lily. This is my friend, Madeline. I have some changes in my schedule. Could you cancel my meetings in France for the next couple of days? Ask Lindsay to address all questions."

"Yes, Ciaran." Lily typed quickly on the computer.

"And take the dog to the pound," Ciaran said, wrapping his arm around Madeline's waist to lead her to his office.

"Excuse me? Ciaran!" Lily asked.

Ciaran stopped on the way and turned around, "I said, take the dog to the pound. I don't want to see it anymore."

Lily's eyes teared up. "Yes, Ciaran."

When the office door had closed behind him, Ciaran went to the desk and made a call. Madeline sat down in a chair and waited. Ciaran finished the call.

"Would you like something to drink? I've arranged a car. We can go to Robert's and then drop by Mortlake to visit Mrs. Hanson."

Then he saw the look on Madeline's face. "What, Madeline?"

"If you want Lily to adopt the dog, you should just ask her. I'm sure she will."

Ciaran sat down at this desk. He didn't smile, but his eyes twinkled.

He's intrigued. Madeline smiled and patted herself on the back.

"I prefer flexibility." He smiled now and stood up from his chair to move around to the other side of his desk. Her stomach quivered and spasmed at an alarming level. Then he stopped on his way.

The computer screen on his desk flashed and turned itself on. He frowned. Madeline stood up, came around to where he was, and looked at the monitor. The screen was filled with static symbols. It flashed once, twice, and then some text appeared. *"It's time, Ciaran. The enemies are nearby."* Then the screen flashed again and turned itself off.

Ciaran dove at the keyboard and typed frantically. For a while, he sank into his work and didn't look up once. Madeline sat in the chair, waiting. Then he stopped, turned it off, and stared at the blank screen.

"Hacker?" Madeline asked.

He shook his head.

"So it's internal then?"

He swivelled his chair around, looking at her. His intense gray eyes were darkened, but he said nothing.

"Police?" Madeline guessed. "Spy? Cyber terrorist? Fanatic? Serial killer?" Madeline had her hands on her hips. "Vampire? Witch? Werewolf? Angel? Or demon? Come on, Ciaran!"

Ciaran gazed at the computer screen. "Extraterrestrial," he said.

"It's . . . it's from aliens?"

Ciaran approached the cabinet at corner of the room and opened it. He drew out a decanter of scotch, and poured it into a crystal glass. He gestured to ask if Madeline wanted some. She shook her head.

"You knew this? You weren't surprised?" she asked.

Ciaran sipped the spirits and stared out the window.

"You said your rage wasn't psychological. Are you—?"

"No, I'm human, if that's what you're asking."

Madeline nodded. "Why did the aliens say I'm your enemy?" She raised her voice.

"What? No. They weren't referring to you." Ciaran put the glass down and walked around the desk to approach Madeline.

"It has to be me. Someone gave me a mysterious note. Then I

ran into you. Then you got shot, and Robert got killed. Disaster. I can only bring you disaster." A tear rolled down her face. "I have to leave."

Ciaran blocked her at the door. He grabbed her shoulders and directed her back inside. He lifted her and sat her on his desk. Then he embraced her, hard. His arms were like a vice—there was no way she could wriggle her way out of his grasp. For a while, she could feel his muscles vibrating along with her emotions.

Then he released her. He kissed her forehead, lifted her chin up, and looked into her eyes. "You're not my enemy, Madeline. I have many of them, and you're not on the list."

"I lied to you about the game hacking."

He snorted. "You're an amateur when it comes to lying, Madeline. I trust you, and I don't trust people easily."

"Why?"

"Because no one that I've taken to One Hyde Park before has ever noticed I don't have a TV, and that the apartment wasn't my home."

She smiled.

"Not a single woman before you has ever noticed that the meals I served them were takeout. All they saw in that apartment was the shine and the attraction of money and power."

She laughed. "Exactly how many girls have you taken there?"

He smiled. "And none of them have ever cared how many others I've taken there." He kissed her lips lightly. "You know very well I could have forced myself on you last night. You know I could have done the unthinkable. Yet you stayed with me."

He deepened their kiss, and her head started to spin. She spoke, her breath quickening. "Because you asked me . . ."

He roamed his hands up and down her arms. "What else?"

"You needed a hugging pillow . . ."

His hands were under her blouse. She pulled at his shirt, untucking it from his waist. "What else?" he asked.

"Because . . . you let a puppy into your car!"

He stopped kissing her and started laughing. When his

laughter finally subsided to chuckles, he said, "I have many secrets, Madeline. A lot of them you're better off not knowing. But if any of my secrets got you tangled up in my mess, I won't let anything happen to you." He tucked a stray hair behind her ear and rubbed his thumb on her dimple.

"So if all this wasn't because of your secrets, I'll be just another girl you took into your luxurious apartment?" She hopped down to the floor.

He grabbed her and put her back up on the desk.

"Without my mess, I'm sure I don't have anything to hold you, Madeline."

She frowned.

"You're a very complicated woman."

"It comes with the job." She saw his eyes twinkle again.

"I won't let anything happen to you," he repeated.

"Same goes for me." She hopped off his desk once again and strode toward the door. She didn't look back, but she knew she had made his eyes twinkle again. She hadn't intended to do that to impress him. But somehow, there was a rhythm in this thought and his emotion that she could tap into.

She felt him. And somehow, she knew he felt her, too.

24

The town was charming, but she just felt something wrong was about to crash down on Ciaran and her. Ciaran parked his car in the yard of a cottage in Stow-on-the-Wold. The house was as cozy and charming as the ancient town in which it was located. Ciaran pushed the door open and walked straight into the house.

This used to be his home! Madeline thought.

A woman stormed out from the side room. She clung to Ciaran and sobbed. Ciaran embraced her and murmured something that Madeline knew was more than typical condolences. There was no formality between them. He held the woman tightly and said nothing until her weeping abated.

"This is my friend, Madeline Roux. Laurent Chandler, Robert's wife." Laurent Chandler was in her late thirties and quietly attractive.

"I'm very sorry for your loss, Mrs. Chandler."

Laurent smiled. "Laurent, it is! Would you like a cup of tea?"

Laurent led them to the room at the back of the house. The room was warm with candlelight. The winter sun didn't shed much light into the room, particularly on a grim day like this. Robert's coffin lay in the middle, and his picture stood quietly on a stand next to it. Robert Chandler was a sturdy looking man in his early forties. He looked formidable with a strong face, brown hair, and honest eyes. Ciaran stood still, looking at the picture. Beneath his calm expression was the unspeakable pain that Madeline understood.

Laurent came into the room with the baby in her arms. She gave her to Ciaran. He held the baby gently, kissing her forehead as if she would break like crystal. Then he gave the baby back to Laurent.

"Were you comfortable with Lindsay's arrangements?" Ciaran asked.

Laurent looked at Ciaran. Her eyes were dry now and filled with the affection of a sister. "That was all Robert would have wished for. He'd be pleased. Doctor Thomas put through an official record of accidental death. Everything was handled smoothly. Thank you."

"You thank me for this?"

"Yes. And Robert would thank you for what you've done for us."

"I'll find the answer, Laurent. I will find the answer for all of this."

"Please don't mix it with vengeance, Ciaran. Robert's death was part of the job he took on with you."

"He had no such duty, Laurent. There is no money in the world that could give his girl back her father, give you back your husband ... and me ... back my friend. Had I known ..."

"You didn't know, Ciaran. You didn't know, and let's keep it at that."

Laurent looked at Madeline. Madeline couldn't understand how a newly grieving widow could have had such warmth in her eyes. *If she knew it was me who had caused Ciaran to go to Fosse Way—and hence the death of her husband—would she still have that warmth in her eyes right now?*

"Ciaran," Laurent continued, "Robert would have been happy to see you open up for a new life. Ten years is enough to forgive."

"But not enough to forget, Laurent. Never enough," Ciaran growled and sounded as if he didn't care the conversation to go further in that direction.

Just before Ciaran and Madeline left, she saw the blue dots hovering in the air. She wasn't sure whether they hovered around her, Ciaran, Laurent, or the coffin.

She hadn't told Ciaran about her psychic ability. *Why were the blue dots hovering here?* Madeline shook her head, trying to will the thought out of her head.

"What's the matter, Madeline?"

"Huh?" she asked and realized they had left the house and now were standing in front of Ciaran's car. She didn't know where to begin to tell Ciaran about the blue dots.

Whenever she saw the blue dots, something unfortunate would happen.

Just let it slide for now, she thought, shook her head, and got into the car.

25

*T*he street was just the same as it was when Madeline had last seen it. Ciaran parked a block away from Mrs. Hanson's cottage. Madeline knew he could park right at the front, but she had trained herself not to ask questions.

As soon as they entered the front yard of the cottage, Mrs. Hanson appeared mysteriously on the doorstep. Had she known they were coming?

"It's good to see you again, Ciaran. What did this old woman do to deserve a visit?"

She stepped down from the steps to the lawn. Her weird earrings jingled, making an unpleasant sound with her every step. Madeline wished it would stop as it made her head ring.

The woman looked at Madeline. "I'm glad to see you again, too!"

"You know why we're here, Mrs. Hanson. I know you're disappointed to see her alive."

"I don't know what you're talking about, Ciaran. This young lady was just here asking for directions a couple of days ago. She must have found what she wanted, given my instructions. Aren't you grateful for my help, Madeline?"

"How do you know my name? I didn't introduce myself."

Madeline remembered the jingle of Mrs. Hanson's earrings now. She had heard that sound when she'd hallucinated about the Roman soldiers. They were the sounds that made her head ring, her eyes droop, and ended up with her driving into the walls.

Madeline grabbed Ciaran's arm, pulling him backward. "Her earrings, the sound of her earrings is what caused my hallucination at the walls. Don't listen to it."

Mrs. Hanson grinned widely, showing her black and rotting teeth.

"They contacted you, didn't they Mrs. Hanson? They've made an appearance." Ciaran advanced on the woman.

Mrs. Hanson grunted out her words. "Greedy people are supposed to die!"

"You don't care about those greedy people. I know what you want. You're as greedy as they are. They killed my friend. Tell me where they are."

The woman laughed. "If I don't tell you, what will you do? Kill this old woman? So much for the gentlemen I used to know? And all that because of this *bitch*?"

"Don't call her names!" Ciaran growled. "Tell me where they are, and I'll leave you in peace."

Mrs. Hanson laughed—a crooked laugh that pulled at the muscles on her face and made it look as if she was in pain. "You think you can blackmail me?"

"I don't think it. I do it. I know where you get the supplies to make your evil drugs. I can stop it right now. With one phone call."

"Don't you dare!" The woman flew at Ciaran and shoved him backward. Madeline darted in front of him and shoved the woman away.

She gave the old woman a stern stare. "He wouldn't hit a woman, but I wouldn't mind a cat fight."

"Try me!" she screamed, but the scream came out more like a

croak. She swung her head so that her earrings jingled loudly. Madeline grabbed her ears and stepped back.

Mrs. Hanson shook her arms so that the bells dangling on her beaded wristbands sang as well. The sound from the earrings was the worst, though. Mrs. Hanson looked as if she was dancing.

Ciaran stepped in front of Madeline. "Go to the car and wait for me there," he directed.

"No."

"Go, Madeline!"

Mrs. Hanson swung her earrings more violently. Madeline thought her nose and ears would bleed. She heard Mrs. Hanson laughing. Her laugh was loud now, and the ringing noise pierced her brain like a well-sharpened knife. Thousands of knives. Madeline heard Ciaran calling to her, asking her to leave. She could feel him grabbing her, pulling her away.

The noise was pounding in her head.

No, she wouldn't run. Not from an old woman with weird earrings. The old woman had killed Robert. His blood was on her hands, as well as on Madeline's. In her mind, Madeline saw Robert's widow and his orphan. She remembered now what happened at Fosse Way. What she had seen were not Roman soldiers. They were men with rifles wearing masks. They had bells on their rifles, and clothes that made the same sound.

Madeline shrugged off Ciaran's grip and rushed toward the old woman. She grabbed her dangling earrings and pulled hard. The sound stopped. The woman screamed in pain as blood poured out of her torn ear lobes. Then the old woman grunted, and the sound coming out of her mouth was deep and demonic.

She pulled a knife from beneath her clothing and ran back toward Madeline.

Seeing the flash of the knife, Madeline stepped back, and Ciaran darted toward her from behind. Madeline tripped on a small stone, tumbled, and fell on her back. The old woman growled and jumped on top of Madeline, arcing the knife up in the air and preparing to stab downward.

Ciaran grabbed the old woman's hand. The old woman looked at him as if she had been waiting for just that moment. She didn't jerk her hand out of Ciaran's. It happened in front of Madeline's eyes as if it were a slow-motion movie. The old woman turned the knife and pulled it toward herself, along with Ciaran's hand.

She stabbed the knife deep into her chest.

From the back, Shaun, the gardener, walked out and saw Ciaran's hand still on the hilt of the knife which had been plunged into Mrs. Hanson's body.

"Oh, God! Oh, my God! Mrs. Hanson!" He stumbled backward, fell, and then stood up and ran.

Madeline rolled away. Mrs. Hanson lay on the ground, grinning ghoulishly back at Madeline and Ciaran. She reached her hand up, grabbed Ciaran's shirt, and pulled him down.

"Blood on your hands. Blood in your soul. I curse you, Ciaran . . . for the young soul that died for you . . . It's time. The enemies are coming . . ."

The old woman stared into nothing. Dead eyes.

Ciaran yanked himself free of the woman's grip. Then he just stood there, looking incredulously at the blood on his hands.

26

"*A*re you okay?" Ciaran held Madeline's shoulders and looked into her eyes while they waited for the elevator in the foyer of One Hyde Park. "You were very quiet on the way back."

She could give him a white lie to get this over and done with, but he had figured out she was lousy in that regard. And those intense gray eyes were so filled with genuine concern and emotion that she would feel like a bitch lying to him.

"Well, it's not every day that I see someone die in front of me. You were shakier than me, though. I pulled *you* from the scene, remember?" She sighed. *I lied to him anyway*, she thought.

He lifted her chin. "On the contrary, you were *too* steady for the situation. And that's what I'm concerned about."

"Hey!" She pushed his hand away. "You think I eat people for breakfast?" She put her hands defensively on her hips. *Damn, should have known he would see that.*

"One day, you'll have to tell me about what happened to you, Madeline."

"Who the hell do you think you are?"

He shrugged.

"My personal life is none of your business." She jabbed a finger at his shoulder.

Ciaran nodded. "Someone is using you to get to me. That's my business, and I'm entitled to know what's relevant. If you don't want me to know about your past, I won't ask again."

She nodded and looked away.

"Lindsay will have a car picking us up in ten minutes. We're going to the police station to give information as witnesses."

"These police, are they yours?"

Ciaran chuckled. "If you mean do they live in our pocket, no. Detective Adamson is a good friend of Lindsay's. We don't bribe, Madeline."

"Why did Mrs. Hanson kill herself? Just for a chance to frame us?"

"It's not her we talked to. Remember how I threatened to cut her supplies with a phone call?"

Madeline nodded.

"I did that to her ten years ago. She no longer makes medicines that require those supplies. So what's running in her head now is like an old tape recorder of behaviour and thought patterns."

Madeline's eyes widened. "You knew it back there? You were testing her?"

"That used to be a woman. But it's not anymore, I'm afraid."

"What? She was abducted by aliens, and they replaced her human brain with a robotic one?"

Ciaran chuckled and shook his head.

"She was possessed by a demon of her past?"

Ciaran grinned. "You have a very unusual thought process, Madeline."

"So tell me!"

"You don't want me to know your stories, so you don't get to know mine."

Damn, Madeline cursed silently.

The elevator opened. At the same time, Madeline's phone buzzed. She glanced at the screen. Unknown ID.

Ciaran nodded. She picked up, and Zen's voice oozed out from the other end of the line, "Hello, old friend. Remember me?"

Ciaran shook his head.

"Look, Zen, I'm in the middle of something right now. Call me back later, okay?" She hung up. Then she saw the look on Ciaran's face. "What?"

"You're quite good dealing with criminal minds." He smiled. "I'm impressed."

"It comes with the job," she muttered. They walked into the elevator and ignored the buzzing phone.

MADELINE AND CIARAN entered the grand hallway of the apartment to find a man standing there with his back to Madeline and Ciaran. He was looking out the window, down to the city.

"I thought you were in Australia," Ciaran said.

The man turned around. He was maybe an inch or so shorter than Ciaran, but they shared so many similarities that it didn't take much thought for Madeline to guess they were brothers.

"I was. I'm sorry, I didn't bring home any kangaroos or boomerangs as souvenirs. Plus, I went back to Spain last week, and then to Rome, and so forth . . ."

"I must have lost track of your extensive travel."

The man winked at Madeline. "So as I've heard, this must be the lady, Madeline Roux!"

"I'm no lady, but you've got the name right. You're Ciaran's brother?"

"I hope he's said nice things about me."

"If you assume nothing is a nice thing," Ciaran responded. "This is Tadgh, my brother. I'm sure you could tell. Apart from some physical similarities, I don't believe we have much in common."

"Oh, come on, Ciaran. We share our parents. Isn't that enough?"

Tadgh came forward, took Madeline's hand in his, and kissed her knuckles before she could react. Then he rushed forward quickly and gave Ciaran a bear hug that took him totally by surprise.

Apparently embarrassed, Ciaran shoved Tadgh aside, saying, "Grow up."

Tadgh turned to Madeline. "I took off without saying goodbye to him, so he's a bit testy at the moment."

Madeline merely smiled.

"Mother would be very pleased to see you," Ciaran said.

"I'm sure of it. I'm her favorite. But I'd like to flop on the couch here for a couple of days before I head to Dublin. That is, if it's okay with you?"

"Don't even ask," Ciaran responded sarcastically. "Tadgh, Madeline and I have to run. But before we do, what do you want, really, apart from my couch?"

Tadgh looked at Madeline.

Ciaran said, "She's in. So you can spill it. What is it that you want?"

"In? How far in?" Tadgh asked.

"All the way in," Madeline responded. *Too fast, damn it,* she thought, judging by Ciaran's reaction—or lack thereof.

Tadgh looked at Ciaran for a confirmation, but nothing came from him. "I've heard about Robert."

"If that's your main concern, you know where they live. Pay them a visit."

"I saw a record of an entry at Mon Ciel lab." Tadgh stared at Ciaran.

"It was me. Since when do you read security reports?"

"You haven't used it for years. What could you possibly do in that rusty old lab except dig up your dead and buried problems?"

"You have no say in this. Get back to your travel extravaganza and leave the family business to those who are responsible," Ciaran snarled.

Tadgh laughed and spoke to Madeline, "You see how lucky I am to have this big brother to take care of everything!"

"Then leave if you have a problem," Ciaran growled. His migraine was coming back in waves.

Tadgh flopped onto the couch and stretched his arms out. "The thing is, Madeline, he's only good ninety-nine percent of the time. When it's time for the other one percent to take charge, he's hopeless."

Ciaran snatched Tadgh off the couch and threw him to the wall. A framed painting nearby dropped on the floor, and glass shattered everywhere.

"The computer said, '*It's time*,'" Madeline said.

"Madeline!" Ciaran growled.

Tadgh narrowed his eyes. "Say again, Madeline?"

"Madeline . . ." Ciaran objected, but his vision blurred with the headache. He strode toward the medicine cabinet to take his painkillers.

Seizing the opportunity, Madeline spilled, "The computer in Ciaran's office turned itself on and said, '*It's time, Ciaran. Enemies are nearby.*' Ciaran said Mrs. Hanson was replaying information in her dialogue that was ten years old—without even knowing it. And she stabbed herself to frame us."

Ciaran had his eyes closed and was bracing his hands on the bench, waiting for the medication to take effect. Beads of sweat ran down his forehead. He said nothing.

"You're going back to Mon Ceil, Ciaran," Tadgh growled.

Ciaran opened his eyes. "I don't need you to tell me what to do."

"I don't know what and where Mon Ciel is, but I have a problem here. Before my friend is safe and sound, I can't go anywhere" Madeline said.

"They kidnapped her friend and used her to get to me," Ciaran said.

"Oh, I see, they've gotten smarter!" Tadgh said.

"You're saying my friend's kidnapping was just a manipulation to get to you? You knew the whole time? And my friend's life is just a pawn for someone to get in touch with your family?" Madeline waved her arms in the air, frustrated. "For what? I don't care how important your family is. Jo is everything to me. I'm done with this." Madeline turned on her heel and strode toward the door.

Ciaran darted toward her and grabbed her arm. "I didn't know at the beginning, Madeline. You have to trust me."

"You don't trust anyone. Why should I trust you?"

"My family has a lot at stake here. I understand your friend is important and I don't take her kidnapping lightly. But I do think that there is a connection between that and our family business. If you stay with me, we can work things out."

Madeline hesitated.

"You don't have anything to give Zen, and he'll be calling back any minute!"

"You're not lying to me?"

"No. And we have to go to the police station now."

Madeline nodded. Ciaran pulled Madeline into his arms and embraced her. In the background, Tadgh rolled his eyes.

27

*C*iaran glanced quickly at Madeline on the passenger side of the car. She looked calm and collected. Her hand slid inside her handbag. He shook his head and reached over, gently taking the phone from her hand.

"We'll sort this out and get Jo back, Madeline."

"I know." She smiled at him, but the smile didn't quite reach her eyes.

"Thank you for your help at the police station." Ciaran tried to break the silence.

"I didn't really do anything. You had everything organized. Even if the gardener had gone to the police, he wouldn't have had a leg to stand on."

Ciaran smiled. "It's not me. Lindsay had it organized."

Madeline nodded and remained silent. She didn't seem to want to talk any further. The closer to the time Zen would call, the more Ciaran saw her wits leaving her.

He looked at the road. The business traffic was heading toward the city while they were going in the opposite direction. The traffic movement was a metaphor for his life and his family—always against the odds.

Very soon, he'd open his home to Madeline. He barely knew her, but he couldn't deny the comfort he felt when he was around her. Still, he didn't need comfort, didn't need safety, and didn't need anyone's protection. Hell, he'd let someone into his comfort zone once, and it had been a mistake he'd sworn he would never repeat.

For now, Madeline was a victim, tangled in the mess he'd created in the past. So protecting her was a mission. Happy with his reasoning, he pressed the accelerator.

The phone rang.

"Let it ring a few times," Ciaran said quickly. He veered to the side of the road and parked. Then he signaled.

He could see the screen flash on, and he cursed. He should have turned that video function off. Jo's face was pressed against the screen at first, and then she was pulled back a bit by her hair, revealing a large bruise on her forehead and a black eye. She was barely conscious.

Ciaran felt his blood boil, and he saw that Madeline had lost it. Her hands shook, her lips trembled, and tears streamed down her face. She was in no condition to negotiate.

Ciaran grabbed the phone, pointed it to the floor, and twisted it around quickly to disorient the view at the other end. Then he turned the video off.

Zen's voice came across. "Hello, sweet pea."

"Who's that?" Ciaran cleared his throat.

Zen's voice came across reluctantly. "Uhmm . . . Maddie . . . are you there?"

"She's busy. Who are you?"

"I need to talk to Madeline."

"Why?" Ciaran snapped.

"Who the fuck are you?" Zen snarled.

Ciaran cut off the call.

Zen immediately called back. Ciaran picked up, "This is our

company's phone. One more harassing call to Madeline, and I'll hand you over to the police."

"Harassment? I ain't harassing anyone. She promised me something. We had a deal. If I don't get to talk to her, she'll regret it."

"Who are you?"

There was a pause. "Zen."

"Ahhh, the idiot who wanted to talk to White Knight."

"Who am I talking to?"

"Ciaran."

"Ciaran LeBlanc? Are you fucking with me?"

Ciaran cut off the phone again. Zen called back. Ciaran let it ring a few times before picking it up. "Last chance, Zen. What do you want?"

"I want to talk to White Knight."

"Talking."

"I want White Knight, the avatar in hologames."

"What part of 'I am talking' don't you understand?"

"I can't believe . . ."

"You're wasting my time. You had a deal with Madeline, not with me. If you have White Knight, what's in it for me?"

"I didn't know I'd be dealing with you. I have her little friend with me. If Madeline is with you as she claimed, then her concern should be your concern."

"That's a long shot, but go ahead."

"Well, if you *are* White Knight, then you know how to complete the other half of the program Jo developed. There is an artifact buried with John Dee. A crucifix. I want that, too. If I have those two things, then Madeline will get her little friend back."

"If that's all you want, call me back tomorrow. I'll let you know the location of John Dee's tomb."

"Why can't you tell me now?"

"I don't think a scumbag like you would honor your promises. Call me tomorrow. We'll work out a place for an exchange. We get Jo back, and you get the artifact."

"I . . ."

"You don't have a choice, Zen. As you can see, there's nothing in this for me."

"All right. I'll call you back tomorrow." Then there was the sound of a gun shot from the other end of the line. Madeline nearly passed out. She opened the car door and got out. "Hear that?" Zen taunted. "That's a real gun. Next time, I'll be aiming it at Jo's head. So don't fool around, Ciaran."

"Fuck you, Zen." Ciaran cut off the call. He opened a small compartment below the dashboard and pulled out a small box. Tipping a couple of pills onto his hand and grabbing a bottle of water, he rushed out after Madeline.

She was walking aimlessly at the shoulder of the highway. Ciaran darted forward, pulling her back and into his arms. Her body was cold, she looked at him blankly. She was going into shock. He knew the symptoms too well. She wriggled from his arms, but he was squeezing her too tight for her to break free.

"Shhhh, listen to me, Madeline. Look at me, please."

"Is Jo dead?"

"No."

"She's dead, isn't she? It's my fault."

"Don't talk. Listen to me."

"Gunshot . . . he shot her. . . I heard it . . ." She shoved Ciaran away.

He grabbed her again and shoved the pills into her mouth. He held her tight and pushed the water bottle into her mouth. "Drink this." She wriggled. "Drink, and I'll let you go." She swallowed. Then he swept her off her feet and carried her back to the car. He put her in the back seat and climbed in.

Madeline opened the car door on the other side, trying to get out. Ciaran pulled her back in and held her in his arms. After struggling for a while without success, she started to sob. Ciaran held her and rocked. And her weeping came like a storm.

Then she lay on his lap, looking up at him and grinning foolishly. "Ciaran LeBlanc." Her sultry voice was slurred with drugs. She touched his face. "Do you know how beautiful you are?"

"People don't normally refer to a man as beautiful, but I'll take that as a compliment."

She grinned. "Do you know how many men I've been with?"

"No, I don't."

"I don't have enough fingers and toes to count them."

He smiled at her as she played with his thick, dark hair.

"Do you mind?"

"Mind what?"

"That I've been with many men."

"No." He chuckled. "No, Madeline. You're a beautiful woman. It's only natural that men admire you."

She was giddy. "Got ya . . . Got ya . . ." Then her laughter slipped away. Her eyes were dreamy as she traced her fingertip across his Adam's apple, along his throat, and down his chest. "I haven't really been with that many men. I wasn't trying to be selective or anything. I've just never been drawn to anyone . . ." Her hand was on his chest now, circling, teasing. "I've never met anyone as powerful as you are."

His breath quickened and his heart skipped a beat.

"Do you know you have that power? You draw people in. Not just women. Everyone. People just love you."

"No, I don't think I have such power, Madeline."

"How many women have you been with?"

"Can you guess?"

"Many, many, many . . ." She almost sang it. Then she cupped his face in her hands. "I'd be surprised if it's not many . . ."

He looked into her big brown eyes. "Not many," he said.

She reached up and pulled him down so he lay on his back. She traced his jawline with her fingers. "You look like a dark angel, Ciaran. The moment I saw you at the park, I wanted to taste these lips." She rubbed her thumb on his lips, parting them. He bit her thumb and sucked. She yelped, delirious, and devoured his mouth with hers. Her hands traveled down his body.

He felt like he was going to explode. The blood was coursing furiously through his veins. He saw stars in his eyes. His body was tensed like a bow at a maximum stretch.

She wouldn't let go, wouldn't ease off. Her passion attacked his body without mercy. Her tenacity occupied every corner of his mind. She consumed every life force he could summon. Her energy pulsed into him like tidal waves and withdrew like a strong current.

In a very short moment, they were going to become one. They were going to invade each other's lives.

Yet he barely knew her.

He pushed her up then propped himself up, still breathing heavily. "I can't do this to you. We can't do it, here and now. You're doped up with the medicine I gave you, Madeline."

"Why not?" she murmured sleepily. He brushed the hair back from her face and kissed her forehead as she fell asleep. Then he climbed into the driver's seat and drove her home to the mansion at Henley-on-Thames, Oxfordshire.

28

The sound of the tires rolling over the gravel on the long driveway woke Madeline. She sat up in the back seat and beheld the magnificence of Mon Ciel. It was a palace—Ciaran's home. She didn't need an introduction to know where she was and what she was seeing. This place was a world in itself—separated from the outside world.

It was more than a castle, Madeline thought. This palace had the warm feeling of a home. This was the place that Ciaran called home, the place that he would not share with outsiders. But wasn't he sharing it with her by bringing her here, though? *Don't flatter yourself,* she thought. Who knew how many women had shared his bed in this palace?

She rubbed her forehead. Her head was pounding. As Ciaran stopped the car, Madeline recalled what had happened before. She stormed out of the car.

As quick as a cat, Ciaran was out of the driver's seat and after her.

"Jo?" Madeline asked.

"She's fine. Fine for now. The gun shot was just a warning. Zen didn't shoot Jo. He'll call again tomorrow." Ciaran spoke as quickly as he could.

Madeline stared at him. Then she nodded. "Oh. That's all right then. We'll have another night to prepare."

He smiled.

"Is this your home?"

Ciaran nodded. He wrapped his arm around her waist to guide her inside.

"Why was I sleeping in the back seat of the car?"

"You were tired," Ciaran explained. "The back seat is more comfortable than the front seat."

She frowned. "I remember you in the back seat as well?"

"Then who was driving?"

"Right. You're right. I must have been hallucinating. The back seat of your car is very comfortable."

"Is that so? I'll have to try it out sometime." He grinned and then yelped as she poked his side.

It surprised her that Ciaran seemed to have no live-in staff to maintain such an enormous place.

"Be careful when you walk around. There are security cameras everywhere."

She frowned and glanced around. "Where?"

Ciaran smiled. "You won't see them, but they see your every movement."

She figured that behind the antique interior made up of endless expanses of polished wood, glass, stone, and sculptures, there was an ultra-modern technology that controlled everything—from light switches to security doors.

There was not a trace of violence, death, or sorrow in this place, Madeline noticed. Unlike what Madeline had seen in other castles, towers, and even in churches, the paintings, artwork, sculptures, and tapestries in this palace did not bear a hint of blood, weapons, war, or any historical or religious activities involving blood and sacrifices.

This was a *home*.

"There are two parts of the house," Ciaran explained at they stood at the junction of two marble corridors. "The old section used to be a castle, and the new part my father added when we moved in."

"You were born here?"

He nodded and gestured toward the left wing. "In the new part of the house." Before they headed up the set of stairs, Madeline saw a group of blue dots hovering at the corridor Ciaran had referred to as the old part.

A hollow female voice echoed in the air, "Ciaran!"

Madeline turned to look toward the dots.

"Ciaran, you're home! Welcome home!" She heard the voice again from the same direction.

Noticing Madeline had stopped walking, Ciaran turned around. "There are rooms in the old wing, but they're not as nice as those in the new one."

"Did you hear that?" she asked.

"Hear what?"

Madeline looked again. The blue dots had disappeared. "Never mind," she said and followed Ciaran up the stairs.

29

*M*adeline buried her bare feet in the lush carpet. She loved the softness and texture of the carpet on the soles of her feet. She smiled at the sunshine and went over to the window. In front of her was the endless lawn of the magnificent Mon Ciel. She felt like a princess in a castle. Except she wasn't waiting for a prince to climb up the tower to rescue her. Her prince was going to knock on her door any minute.

There was a knock on the door.

Ciaran stood leaning against the door frame, smiling. *The LeBlancs trademark their eyes and smiles,* Madeline thought. She had seen the same qualities in Tadgh. Striking eyes and warm smiles.

"I'm afraid I can't arrange room service," he told her. "If you want breakfast, you'll have to come downstairs with me," he said.

"All right. Let me put some clothes on." She closed the door.

As soon as she had dropped her robe to the floor, a cold wedge of air brushed over her body. Blue dots appeared in a flock. They swirled around her body, moving up and down.

Madeline froze. She heard the humming sound and the singsong voice of the woman who had called Ciaran last night.

Don't freak out. She could see people's minds, their thoughts. That meant someone with some sort of connection to her is looking at her body right now.

She put her clothes on. The flock of blue dots hovered toward a side door tucked at the corner.

"You know what, people in movies would probably follow you to their death. But I'm not that stupid. You have a good day!"

She strode to the door, opened it, and smiled at Ciaran.

"What is that?" Ciaran asked.

"What is what?"

"The brilliant smile on your face."

"Apparently I'm in a very good mood."

UNLIKE WHAT SHE HAD EXPECTED, the house was quiet. In fact, no one seemed to be around. In a large kitchen that opened onto a back garden, there was no breakfast waiting for them.

Ciaran turned on the coffee machine. He opened the cabinet to search for food. Sensing Madeline's confusion, he grinned. "I'd told my staff not to stock any food. But we might get lucky and find something."

Madeline nodded. "So you don't hang around here much."

"I used to. I grew up here." He pointed to a headless statue of something looking like a woman in the garden. "You can see my mark right there!"

"You beheaded the woman!"

"It was the Goddess of Kindness. I experimented with some explosive compound. I didn't know it would be such a success! My father was less than happy about it. He left the statue there to remind me of my sin."

"How old were you when you committed such a crime?"

"Very young. Way before school age. I was home schooled in my early years, and even at that age, I was reading advanced chemistry books."

So you didn't actually have a childhood, Madeline mused. *Where is his family now? Where is his father?* Madeline had the feeling Ciaran's father had passed away, but her reporter instincts told her that trying to dig for more information on that would be a deal breaker. When Ciaran was ready, he would tell her.

"That looks promising," Madeline commented, scanning a couple of boxes of something that appeared to be breakfast cereal.

Ciaran looked at the box. "Promising, indeed. And still within the use-by date!"

"Even if it was expired, I'd risk my life. I'm starving!"

"Oh, here you are! Oh, my dearest boy!" A cheery voice echoed in from the side door.

Ciaran dropped the cereal boxes on the bench and rushed toward the voice. An elderly woman with two armfuls of bags stood in the doorway.

Ciaran grabbed the bags, put them on the floor, and hugged the woman tightly, almost lifting her off the floor. "Mrs. Rutherford. It's so good to see you. You look wonderful!"

"Let me take a look at you!" She cupped Ciaran's face. "You look so pale. Doctor Thomas said you were injured. He was so right to worry about you. What have you done to yourself? And now, you're about to eat this stale food." Mrs. Rutherford's voice trailed off when she saw Madeline. "You're not going to force your very pretty friend here to have breakfast-in-a-box, are you?"

"This is Madeline Roux. She's a reporter from New York. Boxed meals are quite normal in her line of work."

"You're making too big of an assumption, Ciaran. I have my own chef. Ask my co-editor," Madeline corrected him.

"A reporter! You must be smart, just like—"

"Mrs. Rutherford . . ." Ciaran cut in.

"Uhmm . . ." She caught herself. "No one is going to have any meal in any box in *my* kitchen!" Mrs. Rutherford put the bags on the counter and started to unpack eggs, butter, orange juice, milk, and other assorted grocery items.

"You don't have to do this. We'll only be here very briefly,"

Ciaran said.

"I have to use all the chances that I have to cook for you! When Lindsay and the security boy told me you were here, I was so happy, Ciaran. I don't care how short your stay is, when you're here, you eat my food."

For a moment, Madeline saw Ciaran as a nine-year-old boy under Mrs. Rutherford's care. She envied him, then felt guilty about it. She distracted herself with a cup of black coffee.

They heard the buzz of the front door and some high-heeled footsteps.

Mrs. Rutherford looked disappointed, as if she might not have a chance to feed Ciaran after all. Ciaran's eyes darkened as if he knew what was coming.

"How about some orange juice to please this old woman?"

Ciaran took the glass from Mrs. Rutherford and drained the contents. He kissed her lightly on the cheek and then left the kitchen.

Madeline followed him. When she passed Mrs. Rutherford, the old woman murmured to her, "I can tell he likes you very much. He's never brought anyone else home since . . ."

Madeline arched an eyebrow, waiting.

"But it's not my tale to tell. He's a very good man, Madeline. He doesn't deserve to be hurt."

"Ciaran is a man with strong will. I can't protect him. But I can promise, if he gets hurt, it won't be on my account."

Mrs. Rutherford nodded.

"I envy him for having you, Mrs. Rutherford." Madeline left the kitchen.

"Madeline!" Mrs. Rutherford called from behind her.

She turned around. "Yes."

"... The LeBlancs are good people..."

"I'm not judging."

The old woman looked as if she wanted to say a lot more, but decided not to. Madeline gave her a courtesy nod and followed Ciaran.

30

They exited a long hallway that led to a large reception room. A tall woman waited there. Madeline didn't need an introduction to know that she was Ciaran's mother. It wasn't just her beauty that Madeline wished she could have a fraction of when she got to that age, but her formidability.

The woman's long, dark hair was tied at the nape of her neck. Her lean, oval face was lit up with striking almond eyes, as sharp as a laser. Madeline could see that hidden somewhere in those cold eyes was the love, care, and warmth of a mother. But her affection was controlled, masked, and disguised so skillfully that had she not had years of experience in a job where she had to see through layers of lies, Madeline wouldn't have been able to see it.

"You were injured because of this girl, or so I was told?" her voice sounded like beautiful music.

"Doctor Thomas worries too much, Mother. You shouldn't have come all the way from Dublin. This is Madeline Roux. I wasn't injured *because* of her. I was injured because someone shot at me."

"You are as pretty as Tadgh described. My younger boy has exquisite taste for women. He praised your beauty."

"I don't make a living with my appearance, Mrs. LeBlanc, although it might be pleasing to people's eyes when I talk to them."

"And a smart cookie, you are! Call me Jennifer, please. I've been married to the LeBlancs my whole life, so there's no need to remind me of the association." Jennifer glanced at Ciaran.

"Please send my regards to Robert's poor family. What is your plan regarding security?"

"You don't have to worry about that, Mother. Mon Ciel should be fine."

"Is that so?" Jennifer walked toward a chair at the end of a long table and sat down, taking the most powerful position in the room. She spoke to Madeline. "My family has a lot at stake here, Madeline, just in case you wonder why we are strict with security. We know to the DNA of every staff member who ever set foot in this household." She stood up and approached Madeline. "No stranger is ever allowed in."

"Madeline is not a stranger, Mother," Ciaran growled.

"Did you scan her before she came here?"

"There was no need."

"Are you sure? Or have you just gone soft? I can see the resemblance, Ciaran."

"Resemblance of what?" Madeline asked.

"I am in charge of the family business, Mother. I can bring anyone in as I see fit."

"I don't like your tone, Ciaran."

"You wouldn't have to hear it if you stayed in Dublin."

Jennifer laughed. Her voice was like bell. "Listen to yourself, Ciaran. You sound like your father. A woman's place is in the home."

"And Father was correct."

"The protection your father built for Mon Ciel was to keep *all* of us safe. Tadgh told me you received a message about the timing. So I suggest you stay put inside Mon Ciel."

"I have things to do outside."

"You can keep her here, if it's what it takes."

"With all due respect, Jennifer, I can't stay here and be a piece of furniture. Like Ciaran, I have things to do. In fact, we have to leave now." Madeline looked at Ciaran, gesturing at her phone. Ciaran nodded.

Jennifer arched an eyebrow.

She probably isn't used to anyone talking back to her, Madeline thought.

"Very well." Jennifer sighed.

"In regard to your incidental exposure, I've gone beyond anger. I can never stay angry at you for long, Ciaran. I just wanted to see that you were safe and sound."

"Incidental exposure?"

"Oh, so you're not as totally on top of everything as you might think." Jennifer put a stack of newspapers on the table. "Don't take this family for granted, Ciaran."

"I'd never . . ." It came out in a raised voice, more like a hiss. Madeline knew it was a snap of Ciaran's control. He calmed down instantly. "I know what I have to do. It will be business as usual by the end of the week. Should I call the staff in, Mother?"

"Do as you see fit." She walked for a few steps and turned around. "One more thing, your cousin George—someone trashed his place a couple of weeks ago, looking for the artifact. He and his family were fine. Just had a bit of a fright."

Ciaran narrowed his eyes. "A couple of weeks ago? Why wasn't I informed?"

"You're not exactly on good terms with George, Ciaran. He told Tadgh. It wasn't just any artifact they were looking for. They identified the specific item."

"Is that why Tadgh came back to London?"

Jennifer smiled. "You really should talk to you brother more." Jennifer nodded a goodbye to Madeline and exited the room.

Madeline grabbed the stack of newspapers while Ciaran pulled out his cell phone and called Tadgh. He wandered over to the window, looking outside. Tadgh wasn't picking up his phone.

Madeline flicked through the pages of the paper. The two of

them had made the front page of all the newspapers in the UK. Pictures of Ciaran with his arm wrapped protectively around Madeline's waist as they left the police station and when they had entered One Hyde Park were prominently displayed. All associated articles speculated about the rare public appearance of a LeBlanc at a police station in London, and about Madeline's role.

"Bloodthirsty media hounds," Madeline mumbled to herself. That's what Jennifer had meant by the unwanted exposure. The LeBlancs had never been exposed to the media.

Ciaran gave up on calling Tadgh. Madeline put the article on the table for him to see. He glanced at it.

"Robert would have never let this happen," he muttered and made himself a cup of coffee.

As she flipped randomly through the pages of the newspaper, she saw a small article on page four. "Two mysterious deaths in Mortlake." She shuffled through the other papers. On pages four and five, a series of small articles about Mrs. Hanson and Shaun the gardener. Mysterious deaths by stab wounds. No weapon found.

The exhale of breath came out of her mouth so loudly that it captured Ciaran's attention. He turned toward her, looking as if he was waiting for whatever might be coming at him next.

31

"What's your family, Ciaran? Mafia?"

"I beg your pardon?"

"Anyone who goes against your family will get themselves killed," Madeline said.

"Madeline!" Ciaran's voice came out in a warning growl.

That was a pack reaction. She should have known. One of them got attacked, and the whole pack would kill to protect. She got that. She understood pack mentality. She had encountered many in her line of work. *Wolves.* Madeline could hear the word roaring in her head. Her heart pounded, and her blood pumped so hard that it felt as if her head would explode.

"Did you kill Peter?"

"Peter who?"

"The man who pulled me off the bus in front of your headquarters."

Ciaran smiled. "Ah, when we saw the news at One Hyde Park, I asked if you knew him, and you said no. You lied to me, Madeline."

"I didn't know you at that point."

"You still don't know me, Madeline. Otherwise, you wouldn't have asked me that question."

"Did you kill Shaun, the gardener?"

Ciaran shoved his hands in his pockets and stared at Madeline. "Do you really want me to answer those questions?"

Madeline stared back. *He was right.* She didn't really want him to answer because if he admitted to it, she didn't know how she could live with herself. But it his answers were no, she had revealed her distrust.

She withdrew a step and stormed out of the room.

"If you want to call a taxi, there's a phone in the hallway with a direct number," Ciaran called after her.

She raced along the corridor. She had to get out. She didn't hear Ciaran coming after her. Of course, he wouldn't. He'd shown her the door. She had questioned his family. His pack. Would she have done the same if she were in his situation?

At the front door of the house, she came to a skidding halt.

She would and could do worse.

She'd killed before. She wasn't innocent. It was a secret she'd shared with Jo, but it wasn't the reason they had built a relationship. Jo's family was hers, and she would do anything to protect them. Anything.

A short moment later, Madeline stood at the doorway. A tear trickled down her face, but she didn't bother to wipe it away. "This place does not qualify as a household in its current state."

Ciaran sat in a reading chair in the corner of the room, sipping his coffee quietly and watching Madeline over the rim. "It's waiting for the rightful and deserving owners to make it a household."

Another tear escaped Madeline's eyes. "I know you didn't do it."

"Neither did my family, Madeline. You were right—we could kill, but we wouldn't. It's not our way."

Madeline nodded. "I believe you."

She rushed in and all but fell into his arms. There, she felt his muscles quiver and his body vibrate with emotions. "Don't ever walk away from me like that again!" he said as he kissed her forehead.

"Okay, I promise. I have a temper, and sometimes, I can throw a tantrum."

"I noticed!" Ciaran chuckled. "I'll arrange a location to meet Zen and get Jo back tonight. To avoid further *misunderstanding* with law enforcement, could you liaise with your Stephen to get the police on site? If he's here."

"He's not *my* Stephen. And yes, he's here. He messaged me last night." Then she frowned. "You can do this easily with a phone call to detective Adamson, I'd imagine?"

Ciaran smiled. "Adamson is as straight as an arrow. We reported the incident at Mrs. Hanson's to him but mentioned nothing about Jo and the kidnapping, which occurred at the same time. I can go back to him with reasons for not reporting it, but regardless of how much wheeling and dealing I do, he'll suspect we have something to hide."

Madeline arched an eyebrow.

"My family doesn't deal with media and the police when it comes to our internal business. And you didn't go to the police in the first place when Jo was kidnapped—for a reason that you will one day tell me."

"Hey, I didn't call the cops because Zen threatened to . . ."

"That's the reason you'd give Stephen, but not me, Madeline."

Damn! He didn't manage a gigantic conglomerate for nothing. "Right, I have something to hide. But you have to admit that you need Stephen now to make arrangement with the police? Because he came here as my friend, not as a cop. He's not a big deal FBI agent or anything. He just catches small timers."

Ciaran laughed. "Madeline, don't worry. I'll be gentle with him. Okay?"

Damn, again! Am I that obvious? "Okay, I'll call Stephen," Madeline muttered and scurried out of the room.

～

TEN RINGS and Stephen had not yet picked up. Madeline walked up and down the hallway, waiting. There was no natural light although the down light was lit twenty-four/seven. The floor was covered in black stone tiles which were slightly uneven and difficult to walk on. Madeline's shoes had a bit of a heel, and they tended to slide into the gaps between the stone tiles. In addition, the hard soles of her shoes made clicks that seemed to echo through the area even though Madeline was very sure that she was walking lightly and not stomping.

Along the hallway, there were twelve white statues of what Madeline guessed must be Greek Gods. They all had kind and caring faces and looked like the sort of gods one would feel comfortable talking to—or maybe *praying* was more appropriate.

Madeline thought it a good idea to stop pacing up and down the hallway. The noise she was making might annoy those gods. Just then, one of Madeline's pointy heels got stuck in a gap between two stones. The walking momentum made Madeline fall forward, punching her palm against the toe of a god's statue. For a moment, Madeline thought she had broken a bone in her hand or dislocated her shoulder. But no, she took a quick inventory, and she was not hurt—but the god was. The toe had broken off. She caught it before it slid off and shattered on the stone floor.

"Oh, my God! Oh, dear, sweet Jesus God, please forgive me!"

"What's that, Madeline?" Stephen's voice piped up from the other end of the line.

Madeline finished her phone call with Stephen, making an appointment to meet with him at the bakery café at the London Eyes.

She walked into the great hall, and Ciaran looked as if he was ready to go out with her to meet Stephen.

"I broke a god's toe."

Ciaran cocked an eyebrow in question.

"I broke his toe, but I'm going to fix it. All I need is some super glue."

Madeline showed him the toe in her palm.

Ciaran had a blank look, glancing at the toe and back at Madeline's expression. Then he had a fit of laughing. He looked at her standing there with a toe in her hand and thought about how much he adored her.

"Don't worry about it. I'll get someone to fix it for you!"

"No, no, it's my doing. I broke the god's toe, so I'll fix it."

Ciaran smiled. "As you like. I'm sure he won't mind having a toe missing for a few hours. But we've got to go now."

On the way out of the house, Madeline asked, "Why don't you have marble statues, or metal ones that would be sturdier and last forever? I hope these statues didn't cost a fortune."

"Nah, I bought them cheap. Just a couple of million each."

Seeing the appalled look on Madeline's face, Ciaran laughed.

"I was just kidding. The statues aren't antique or anything like that. They aren't expensive at all. That hallway connects to a new extension of the house—it was built ten years ago. The statues were added to blend the décor with the old section. The statues in the old part were all antique. I blew the head off of one of them."

"I'm sure you're the favorite child in the family!"

"That's a safe bet." Ciaran grinned.

In London, Ciaran swapped the car for a long black limousine. He asked Madeline to call Stephen and request that he walk across the bridge to the opposite side of the river from the London Eyes.

Before Stephen reached the car, Ciaran asked Madeline not to mention the location of his house.

A moment later, Stephen opened the limousine's door and got in. After the standard greeting, Ciaran offered Stephen some scotch. Stephen accepted and grinned at Madeline's stare.

"What? I'm not on duty."

"Please excuse this moving office. I trust you understand."

"Of course. I was surprised when you'd agreed to meet at a

café." He looked at Madeline. "I'm so sorry for messing up your plan, Madeline."

"No, I appreciate your help, and I'm glad you stopped by Zen's place. It turned out to be a positive thing, actually. He thought I could play hardball."

"Could you?" Stephen asked.

"Yes, with Ciaran's help."

Stephen looked at Ciaran suspiciously.

Ciaran sipped some scotch. "Stephen, what's in this for you? I just don't believe that a normal friendship would make you travel all the way from New York to London. I don't believe in sentimental reasons, either, and am therefore assuming you have a crush on Madeline."

Stephen choked on his scotch. "Then . . . I . . . I don't have a reason."

Madeline glanced at Ciaran, warning him not be too harsh on Stephen.

"So then, what's your plan to help Madeline?"

"I'll talk to Zen and get Jo back."

"What do you have to give him?"

"Nothing. But he knows I'm a cop and I could cause him trouble."

"And you think that this is sufficient to scare Zen and get Jo back?"

Stephen looked at Madeline as if asking for a rescue.

Madeline spoke gently. "I know that London is out of your jurisdiction. But could you get some collaboration here if action is needed?"

"Depends on what kind of action. I'm on vacation. I'm not even carrying a weapon."

"So you were just being a sentimental fool, jumping on an airplane to come here without any idea what you were going to do?"

"Ciaran," Madeline warned again.

Ciaran stared at Stephen. He cocked an eyebrow and waited for

Stephen to respond. Madeline knew Stephen was doing his best not to stutter under the pressure.

"Stephen, you might think that I am in no position to judge your motives or interrogate you about your actions. And you're right. You and I are in competition for the same woman, and on that ground, we are equal."

"Excuse me, do I need to get out of here?" Madeline asked, astonished.

Ciaran continued, "However, when it comes to solving the problem Madeline has at hand, I now have a stake in it more than you do. I am involved. Blood has been spilled, and I have lost a friend in the process. On top of that, I have my family and my business interests to protect. So I do hope you understand why I have to ask these hard questions."

"Yeah, yeah, sure." Stephen cleared his throat. "I understand. So what do you want me to do to help? I assume you have a plan?"

"I'm not asking you to do or give us anything. On the contrary, we're going to give you the collar."

"What?"

"We will trap Zen, and you'll catch him. Simple. But you have to make it official. You have to liaise with the cops here. How you play it out is totally up to you. I'll notify you with Zen's location when we get to it. How does that sound?"

"Ah . . . ah . . . perfect . . . I didn't expect this . . ." Stephen nodded.

"How fast can you get a team together?" Ciaran asked.

"I don't know. I've never worked with British partners before."

Ciaran pulled out a card and gave it to Stephen.

"Detective Adamson is a good man to talk to. Can you get something together soon?"

"How soon?"

"Let's say a couple of hours."

"Jesus . . ."

"Can you do it or not?"

Stephen nodded somewhat doubtfully and got out of the car.

Ciaran smiled at Madeline's astonishment.

"Two hours?" she asked.

"Well, he didn't ask for more, did he?"

Madeline shook her head and sighed. "What about your promise to me?"

"I don't think I was too harsh on him."

"He's harmless, Ciaran!"

Ciaran turned at Madeline. He rubbed his thumb on the dimple on her left cheek. "He's too good to be true, Madeline."

*a*s soon as the screen of the video call flashed, Ciaran reached over and turned the video function off.

"Put the video on, Ciaran," Zen's voice croaked.

"You don't have anything I want to see. Do you want the location or not?" Ciaran asked.

They were sitting at a table in a private room at an exclusive restaurant in Knightsbridge. Madeline sat next to Ciaran, her eyes glued to the phone on the table, listening to his voice coming out of the speaker.

"This isn't my turf. I ain't going to fall into one your traps. I'll give *you* the location, and you bring the crucifix. I'll have equipment on site—you'll code the program for me, and then I will give you Jo."

"No. I'm not digging a grave for you. Let's meet halfway. We'll go to the tomb, and while you dig for your crucifix, I'll finish the program for you."

"And what if you set a trap for me? Call the cops or something?"

"I can do the same thing if we meet at *your* location! Look, I don't have time to play around. I want Jo back. I don't care about the crucifix and your little program, whatever it does."

"All right . . . what's the location?"

"We'll see you tonight at seven at Rufford Abbey."

There was sound of tapping on computer keyboard. And then, "Mr. LeBlanc, you think I'm an idiot?"

"As you like!"

"Fuck you, Ciaran! That's a tourist park."

"If the tomb is at Mortlake where everyone thinks it is, do you really think whatever you want to find in it would still be there?"

Zen hesitated. "It's like three hours' drive from London . . ."

"Then you'd better start driving. Remember, you better bring Jo. Without her being safe and sound, the deal will be off. I won't give you a second chance." Ciaran hung up the phone.

When Ciaran turned to look at Madeline, her heart sank. His eyes were too dark.

"What, Ciaran?"

He gestured for silence, then dialed on his cell phone. "Lindsay, I need the chopper at the London headquarters right now. Arrange two handguns for me. Send twenty of Robert's best men to Mon Ciel. Get my mother out of there. Tie her up and drug her if you have to. I'll deal with her wrath afterward. No civilian staff in Mon Ciel tonight."

He hung up the phone, pulled out his painkiller box, and popped two pills in his mouth. Then he rubbed at his temples. Madeline pulled a chair over and sat opposite Ciaran. "Let me," she said and rubbed her thumbs on his temples. Ciaran closed his eyes, then he reached over, pulling Madeline onto his lap and nuzzling into the crook of her neck. She wrapped her arms around his shoulders and found the muscles there tightened up in knots. She pressed and kneaded them, trying to relax him.

Ciaran released her but still held on his lap. "Zen is simply too stupid to handle this by himself. Do you know what a hologame is?"

Madeline shook her head.

"It's the most advanced game technology on Earth. Jo finished only the front end of it because she doesn't have the technological resources to complete it. For Zen to say he'll arrange a computer for me on site—that suggests he knows nothing about this technology and what he's dealing with."

"You're saying that the person Zen is working for wants whatever is inside Mon Ciel?"

"I hope I'm wrong and Zen is only a stupid gold digger."

Madeline hopped up and kissed Ciaran's forehead, then grinned as she saw the twinkle return to his eyes. "What if they send more than twenty men to Mon Ciel?"

Ciaran laughed. "It's not the numbers, it's the technology we have that protects the place." He kissed her dimple. "All you need to know is that we'll get Jo back tonight, regardless of whether Zen is stupid or not. Okay?"

She nodded and got off his lap.

HALF AN HOUR LATER, Madeline and Ciaran finished the last part of the security check and headed toward a dispatch platform at the back of the building. The helicopter pilot started the engine as soon as he saw Ciaran's shadow at the door. Ciaran got into the helicopter and helped Madeline in.

Tadgh was sitting in one of the front seats, grinning at them. "Thank you for asking Lindsay to arrange a gun for me. You know me well, brother."

"It wasn't for you," Ciaran growled.

"You weren't intending Madeline to carry, were you? Don't worry, she can handle this." Tadgh reached over and handed Madeline a gun so small that it would fit nicely into her purse, if she had one.

"Tadgh!" Ciaran warned.

"This could come in handy. Put it in your pocket. I don't think

Ciaran intended to give you a weapon. He's a two-hand shooter. But he'll have to manage with one gun for tonight."

"What? Are you both combat trained?"

"No. We just bluff." Tadgh grinned again.

"If you know about tonight, then you should be at Mon Ciel," Ciaran scolded.

"No." Tadgh's grin faded. When he was serious, his eyes were as intense as Ciaran's. "Mon Ciel is only a house. *You* are my brother."

"Then don't be my burden. I don't have time to watch your ass."

"You have to. That's your responsibility." Tadgh sank deep into his chair, relaxing as if he was going to take a nap. Ciaran swallowed a snarl and asked the pilot to take off.

AT FIVE THIRTY p.m. in the winter, Rufford Abbey had already been deserted by staff and visitors. *What a magnificent sight,* Madeline thought. She was wondering how many people visited during the day. Under the very limited sunlight that was left, the abbey sat quietly as praying for the monks who had lived and died here in the twelfth century.

Once the helicopter had landed, Tadgh whined, "I hope we make it for dinner tonight."

The area was surrounded by national parks and bushland. There would be no hope for civilized comforts such as meals and accommodations in nearby locations.

"I didn't twist your arm to make you come here. We need to set up." Ciaran pointed to the parking lot. "You see that lot? We'll make the guy park there and show us clearly that he has Jo with him. Then Madeline and I will distract him and make him work to find the crucifix.

"Crucifix?" Tadgh frowned. He shot a very quick glance at Madeline, and Madeline knew he didn't realize she had caught his look. She kept her face blank, focusing on Ciaran's plan.

33

*C*iaran assured Tadgh with an easy tone. "He mentioned John Dee's tomb, then an artifact, then a crucifix. I don't think he knew exactly what he was talking about."

"A gold digger you've got there." Tadgh smiled.

Ciaran nodded.

"So you want to lure him away from the car, and then we can jump in and rescue the girl?" Tadgh asked.

"That's the ideal scenario. I don't think Zen is very smart, but he might not be totally stupid, either. If he figures it out before we get to Jo, then our plan is doomed."

"You have to help us guide the cops in here to get Zen, Tadgh," Madeline said. She pulled out her phone and shared Stephen's number with Tadgh. "This is my friend, Stephen. He's a New York cop. Zen is apparently wanted by the police internationally, so Ciaran thought we might give Stephen a sexy collar on this case."

Tadgh shook Ciaran's shoulders. "Nice!"

Then they went about setting up the venue while Madeline followed up with Stephen on his progress. Everything seemed to be going as planned.

Just after seven, a car drove slowly into the dark parking lot. As soon as the headlights went off, Madeline's phone buzzed, and Zen's voice was broadcast on speaker.

"Well, we're here. Got lost a bit but didn't kill myself by driving on the wrong side of the road."

"Where's Jo?" Madeline asked.

Zen switched on the internal light of the car. Jo was leaning back, sleeping in the back seat of the car.

Tadgh gasped. "Oh, sweet Jesus Christ, what a sleeping beauty!"

Both Madeline and Ciaran turned around, their eyes commanding silence. He made an apologetic zipping gesture across his lips and shut up.

"I had to give her a sedative. She wasn't exactly cooperating, as you might realize, Madeline. She should wake up in a couple of hours. So what's next?"

Ciaran leaned toward the phone while he signaled to Tadgh to go away. "All right, we're in the main abbey. I'll meet you at the door."

Five minutes later, Zen appeared at the entrance to the abbey. Madeline and Ciaran met him at a stone door to the side. The door was small, and Ciaran had to bend down to go past it. Zen followed and then Madeline. Madeline checked behind her before entering the chapel area and caught a flash of Tadgh's shadow running between the trees. She smiled to herself. Just like his brother, he was as quick as a cat.

The chapel was made entirely of stone, and thus it was freezing. Some burning torches mounted on the walls dimly lit the interior, and it was just enough to give light and keep the ambience of the old place of worship. An old altar, consisting of a non-operating platform that looked as if it was now used as a fireplace, was located at the far end of the room. Paintings and information about the history of the abbey covered part of the cold stone walls.

Along with the noise of birds and wild animals from the nearby lake and bushland, the quivering shadows and the feeling in the air inside the abbey caused a chill to run up Madeline's spine. If anyone had told her that the ghost of an ancient monk haunted this place, she would have believed it. Madeline admired Ciaran for choosing such a place for their setup. Still, Madeline wished she wasn't standing in one of King Henry VIII's ruined abbeys. Surely some of the ghostly things people talked about occurring in these dark and mysterious abbeys were real.

"What the hell is this?" Zen broke the silence.

"This is where the crucifix is possibly buried," Ciaran answered.

"How could the tomb possibly be in here?"

"You confuse me, Zen." Ciaran spoke sternly.

"What?"

"First you said crucifix, but now you say tomb." Ciaran shoved his hands into his pockets as if annoyed.

"Don't fuck around with me."

"Although I'm not religious, I would expect that it's disrespectful to swear at a place of worship. But given you're going to dig around, I suppose that's much worse than swearing, so I'll save my comments. Now, please clarify for me . . . do you want to dig up a tomb? Or do you want to find a crucifix?"

"Are you trying to mess with my head? I want the crucifix, of course. Why would I want to dig up a grave?"

"I certainly wouldn't want to," Ciaran muttered.

Madeline waited for a buzz on her phone—the agreed-upon signal of good news from Tadgh. There was nothing.

"There are two possible locations of the crucifix—one is here, and the other one is in the ruined compartment around the corner. That part has not been restored, thus there is no light of any sort inside. I thought you might want to dig in here first, as it's warm and cozy."

"Dig? I thought you said no tomb digging?"

"No, I said no *tomb*. I didn't say anything about no digging."

Madeline felt as if her head was about to burst. *Tadgh, Tadgh, Tadgh!!! What is he doing? What about Stephen? Where is he? How long can Ciaran drag this out?*

"What the fuck are you doing? You really want to mess me up?" Zen's face started to turn red.

"I want to get out of here more than you do, Zen. If you want your reward, you're going to have to work for it. You want the crucifix? Then you've got to dig," Ciaran stated firmly.

"I won't do any digging. *You'll* have to dig." Zen threw a tantrum.

Ciaran smiled. "It's bad luck to disturb spirits in a place like this. So no, I won't be doing any digging."

The phone in Madeline's pocket buzzed. At the same time, a car alarm sang loudly from the distance.

"I knew it! I fucking knew it!" Zen screamed and rushed outside the room. Ciaran stopped him with a kick. Zen rolled over, falling back inside the abbey. Ciaran pulled his gun and pointed it at Zen.

On the ground, Zen grabbed a wooden bow, an exhibit item next to a statue of a monk praying, and blasted dust at Ciaran's face. He followed with a kick to Ciaran's gun, and before Ciaran knew it, Zen swung a displayed scepter at Ciaran's head. Ciaran dropped to the floor. Madeline pulled her little gun out, and at the same time, Zen pulled his gun.

They stood facing each other, at point blank range. Saying nothing, Madeline pulled the trigger, aiming straight at Zen. Zen did the same thing. Ciaran pulled at Madeline from the ground, and she fell over and out of the bullet's range. The bullet put a large ding on the wall behind her.

Zen took the opportunity to run from of the chapel. Then from the outside, Zen kicked the heavy oak door closed and jammed the outside with some wood logs.

"Goddamn it!" Ciaran kicked at the door although he knew it wouldn't help. Madeline tried to call Tadgh, but the signal wouldn't pierce the thick stone walls.

There was a display table showing visitors how the abbey was built and the process used to make the stone walls. Ciaran grabbed the steel hammer from the display and used it to hit at the door handle until the wood logs on the outside gave way.

Cold wind slapped at their faces when they ran outside. "This way." Ciaran pointed toward the bush.

Madeline didn't know where the light was coming from, but she could see the shadows of weird-looking tree branches reaching out across the ground from the darkness, twining together as if they were holding hands to create an evil web in which to ensnare them. She kept running and trying to work the phone at the same time.

They could see Zen stumbling in the bushes. Madeline heard water splashing against the shore. The unmistakable sound of water, a lot of it. Then she remembered—there was a lake, a very large one, and there might be some swampy areas.

They seemed to be walking along a small bridge. It was really dark. Something that looked like an enormous bat flew at her. Madeline yelped and lost her balance, but Ciaran caught her.

Zen's turned. He saw them. He spun around again, then stumbled over something and fell. He stood up quickly and ran.

In another direction, they could see Tadgh approaching. He sprinted quickly in the dark. Madeline didn't think Tadgh saw them, but he certainly caught sight of Zen. He charged toward him.

Ciaran took off as fast as he could. Madeline couldn't keep up.

Then there was another set of footsteps, loud and clear. Madeline looked around, but she couldn't see who it was.

Ciaran had disappeared into the darkness. She had to follow him. She kept running.

She was soon catching up with Ciaran and could see him approaching Zen from behind. Tadgh was running straight toward Zen. It was so dark. The shadows kept switching on and off and jumping around from the dim light shining down from somewhere in the sky. It felt as if there was moonlight, but it was too hard to tell.

Tadgh just realized he was running straight for Zen when Zen raised his gun. It was too late for Tadgh. There wasn't much he could do. It was too dark to seek something to hide behind. The only thing around Tadgh was shadow filled with thin, chilly air. For a moment, looking straight at the gun muzzle, Tadgh could feel the brush of death.

A gunshot echoed in the air.

Zen's body slumped down to the cold mud, his gun still in his hand. Tadgh could see Ciaran standing tall behind Zen's body.

Ciaran had shot Zen.

Madeline approached from behind Ciaran, and then from the side, Stephen appeared. Stephen saw Ciaran holding the gun. The scent of gunpowder still hovered in the air. Stephen approached, holding his hand out for Ciaran's gun.

"He would have shot Tadgh if Ciaran hadn't shot him first." Madeline cried, grabbing Stephen's arm. Stephen shrugged her hands off. This was the first time since they had known each other that Stephen had acted like this.

"Ciaran's a civilian. He has no right to execute another man, criminal or not. And it *wasn't* in self-defense," Stephen stated clearly.

Ciaran said nothing. He gave Stephen his gun.

"No, no . . ." Tadgh charged forward as if he was going to take Stephen down.

Ciaran grabbed Tadgh, stopping him from attacking Stephen.

"Jo." Ciaran snapped back to reality and ran back to the car.

34

*T*he car park was dark. The air was deadly quiet. Ciaran ran, and in front of him was one vision—Jo lying in the car, dead. It was too dark to tell, and much too quiet for his liking. The others were calling him from far back, but he ignored them. If anything had happened to Jo, it would be his fault.

He had severely underestimated Zen. Sometimes his arrogance was his worst enemy. He'd had no right to assume that Zen was stupid.

The car stood lonely in the car park.

He reached the car before Madeline and opened the car door. It was totally empty.

Stephen approached and shined a light into the car.

"The car is empty, Ciaran. Jo isn't here," Stephen said.

"But we saw her!" Madeline asked.

Ciaran looked at the car floor. He saw a box that looked like a mini projector. "Oh, fuck me . . . it was a fucking hologram!" Ciaran grunted out the words in frustration. He kicked the car. He could feel his blood boiling, and soon his rage would come. He turned around, looking for Madeline. For the first time in his life, during a chaotic moment when he was confused and afraid of his own rage, he needed to hold on to her.

She was his constant.

Before he could say anything, and before the rage he was afraid of flooded his mind like tidal waves, Madeline interlaced the small delicate fingers of her hand with his. Warm. Steady. And she just looked at him. And somehow, he just knew his rage wouldn't surface this time.

From the far end of the car park, the deep voice of Detective Adamson yelled, "I'm calling the crew back. We should wrap up here."

Stephen, Madeline, and Ciaran walked toward Adamson. The detective continued. "What's with Zen? Bullet in the head!"

Stephen looked at Ciaran. Madeline looked at Stephen. Ciaran said nothing.

Stephen's eyes paused on Ciaran's face for a moment, and then he pulled Ciaran's gun out. Stephen said calmly, "I announced myself and asked the offender to put his weapon down. He was aiming at Ciaran. Then he swung the gun at me. So I had to get the gun off him. We struggled. Then Ciaran jumped in, and the gun went off. Apparently, Zen took the stray bullet. I followed protocol, detective."

Adamson nodded. "I need the report in writing."

Stephen nodded.

As Adamson gathered his team together, Ciaran approached Stephen. "Thank you. I owe you one."

"Was the gun registered under your name?" Stephen asked.

Ciaran shook his head, and Stephen nodded.

Madeline approached and looked at Stephen with appreciation.

Ciaran glanced around, looking for his brother, and saw Tadgh approaching the car. He could see a small dot of red light flashing from under the car, close to the rear wheel.

"Tadgh, the car is rigged," Ciaran screamed.

Tadgh turned and ran from the car. But it seemed he was too late. The car exploded. The loud explosion tore through the quiet air. Birds darted out from their sleeping nests, and wild animals leaped from nearby bushes. The car was in flames. Fire shot out from it in waves.

Tadgh's body was thrown in the air and landed with a thud in the cold grass.

Ciaran darted toward him. That was his stubborn brother lying in the mud, the one he promised his father he would look after.

"Come on, bastard, breathe! Answer me! Open your eyes! Come on!" Ciaran thrust the phone toward Madeline, saying, "Call Doctor Thomas."

He took Tadgh's pulse. "Come on, come on! Keep breathing!" Then he shook Tadgh's shoulders. "Open your eyes and look at me!"

No response.

"Open your eyes, for fuck's sake!". Ciaran peeled off his coat and jacket quickly, leaving himself with only a white business shirt. He rolled his jacket and tucked it under his brother's head to stabilize his neck. Then he covered Tadgh with his coat.

"Now that you're warm and comfortable, open your eyes and look at your brother!"

Doctor Thomas and Lindsay arrived in the helicopter.

"He landed badly, but I think his neck is fine," Ciaran said to Doctor Thomas. The doctor did a quick visual check and cleared Tadgh to be airlifted. Madeline jumped on the helicopter with Ciaran.

Before taking off, Madeline looked at Stephen, miming her thanks. Stephen nodded and smiled. Madeline saw the gentle look in his soft green eyes, and at that moment, she understood why she hadn't given him a chance before—he was too good for her.

The helicopter went straight to Ciaran's house at Hanley-on-Thames. A large section of the new quarter had been lit up in anticipation of their arrival. After passing through layers and layers of doors, Tadgh was finally pushed inside a room that looked like an operating room.

"Why not bring him to the hospital, Ciaran?" Madeline asked.

"We have the best equipment here, and Doctor Thomas is one of the best surgeons in the country. Please wait here," Ciaran said to Madeline. "And you, too." Then he disappeared into the operation room.

At that moment, Madeline realized she was standing next to Ciaran's mother, and that he had just told his mother to wait outside the operating room.

THE LONGER MADELINE STOOD WAITING, the more her brain went numb. For the entire trip in the helicopter, Ciaran's universe had revolved around Tadgh. He hadn't responded to her questions. He didn't hear her at all. She could see the emotion blasting at him, even bigger than the bomb that had blasted at Tadgh. The scene of Ciaran kneeling next to Tadgh's lifeless body kept replaying in her head. He looked as if his own life depended upon Tadgh's survival —so much so that she dare not ask any *what if* questions. He hadn't touched her at all during the trip home. Not a hold of the hand. Not a single look. He was completely alone in his grief and concern for his brother. And so was she.

Where was Jo?

Was she okay?

Had she escaped?

Will Tadgh be okay?

Madeline shuddered in the chill air. Maybe there was an open window somewhere causing this cold atmosphere. She was standing in the corridor with the god statues, one of them still with a missing toe. She must have made them angry.

The blue dots appeared again, gathered in the corner. If she wasn't mistaken, they were dancing at her despair.

Then she looked at Ciaran's mother and realized that the chill she felt was not from an open window—it was from Jennifer. The woman could shatter her bones just by her stare.

She approached Madeline slowly, like a snow leopard

observing its wounded prey before cutting its life short. With a calm voice, she stated, "You brought my older son a bullet. Now you brought my younger one a bomb. What will you bring next to this family, Ms. Roux?"

It was weird to hear her last name spoken in that way. She gave it an emphasis, an accent that brought a totally different meaning to the ordinary word. Her last name. His family. Disaster after disaster. She was going from bad to worse. It was she who had brought bad luck. It was her responsibility.

It was because of what she had done in the past.

It was her fault.

Madeline looked at the door to the operating room. It had been a while. The door was still closed. "Can I stay to make sure that Tadgh is okay?" she asked.

"No. My son, my worries. You've done enough harm. Let us live in peace!"

She was right. Madeline had no place here, in this magnificent palace.

She had to find Jo.

Madeline stormed out of the room, walking down the hallway with the line of statues.

efore she knew it, Madeline was outside the high stone walls of the estate. The steel door shut behind her, and the darkness opened in front of her.

Madeline walked. She was chilled-to-the-bone cold. She should call a taxi. She pulled out her phone and found herself dialing Stephen's number. The only number in her address book. The only person she could call for help.

She walked along a main road outside the estate. It was a tree-lined street, but she wasn't sure it could be called a road. If she called a taxi, she wouldn't even know where to ask them pick her up. Madeline realized that she was in the middle of nowhere.

She wondered how Stephen could find her. She turned on the Internet to search for maps. She needed to navigate for herself. She was close to a national park and was indeed in the middle of nowhere. She kept walking. Her teeth started to chatter. The cold air crept through her clothes and brushed her skin. She realized that she had left her beloved red leather jacket at Mon Ciel.

And then she heard the jingles—those from Mrs. Hanson's earrings. But the old woman was dead, Madeline reminded herself.

She looked around. The Roman soldiers on Fosse Way had had bells that made the same noise. But she saw no one. Nothing but darkness. She was sure she was awake.

"Roman soldiers, my ass," she cursed.

The cold air started cutting into her flesh, so she walked faster. Before she realized it, she was galloping down the road. The ground seemed to slope downward. She was going down a hill, but she wasn't sure she was following a path. It was much too dark to see.

In the distance, she saw a flash of car headlights. That had to be Stephen. It had to be. The light was so dim and far away. It was so small that Madeline felt as if she was running through an endless tunnel, and the light was always just out of reach at the end. It might take her a lifetime to get there.

She called Stephen. "I think I can see you. I can see your car headlights."

Stephen turned on his speaker and held the phone in one hand while he steered the car using the other. "I can't see you, Madeline. I can't see anything. It's too dark. I guess I'm driving toward you if you can see my headlights. I'll blink. Okay? Tell me if you can see it."

Stephen switched the headlights on and off three times.

"Yes, I can see it. From a very long distance, though. Keep on the road. I know it's hard to see."

"Tell me about it!"

Madeline yelped and dropped her phone on the ground. A searing pain had cut through her right arm. She grabbed at it. She couldn't see, but she could feel what she knew was warm blood running out from what felt like a gash. She heard the sound of something hitting a tree trunk right next to her. From her experience at Fosse Way, Madeline knew it was a gunshot.

She grabbed the phone she'd dropped on the ground. It was still working, and Stephen's voice was coming out from it. "Madeline? Madeline, what happened? Did you fall?"

"I was shot," she said.

Madeline ran toward Stephen's headlights. She could see the lights moving a lot more quickly, as if Stephen had accelerated.

One more shot missed her and went past. She could hear footsteps in the mud and shallow water behind her. She couldn't tell how many people were chasing her. "I think they shot at the LED light of the phone. I have to turn it off."

"Don't. I can't find you if you turn it off."

"Bluetooth is on," she said and slipped the phone into her back pocket, running for her life.

Without the light on the phone, the bullets missed her widely. But Madeline knew she wouldn't be able to keep on like this for long. If they sprayed, that would be the end of her. She dodged and zigzagged as much as possible. She felt dizzy. She must be bleeding badly.

Stephen's headlights got closer and closer, and she could hear the car engine. Madeline ran straight toward the light.

She heard a grunt and saw a shadow flying at her, tackling her. She fell, sliding on slippery grass and rocks.

The shadow howled. It had to be chimpanzee, she thought, by the shape of it. It tried to strangle her. She heard more footsteps. Maybe from those with guns. Madeline knew if she couldn't get rid of this monkey, she was doomed. She grabbed a rock near her hand and gave a hard blow to the head of the chimp. It roared and slapped at her so hard that she thought her neck would snap. Madeline flipped and pushed the chimp aside.

Stephen's car stopped right in front of her. Its headlights shone straight onto the creature—a tall, bearded, strange-looking man who was grabbing his head. His eye was bleeding severely. Madeline must have taken his eye out with the rock. He stood up, growled, and fled into the bush. She could hear the other footsteps running away.

Stephen jumped out of the car and charged toward Madeline. "Are you hit again?" he asked.

"No," she replied and helped her into the car. The he turned around and drove away quickly.

It was nearly dawn, but the winter sun was in no way near to giving them any sign of daylight. The car's headlights showed just enough of the road ahead so that they didn't veer off into the bushes. They hadn't driven far before an extreme flash of light beamed at them from ahead. An engine roared loudly, and a truck charged straight at their pitiful rented car. From the shape, the sound, and the speed of the truck, Madeline knew they were no competition.

The truck hit their car head on. One hit, and their headlights were gone. A second hit and the hood of their car gave in, the engine hissed, and the windows cracked.

Stephen backed the car away quickly. He tried to keep it straight, but the road they were driving on was not exactly straight. Madeline knew their car couldn't handle another hit. Stephen kept reversing the car quickly. They slid off the road and flew through the air. The car landed on the fast-running creek.

"Get out." Stephen pulled Madeline out of the car. They held on to each other, trying to stay afloat and letting the water carry them downstream.

Madeline saw the crack of dawn before her world went black.

36

*D*octor Thomas turned off the operation light, pulled his medical mask off, and smiled. Ciaran released a sigh of relief. He had the same medical knowledge as Doctor Thomas did, so the doctor didn't bother explain to Ciaran about Tadgh's condition. "Well, I don't think he'd need to be sedated any longer. I'll give him some painkillers when he's up," the doctor said.

"Lucky bastard," Ciaran muttered and grinned. He pulled out his cell phone and turned it on when he saw a message from Detective Adamson flashing. He didn't check the message but called straight back.

"Adamson," the greeting was brusque and almost grumpy. Then Ciaran noticed the time—it was five in the morning.

"I apologize, Detective. I lost track of time."

Adamson snorted. "That's all right. Doctors and cops don't work by the clock. I've got good news for you. On the way back from Rufford Abbey, I got a call. Turns out Jo ran to a police station and reported the kidnapping. She put down your name as the contact person. Very smart girl. Because of the case at Mortlake, your name is in my file and high priority, so the station tagged me."

"Is she all right? Where is she now?"

"She's fine and at the station. I'll call you back later to confirm the status. Is that okay?"

"That's perfect. Thank you very much, Detective. I'll give Madeline the good news."

Ciaran hung up the phone and walked a couple of steps when it hit him—tidal waves of pain in his brain. He grunted, doubled over, and grabbed his head. Doctor Thomas darted over.

Ciaran couldn't hear anything except a robotic voice from a hollow distance, "It's time, Ciaran. The enemies are coming." The pain was excruciating, and blood trickled from his nose. All the monitors in the room flashed, and text came across all of them —"It's time, Ciaran. The enemies are coming." Doctor Thomas helped Ciaran to stand. Ciaran stood to his full height, towering over the doctor, then slumped to the floor and blacked out.

He awoke, lying on the floor, with Doctor Thomas crouched next to him. "How long was I out?" he asked.

"About thirty seconds. How often does this happen, Ciaran?"

Ciaran sat up. "It was thirty-*three* seconds that I blacked out, wasn't it?"

Doctor Thomas glanced at his watch. "Perhaps. What does that mean, Ciaran?"

Ciaran stood up, leaning on a bench for a moment to regain his balance. "A long time ago when I was developing a computer program, I came across a cross-over point between alchemy, astrology, and string theory."

"String theory? As in the context of parallel universes?"

Ciaran nodded.

"It's a very strange logic to combine these areas together! Like marrying a horse to a kitten."

Ciaran winced. "Well, it would definitely require creativity when it comes to their physical incompatibility. But anyway, my strange combination of theories suggested that a major galactic event would occur every thirty three years, where exchanges would be made between universes."

"What sort of exchanges?"

"Energy. Power. Before Father died, he told me that a man has to live up to his duty. But if I ever decided against my duty, he would understand. Then he told me to pay attention to thirty-three. I didn't know what he meant. But in the last two weeks, with all the migraines and strange static occurrences on computers, I think it has something to do with the theory." Ciaran shrugged. "Thirty-three has some theological meaning. But thirty-three what? Months? Days? Seconds?"

Doctor Thomas approached Ciaran and looked straight into his eyes. "It's thirty three *years*, Ciaran. It has been exactly that many years since you blew up the head of the Goddess of Kindness."

"It was only a statue."

"Yes, but it was the first time your trait of violence surfaced, Ciaran. Your father consulted me on that. I told him it was a violent trait, but he believed otherwise. He called it demon."

Ciaran shook his head. "It's Daimon, not demon, Doctor Thomas. The first is philosophical, and the second is theological."

"Philosophy of what?"

"A virtuous life," Ciaran headed toward the door. "Please don't tell my mother anything until I figure this out."

A BLAST of cold air greeted Ciaran when he walked out of the operation room. Jennifer rushed over from a corner.

"Tadgh is fine, Mother. He has some internal bleeding, but he's fine now. He'll be up and running around in no time," he said and saw some relief on his mother's face. He knew he had worried her, and he regretted that. He wanted to embrace her, but then he thought better of it and let the thought pass.

Tadgh would have dived right in, hugging and kissing his mother without any hesitance, not giving a flying thought to who might be watching him. His brother had a warm personality that Ciaran liked, but he would never admit it. That was his problem.

He'd never admitted his emotions. Ciaran could count exactly the handful of occasions in his life when he'd embraced his mother.

Then he glanced around. It wasn't the cold breeze that had blasted him, it was the emptiness of the space.

"Where's Madeline?" he asked.

Jennifer stopped on the way into the operation room. "She left." She turned to proceed into the operating room, but Ciaran darted forward, blocking her way.

"What did you say to her?" His voice was so low that it was hardly audible. But he knew his mother had heard him well enough.

"Nothing. She just left."

"Even when she wasn't sure if I was a murderer, she came back to me. She stayed with me during my rage, Mother! What did you say to make her leave me?"

"I reminded her that she brought you a bullet and Tadgh a bomb. I just asked her what she would bring us next."

Ciaran withdrew a step because he wasn't sure of the consequences if he didn't.

"Don't look at me like that, Ciaran!"

He turned around and strode down the hall. He heard his mother asking from behind, "Which part of what I said to her wasn't true?"

Ciaran galloped up the stairs to his office and stormed into the control room. He activated the control panel with one hand, and with the other hand he flipped the telecom on and called his security.

On the control panel, a large round circle appeared. He coded in and activated the chip in Madeline's cell phone. His hands shook a bit as he finished. He stared at the screen. Within seconds, a small, green blinking dot appeared. The round circle on the screen spun like a compass, and the location of the green dot appeared on the screen. Ciaran transferred the data to a portable device and hurried down the stairs to the front where his men had the helicopter ready for him.

The creek was cold at dawn. The natural light was just enough for Ciaran to see Madeline and Stephen hanging on to a rock in the middle of the fast-moving water. He wanted to go down there to lift Madeline up. He wanted to touch her, to feel that she was alive. But he knew better.

He stood aside and let the rescue team go down to the creek with their stretchers. As soon as they had loaded her onto the helicopter, he grabbed her wrist to check for a pulse and was almost giddy when he found it was strong and steady.

She was a hell of a fighter when it came to survival. Ciaran checked Stephen and found the same strong, steady pulse. Neither were conscious, and the fact they'd clung to the rock in the freezing water amazed Ciaran. He took them home.

37

*A*n hour seemed like an eternity to Ciaran. Finally, he saw Madeline open her eyes. It amazed him that he had been able to totally control his emotional reactions—the urge to hold her in his arms, to hear her heartbeat, and to feel the vibration of her emotions inside that delicate body assaulted him without mercy and left him defenceless.

He rushed to the bed, pulled her up, and let her body melt into his arms.

Then he released her and said, "Yesterday you promised me you wouldn't walk away from me."

"I might have to break that promise. I only bring you disaster, Ciaran. Nothing good is going to come from you staying with me."

"If you come with a package, I'll take all of it. Why don't you give us a chance?"

She shook her head. "I have to find Jo."

"If we find Jo, will you stay with me, or will you go back to New York?" The question came as a surprise to her, and to him as well. Madeline gave no answer.

"Is Stephen okay?" she asked.

"Yes. Doctor Thomas has taken care of him. He had some minor external injuries. But he's fine. He'd already told me about the attack from his end. He didn't know what happened before he got to you."

"Just after I left Mon Ciel, they attacked me. I don't know how many of them were there—or who they were. I think it was the same people who attacked me at Fosse Way. They shot at me again." She looked down to her injured arm, and frowned.

"You don't feel any pain now because of the painkillers. We make the best." He smiled and sat on the side of her bed. "Madeline, I have a very complicated family."

"Tell me about it!"

"After we find Jo, and if you decide to stay, I'll tell you what you want to know."

His phone buzzed.

"We have to find Jo first," Madeline said emphatically.

Ciaran looked up from his phone and grinned. On the computer screen, Jo looked at Madeline with a big, bright smile on her face. Her catlike, green eyes glittered, and her long black hair was pulled back in a ponytail. "Madeline!" Jo yelped in joy.

Madeline was speechless, and tears flowed.

"Come on, Madeline, don't do that. I'm good now. I could do a somersault right now, but I don't think it's very ladylike to do so, and I might frighten Mr. Serious Detective here." Jo turned aside and winked at him. "I need to cheer her up."

"Keep talking, Jo," Madeline said.

"I got really lucky. In the afternoon, after Zen talked to you, a couple—I don't even know their names—broke into the hotel. They beat Zen up pretty bad and let me go."

Madeline smiled but her tears kept falling.

"The couple told me to hide for a bit before going to the police. So I did. I went to the police early in the evening. Then late that night, Detective Adamson contacted the station and picked me up. I'm in his office right now."

"Last night, I thought—"

"I know. Michael— Detective Adamson told me. It must have been hard on you and everyone involved. I'm so sorry. But I'm fine now. When we finish with the paperwork here, he's going to take me right over to your place . . ." Jo turned sideways. "What? You don't know where she is?"

Ciaran walked over and hopped onto the bed. "Jo, I'll send someone to pick you up."

Jo stared at the screen and cooed, "You must be Ciaran. Thank you for everything you've done for me."

"I didn't do a thing. You saved yourself, Jo. And it was a very smart move to name me as your contact person. You know how to pull strings."

Jo grinned. "You set the strings up first. Otherwise, I'd have had nothing to pull."

"Have you been to England before?"

"Haven't had the pleasure."

"Why don't you stay for a few days? There are many wonderful places to see."

"You made my dreams come true, Ciaran." Jo beamed at the screen. "Madeline and I can finally do our girl shopping in London!"

Madeline nodded. They heard Detective Adamson calling out for Jo. She rolled her eyes. "Paperwork. See you soon. Love you both." She grinned at Madeline and Ciaran and disconnected the call.

"Inviting Jo to stay . . . Very clever, Ciaran. Thank you." She smiled and linked her fingers with his.

As soon as she touched him, he felt the comfort he'd been longing for. Not the comfort, perhaps, but the fear of having it and then losing it—the fear of what came afterward. Something wasn't right. Ciaran shook the thoughts out of his mind.

"Hungry?" he asked.

"Famished."

"Then let's fix that."

Ciaran and Madeline left the room and found Tadgh standing

in the hallway, leaning against the opposite wall with a big grin on his face.

"What are you doing up here?" Ciaran asked.

"Rumor has it that our princess was up, so I just wanted to come to say hello."

Madeline smiled, approaching to give Tadgh a kiss. "How are you, Tadgh?"

"Better than you were at dawn. You scared the hell out of my big brother." Tadgh paused, making a humming noise, then pressed on. "You're still mad at Mother, aren't you?" he said to Ciaran. "Come on, she doesn't deserve your wrath. Be mad at me. You can punch me, if you like."

"Grow up, Tadgh."

"This is as grown up as I can be at the moment. Give me a few more years, will you?"

"Take your time. Mrs. Rutherford is in, and I'm going to introduce Madeline to her famous jam and scones." Ciaran slid his arm around Madeline's back to lead her down the hallway.

"Ah . . ." Tadgh mumbled something.

"What?" Ciaran asked, without turning back.

"Mum is waiting for you in the Great Reception."

Ciaran slowly turned around as if accepting a challenge. "Very well. Would you accompany Madeline to the kitchen?"

"Ah . . . mum asked for *both* of you, actually."

Ciaran knew what was coming and opened his mouth with the intention of asking Madeline to go to the kitchen to stay out of this, but she had already grabbed his arm. "Come on. Let's go have a chat with her."

He had no choice but take her with him. Tadgh followed without making a sound.

38

*T*he Great Reception room was used for family gatherings. Jennifer remembered vividly Conan sitting in the chair in front of the fireplace. Her husband had loved to watch her teach baby Tadgh to walk—he fell so many times trying to run. Conan had gotten a thrill out of a young Ciaran presenting him with new chemical formulas that he had mixed from his mother's cooking recipes.

Ciaran had been only four turning five, but he'd been able to heal many injured wild animals he found in their yard by using things he found in the kitchen and the garden. That pleased Conan tremendously, inasmuch as he was devastated when Ciaran mixed his first explosive compound and blew up the head of the Goddess of Kindness statue. Conan had then put the statue in the middle of the yard to remind Ciaran of the consequences of violence. But Jennifer knew that wouldn't work for Ciaran.

She knew her son.

And she would do whatever it took to keep him safe and to keep this family together under the roof of Mon Ciel. They couldn't afford mistakes this year. She couldn't allow strangers in the house this year.

She knew what was behind the number thirty-three. But she would take the secret to her grave. Revealing it to Ciaran would undo his life. She would rather rot in Hell than doing that.

So for now, she had to eliminate the immediate threat—those strangers in their home—and she had to live with Ciaran's resultant wrath.

Ciaran and Madeline walked in, followed by Tadgh.

Jennifer sat on a chair at the top of a long dining table. "I'm sorry about what happened to you last night, Madeline," she spoke gently.

"They couldn't get to me last night, whoever they were, but I'm sure they'll find another opportunity."

"You're a reasonable girl, Madeline. I'm sure you won't mind me arranging a late breakfast here. I feel like a morning tea myself. Then we can discuss some family business."

"Your house, your rules, Jennifer."

"That's a good sign. We're starting to understand each other a bit better now. Why don't you all sit down?"

Tadgh didn't need a second invitation. He grabbed a chair and settled in.

"Tadgh travels extensively and has experienced great foods all over the world, but he always craves Mrs. Rutherford's scones and jam. At one point, he asked me to express post them to him when he was in Africa!" Jennifer smiled.

"Mother, that's not to be spread around. You promised me," Tadgh protested.

"You were lucky you didn't ask *me* to do that." Ciaran smiled slightly.

"That wasn't luck. I was being smart."

"You know, Madeline, Ciaran's father called this place 'Mon Ciel,' as if this was his blue sky, his heaven, his world. And he wasn't talking about the palace. He meant the family that he loved with all of his heart. Am I correct, Ciaran?"

"What are you getting at, Mother?" Ciaran lowered his voice.

"The LeBlancs were blessed with their fortune, but they were also cursed with secrets, Madeline," Jennifer said.

"She doesn't need to know any of that," Ciaran growled out in protest.

"As you can see, like his father, my son will do whatever it takes to protect the family secrets . . ."

"Mother!" Ciaran stood up.

"And as you can see, he was about to bully his mother out of her place."

"I would never—"

"Then you will give me a fair chance to speak to Madeline. I think she cares for you, so she should hear what I have to say. Don't you agree, Madeline?"

Madeline nodded. "I'll listen, but I'll reserve judgment. There's nothing you can do or say to influence me."

"Naturally! And Ciaran, I will only speak the truth, and if you think otherwise, you can have your say. Of course, that will only happen if you stay. Would you rather stay or leave the room, Ciaran?"

Ciaran sat down slowly, giving Jennifer a warning look.

Jennifer smiled. "Yes, I'd rather you stay. Madeline, Ciaran loved his father—no, more precisely, he worshipped his father. Before you object, Ciaran, let's say you loved your father very much. Is that better?"

No response from Ciaran.

"Yes or no, Ciaran?"

"Yes, I loved Father," Ciaran snarled.

"So much so that your world seemed to stop when he died. So much so that you would not accept his death, although he died from natural causes. So much so that you immersed yourself in natural medicines, exotic pharmaceutical compounds, and any and all computer gimmicks that helped you to fantasize about bringing your father back."

"No, Mother. That's not true. We're finished here, Madeline."

Ciaran stood again, grabbing Madeline's hand so that she would come with him.

"Did you or did you not create the computer character called White Knight?" Jennifer spat out the question.

"What?" Tadgh was astonished.

Madeline stared blankly at Jennifer, and then she turned around to observe Ciaran.

Jennifer continued, "You think your old mother knows nothing about what you do? You think you are in charge of the family, and I am living in oblivion in Dublin?"

"*Create*? So you are *the* White Knight?" Madeline asked, shocked.

"White Knight is a very critical and advanced program that could change the landscape of science, Madeline," Ciaran said.

Madeline stared at him. "I don't question your motives for creating such program. I am sure it will benefit humankind and more. But I *am* questioning your motives toward me. Did you arrange our *coincidental* meeting at Hyde Park?"

"No. I didn't know you before that."

"So did you know what I needed to do at our dinner?"

"Yes, but I only had general information. I didn't know your intentions."

"So that's why you let me into your headquarters so easily. You wanted to scope me out!" Tears welled in Madeline's eyes.

"Madeline!" Ciaran approached, "It's not what it looks like."

"Why didn't you tell me you were *the* White Knight, Ciaran?"

"I . . . I didn't say I wasn't."

"It's the same as a lie. And I lied to you, too. We can't start a relationship based on lies. We aren't meant to be together, are we?" Tears were streaming down Madeline's face now.

"I would never tell a woman I worked with those programs. They're violent games. If she didn't know me, she'd think I was a serial killer," Tadgh chimed in and received a scolding glare from Jennifer.

Madeline stood up and headed toward the door. Ciaran

grabbed her arms. "You said you'd give us a chance, Madeline. We need time." His voice was gentle but firm.

"Will you tell me everything? There can't be any secrets between us—" Madeline said.

"Everyone has secrets they can't share, no matter what," Jennifer cut in.

"Mother!" Ciaran growled, turning toward Jennifer.

"Let me help you elaborate on that, Ciaran. Can you honestly say that your wife did not die because of one of your secrets, Ciaran?"

"Juliette didn't die because of my secrets." Ciaran's voice quieted, but Jennifer could see the anger oozing from his pores. His eyes were red, and a vein on his forehead throbbed. She remained seated, staring at Ciaran while Tadgh stood.

"Perhaps not. Because she died *for* them. She robbed you of your heart, your life, and your secrets. She died for her greed," Jennifer continued.

"Why would you say that, Mother? Why do you hate me?" Ciaran flew in Jennifer's direction. Tadgh darted after him, but he was too slow. Ciaran punched the leg of a statue standing on a head-height column behind Jennifer. It cracked, crumbled, and collapsed to the floor. He braced his hands on the column, trying to suppress his anger.

Jennifer didn't even blink. She didn't need to look behind her to see Ciaran's expression because she could read that on Madeline's face. Madeline stepped back, tears rolling down her face. She turned around and headed toward the door.

Stephen entered the room just then and saw Madeline. He glanced at the scene before him and gently touched Madeline's shoulders. "Madeline, what's the matter?"

"I need to leave. Could you take me out of here, please?"

"You were attacked last night just outside this house. We have to be careful. We haven't found Jo. We could use some help."

"We found her. She got away yesterday and is with Detective

Adamson. Please take me out of here. We can pick her up on the way."

"On the way to where? The car was trashed last night. Could you calm down? Stay here for a bit, and we can sort things out?" Stephen spoke gently.

"I can arrange transportation for you right now, if that's of any help." Jennifer's voice was as cold as steel.

"Lady LeBlanc, if you or your boys do anything to hurt Madeline, I will not let it slide," Stephen growled.

Ciaran turned his gaze from the ruined statue and directed it toward Stephen. Tadgh inched forward. Jennifer knew the sight of her sons would intimidate the hell out of Stephen, so she remained silent.

"They didn't hurt me or anything, Stephen."

"So why the hell do you look like this?"

"I just need to leave. Right now."

"Not until you tell me what happened. What did they do to make you cry?" Stephen threw a lethal stare at Ciaran.

"Nothing happened. It's my problem. Let's go get Jo and head back to New York. I don't belong here."

Stephen shook his head and stiffened his stance.

Madeline huffed out a breath. "Stephen, if you want to stay and pick a fight, feel free to do so—it seems there's enough testosterone in the room to do that—but I will leave here by myself."

The cheery sound of Mrs. Rutherford humming a country song as she pushed her teacart echoed into the room.

"Madeline, please stay a bit longer. The people who attacked you last night might still be out there waiting. If anything happens, I don't think I'm in any shape to help you."

Mrs. Rutherford entered the room, the aroma of her famous scones with jam and freshly brewed jasmine tea filled the room. She stood at the door and noticed the tension in the room right away, saw Madeline's tears.

"Morning tea, everyone." Her voice trembled a bit and sank into an awkward silence.

"Madeline . . ." Ciaran approached.

"Stay the fuck right there, Ciaran," Stephen yelled and stopped Ciaran in his tracks.

Madeline continued to head toward the door and had to step around the teacart.

"You, too! I said stay, Madeline!" Stephen growled.

Madeline took one more step and Stephen ran to her. He grabbed her shoulders violently and threw her back into the room. Madeline fell, rolling on the floor. Ciaran rushed to her, and Jennifer stood up from her chair.

Stephen grabbed Mrs. Rutherford, pulled out his gun, and pointed it at her head. "Stay still," he commanded the room.

Everyone froze.

"Lady LeBlanc, may I ask for your permission to stay thirty minutes longer at your palace?" Stephen asked, a sarcastic smirk on his face.

Ciaran inched closer to Madeline.

"I said, stay still, Ciaran. Or I'll put a bullet in her head." Stephen pressed the gun against Mrs. Rutherford's head.

"Stephen, what's going on?" Madeline asked.

"I wouldn't have had to do this if you'd behaved and done what I said. But you preferred to go about it the hard way."

"Let her go, Stephen. If I did anything to offend you, then take it out on me," Madeline pleaded.

"I would never hurt you, Madeline."

"I know you wouldn't. So let Mrs. Rutherford go. I'll do whatever you say. If you want me to stay here, I will."

"You will?"

"Yes."

"Liar!" Stephen screamed. "She's a stranger. She's nothing to you. I'm your *friend*, Madeline. Have you ever thought of me? Would you do anything for *me?*" Stephen's eyes sparked with insanity.

"You never asked for anything. If you'd asked, I'd have done anything for you." She tried to approach him.

"Stay right there." Stephen raised his gun, aiming at Madeline now. Tadgh and Ciaran rushed Stephen at the same time. Two gun shots discharged from the silencer on the gun muzzle, and both Ciaran and Tadgh slumped to the floor.

39

The sound of the two bullets tore at her heart. Madeline turned around slowly. She knew Ciaran couldn't be dead, but she had to see with her own eyes. Ciaran and Tadgh pulled themselves up from the floor. A bullet had hit Ciaran's left shoulder and Tadgh's right leg. Madeline looked again at Stephen. He shrugged.

"I warned them to stay still." Stephen smirked. "I didn't mean to scare you, Madeline."

"Whatever it is that you want, we can talk about it. Let the women go," Ciaran said.

An insane peal of laughter came from Stephen. "Let the women go? What a gentlemen you are! So why didn't you give Juliette that chance?"

"Who the fuck are you?" Tadgh asked.

Stephen released Mrs. Rutherford, but still held on to her hair. "You don't even know your brother-in-law, Stefan? What kind of husband are you?"

"Juliette never mentioned your name. She must have been embarrassed by your very existence," Ciaran said with scorn.

"She told me enough. How do you think I knew about your technology and was able to get my weapon past it?"

Ciaran smiled. "It's obvious she didn't tell you enough. There is nothing here. You wasted your time and effort to get in."

"You think my sister married you for love?" Stefan laughed.

"What Juliette and I had, a scumbag like you could never understand. If she had married me for our family secrets, you wouldn't be here, threatening women to get what you want. You're pathetic!" Ciaran taunted.

Stefan angrily thrust the gun in Ciaran's direction. Madeline could see he was provoked enough to pull the trigger at any time. Despite the look of insanity on his face now, his eyes were still the same. They were still the eyes of the Stephen who fumbled his words whenever she smiled at him.

"What about *me*? What about *us*? Did you ever have any real feelings for me? I have nothing! I don't have any gold or secrets you could profit from." Madeline stepped toward Stefan.

Stefan's eyes softened a bit. "Of course I have feelings for you, Madeline. It took me years of digging around to find the last line of the Kelleys."

"Me? I'm a Kelley?" Madeline frantically searched in her head for a Kelley in her life. No, it rang no bell.

"Oh yeah! You're powerful when it comes to that. Don't you have any idea where your psychic ability comes from?"

"If you planned this whole thing, then tell me what you want from me."

"You got me inside Mon Ciel. That's all I needed."

"If that's all you needed, why bother with the kidnapping?"

Stefan laughed. "That was Zen's stupid idea. I paid him to design the kidnap and create a scare big enough so that you would call for my help. But then he got fancy. He wanted the stupid hologame program and White Knight and all of that crap. He got tips from the wrong people and did everything *except* getting me what I'd paid him for. Then I had to pay someone else to get Jo off him so that he got nothing to give you at Rufford Abbey..."

Madeline cut in, "You wanted me to call you for help. I did. Now you are here, so do you want me to help you find the crucifix?"

"Oh no, sweetie, you stay right there. You're falling too deeply for that guy." He pointed toward Ciaran with the gun. "Just like Juliette. My feelings for you pretty much guarantee that I won't shoot you . . . unless you provoke me. Now, let's go and get the crucifix. You, come here." Stefan pointed the gun at Jennifer, waving her over.

"Oh, no, no! Don't do that to the lady," Mrs. Rutherford cried out. "Take me."

"Don't provoke him, Mrs. Rutherford." Jennifer walked toward Stefan.

"No, Mother." Ciaran and Tadgh walked toward Jennifer to stop her.

"Don't make me prove myself again!" Stefan yelled out.

"Please don't hurt the lady." Mrs. Rutherford charged toward Stefan. Madeline tried to grab her.

Stefan waved the gun. "Step back! Step back, you two."

A voice on the intercom announced, "Doctor Thomas has just arrived at the gate. He is on his way in."

Stefan was distracted momentarily, and Mrs. Rutherford charged toward the intercom corner and hit the panic button. Madeline tried to pull her back, but it was too late. Stefan fired his gun. The single bullet pierced Mrs. Rutherford's chest. She fell back into Madeline's arms, dead.

Alarm bells rang all over the building, and Madeline deduced that it would alert the central security system and all related parties in the LeBlanc's security network.

Stefan laughed. He pointed the gun at Jennifer.

Ciaran and Tadgh stood up to protect their mother. But they stood at a distance, and Stefan could take them down, one by one.

Ciaran stepped forward. He looked as if he could grind Stefan into dust with his bare hands. Stefan pointed the gun at Ciaran. "Don't be foolish."

Suddenly it felt as if a whole army of security guards was

charging toward the Great Reception. Madeline could feel the motion of many approaching people. She was sure Stefan knew it, too.

Jennifer cried out and slumped down, gasping for air. She was as white as a sheet. Ciaran ran over and held his mother. "She has asthma. She needs her medicine."

"I'll get it." Tadgh stood up.

"No one goes anywhere." Stefan waved his gun. "The faster you give me what I want, the faster she'll get her meds. Now come here."

"She can hardly stand Stefan," Madeline scolded.

"Then you ought to help her."

Madeline went toward Jennifer. "Can you hold up a little longer?" Jennifer was gasping but nodded. Madeline helped her up. "Now what?" Madeline asked.

"All right, the crucifix was in one of the statues. Given that you have so many in this house, where do you want to start? Be strategic, as Lady LeBlanc here doesn't look as if she can last long," Stefan said coldly.

"Right here, then," Ciaran responded.

The Great Reception was at the far end of the old section of the house. Madeline knew the old statues were marble or stone, and it would be really hard to hide anything in there. It would more likely be in the new extension of the house. Ciaran said it had been built around ten years ago. That must have been when he had married Juliette. So Ciaran was hoping to bide some time, Madeline thought. She took Jennifer to the chair.

"Well, then." Stefan signaled a go ahead. "Lead the way."

"What do you want me to do? Hammer the statues?" asked Ciaran.

"That won't be necessary. My little sister was a smart cookie. She would have tagged it with electronic chips. Do a scan. And do it carefully." He put his portable scanner on the floor and kicked it toward Ciaran.

Stefan was standing very close to Jennifer and Madeline, his back against the wall. That way, he had a full view of the entire room, the door, and the security team in the hallway.

The team apparently didn't know what to do, Madeline thought. She doubted Ciaran had had any time to replace Robert, and now with both Ciaran and Tadgh in this room, security clearly didn't have any leadership.

The warm and friendly voice of Doctor Thomas came across the room from the door. "Stephen, this is Doctor Thomas. I examined you this morning."

"Yes, I remember you. And it's Stefan. What do you want?"

"Could I please bring some water and medicine in for Jennifer, and check the bleeding on the boys' gunshot wounds?"

"Water and meds for the woman is okay. Nothing for the boys. Don't try anything silly, Doctor Thomas. See for yourself." Stefan nodded toward Mrs. Rutherford's dead body. Madeline could see the doctor's eyes waver with pity and sorrow for a fraction of a second, then he was calm again.

"Yes, Stefan. I can see clearly. May I come in now?"

Stefan waved his gun to signal Doctor Thomas to come in.

By the time they had finished scanning all the statues in the old quarter, the sun had begun setting, and the lights in the building had illuminated. They moved on toward the new quarter.

As soon as they entered the long corridor where the twelve statues stood, including the one with the missing toe, Madeline knew that what Stefan wanted was there. She shifted and felt the broken toe still in her jacket pocket. She swore to herself that if there was truly the spirit of a god in that statue, and if he helped her solve this disaster, not only she would put his toe back, but she would also name her first son after him.

The first statue Ciaran scanned resulted in a positive beeping signal. Stefan's face brightened. Ciaran slid his fingers along the edge of the marble base where the signal was the strongest. It was one solid piece of marble—no handle, button, or compartment of any kind. Then he stopped at a small copper plaque. That had to be it.

Stefan grabbed Jennifer and pulled her with him. Using a hunting knife, he gave the edge of the plaque a nudge. Nothing. He stabbed hard into the niche around the plaque until the copper piece gave way and dropped to the floor. Inside was a computer disc, neatly tucked away in plastic.

Stefan grabbed the disc and mumbled to himself. "What the fuck?"

"Do you want to read the disc?" Ciaran asked.

"You think I'm stupid? You want me to use your computer so you can copy it?"

Ciaran shrugged. "I'm curious, of course."

Stefan swung a hard kick at Ciaran's abdomen. Ciaran slumped to the floor, heaving in pain. His shoulder bled.

Jennifer cried out, "What else do you want? The crucifix apparently isn't here."

"I know!" Stefan screamed, giving Jennifer a hard push so that she fell into Madeline's arm.

Stefan pulled Ciaran up from the floor. As Ciaran was much taller than Stefan, he made a nice human shield. "I need to go now, and your master will escort me to safety." Stefan addressed the hopeless security team. "One wrong move from you, and he will eat my bullets. Now get out of my way."

The security backed off. Madeline could see that they have absolutely no idea how to handle the situation.

Stefan pulled Ciaran with him, backing out the door.

Madeline followed. "Stefan, you're a smart man, and you know better than anyone that your sister would have coded the disc, and that Ciaran might be the only person who can decode it for you."

Stefan laughed. "You've definitely fallen head over heels for this guy. You just don't want me to kill him, do you?"

"They were married, Stefan. You might not want to hear this, but their marriage was far more important to her than your brother-sister relationship. Otherwise, she would have given you the information. If she coded something in that disc, who do you thing she would let read it? You can barely turn a computer on."

"You'd better stop talking and stay right there."

"That's enough. You want to go, let's go," Ciaran cut in.

"I hate to repeat myself, but don't move. You won't like the consequences." Stefan threw out his last threat, addressing everyone, and pulled Ciaran away into a waiting car.

At the entrance of the house, Madeline watched as the car zoomed into the darkness. She heard a rumbling, chaotic movement behind her. Then there was a click and a humming sound, and a blue wave of light flashed outside and blanketed the entire Mon Ciel estate. Then the light disappeared, and Mon Ciel returned to its normal magnificence.

Jennifer cried out and slumped to the floor. Tadgh held his mother, a tear rolling down his face. Madeline could see his body shaking with emotion, but he tried to remain calm, perhaps to hang on to a thread of hope.

There was nothing in Jennifer's eyes but devastation.

Madeline approached and crouched next to Jennifer. In front of her was a desperate mother. "What was that blue light?" she asked, knowing that whatever the answer was, it wouldn't be good news.

"Ciaran put Mon Ciel in lockdown mode." Tears streamed down Jennifer's face.

Madeline frowned and looked at Tadgh.

"That means all weapons and machinery will be neutralized at the contact point outside the protective shield. No one can attack us from the outside," Tadgh explained.

"Can we take weapons out from the inside?" Madeline asked.

Tadgh shook his head. "You can't even drive a car out."

"Can you unlock it?"

Tadgh shook his head again. "Ciaran coded the lock. No one has access."

"Does that mean none of us can go out and help him if we need to?" Madeline asked.

"The shield doesn't stop human passing," Tadgh said.

They saw a flash flare up in the distant darkness and the sound of an explosion which was muffled by the thick foggy air. Jennifer was pale and numb with pain.

"I'm going after Ciaran," Madeline said and stood up.

"I'll go with you," Tadgh said.

"Not with that leg," Madeline snarled and strode to the kitchen. She grabbed a couple of knives and tucked them into her belt. When she returned to the hall, Tadgh had already patched up his wound. He had a combat knife tucked at his waist.

Seeing Madeline enter, Tadgh grinned. "If you can go out there in the dark on foot with those kitchen knives, I can do it with one good leg. Doctor Thomas patched up this stupid wound—and Ciaran's kick-ass painkillers will come in handy."

Madeline nodded. When she walked past, Jennifer grabbed her arm. "I'm in debt to you for this," she said. The tears had dried on her face, but the worry and exhaustion haunted her eyes.

"Ciaran went out to Fosse Way for me. This is the least I can do for him." She turned on her heel. Tadgh finished giving instructions to the troops staying behind, and then he followed Madeline out the door.

40

*C*iaran clung to the steering wheel and focused on the dark road ahead. He could drive this road with his eyes closed, but at the moment, the more Stefan thought he was struggling, the better it was for him. Stefan didn't notice he had flicked on the protective shield to put Mon Ciel on lockdown. Those he loved would be safe inside the shield. Stefan wouldn't be working alone, and Ciaran wasn't sure how many he had left behind to attack Mon Ciel.

They were approaching the bridge over the creek where he had picked Madeline up this morning. He knew this creek well. Fast running water hit the rocks and created strange sounds that could sometimes be calming and therapeutic. But not now. Going down there with a bleeding wound on his shoulder was probably a dumb move, but it might be the only option he had.

Ciaran swung the steering wheel hard to lift the car over the rail. The bullet in his left shoulder was damn inconvenient. Instead of going over, the car smashed into the cement rail. The air bag assaulted his face and almost made him black out although he had anticipated the impact and turned sideways.

When the car grinded to a stop, there was no movement from Stefan. Ciaran unbuckled himself and exited the car, but before he could get to the other side to get Stefan's gun, strong headlights flashed at him. A truck and an armed group of men stood waiting at the bridge. They raised their guns and stopped Ciaran in his tracks.

From the passenger side of the car, Stefan emerged, rubbing his head. "Where the fuck have you been? I messaged you from the house!"

A man from the group stepped forward. "We didn't have a signal," he told Stefan.

Stefan pulled out a portable device and looked at the screen. "The gun works, but this piece of shit sure doesn't."

"Did you get what you need?"

"Not quite."

"So you still need him?" The man pointed his gun toward Ciaran.

Stefan shrugged. "Yes. Take him. Let's go." He walked toward the truck. Blood streamed from Ciaran's wound. He swayed and slumped to the ground. Stefan glanced back. "Take him with us. I need him."

The man nodded and approached Ciaran. But as soon as he touched Ciaran's arms, Ciaran jumped to his feet, stepped around him, and before he could do anything in retaliation, confiscated his gun. Ciaran stood behind him, using him as a shield, and pointed the gun at the man's temple.

Stefan turned back and cocked an eyebrow. "Only I use tricks like that, Ciaran. You think that will work on me?"

Stefan shot straight at the man's head. His brain splattered all over Ciaran.

Ciaran felt a force coming up from behind him and could see all the men standing next to the truck in front of him raising their guns. Stefan dove behind the truck. Ciaran swiveled to the side of the bridge toward the car.

The group of men behind him marched head on to those

standing next to the truck. Guns discharged, and bullets sprayed from both sides.

A man behind him covered Ciaran. Bullets rained and punched holes in the man's body. He fell and squashed Ciaran to the ground. Men around him slumped to the ground like tree trunks. Ciaran heard the sounds of car tires squealing, and then everything went quiet.

He flipped the dead man on top of him over, steam still wafting from the bullet holes in his body. Ciaran observed a large hole in the man. "Wires," he muttered.

The thing on top of him was not a man.

Ciaran stood. There were about a dozen men-like beings in the group that had just rescued him. Before they could get too close, Ciaran hurled himself at the cement rail and threw his body over the bridge and into the rapids. If he wasn't mistaken, those men on the bridge were there to take him. *Thirty-three year cycle*, he thought. Was this the end of his human life?

His father had worked until the day he died to prevent this from happening. If this meant his death, he was fine with it. Everyone had to die someday. But his father had called this his *duty*—and he had said that he could deny it.

But what kind of duty? And if he had to go somewhere, what about his family here? And what about Madeline? She hadn't answered him when he'd asked if she would stay with him or go back to New York. He hadn't had a chance to explain to her that he had never meant to lie to her or hurt her in any way.

The icy water was pulling him with incredible speed, freezing every blood cell of whatever blood he had left in his body. He saw a large clump of tree branches floating in the water. The force of the water was going to slam him into the tree branches, impaling his body on those giant claws. Ciaran used every ounce of his leftover strength and flipped his body sideways before he hit the branches.

The blow was like an explosion in his brain. He remained still for a moment, and then began to follow the tangle of tree branches to the bank of the creek. He slumped to the ground, trying to catch his breath and shivering with the cold. Then he felt a movement in front of him, and when he looked up, the group of men-like things from the bridge were surrounding him.

One of them spoke, "We're here to help you and mark your entry." Its voice was surprisingly human.

"Entry to what?" Ciaran's vision started to blur with his fatigue.

"Entry to the realm of righteousness and fulfilling your duty."

"Stop the bullshit. Who wants me? For what and where?"

Silence.

Ciaran chuckled. He wanted to laugh heartily but didn't have the energy to do so. In front of him stood a bunch of advanced artificial creatures with hardwired brains. His questions hadn't been previously programmed, so there was no way they could give him an answer.

"We are here to help you and mark your entry," the robot repeated.

"No. I reject your request." Ciaran used language that he speculated the robot would understand. "Go back to your commander and request him to contact me directly."

The eyes of the robot flashed as if processing the information. "We are here to help you and mark your entry," it repeated again.

Shit. This is their one-off mission. Ciaran turned to run but only made a couple of steps before he was surrounded. He felt a puncture at the back of his neck, and the world went black.

41

*W*ith Tadgh trailing behind, Madeline ran in the dark, the bitter winter breeze slapping at her face and crawling under her skin. It might not be the chill but the fear of losing Ciaran that was clawing at her heart. She wanted one last chance to tell him she understood him, and that she was forever in his debt for going after her and protecting her at Fosse Way.

The moment the basket with four-week-old Madeline had landed in front of a random house, she'd had no protection from either those who had created her or those who raised her. Her soul was damaged. The thought that she was unwanted, and that she had been a mistake in this world had created a void in her that had never been filled.

Until, that is, she'd felt Ciaran's arms wrapped around her shoulders, protecting her from the bullets at Fosse Way. But it wasn't his heroic action that moved her. It was his genuine intent to protect her.

The man trusted no one. But in his most vulnerable moment during his rage, a flaw he wouldn't reveal to anyone, he had reached out to her. When their fingers had linked, when their hands were joined, she found the connection she had always longed for.

He filled her void. And somehow, she thought she filled his.

They approached the bridge, and the scene tore at her heart. Ciaran's car was severely smashed, crashed into the side of the bridge. But it hadn't gone over into the water. There were smear of blood, pools of red, and skid marks of larger vehicles. It looked like a war zone. But there was no sign of Ciaran.

Her heart thundered, and her blood boiled with fear. The winter air didn't seem cold anymore.

Where is he?

Tadgh was saying something, but she couldn't hear him. If her psychic ability was real and of any use, she needed it to work right now. But the signal was only strong if it was sent both ways. She could track him, but it might take forever, and it might not be accurate at all.

Help me, Ciaran, where are you? All you have to do is to think about me. Please!

And then it came. A flock of blue dots flashing at her from down the creek. She charged toward them as if her life depended on it.

There he was. Madeline saw the shape of his body sprawled on the ground. She trampled tree branches, rocks, and whatever poor wild animals were in her way. She hurried toward his body and knelt down. From the ground, Ciaran smiled up at her.

"Thank you for thinking of me. I couldn't do it without you," Madeline said to him while tears rolled down her face. She brushed the hair from his face. He was shivering, soaking wet, and there was blood everywhere.

She took her jacket off, but Tadgh pushed her aside. "Your jacket is just for show, Madeline." Tadgh took his thick coat off and wrapped it around Ciaran. "You've done a good job locking Mon Ciel down, Ciaran. Now we have no car, no chopper, and no men. Are you okay to stay here by yourself, Madeline? I'll run back to get more men to help carry him back."

"I can walk," Ciaran said weakly.

"Walk, my ass."

Ciaran tried to sit up, but he flopped back down and passed out.

"I rest my case," Tadgh mumbled and stood up to leave. Then they saw Mon Ciel's shield flash up in a brilliant blue light and turn off.

"Holy fu—," Tadgh muttered. "How you do that, Mother?" he asked the air.

The helicopter dispatched from Mon Ciel and, in a short moment, the search light swept over the spot where they were waiting.

42

*S*he couldn't restrain herself. She flew to the bed and panted a hard kiss on Ciaran's cheek as soon as he opened his smoky gray eyes. He smiled at her. They heard a protesting moan from the corner of the room.

"He's jealous." Madeline grinned. "Come here!" She patted her hand on the bed next to Ciaran. From the corner of the room, the puppy darted forward and leaped onto the bed.

"This is TJ," Madeline said.

"TJ?" Ciaran asked, ignoring the dog sitting on the bed with his pink tongue poking out and his tail waving frantically.

"It's for traffic jam. Isn't it how you got him?"

"I didn't *get* him. He picked me because my car was the best looking one in the line."

"Is that right, TJ?" Madeline asked.

TJ lowered his head and snuggled against Ciaran's hip.

"Lily couldn't take care of him. She and her husband have a small apartment and are planning to have a family. So if you don't take TJ in, he really will have to go to the pound."

"I'll ask Laurent."

TJ gave Ciaran his most pathetic puppy look.

"Come on, if the magnificent Mon Ciel can't accommodate a puppy, how can it accommodate me and my friend Jo?"

"Laurent's place is more appropriate. She has a yard and she loves . . . Wait, what did you just say?"

"I wondered whether Mon Ciel has room for me and Jo. I talked to her just a few hours ago. She's on her way to the London head-quarters, and Lindsay will take her here."

Ciaran sat up. "TJ, I'll build you a doghouse, find you a girl-friend, and make sure you have plenty to eat for the rest of your natural dog life. Now, get out of the room—and close the door behind you."

TJ kept his puppy eyes fixed on Ciaran.

"That's all I can give you for now."

TJ licked Ciaran's hand then hopped off the bed and exited the room.

Ciaran held Madeline's hand and played with her long fingers. She interlocked her fingers with his.

"How long was I out?"

"Long enough. You're not in pain now, are you?"

Ciaran shook his head. "No. We make top of the line painkillers." He lifted his blanket and looked at his body—he was wearing nothing but bandages. Then he chuckled when he saw the smug look on Madeline's face.

"Sorry, I couldn't help it."

"Not fair," Ciaran said and pulled Madeline into his arms.

"I don't want to squash your injuries."

"I'll risk it." He kissed her.

"Seriously, Ciaran. You have cracked and bruised ribs, three gashes on your legs, one on your right arm, and one on your back. I highly suggest that you limit the number of bullets you take in your left shoulder. Next time, switch to the other side."

"Thanks for the suggestion."

"Now, you might want to tell me how you seem to have left a war zone behind you on the bridge. How many men did you have to fight off to sustain the amount of injuries you've got, and among those you killed, was Stefan included?"

Ciaran winced when reality hit him, along with all of the issues he now had to confront.

"Stefan got away. And I didn't kill any men. There were two groups—one helped Stefan, and the other helped me. They canceled each other out."

"The group that helped you, are they the ones who gave you the tattoo?"

Ciaran frowned. Madeline peeled off a bandage on his left forearm, revealing a small tattoo of a crucifix.

The image glared back at Ciaran, another reminder of a brutal reality. Ciaran sat, leaning against the headboard. "Juliette and I shared a passion for alchemy. After we were married, she moved in here and started to work on a lot of alchemy-based medical formulas. Mother never trusted her. She said Juliette married me for reasons other than love."

Madeline laid her head on Ciaran's chest and kept their hands linked. He kissed her hair and stroked her back with his free hand.

"You loved her." She made a mental note but didn't realize that she had spoken out loud.

Ciaran nodded. He tilted Madeline's face up and looked into her eyes. "Yes, I love her and I always will."

"How did she die?"

"She was working on an important formula. She was confident, and I was young, foolish, and ambitious. She tested the formula on herself, and I didn't stop her. It didn't work. She died in my arms." His voice was hollow with the pain from the haunting past.

Madeline shifted and pushed Ciaran down to his pillow, kissing him lightly. "It wasn't your fault." She hoped her sultry voice melted into his mind and would have some soothing effect.

"It's a longer story than I care to tell. But she wouldn't have died if it wasn't for me. The most painful part was that Mother got the information that Juliette had taken a secret formula from our family and had hidden it in an artifact, a crucifix. I don't know where Mother got that information, but at the time, I didn't want to know—or believe it."

Ciaran tried to sit up, but Madeline held him down firmly.

"We scanned the house anyway and found nothing." Ciaran sighed and closed his eyes. "I later found a copy of our secret formula in the lab—that's the living proof of an attempt to duplicate it. My mother had been right all along. I never told her about what I'd found. But she always, despite the lack of evidence, believed that Juliette had an agenda in marrying me."

"And you love them both."

"What Juliette and I had was love, Madeline. I can't lie to you about that . . ."

Madeline covered his mouth with hers. She loved a man who knew how to love. If there wasn't any more room for love in his heart, then the current companionship they shared would be enough for her. . . Or maybe not. That last thought stopped her kiss and pulled a tear from her eye. It fell onto Ciaran's lips.

He swapped their positions so that she was beneath him. He gazed into her big brown eyes and rubbed his thumb at the dimple on her left cheek. "What I found in you is more important than the passionate love people have in their twenties. I don't know what you expect or look for in a relationship, but if the love that I had for Juliette is what you want, then I don't have that left in me."

Madeline tried to sit up, but Ciaran held her down firmly. He wiped a tear that escaped from her eye. "I can't speak for you. But let me be very selfish by telling you this. What I found in you is a missing part of me that I never thought I would find again. A part of me that I didn't even know I had lost. When I lost it, I simply didn't exist anymore. But now that part makes me whole. *You* make me whole."

She pulled him down to the bed so they lay face to face and traced her fingers along his jawline. "I've never been important to anyone."

"Then you start now." Ciaran pulled her toward him and devoured her lips. "Be a part of my life. Let me explore you." The sound came from deep in his throat. The words, the tone, and the meaning flew deliciously into her ears and into her soul as he whispered them. She reached up, kissing his throat, and at the same time, she yanked off her blouse.

He pleasured her jaw with small kisses, working his way down to her throat and then to her breasts. Her hands fumbled with the button of her pants, and she gasped and clawed at the bed sheet for purchase as he pulled them off in one swift move. His mouth assaulted her without mercy.

She hadn't been touched like this.

Hadn't been loved like this.

And hadn't been needed like this.

By anyone.

Every move he made was full of thought, care, love, and desire.

She was more than a woman. She was the one he needed.

And she was the one who reciprocated.

She flipped him over so she was on top of him. And what she had received from him, she gave back. And more.

More.

She locked her hands with his.

She was drunk in his pleasure as he did hers.

They moved in rhythm, in sync with their hearts and their minds. They took each other to another place that only they knew.

Their secret place.

A LONG WHILE LATER, Madeline nuzzled in Ciaran's arms, looking at the deep color of the feature wall and the elegant detail of the furniture in the room. She didn't want to stir as she might wake him. She loved to watch him sleep, to hear his heartbeat, and to feel the virility seeping out of his skin.

How long would this last? Hell, she didn't care. At the moment, she was on top of the world.

Ciaran's phone buzzed. She ignored it, but it had wakened Ciaran.

Damn!

Ciaran opened his eyes groggily and grabbed the phone. "Lindsay?" Ciaran's eyes switched to full alert mode instantly. He then grabbed the remote control and pointed it at the wall. The "wall" pulled up, revealing a gigantic screen.

On the screen was breaking news about Detective Adamson who had been killed in his own apartment.

Madeline's phone buzzed. She jumped off the bed and grabbed it.

"Jo?" Madeline gasped and held up the screen of her phone for Ciaran to see. There was no caller ID.

Ciaran shook his head. "It's not Jo. It's Stefan."

THE MULTIVERSE COLLECTION

A SHADE OF MIND
by D.N Leo

RANDOM PSYCHIC
FOREVER MORTAL
ELUSIVE BEINGS
IMPERFECT DIVINE

>>>SERIES HOME PAGE<<<

AFTERWORD

Thank you for reading.

If you enjoyed reading **Random Psychic**, I would appreciate it if you would help others enjoy this book, too.

Recommend it. Please help other readers find this book by recommending it to friends, readers' groups and discussion boards.

Review it. Please tell other readers why you liked this book by reviewing it. A few sentences will make a significant difference to me. If you do write a review, please send me an email at info@dnleo.com so I can thank you with a personal email.

Connect with me online:

Web: http://dnleo.com ; Twitter: @dnleostory

Facebook page of the Outlanders of the Multiverse series

https://www.facebook.com/dnleomultiverse/

FOREVER MORTAL

SYNOPSIS

Forever Mortal - A Shade of Mind - Book 2

Synopsis

Thirty-three years' worth of secrets fall on the shoulders of Ciaran and Madeline with a force that even their enduring love for each other might not help them survive. How much will they give, take, and sacrifice for each other and for those they love?

This second installment in an urban fantasy thriller series, filled with romance and science fiction twists and turns, will take you to the deepest corners of the minds of those who dare to love against all odds.

A drop of blood leaked from the center of the flower, ran down a petal, and dropped onto the wooden bench. The sound of it hitting the bench was in harmony with the raindrops tapping on the tin roof of the small shed.

Ciaran blinked.

The drop of blood vanished before his eyes.

"Ciaran!"

The voice came from Mrs. Hanson, an old gypsy, who approached him from behind. He almost jumped out of his skin. Almost. He cleared his throat, loosened up his tie and smiled. "Mrs. Hanson, I am here for the flowers."

"Certainly." Her smile was crooked. Ciaran thought she had probably been a mysterious and very beautiful woman before things had gone wrong with her alchemical practice. She had crossed the dangerous grounds of natural medicine and had paid a dear price. "I'll get the ribbons and wrap them for you."

Ciaran nodded in appreciation and returned to examine the flowers.

The purple strikes and swirls on the white petals of the Mountain Avens he had chemically engineered looked perfect. He understood why Juliette liked these wild flowers. They were plain, free, and determined, just like her spirit. He had created the purple strikes on the petals to make the flowers uniquely hers. Or maybe, to reflect her in his mind.

She had fallen in love with the flowers when they were on their honeymoon in Ireland over a year ago.

She'd intrigued him since the very first time they met. He was checking out a rare book in the library at Oxford University. She approached him, a total stranger, and asked if she could borrow a few dollars for a cup of pumpkin soup. Who could say no to her brilliant smile, magnificent flaming red hair, and eyes that contained a sea of innocence.

She did have a perfect explanation for asking. She wanted the soup. The shop was closing, so there wasn't enough time for her to run back to her dorm for the money. And after she got her soup, he walked her home to get his money back. At least, that was his excuse.

One thing led to another, and the next thing he knew, he married her despite his mother's objection.

"These flowers are cursed." Mrs. Hanson's voice interrupted Ciaran's concentration.

"I beg your pardon?" Ciaran had never raised his voice to Mrs. Hanson, or to anyone, but this statement not only demeaned his work and his belief in science but also his intentions to Juliette.

Mrs. Hanson shrugged as she wrapped a sheet of tissue paper around a pot of Mountain Avens and affixed a bow to it.

"I'm not a believer, Mrs. Hanson."

"Then you should start believing."

"You're wasting my time. What's the problem with the flowers?"

"You and Juliette are my good students. I don't want one of you to end up dead. I've been watching these flowers grow every day in my lab. They aren't normal. A couple of them turned red and bled drops of blood before they died yesterday."

"And you didn't think to let me know?"

"I'm letting you know now. You think I should have called your headquarters and wormed my way through an army of your minions just to tell you your little flowers died under tragic circumstances?"

Ciaran shrugged and pushed the pot of flowers away.

"So you don't want the flowers now? You believe me that they're cursed?"

"Of course I don't believe you. But you've said it now, and I don't feel comfortable giving them to Juliette anymore."

"Very well then. It's your decision." Mrs. Hanson smiled and turned on her heel to leave.

"Mrs. Hanson!"

"Yes."

"Never mind." Ciaran turned and strode out of Mrs. Hanson's little lab. There was no way in hell he was going to ask her whether the curse would still have an effect even if he didn't touch the flowers. *Ciaran LeBlanc is not superstitious,* he scolded himself.

He invented medicine that could change the landscape of science. He understood and accepted the fine line between science and fiction. He understood the human cognitive system and how theology worked on the human mind.

People had different beliefs. He could tolerate the differences. *But a curse? Hell no.* He wouldn't even mention it to Juliette because it was ludicrous. Juliette was a scientist.

He accidentally stepped on a bunch of wild daisies on his way out. As he moved his foot away, he saw trace of blood.

He jumped off the flowers, but the blood vanished right in front of him.

What the hell? He shook his head. He had been working way too hard in the last couple of weeks on a new project. It must be fatigue. Ciaran left Mrs. Hanson's house in a hurry.

He needed to go home.

2

---

*T*he familiar scent of vanilla and roses greeted Ciaran. He kicked his shoes off on the lush carpet of his master suite at Mon Ciel, the palace belonging to his family.

He might tell Juliette about the blood flowers. Whether or not he believed in superstition, what happened bothered him more than a little.

He pulled the tie from his collar and walked into the closet when a cool hand covered his eyes from behind. A voice as light and colorful as an Irish lullaby whispered into his ear, "Hello, stranger. My husband won't be happy at all when he finds out about you."

He turned around. "Your husband shouldn't be surprised. He married such a beautiful woman, he should know he's got competition."

He lifted her up. Juliette wrapped her long legs around his waist and let him carry her to bed. He lay her down on the bed and ravished her mouth. He hadn't seen her all day long—he was starved for her. He could comfortably justify it as the lust of newlyweds.

His hands stopped on her flaming red gown. She was wearing artfully applied makeup and her favorite perfume.

"Is there an occasion I have forgotten?" he asked, searching his mind frantically but coming up with nothing of significance attached to this particular day.

Juliette sat up, adjusted her hair, and smiled at him. "Do you like the dress?"

"Only if you wear it . . . and then take it off when appropriate . . ." He grinned.

He stood next to the bed, preparing for whatever might be coming at him. She still lay down, lazily rubbing her bare foot against his thighs.

"You've got to have an opinion about the dress as I'm wearing it to a very important function in a couple of weeks." She smiled.

Ciaran rolled his eyes and flopped face down on the bed. Juliette rubbed his back and wrapped her long legs around him. "I don't care what your forever-extended family will do for your birthday. But I have to have my private time with you. Also you have to open my presents before you deal with everyone else."

"I'm not dealing with anyone." His voice was muffled in the mattress.

"Darling, you're turning thirty. You've got to grow up at some point."

He sat up, leaning against the headboard. "This is my room, and you are my wife. That's all I want to know right now. I don't want to bring my family or anyone else into this bedroom."

She stood up. "And that's why we're celebrating your birthday here and now, just the two of us!"

He laughed. "It's a very attractive proposition. But it would be even better if you didn't wear any dress at all."

She winked. "I've got to wear something for you to take off." She went to the wall cabinet and opened it. Inside was a tray with appetizers, a small birthday cake, champagne, and a small box wrapped in a bright purple ribbon. She poured champagne into some tall, slender glasses and brought them over to the bed.

She was stunning. He took his glass, still sitting on the bed, his eyes fixed on her face. He just wanted to ravish those lips that were made for sex. He hopped off the bed.

"No. You stay right there, birthday boy." She used a single finger to push him back to a sitting position on the bed. She climbed onto him and straddled his lap, facing him. As she gazed at him, he caught a brief glimpse of something strange in her eyes, but he was too distracted to dwell on it.

She drained her champagne. When he reached to kiss her lips, she stopped him. She yanked his shirt open and moved her lips to his chest. His pulse quickened, but just when his hands started to roam over her body, she whispered, "Let's look at your presents first." She put a small box in his hand.

He smiled and opened it. It was a small vial containing a clear liquid. He opened his mouth to say something, but she put a finger on his lips to stop his words. "You don't have to take it. But if your migraines turn bad, promise me you'll give this a try."

"Juliette!"

"Unless you don't trust me."

"You're one of the most competent engineers I've ever met. But I don't believe in Mrs. Hanson's natural medicines. I know you use her ingredients."

Juliette smiled. "I understand. And as I said, you don't have to take it."

He touched her cheek. "I don't want to disappoint you. Let's not argue over a headache medicine."

"What about something grander? Life, for example." She hummed the tune of a song she had written during their honeymoon, "Little hummingbird, do you see the sky? It is free. It is yours. Fly. Past the mountains. Past the oceans. There you will find love . . ."

"Juliette, what have you done?" He was beginning to understand the strange look in her eyes before. What he had seen was a shade of dark satisfaction. "Have you been working on the Golden Life?" he asked, knowing the answer already.

It was a project they'd started together before they got married —a medicine that could revive the newly dead. If successful, it would change the landscape of modern medicine. Only that would give Juliette this look of accomplishment.

"You have to be happy with this present, Ciaran. We've got it. We've made it. The Golden Life. I revived the lab rat. It didn't just come back as it was before—it was *better* than before death."

He had guessed the answer, but it still felt as if she had pulled the rug out from under him. "Are you out of your mind, Juliette?"

"You've worked on it your whole life, Ciaran. Why do you suddenly want to stop? Is it because it needs one ingredient you don't approve of?"

"And you've gone ahead and put it in apparently!" he could feel his rage coming. *Control*, he warned himself.

She smiled, a warm smile that was fading by the second. "You were right. That ingredient enabled the completion of the medicine. But it works. It's cruel, but it *works*, Ciaran." The smile had faded from her face, and she swayed. He caught her in his arms and carried her to the bed.

"Jesus Christ, don't tell me you tried it on yourself."

"Not yet."

"What did you take?"

She was almost out of breath. "My potion. There's nothing you can do, Ciaran. It was in my champagne glass." She smiled again.

"I can't believe you would do this to me, Juliette. Where's the damn drug?"

"In the cabinet."

He scrambled to the cabinet and saw another present dressed in purple ribbon. Opening it, he found a syringe in a box. He grabbed it and darted toward his wife.

Juliette lay in the bed, her eyes glassed over, but she still hummed her song. "Little hummingbird, do you see the sky?"

She grabbed his hand when he wanted to inject the medicine into her. "Not yet, Ciaran. If you do it now, it won't work."

"I can't wait until you die. I can't do that . . ."

"You have to. You should be happy, Ciaran, for what we have accomplished."

"I don't care . . ." He gathered her into his arms and rocked her. Regardless of whether he liked it or not, he knew she had to die for the medicine to work. She had to die so he could revive her. "Tell me you're not in pain, please . . ." he whispered.

"You were born to do this, Ciaran. You will change people's lives. You're a crusader."

"You don't know what it means to me, so don't say that."

"I know what it means to you. I know what it's like to do something that's larger than life. If I could be a part of your journey, I'll be happy."

"Please tell me you're not in pain . . ."

"I love you, Ciaran . . ." She closed her eyes and drew in her last breath.

He felt the vibration of emotion ready to burst out from him. His uncontrollable rage was coming. He was furious at himself and at the life's mission he'd set himself up with. He was angry it had caught up to the woman he loved. But there was no time to wallow in self-pity now. He held his breath and steadied his hands. He couldn't make mistakes now. He had to stay calm. He put Juliette down on the bed and checked the syringe. Then he injected the golden liquid into her.

He waited.

Ten seconds.

Thirty seconds.

Sixty seconds.

His head was pounding with a migraine, but he ignored it and concentrated on Juliette. There were no vital signs indicating she was coming back.

Stay calm! He stood from the bed and took the syringe. He would go to the lab, check the sample, and find the solution. He always found a way to get himself out of impossible situations. He had taken only two steps when the room exploded with light. Ciaran was thrown against the wall like a rag doll.

When he pulled himself up, he saw a man in his late fifties with flowing white hair, standing in a circle of white and blue light in the middle of the room. He looked quite formidable in his long black robe. "You killed her," said the man.

"No, I didn't. But if I don't get to the medicine, she will die."

The man looked Ciaran up and down. "I thought you were better than this. If it was possible to make the Golden Life, you would have made it."

The Golden Life was his deepest secret—only people in his family would know about it. His mind raced hundreds of possibilities why this stranger knew his secret. But he had to tend to Juliette. "I have to get to the lab!" Ciaran rushed toward the door.

An invisible force grabbed at him and threw him to the wall again. "No point. She's dead, and that's your fault."

The man stared at Ciaran. The man didn't making any physical movement except for a slight narrowing of his eyes. The invisible force squeezed around Ciaran's neck, choking him.

"Air bending. Who are you?" Ciaran gasped for air.

The man smirked. "You're knowledgeable, Ciaran, but not enough to save yourself."

The migraine was nothing compared to the pain the force was causing him right now. His life was drifting away from him. "Who .. . are ... you?"

"Mon Ciel isn't as safe as your mother thought. All I need is a channel to get in here." The man narrowed his eyes even more, and the force squeezed harder at Ciaran's neck and crushed his body. Then Ciaran heard the door burst open. People stormed into the room. There was the sound of a gunshot and a struggle.

And then he didn't remember anything else.

 *even years later.*

THE PHONE BUZZED for the third time. A news reporter on the wall screen in front of the bed was still elaborating on the death of Detective Adamson.

Madeline stared at the phone. 'No Caller ID' appeared on its small screen. "How do you know it's Stefan? It could be Jo."

On the other side of the bed, Ciaran tossed his clothes on. Madeline winced. The two bullet wounds and the five gashes on his body hadn't had a chance to heal. Not that she was one to complain about the explosive sex they'd just had—that certainly hadn't helped his recovery—but she wished they had more time to let him rest.

"If it's Jo, she'll leave a message," Ciaran said.

"Jo said she was going to your London headquarters. We don't know if she was with Adamson when Stefan killed him." She knew she was talking nonsense again. She tended to babble when she was nervous. And she had every right to be.

Ten years in journalism should have taught her better than letting herself be used by Stefan to get inside Mon Ciel. Stefan had killed Mrs. Rutherford and had shot Ciaran and Tadgh and then fled without getting what he wanted.

Stefan had arranged the kidnapping of Jo. Madeline should have anticipated what he would do when blackmailing Ciaran didn't help him obtain the information he wanted. He would kidnap Jo again. *Damn it!* Madeline cursed to herself.

"If he hasn't had a chance to talk to me, he won't get to demand anything. He will keep Jo alive because she's his currency now, am I right?" she asked Ciaran again, more to reassure herself that she was doing the right thing.

Ciaran headed toward the door, and she trailed behind him. He said nothing but headed down the hall toward the old section of Mon Ciel. The phone in Madeline's hand had stopped buzzing.

Ciaran stopped in front of a double-doored room. The rusty handles suggested it hadn't had visitors for a while. He gazed briefly at the handles. A flash of pain crossed his eyes, so quickly that Madeline didn't notice.

Ciaran cleared his throat, a tell-tale sign that he was about to say something difficult for him. "This used to be my room," Ciaran said and shoved his hands in his pockets.

She nodded and waited patiently for the next bit of information.

"Juliette died in here. I left Mon Ciel after that incident. The room—the whole place, in fact—was deserted after that. We still have maintenance staff. But the family rarely comes back here."

She pulled one of his hands from his pocket and rubbed her thumb in his palm. She didn't know when or why she had developed that habit, but she often did it to herself whenever she needed to stay calm. She hadn't realized she was doing it to Ciaran, but by the time she noticed, it was too late. He was watching her gesture with a twinkle in his eyes.

"If the memories are too painful, why dig them up? What are you looking for here, Ciaran?"

She pulled her hand away. But he grabbed it and held on for a short moment before giving it a slight squeeze. Then he sighed and let her hand go.

"There are two places in the house that Stefan didn't search. One is this room, and the other is the old lab. He believed Juliette hid the crucifix in a statue, which suggests she didn't tell him much."

Ciaran turned, facing her now. "Before we enter this room, I need to tell you something."

He proceeded to tell her about the incident in which Juliette died.

"I didn't return to the room afterward. Mother told me it hadn't been cleaned up because she thought I wouldn't care for that. What I'm looking for in the room is a trace of the air bender. He had some kind of connection to Juliette. Maybe he controlled her in some way to learn our family secrets. He might be controlling Stefan now. If we can trace him, we'll have the upper hand when we talk to Stefan."

Madeline nodded. "I didn't realize Stefan had anything to do with aliens. Not that I know anything about him . . ."

Ciaran smiled. "An air bender doesn't necessarily have anything to do with extraterrestrials. It could be some kind of an earthly talent."

Madeline scowled. "I feel so stupid."

"Don't. It would be strange for you to know about these sort of things." Ciaran chuckled. "I know because it's my field of interest, and I research the topic quite extensively."

"I know, but it still doesn't make me feel any less stupid."

"Humm. How about this explanation? It has to do with dimensions. You know our standard three-dimensional world."

"Yes—vertical, horizontal, depth. And time is another dimension, I hear." She grinned.

"You see, you're not too bad after all. Anything with a status of being that changes constitutes a dimension. Our mind is a dimension, for example."

"Like we are changing our minds all the time?"

Ciaran laughed. "No. That's an ingrained human psychological problem. Status of mind is more like a perception of the world in general. Let's say you believe this world is heaven, and you behave accordingly. That's your status of mind. When that status changes, it constitutes a dimension."

"Okay. I get it."

"There are people who have the ability to influence other people's status of mind. They can use their talent to manipulate people and drive their behavior."

"Like hypnotizing people?"

Ciaran shook his head. "I'd call people with that talent mind benders. They can change your mind's dimension by simply wanting you to do so. They can *see* your mind."

"See it?"

"Yes. If it's their talent, the minds of others become tangible to them. They manipulate it however they want, just like you steer a car. The same deal with the air bender. He can *see* the air and manipulate it. That man turned the air into hands, and it did whatever he wanted it to do. It almost strangled me."

Madeline nodded, thinking about her psychic blue dots. "Are there many like that around?"

"I don't know, Madeline. But this air bender had a light circle around him . . ." He shook his head. "I haven't given it much thought. I didn't know much back then, but maybe the light circle was a holocast."

"A what?"

"It's like a broadcast of a hologram"

"Like in *Star Wars*?"

Ciaran chuckled. "Not quite. But yes, I can accept that explanation for now. Anyway, I think we have enough information to go inside the room."

She nodded. She wasn't nervous or anything, but Ciaran wrapped his arm around her protectively and pushed the doors open.

Holy cow! That was all she could think of. She froze.

4

*T*housands of glaring, bright, blinking blue dots flooded the room. They hovered and swayed like waves in the ocean. They hummed. *"Little hummingbird, do you see the sky . . . ?"*

The dusty room swiveled and swung back and forth, zooming in and then back out again.

The dots kept humming. *". . . It is free. It is yours. Fly. Past the mountains. Past the oceans . . ."* Madeline's vision blurred with the glare of the blue shade.

". . . There. You will find love . . ."

She couldn't get a word past her mouth. She just wanted to tell Ciaran she saw the blue dots and they were singing to her.

"Madeline!"

She heard Ciaran calling out for her. But then she was flying. She tried to regain her footing, but she kept flying.

When the world stopped spinning, she realized that Ciaran was carrying her. They were at the far end of the hall, almost out of the old quarter of the house.

"Put me down, Ciaran."

He stopped walking and set her on her feet but still held on to her shoulders firmly.

"I'm okay."

"You fainted, Madeline. That's not okay. Was it because you spent a couple of nights down at the creek?" He put his hand on her forehead. "You don't have a fever."

He gazed at her, searching for an answer. The worry in those intense gray eyes bothered her. Should she tell him? After all, he'd just told her a secret that he had refused to revisit for many years.

Hell, forget this! "Please don't think I'm crazy, Ciaran," she began. "I don't have any magical talent. But I do see things. It's very random. I don't have a theory of what it is that I can and can't see, or even what I'm going to see. Sometimes I hear things. But most of the time, I just feel things."

He pulled her into his arms and kissed her. She didn't think romance was the reason for the kiss, rather that it was the only way he could stop her from ranting. She was babbling nonsense again, and she knew it. But then nothing was making sense to her at the moment.

When he finished with the kiss, he spoke gently, "Now, tell me one thing at a time, Madeline. What do you think you can see sometimes, and what did you see in that room?"

She drew in a breath. "I think I can see people's thoughts. They appear as blue dots. I don't know their meaning—they just hover in front of me. That's how I found you at the creek. You thought of me, and I followed the blue dots, the trail of your thoughts."

Ciaran lifted her chin up and looked into her eyes. His intense gray eyes filled with curiosity and his face lit up with fascination. "You're a . . ."

"Don't label me, Ciaran. I'm not one of your science projects." She turned around and walked away. He grabbed her elbow to stop her.

"I'm sorry. I'll never do it again. Please calm down. Stefan will ring again at any time. We should try to see if we can do something to prepare."

She stopped walking. He was right. "I'm sorry. My head just scrambled a bit. Let's get back to the room," she said.

"Not until I'm sure you'll be okay. Tell me what you saw in the room?"

"Lots of blue dots." She looked straight into his eyes. "I don't think you want to hear this, but if what I saw were thoughts, they had to be Juliette's."

"Only living people have thoughts, Madeline."

"Well, it can't be the air bender because I haven't met him. But I do have a connection with Juliette via you."

"It's not possible."

"Now you think I hallucinated it?"

"No . . ."

"When you brought me here the first night, as soon as I walked into the house, I not only saw the blue dots heading toward the old quarter, but I heard a woman's voice welcoming you home."

Ciaran raked his hands through his hair. "Juliette died in my arms. I wish it were a mistake. But it wasn't . . ."

"Does she have an Irish accent?"

Ciaran simply stared at her.

Madeline hummed the tune. *"Little hummingbird, do you see the sky . . ."*

Ciaran gestured for silence. He braced his hands on the wall. She couldn't see his face, but she guessed he was wanting to bang his head against that wall. She must have gotten it right.

He hadn't told her anything about Juliette apart from what had happened in that room, and he certainly had never mentioned her accent. And the song did it. It was Juliette's song.

"Ciaran, you asked me what I saw . . ."

"Yes, I know. I'm sorry. It was just . . ." He turned around. "Okay. Let's just go back to the room. We'll figure out what's what later. But you have to let me know right away if you feel uneasy."

She nodded and headed toward the room. When they entered again, there were no more blue dots.

Damn!

The room was a mess as a result of what appeared to have been a massive fight, and nobody had cleaned up a thing. Ciaran glanced at the bed and then focused on the floor in front of it. He deliberately avoided looking at Madeline. She knew he was trying to control his emotions and didn't want to create any awkward moments, so she kept silent.

He crouched and pointed to the floor. "You see the circle here? This is where the light circle landed. It must have scarred the wood . . ."

"Ciaran!"

He traced his fingers on the floor in circles.

"Ciaran!"

"Yes?" He looked up.

"I don't see any circle marks on the floor."

"You can't see these?" He pointed.

"No."

He frowned.

Then she saw a single lonely blue dot blinking in the corner of the room. She pulled at Ciaran's sleeve and nodded her head in the direction of the dot. Ciaran looked and obviously saw nothing except a sturdy cabinet standing there.

"Over there?" He pointed.

She nodded and felt a chill run up and down her spine. The air seemed to have become hollow. She heard the voice of the woman again but couldn't make sense of what she was saying. It was more like weeping or chanting of some sort.

Madeline stood up and saw Ciaran examining the cabinet without any hope of finding anything. The temperature in the room seemed to suddenly drop several degrees. She was trying to tell Ciaran to get out, but she had a feeling if she spoke, he wouldn't be able to hear her. It seemed as if they were in two different worlds.

The weeping sound still echoed in her mind.

Ciaran approached her and looked at her face. He said something, but she couldn't quite hear him. He seemed to know she was in trouble. He held her shoulder gently. And then reality suddenly blasted back at them.

"Ciaran!" a voice came from behind them.

Madeline and Ciaran both jumped out of their skin. Ciaran turned toward the voice and saw Tadgh standing at the door.

"Don't you knock?" Ciaran growled.

Tadgh raised an eyebrow. "This isn't your room anymore. Why do I need to knock? What are you two doing in here? Doctor Thomas asked for you. He wants to check up on you. Your painkillers are running out soon."

Ciaran glanced around one last time then led Madeline out of the room. "Where's Mother?" Ciaran asked Tadgh.

"I have no idea. She doesn't usually report her whereabouts to me. And after last night, I don't think she's ever told us anything real."

"What do you mean?" Ciaran asked.

"How do you think we got you back home?"

Ciaran shrugged. "I haven't thought about it. We've been busy!"

"I see." Tadgh shot a glance at Madeline and rolled his eyes. "You put Mon Ciel on lockdown, remember? She unlocked the shield. We got you onto a chopper."

Ciaran stared at Tadgh for a moment then strode down the hallway. Madeline trailed right behind. "There are only two people who have the key, and she isn't one of them. Mother didn't unlock it by herself."

"You mean Father helped her?" Tadgh asked.

"I don't want to hear about two ghosts in one day, Tadgh!" Ciaran growled and punched a code into the security pad of a room that looked like some kind of control room.

Ciaran's phone buzzed. A text message read, "Meet at British museum in one hour." The caller ID was Sciphil Two.

"What that hell is Sciphil Two?" Tadgh asked. Ciaran shook his head. At the same time, Madeline's phone buzzed.

"It's the same No Caller ID," she said, looking at Ciaran.

Ciaran nodded. She picked up the phone. From the other end of the line came Jo's voice. "Madeline?"

"Oh my God, Jo, are you okay? Where are you now?"

"I'm fine. I ran. Stephen—no Stefan—got me, but I ran."

"Where are you now?"

"In London . . . where are you?"

"Can you find your way to the British museum? We'll be there in an hour."

"I'll be there. I never get lost in a big city, and I always find you." Jo hung up.

Madeline stared at Ciaran and Tadgh.

"What's the matter?" Ciaran asked.

"I'm so sorry."

"Why? Didn't you just talk to Jo? She escaped? Why isn't that good?" Tadgh asked.

"You don't think Jo ran again, Madeline?" Ciaran asked.

She shook her head. "I'm so sorry. I think I've just given Stefan our location in the next hour. Jo makes fun of people who use the words *never* and *always*. She wouldn't say *always* with an emphasis. I didn't catch it when we spoke. I'm sorry."

"It's okay, Madeline. Stefan will be at the museum. We'll get him and bring Jo back," Ciaran said. But she caught the way he glanced at Tadgh. His eyes were too dark—they scared her.

5

The British museum looked exactly the same as Madeline found it the week before. Groups of tourists were scattered around. It was an awfully busy place for a secret meeting with the person called Sciphil Two. Perhaps it wasn't a secret meeting at all.

She caught sight of Ciaran nodding at Tadgh. Tadgh responded with a wink and patted his pocket.

"Jesus Christ, are you carrying guns?" Madeline spoke between her teeth.

Ciaran smiled. "I like to refer to them as weapons. Guns sound too primitive."

"You can't have them here! This is a museum!"

"Says who?" Tadgh asked.

"We won't use them unless absolutely necessary. I don't care to be at a disadvantage when we don't know who we're dealing with," Ciaran said.

They walked further into the ancient history section. Ciaran checked his phone and found no messages.

Suddenly, the air seemed to stop flowing. Their hearts skipped a beat. Everyone else in the museum seemed to be oblivious to it.

Madeline, Ciaran, and Tadgh seemed to be in a different world—a very quiet one. They could hear their own heartbeats.

"John Dee's glass! Look!" Madeline pointed toward a display of a golden plate. As they walked closer, the air around them seemed to thicken.

Ciaran grabbed Madeline and Tadgh to stop their movement toward the display. Ciaran asked them, "You hear anything strange? Like an echo in the air?" Ciaran shook his head as if shaking away the noise in his ears.

"No, I just feel strange, like the air is thick as gel and lacking in oxygen," Madeline said.

"It feels like the air has been vacuumed out of the room to me," Tadgh said.

Ciaran approached the glass cabinet of John Dee's exhibit with caution. The thick air seemed to follow him. Ciaran spoke to no one in particular. "We haven't the time nor inclination to play hide and seek. Show yourself, or we'll leave."

In the air right in front of them, a white and blue beam flashed straight to the plate. The light bounced back from it, forming a cone shape in which text appeared. *"Hello,"* it said.

"This is a very primitive model of the hologame technology," Ciaran said.

"Yes," the text printed.

"Can we talk elsewhere if all you need is a shiny plate to reflect your light on? What if people walk in and see?" Madeline asked.

"Other people's vision in the same space with you has been blocked. You are fine where you stand. The plate reflects the correct frequency," the text read.

"What do you want?" Ciaran asked.

"We need to warn you that the LeBlancs are in danger."

"Who are you, and what sort of danger are we facing?" asked Ciaran.

"We are your council and your guards when your position is active. At the moment, we can only alert you of possible danger. The danger is

coming. It's time . . ." The text flickered, faded away, flickered again, and then was totally gone.

"What position?" Ciaran asked.

"Damn it. That wasn't very helpful," Tadgh snarled at the air.

Ciaran grunted in pain and held his ears. A drop of blood trickled from his nose. Madeline tried to hold him steady as he swayed. When Tadgh approached to help, Ciaran said, "Time me." And then he fell to the floor, unconscious.

Madeline shook his shoulders and got no response.

"Tadgh!" she called out.

Tadgh stood frozen. He shoved his hands in his pockets, looking as if he was somewhere else. Madeline shook Ciaran's shoulders again. "Come on, you're scaring me." Then she looked up as Stefan walked into the room with Jo at his side. He had his arm around Jo's waist. Madeline knew that underneath Jo's jacket, Stefan was holding a weapon to her.

"Tadgh!" she called out, but the only difference between he and Ciaran was that Ciaran was on the floor and Tadgh still stood, looking like a statue. The text had said that other people couldn't see them. That was the hope Madeline held on to.

Stefan glanced around the room. Jo did the same.

"Nobody's here. Let's go," Jo said.

Madeline caught an unusual sign in Jo's eyes. Jo saw something, Madeline thought.

"Be quiet. If you can decode my sister's disk, I don't need Ciaran. I shot at him before, so I can't just come back and ask him nicely. But you can use your charm to get what we need," Stefan told Jo.

On the floor, Ciaran stirred and opened his eyes. Tadgh immediately switched back to reality. Madeline helped Ciaran sit up. "How long was I out?" he asked Tadgh.

"Precisely thirty-three seconds."

She could see Tadgh wore no watch and had nothing with which to track the time.

Ciaran saw Stefan and Jo now. So did Tadgh. Tadgh growled

and turned to walk toward Stefan, his hand ready on his pocket. Ciaran grabbed at Tadgh.

"Wait. I can't fight yet. I don't think they can see or hear us." Ciaran stood up.

Jo gazed straight in their direction.

"Are you sure they can't see or hear us?" Tadgh asked.

"Jo has very good instincts. She might be able to feel us," Madeline said.

Stefan steered Jo in their direction, keeping his hand on her back.

"He has a knife on her," Ciaran said. Both Ciaran and Tadgh had their hands in their pockets. Ciaran moved Madeline behind him.

"Are they going to bump into us?" Madeline asked.

"I'm not sure what will happen," Ciaran said.

Jo gazed in their direction and stopped walking. "I need to go, Stefan."

Stefan stopped on his tracks. "Go where?"

"The girl's room. You can come with me if you like."

"Don't fuck around with me, Jo. You stay right here. They'll turn up sooner or later unless you gave them a hint over the phone." Stefan glared at Jo.

"Look, Stefan, I want to go home. I told you I can decode the disk for you. You don't have to wait for them."

"What are they saying?" Tadgh asked.

"Can't you hear them?" Madeline asked.

Tadgh shook his head.

"Can you, Madeline?" Ciaran asked.

Madeline nodded.

"You tried for hours, and you've got nothing," Stefan raised his voice.

"If you knew a scrap of computer programming, you would know it takes an awful lot of time to decode a program at that level. I could have been faster if you'd put me in a habitable place. Not that dingy little hole in the wall you call a house. And if you'd pulled down those silly distracting bells on the veranda, stopped the flutes in the garden, and let me work in the actual house rather than a basement . . ."

"Lower your voice or I'll hurt you," Stefan growled. Jo stiffened. Stefan must have pushed his knife harder into her back.

"Coward," Tadgh snarled and moved forward. Ciaran grabbed at him, pulling him back.

"I can take him. I'm a good shot. I'll blow his brains out before he even knows what hit him," Tadgh said.

"Do you know how long it takes to slit someone's throat, Tadgh? One second. He's closer to Jo than you are. You haven't seen what Stefan is capable of. He blew a man's head off without a thought."

Tadgh shoved Ciaran away from him.

"As long as Jo behaves, he won't hurt her," Ciaran continued. "What did Jo just say, Madeline?"

She repeated it to Ciaran. "She must sense someone is listening. She's giving us the location of the house."

Ciaran nodded. "And I know exactly where it is."

Stefan seemed convinced that there was no point in waiting for Ciaran. He took Jo out of the room.

The text flicked and appeared in front of them again. *"Your enemies are attempting to obtain our frequency. If they can get to us, they can get to you. The disk contains the frequency."* A number appeared—a countdown from five seconds.

Five. Four. Three. Two. One.

Ciaran grabbed at Madeline and Tadgh, pulling them back toward the far end of the room. The air stretched, following them like a rubber band.

6

---

*I*f Madeline wasn't mistaken, they were exceeding the speed limit on the highway. From behind the steering wheel, Ciaran gazed at the road ahead of him. He didn't look as if he wanted to talk, but she asked anyway.

"Did you expect an explosion from the five-second countdown at the museum?"

"Better to be safe than sorry. We don't know who Sciphil Two is yet," Ciaran warned,

"I still feel sorry for those visitors. We appeared in front of them out of nowhere. They must have gotten the fright of their lives," Tadgh said.

"I guess we would be sorrier if it had been an actual explosion." Madeline smiled.

Ciaran didn't say anything further. *Mind reading would be a handy talent to have right now,* Madeline thought. She'd love to get inside his head and know what he was thinking about.

"Where are we going?" she asked.

"Mortlake. Mrs. Hanson's house. You've been there," Ciaran said.

"I don't care where we're going as long as I arrive with all of my organs intact," Tadgh blurted from the back seat. Madeline turned around and saw beads of sweat running down his forehead.

"Have I ever gotten you into a car accident, Tadgh?" Ciaran asked.

"I don't want you to break your record, Ciaran. Slow down, will you?"

"Madeline isn't complaining. Neither should you."

"How can you be so sure Jo was talking about Mrs. Hanson's house?" she asked.

"I spent a lot of time in the part of the house she described. The bells, the flutes, the basement underneath the kitchen. It has to be her place."

"Ciaran studied flowers there for years," Tadgh added.

"It was natural medicine, not flowers. And I consulted with her. I didn't study anything with her," Ciaran snarled. His voice and his eyes were disturbingly cold. He reached over, touched Madeline's hand. He felt her brace herself, and he slammed on the brakes then stomped on the accelerator. The movements threw Tadgh sideways and back.

"Hey! I know you're a tough guy, you don't have to prove it. If you're mad about the number thirty-three, it isn't my fault. You asked me to time you!" Tadgh yelled.

"You know nothing about it, Tadgh. Let it be."

"I don't know much. But I can always ask Mother. I'm sure she knows. Just like the way she knows how to unlock Mon Ciel's shield that you think is invincible."

"Leave her out of this."

"The hell I will. Sciphil Two, whoever that was, said our family is in trouble. You don't have the right to speak for all of us, Ciaran. Not only I am talking to Mother, I'm going to talk to everyone in the family."

Ciaran swung the car over to the emergency shoulder of the highway and stopped. "Get out," he said.

"You don't get to kick everyone out of your life at your leisure, Ciaran."

"It's my car that I'm kicking you out of. Get out before I cause you bodily damage."

Madeline turned around and looked at Tadgh, while Ciaran stared at him from the reflective mirror. Tadgh put on a stern face and sat unmoving.

Ciaran slammed the heel of one hand on the steering wheel and got out of the car. He strode along the shoulder of highway. Madeline got out and went after him.

"Ciaran, talk to me, please. What's happening?"

"You don't have to worry about this. I don't want you to get tangled up in my mess."

"As far as I'm concerned, I don't have a choice. I know you and your family have a lot going on, but I brought Stefan into your home, and it seemed to stir up a lot of dust from the past. But I have my friend to save, and whether I like it or not, I'm a part of this mess now."

Ciaran looked away. She grabbed him and spun him around to face her. "Please. Tell me."

"I just recalled now—the air bender said the thirty-three year cycle would come. He said I broke his family, and he will break mine."

"How did you remember it just now but not before? Are you sure the memories are there, or did one of those talented mind benders you told me about put them in your head?"

He looked at her in surprise. "You're very good Madeline. Not everyone catches on to the idea so easily."

"It comes with the job. I've seen enough weird things." She touched his face gently, the face God had created when he was in a very good mood. "If you feel anything, just tell me. A man is allowed to have emotions, Ciaran. You can be out there, saving the world, being a crusader, changing people's lives. But once in a while, when you just need to talk, I'll listen."

He nodded. "The information must be in my subconscious. He said that after I'd passed out. I didn't remember it before because the triggers weren't strong enough, and I don't think I wanted to remember." He held her hands. "I still don't know how the thirty-three year cycle resonates with my family's affairs. But the man came back because he thought I had killed Juliette, and that Juliette was the cause of all this, so I am responsible for what happens to my family."

"I have to agree with Tadgh on this point. You can't take all the responsibility. And kicking everyone out of your life isn't a very good way to deal with it."

"My family is vulnerable now. I don't know what will come for us or how to deal with it." Ciaran turned to look at Tadgh, who was stepping out of the car.

"But as you said, I'm in this with you. Whatever it is, you won't deal with it alone—like it or not." She smiled at him.

He tilted her face up, rubbing his thumb over the dimple on her left cheek. "When you said you'd take care of me, you meant it!"

"I'm in it for the long haul."

"And you'll let me do the same for you?"

She nodded.

"You promise to tell me everything? I've told you everything I know. But I don't know anything about you, Madeline."

"Didn't you say you have access to one of the most secretive and powerful databases on Earth?" She chucked.

"The things I want to know are not in the database."

She tucked a strand of stray hair away, tiptoed, and kissed him.

"Promise me?" he asked again.

She smiled and nodded. Then he kissed her as if it was the first time they'd ever kissed. He hands gripped at the dip in her back and her neck, lifting her off the ground.

"I don't have all day. We have places to be!" Tadgh tapped the side of the car.

Ciaran ended the kiss and chuckled. He walked back toward the car. "All right, you don't have to hurt my car. We're leaving."

As she began to walk toward the car, Madeline saw a handful of blue dots at the corner of her eyes. A chill shot up through her spine and numbed her brain. The dots weren't hovering like they usually did, but they stayed fixed on the road, forming the number thirty-three. Some of them weren't the usual haunting blue color but were instead a grainy blood red .

"Go away. I have nothing to do with this," she scolded. The dots stared back silently at her.

"I have no idea what thirty-three means," she said. She looked toward the car and saw Ciaran had climbed in behind the steering wheel.

The dots flashed at her. Flashed. Flashed. Flashed. Then disappeared.

She glared at the road where the dots had been one last time before turning on her heel and heading back to the car. Suddenly a pain stabbed at her heart as an old emotional wound just broke open and started bleeding.

She might know what thirty-three meant. She hoped she was wrong. But if not, she might have to let go of the relationship she had just found with Ciaran.

7

*J*ust before dusk, Ciaran, Madeline, and Tadgh arrived at Mrs Hanson's house. Ciaran parked a block away. As they approached the house, they could see Stefan driving away with Jo in the passenger seat.

"We missed them again," Madeline muttered.

"They might come back," Ciaran said. "We should take the opportunity to see what he's got set up inside."

They neared the front of the house. The police had sealed the place up after clearing away Mrs. Hanson's body.

"How on Earth did he get in here with the police seal intact?" Tadgh asked, looking at the front door.

"He's a cop himself. Don't you think he could figure that out?" Madeline asked somewhat sarcastically.

Ciaran said nothing but moved directly to the back of the house. The back door wasn't sealed but locked by an old padlock on a rusty handle. Tadgh chuckled. "Apparently, the cops didn't think this was a major crime scene." Tadgh pulled out his pocket knife to work on the lock.

"No need to do that," Ciaran said and walked toward the side of the house. He opened a small window, gestured for Tadgh and Madeline to stay back and hopped inside.

Moving to the living room, Ciaran scanned the area. Everything looked the same. He had spent a considerable amount of time here with Juliette. It was all too familiar, and he didn't care for it.

What had happened in the last couple of weeks had turned an old emotional scar into an open wound—fresh, raw, and bleeding. The wound had never really healed, and it now needed his attention.

He came back to the window and reached out a hand to help Madeline in. "No one else is here," Ciaran said. "Stefan wouldn't rig this place or lay traps. He only needed a place to stay, and the cops would be all over him."

"How do the police know?" Madeline asked.

"I asked Lindsay to give the police an anonymous tip," Ciaran answered as he moved to the kitchen that could barely accommodate three people.

The flutes hanging from the trees in the garden and the bells dangling on the veranda composed strange melodies, and the haunting sounds poured into the room from the window.

Ciaran approached a small cabinet that looked as if it would crumble into pieces if he opened its door too quickly. Inside were rows of ceramic cups and plates and a teapot. He grabbed the teapot handle and turned slightly. The dining table slid aside to reveal a rickety wooden staircase that led to the basement.

Tadgh grabbed Ciaran and Madeline, pulling them backward. "If someone's hiding down there, we'll be shot in places we won't much care for."

"You're not going down there, Tadgh. I am. You stay here and keep watch in case Stefan comes back."

"You always get to do the fun bit," Tadgh muttered and sat down on a chair at the kitchen table.

"Don't touch anything," Ciaran said as he started to descend a small set of stairs. Madeline followed.

The basement was spacious. It looked like the entire house was built on top of it. It wasn't a lab—there were no vials, jars, or chemical compounds of any kind. The room was almost empty with a large rectangular table in one corner and projector-like equipment hanging from all four corners.

There were shiny panels that looked like black mirrors lining the walls, angled in no particular logical order. Some of the panels were shattered, and an apparently damaged projector dangled from the ceiling.

"This is a holocast room, a primitive model," Ciaran said. "Stefan must have taken the control center with him. Without it, I can't make any sense of the setup here. Especially, this . . ." Ciaran pointed toward a round reflective plate sitting in a corner. "I don't know what that does."

"It looks like John Dee's glass, the one we saw at the museum," Madeline commented. She looked at the round plate but didn't touch it. There were no cords or electrical connections of any kind attached to the object. "Could it simply be an artifact? A symbol, or some kind of worship thing?" Madeline suggested.

"It's a communication center. One that gathers channels, frequency and connections of different dimensions. But what we have here is too primitive to do anything like that."

"You means this room can facilitate communication between extraterrestrial agents?"

Ciaran nodded. "Very likely."

Madeline sneered. "I can't imagine a ninety-year-old gypsy handling this technology."

"It's not her, Madeline. We talked about this. What we met here wasn't her."

"Right. You said they rewired her brain. It was a robot lookalike."

He couldn't help but chuckle. Madeline always had a very interesting way of interpret things. Sometimes her interpretation was simple and basic, but most of the time, it was frighteningly relevant to the core of the matter. He wondered if it was the quality of a good journalist or simply her unique intuition.

"You said on the bridge there were two groups of people—or robot lookalikes—fighting. One group was on your side, and the other was on Stefan's. Before Stefan revealed his intention to get inside Mon Ciel, he was on my side. Mrs. Hanson wanted to kill me, so she couldn't possibly be my friend. And now Stefan is using her house. So who are our friends and who are our foes here, Ciaran?"

"Stefan may be on the side of the people who neurologically killed Mrs. Hanson—or rewired her brain, in your terms. That was why he knew this place. He may have manipulated Mrs. Hanson to send you to Fosse Way to intentionally put you in danger so that you would call for his help."

"But he got lucky, I got you in the process."

Ciaran smiled. "Yes, it was lucky that he was able to skip a couple of steps to get inside Mon Ciel. But even if he hadn't, he would have found another way and put you in further danger."

She stared at him in a way that let Ciaran know she was about to ask an important question. "What's in the crucifix, Ciaran? Why would Stefan kill to get it?"

"A powerful spell that would cause an apocalypse." Tadgh stuck his head down from the top of the stairs and grinned. "Okay, okay. I know that's lame. But come on, if there's nothing useful down there, we'd better leave."

Madeline raised an eyebrow, looking at Ciaran.

"I'll tell you about it later. Not about Tadgh's flawed theory about the spell and the apocalypse, but about what I think Stefan is looking for in the crucifix. Let's go," Ciaran said and climbed back up the stairs. His head was pounding now. In the rush of the morning's events, he had forgotten to take his painkillers. Now the bullets and stab wounds were punishing him for it.

There was the sound of silenced guns shooting at the shelves in the kitchen, and cups and plate in the opened cabinet came crashing to the floor. Ciaran flew up from the basement.

"Tadgh!" he called out.

8

Ciaran saw Tadgh's shadow chasing someone outside in the garden. He glanced at the damage the bullets had wreaked on the kitchen furniture. If Tadgh hadn't been quick, the consequences could have been unimaginable.

Madeline and Ciaran heard a crash from the shed where Mrs. Hanson had kept her botanical lab to make natural medicines. Ciaran pushed Madeline behind him as they approached and held his gun tightly. They approached the shed slowly. Ciaran pointed his gun at the lock on the door and fired. Ciaran pushed the door open little by little.

All was quiet inside the shed. Ciaran pushed the door open a bit wider. A furry black shadow leaped through the gap and landed outside. Ciaran aimed, ready to shoot. In front of Ciaran and Madeline was an enormous black cat, nearly the size of a small leopard. The cat blinked its bright yellow eyes and darted at Ciaran.

"Be careful!" Madeline squealed.

"Don't worry. This is Migi. She's very gentle."

Migi meowed and waved her tail contentedly as she rubbed against Ciaran's legs.

"Oh my God, there are two tails," Madeline gasped.

Ciaran chuckled. "She originally had only one tail, and she was a very tiny kitten. Mrs. Hanson manipulated her appearance using her magic and natural medicine." Ciaran patted and scratched the cat below the jaw and elicited a loud purring. "So Migi became quite big and very intelligent, but she still doesn't speak, I'm afraid."

Madeline reached her hand out nervously.

"She doesn't bite," Ciaran said.

"Just in case she changes her mind, I'd like to keep my fingers," she said, curling her fingers into her fist.

Migi licked Madeline's hand and rubbed her head against it.

"Among other things, I didn't approve of Mrs. Hanson's practice on animals. Her alchemical practice was so distorted that often she turned transmutation into mutilation."

"Transmutation?"

"It's an alchemical term. The less you know, the better, Madeline." The cat came back to rub at Ciaran's legs.

"Who's feeding her now?" Madeline asked.

"I don't know. I think she's very self-sufficient."

They heard footsteps, and then Tadgh appeared, pushing a man in front of him. Tadgh kept his gun pressed to the man's back.

"He won't say a word," Tadgh said. "Do you have any special mouth-opening techniques, Madeline? We boys only have our fists."

The man's eyes were bizarre—a feline green.

"Who are you?" Ciaran asked. The man stared at him but made no move to answer. Ciaran circled the man, observing him. He had seen these eyes before. He remembered now, on the bridge, the robot who had shielded him from the bullets. Its eyes had flashed the same bright green shade before it shut down.

If his speculation was correct, these robots didn't appear to have high levels of problem-solving abilities. They were merely soldier robots. That was why they couldn't get him to talk.

"Did Sciphil Two send you?"

The man nodded.

"Oh, so he can understand simple questions," Tadgh said.

"It's a robot, Tadgh. Very low level. Not programmed to do anything complicated," Ciaran explained to his brother.

"But it shot at me. Is killing such a simple task?" Tadgh muttered.

"Your mission is to kill Stefan?" Ciaran asked.

No response.

"It probably wouldn't know Stefan or Stephen," Madeline said.

"Your mission is to target residents of this house?" Ciaran asked.

The man nodded.

Tadgh rolled his eyes. "This is ridiculous. Now we have to speak robot?"

Suddenly Migi stepped out from the darkness and hissed. Tadgh jumped and pointed his gun.

"No, no ... it's a cat. Don't shoot, Tadgh!" Ciaran yelled.

"Fuck me, it's a *hell* of a cat!" Tadgh grumbled and glared at the animal.

Migi kept hissing at the air, her tails waving frantically in different directions.

They heard a faint movement in the air, but before they could make sense of it, the man they had captured flew at Ciaran, pressing him to the ground. Two small darts appeared on the man's back, and Tadgh shot in the direction of a shadow in the bush and gave chase.

Ciaran pushed the robot off of him. The man's eyes filmed over instantly, and his body started to melt, turning into yellow liquid. The liquid pooled on the grass, smoking and sending the stench of burning flesh into the air. Then the liquid evaporated and, except for a burned patch on the grass, there was no sign of the dead man.

Madeline helped Ciaran stand up. "You're burning up, Ciaran."

"I'm running out of painkillers."

Tadgh returned, puffing. "Lost him." Then he saw the patch on the grass. "Where did he go?"

"He evaporated," Madeline said.

"Look out!" Ciaran flew at Tadgh, shooting at a shadow on the way down. A dart stuck into a wood panel behind Tadgh. The three of them rushed to the side of the garden where they saw the shadow drop after Ciaran's shot.

A man lay on the ground, looking up at them. He said nothing but pulled out a small dart.

"Stop!" Ciaran yelled and grabbed the man's hand. The man struggled and waved the point of the dart dangerously close to Ciaran's hand.

Madeline grabbed Ciaran from behind, pulling him off the man. "Let him go, Ciaran." They both fell backward onto the ground.

The man took the opportunity to stab the dart into his heart before he could be questioned. Like had happened before, this man evaporated into thin air.

"What's with this place? A two-tailed cat, and now evaporating men. Will we see the dragons next?" Tadgh mumbled.

"We should go before more of them show up. The robots, not the dragons," Ciaran said. He stood and helped Madeline to her feet.

"Thanks. I shouldn't have hung on to a robot programmed to self-destruct when caught," Ciaran said.

"You're welcome. I make it my life's mission to keep you alive." She grinned and kissed him lightly.

"Likewise," Ciaran said. Before they left, he turned and flicked his fingers at Migi. "Come on. You too."

"You're kidding me," Tadgh protested.

"I didn't know you were allergic to cats," Ciaran said.

"People are allergic to anesthesia. I simply don't like cats. It's a matter of choice."

"Come on, Tadgh. She's a nice and gentle cat," Madeline said.

Tadgh rolled his eyes. "Look at the size of her. I'd feel safer with TJ."

"TJ is a puppy, Tadgh. Don't embarrass yourself. Man up. You can handle a cat," Ciaran said and strode away.

Migi rushed over, rubbing against Tadgh's legs and purring. Tadgh rolled his eyes and walked away. Before reaching the car,

Tadgh turned around and glared at Migi a couple of times, but she continued to follow him.

"Don't grin at me, cat, I'm not that friendly," Tadgh addressed Migi before he got into the car, knowing full well the gigantic cat would be sitting right next to him.

9

It was rare that Ciaran found the air in his master bedroom stuffy. He got off the bed and raised the window slightly. The cold winter breeze rushed into the room. He shut it quickly.

The combination of painkillers and his company's anti-inflammatory medication wasn't pleasant, but it was a lot better than the anesthesia Doctor Thomas had threatened to put him under if he had to perform a surgery to remove the fragment of the bullet Stefan had put in his shoulder the day before.

He turned and looked at Madeline. This beautiful woman had walked into his life in much the same way Juliette had. Except Madeline had no agenda that he knew of. Would his secrets hurt her? Would she still think of him in the same way if she knew what he had done?

Madeline stirred and opened her beautiful brown eyes. They smiled at him even before she realized he was watching her.

He sat down on the side of the bed. "Go back to sleep," he said and rubbed his thumb over the dimple on her left cheek.

"How's the pain?" she asked groggily.

"Totally gone." He smiled as she rolled her eyes. She pulled him down to kiss him but suddenly stiffened and sat straight up, staring at a corner of the room.

"What is it?" he asked.

"The dots." She jumped off the bed.

"Just ignore them." He tried to pull her back to the bed, but Madeline grabbed her robe and put it on.

"It's the middle of the night," he said, but he could see she wasn't listening to him. Her eyes were fixated on a corner of the room, following what he knew were her psychic blue dots.

"Madeline," he called and grabbed her arm, but she shrugged him off. Ciaran staggered back. She had incredible strength. It didn't even seem like her. Madeline walked along the hall toward the old quarter.

"If you don't talk to me, I won't let you take another step, Madeline." He darted in front of her and blocked her way.

"There are hundreds of blue dots around you, Ciaran. They want me to follow them."

"You've seen them before. Just ignore them."

But instead, she ignored him and kept walking.

"No," he said firmly and held her shoulders. "I want you to go back to the room." Madeline didn't even look like herself anymore. She kept walking, and a moment later, she stood precisely at the place he feared the most—the old lab.

The steel door glared at him in challenge.

"The blue dots showed me the code. If you don't punch it in, I will," she said.

The look in her eyes weakened his knees. Ciaran stared at the door for a long time and then entered a code and the door slid open.

The lights turned on automatically. It was a massive abandoned lab. Vials and jars were scattered on a long, stainless steel workbench. A row of computers sat quietly, gathering dust in a corner of the room. In another corner, there was an enormous steel box that looked like a computer mainframe. Layers of dust coated everything in the room.

He gestured widely at the room. "Well, there it is. The secret place. Are you happy now?" He was nervous, but he didn't know why. A strange, anxious feeling washed over him.

"What are you seeing now, Madeline?"

She smiled. "I saw the blue dots, but they've gone now."

He narrowed his eyes. "So they woke you in the middle of the night, led you here, and then disappeared?"

She shrugged. "Totally random, weren't they?" She glanced around. "What a setup you have here."

He didn't believe her that the dots had gone. He didn't know what game she was playing, but he didn't like it.

"If there's nothing else to see, shall we leave?" he said and headed toward the door.

"What's in the crucifix, and exactly what's in the Golden Life?" she asked.

"They are not related."

"The Golden Life killed Juliette and upset the air bender. He sent Stefan to go after you and the crucifix. As far as I'm concerned, they're related."

The determination in her eyes told him she would find out one way or another. He nodded. "Okay . . . Juliette and I used this lab to create medicine and engineer a lot of unimaginable drugs. Golden Life was a failure, and that's why Juliette died."

"You mentioned you both loved alchemy. Immortality is one of the goals of alchemy, is it not?"

He didn't like where her questions were heading. She couldn't have known this much about the nature of alchemy. "What I wanted wasn't immortality but a medicine that healed all kind of diseases. Reviving a person from death was just the first step."

"So why did you stop?"

"There was one ingredient I didn't approve of—the blood of the living."

Madeline raised an eyebrow. "Have you heard of a blood bank? A lot of people donate blood for medical uses, Ciaran. Why is that such a big deal?"

He shook his head. "Nothing comes cheaply when it comes to saving lives, Madeline. To make a single dose of the medicine to save one life required sacrificial blood from another. That is, the blood had to be drawn from a person until that person died from blood loss. The blood was then distilled into one dose." He was angry now. He could feel his uncontrollable rage coming. He inhaled slowly and lowered his voice. He needed to end the conversation quickly. "Organ donations generally occur *after* the donor dies. With this medicine, even if people consented, removing their blood is an execution. There's no other way to look at it."

He looked at Madeline. "Feel free to judge me, Madeline."

She just looked at him and said nothing.

"I was young and ambitious. I was smart enough to put together an argument that would make the project appear to be morally acceptable. And you know who was my biggest fan and believer?"

She nodded. "Juliette."

"But I couldn't go through with it. I could make the whole world believe in me. I could create a legend. I could change the landscape of science and crap like that. But I wouldn't be able to live with myself. So I pulled the plug on the project."

"It was too late for Juliette?"

He nodded. He raked his hands through his hair. He needed to punch something. "My ambition was contagious. It ate her up like cancer. And you know the rest. So effectually, I killed Juliette."

"No, that's wrong."

"I know what's right and what's wrong, Madeline. I don't care what people think of me or how they judge me. Juliette might have had another agenda when she married me. But she died because of me, and I really don't want the past to be dug up, whatever we might find."

"What about the crucifix?"

"You won't let this go, will you?"

"No."

"If there was a crucifix, and if Juliette did what people claimed she did, she hid some sample gold in the crucifix. Why she chose to use a crucifix rather than other artifacts, I don't know."

"Sample gold?"

"Rumor has it that our family fortune for generations was built on the fact that we have the John Dee's formula to make gold. As far as I know, the rumor is partially incorrect."

"So what's the correct part?"

"Our fortune has something to do with gold, but not until more recently. And we have no ties to John Dee."

"How recent?"

He turned and looked at her. "The attempt to make gold spanned generations of the LeBlancs, but my family was never able to make gold until my time. My father trained me, but I was the one to complete the formula."

"So you can make gold?"

He shrugged. "It was a part of the process I stumbled across in trying to make the Golden Life. It didn't mean much to me, but apparently being able to make gold means a lot to many greedy people. So if the rumor was ever confirmed to be correct, those people would crush our family to dust to get the formula."

"I can imagine."

"We don't exactly make pure gold. Rather, it's a replica of a material that has the same if not better properties. At the end of the day, the gold you dig up from the ground and the gold we make is just a material, a thing. It's valuable because of its properties."

"If Juliette got a sample of your gold and gave it to someone, could they replicate it?"

Ciaran chuckled. "I wouldn't think so. It's not just a formula. It's an alchemical practice."

"Could Juliette do it if she had the formula?"

He nodded. "Maybe. But we'll never know, will we? That's why the air bender was upset when she died. Because even if they had the formula, without her, they couldn't do anything with it."

"So why is Stefan so insistent about finding the crucifix?"

Ciaran shook his head. "I have no idea. Maybe he has no idea that the formula is worthless without the right person to aid in the process. I don't think Stefan exists at the upper end of the food chain. But whoever is paying him might know how to use the formula. Regardless, I don't intend to investigate. We can't change what happened."

Madeline smiled. Strangely, he didn't think she was smiling at him. It wasn't a smile, but more like a look of smugness.

"Do you hear that?" she asked, seeming to look straight through him.

"Hear what?" he asked and turned around to look. No one stood behind him.

"So he said your death was accidental. He cares for you. Whatever your game is, take it elsewhere. Call off your minions." Madeline was talking to the air.

"You can't be talking to Juliette, Madeline. She's dead. Whatever is claiming to be Juliette and talking to you now, it's lying."

"Get the hell out of his life! Out of his home!" Madeline raised her voice.

"This is ludicrous, Madeline. Talk to me!" He tried to get her attention without success. Madeline paced back and forth in the room. He tried to drag her out, but she shoved him away. It was so sudden he wasn't prepared. He staggered back, off balance.

He approached her again but the air grew thicker and seemed to hold him at a distance.

"Air bending. Who are you? Show yourself. Show yourself to me, coward!" Ciaran snarled. "You picked on Madeline because she doesn't know. If you claim to be Juliette, show yourself to me. If you can't, then you are a liar." Nothing happened. "You see, Madeline. Whoever you are talking to is lying." He tried to get to her, but he couldn't even move an inch toward her.

Madeline still paced and ranted. He could hear part of what she was saying but not all.

"Madeline!" he called out.

Madeline waved her arms in the air. "You want to negotiate? All right!" She darted toward the medicine cabinet. Inside, there was a row of vials. "Which one?" she asked.

"No!" Ciaran yelled at her, but she didn't seem to hear him.

She grabbed one of the tubes and smashed it on the floor. A stream of smoke rose up from the substance and flooded the room.

And that was all he could remember.

_M_adeline flopped onto a cold stone floor so hard the she could hear her bones rattle. She couldn't remember much except for some flashes of light and feeling as if she was flying through a tunnel of bright light. Then she awoke here, in a stone chapel.

She glanced around. This wasn't the lab, and Ciaran was nowhere to be seen. She wasn't sure she was even in the same century. She was conscious, and she didn't need to pinch herself to know that. The bone-crushing fall pained her, and it wasn't the sort of pain she would experience in a dream.

She knew the pain of nightmares. She'd had too many of them to count, and this chapel, the air around her, and the feel of the cold breezes and the vivid stench of rotting flesh was much more real than what she would experience in nightmares.

She walked along the dark hall of the chapel, approaching the altar at the far end. Or maybe it was a stone bench rather than an altar. When Madeline got closer, she could see the shadow of someone praying. Hearing Madeline's footsteps, the person turned around. At the same time, large candles on the stone base and torches on the wall lit up.

The woman was stunning. Her long, flaming red hair hung down to her waist. Her milky skin glowed in the flickering light. Her almond-shaped blue eyes gazed at Madeline.

Madeline's instincts told her this was Juliette. A primal corner of her mind whispered to her that this was the woman with whom she was in competition, the woman who held a permanent place in Ciaran's heart.

"Hello, sister," the woman said.

"Hello back."

The woman stepped closer to Madeline, sweeping her long dress across the floor. "I'm Juliette."

She smiled. "I knew that."

"You're smart. Ciaran is always attracted to smart women."

"You studied him thoroughly before you met and married him."

Juliette smiled. "Do you mean I married him with an agenda, as everyone else says?"

"It was a statement, not a question. You don't have to confirm or deny. Ciaran wouldn't care for that. You called, and I responded. Let's talk this out."

"You can see me. That means you have a talent."

"You heard Ciaran. He didn't mean you any harm. Why didn't you leave him alone?"

"Well, I didn't do anything to him, did I? He doesn't have your talent. He can't see me. What can I possibly have done to him?"

"Your brother, Stefan, claimed you sent him a crucifix with Ciaran's family secrets in it. Is that true?"

Juliette smiled. "You're very direct, Madeline."

"It comes with the job."

"Do you love Ciaran?"

"Look, if you are who you say you are, I need answers. Your brother took my best friend, Jo, and if we can't figure out the location of the crucifix, he's going to kill more people, including my friend."

"I no longer have a connection with Stefan. But yes, I did hide away a crucifix for my long-lost family."

"Where?"

"Why do you expect to get things the easy way? The short time I spent with Ciaran, I barely had any of his love. It was all about work. I worked hard, and I devoted myself to him and to his work. I dealt with his mother's harsh judgment and lived in hell for six long months. And I got nothing from it. Why would I want to tell you anything?"

"This isn't a competition, Juliette. Look at you. You're stunning. You're smart. You went to Oxford. I'm a nobody, a reporter from New York. I have no qualifications of the LeBlanc's caliber. Ciaran loved you. He told me so. Your death scarred him for life. Look, all I need is the location of the crucifix so I can rescue my friend from your brother. Then we can go back to New York, and Ciaran will be yours forever."

"Sister! Oh, sister! Talk is so cheap." Juliette walked around, pacing back and forth like an angry cat. "It was his fault for not believing in me. He never believed I loved him."

"Did you? You didn't dig for his family secrets? You didn't scam your way in?"

Juliette looked at Madeline with tears in her eyes. "Yes, I did. I did scam my way in. I was nineteen, and I was raised to do just that, to get inside the LeBlancs. What did you expect me to do?"

"I can't say. I can't speak for you. But just this once, if you've ever loved Ciaran, tell me where the crucifix is."

Juliette laughed bitterly. "And what do I get for telling you?"

"What do you want?" Madeline asked.

"Be careful what you ask for."

"I'll keep my promises. Whatever you think is fair."

Juliette laughed again. "I lived for fairness and believed in good karma. And that is why I ended up dead. What do you think, sister?" Juliette gestured widely at the unflattering chapel in which she resided.

"Just tell me what you want, and I'll see if I can help."

Juliette looked Madeline up and down, and she put on a gracious smile. "If you want to know where the crucifix is, come here. I'll show you." She waved her arm and a ring of fire burst up from the floor, surrounding her. She looked at Madeline and smiled. "I don't have to tell you that the fire is quite hot, do I?"

This can't be real, Madeline thought. She stepped toward the fire. Juliette was right. The fire released a terrifying heat.

"This is not a fair fight," she said.

Juliette laughed. "No, it's not. You can have the weapon of your choice. What would you like?"

"A sword." She didn't have to think hard about that one. Fencing was her favourite sport, and she did quite well at it, depending on the type of sword. She'd fare a lot better with a sword in her hand than clawing at Juliette through the fire.

Juliette flicked her finger and a sword dropped down at Madeline's feet. *Where the hell am I? This has to be a dream.* Surely she couldn't die in a dream.

She picked the sword up. It was perfect as if tailored for her.

Madeline looked at Juliette who still stood smiling from the other side of the firewall. Madeline approached the fire and walked through it. The flames were thick and hot. The pain was excruciating. She didn't understand how a dream could hurt so much. Her clothes, her flesh, her bones were burning. A fireball exploded on her chest. She could feel her heart searing.

Madeline couldn't comprehend the pain and didn't think she could make it to the other side, she didn't believe she could survive this fire. If she died in a dream, would she remain in oblivion forever?

Amazed that she was past the fire, she raised the sword and charged at Juliette. Juliette raised her arm, and a sword appeared in her hand. She blocked Madeline's blow. The force of the swords' clash was like an explosion, sending numbing pain straight to Madeline's brain. She was sure it had the same effect on Juliette, as she staggered back and look stunned. Like an angry wolf, Juliette charged at her. She dodged, slashed, swiped, and was surprised that her fighting skills weren't rusty in the least.

Juliette's had what looked like supernatural power. It was not a fair fight. Madeline traded a blow for a blow, a kick for a kick, and a slash for a slash. Juliette raised her sword and charged straight at her without guarding. She was fighting to the death.

Madeline did the same. Her sword stabbed into Juliette's chest, and Juliette's sword did the same to her. The pain was excruciating. The difference between the two of them was that Juliette screamed, and she didn't.

As far as she was concerned, she had won the contest.

Juliette pulled her sword back and waved her arm. Both the fire and the swords vanished. Madeline looked down to see that the wounds on her body had disappeared. But the pain still lingered.

"We're such fools, sister. After all I have done for Ciaran, he has never said he loved me. He has never said the word. He burned my heart. And now he'll burn yours."

"Do you want his love, or do you want him merely to say it? I know men who would say without hesitation that they'd die for their women. But do you think any of them would actually do what they say? None that I know of."

Juliette sneered.

Madeline continued. "As for Ciaran, when he says something to me, I know he means it. He said he loved you, and he said I mattered to him. So how are we stacking up on this love ladder?"

"He was my first, and my last. Why does it matter now?" Juliette laughed until her eyes watered. Then she waved her arm absently. "The crucifix was at Fountains Abbey . . ." Juliette's image flickered, and her expression changed. There were intense emotions in her eyes, very different from what had been there before. "Do not let him find the crucifix. It's not meant for him," Juliette said. Her image flickered again and again. Then her expression returned to what it was before, staged.

Madeline frowned at the inconsistencies in Juliette's statements and expressions. What was going on? "If the crucifix is not meant for Ciaran, who is it for?"

Juliette stared at her blankly. "When did I say it wasn't for Ciaran?"

You just did. What's with the inconsistency? "Oh, I had thought you might want to give the crucifix to your brother. Why would Ciaran want it? If I just tell Stefan where it is, would he leave all of us alone?"

Juliette frowned. "Stefan! Yes. My poor brother. He knows nothing. Father wasn't nice to him."

"Where's your father now?"

Juliette looked as if she was daydreaming, and her image flickered so much it almost dissolved. Madeline had a feeling she was talking to two different versions of Juliette, and the flickering one before her was the real one. "Tell me why Ciaran shouldn't find the crucifix?"

"It will kill him. Please don't let him do it. I love him. I never want to harm him."

The image flickered again and again, and then the cold, emotionless Juliette returned. She wiped at a tear running down her face and observed the teardrop on her fingertip. Then she glanced up at Madeline.

"What did you just say?" Juliette asked.

"Nothing. Is this a dream? Am I conscious?" She couldn't think of any other questions to defuse this Juliette's suspicion.

"You're not dreaming. This is my world. It's more real than anything you can ever imagine. This is a hologame."

"A what?"

"A world where I can kill without consequences." Juliette swung her arm, and a dagger appeared out of nowhere. Madeline didn't have time to react before the dagger stabbed her heart.

A hologame? She wasn't sure what that meant, but the blood gushing from her body was definitely real. It wasn't nearly as painful as before. But she could feel her life drifting away. She slumped to the floor.

If this was the last time she would be able think as a human, she might be tempted to use her remaining drop of consciousness to think of Ciaran. But she refused to give up that easily. "For the rest of his life, Ciaran will feel responsible for your death. But that means you're dead to him. Killing me isn't going to help you. And I am not going to die here in your stupid hologame."

Juliette touched Madeline's cheek. Her hands felt cool but very real. "You're a fighter. And I have underestimated you. I haven't set the rules for the game, so I can't kill you now. I'll see you next time, when I set up the game properly and kill you both."

"Whatever you do, you're dead to Ciaran."

"If Ciaran thinks I'm dead, he's mistaken." Her image flickered again and then disappeared into the darkness.

11

"*A*re you sure, Lindsay?"

"Very. I'll get the file delivered to you right after Stefan finishes with it."

"Thank you. I will be at Mon Ciel this morning."

Ciaran put the phone away. Stefan was searching for old records of Juliette's addresses before they were married. *What an idiot!* He should have known Ciaran had tagged all information channels of anything related to Juliette. As soon as Stefan triggered a search, his people would be alerted.

He gazed out at the endless lawn of the manicured back garden, squinting at the sunshine on the beheaded statue of the Goddess of Kindness, the missing head a product of his youth. His father had placed the statue in the garden to remind him of his careless action.

But he was four when it had happened. What would a child of that age know about violence and justice? As far as his four-year-old mind had been concerned, a pack of wild dogs had attacked and killed Dew, his German shepherd, and in retaliation—to blow that pack into pieces—he had mixed the explosive and tested it on the statue. His father had grounded him for a week because of that, and the wild dogs had migrated away from the hillside—a peaceful escape for them, a week of nonviolent activities for him, and injustice for Dew.

It had taken him years to regain the balance of his life after Juliette's death and to find a person who understood him. It had been a lifetime since he was able to fill the void in his soul. And the woman who now completed him was lying on the bed while he stood helpless.

Ciaran glanced back at the bed and saw bead of sweat run down Madeline's forehead. He scrambled back to the bed and wiped the sweat away, and her body began shaking violently as if she was fighting in her dream. He gathered her into his arms and rocked her. If he could take her pain away or fight for her, he would do it.

The compound had exploded in the lab. He didn't know how long it had taken the others to find them lying on the dusty floor. The anesthesia in the compound hadn't agreed with him, and it had taken him hours to regain his consciousness. By the time he awakened, Doctor Thomas was there, telling him there was nothing he could do to wake Madeline.

Her eyes fluttered and opened. She was back. He needed to control his temper and keep his sanity in check. He rubbed his thumb at the dimple on her left cheek and spoke as gently as he could. "Hello there!"

She smiled. "How long have I been out?"

"All night." Ciaran smiled.

"And you didn't sleep?"

"I didn't know when you'd wake." He rubbed at the stubble on his unshaven face and tucked his loose hair back behind his ear. "How are you feeling?"

"I scared you, didn't I?"

"You had a fever. That was all. But you're okay now." He checked the temperature on her forehead with the back of his hand.

"I'm sorry," she said.

"What for?"

"I shouldn't have insisted on seeing the lab and shouldn't have smashed that tube."

He gazed into her eyes and saw a sea of secrets. She was withholding information from him. "Exactly what did you dream about, Madeline?"

She grinned. "I saw us having wild sex in the middle of a jungle, and we somehow ended up on a mountain with lots of naked women running around, and you were the only man there. Then we flew like birds and landed on a tropical beach in Asia. I was drinking fresh coconut juice and you were wearing a Hawaiian shirt."

He brushed a strand of hair from her cheek. "I don't wear Hawaiian shirts."

Madeline laughed. "I feel really good right now and could do with some breakfast. What do you have?"

"I can make you an omelette."

"Sounds wonderful. I'm starving!"

He smiled and nodded. Both he *and* Madeline were lying. He knew it, but he needed a bit more time to get over this hurdle. *What did Juliette want?* He wasn't really sure when she had been alive, and he certainly didn't know now that she was dead.

While Madeline was in the bathroom, he entered a code into a small cabinet in his closet. A small door slid open. He pulled out a watch and snapped a small disk onto its back before putting it on.

This device wasn't finished and hadn't been tested. But if the air bender was the one who had broken into Mon Ciel and caused all the problems, it would be no different from the pack of wolves that had killed his Dew. The big difference was that his father was no longer around to prevent Ciaran from doing what he considered fair and justified. He intended to give a tit for a tat. And if that took violence, so be it.

Suddenly the air thickened as it had in the museum.

"Air bender," he growled. "The only part of Mon Ciel you get a channel into is my old bedroom. Is this the most you can do here?"

The thick air wrapped around him, but it couldn't create any pressure. Ciaran smiled.

"You believe you opened a hole in Mon Ciel's security. In your dreams! Why don't you show yourself, and then we can talk. Or are you too weak?"

The thick air closed in and tightened around him.

"All right, let's end this."

He raised his watch and turned a small handle. A fan of electric blue light shone out, cutting through the thick air and lighting the entire room. When the light lit up the far wall, instead of seeing the old man as he had expected, he saw the shape of a woman.

Juliette.

Ciaran jerked his arm back, and the electric light swung in the air, hit the ceiling, and bounced back to him. He was thrown against the cabinet door, collapsing a shelf.

He must have hit his head because he saw stars. His vision was blurry. He heard Juliette's voice, "Try the Primer. I want to talk to you. I miss you, Ciaran."

He shook his head. "You're dead, Juliette."

"I want to see you again, Ciaran. Take the Primer . . ."

The voice echoed away and vanished. He knew he'd been lucky. If the device had been perfected, he could have electrocuted himself. He must have a concussion as it was. But it was better than being dead.

Madeline rushed into the closet. "What happened? Are you okay?"

"Just a stupid accident." He sat up and wrapped his arm around her shoulders so that she could haul him up from the floor.

Madeline glanced around. "You accidentally flew into the cabinet?"

Ciaran shook his head. "I've got some information about Stefan's whereabouts. We might be able to track him precisely in a few hours."

"That's great news. Can you walk? Should I call Doctor Thomas?"

"I'm okay." He glanced at the corner of the room where he had seen the shape of Juliette and saw nothing. Then he caught the faint scent of vanilla and roses in the air.

"Do you smell that?" he asked.

"Yes. It wasn't here before. What just happened, Ciaran?"

He shook his head. "I don't know."

"Oh, no." Madeline held her ears and winced. "It's Juliette's voice. She's in the old lab."

12

---

*I*n the hallway in the new quarter, Tadgh was negotiating with Migi. "Okay, listen sweetheart, I'm about to go into the men's room. And you are *not* following me there!"

The cat waved her twin tails patiently in different directions, then sat down and thumped them on the floor.

"Come on. Be patient. When Doctor Thomas brings TJ back from the vet, you can be friends with him and leave me alone. He's only a puppy, but he's a lot of fun."

Thump. Thump.

"Cats don't thump their tails. And could you try to be a bit more ladylike?"

Thump. Thump. Thump.

"All right, I'll ignore you then."

Before Tadgh could leave for the bathroom with the intention of sneaking out the other side and going straight to the kitchen for a quick breakfast, Migi jumped up. Her hair stood on end, and her tails pointed straight to the ceiling, the tips waving rapidly. The cat hissed and meowed and slapped the air with her paws, talons unsheathed.

"Come on. Don't act like that or people will think I hit you."

The cat continued to hiss.

"We might disagree on things, but this is completely unnecessary. What do you want?"

Tadgh felt a chill run up his spine. He turned around and saw only the empty hallway. But someone was calling his name. He couldn't see anyone.

He felt an urge to do something, go somewhere. Tadgh glanced around again.

The hallway lit up toward the old quarter of the house. He followed the light. Part of him didn't want to, but it seemed natural to go.

Migi clawed at his jeans and meowed loudly.

Why is she doing that? Tadgh shook his head and kept walking.

In no time, he stood in front of the old lab. His mind went blank, and he had no idea what the code was to get in. He had never entered the lab by himself. Ever.

Suddenly, the security pad lit up by itself. The code was right there, highlighted for him. In the back of his mind, something was screaming for him to stop.

It had to be the cat. Tadgh sneered and pushed the door open. He walked along the shelves, tracing his finger over rows and rows of jars full of chemicals. Ciaran's stuff. Tadgh shook his head.

"How on Earth could anyone find chemicals and potions interesting?" Tadgh muttered to himself. Ciaran was only two years older than he, but his big brother was way too complicated for him to even think about understanding.

Tadgh chuckled. He swayed a bit and felt drunk.

What was he doing in this old lab? His family owned a pharmaceutical company, but when it came to medicine, the most he ever had to deal with was taking a few aspirin when he had a headache.

A jar full of some kind of chemical in front of him caught his eye. He reached his hand out to grab it, ignoring the screaming voice in his head telling him not to.

The cat flew at him and bit his hand. Tadgh dropped the jar, but it didn't break.

"Ouch! You stupid cat." He bent to pick up the jar.

Migi darted at him with the force of a leopard and knocked Tadgh on his backside. "Okay, that's enough, cat. I'll kick you if you come near me again. I really will. Don't tempt me!"

Tadgh grabbed the jar, and the cat slapped at it with her paw, making it fall to the floor again.

"You're pissing me off, Migi!" He scrambled to grab the jar again.

"Come near me, and I'll smash this over your head."

Migi withdrew, hissing from a distance.

Ciaran and Madeline rushed to the door of the lab and stood there, breathing heavily.

"What are you two doing here?" Tadgh grinned.

"Put that jar down," Ciaran said.

"Why?" Tadgh said and pulled the lid off. "I'm making something here. I have a headache." Ciaran gestured for Madeline to stay outside the lab and approached his brother.

"Want to help me?" Tadgh waved the jar.

"Sure," Ciaran said, reaching his hand out. "But give me the jar." Ciaran took the jar from Tadgh and put the lid back on.

Tadgh's vision started to blur. His head wasn't functioning properly. It must be the headache. "Aren't you going to whip something up for me?" Tadgh shook his head, trying to stay alert.

"I will," Ciaran said. "Why don't you go back to your room to rest? I'll bring you some medicine."

Tadgh nodded. He took a couple of steps then turned back to Ciaran. "Hey, you tricked me. You just don't want me to touch your stuff!"

"It's not my stuff, it's Juliette's. You need something for your headache—I'll take care of it. Get out of here, Tadgh."

"Oh, no, no, you don't understand." Tadgh came back in and pointed to the cabinet at the far corner. "The jar you're holding and *this* jar will make a dream potion." Tadgh pulled the cabinet door open.

"No, Tadgh. Don't touch anything in there!" Ciaran approached.

"It's not poison or anything." Tadgh picked up a bottle. "This stuff and that jar will make a primer."

"A what?"

"The Dream Primer. Here, I'll show you."

"No, no. Give me the bottle. I'll do it for you. I promised."

His brother had promised. Ciaran always kept his promises. "All right," he said. But just as he was about to give it to Ciaran, someone was screaming at him in his head, telling him Ciaran was lying. The voice told him to take the bottle and run.

So he ran.

Ciaran grabbed him from behind. "Leave the bottle."

"No."

A scuffled commenced, and the bottle slipped out of his hand. Ciaran grabbed it before it could hit the floor.

"Tadgh, get out of here!" Ciaran shoved him, pushing him out of the lab.

Tadgh shoved back. "Don't you push me around, big brother."

"Out! Out!" Ciaran kept pushing to no avail, so he landed a punch on Tadgh's face.

Tadgh saw stars. But he didn't give in. He charged at Ciaran. Ciaran put the bottle on the lab bench, grabbed his arms, and kicked his legs out from under him.

Tadgh crashed to the floor.

Madeline flew into the lab and sat on him, pinning his arms to the floor, while Ciaran rushed to a cabinet, coming back with a needle.

The two of them were ganging up against him. Tadgh kicked hard but couldn't get free of Madeline's grip.

Ciaran shoved the needle into Tadgh's neck and pumped the fluid into his vein. Tadgh wriggled and threw Madeline off. He sprung up to his feet and ran. But he only made it a couple of steps before his world went dark.

He screamed and turned around. There, he saw Juliette. "Juliette!" Tadgh cried out.

She reached her arms out to him, but they turned into giant snakes, wrapping around his neck and strangling him.

adgh yelled out Juliette's name and sat up on his bed abruptly, panting. Madeline rushed to the bed and grabbed his hands, pulling them away from his neck as he gasped for air. She understood very well how disoriented he must feel coming out of unconsciousness.

He looked at Madeline then glanced around his bedroom. Madeline pulled him in to her arms for an embrace. She held him until the vibration of emotion in his body settled. "You're okay now. Ciaran has just gone to talk to Doctor Thomas. He'll be back soon."

Tadgh eased out of Madeline's hug.

"What happened?" he asked.

"You went into the old lab, apparently trying to mix something up. Ciaran had to knock you out before you intoxicated yourself."

Tadgh rubbed at his forehead, trying to recall. He shook his head and flopped back to the bed on his back. "I can't remember any of it."

"It'll take time. But it will come back to you."

"Can I have some coffee?"

"I'm not sure if that's good for you right now. I'll ask Ciaran."

Tadgh sat up, arching an eyebrow. Madeline laughed. "All right, all right. I'll get you some coffee." She stood to leave the room.

"No need to go to the kitchen, Madeline." Tadgh got off the bed. He held onto the bed post for a short moment to steady himself. Madeline rushed over to help him, but he waved his arm absently. "I've got it. Thanks."

He opened a wall cabinet, revealing a coffeemaker and several containers of biscuits and sweet treats. He turned around and grinned at her.

"Ciaran stocks spirits and wine and you stockpile coffee and sweet treats."

Tadgh laughed. "I don't have gadgets in my room like he does."

Madeline glanced around. Ciaran had a gigantic wall-sized screen in his room, but Tadgh didn't even have a TV. Ciaran had a computer system set up in a corner of his room, so complicated that Madeline didn't even know how to turn it on. But in here, Madeline couldn't even see a remote control.

"I'm not anti-technology, if that's what you're thinking. I travel a lot and just don't generally need gadgets. Coffee?"

Madeline nodded.

Tadgh brought the coffee over to the bed. He climbed onto it and sat cross-legged. He placed a small plate of cookies in the middle of the bed and pushed it toward Madeline.

"How are you feeling, Tadgh?"

"Still a bit queasy. But I'll be fine after this." He raised his mug of coffee.

"What did you see? You can tell me, and then I'll tell you what I saw."

"What you saw last night when you scared the hell out of Ciaran?"

"What?"

"We found you both in the lab, unconscious. When Ciaran was up and Doctor Thomas told him there was nothing he could do to wake you, man, I've never seen him like that before."

"Like what?"

Tadgh shook his head and bit his cookie. "When Juliette died, he was devastated. But it was more like sorrow, or maybe regret. But he seemed to accept her death. But last night, he was furious. He wouldn't consider even the slightest possibility that he might lose you. It was madness."

"He didn't say much this morning."

"I'd be surprised if he had. He's a control freak. I should ask Mother if he even cried as a baby. I doubt it very much."

"Have you heard from Jennifer?"

"Yes. She called. She'd back to Dublin now. Wouldn't talk to Ciaran! You can see where Ciaran got his hard head."

From the door, Migi walked in graciously in and hopped on to the bed. She lay down next to Tadgh and purred loudly.

"You haven't asked for permission to come in, let alone to get in bed with me, lady."

Madeline laughed. Migi moved over to lay next to Madeline. She scratched the cat's ears, making her purr louder. Tadgh shook his head and sipped his coffee.

"Do you like Juliette?"

"What?" Tadgh choked on his coffee.

"You heard me, Tadgh."

Tadgh reached to Migi to scratch her ears, but she inched out of Tadgh's reach. Madeline looked at Tadgh, waiting for an answer.

Tadgh cleared his throat. That was exactly what Ciaran did before he said anything difficult, Madeline thought.

"Ciaran is the smart guy in the family. He was home schooled, but by about fourteen, he had mastered all the subjects—chemistry, medicine, artificial intelligence, computer science, you name it— at a university level. And at sixteen, he ran our business empire. Our family business had grown tenfold since he took it over..."

Tadgh leaned back and stretched his legs out. "You might think our parents forced him to study. But that wasn't the case. And look at me! I went to college just to keep up appearances." Tadgh sipped his coffee and looked at Madeline over the rim. "Ciaran has loved to learn ever since he was a kid. He's always been hungry for knowledge. And not just learning and accepting things the way they are. He loves to *create*." Tadgh gazed at Madeline. "You might not like this, Madeline, but in that regard, Ciaran and Juliette were a perfect match."

"And how can you be so sure I don't love knowledge and creation?"

Tadgh shook his head. "Apart from a slight physical resemblance, Ciaran and I have nothing in common. I'm not perfect and never try to be. Ciaran thinks he has to be perfect and has to be responsible for everything."

Madeline nodded and leaned against the bedpost.

"Juliette was a perfect match for Ciaran. She was almost a mirror image of him, just in a different gender."

"And isn't a perfect match a good thing?"

Tadgh shook his head again. "It's like having two right shoes."

Madeline chuckled. "Interesting analogy."

"You haven't been with him for a long time, Madeline. And I don't know you at all. But I'm telling you this even though Ciaran will shoot me if he finds out. When Doctor Thomas said he couldn't wake you, I swear I saw tears in Ciaran's eyes."

Madeline nodded. "I appreciate you telling me."

"It's more for me than for you. It's nice to see my brother has some feelings again," Tadgh muttered. "I knew Juliette was using my brother. But there's nothing I can do about it because she's dead now . . ."

"I don't think so."

"Excuse me?"

Then she explained to him about the blue dots.

"When I was in the coma, I talked to Juliette, and she told me she might not have died."

Tadgh narrowed his eyes. "You dreamed about Juliette, and she said she didn't die?"

"It wasn't just a dream. I intentionally inhaled the drug so that I could talk to her. Don't question it, Tadgh, just accept it. She haunted Ciaran, and I wanted to know what was going on."

Tadgh stared blankly. "I think I need more coffee." He rushed to the cabinet to get some more brewing.

"It wasn't a dream. I fought with Juliette, and there was this." Madeline opened a button on her shirt and pulled the collar aside. On the left side of her chest, there was a nasty red scar from a stab wound.

Tadgh stared, speechless at the sight of the raw wound.

"There were more, but they all vanished except for this one. I was supposed to die from this wound. It wasn't a dream, Tadgh. She said she would come back for Ciaran. The thing is, though, it seemed as if I was talking to two different versions of Juliette. One was cold and calculated, and the other one was sad."

"I bet it was the cold bitch who stabbed you."

"That's not what I'm concerned about. She told me the location of the crucifix."

Tadgh choked badly on his coffee. When he got his breath back, he asked, "Where?"

"It's at Fountains Abbey."

"What?"

"Fountains Abbey."

"Do you know anything about that place?"

"No."

"There are miles and miles of national parks and tourist attractions. You've got to be kidding me!"

"I'm not making it up. And that's not my main concern."

"So what is?"

"After the cold Juliette revealed the location of the crucifix, the sad one told me not to let Ciaran find it, that it wasn't meant for him."

"So who is it for then? Stefan?"

"She said if Ciaran found the crucifix, it would kill him."

"Why? Is there a bomb in it?"

"I don't know. Poison maybe? A toxic chemical? Whatever it is, I'm not telling him until I figure out what she meant."

"Agreed. If he knows, he'll be the first one there. And then we'll need a bulldozer to get him off the issue. That's no good if we need to defuse a bomb at the same time. But how do you plan to find out what's going on? Talk to Juliette?"

"No, I'm not ready to do that again. I'll take a look at the site myself."

"I'll go with you."

"Go where?" Ciaran asked from the doorway.

14

*M*adeline pushed at Ciaran's chest, backing him into his office. The sunlight poured in via a tall window at the far end of the room. The frame of the window and the light haloed behind Ciaran, making him look to her like a doomed angel. The sight of him made her stomach churn.

He smiled at her. "Explain to me why you suddenly want to have a picnic at a national park with Tadgh?"

Needing to distract him from the current issue of the crucifix, she turned on her best weapon, her sultry voice. "And why not?" She wrapped her arms around his neck. "I'll take Migi, TJ, and you as well, if you're interested."

Ciaran's voice was already muffled with the kiss. "It's quite convenient actually. Stefan just called your phone. I picked up, so he was a bit disappointed. He wanted to meet at a national park."

She stopped the kiss. "Which one?"

"The national park next to Rufford Abbey."

She withheld a sigh of relief. If the crucifix was actually at Fountains Abbey, Ciaran wouldn't accidentally stumble upon it at Rufford Abbey. "All right. Is Jo okay?"

"Yes. She sounded fine."

"Stefan let you talk to her?"

"Not voluntarily. But a man has to know how to negotiate, doesn't he? The meeting isn't on for another few hours. So we have time."

"Why didn't you tell me in front of Tadgh?"

"I don't want to have to worry about him."

"He looked all right in the room. You're worried about what happened in the lab?"

Ciaran nodded.

"Wouldn't it be better to have him by your side than leaving him at home?"

Ciaran shook his head. "I'm sending him to our Paris headquarters. It will keep him busy. He gets along well with my cousin, George, there."

"You'll need a bulldozer," Madeline muttered.

"I beg your pardon?"

She smiled and kissed him again until all of the knotted muscles in his body loosened. With just a slight push, he was on the couch with her on top. She tugged at his shirt, pulling it, desperately getting to the flesh and the firmness of his toned muscles.

This man knew how to touch a woman. All of her senses exploded, her body relaxed, and she felt as if she'd melt under his touch and evaporate into thin air. He ravished her mouth then tugged at her shirt and pulled it off.

And that was when he saw it—a big red scar on the left side of her chest.

Damn! Madeline cursed to herself. She had totally forgotten about the mark.

"What's this? It wasn't there the night before."

"It's a burn."

"This is a scar, Madeline, not a new wound. How did it happen?"

Madeline pulled her shirt down to cover her exposed breast. "I fought with Juliette during the coma. She stabbed me, and I didn't duck fast enough. I gave her a few good blows, though."

Ciaran sat up on the couch. "Say that again, please!"

"I fought with Juliette. She told me it wasn't a dream. It was a hologame, whatever that means."

Ciaran narrowed his eyes. "She told you that she got you into a hologame?"

"That's what she said. What's a hologame, Ciaran?"

Ciaran smiled and teased Madeline hair. "You've seen a hologram, haven't you?"

She nodded.

"At a very advanced level of technology, instead of using telephone, we use holograms to communicate, and we call it holocast. A holocast can not only send hologram images but can actually teleport a person as well. That is, if the communicators *choose* to step out of a holocast."

Madeline blinked. "Better than *Star Wars!*"

Ciaran chuckled. "A hologame uses the same technology to allow players to compete in a virtual environment. I'm testing the technology at the moment."

"You invented it?"

Ciaran laughed. "I invented my own version of it. But there are others who have their own technology."

"How many others?"

"There are a handful of manufacturers in the world. It's very cost-prohibitive."

Madeline chuckled. "I'm sure it takes more than money."

Ciaran nodded. "But what you experienced—if it truly was a hologame—is unheard of. It was played under subconscious conditions—that's like playing using your mind. Any technology that plays with the mind is dangerous and immoral. Especially, when it's done without your consent."

His eyes darkened now. She recalled Tadgh telling her how helpless Ciaran had felt when she didn't wake. "Juliette had my partial consent. Please don't make her angrier with you."

"What do you mean?"

"Her blue dots and her voice kept accusing you of killing her. I just wanted her to stop haunting you and this house. I agreed to talk to her, and she told me to smash the tube in the lab."

The fury shooting from his eyes was like a laser. Ciaran stood and strode toward the window, staring outside. She knew he was trying to control his temper. She said nothing else.

When he turned around, his eyes were completely dark, and his voice was so low that it sounded like a growl. "Don't you ever put yourself between me and my problem. Juliette is *my* problem. I alone will deal with her, just as I have in the past I don't know how many years."

"Well, you didn't exactly do a good job."

"I'm handling it."

"How? By not talking about it? By stopping everyone in your family from discussing it or helping you?"

"I don't need your help. Or anyone else's."

"I'm sorry I hurt your ego." She put her hands on her hips.

"Ego! You think this has to do with my *ego*?"

"Give me a better explanation then, Ciaran."

"You don't know what Juliette was capable of when she was alive. And she's worse now that she's dead. The people you're talking to are Juliette's allies, and they can crush you before you even know what's happening. You're far too important for me to lose. And if you take that lightly, then *that* hurts my ego!" He hit a vase. It flew to the wall and fell shattered to the floor, along with her nerves. "I'm sorry I've scared you." He flopped down to the couch and put his head in his hands.

She embraced him from behind. "Please tell me you forgive me."

He turned around and pulled her into his arms. "There is nothing to forgive, Madeline. I'm sorry, I didn't mean to yell."

"Say sorry to the vase!"

He smiled, although it didn't quite travel to his eyes. "It would take a load off me if you could refrain yourself from any drastic action toward people you don't know."

She tucked his long hair behind his ears, reached up, and kissed his cheek. "I promise."

Ciaran's phone buzzed. "Lindsay . . . All right. Thanks." He hung up the phone and rushed toward his computer. Madeline followed.

Opening a file, he skimmed through rows and rows of data and codes. Then he turned off the computer and stood up.

"We need to leave now. We are going to Laurent's place and then off to Rufford Abbey."

"What just happened, Ciaran?"

"I'll explain on the way. The data is Stefan's computer search pattern. He just tapped into Laurent's home computer. I want to make sure everything is okay."

"Why Laurent?"

"She was Juliette's best friend."

Before they reached the door, Tadgh approached with a grin on his face. "Going to a picnic without me?"

15

*A*n hour later, they arrived at Stow-on-the-Wold. They had been here before for Robert's funeral, the day after the Fosse Way saga. Madeline remembered the lawn, the house, and the sad aura it had had at the time.

She was sure that, as the head of the LeBlancs' security, Robert's death wouldn't have left his own family in limbo. But after what had happened at Mon Ciel, she thought they would be able to leave this behind them. But no, here they were here again, seeing the widow and the child.

But things had indeed changed since the funeral. The sad aura was gone. The widow Laurent greeted them at the front door. Her eyes were warm and contented. Laurent had had to get on with life for her daughter's sake, Madeline thought.

"Oh, Tadgh, you look so well! It's so good to see you."

"You are beautiful, as always. I am desperate to see the baby Bella!"

"She's asleep, but she'll be up soon. Come on in."

When everyone had settled around the coffee table, Laurent asked Ciaran, "Why now, Ciaran? For so many years, you refused to touch any of her belongings. Is it worth it to dig up old memories now?"

"It's a long story. I need to have a look at her journals, or anything about what she did before we got married. Also, I've reserved a very nice holiday home overseas where you can stay. You need a break from all this."

"Are you evacuating us, Ciaran? What's going on?"

"I've lost Robert, and there's nothing I can do to bring him back. But I can't let anything happen to you and Bella. Just go for a short time. It would give me peace of mind. Please."

Laurent sighed. "All right, very well then. The room is intact. Help yourself to anything in it."

"You kept her room all these years?" Ciaran was astonished.

"We were like sisters. You're not the only one who can't let go, Ciaran. She used it occasionally after you got married as well. Whenever she was confused, desperate, lonely, or just needed a shoulder, she'd come here."

"I'm sorry . . ." Ciaran began.

Tadgh cleared his throat. "I think the baby is crying. Could I please see her, Laurent? I'm good with kids. I promise I won't scare her or anything."

Madeline knew there was no baby crying. Tadgh was a master at distraction. As his mother had said, he knew Ciaran's weakness.

Laurent stood and smiled at Ciaran and Madeline. "All right then, you two can head to the room. You know where it is, Ciaran. I'll take Tadgh to see the baby so he'll stop nagging. I have something else for you, too, Ciaran."

They parted ways.

Juliette's room was neat, tidy, and minimal. There was nothing nonessential. No flowers, vases, paintings, or decorative items. A single bed was tucked into a corner, and a desk sat in front of a small window.

On the desk was a small computer, books, journals, and other reading material, all neatly arranged. The room was well-maintained, so much so that Madeline wagered she wouldn't be able to find a single speck of dust in here.

On a small shelf, there were more books and a picture of Ciaran and Juliette that had been taken in front of the Bodleian Library at the University of Oxford. They looked so happy. Ciaran looked exactly the same, his long black hair swept back, almost touching his shoulders.

Ciaran muttered something and was about to remove the picture from the shelf, but Madeline stepped in and grabbed it before he could. "Look at you! You wore your hair long, even back then." Ciaran just smiled and continued to scour the room for notebooks and journals.

Madeline found a large wooden box and opened it. Inside, there she found tiny jars and tubes containing eye shadows, lipsticks, and lip balms. It looked like Juliette was trying to create her own line of makeup. There was also a small bottle of perfume. Madeline thought Juliette had probably made that, as well.

The box looked as if it had another layer. She dug her fingernails in and tried to lift the surface shelf. The velvet-covered bottom popped up. "What do we have here?"

Ciaran turned around and came closer to take a look. Peeling the fake bottom off, they found a smaller box with a rusty lid underneath. Ciaran rubbed the rust off to see what was written there. It read "Dream Primer."

Ciaran put the box down on the bed quickly and pulled Madeline away from it. "It's a primer. She had been making this all along. What's it for?" Ciaran asked, mostly to himself.

Ciaran grabbed a large folder from the shelf. Inside, there were several articles, pictures, and notes. He picked up an article. The title read, "Susceptibility to Hypnosis." He picked up another one. "Neurological Fantasy." Ciaran shook his head and muttered, "I didn't know she was into these subjects."

Then he picked up a note with her handwritten text and a diagram. The diagram looked like a flow chart and had many wavy lines coming in and out of boxes and bubbles. "Electrical waves . . . Brain waves . . ." Ciaran talked to himself. He turned the note aside to read the tiny print. "Dreamer Primer," Ciaran read out loud.

They heard a loud bang and saw a fireball hit the glass window. The glass shattered. The curtain and the rod collapsed on Ciaran and Madeline. Ciaran dropped everything he was holding, pulling Madeline aside.

They both dropped to the floor as another fireball flew in and hit the bed. The linens caught on fire and spread with lightning speed. Ciaran grabbed Madeline and pulled her with him out of the room.

They heard Tadgh shouting to get out from the other end of the house. At the end of the hallway, they could see him helping Laurent, who was carrying the baby.

It looked as if the back room of the house and the kitchen was on fire. They could hear the footsteps of people running outside and some on the roof. They met in the living room.

Both Ciaran and Tadgh pulled out their guns and pushed the women protectively behind them. Ciaran looked toward the kitchen and saw a spark. They kicked the door open and stormed outside. The gas tank in the kitchen exploded behind them, and the house burst into flames.

"Get in the car," Ciaran said. As they ran toward the car, a fireball dropped and exploded in front of it, stopping them from getting inside.

They withdrew from the vehicle.

Three men in black, all wearing masks, ran after them from the back of the house.

The house was quite remote and did not have any next-door neighbors. But it did sit close to the road. A car passing by approached and stopped when the driver saw the house on fire. A couple got out. Two men in masks rushed out from the side of the house to shoot at them. A series of small darts flew out and hit the car's passengers.

Ciaran, Madeline, and Tadgh had seen this weapon before at

Mrs. Hanson's place. The tourists evaporated into thin air, leaving only piles of empty clothes behind.

Ciaran shot at a man approaching them. Tadgh took another one down.

The third one pointed his gun right at Madeline. But when he saw her face clearly, he didn't shoot. Taking the opportunity, Ciaran put a bullet in the man's head.

The baby cried in Laurent's arms.

The two who had just shot the couple took shelter behind a tree so that Ciaran and Tadgh couldn't get a good shot. Despite Ciaran yelling at her, Madeline ran out and grabbed two wood panels standing against the garden fences.

They could use these as shields against the darts, Madeline thought. Whoever those people were, they apparently wouldn't shoot her.

Ciaran cursed and grabbed the panels, pushing Madeline behind him. Tadgh grabbed the other panel, and blocked Laurent and the baby.

Five men appeared from the left and five from the right. They charged forward, kicking at the panels. But they didn't shoot.

Ciaran took down two more, and Tadgh fired at one of them.

There were more men coming. The masked men kept charging at the panels until one of them got past. He grabbed Ciaran and kneed him in his cracked rib. Ciaran slumped to the ground, heaving in pain.

Tadgh turned around and received a kick that sent him to the ground as well.

The five men in masks charged toward the women and children.

Madeline picked up a steel bar lying nearby and whacked at the coming men without mercy. She sent three of them to the ground, perhaps with cracked skulls.

The other two were grabbed from behind by Ciaran and Tadgh. While the men fought, Madeline guided Laurent, still carrying the baby, to the car.

They traveled only a short distance before five more men charged over from the other side of the road. These five had the dart guns in their hands.

Ciaran could see it was too far to reach the women before they were shot. One man gave Madeline a kick, sending her skidding away on the ground.

Ciaran and Tadgh pulled their guns and fired at the five men. Four went down, and the last one shot at Laurent and the baby before was killed by Ciaran.

Ciaran and Tadgh hurried over, and Ciaran helped Madeline up. "Were you shot?" he asked.

"No, I'm fine," she said.

Then Ciaran ran over to Laurent and the baby.

"No, no, no, please no!" Ciaran looked helplessly at the two of them, who were fast fading away. Soon, like the others, mother and daughter became just piles of clothes.

Lying next to Laurent's clothes was a book, Juliette's diary. Laurent had kept the diary in her own room and wanted to give it to Ciaran. Luckily, it had not been destroyed in the fire.

Madeline grabbed Ciaran and hugged him tightly while his body shook in uncontrollable grief.

Tadgh kicked the fence furiously. "Who the fuck were those people? What the fuck do they want?"

There was nothing more here for them to see or do. There was nothing left except for piles of clothes where people used to exist. Ciaran stood up, grabbed the diary, and moved numbly toward his car. His face was cold, his eyes burned with anger.

Five more men appeared across the road.

"You've got to be fucking kidding me," Tadgh said.

Ciaran said nothing. He pulled out his gun and shot three men down at once. The other two charged forward with lightning speed, leaping onto Ciaran's car, one of them giving Ciaran a flying kick on his way down. Ciaran slid away on the ground. The diary dropped out of his hand. The other man attacked Tadgh.

The one who had just kicked Ciaran walked toward the diary to pick it up. Before he could reach it, he copped a metal bar in the head from Madeline.

He was down and stayed down.

The last man had been incapacitated by Tadgh.

Ciaran picked up the diary, put it in his jacket pocket, and walked to the car. Madeline and Tadgh followed.

16

Ciaran got behind the wheel. Madeline was in the front seat, and Tadgh was in the back.

Ciaran had just started the car up when they heard the roar of an engine and saw a car hurtling toward them. Ciaran gave a half smile and geared up his car.

Tadgh was silent. He braced himself and did his best to hold his organs in place.

Ciaran's car zoomed out to the road, fishtailed at the corner of the driveway, and left behind nothing but smoke for the other car.

Madeline looked in the rear view mirror and saw Tadgh was sweating as if just out of a shower. His eyes were shut tight. Ciaran smiled. "Speed is Tadgh's worst nightmare."

The chasing car didn't give up easily. Ciaran drove to a back road and continued in a direction which led away from Rufford Abbey.

The back country roads were not kind to Tadgh as Ciaran drove with highway speed on rural, two-way country roads meant to hold only one car at a time. Madeline thought she had a strong stomach, but sometimes she felt her organs might just erupt through her ribcage.

Ciaran kept his eyes fixed straight ahead, shifting gears and turning corners as if he was driving in a grand prix. His face was cold as steel. Sometimes, inches from hitting stone fences or trees, Madeline gasped. But Ciaran didn't even blink.

Ciaran knew these roads well. At an approaching sharp corner, he hit the brake, veered to the other side of the road, and smoothly turned. The other car went straight through the corner and into a fast flowing creek.

"Farewell," Ciaran said dryly and drove back in the direction of Rufford Abbey.

Shortly afterward, Madeline, Ciaran, and Tadgh approached a small rest stop in the middle of deer hunting ground. They found Stefan and Jo waiting.

As they entered, Madeline could see that Tadgh was dazzled by Jo. She was a petite girl, barely reaching his shoulder. Her long, black hair framed a foxy face, mysteriously brightened by her large green eyes.

Jo's eyes widened when she saw Ciaran. "White Knight," she said.

"Hello, Jo. It's a pleasure to meet you face to face." Ciaran nodded in greeting.

Madeline smiled at Jo in reassurance. They didn't need to talk to communicate.

"I'm Tadgh, Ciaran's brother." Tadgh approached to shake hands with Jo, but Stefan waved his finger to stop his motion.

"This is not a party."

Jo gave Tadgh a bright smile that weakened his knees.

"Very nice to meet you, Tadgh. I can tell you're Ciaran's brother. Do you play hologames?"

"I said, this is not a party," Stefan cut in.

Jo winked at Tadgh. "We'll play later."

Ciaran couldn't hide a smile. "All right, we're here. Now tell us what you want, Stefan."

Let the opponent draw blood first, Madeline thought. That was the Ciaran approach she admired.

"Jo can only decode half the disk. I want you to do the other half for me. Otherwise . . ." Stefan turned Jo's shoulder slightly so that everyone could see the gun he had pointed at her back. "Let's move it up a bit." He shifted the gun up, pointing it at the back of Jo's head. "And now let's get cozy." He pulled Jo with his left hand, pressing her body against his and wrapping his left arm around her. He pointed the gun at her temple. "One wrong move, and I'll blow her head off."

Jo smiled. "He's been saying that for two days."

Stefan pressed the gun harder against her head.

"Hey, hey, hang on," Tadgh interrupted. "You want us to do something, right? I don't know shit about computers. Which half did Jo translate or decode or whatever you call it? Was it the first half or the second half, or did she translate every second word?"

Stefan's face reddened. "You think this is a joke?"

Madeline swallowed her laugh.

"It's the last one . . . unfortunately," Jo spoke gently.

"What the fuck do you mean by that? You told me you've got fifty percent done," Stefan fumed.

"I did, but I did bits and pieces," Jo explained.

"Program coding is complicated, Stefan. I'm sure Juliette told you that. There will be a part that Jo has enough experience to decode. But there will be part that only I can decode because I have the experience in that area. It's not necessarily about who has better skills. It's the experience that makes the difference." Ciaran smiled at Jo.

"I don't give a shit. I don't care how you do it. I want the information in one piece—and in English."

"Stefan, Ciaran and Jo have to work together to decode the document for you. I'm sure you understand that," Madeline added.

"Then you'll all have to come with me," Stefan said.

"We need *real* computers to do it. Remember, Stefan, Juliette used my computer to code this disk. Our technology is the most sophisticated in this country. So can you arrange that?"

"He has a piece of junk in his room he calls a computer," Jo teased.

"You think I'm stupid? You think I'm just going to give you the disk and let you go? Or follow you back to your place so that you can pull a gun on me?"

Ciaran responded. "I'm not suggesting any such thing. And besides, you're the one pulling guns here. The crucifix isn't even what you really want. You want the gold—and you think my family can make gold, maybe out of thin air. You believe that Juliette got some gold somehow —or the know-how from our family—and sent it to you in the crucifix. The truth is, we don't make gold, and no such method to do it exists. Look, why don't we just give you some money..."

Tadgh interrupted, "No shit. I'm not giving him any money. You can hang on to the disk and half of the information, if you want. I could care less. But that very beautiful person standing next to you is a good friend of Madeline, and Madeline is almost my sister-in-law..."

"What?" Jo and Madeline said at the same time.

Ciaran looked at Tadgh. "Now you *are* talking shit."

"You married her because you had sex with her," Tadgh sneered.

"You don't think I'd marry just anyone I've had sex with, do you?" Ciaran scolded.

"Come on, bro. You get too serious about casual sex."

"Casual sex?" Ciaran raised his voice.

"Sorry, it was me. I'm the one-night-stander. But I've already given Juliette some money. She was smoking hot. I've already spent a lot of money on her. So no more money for him." Tadgh pointed at Stefan.

"What the fuck do you mean by that?" Ciaran snarled.

"It was before you got married. Come on! A pretty girl like Juliette? You were out and about with your big deal business. You thought she'd sit around and wait for you?"

"Tadgh!"

"Oh, don't tell me you thought she was a virgin, bro. She . . ."

Stefan screamed, "Shut up, shut up! Don't you two fuck around with me!"

He was so angry he swung the gun, pointing it at Tadgh, and thus took it away from Jo's head. At the same time, Ciaran and Tadgh pulled their guns and pointed them at Stefan.

"Don't move," Ciaran said.

"Two of us and one of you—better keep the gun there. Don't move an inch, you stupid son-of-a-bitch," Tadgh said with satisfaction. "You don't want to make my brother shoot. He doesn't miss. Keep the gun on me. But if you shoot me, your head will eat a bullet, I guarantee you."

"Come here, Jo," Madeline said.

Jo moved away from Stefan, inch by inch. She could hear him breathing heavily with anger. She ran toward Madeline.

They hugged at each other.

"Sorry about the stupid sex talk, Madeline. I need to improve my improvisational technique. Ciaran played along well, though." Tadgh grinned, his eyes still focused on Stefan.

Ciaran smiled slightly. "Find a better angle next time, brat. You've got a lot to learn."

"What was your code?" Jo asked.

"'Talking shit'. We've always used that one, haven't we?" Tadgh laughed.

"Nice." Jo let out a short laugh.

Ciaran waved at Stefan with his free hand. "Now, the disk, Stefan. Take it out."

Stefan pulled it out and held it in his hand.

"I really want to be fair to you, Stefan, since you worked hard for whatever it is that Juliette sent you. But Mrs. Rutherford was our family. You can't kill one of us and get away with it," Ciaran said.

"But you killed one of ours. You killed Juliette."

"No, I didn't. She might have died because of me, but I did not kill her. She was my wife."

"Mrs. Rutherford died because she called the security on me. She might have died because of me, but I didn't mean to kill her!"

"Good point. Okay, I'll let you go—but only because you're Juliette's brother. I didn't kill her, and I won't kill her family, either. But you have to leave the disk," Ciaran stated firmly.

"No," Stefan protested.

"You don't have a choice. We can keep you posted on what's in it," Tadgh added.

"I'm not a patient man, Stefan. Put the disk down and leave. There's no point dying for this. There is no crucifix or formula for you to find," said Ciaran.

They could see Stefan's body shaking with anger. He kept his grip on the disk.

They heard a shifting sound outside as if a very large bird had just taken off. Then there was a thunk on the roof and a flash of someone's legs flitting across the outside of the window, almost like the person was flying.

Madeline could see outside. A man in black, hanging from a rope, was swinging at the top of the trees. He swung past the window again and threw a small ball inside.

The ball rolled and stopped in the middle of the room. Stefan, Ciaran, and Tadgh were frozen in gun-pointing positions. None of them wanted to take their guns off of their targets.

Jo and Madeline rushed toward the ball to grab it, with the intention of throwing it outside. But before they could reach it, the ball exploded in thick red smoke.

17

*T*he stench of rotten bodies blasted at him. Ciaran winced. He was standing in a different world, a world he had visited many times.

Hologame.

The dark gray sky was scarred with cuts and bruises from the attack of demons' claws and fangs. Haunting trees were clumped together, and there were enough to make running difficult but not enough to form a forest.

He glanced around. Images of Madeline, Tadgh, Jo, and Stefan flickered and appeared.

Only Jo knew where they were. "Hologame," she muttered.

Ciaran strode toward Madeline and Tadgh. "Don't be alarmed. We'll be fine. It's just like playing a computer game. Except we're in it."

They still wore their normal clothes. Ciaran and Tadgh were in their long black coats. Madeline was in her long red leather jacket. Jo was in her leather pants and short furry coat.

Stefan stood by himself, confused.

None of them had their weapons.

The cold wind blew in bizarre sounds from the distance, the

sound of demons calling from hell. Wolves were crying for their pack somewhere among the trees. There was the sound of running water. The water was perhaps the most familiar sound. But they couldn't see water anywhere.

"If this is a game, do we get to specify the expertise level?" Madeline asked.

"I don't think so," Jo guessed.

"If we got beaten up in here, would it be the same as on the outside?" Tadgh asked.

"Are you asking if we die in here, will we die out there? In theory, the answer is no. It's a game. But in reality, I really don't know. The designer of this game violated the rules. We didn't consent to be in here. My guess is that we're lying unconscious somewhere back there and will be eaten by wild animals by the time we get back."

"*If* we get back," Stefan sneered.

A laugh echoed behind them. Beyond the trees, a small stone bridge appeared.

Now they could see a small creek. Juliette stood on the bridge, looking magnificent. Her long red hair blew in the wind, and her bright blue eyes were clear through the thick fog.

She looked the same, Ciaran thought. But she might not be his Juliette.

"You look like Juliette," he said.

"Ten years older, though," Tadgh added.

Juliette waved her arm and sent a lightning bolt at Tadgh, hitting him and sending him flying to the ground behind him.

"I can see that you still haven't grown up. You don't mock a woman's age, Tadgh. Especially one who has total control of your environment, your life, and your death. Out there, your family can have whatever they want. But in here, in my world, you will play by my rules. You will do what I say. I alone will decide whether you live or die."

Juliette laughed. An insane laugh.

"So how do you want to play, Juliette?" Ciaran asked.

"Oh, my dear Ciaran, you're just the same as you were. Even after ten long years, you still love games, and let me guess, you still love winning."

"Who wouldn't?"

"That's exactly right. Who wouldn't want to win? So let's play the game you all wanted to play in your world. Let's play crucifix hunting. All of you against me. Here are the rules. The crucifix is in this park. You are to find it and bring it to the other end of the park for me. You will fight as a group. If you lose one person, you lose the game."

"What will happen if we lose the game?" Madeline asked.

Juliette looked at her and smiled mysteriously. "You do not want to lose, sister!"

Juliette turned around to look at Stefan.

"I thought you were dead," Stefan whispered in disbelief.

"I'm not. Win the game, and we can see each other again, brother. I'm sure you missed me."

"Why can't you tell me where it is? We don't need them," Stefan said.

"Oh, no, no! That's no fun at all. I hid it, and I traded my life for it. Now you will have to work hard to find it. Isn't that fair?" Juliette waved her arm in the air and disappeared into the darkness.

A roar of wind blew at them. "That's not wind. Wind doesn't sound like that," Tadgh said.

They looked to the sky. In the distance, a flock of half dragon-half bat creatures was flying toward them.

"Get some ammo!" Ciaran shouted.

"Tree. Tree gives life." Jo ran toward a huge tree.

"What?" Tadgh asked.

Madeline ran toward Ciaran and Jo. Stefan reluctantly followed.

Jo put her right hand on her hip. "Knife." A belt appeared, wrapping around her waist, a hunting knife in a side pocket.

"All right, so we've got the basic package. Get what you want," Ciaran instructed the others. Ciaran asked for a sword, and a gigantic sword appeared in his hand.

Tadgh, Stefan, and Madeline asked for handguns.

And suddenly, they all had guns.

The flying animals were closing in fast. Ciaran used his sword and Jo used her knife to dig into the roots of the tree, but it wouldn't budge an inch.

"Got to lose some blood here." She held the knife against her wrist.

Ciaran stopped her. "No, let me." He sliced his arm, and blood droplets fell onto the tree. Its roots pulled up like arms, revealing boxes of machine guns.

Tadgh gasped. Ciaran grabbed a gun, and everyone else followed his lead.

Ciaran and Jo pointed the machine guns to the sky and sprayed a barrage of bullets at the weird flying animals. They screamed and hissed with pain and exploded into black dust and ashes.

"Awesome!" Tadgh was enjoying this.

They heard a hiss, a shift, and a roar behind them. A leopard with horns jumped out from the bush at them. Madeline turned quickly, stood her ground, and punched it full of bullet holes.

Ciaran looked at Madeline and smiled. "Magnificent warrior."

In the distance, a dragon raised up from the ground.

Tadgh lifted his gun and took aim.

Ciaran dropped his machine gun to the ground and charged toward the dragon. "He's mine, brother. I want my blood back."

Ciaran ran, grabbed a low tree branch, and swung himself up high. He flew from one tree to another. The dragon greeted him with waves of fire. Ciaran leaped over the flames, pulled his sword, and stabbed it straight into the dragon's heart. The dragon disintegrated and crumbled to the ground. The blood that spurted from its heart was absorbed by Ciaran's hand.

When he rejoined the group, Jo gave him an admiring salute. "White Knight!"

"We have to move," Ciaran said.

They looked around, gauging their surroundings.

"She said this is a park. If it's manmade, there will likely be a lake in the middle. The trees will be surrounding it. And the hiding place will be somewhere in the center. Center of the road, middle of the lake. It has to have some kind of central logic to it," Stefan said.

"Could it be in the water?" Tadgh asked.

"Maybe. It depends," Stefan responded.

"Let's head that way to see if we can find a lake," Madeline said, pointing.

They walked for a while, and a lake appeared in front of them. They followed a path along the water, and they came upon a small island with a statue in the middle of the lake.

"That looks quite central," Jo commented.

Ciaran asked for some rope, a boat, and a waterproof weapon. He didn't get anything. "I forgot. We've got a basic package."

"I'll go out there," Stefan said and dove into the water. He reached the island, looked around, dove underneath again. He looked on top of the statue and found nothing, so he headed back to the bank of the lake. But before he could get out of the water, two long arms of a gigantic octopus wrapped around his legs to drag him down.

Madeline and Jo tried to pull him back, and Ciaran and Tadgh shot at the octopus. Bullets didn't seem to do much harm to the animal. Madeline and Jo were losing ground.

Stefan looked at Madeline. "Let go of my arm."

"No."

"Just let go, Madeline." She released him.

Stefan pulled the hunting knife out and swung at his leg. He almost passed out with the pain. The octopus was happy with what it had, however, so it went away, carrying with it Stefan's leg from the shin down.

Tadgh took his coat off and tore the fabric to stop the bleeding. "Can you keep going?" Tadgh asked.

"Do I have a choice?" Stefan winced. He was losing blood badly.

Tadgh put Stefan's arm over his shoulders and carried as much of Stefan's weight as possible.

The group kept going, searching every possible place along the lake where the crucifix could be hidden.

They approached a small bridge. They had to cross it—there was nowhere else to go on this side.

"Wait here," Ciaran said. He cautiously crossed the bridge by himself. When it seemed to be relatively safe, he came back again to escort the group over.

They soon arrived at a small temple.

"Maybe this is it," Madeline said.

"It does look like a good hiding place." Tadgh set Stefan down. "I'll have a quick check inside," Tadgh said.

"I'll look go around the back. Jo, check out the side please, and Madeline, if you could stay with Stefan?" Ciaran asked.

Tadgh cautiously pushed open the door of the temple.

Ciaran had walked around the corner, looking at the temple from the outside. Running back to the front, he yelled, "Tadgh, get out!"

But it was too late.

18

*T*he chunky wooden door of the small temple closed Tadgh in as soon as he heard Ciaran's yelling.

"Fuck!" he muttered.

Tadgh yanked the door handle, but it wouldn't budge. He could hear the others banging from the outside, trying to knock it down.

He looked around. Nothing suspicious. He move further inside and inspected all the corners of the temple. There was no sign of the crucifix.

"Get out of the way, Tadgh!" It was Ciaran. Tadgh dove aside just before a machine gun sprayed the door and it collapsed.

As he headed toward the open doorway to leave the temple, a line of fire shot up from the floor, creating a barrier between Tadgh and the outside. The curtain of fire burned with incredible heat. The temple was small with thick brick walls and no windows. If he wasn't burned to death, he would die from lack of oxygen or smoke inhalation.

Tadgh yelled over the top of the fire. "I'm going to run through this. It's only a game, right? Should be okay."

Madeline screamed at him, "No! You'll die! You can't cross it."

She knew better. Been there and done that. She knew how

much it hurt. She'd made it through the fire, but it was only because Juliette hadn't set the rules. In their current game, Juliette had set things up, and she was almost positive Tadgh couldn't cross the fire and live.

Ciaran and Jo tried every object they could find to suppress the fire for a few seconds so that Tadgh could cross. Nothing worked.

The heat inside the temple was incredible. It seemed hot enough to boil blood. The air was growing thicker and thicker. Tadgh slumped to the floor.

Madeline looked at him and knew what he was thinking. She yelled to him over the fire. "Don't cross! I'll fix this!"

But Tadgh had already lain down on the floor and didn't appear to hear what Madeline was saying to him.

Madeline ran to a nearby tree. "Tree gives life. Jo said, tree gives life. Must be some kind of game code." Madeline was thinking out loud.

She pulled out her hunting knife and cut her arms. Blood streamed onto the tree. Ciaran saw what she was doing, but he understood the reasoning behind her actions. He didn't stop her.

"Tree gives life. Okay, you have enough of my blood now, so I'm asking you to fall down and make a bridge."

Madeline pushed the tree lightly. It lifted easily from its roots and fell across the wall of fire.

Ciaran stormed inside the temple. Tadgh was no longer conscious. He carried his brother outside and lay him on the grass, Jo darted over and performed CPR. Tadgh coughed and opened his eyes. He blinked and looked up at Jo, who was sitting on top of him.

"That was smoking hot!" he managed to say teasingly.

"Thank you." Jo smiled.

The group made it to the end of the lake but still had found no crucifix.

In front of them now was something that looked like the ruins of an ancient castle. Tall stone walls with glassless arched windows towered above them. Gothic rooflines shaped like towers pointed to the bruised sky. It was a magnificent and imposing structure—in the middle of nowhere.

Juliette stepped out of the fog. "I'm disappointed. I thought you were much better than this."

"So who's going to punish us if we lose the game?" Ciaran asked.

"My game, my rules, and my execution." Juliette smiled menacingly.

"But we haven't lost yet. We still have the final round."

Juliette's grin widened. She lifted her arm up, and a sword appeared in her hand. "You asked for it, my husband."

She swung her sword at Ciaran. He blocked with his. The clash of metal against metal sang in the air. The force of the contact pushed Ciaran a few steps backward.

Ciaran could see the shadow of dragon wings behind Juliette. Each blow of her sword carried an incredible amount of supernatural force. She was cheating.

Ciaran swung and attacked her, pushing her back several steps. His sword, however, was obviously inferior to hers.

Madeline asked Jo. "What kind of sword does he need to win?"

"One soaked in angel blood."

"What does that mean? I don't have angel's blood." She ran to a tree. She cut her hand again. "Here is my blood. I need that sword."

Nothing.

Still engrossed in their swordfight, Juliette gave Ciaran a hard kick, sending him down to his knees. In this hologame world, gender held no power and gave no advantage. Only the power of the game mattered. Ciaran knew that.

He had power, but his weapon was inferior. His sword had already been chipped and would break soon.

Tadgh grabbed his knife and rushed forward. He hit hard against an invisible wall and slumped to the ground.

"Game rules, Tadgh. Their fight is one-on-one. You can't get in," Jo said.

"But that bitch has a better weapon. How is that fair?"

Jo darted toward the tree where Madeline was still trying to get the sword. "Nothing yet?" Jo asked.

"No, I've given my blood. What else can I do?"

Jo took her own knife and cut herself. "Here is my blood, too. We give you our sister blood. Pure blood. Pure love. Give us strength. Give us the sword."

There was a rumble from within the tree trunk. Then it opened, revealing a knight's sword with a blood red blade.

Madeline grabbed the sword and ran toward Ciaran and Juliette.

Before Jo could warn her, she heard the thunk of Madeline hitting the wall as Tadgh did.

"I can't get in!" she yelled. "Jo, what do I do?"

"Ciaran has to ask for it himself. You can't bring the sword to him."

Ciaran's sword broke in half, and he tossed it away.

Juliette laughed. "Well, my warrior. I don't want you to be disadvantaged."

She opened her palm, and her sword disappeared.

They now fought hand to hand.

Juliette's arms were as hard as steel, and her strength was superhuman. As soon as she made contact with him, Ciaran knew her game strength was abnormal. She was cheating again. He wondered if she had been all along and not a single moment between them had been genuine.

His lack of concentration caused him to take a few blows from Juliette's steely arms. Whatever this was in front of him was a monster, not a woman.

Concentrate. Look into her eyes, he told himself. She was a monster. And he was White Knight. It was his mission to destroy all evil.

Ciaran clenched his fists and went head-on with Juliette. He blocked her steel blows with his kicks. The sheer force of will from him was something she could not defeat.

Ciaran pounded on her. Blows and kicks until she fell, tumbling across the ground. He wouldn't stop until he defeated this evil force.

He charged.

Ciaran could see Madeline holding the sword outside the fighting arena. He knew what she had done to get it.

He continued his attack on the woman. She roared with a demonic thunder of anger and frustration. Her power was abating. From the ground, she looked up at Ciaran, who was walking toward her to finish the job.

She looked at him with Juliette's eyes.

Those innocent, bright eyes he had loved years ago. Was this Juliette he was about to kill? It couldn't be. But how could a demon have her eyes?

She started humming the tune of the song she had written on their honeymoon, the song she sang before she died. "Little hummingbird, do you see the sky? It is free. It is yours. Fly. Past the mountains. Past the oceans. There. You will find love . . ."

Kneeling on the ground, Juliette looked at him with tearful eyes containing a sea of innocence, those he had fallen for when they first met at Oxford University. She had died for him. How could he now execute her?

That single moment of hesitation was what Juliette had been waiting for.

She flexed and turned her fist. It morphed into a blade which she stabbed straight into Ciaran's body.

He heard Madeline scream as he fell. *Is this the end?* he wondered.

He couldn't kill Juliette, regardless of what she did to him.

As Juliette withdrew her steel arm from him, Ciaran slumped to the ground.

Juliette raised up with a devil's smile. "Ever lost a game, Ciaran?"

"I don't like losing, and I've never lost."

"So this will be your first loss. Your first, and your last." Juliette extended her arm, and her sword returned.

She was going to kill Ciaran.

From the ground, Ciaran looked up at a demon.

"You're not Juliette!"

Ciaran reached up. The sword in Madeline's hands vibrated and then flew toward Ciaran. He grabbed it and swung quickly, beheading the woman in front of him.

She screamed even as her head fell from her shoulders. Then her entire body shattered like crystal and vanished into thin air.

Ciaran muttered, "If you were Juliette, you would know that I lost my first game to her. The *real* Juliette. Demon bitch!"

19

Tadgh winced as the cold moisture from the ground seeped into his skin. He opened his eyes groggily and immediately registered the reality of the situation. He scrambled to reach for his gun and saw the muzzle of Stefan's pointing at his face.

"Hey, hey, stay still," Stefan said.

Tadgh quickly took inventory of the scene as he stood up. They were back at the rest stop. Madeline and Jo had just gotten up. Ciaran was still on the ground.

Stefan limped badly, but he managed to reach over and grab Madeline. He pointed the gun at her.

"Without Ciaran, no one can work on your disk, Stefan," Tadgh said. "And he doesn't look as if he's coming back soon."

"I can see that," Stefan scolded. "Here's my solution. I'll take Madeline with me. When our White Knight here wakes up, he and Jo will decode the disk for me. Then we'll talk again."

"Let me try again. I'll go with you," Jo said.

"No, it's better you stay with Ciaran and Tadgh. I can handle this, Jo," Madeline told her.

"Hear that, Jo? Your big sister wants you to do your job and be a good girl." Stefan smirked.

"When we sort out the disk, how can we find you?" Tadgh asked.

Stefan laughed. "Why don't you just come right out and ask where I'm hiding?" he mocked. "I'll contact you. Remember, I like Madeline, but I like what's in the disk much more. Don't disappoint me."

Stefan pulled Madeline out the door.

Jo stomped her feet on the floor. "Damn it!"

"Careful—you'll punch holes on the floor with those heels. Damaging national park property will land us in jail."

Jo glared at Tadgh. "That's not funny."

"I'm not trying to be funny. But I have to entertain us somehow because we're going to be here for hours."

"Why?"

Tadgh nodded at Ciaran. "He'll be out for that long."

Jo looked at Ciaran. "Because of the stab wound?" Jo ripped Ciaran's shirt open and saw a large red scar where the demon had stabbed him.

"You're just checking out his abs, aren't you?"

"What's your problem, Tadgh? Why you keep making stupid comments?"

Tadgh crouched so that his eyes were level with Jo's. "It's because I'm feeling completely stupid right now. We did everything we could to rescue you. And then things got so messed up. People we care for died. Now we got you back. And he took Madeline. When will this end? How many more people will be killed?"

"You care for Madeline."

"Not as much he does." Tadgh pointed at Ciaran. "In fact, I don't think I've seen him care that much for anyone in years. Now he's out, and I couldn't even keep Madeline safe for him." Tadgh shook his head.

"You couldn't help it. Stefan is a trained soldier. He had a gun on you."

"So you're saying I was scared shitless when he pointed the gun at me?"

"Why do you have twist everything I say the wrong way? What did I do to offend you?" Jo jabbed her finger at Tadgh's chest.

He shook his head. "It's just me. I'm sorry."

Ciaran stirred.

Tadgh tapped his shoulder. "Okay, get up Ciaran."

"Why does he take such a long time to wake up?"

"He's allergic to anesthesia. It must have been in the smoke bomb they threw at us. It knocks him out for hours. And it'll get worse."

"How?" Jo asked and picked up the sleeve that contained the disk from the ground. It was empty. She showed it to Tadgh.

"Shit!" he exclaimed.

"Okay, so we have no disk. Stefan thought we had it. I don't know what to do now. Who were those men with the red bombs?" Jo said.

"Probably the same ones who attacked us at Robert's house just before we came here. They burned his house down and killed his wife and daughter." He searched Ciaran's jacket pocket. "Holy fuck . . . Juliette's diary is gone, too." Tadgh pulled at his hair as if it would help him find a solution.

Jo's eyes teared up.

"Oh, no, that's the last thing I need here. Girl crying."

"I don't cry." Jo ground her teeth. "I'm female, and this is a normal biological reaction of the female body in situations of distress."

Tadgh stared. "Why can't you just say girls cry when they're stressed?" he grumbled. "Never mind."

Ciaran opened his eyes. He was too groggy to make any sense of what was going on. Tadgh pulled him up.

"All right, let's go." Tadgh pulled Ciaran's arm over his shoulders to help him walk. Ciaran pushed him away.

"All right, all right. I've got it. You don't have to carry me."

Tadgh released him, and Ciaran slumped to the floor again.

"I'm going to help you whether you like it or not." Tadgh pulled his arm over his shoulders again and started walking.

"Back to the car, this way," Tadgh said, steering his brother.

Ciaran pulled away from him, and ran to a tree and vomited violently.

Tadgh looked at Jo. "That's what I meant by it gets worse. He does that all the time. And if you ever tell him you've seen him like that, you'll never be his friend!"

Jo rolled her eyes. "Men and their dicks!"

"Excuse me?"

"You wanted me to put things simply. Or would you rather me analyze the neurological system of the male species when it comes to their so-called sexual organs?"

"No, thank you. Let me keep my sanity."

When Ciaran had emptied the contents of his stomach, his brother half dragged, half carried him to the car. He put Ciaran in the backseat and got behind the wheel.

Tadgh sat for a long moment, staring at the dashboard.

"Out of gas?" Jo asked.

"I can't believe I have to drive this stupid machine!"

"You don't know how to drive?"

"Of course I do, excuse me! But I drive normal cars like normal people. Not this piece of shit."

"This is a very expensive sports car. It's supposed to be every man's wet dream."

"Well, it's not my dream, okay?"

"I can drive," Jo offered.

"Oh, no, thank you. You Americans drive on the wrong side of the road. This is not a hologame. If we die here, it's going to be very real!"

"We Americans think you British drive on the wrong side of the road."

"Stop babbling and let me concentrate."

Tadgh focused and started the car while Jo rolled her eyes and swallowed a laugh.

The car jerked, roared up, accelerated, stopped, and stalled.

"Don't tell me—you drive an automatic."

"Just shut up." Tadgh tried again, and this time he succeeded. They made it to the highway.

"You might get a ticket for driving too slow."

"Just shut up."

20

The stuffy air of a small hotel room greeted Madeline and Stefan as soon as he opened the door. "Sorry, it's all I could find on such short notice. The location is the best, though," Stefan said and shoved her into the room.

He locked the door and limped toward the only bed in the room. He flopped onto it, wincing with pain. He pulled his jeans up to the knee, and saw a bright red scar around his leg where he had chopped it off in the hologame. The scar was swollen and looked infected.

"Fucking stupid game," he mumbled to himself.

Madeline walked over. Stefan immediately grabbed his gun.

"I just want to have a look at your injury. Are you going to hold me at gunpoint all night long? We used to be friends, Stefan."

"You're good with words, Madeline. But you need to check the dictionary for the definition of friendship."

If this continued, getting away from Stefan would be difficult, Madeline mused. She glanced at his wound. "It's badly infected. You might need medical treatment. If it gets any worse, you'll lose your leg for real."

"I'll take care of this little scratch."

"You can't do what you want to do if you can't walk. I won't be able to carry you, even metaphorically."

"I said I'll figure it out."

"All right then. I have to give it to you, though. Chopping your leg off was very brave, even if it was just in a game."

Stefan smiled slightly. "I can do a lot better than that."

"I bet."

There was a knock on the door. Stefan grabbed the gun. They waited, and an envelope was slipped under the door. Stefan waited another moment and then picked up the envelope.

He opened the envelope to find a fancy card. He glanced at the card and gave it to Madeline. "For you," he said.

The card read:

"Dear Madeline,

It is my pleasure to invite you to visit our residence. I trust you will find this meeting beneficial. We had a brief encounter earlier. Thus you know the resources I can provide to help you to achieve what you want. Should you accept the invitation, your transportation is ready now.

Sincerely yours, Mr. Kelley.

P.S. Your friend Stefan may accompany you. Should he keep you against your will or cause you any harm, I assure you he will not make it out of that hotel alive."

She gave the note back to Stefan, trying to look as smug as she could. She had nothing to lose. Being captured here or there. She remembered the encounter at Robert's place. The men had drawn their guns on her but hadn't fired.

Who is her ally?

"Friendly and helpful people, aren't they?" Madeline said.

"Who are they?"

"I have no idea. They sent about fifteen men to burn down a house, and they killed four people, including two innocent bystanders and a woman and her baby. So I guess they'll give you the same if you stop me from accepting their invitation. If you can call it an invitation."

"So you want to go?"

"Well, both you and they have pointed guns at me. What do you think I'm going to do?"

Madeline grabbed her jacket and left the room. Stefan followed like a meek dog. As they walked along the sidewalk, a car approached them and stopped. The uniformed driver spoke to Madeline. "Ms. Madeline Roux?"

"Yes?"

He gestured toward the car. "Your transport, ma'am."

Madeline nodded toward Stefan. "He's with me."

"Yes, ma'am."

They arrived at a private villa outside London. The house sat back almost a mile from the road and was surrounded by nothing but green fields. It looked like a converted barn. She was sure it held a world of surprises inside.

The door swung open as they approached and text images floated in the air. "Welcome."

"You can't afford a screen? Or a voice announcement? I don't want to walk into your *words*," Madeline said.

They entered a large foyer. A robotic voice directed, "Please sit. Someone will be with you shortly."

For a moment, it seemed oddly quiet. Then the air thickened, and Madeline knew what it was. It was the holocast she'd experienced at the museum.

"Mr. Kelley, if you're there, I'd like to talk to you. After all, you're the one who summoned us here."

A hologram of a man in his sixties appeared. He was sitting on the sofa opposite Madeline and Stefan.

"Welcome back to the family, Madeline."

"Thank you. But I'm happy with who I am now—and with the people I'm with."

"Family is important."

"Well, I've had a decent life without having family. I have no plans to change that."

"I'm sorry you've been down here all this time by yourself. But thirty-three years is long enough. It's time to come back."

A chill shot up her spine.

Fear crossed her mind. Did her age coincide with the number that had bothered Ciaran and his family so much? She decided it was purely coincidental because she didn't even know the exact date she was born. Someone had dumped her in a basket and left her on the doorstep of a stranger when she was only four weeks old. But even age was a speculation. She hadn't said anything to Ciaran.

Based on the note this man had sent her, he had organized the attack at Robert's place and had sent them into the hologame with the demonic version of Juliette.

This man had some kind of connection to Juliette. And now it seemed he had ties with her as well. In addition, he'd confirmed she was thirty-three years of age. If she still believed all of this was just coincidental, she would have to be an idiot.

"Madeline!" Stefan called.

"Huh?"

"You okay?"

She nodded and turned toward the man. "Who are you?"

"I'm Richard Kelley, your grandfather. Your parents died in a battle, and you were stolen from them."

"A battle?"

"A battle between us and our enemies. We don't live on Earth."

"So you're alien?" Stefan muffled a laugh and became quiet when he received a cold stare from the old man.

"We're human. We just took residence in a place that is far more supreme than this filthy, polluted, and overpopulated planet."

"What do you want from me, apart from a family reunion?" Madeline asked.

"The crucifix. The sample gold inside the crucifix, to be precise."

"The crucifix has been where it is for a long time. Why do you want it now?" Madeline asked.

"The thirty-three-year cycle is very important to us. Your parents fought and died in that battle. We never regained our strength after that. And now, the critical time is back again, and if we don't have the gold, we will be destroyed forever."

"I'm only a journalist. What can I possibly do to help you fight battles that aren't even my own?"

"I'm certainly not going to fight any of your battles, wherever they are!" Stefan raised his voice.

"Your father was my ally. It was a shame he passed away because of the mishaps of Juliette. But we continued his work."

"What the hell are you talking about?"

"Your father was going to tell you his plan for you. But he didn't have a chance. Apparently, he didn't tell you much beforehand."

"I don't care about any of this, and I have no intention of being friends with you." Stefan stood up.

"Because you want the gold, you kill women and children, and burn down houses?" Madeline asked.

"Collateral damage . . ."

"Who the hell do you think you are? Collateral damage? They were innocent people!" Madeline stood, enraged.

"I regret it, but it couldn't be helped. As I said, Juliette is the key to our technology. I can't let anyone get their hands on any trace of her material—including the disk and the diary."

"She's my sister! So fuck your technology, fuck your people, and fuck your gold. I'm done with this." Stefan grabbed Madeline and turned to leave.

"When your father retrieved Juliette, she was effectively a corpse. He lost his life because of that. I can only revive a part of Juliette's mind, and to fulfill your father's dying wish, we need to get the crucifix which is somewhere in Fountains Abbey. Don't you want to fight for your father's legacy, Stefan?"

Stefan and Madeline looked out the door. Dozens of men in black were lurking.

"What exactly do you want from me?" Stefan asked.

"I came in peace. I just wanted to meet my granddaughter. Besides, I'm going to help you get the crucifix, and you can keep it."

Stefan narrowed his eyes. "And what do you want in return?"

"I only ask for a sample. You can keep the rest. It's a win-win solution, and a very generous offer from our end."

"Why can't you just ask Juliette where the crucifix is?"

"Her mind is very unstable. We get very limited information from her. The most I can do is simulate her image—the one you saw in the hologame."

So Richard had no idea Juliette had spoken to her at the chapel, Madeline thought. And he certainly didn't know about the warning that the crucifix killed. Maybe she should just play along and help Stefan obtain the crucifix.

"What support will you give me?" Stefan asked.

"You will have my men. They are well-trained and well-equipped."

Stefan nodded. "That should do for now. When can we start?"

"Our people are ready to go as soon as you're ready. We just need to wait until my people finish decoding Juliette's disk. I want to be sure there is no additional information we need to know in order to plan accordingly. Once that's confirmed, you're good to go."

"The disk?" Madeline asked.

"Yes, my men took the disk and the diary from you while you were out and about in your hologame world. You think I sent you to the game for fun? It was a practice round for your show and a test of your skills. Apparently you both passed."

"Test for what?"

"You're our family. You're a warrior, Madeline. But you were stuck on this planet for a long time. I've got to make sure you can be trained. You can't be a part of us if the only skill you have is cooking."

"I don't cook. But I can kill. I believe you know that," Madeline muttered.

"Indeed." The old man laughed. "One other thing. You can't go back to the LeBlancs after this is done."

"Why not?" Madeline was astonished.

"We're not exactly on friendly terms with them and haven't

been for generations. So if you're involved with them, you cannot be with us."

"Then I don't want any of this." She turned to leave.

The grandfather cleared his throat. "If you don't want this family, that is fine. However, you know quite a bit of our plans, so I'm afraid I'll have to hold you until things are finished. If you ruin our plan—and I hope you don't—I won't leave the LeBlanc boys alive."

If she refused, they would keep her, and Ciaran would try to find her. Ciaran was in the dark about all this. But if she agreed, then she would have control over the situation and could communicate with Ciaran to ensure he didn't get involved in the crucifix hunt.

Once things were over, she could go back to Ciaran and break her promise with this Kelley family. Considering this a good plan, she nodded. "All right, I'll stay and help. Don't hurt any of the LeBlancs," Madeline said.

The grandfather smiled warmly. "Good news for the whole family! Remember, Madeline, don't take your promise lightly. If you return to the LeBlancs after this, I'll hunt you down wherever you are, no matter how long it takes."

She couldn't let Ciaran walk blindly into this trap trying to find her.

"Do I have your word?" the grandfather asked.

"Yes," Madeline said.

Stefan laughed in disbelief. "So Ciaran gets nothing! Absolutely nothing! I'm excited now. When can we begin this hunting game?

"Tomorrow at the latest."

The holocast disappeared.

21

*C*iaran used the computer in his bedroom instead of the one in his office. He needed to be here, in this corner of the house. He stared at the screen, not knowing where to start his search. This had never happened before.

This master suite was in the new part of the house, and it was supposed to have been a new start to his life. This room was where he had begun his connection with Madeline, the woman who made him think he could love again.

And now, she was gone.

The wait was torturous, and he needed all the time he could get. He didn't have the disk. He couldn't make anything up because he had no idea what Juliette had put on it. When Stefan called to bargain for Madeline's life, he would have nothing to offer.

He sat, brooding. It was very unlike him.

But he knew a dangerous storm was heading his way. He didn't know what kind of storm it would be. But this time, he would be defeated.

Stefan called. Ciaran frowned at the number. It was too soon. He needed more time. But he needed Stefan's confirmation that Madeline was okay. He answered.

"Hello, there. I've got some good news, and I can't wait until tomorrow to let you know." Stefan's smugness oozed out of receiver.

"Say it quickly, Stefan. I'm expecting a phone call," Ciaran snapped.

"Okay, then. I—no, *we*—have some new developments on our end and would like to let you know that you don't have to bother with the disk anymore."

"What do you mean by that?"

"There's no need to play games with me anymore, Ciaran. You don't have the disk, do you?"

Ciaran didn't know what to say. His brain was simply not working at the moment.

Stefan continued. "Madeline and I have some news for you."

He felt sweat running down his spine. "I'll only hear it from Madeline. Put her on the phone."

Stefan laughed. "She's in the bathroom right now. I'll get her for you. But the exciting news is that she found her grandfather."

"That's great news. But I can't imagine it would make you very excited."

"Crucifix aside, I do like her, you know. Her grandfather is going to help us find the crucifix and the gold. Madeline is happy, and I'm happy, too. Thing is, her grandfather doesn't like you much. I tried to put in a good word for you. I really did. But he forbade Madeline to come back to you."

"Put Madeline on the phone."

"Sure. Oh, and just between us men, he said he'd kill her if you come near her. So if you care for her, my advice is to leave her alone."

Fury rolled over him in waves. "Brag on, Stefan. You know I won't believe a thing you say."

"My bad, but I'm not bragging! I'm willing to forgive you for killing my sister. I did kill a few people on your end. So let's call it even. Let bygones be bygones. You don't have to worry about the crucifix, about Madeline, about the disk, or about anything else for that matter . . ."

"Put Madeline on the phone, or I will hang up."

Stefan clucked his tongue. "Richard Kelly has an army of people. He's been waiting for thirty-three years, and he's not going to let Madeline go that easily. She's important to him, just as my sister is important to me. Somehow you ended up with both women. But your time is up. You're done, Ciaran."

Ciaran's blood ran cold. He gripped the letter opener so hard that it cut into his hand. Blood dripped on the piece of elegant white paper in front of him.

Stefan's voice suddenly became cheery. "Here she is!"

"Hello," Madeline's sultry voice came across. "Hello? Who is this? Grandfather? Who am I talking to, Stefan?"

"It's me, Madeline."

There was silence on the other end of the phone.

"Ciaran . . . how . . . how are you?"

"Have you found your grandfather?"

"No, he found me. I . . . I didn't know anything about him before."

"How old are you? You should know that answer."

"I . . ."

"It's not a trick question, Madeline."

"Thirty-three, but I can explain."

"Did he threaten you?"

An instant message signaled an alert sound. Ciaran switched the screen. The message said, *Spot the hotel, Lindsay.*

"I know where you are now, Madeline. I can come and get you right now."

"No."

"I know he's threatened you, but I . . ."

"No. I said no, Ciaran."

"I can help you and your grandfather find the crucifix. If that's what you want . . ."

"I don't need you, Ciaran. We can take care of it. I don't need you at all. Bye, Ciaran."

Madeline hung up.

He stood looking out the window for a long moment, trying to make sense of what just happened. He wanted to throw his phone at the wall. But he didn't. What good would it do?

He walked back and forth in the room, thinking. He leaned against his desk. He wasn't sure how long he stood there before he heard footsteps in the hallway. Tadgh, Jo, and the cat Migi appeared at the door.

Ciaran smiled at Jo.

"Jo has an idea. Given that Stefan has never seen the contents of the disk, she could make up a . . ." Tadgh trailed off when he saw the blank stare on Ciaran's face.

"Ahh . . . any news?" Tadgh asked.

Ciaran shrugged. "It's over, Tadgh."

"What do you mean?"

"Madeline said she found her grandfather and will use his help to find the crucifix herself. She won't be needing us anymore. Jo, I can make arrangements for you to go back to New York."

"I . . . can I talk to her, Ciaran?" Jo asked.

"I'm sure you can. But you'll have to call her yourself. She finished her conversation with me. Now if you'll both excuse me, I have some work to see to."

"Of course. I'll talk to you later. Let's go, Jo."

TADGH DRAGGED Jo away from Ciaran's room and strode downstairs. "You said you'd teach me how to play computer games, right?" Tadgh asked.

"Sure," Jo raised an eyebrow.

"Let's go to the game room. Ciaran's got truckloads of them."

They entered the game room. Rows of computers were lined up in the room, all different sizes and models. Tadgh gestured widely. "See? All ours. We're free now. We have nothing to do. Let's play!"

Jo chose the most basic computer. "What do you want to play? Tennis, ping-pong, car racing?"

"I want to fight."

Jo showed Tadgh how to play some basic fighting games, then they role played in a game.

In the game, Tadgh pounded at Jo. "Wow, you're too aggressive for a beginner!"

"It's a game, right? I wouldn't do that in real life." Then he picked up the weapons in the game and fought like a mad man, killing all the other characters, including Jo's.

On the computer screen, a triumphant jingle came out with the words, "Congratulations, you won!"

Tadgh stood up, pulled the keyboard out, and whacked at the computer monitor. "Win, my ass." He pounded the computer until it was just a pile of scrap metal. Finally, he slumped to the floor, breathing heavily.

Jo waited, then she went over and hugged him. "Okay, there now, tell me what's going on."

Tadgh sat on the floor, leaning against the wall. "Just shoot me!"

"You broke the computer. Want to play a more advanced game?"

Tadgh put his head between his knees. "Oh shit!"

Jo waited patiently.

"I've only seen my brother like that once. After Juliette died. He didn't have the answer—and still doesn't—about her death. It was painful for him. But when he finally accepted her death, he looked just like that."

"If she's dead, and he accepted it, isn't that a good thing?"

"It was. But the other night when he thought he would lose Madeline, he wouldn't accept it. He would fight for her. He'd never accept defeat."

"You mean he loves her."

"I don't think he'd use the 'L' word."

"So what's wrong with him?"

"He thinks he's responsible for Juliette's death. We all knew she just used him. But he still wants to believe they had a fairy tale, that she at least loved him for real at one time."

"Okay, once bitten, twice shy. He doesn't think he can use the 'L' word with Madeline. And now Madeline's told him she doesn't need him. I know that hurts. But it's not worth you destroying all of these very innocent computers."

"I think Madeline loves him, too."

"Only need half a brain and one eye to see that, Tadgh. I'm not stupid. I saw that in the hologame."

Tadgh yanked at his hair. "Madeline believes the crucifix kills. It has explosives, poison, or something in it. She wasn't going to let Ciaran go anywhere near it. But Ciaran is stubborn. If you tell him that the crucifix has explosives in it, he's definitely going to go looking for it. So if I were Madeline, I'd do my best to *help* Stefan find the crucifix so he can blow *himself* up."

"How did you come to that conclusion?"

"She told me about the crucifix. I think the whole grandfather deal was bogus. The fact that she's not coming back here, maybe it's part of a deal she has with Stefan. That guy is a nasty piece of shit."

"So why can't we tell Ciaran and try to figure the whole thing out? We can't let Madeline do it on her own."

"I promised her I wouldn't tell. I also want to keep my brother out of danger."

"You know what Tadgh, if I were Ciaran, I would beat you up." Jo stood up and marched out of the room.

Tadgh trailed behind submissively and asked, "Where are you going?"

"I'm telling Ciaran. And if you don't like it, bite me!"

22

The real Fountains Abbey greeted Madeline with the magnificence of a place that had housed hundreds of monks who lived and died there centuries ago. Located in the endless and mysterious national park, the history and the beauty of the place attracted so many tourists that searching for a crucifix during the daytime hours was almost impossible.

"Can you ask your men to be a little less conspicuous? All they need are dark sunglasses and people will pick them out as member of the mafia," Madeline complained.

"They're not *my* men," Stefan said between his teeth, glancing at the five fighters Richard had sent along with them.

They walked down to the valley from the visitor center and recognized the grounds. It was the setting from the hologame they had played the day before.

Madeline looked around—miles of trees, a gigantic manmade lake, and the ruined sites of abbeys and graveyards.

"This is just great. We may have to spend a lifetime here, digging," Stefan muttered.

"We need more information," Madeline said.

She turned around, asking Douglas, the head of the group, "Is there anything we can do to speed this up?"

Douglas shook his head.

"Can we at least have a dog to scent something out?" Stefan asked.

"We have a scanner," Douglas offered. "Would that help?"

"A scanner for what? Metals? Explosives?"

"It doesn't detect. It just provides visuals of objects up to six feet underground."

"Great, I'm looking forward to scanning the graveyard," Madeline muttered. "We'll start at the far end of the lake and work our way up to the abbeys. There are too many tourists in the abbeys right now. They'd be alarmed if we looked like we were scanning for a bomb."

The group walked along the lake's edge to approach the park at the far end. Halfway there, they saw Ciaran, Tadgh, and Jo on the other side.

"Just great. They sniffed this out already," Stefan moaned.

All the men had their hands in their pockets, ready for necessary action. Madeline knew they were packing the dart guns.

"No fighting," she said. "No need to fight. None of you will draw a weapon here. Let me talk to them." Madeline approached the narrow, railing-less bridge that led over the water. At the other side, Ciaran approached. They both accessed the bridge but kept their distance from one another.

"Madeline." Ciaran nodded an aloof greeting. His raven black hair was tied back, revealing that face graced by God that she had fallen for at first sight. His smoky gray eyes no longer looked at her with passion but with calculated strategies. His hands were shoved his pockets as if he was about to negotiate with an adversary that he considered lesser than him.

"You don't own this park, do you?"

"No, it's a public place. A very beautiful historic site that anyone with an appreciation for history and nature can visit."

"And that's what you're doing here?"

"Of course. Jo is going back to New York soon. It would be a shame if she missed seeing this site. She might not have a chance to come back. We would love it to become one of her fond memories."

Damn his fancy words and damn his fancy accent, Madeline thought.

Ciaran gazed at her. The intensity in his eyes was so strong she thought it could punch holes through her body. There were so many questions in them. Questions that had neither been asked nor answered.

Hadn't last night's conversation been uncomfortable enough? Did he have to cause more pain? What had Tadgh told him? He'd promised he wouldn't open his mouth. But here was Ciaran, standing right in front of her. So best guess, Tadgh had spilled the beans.

Ciaran was here, searching for the crucifix like everybody else. She didn't think he'd go for the gold. Rather, he was looking for an answer about Juliette. If Tadgh had told him about the possible danger of the crucifix, then that would motivate him even more.

"I have friends with me as well." Madeline gestured toward the fighters. "So I'm playing the tour guide."

"I see."

A small group of visitors went past.

"It's a big place. There are a lot of things to see here," Madeline continued.

Ciaran stepped forward. Madeline stepped backward.

"Madeline, we don't have all day. Our friends are 'dying' to see the entire site here," Stefan called out.

Ciaran stepped forward. Madeline backed down off the bridge.

"Don't." She grunted out the word to Ciaran between her teeth. The fighters moved in.

"Ciaran, we're late. Let's go. The party is waiting at home," Tadgh yelled out.

Ciaran grinned. "I invited you to our party, but you declined. If you change your mind, our home is always open for you, Madeline."

Two tourists walked past.

"That's enough, Madeline. We're very late. Our friends need to get home. Their families are waiting." Stefan grabbed her arm.

Madeline could see Ciaran's eyes burning with anger. But he said nothing more. Another group of tourists walked past the bridge.

"Ciaran, I have to go . . ."

Ciaran reached out for her elbow. She saw the men with their hands at their back pockets.

"No." She glared at them, warning them. "Please let go, Ciaran."

"All you have to do is to say you've changed your mind, and I'll take you home right now," he growled.

"Hey!" Stefan came over and shoved Ciaran back. "Don't you touch her. She said no."

"She said no to those scumbags over there to stop them from pulling their weapons out in a public place," Ciaran snarled back.

"You think I won't?" Stefan grabbed Ciaran's collar. Ciaran grabbed him back.

"Don't, you two." Madeline pulled Stefan back. Another group of tourists ambled past. Stefan grumbled some profanity.

"I want you to leave, Ciaran. Please."

"You hear that? She doesn't want you anymore." Stefan sneered.

Ciaran moved one step forward and swung a punch right at the side of Stefan's face, knocking him to the ground. Five men pulled their weapons, and Madeline jumped front of Ciaran. "Put your weapons away. I'm in charge. I'll tell my grandfather."

Stefan stood up and looked about to charge at Ciaran.

"No, Stefan," she said then turned around, looking at Ciaran. "How much more do you want to punish me, Ciaran?"

"I don't . . ."

"Then go, please."

Ciaran looked at her one last time, then left. She wasn't sure who was hurting more when they parted, but she had to move on and finish this.

There was a killer crucifix to find.

She shoved her hands into the pockets of her leather jacket, and they hit something.

"You lose something?" Stefan frowned, looking at the expression on her face.

"No. I just need some tissues." She sniffled.

Stefan rolled his eyes and walked toward the fighters. "Anyone have any tissue?"

23

A moment later, Ciaran drove out of the national park, headed toward Mortlake. Both Tadgh and Jo sat in the back seat.

Ciaran glanced at Tadgh in the mirror. "Okay, if you have anything on your mind, speak now."

"You couldn't refrain from punching Stefan? What if those guys had actually shot at you?" Tadgh scolded.

"They didn't."

"Is that all you have to say? I thought I was the reckless one in this family!" Tadgh exclaimed.

"It's done. There's no point arguing about it. Where did you plant the bug, Ciaran?" Jo asked.

"In Madeline's pocket. I slipped her a pocket knife, too."

Tadgh shook his head. "Why didn't you give her a gun?"

"The biggest compromise I made was to agree to go along with you two and let Madeline handle this by herself. I can't offer more than that."

Tadgh grumbled some profanity and then shut up, looking out the window.

Mrs. Hanson's house still wore the police security banners.

Apparently, nothing much had been done here by the police since their last visit. Ciaran walked straight in, peeling the police seal off.

"Are you going to be okay going in there?" Tadgh asked Jo, concern filling his eyes. Jo smiled, and her green cat eyes almost glittered.

"Very sweet of you to think of me, Tadgh. But Stefan didn't do anything in here that traumatized me. Plus, I don't get scared easily."

Ciaran looked around, pulling some projectors and leftover computer equipment together.

"How did Stefan have it set it up, Jo?"

"He didn't exactly set anything up here. He gave me a piece of junk called a computer and asked me to decode the disk. I think he knew this was a communication center for whoever he was working for, but he really had no idea how to operate it."

Ciaran nodded and concentrated on a couple of broken wires.

"What medium do you think they're using?" asked Jo.

"The most primitive holocast model uses sound frequency. Why don't we try that?"

"You think we can get a frequency in here?" Tadgh asked.

Ciaran nodded. Jo approached a computer. "I'll work on this one," she said and sat down in front of the monitor. Tadgh stood behind, rocking back and forth from his heels to his toes. Ciaran put in the code, and the computer screen popped up an authorization box.

"Okay," Jo smiled. "Stefan always asked me to type in this key he had written on a piece of paper. 524HJUP12.653.212.OZR."

The computer flashed, "Authorized."

"How did you remember that?" Tadgh asked.

"Photographic memory." Jo grinned.

"Did you get it working for Stefan?" Tadgh asked.

"No! I always seemed to call up a wrong authorisation box for Stefan. What a shame!"

"All right. Let's start the search," Ciaran said and took over computer duty. A while later, there was a diagram on the computer monitor and a needle hitched up. "That's it!" Ciaran said and pointed at the diagram.

Both Ciaran and Jo typed lines of codes and commands into the computer.

"Stupid lightwaves," Ciaran muttered, more to himself than to anyone else.

A moment later, Jo yelped in delight.

And then, "Got you, bitch," Ciaran muttered.

Tadgh cocked an eyebrow, amused by the fact that Ciaran did not realize that he was streaming profanity as he worked.

They heard static on the speaker. Then a robotic female voice spoke. "Verification affirmative. Ciaran LeBlanc. This is TK5467.23.7 channel authorized by Sciphil Central."

"Sounds friendly," Tadgh said.

"I'd like to talk to Sciphil Two," Ciaran directed.

"Sciphil Two is not available. I am authorized to give you necessary assistance."

"Last week, there was a troop helping me at the creek in Henley on Thames. Did Sciphil Two send them?"

"Affirmative."

"Can I have access to them?"

"Affirmative. How many do you need?"

"As many as you can give."

"The direct contact will be sent to you. This channel can only be used for three minutes, Earth time. What is the next task?"

"Earth time? Where are you exactly?" Tadgh asked.

"Aphiemi, AKA Aphi, satellite station of Eudaiz."

"How far from here?" Jo said.

"We're not in the same dimension. There is no available data on physical distances."

Ciaran nodded. "Dimensional travel," he muttered. Then he asked, "The people attacking us were using dart guns that could turn organic objects into thin air. Any idea who they are and where they come from?"

"That weapon is used exclusively by the Kelleys."

Ciaran paused. "What's the relationship between Madeline Roux and the Kelleys?"

The computer monotoned the answer. "Madeline Kelley, age thirty-three, the only daughter of Thomas Kelley and Diana Kelley. Lost on planet at four weeks of age. Recently found by grandfather Richard Kelley . . ."

"Yet she doesn't have green skin and a big malformed head," Tadgh said.

"You are referring to extraterrestrial creatures in your dimension. Eudaizian's complexion is . . ."

"That's enough." Ciaran cut the computer off. "Is Juliette one of yours?"

"Please elaborate on the term *yours*."

"Is she like Madeline?"

"Negative."

"So she is human?"

"Negative."

"Damnit, so what is she?"

"Please elaborate on the term *damnit*."

"What is she?"

"That information is not available."

"What about Stefan Dubois?"

"Stefan Dubois is not in our database."

"Why does Richard want the crucifix?"

"We cannot identify an association between Richard Kelly and the object crucifix."

Ciaran shook his head. "Why did Sciphil Two's troop tattoo a crucifix on my arm?"

"Negative. We do not have the record of them performing such task. You have three seconds left."

Three loud beeps were emitted by the computer, and the voice died out.

Silence.

Ciaran paced, contemplating the plans.

"This is so fucked up. So the grandfather deal wasn't bogus," Tadgh said.

"Ciaran, do you think the crucifix at Fountains Abbey is fake?" Jo asked.

Ciaran shook his head, still circling the room.

"You're make me dizzy, Ciaran. Say something," Tadgh said.

Ciaran deduced aloud. "All right, we have too much information about one thing and not enough of another. Let's tackle this one thing at a time. I think Richard Kelley, Madeline's grandfather, is onto something bigger than a crucifix. But I think the crucifix is real."

He pulled his left sleeve up and studied at the tattoo the robotic soldiers had inked him with at the creek. Jo and Tadgh looked at it, turned their heads sideways and upside down to look at it from all angles.

"It looks like a key from this angle," Jo said.

"Yeah!" Tadgh agreed.

"Key? To what?" Ciaran muttered the question to himself. His phone buzzed. On the screen, a line of text appeared, *"Your troops are ready at Henley on Thames. Specific locations will be indicated on maps."*

"Let's go." Ciaran said.

In the car, the device Ciaran had in his pocket buzzed. He pulled it out and gave it to Jo. "Okay, the bug in Madeline's pocket has received signals," she said and adjusted the speaker volume.

They heard voices at the other end.

"How much further have we got to go?" a male voice asked.

"Douglas, we've only scanned halfway and on one side. This isn't going to work," Stefan said.

"Then ask for more scanners and get them to do the scanning," Madeline said.

"Call Richard," Stefan commanded.

Stefan continued, "Ten more scanners . . . give me the phone . . . Mr. Kelley, if you were online this morning, you heard Ciaran. They've sniffed this site out. That means we can't stop now. Do you

think he really went home to dance at a party? I need more men
here to sweep the site fast. As many as possible. They have to be
able to fight, if necessary. I don't know what sort of manpower
Ciaran has access to. But we have to be prepared for the worst-case
scenario if you don't want to lose the crucifix . . .

"How many can you spare?" Stefan laughed. "You've never been
to this planet, have you? You can't send hundreds of your men here
to run around civilian areas with guns and scanners and not alert
the cops. I've already killed a cop, and Ciaran would turn me in to
the police in a heartbeat. I need men strong enough to go against
Ciaran but subtle enough to stay off the police radar . . .

"I'll take fifty. Ten on the ground and forty to back them up. Can
you provide that?" Stefan asked. "I'll need to talk to them, but not
here." Stefan seemed to finish his conversation with Richard.
"Madeline," he said, "we need to go back to the villa . . . take . . .
what's this?"

"I don't know," Madeline said.

"It's a bug. Douglas, do you know what this is? It was in her
pocket."

Ciaran hit the brakes, and the car fishtailed as he swung to the
side of the road and stopped. They heard struggling—and then
static.

"Let go of my arm, Stefan," Madeline said.

"She bugged us. Probably sent signals straight to Ciaran. Give
me that rope," Stefan said.

"Don't you dare, Stefan! Douglas, you work for my grandfather.
If I lose a hair, you'll answer to him."

"Take your hand off her," a male voice said.

"Let go of me!" Madeline yelled.

"Weapons down. Put them away," the male voice commanded.
"She's right, we don't work for you. Let's get back to the villa, and
then we can work things out."

The signal died.

Ciaran stepped out of the car. He needed some fresh air. His world had stopped and started so many times in the last two minutes.

He couldn't make that mistake again. He couldn't let that happen to the woman he loved . . . again. Then it dawned on him that he'd never told Madeline he loved her.

He wasn't sure he was capable of delivering that emotion.

He inhaled deeply, scolding himself, then regained control of his temper and stepped back into the car.

24

*T*he dusk was settling on the horizon when Ciaran and his troops got back to Fountains Abbey site. The soldiers came equipped with a lot of rope.

Ciaran spoke softly but firmly to the robotic soldiers. "I remind you again, only discharge your weapon if it is absolutely necessary. The best-case scenario is that we do not have to kill anyone. However, casualties might be unavoidable. Our opponents are dangerous, and they are trained to kill. I believe we will be outnumbered. Within the best of my capability, I promise to return you to your employer, as much as possible in the same condition that I received you. Am I understood?" They all nodded.

Ciaran spoke to James, the leader of the soldier group. "Can these soldiers perform advanced tasks?"

James shook his head. "Unfortunately not. But they're very stable and expendable."

"How long have you been working for these people?"

"Five years. I have enough experience, if that's what you're concerned about."

"No. I'm not concern about your experience. But we are going against robotic soldiers, and I don't care to have any human casualties."

"I signed up for it. It's the same at the other end. The commander is going to be human. They don't have robots that can carry out complicated tasks yet."

Ciaran nodded. "Is twenty the maximum number we can get."

James nodded. "For now."

"This morning, they scanned half of the right-hand side of the lake, looking down from the abbeys. So we'll set our people up on the left-hand side only. My prediction, however, is that the crucifix is not lakeside but somewhere in the abbeys. Thus, when they get there, I want only their key people left. By key people, I mean Madeline and Stefan. It might not be possible. But that's the best scenario."

James nodded.

"Focus on parts of the lake that have hillsides as close to the water as possible. Get your men up as high as they can go, and work in groups of three."

"Why?"

"Have you ever read Sun Tzu's *Art of War*?"

James shook his head.

Ciaran smiled. "You don't need to. You're practicing it now."

AT THE VILLA outside of London where they had received the holo-cast of Richard Kelley, Madeline and Stefan stared blankly at a group of fifty men in heavy-duty military uniforms.

Stefan yelled, "Michael!"

Five soldiers stomped their feet in a military style and saluted.

"Yes, sir," they responded.

"Oh, yes. Dandy. Ten percent of our troop is called Michael." Stefan laughed. Then he grabbed the phone again. "Richard, on which planet are you living?"

"You wanted fifty men, I gave you fifty," Richard responded.

"I told you, I need soldiers that can fight. Not these meatballs."

The head of the fighter group, Douglas, looked angry at Stefan's comment.

Madeline knew they needed the fighters used at Robert's place —the flying and dart-throwing men. But she wasn't going to help Stefan get better men to fight against Ciaran. She just wanted Stefan to march in there and get the crucifix. Ideally, there would be no fighting.

"Let's get to work," Stefan said and pointed at Douglas. "You, with me." Then he stomped off.

Madeline saw the look on Douglas's face. *Keep that going, Stefan, and you'll catch a bullet very soon*, Madeline thought.

"The five of you with me this morning? You will be right behind Madeline and myself. We'll get ten men to do the scanning. The other forty will surround us from the outside. We'll be working our way from the lake up to the abbeys, as planned. My guess is that if they attack us, it will be lakeside. The abbeys are too confined for large numbers of men. So I want you five to stick with us, all the way to the abbeys. These meatballs? They're expendable. Got that?" Stefan commanded.

Douglas nodded coldly.

"The forty surrounding men, tell them to shoot at anything moving," Stefan directed.

"They were hired for you. Why don't *you* tell them? I only handle my four fighters," Douglas responded.

Stefan glared at Douglas. Then he nodded and walked toward the hired soldiers.

∾

LATER AT FOUNTAINS ABBEY, Madeline looked at the site. Cold wind twisted between thousands of trees, making an eerie chanting sound. Despite the wind, the water in the lake looked calm—too calm, as if there were legions of ancient soldiers hiding underneath that would rise up and charge at them at any moment.

It was getting colder the later in the night it got. Ten of Stefan's soldiers were hunched down behind some small bushes. They needed to have a clear view of the lake and the team down there. They could see ten men with scanners, working slowly in a line on the left bank of the lake. Madeline and Stefan walked behind them, followed by the five fighters.

Except for the eerie sounds from the bush and the crackle of occasional movements from wild animals through the forested area, it was quiet and seemed as if there was nothing much to worry about.

At a distance, on much higher ground and far behind Stefan's men, were Ciaran's people. There were many trees around that blocked their view. However, Ciaran was certain that they had the ground covered.

He moved stealthily between the trees. He wanted to get closer to keep an eye on Madeline, but to do so, he would have to get rid of the first line of Stefan's men.

Ciaran signaled. His flashlight revealed a very small white dot. In the night, it looked like a reflection from an animal eye. He flashed three times.

A bird was released. It made a quacking sound and flew into the bush, flapping its wings and rustling leaves and tree branches.

A couple of men in Stefan's troop looked up. Seeing nothing, they focused once again on the team down at the lake. They did not realize that the last two men in their line had been taken when the bird distracted them.

From the back, Ciaran asked James, "How many men are down there?"

"Forty in the bush, ten scanning at the lake, and five walking with Madeline and Stefan."

Ciaran nodded. "Those five will be tough to get rid of. They're real fighters. And we don't have enough tranquilizers for the rest.

So some of them will have to be taken down by force. How far along are they in the scanning of the lakeshore?"

"About twenty percent complete."

Ciaran contemplated. Then he said, "I'm changing the plan a bit. I need a direct path to get down there, and this line of ten has to be taken down quickly. We only got two of them, and they haven't figured they're missing guys yet. If you give me another three men from the north corner, I'll take down the remaining eight at once."

"Will do, right now," James responded and disappeared into the trees.

Stefan's eight remaining men were watching the team down by the lake. The last man looked behind him and found that the last two men in line were missing. He turned to alert the others. But before he could say anything, Ciaran's men released a cage full of bats. They flew straight into the group of soldiers. The men jumped, and some yelped.

Stefan looked up at the chaotic sounds coming from above the lake and saw soldiers dodging the bats. He rolled his eyes and said to Madeline, "Like I said, meatballs."

Madeline merely smiled and said nothing. She looked up and saw a white dot blinking three times. She smiled again and kept on walking.

While the men danced amid the cloud of bats, lines of rope dropped down at them and hoisted them up to the trees. Tranquilizers worked very efficiently, and the eight soldiers were quickly tied up, gagged, and put snugly to sleep among the small bushes.

Ciaran closed the gap and moved to a closer position. There, he could see Madeline clearly.

They were getting close to the temple. Ciaran wanted the next group of ten taken down as they were standing right behind it. He used his flashlight to signal again. A blue dot blinked three times in response.

Tadgh got Ciaran's signal. He was to take down the second line of ten men. He had three men, including himself. It would be four against ten.

Tadgh held two tranquilizer guns, one in each hand. The four men approached the line of ten from behind. On Tadgh's signal, they shot tranquilizers into five of the men. As soon as they were down, Tadgh charged forward, and with two kicks, he knocked the gun away from one of the soldiers. Tadgh's three other men threw ropes around the remaining soldiers' arms, effectively incapacitating their ability to shoot. They wanted to avoid any gun discharge as much as possible because they were still outnumbered by a large proportion.

Tadgh went one-on-one with the soldier and lost his gun. He took the soldier down very quickly. Looking around, he saw his men had restrained the other four. Tadgh said, "Let's just gag them and save the rest of the tranquilizers for the others." They secured the captured soldiers, and Tadgh signaled Ciaran.

Seeing Tadgh's signal, Ciaran smiled and moved down closer to the temple.

Ciaran could see the scanners had gone inside. He'd wanted that, however, the fighters were still behind Madeline and Stefan. He could see them approaching the temple.

Ciaran signaled.

Jo was at the far end with a remote control. As soon as she saw Ciaran's signal, she pressed a button. Smoke exploded from inside the temple just before Madeline and Stefan walked in. Five of the scanning soldiers collapsed, and the other five hurried outside.

Douglas darted to the temple. He looked inside, and when the smoke subsided, he stepped in.

Stefan looked around the hillside. He saw no one but his men.

Douglas exited the old building. "It wasn't a bomb. Just tranquilization," he reported.

Madeline smiled.

Stefan walked around. "So this is how he wants to play. Smoke people to sleep. I know he's up there. Where are my men? Go check on them."

Douglas raised an eyebrow. "Me? You want me to leave you?"

Stefan waved his hand absently. "No, you stay here. Send one of your fighters."

Douglas nodded and sent a man up the hill to check on the supporting soldiers.

Ciaran signaled Tadgh. Tadgh prepared his men. But when he looked back again, the fighter had disappeared.

25

*C*iaran's view was blocked. He didn't see Tadgh's signal that he had lost sight of the fighter. It was way too quiet from Tadgh's direction. Ciaran moved a bit closer.

From the darkness, the fighter flew out with a forceful kick. Ciaran dropped his gun, fell, rolled down the hillside, and dropped onto the stone below. The fighter raised his gun to shoot at Ciaran.

Tadgh jumped out from behind the tree and kicked away the enemy's gun. The encounter was too close to use handguns, so they used their fists instead.

Tadgh was a skilled fighter and quickly dominated the fight as Ciaran climbed back up. With one last kick, Tadgh sent the fighter down. He stayed down. Tadgh moved to grab him and restrain him, but the fighter suddenly swung at him with a knife.

Ciaran saw the flash of the blade, but it was too late for Tadgh. He ducked, but the knife still slashed through his side.

Tadgh was on the ground. Ciaran flew at the fighter and pounded him. He had to take the man quickly. He took the knife and restrained him. The man pulled out a dart, and Ciaran knew exactly what it was. With lightning speed, Ciaran's fist landed on the fighter's neck. There was a snapping sound, and the fighter went limp.

Ciaran ran forward, pulling Tadgh up. Tadgh puffed out the words, "No worries, just a flesh wound."

Jo rushed toward them. She touched Tadgh's side. "Jesus Christ, this is a lot of blood," Jo said.

"It's a flesh wound," Tadgh grumbled again.

"You're going back to the van," Ciaran said. "Jo, he's all yours. Please take him back to the van and do what you can to stop that bleeding."

Jo pulled Tadgh up, ignoring his protests.

At the lake, the head of the fighters looked up the hill. "Fighter down," Douglas said dryly.

"What about the rest?" Stefan asked.

Douglas shrugged. "I don't know. They're your men. Who did you set to report?"

"I thought it was you," Stefan said.

"No, I told you, I only handle these men. I have one man down now, and I won't send more up there to get killed."

"Isn't it your job to protect us?" Stefan asked.

"No, we work for Richard Kelley. We're here to protect Madeline. He hired these soldiers for you. They won't listen to me."

"Son of a bitch," Stefan growled and grabbed Douglas's collar, barely moving him an inch.

"This is your first and the last warning. Take your hands off me," Douglas said.

Stefan released him.

"We should keep going," Madeline said. "If Ciaran has us surrounded, we need to keep these fighters with us to get to the crucifix and get out of here. There's no time for you to throw a tantrum."

"Throw a tantrum? I'll show you what it's like when I throw a tantrum."

Stefan grabbed Madeline at the back of her jacket and dragged her close to the edge of the lake. He held her in front of him to block any shots from the hillside.

Stefan yelled out, "Ciaran, I know you can see me. I want to play nice, but you're playing some psycho game with me. Ciaran!"

Silence.

"Ciaran!" Stefan yelled again. "If you don't come out, I'll put a bullet in her head. You hear me?" Stefan's voice bounced off the water, to the hillside, and through the trees. He could hear his echo clearly.

Silence.

Stefan fired into the air. The loud boom from the gun discharge tore through the darkness. Birds flew out from the trees, and some wild animals leaped from the bush.

Sounds came from a tree right in front of them. Ciaran stepped out. "You have to give me time to move from one place to another. I don't fly, Stefan."

Madeline could see disaster coming. She could smell the hot blood in Stefan's breath. And there stood Ciaran, alone, against ten armed soldiers, one of them a mad man who was holding her captive. She had done all this to prevent Ciaran from getting to the stupid crucifix, and she could not let him finish in this way.

"My grandfather won't be happy with this," Madeline spoke to Douglas. She could see him straining against Stefan when he grabbed her. But he was in the same boat with Ciaran because Stefan was using her as his human shield.

Madeline was angry. How many times had Stefan used her in this manner? What a coward.

"Let her go. As you can see, I'm unarmed, Stefan," Ciaran said.

Stefan laughed. "I don't think you're stupid enough to come here unarmed, Ciaran. How many of your men are up there? How many bombs did you plant down here?"

Madeline's body was pressed against Stefan's. She could hardly breathe. He held her so tightly and had his gun pressed right against her temple. Madeline thought if he didn't shoot her, the pressure from the gun would punch a hole in her head anyway.

"If you want to find the crucifix, go find it yourself. Why do you always hide behind women? First Juliette, and now Madeline," Ciaran said.

"I don't hide behind women!" Stefan screamed out the words and moved the gun to shoot at Ciaran.

Ciaran dodged. The bullet grazed his left arm.

When Stefan took the gun off her, Madeline tilted her head forward and then flipped it back as hard as she could, hitting Stefan on the nose. When he staggered, she turned around and shoved him full force into the lake.

Madeline ran toward Ciaran. He grabbed her hand, and they both took off into the bush, disappearing into the shadowy recesses among the trees.

❧

THEY RAN. Ciaran helped Madeline climb the hills. He held her hand in his, and he could feel her energy, her breathing. On a stone platform behind the trees, when he was sure they were alone, he stopped, cupping her face. "Don't ever leave me again," he said. And he kissed her.

A few hours ago, he couldn't even think about how it would feel to have her in his arms again. And now, he would breathe her in if he could.

When they turned to leave, a fireball dropped to the ground near them. A couple of trees burst into flame. He protectively pushed Madeline behind him.

From the darkness behind some trees, four fighters jumped out.

Ciaran glanced up the hill and saw the shadows of his people closing in. But before they would be close enough to give him assistance, he had to handle these men.

They were good fighters and moved extremely fast. They

knocked his gun from his hand and pounded on him. Two fighters kicked Ciaran at once. He fell on the ground and rolled away. His head hit the stone base behind, leaving him dazed.

Douglas pulled out his gun.

Madeline jumped in front of him. "Please, don't shoot. Please, for God's sake. I'm going with you."

Douglas thrust his gun forward. Madeline stood in front of the muzzle. "I'll go with you and get the crucifix. You will have all of my grandfather's praise and glory. Stefan is down there looking for the crucifix himself. If you shoot Ciaran, nobody will stop Stefan. Please, don't!"

Douglas did not hesitate for long. He grabbed Madeline and fled down the hill.

Ciaran tried to reach for her, but his vision was still blurry, and his body was not cooperating. Tadgh and Jo arrived. Tadgh pulled his brother to his feet.

"You should be in the van," Ciaran scolded.

"Look who's talking," Tadgh responded.

Ciaran kicked a tree in frustration and anger. "They took her again! I'll get the crucifix, and I'll get Madeline. Fuck them all!" Ciaran charged away toward his men.

Another fireball dropped down right in front of Ciaran. The bright flash of light revealed the positions of all the soldiers from both sides.

They were only meters from one another.

Stefan had told them to shoot at anything moving, so his soldiers pulled their guns, prepared for a massacre.

Ciaran yelled at his men, "Use your weapons! Fight!"

The two sides charged at one another. At that moment, they were even-numbered.

26

When Madeline and the fighters got down the hillside to level ground, Stefan had recovered the five soldiers who had done the scanning previously. They were waiting by the graveyard flanking the abbey. They had scanned quickly, working their way through the graveyard.

Madeline guessed they'd found nothing except the remains of dead bodies, both human and animal.

Stefan's nose was bleeding, and his clothes were soaking wet.

Douglas asked her, "What do you want to do? We don't have scanners. And I can't go back to Mr. Kelley with only you after losing so many of his men."

"We have to negotiate with Stefan then. You have the real fighters. Stefan will need them when he's up against Ciaran. I appreciate that you didn't shoot Ciaran. I'll make it up to you." Douglas nodded.

They headed up the hill toward the graveyard. Seeing Madeline, Stefan pulled his gun. "You bitch."

She just glared daringly at him, and the group of fighters pointed guns at him. Madeline cocked an eyebrow, waiting. Stefan was a smart man. He would work it out. Five of the so-called soldiers against the strong fighter group was not good odds.

"What do you want now?" Stefan asked.

"Same deal. They need me and a sample of the gold you'll find in the crucifix. So they still need you and your scanners. Ciaran and his men are coming down. All of your men up the hill are gone. You'll need these fighters or you won't get out of here alive. Your choice," Madeline responded.

"All of my men are gone?" Stefan asked Douglas.

"I could only manage to get her back. I can't protect your men. They didn't have any leadership up there. As a result, they were slaughtered."

He lied without a blink, Madeline thought. That had to work.

It did.

"Then dig in," Stefan said. "And don't be a fool. You won't get lucky again," he warned Madeline.

UP ON THE HILL, the fight had finished. Ciaran, Tadgh, and Jo were taking inventory. "I'm sorry, we've lost ten," Ciaran spoke to James.

James said firmly, "It was still a win. We took out twenty of them. There were ten more down the lake. But taking the fighters will not be easy."

Ciaran asked Tadgh, "How is your injury?"

"Do I need to say it? I'm alive and kicking. Told you it was just a flesh wound. But you'll have to fix Jo's dislocated shoulder." Tadgh gingerly led Jo to Ciaran.

"May I look?" Ciaran asked. Jo nodded.

Ciaran held her left arm up gently. Holding Jo's arm with his left hand, his right hand touching her shoulder lightly and very gently, he snapped it back.

Jo yelped in pain, and tears escaped from her eyes. Ciaran held her and kissed her forehead. "I know it hurt. I'm sorry. We'll get you a sling to wear, but for now, try not to move your shoulder too much." Jo nodded.

He handed her off to Tadgh and headed down the hill.

STEFAN LED the way to the abbey via the courtyard. It had started to rain. They walked through the wet grass and muddy areas between the graveyard and the abbey. Madeline glanced up to the hill, knowing Ciaran and his people were up there. She knew he would come after her, and there was nothing she could do to prevent that.

As they entered the long courtyard, Stefan asked the fighters to come inside with him, and he left the soldiers at the entrance. They stayed there for a while and then entered to start the scan.

The rain came down even harder.

Madeline caught a smirk on Stefan's face.

What's that about? She'd seen the same thing at the hotel when he'd called Ciaran to tell him about her grandfather. That smirk. She couldn't figure out what it meant.

Then she looked outside.

Through rows and rows of stone columns and arched doorways, the view she had was of a dark and wet canvas and Ciaran's men approaching the abbey.

That very path was where Stefan had been lurking before he entered the hall.

It was not the rain and the thunder.

She had been mistaken.

An explosion tore through the air, the rain, and her heart. The men in front of her were blown into pieces.

"Ciaran!" she heard the scream in her head. Or maybe she screamed out loud.

There was no way anyone could have survived the explosion.

Madeline tore through the rain and the mud, sprinting outside. The wind slapped at her face. She couldn't hear much. Her ears were ringing with fear.

The world was empty. Dark. And quiet.

She would not believe that Ciaran was dead until she saw him for herself.

27

The explosion had left a deep hole in the ground. Despite the rain, there was fire and the acrid smell of burnt flesh. Body pieces were strewn about.

She walked into the middle of the massacre. But she refused to come to any conclusion until she found him.

She scrambled to each body, every body part, on all fours, swimming in the mixture of fresh blood, mud, and rain water.

She would search until she found something that belonged to him.

She kept looking. She didn't know for how long. She wouldn't give up until she had looked at everything she could find.

And then that was the end of it. She had seen everything. She felt like laughing. She was giddy.

She could not find his body or any evidence of it.

Douglas appeared beside her.

He didn't recognize the expression on her face. He must have thought she was grieving. *Keep it up*, Madeline told herself.

Douglas brought her inside. "I'm very sorry," he said.

He thinks Ciaran is dead. Good. Let him think that. Madeline maintained an expression to suit the scene.

They had completed the scanning inside the main hall of the abbey and found nothing. Madeline thought if those cold stone walls could laugh, they would be, watching the bunch of lunatics digging for gold.

The rain had stopped.

They moved out to the central courtyard where magnificent stone columns and arches had witnessed a thousand years of glory, destruction, life, death, and grieving. The roofs were in ruins here and there, cutting the expansive view of the sky into bits and pieces. Madeline thought she could hear monks chanting, but it might have been her imagination.

"I think I've got it," a soldier spoke up.

Stefan and Douglas charged toward a roofless stone tower. The scanner showed them a ten-inch rectangular box buried right in the middle of the tower. They could see through the material of the box.

The prominent shape of a fancy crucifix was prominently displayed.

There was also something in the box that looked like a piece of paper, perhaps a note or a letter of some sort.

This was it. The crucifix everyone had been searching for, lying underneath a roofless tower, surrounded by stone walls and arched gothic windows, and maybe even guarded by thousands of souls and spirits.

"Shovel," Stefan commanded in excitement.

The ground was soft in the roofless tower. Two soldiers came with shovels. In a short moment, the box was revealed. A metal box with a small lock.

The box looked so innocent, Madeline thought. It was like a girl's secret diary box where she would lock away all of her thoughts and dreams of the prince who one day would ride in on a white horse to rescue her from the tower. Who would think it could be rigged with a ton of explosives? But apparently, Stefan and the others were not fools. They had sniffed out such things before they even touched the box.

The box was lowered to the ground. Madeline could see blood in everyone's eyes.

The look of greed.

A soldier reached out for the box. Stefan immediately put a bullet, point blank, into his head. "Touch it and die," he warned.

The other soldiers moved back. Douglas signaled his fighters, still guarding outside. The fighters shot wire to the top of the tower and arches over the courtyard. In the blink of an eye, all three fighters hoisted themselves up, half flying and half walking on the walls like spiders.

They were coming at Stefan and the soldiers. The soldiers were confused. They weren't sure which side they were on, but they drew their weapons.

Stefan reached down for the box, but a hard kick from Douglas pushed him backward. He reached for his gun, but there wasn't enough time. Douglas pounded at him, releasing all of the hatred he had accumulated for him in the last day.

Madeline looked through the line of stone columns that arched across a strip of grass which led toward the stone frame for a missing gate.

A gate to heaven.

She smiled at it.

At the bottom of the large stone frame stood Ciaran. He smiled back. All she had to do now was make a run for him.

Everyone was fighting for the box and whatever treasures it might hold for them. She was unimportant at the moment. They wouldn't pay any attention to her. She backed against a wall, contemplating the shortest route to Ciaran.

She looked again. Ciaran no longer stood under the stone frame. She knew he was coming for her. She should run in that direction.

Madeline glanced around her again. Douglas was in a one-on-one fight with Stefan. Three fighters were struggling against four soldiers. The constraints of space between stonewalls, columns, and arched footpaths did not provide a free shooting range for anyone.

They had to fight and eye the box at the same time.

Madeline stepped backward once more and ran.

Douglas saw her. He called out. "Get the girl!"

The fighter shot up his hanging wire to the top window of the roofless tower, flying away from the fighting scene below.

Madeline ran. She zigzagged around the stone column as much as she could. She ran as fast as she could. Behind her was the fighter, coming down from the sky on his wire and running across the tops of the stone arches and walls like a spider. Madeline looked back and saw him. She ran faster, knowing she probably wouldn't escape.

The fighter was approaching her from behind, hoping to scoop her up by the waist. She ran faster. But there were no more columns for her to dodge around. She kept running, and she could feel the pressure of the air behind her when the fighter approached. He touched her waist.

From inside the long abbey hallway, Ciaran charged out, standing right in front of Madeline's path, his gun pointing at the coming fighter. The fighter instantly pulled his wire up, managed to grab the back of Madeline's jacket.

In the blink of an eye, Madeline was off the ground, dangling below the fighter, who would not let go of her jacket. They dangled above Ciaran.

Ciaran turned and aimed for the fighter's arm that held fast to his wire. The pain startled the fighter, and he dropped Madeline. Ciaran ran forward and caught her. They both fell to the ground, rolling.

Ciaran smiled. "You're not going to leave me, either on the ground or in the air."

They stood up and saw the fighter's body dangling next to a stone window. It appeared that he had lost control of his wire and smashed his head against the rough edge of a broken stone.

Ciaran and Madeline were about to run off when they saw

Tadgh and Jo approaching. They turned to the abbey hallway to leave from the inside. At the other side of the courtyard, it appeared that the fight continued. They ran to the end of the hall and could hear the fight right outside.

Then Douglas darted into the hall and blocked their exit.

"I can't let you go, Madeline," Douglas said.

Ciaran pushed Madeline behind him. "I'll talk to Richard Kelley if you let Madeline go." Douglas glanced at the fight in the courtyard. One of his fighters was losing to Stefan.

They would have to leave the hall by the gateway Douglas was blocking. Ciaran approached slowly, Madeline, Tadgh, and Jo behind him.

"You want the box, go get it. I'll talk to Mr. Kelley regarding Madeline. I promise. You spared me a bullet. I owe you. I'll keep my promise. If you let Stefan abscond with the box, he'll never come back. He doesn't keep promises," Ciaran said.

The fighter who was losing to Stefan pulled out a small explosive device.

Stefan knew what it was. It'd kill everyone in the confined space. He stopped pounding as the fighter picked up the box and threw it toward Douglas. At the same time, Stefan kicked the explosive device away and shot at the fighter.

Douglas dove through the air to catch the box. It was a good catch. He got it. On his landing, a bullet from Stefan's gun tore through air at him, striking him in the head. Douglas's body fell to the floor.

The box slid out from his hand, skidded on the ground, and stopped mere feet away from Ciaran.

Madeline tugged at him. "Get away! Get away from it! I won't let you touch it."

28

*C*iaran turned around. "Don't worry. I know, Madeline." He held her hand so that they could move past Douglas's body to the exit.

Stefan charged to the hallway and stood at the exit. But he was focused on the box and nothing else. It was as if he didn't see anything. He pointed his gun at the lock on the box.

"No, you'll damage the crucifix," Madeline said. She didn't want to be here in case the box exploded.

Stefan looked at Madeline. He nodded his head and smiled strangely. He looked strange—so strange it made her worry about what he might do next. His eyes filled with a strange combination of satisfaction and confusion.

He looked like a vampire, starved for blood, but now that he had found the blood, he didn't know what to do with it.

They heard two loud bangs from outside. It appeared to be the end of the fight. They weren't sure who the victor was.

Then there was the slipping sound of the wired device, and the last fighter flew into the hall like a bird. He snatched the box off the ground, jumping on walls and stone columns so high that he almost hit the ceiling. He pulled himself up again to fly out of the hall via a gigantic window.

Stefan drew his gun and fired at him. The body of the fighter was carried by his wire, swinging outside via the window.

The box slipped from his hand and hit a stone arch on the ceiling. The lock was broken, and the lid swung open. The crucifix slid out, flipped a few rounds, and dropped on the floor with a thudding sound.

The top of the crucifix fell off, and the contents inside spilled out.

It looked like a black powder. The note from the box took its time, fluttering down and landing on the floor like a feather.

Stefan stood over the crucifix, walking around it as if he were a cat inspecting a dead rat, checking to be sure it was really dead.

He looked at Ciaran.

"It's certainly not gold," Stefan said with a strange smile on his face. He kneeled down to examine the strange powder.

Ciaran approached. Madeline pulled him back.

Stefan shoved both of his hands into the pile of black powder and let the grains run through his fingers. Then he let out a short laugh.

"It's dirt. I think it's dirt," Stefan said.

Stefan fingered the pile of dirt, rubbing some of it against his palms. He looked at his palms and laughed a little louder. "I think it's really dirt."

Madeline could not make sense of it. But Ciaran looked astonished, like he instantly knew what it meant as soon as the pile of dirt poured out from the crucifix.

Stefan picked up the note. He glanced at it then laughed some more. He held the note in Ciaran's direction.

"Recognize this handwriting?" Stefan asked. He read the note out loud, his eyes filled with amusement.

"*We came from dirt, we should return to dirt. I've made my choice of destiny. Please forgive and forget me. Consider that what you created was only dirt.*

Your lost daughter and sister,
Juliette."

"She chose me," Ciaran mumbled to himself.

But Stefan heard him. "You're right. As usual, you're always right. You're her prince, she always said, her destiny."

Then Madeline got it. She understood now. It made perfect sense.

Guilt was the worst poison for Ciaran. Juliette had decided to betray her family for him. She was going to tell him. They were going to build a new life together. But she didn't have a chance to tell him any of that.

Madeline couldn't undo what Ciaran had seen and had heard. She knew it was better for him to live his life in doubt rather than knowing this naked truth. But it was too late.

Stefan sat on the floor, grinning like a lunatic.

Ciaran said nothing and did nothing. There was no movement from him at all.

Stefan said, between laughs, "She loved Ireland. She wanted a small cottage in the country. She wanted to be a teacher. How cliché was that? Dad always said she was too smart to do anything ordinary. You just do this one for Daddy, and then we'll set the family up for good. He always pushed her." Stefan began crying. "This big brother felt utterly stupid standing next to her. I couldn't do anything to help. She was nineteen. Met you when she was nineteen—and that was the end of her. I told Dad you were bad news. But he didn't listen to me. And now what? He's dead. She's dead. And all I have is this dirt! How is this fair?" Stefan screamed out the question again. "How is this fair?" while he pulled out his gun and shot at Ciaran.

It was too fast.

Ciaran didn't move, as if he was waiting for the bullet.

Tadgh was faster. He put a bullet in Stefan's head. Stefan's arm jerked, but he still managed to fire his gun.

The impact of the bullet pushed Ciaran a few steps backward, then he slumped to the floor.

Madeline grabbed at him. She knew it was bad. The bullet had hit Ciaran in his chest. Blood streamed from his wound and pooled on the cold floor.

She couldn't stop the blood.

Tadgh was calling for help and doing something else that Madeline didn't understand.

Madeline held Ciaran in her arms, hoping the sitting position would help lessen his blood loss. Ciaran's head lolled on her shoulder. She knew she was weeping. But she couldn't help it.

Ciaran shifted. "Let me see you," he said.

"Shhh, I've got you. Tadgh is getting help. Don't talk."

"Please," Ciaran asked again. His voice was so weak that it could hardly be heard.

Madeline lowered him to the floor. She took her jacket off to roll it under his head. Ciaran looked at her.

"I don't want to see you cry," Ciaran said.

She couldn't say anything. She just wept.

"I knew this day was coming. It's a debt I had to pay sooner or later. Had I made more progress in our relationship and then left you, it would be unfair to you. But if I didn't make any progress, it would be unfair to us. Before I go . . ."

"You're not going anywhere . . ."

"I love you, Madeline." He closed his eyes and didn't say anything more.

The room was filled with footsteps and people. Among these people, there was maybe Tadgh, Jo, Doctor Thomas. Madeline wasn't sure who said what. She just knew that Ciaran was no longer talking to her, or to anyone.

He just lay there silently in a pool of his own blood.

29

*J*ennifer was waiting when they wheeled Ciaran into the operating room. Doctor Thomas hooked up the machine to measure his vital signs.

Ciaran's pulse was extremely weak.

The medical team geared up quickly. No one followed the usual procedure of getting nonmedical personnel outside the room. Everyone stayed—Madeline, Tadgh, Jo, Jennifer, and even Migi.

In front of Madeline was a haze of noise and moving objects, none of which made any sense.

What made most sense to her now was that Doctor Thomas was performing some medical procedures and Ciaran was going to be fine. Doctor Thomas was good at what he did.

He had once told Madeline that neither she nor Ciaran could take responsibility for other's people's actions. Juliette's death had not been Ciaran's fault, regardless of how he felt. She hoped he understood that.

Doctor Thomas held a syringe. *That must be anesthesia,* Madeline thought, knowing Ciaran would pay for it when he awoke. But he would just have to deal with it.

Ciaran seemed like he was saying something. Yes, he'd said

something to Doctor Thomas, so soft that Doctor Thomas had to bend down to listen.

Doctor Thomas turned around. "Jennifer, he wants you." Doctor Thomas waved the medical staff outside the room.

Madeline was confused. Why would he do that?

Jennifer seemed to know what was going on. A wicked mom she was, Madeline thought. No worries. Madeline would wait for her turn to talk to Ciaran. Mothers come first. She understood.

Ciaran was so weak. He couldn't even open his eyes. Jennifer held his hand. She kissed it. She whispered something Madeline couldn't hear.

Ciaran forced his eyes open. Those beautiful gray eyes she knew and loved were now blurry with fatigue. Ciaran looked up at his mother, and he said, "I'm sorry."

He kept looking at her.

Madeline was getting more confused. *Why did he keep looking at her?*

Then she realized he was no longer looking. His eyes had glassed over. His pulse had stopped, and her world had collapsed.

The monitor displayed a flat line.

Jennifer put his hand down. She closed his eyes and kissed his forehead.

Silence.

Then Tadgh grabbed Doctor Thomas. "Doctor, you have to do something. Can you resuscitate him? He lost a lot of blood, I . . . I know we have a rare blood type, but you can take mine."

Doctor Thomas shook his head. "He's gone, Tadgh."

"What do you mean? You haven't done anything! He hasn't tried, he can't just go . . ." Tadgh didn't realize he was weeping.

"I haven't told him I love him, Jo." Madeline grabbed her friend. "This is so unfair. He told me he loved me. But I didn't say anything. That wasn't right. I was stupid. I didn't respond . . ."

"Madeline, he understands. He's a smart man. Oh for God's sake, could you please cry? I'd rather you cry than look at me like that."

"Like what?" Then she realized her face was dry. There wasn't a tear in her eyes. Madeline's body started to shake, but she couldn't cry. She couldn't understand what was going on.

Tadgh grabbed at Doctor Thomas. "You're a *doctor*! You cure people! Please help him!"

"Tadgh, he was too weak to survive an operation, if he even wanted it."

"What do you mean?" Tadgh cried. "What do you mean? He didn't want it?"

"He knew his time was up, Tadgh. I loved him like my son. If I could have, don't you think I would have done something for him? You know that when Ciaran didn't want to fight, nobody could make him."

"Nobody?" Madeline's head poked up from Jo's shoulder. "Nobody?" Madeline repeated. "Look at him. He looks so peaceful. Wherever he is, he's enjoying this. He left us in this shit with all of our questions unanswered, with things he promised but didn't do, and he thinks he can get away with it? Everyone has to try. You have to try, Doctor Thomas. The LeBlancs make drugs. You save lives. How can this be so difficult?"

Jo pulled Madeline back when Madeline started to cry. She had started to realize the reality of the situation. But she wasn't sure if she would be able to accept it.

Jennifer stood silently next to Ciaran during the commotion in the room. Then she turned around and said, "May I have a moment with my family, please?"

Doctor Thomas, Jo, and Madeline left the room.

"Please stay, Madeline," Jennifer said, stopping Madeline in her tracks.

Madeline approached Jennifer.

There was not a single tear on the mother's face. Madeline felt pity for the woman. She felt pity for herself, too. She looked at Jennifer and waited.

"I believe you love my son, and he loves you."

Madeline nodded. What was the point of this, Madeline thought. Why did she use the present tense? *Loves.*

"Can you promise me that you would love and take care of Ciaran whenever you could manage it?"

Whenever she could manage it? Madeline didn't have to even promise to love him for the rest of her life? What was this woman doing? Madeline had just lost her true love, and Jennifer had lost her son. Madeline wanted to scream and leave this place. She wanted to grieve.

But now she was stuck here with this woman, feeling ridiculous.

Madeline realized she had never loved anyone before Ciaran. Yes, she'd had relationships with men, on and off, here and there.

But love is a sacred word, and if it used with the meaning it deserves, now was the time. It was for Ciaran.

"I'll always love him, whether he's dead or alive. But if you can bring him back, I'll be with him for the rest of my life, as long as he wants me. How's that for a promise?"

Tadgh approached. "Mother, what's going on?" he asked, the tears still damp on his face.

Jennifer held up a hand for silence. Then she pulled out a syringe with a golden liquid in it.

"Mother, what are you doing?"

Jennifer didn't answer. She checked the needle, and then she injected the liquid into a vein in Ciaran's neck.

Then she watched the monitor.

Nothing.

One moment.

Two moments.

Then the line jumped once.

And then again.

A line showing a healthy pulse ran across the monitor.

Jennifer nodded with satisfaction. "It's Ciaran's Golden Life. Apparently, it works."

Tadgh gasped. "Oh my God, oh Jesus Christ. You . . . you killed Juliette for this?"

"I didn't kill her. I wanted to teach her a lesson. I wanted their Golden Life to fail. I didn't know she was going to test the drug on herself. I swapped the drug. When I knew of the testing, it was too late."

Madeline was too stunned to speak.

"How will Ciaran live with this in his body?" Tadgh asked.

"It's up to you to tell him—or not. I'll lose him anyway, one way or another. But this way, I would lose him, but he would live." Jennifer looked at Tadgh and Madeline.

"If Ciaran were to never talk to me again for the rest of his life, I'd understand. I've never blamed anyone for this but myself." Jennifer opened the door and found Doctor Thomas waiting outside.

"Doctor Thomas, Ciaran's pulse is back. Could you please perform the operation now?" And with that, Jennifer walked away.

Doctor Thomas stormed into the room and looked at the monitor incredulously. He called out for his medical staff.

This time, everyone who was not on staff was sent from the room.

$\mathcal{M}$adeline found Jennifer at the end of the hallway in the new quarter of Mon Ciel. Ciaran's mother looked as if she had aged twenty years since she had walked out of the operating room.

Madeline gave her a moment before she spoke. "I'll keep my promise, Jennifer. Thank you for bringing Ciaran back. I owe you my life."

Madeline gave Jennifer another moment to digest what she had just said. Then she hugged Jennifer.

Then and there, Jennifer cried.

The woman probably had not cried for years. Now, she probably felt old. She probably felt like a mother. Madeline held her for a long moment and let her weep.

When Jennifer's emotion subsided, Madeline asked, "Do you really want me to keep this information from Ciaran?"

Jennifer thought for a moment, then shook her head.

"He'll figure it out. I'd rather it come from you. I want you to add your perspective to the story when you tell him."

"Why me?"

"Because you love him like a soul mate. One day, I'd like to see you be the mother of his children."

"As far as I'm concerned, Juliette loved him, too."

Jennifer shook her head. "Have you ever considered leaving Ciaran if you knew your love could harm him?"

Madeline remembered it vividly. When she saw the number thirty-three written on the road and made the possible connection to her age, she had considered leaving him. She would have gone away with her grandfather if it would have spared Ciaran what just happened.

Madeline nodded.

Jennifer smiled. "If you love someone, you must be prepared to give, to take, and to let go. Out of the three, letting go is the hardest thing to do. Juliette never considered to letting anything go, no matter what it would do to Ciaran. You could argue that one might not understand the concept at twenty-one. But I'd venture to say it's in the nature of the person, not in their age or life experience."

Jennifer took Madeline's hand and continued. "I speak from personal experience. When you become a mother, you'll understand."

Jennifer put a small locket into Madeline's hand. "Juliette was his past. You are his future. As long as he can let his past go, he can have a future with you."

Jennifer turned on her heel and walked away as Madeline returned to the operation room.

THE FAMILIAR SCENT of his room welcomed Ciaran back to the world. Somehow, this world seemed better and much more pleasant than before. Because in spite of all the dark corners, rough edges, and puzzles life had presented to him, Madeline gave him one special thing, the feeling of being loved.

It felt good—being loved.

What happened at Fountains Abbey flooded back to him. But

instead of the pain of regret, guilt, or sundry other dark patches of life, the memory was merely an event in a distant past.

It felt as if a lifetime of grieving had been lifted from him.

Even Juliette. He could think about her now with fond memories of the good times they had had together. He thought about her right now and recalled her brilliant smile and magnificent hair. He remembered the first time they met, and the smell of old paper in the library. The air around them had been so still that he had sworn he could hear her breathing. He remembered how happy she had been when she'd beaten him for the first time in a computer game. And he knew she was too smart not to know he'd let her win. But she'd enjoyed the victory anyway.

But those memories were now genuinely memories.

Previously, they had been mental scars, monuments for him to remember his sins, emotional crimes he had committed which destroyed innocence. A declaration of a lifetime debt to Juliette.

He remembered the sensation of the bullet penetrating his body. Was that it? His debt had been paid, and now he could move on?

Then Madeline entered the room like a fresh breeze in spring. She sat at his bedside.

"Hello!" she said.

"Hello back." He smiled at her. She was beautiful. He sat up, leaning against the headboard, and looked at her.

"Thank you," she said.

"For what?"

"For coming back to me. You wanted to go."

He smiled. "I changed my mind."

She tucked his hair back and kissed him. Then she eased back and looked into his eyes. "I love you, Ciaran."

"That's why I changed my mind. I've let go of whatever happened in the past. I'm hoping to have a future with you—if you'll accept me."

Tears rolled down her face. He wiped them away and rubbed his thumb at the dimple on her left cheek.

"Yes," she said. "Be with me."

He pulled her into his arms and felt the vibration of her emotion, of her love.

Over her shoulder, he saw a pot of Mountain Avens glaring at him from the corner of the room.

"What's with the flowers?" he asked.

She turned around, looking at the bunch of white flowers. "I found them in the back garden. I thought they were very pretty."

"They're Mountain Avens, Madeline."

"They have pretty name, too," she smiled.

"They were Juliette's favourite. This special kind doesn't grow here, so I brought them back from Ireland."

"Oh . . . so . . . do you want me to take them out?"

He smiled and lifted her chin up. "Why? You think they're pretty. You like them. That's what matters now."

They kissed each other.

There was jingle in the air, the merry kind. The flowers must have sung for joy because he let them stay in the room with his precious Madeline.

In the end, they were just flowers. But in a corner of his mind, a tune was playing. "Little hummingbird, do you see the sky? It is free. It is yours. Fly. Past the mountains. Past the oceans. There you will find love . . ."

He smiled to himself. *What a pretty song,* he thought.

ELUSIVE BEINGS

ELUSIVE BEINGS

Synopsis

Ciaran survives the fight for the truth behind the crucifix, but it has triggered an even bigger disaster that might tear Ciaran and Madeline apart forever. The truth behind the crucifix is trivial compared to the catastrophes built into the aftermath. To solve these crises, Ciaran and Madeline face a basic but difficult question—who are they, really?

This third installment in an urban fantasy thriller series, filled with romance and science fiction twists and turns, will take you to the deepest corners of the minds of those who dare to sacrifice.

1

The stench of fresh blood engulfed Madeline. She stormed into the living room of a country house in the middle of the Australian outback. With one hand still clinging to a fish basket and the other gripping a fishing spear, she approached the entrance of the adjacent reception room with caution.

She wanted to call out for Jo but thought that would be unwise.

It had been Jo's idea to travel all the way from New York for an exotic celebration of Jo's eighteenth birthday. Madeline hoped it didn't turn into the last trip of her life.

Madeline went out for the afternoon to take lessons from an Australian Aboriginal on how to catch fish the ancient way. They were going to have a surprise dinner for Jo tonight—a surprise because Jo disliked fish and Madeline didn't cook.

Luckily for them, the dinner was Zach's idea. He was their mutual Australian friend. Zach would turn twenty-one soon and planned to put the cozy kitchen of the small guest house to good use to celebrate a double birthday.

Blood.

It was all she could see in the reception room—amid the broken furniture.

Hesitating no more, Madeline yelled, "Jo!"

A cacophony of sounds—crashing glass, pots, pans, and other kitchen objects and a bloodcurdling scream—came in response, sending Madeline racing toward the kitchen.

More blood.

That was what she found. At the corner of the kitchen, Jo was on the floor, unconscious. Zach stood next to her, guarding her immobile body.

Zach's shirt was soaked in blood. He didn't look like he would be able to stand for long.

Larry, the host of the guest house, brandished a knife with one hand and held the other hand to his ear, screaming as if his head was going to explode. He reeled back and forth, crashing into the kitchen furniture and knocking it over.

There was no sign of his wife and children, but Madeline saw blood trailing out of the kitchen and through the door leading to the family room.

Larry was in his late sixties, a soft-spoken man and kind father and husband who had housed them for three days. That had been Larry before she'd finished her fishing lesson. But it wasn't the Larry before her now.

Zach was cornered. "Run, Madeline," Zach yelled.

She stood right at the door, not moving. She knew what was going on. "Is Jo alive?"

"Yes. Run, Madeline! He's insane. He's not listening, so don't even try to talk to him."

Larry directed his bloodshot eyes at Madeline. There was no humanity in him that she could see. The devil had taken over. An explicable smirk crossed his face as he approached her.

"Run, Madeline!" Zach yelled again and this time he captured Larry's attention. The old man swung his head back toward Zach.

Madeline threw the fish basket at Larry, hitting him in the head.

As soon as the basket left her hand she could smell it—the metallic stench from her ghost.

Larry turned to walk toward her, and Zach took the opportunity to charge him from behind. Larry suddenly swung back, and the knife in his hand slashed at Zach's abdomen. He grabbed Zach's neck with one hand and waved the knife with the other.

He was going to slaughter Zach.

Madeline knew Larry's strength was not his own. It was not his soul inside his body. "Larry, stop!" Madeline said firmly.

He released Zach instantly, dropping him to the floor unconscious to lie next to Jo. Then he turned to Madeline. Smirking, he walked toward her like a zombie. He didn't even threaten her with the knife to give her an excuse to kill him in self-defense. He simply staggered toward her with a crazed smile on his face.

In his eyes, she could still see the pledge of the kind old man who had been their friend for the last three days. She knew he was innocent.

He must have been the one who killed his wife and kids. But his body was only doing what it was being told to do.

The metallic stench of her ghost grew stronger. It was not the first time the ghost had possessed men to kill. All she had to do to end all this was to kill the man in front of her.

Once and for all, it would end.

But the old man was innocent.

She had never been able to do that, to end it, and the ghost kept coming back. Disaster after disaster. And people would continue to be murdered until she killed the host the ghost possessed.

Larry continued to approach Madeline.

"Don't come any closer." She stepped back.

Larry kept coming. She could see his eyes had started to clear. Once that happened, he would return to normal and see what he'd just done. Most often, the men, after being possessed, went insane and eventually killed themselves.

"Your last chance, Madeline. Keep your virtuous soul, and more people will die," an ancient voice echoed in the air.

She had to kill this innocent man for the craziness to end. The ghost had been telling her that for years—it would continue to kill until she killed an innocent man. But no matter how she tried to justify it, in front of her was a helpless man whom she had no right to kill.

Larry took another step toward her.

"Time is running out, Madeline. Next time, it will be worse," the ghost chanted.

"Stop, Larry!"

She yelled at the old man, but he kept advancing. She raised the fishing spear, pointing it at his heart.

2

en years later.

IT WAS after six in the morning, but Madeline couldn't find any sign of the winter sun. She overanalyzed the humidity, the feel of the air, and the sound of the wind, concluding that England winters and New York winters were the same—cold and bleak.

Ciaran turned away from the window and looked at her.

Madeline should have gotten used to the sight of Ciaran by now, but it never happened. God must have been in a very good mood indeed when he created such a gorgeous human being. She could hardly believe that every inch of that six foot three slender yet muscular warrior's body belonged to her. His face—that of a dark angel—continued to make her stomach quiver. Those deep and intense gray eyes focused on her as if for him no one else existed and nothing else in the world mattered.

Suddenly a bullet hit Ciaran's chest, exiting from his back. Blood splattered onto the glass window. Madeline gasped as the image of Ciaran flickered and disappeared.

She shook her head and snapped back to reality. A few days ago, her life had changed forever.

She still remembered the sensation of Ciaran's blood on her hands, the commotion in the operation room, and the emptiness when she thought her world would exist without him in it.

She couldn't get the memory of his beautiful eyes, glassed over and lifeless, out of her mind. And she couldn't ignore the lingering fear that she would have to experience that incident again in the future. Ciaran said he had left the memory behind to move on with life, to be with her. But that was before she told him the truth behind his recovery.

It wasn't a miracle that he was back with her again.

Jennifer had wanted her to tell Ciaran, and she had. But regardless of how much she tried to spin the story and make it golden, the naked truth was that his mother had swapped the drug. And, as a result, Juliette had died, and the real drug had coincidentally saved his life.

Jennifer had told her that Juliette never let go of anything, and Madeline wagered she would cling to Ciaran this time more than at any other time.

This ordeal wasn't over yet. Not by a long shot.

The air seemed to thicken a bit. Madeline spun around, surveying the empty room around her. She didn't care for what she was feeling. This wasn't her familiar psychic blue dots. It wasn't the appearance of Juliette's hologram, either.

It was the unmistakable metallic stench of her long forgotten ghost. *Who was it going to possess now?* Fear rose in her mind like tidal waves.

"Madeline!"

Madeline startled and cried out.

"Are you okay?" Tadgh said from the door. "I knocked." Tadgh stood, puzzled, his hands in his pockets.

"Huh?"

"Can I have a word with you?"

"Of course." Madeline smiled. "Where's Jo?"

"Planning a new game in the game room . . ."

Madeline was a bit disturbed by Tadgh's apparent agitation as he rolled up and down on the balls of his feet. "What's up Tadgh?" she asked.

"I don't know. Something feels strange."

"Why wouldn't it seem that way, especially after all that's happened?"

"I called Dublin. They said Mother hasn't arrived home yet. She left ages ago. Where could she be?"

"Is there anywhere she might go to take some time off? Be by herself? She's been through a lot lately. What about your cousin George's in France? Jennifer mentioned him before."

Tadgh shook his head. "You don't know my mother. She's an authoritative figure in the family. She would never take shelter anywhere or protection from anyone—no matter how mad Ciaran might be at her. I even searched for air traffic info just in case . . ."

"There might have been an accident?"

Tadgh nodded. "Air, road, water . . . I looked everywhere. I even rang George, although I knew it was entirely unlikely that she'd gone to France. I couldn't find a hint of her. What did she say to you?"

"Nothing. She just cried."

"Do you . . ." Tadgh cleared his throat, "Do you think Mother did the right thing, you know, regarding Juliette?"

"I won't judge her, Tadgh. One day, I will be a mother, too, and I don't know what I would do or what I will be capable of when it comes to the welfare of my own children."

Tadgh nodded.

"Let me see what I can do," Madeline said and closed her eyes. She tried to catch a sense of Jennifer's mind—a trace, a feel, a hint of even a single blue dot somewhere.

A dot suddenly appeared at the back of her mind, quickly expanding and exploding like a bomb, spraying dark blood particles all over her. The metallic stench engulfed her senses.

Madeline yelped and slumped to the floor.

"Madeline, are you okay?" Tadgh ran to her, holding her by the shoulders and sitting her up.

"Do you smell anything strange in the room, Tadgh?"

He squinted his nose, sniffed, then shook his head. "Why? What's going on?"

She shook her head. "I can't see your mother, Tadgh."

"That's okay."

"I'll keep looking," Madeline promised.

"Where's Ciaran?" Tadgh asked.

Madeline smiled. "He said he was going out for some fresh air . . ." Her voice trailed off. She could swear that she had just seen the white Mountain Avens flowers she'd picked this morning bleeding. She'd watched as a drop of blood formed at the center of a single flower, rolled down a white petal, and landed on the table. She blinked, looking again closely.

Ciaran had said this was Juliette's favorite kind of flower, and he'd had them brought here from Ireland.

Tadgh frowned. "Are you okay, Madeline? Tell me what's going on."

"What color are those flowers over there, Tadgh?"

"They're white. Why do you ask?"

"Was Juliette by any chance buried near here?"

Tadgh cocked an eyebrow. "You want to buy her flowers?"

"Was she cremated or buried?"

"She was buried. The family's cemetery is nearby. Why?"

She wondered whether her ghost was able to possess an already dead body. Her mind's eye kept seeing the Mountain Avens dropping blood onto the table—it seems like an omen or a warning to her. She closed her eyes, concentrated, and traced Ciaran's thoughts.

Madeline muttered. "Ciaran is at the cemetery at the moment. Trouble's coming. I can feel it. He didn't bring his cell with him. We have to go there right away."

"Can't you channel to him, talk to him in your mind? You know, using your psychic trick."

"It's not a trick, Tadgh, it's an ability. And yes, I can channel and try to communicate with Ciaran. But he's not a psychic—he can't hear me and can't respond."

"Okay. Let's go then. Hope it's not too late. What's he thinking, not bringing his cell with him?"

"Nostalgia," Madeline muttered.

Tadgh led the way, and they rushed out of the room.

3

The bleak morning couldn't possibly weigh down the air at the cemetery any further than it already was. Rows and rows of graves lined up neatly in the grass. Even in death, the LeBlancs protected their privacy, and their private family plots were located at the far corner of the cemetery. Ciaran squinted at the sight of Tadgh and Madeline racing toward the tomb.

It started to drizzle.

Madeline rushed into the tomb and glanced around. She looked nervous—and she should be. He had managed to drag her into the tangled mess of his past in no time. He pulled Madeline into his arms as soon as she ran inside, holding her tightly until every muscle in his body quivered with emotion. In the corner, Tadgh shook rainwater from his coat.

Suddenly, the air thickened. Ciaran knew what it was, and he didn't care for it one bit.

It meant trouble.

"Tadgh, get out of here. Now!" Ciaran called out to his brother.

As the candle in the tomb flickered, and the faint but sharp smell of burning electrical current rushed through the room, a hologram of Juliette appeared. Ciaran wasn't at all surprised to see it—someone had simulated her image, and he had seen it in the hologame.

But he was stunned at how the raw emotion flooded back to him, seeing her this close and this real again.

She wore a red dress and stood next to the altar, smiling graciously at him.

"You killed my brother, Ciaran."

"He nearly killed me, too." Ciaran moved Madeline behind him protectively, almost squashing her against the wall.

"Yes, you're right. You told me that before. But in battle, someone always gets hurt."

"What do you want, whoever you are?"

"I'm Juliette," she said. "*Your* Juliette. Or I was once. I died on Earth because of you. My father traded his life to get me out of here. And now you've killed my brother. So it's only fair to ask you to come back to me, isn't it? All you have to do is to go through the gate."

"What gate?"

"The Daimon Gate. All of the information you need is on the disk I hid at Mon Ciel. Process the disk, and then you'll be able to see the gate. Come here and be with me."

"I don't have the disk."

Juliette nodded. "Oh, it's that old man Richard again, isn't it? He got the disk, didn't he? But he won't know how to decode it. Not everyone is as smart as you and me, Ciaran. You need to find the disk and decode it." She smiled again. "I miss you."

"And what if he won't go through the gate?" Madeline asked.

Juliette laughed. "Oh, sister. Of course, you'd ask such a foolish question. You do think you have a claim on my man."

The holographic Juliette cast an evil eye at Madeline. Ciaran moved forward slightly.

"You're no competition for Madeline," Ciaran told the hologram. "You can't compare yourself with the innocent Juliette I loved years ago. You're an electronic profile. Nothing more. Juliette died. You might be able to simulate her emotions and experiences, but you can't simulate the real love we had for each other."

"I *am* your Juliette! I didn't die!" The hologram whirled back and forth. Its skin grew radiant and red.

"You just told me that you died on Earth because of me. That was a lie?"

"No. I did die on Earth. But I live elsewhere now. You have to be with me. You have to go through the gate."

Tadgh sneered. "So you're in hell now? I would say heaven, but given what you did, I wouldn't think heaven would take you."

"Tadgh!" Ciaran warned him. He didn't want to make the hologram angry. He had a feeling it wasn't just a simple hologram with familiar properties. This hologram was something more, something new and more tangible. It might be able to do some real damage.

Tadgh continued. "As far as I'm concerned, Stefan shot my brother, and he got a bullet in return. That's a tit for a tat. You see, in battle, as you said, someone always gets hurt. If you had told Ciaran your motives from the beginning, you would never have been in a relationship with him, let alone in love and married. You cheated first. Unfortunately—like brother, like sister—you paid a consequence. I can't see that my brother owes you anything. We're done here."

"Tadgh is right. I owe you nothing, Juliette. Let me have my fond memories of you—and you stay wherever you are. I can't—I won't —join you." He tried to be firm, but Ciaran knew it wasn't going to work.

He pushed Madeline toward the door. The burned smell in the air thickened and grew stronger. They heard the faint sound of crackling wires and dry wood burning. "No one walks away from me." Juliette's face turned dark red, and then purple. "Including you." Her eyes filled with rage. "I won't allow it!"

Ciaran grabbed Madeline and called out for Tadgh, "Run!"

Madeline and Ciaran charged out of the tomb.

The hologram whirled and spun. The light circle around it extended until it became a gigantic cylinder.

It grew larger by the second, turning into a small tornado. It stirred the air and sucked everything loose inside the tomb into its vortex. It spun objects around and ejected them randomly in different directions.

It lifted a tombstone and threw it to the ground, breaking it into pieces. It unearthed a coffin and spun the lid away into the air. The tornado grew and exploded the tomb. Shards of rock and concrete rained down on the cemetery grounds.

Madeline, Ciaran, and Tadgh ran. They heard the explosion behind them, but they did not look back.

The tornado built up size and speed quickly. It rose into the darkening sky.

It grew. It chased.

Ciaran looked back and could see the tornado's need to devour. It would indiscriminately suck everyone and everything into it. But he knew its quest—it wanted only him.

4

The funnel of wind and suction followed right behind them. Ciaran knew Juliette wanted him. He slowed down and shoved hard at Tadgh's and Madeline's backs. As they fell forward, the tornado drew him in.

Suddenly, it stopped expanding. It withdrew at high speed, away from Tadgh and Madeline.

Ciaran could feel every bone in his body rattling as he flew around in circles inside the wind tunnel of the tornado. It spun him around, and his body crashed into the various objects whirling around with him—trees, walls, stones.

As he came around each time, he could see Madeline in the distance, trying to run at the tornado. Tadgh held her back.

She yelled, seemingly speaking to the air, "Grandfather, if you are the one who sent Juliette, please stop her! I'll go with you! I'll go wherever you want. Just release Ciaran!"

Ciaran's body dropped to the ground in the center of the funnel after hitting the top of a tree. He spat out blood as he hit the ground hard. His wound had reopened and started to bleed.

Tadgh charged the tornado, trying to get to his brother. The wind wall spun him away, tossing him against a tombstone like he was a mere pebble. There was no way Tadgh would be able to penetrate the circle of wind. It was too powerful.

Ciaran shook his head. "You can't get in, Tadgh. Don't hurt yourself." Ciaran was in the center of the whirling storm. He appeared to be in the eye of the tornado. He leaned on a tree and slowly pulled himself to his feet.

The holographic Juliette appeared next to him and smiled. "Welcome to my world. You're mine now, Ciaran. Forever. Dead or alive." She reached her hand out to grab him.

Her hand would have been cut off had she not withdrawn it quickly enough. A blue lightning bolt struck right between Ciaran and Juliette. Confused and angry, Juliette staggered a few steps backward.

In the middle of the tornado, the woman who stood between Juliette and Ciaran was as beautiful as an angel.

Ciaran stepped closer to the woman. She wore a long, white robe with a furred hood. He could not see her hair, but Ciaran guessed it was long, wavy, and as white as clouds. Her milky skin was almost transparent, and her big blue eyes were striking and oddly familiar.

Ciaran had seen those eyes before.

Unlike Juliette, this woman was not a hologram. The energy coming from her warmed the air around him. He could feel her physical presence.

"Ayana Dee," Juliette grunted with resentment.

Ayana gave Ciaran a warm glance and a gentle smile. Then, she quickly whirled around, snapping at Juliette. "You injured a successor. You are now exiled."

"Since when is he a successor?" Juliette growled.

Ayana grabbed Ciaran's left arm to reveal the golden crucifix tattoo. She pressed her thumb onto Ciaran's left arm. The contact burned his flesh, glowed, and sparked out some flames.

Ciaran grunted in pain. It felt as if his body was going to disintegrate. Every cell seemed to shift, wanting to move away from the cell next to it. He slumped to the ground.

"His successor position has now been sealed." Ayana studied the burn mark on Ciaran's arm with satisfaction. She pulled him up and spun him outside the circle of wind that had imprisoned him.

Ciaran's body rolled across the ground toward Madeline and Tadgh, and they darted toward him. Ciaran sat up and spat out more blood onto the ground. His insides felt like mashed potatoes. Everything around him appeared to be floating in a haze.

"Biological imprint. That's Bran's seal. I am authorized to activate it," Ayana said.

"But Ciaran didn't give his consent," Juliette protested.

"He did."

"When?"

"Before your time. I assume your development stopped when your earthly body died. But even with the mind of a twenty-one-year-old, you should be able to understand that your position comes with great responsibility. Don't be petty about what happened to you on Earth."

"Petty! My life was cut short! You might think it's petty to be angry about that, but for those of us born and raised on this filthy planet, we have only one life. Taking a life is not petty!" Juliette cried.

"So what exactly are you trying to do with Ciaran?"

"He's mine!" Juliette looked like a child having a temper tantrum, like she wanted to stomp her feet in anger. But she was able to refrain from doing so.

Ayana shook her head. "You're still a child, and I am afraid you'll never grow up." Ayana waved her arms in the air. The air pressure crushed Juliette's hologram. She heaved and hissed in anger.

"You don't have the power to exile me."

"Maybe not. But I can certainly constrain all of your power."

"No, you can't!" Juliette yelled.

A spark of white light cut through the air, and the hologram of Richard Kelley appeared.

"We need her," he said. "You can't do this Ayana."

Madeline called out from outside the light circle, "Grandfather!"

"He comes for you, doesn't he? Well, I won't let him take you." Ciaran stood up, pulling Madeline away. He could hardly walk. Each movement he made felt like he was trying to move a mountain. Madeline wrapped her arm around his waist to support him. Tadgh was right behind. They rushed toward the car.

Inside the wind circle, Ayana crushed Juliette harder. Juliette's hologram looked as if it was disintegrating. Richard then swung his white sword and broke through the air pressure around Juliette.

"You need Juliette to balance your power, don't you? You're selfish, Richard."

Richard sneered. "We have no real leadership now. If I don't take care of my power, who will?"

"Eudaiz is a place for everyone. You don't have to overpower the council. The thirty-three-year cycle has come. We will have a new leader."

"No, Ayana. If we can't get stronger, we'll be ruined. I can't let you restrain Juliette."

"She will be the one who ruins us. Every day Ciaran is still on this planet, we're vulnerable. And yet all she can see is her petty resentment."

"But she's a certainty. He's not." Richard pointed at Ciaran. "I'm taking Juliette with me." He approached Juliette.

"You underestimate me, Richard." Ayana turned toward Madeline and waved her arm.

Madeline slumped to the ground and covered her ears. "That jingle, that sound again," she said. It was the same sound she had heard from Mrs. Hanson and the Roman soldiers. It was a sound that made her head feel like it was exploding. And now it was coming from Ayana.

Ciaran grabbed her. He helped to cover her ears, but it didn't seem to help at all. Madeline's nose started to bleed.

Ciaran charged back toward the tornado. "Ayana, tell me what you want and I'll do it."

Ciaran couldn't penetrate the wind wall. He stood there, helpless.

Richard tightened his grip on his sword. Ayana cocked an eyebrow at him in challenge. "Juliette or Madeline. Choose."

"Richard, Madeline is your granddaughter!" Ciaran shouted at Richard.

"You don't know anything, Ciaran."

"Your ally or your granddaughter, Richard?" Ayana said dryly, her face as cold as steel.

Richard turned toward Madeline. "Madeline, I now name you the successor of Sciphil One. Do you accept?"

"Accept what?" Madeline puffed out the question.

Ayana's composure wavered slightly. It was surprise and anger that Ciaran saw on her face. He recalled Ayana telling Juliette before that she could not hurt a successor. It could work. Although they might be jumping out of the frying pan and into the fire, he didn't have any other solution at the moment.

Ciaran staggered back, kneeling next to Madeline. Tadgh cradled her in his arms. She was fading. Blood came out of her nose and trickled from her mouth.

"Madeline, they can't hurt a successor of whatever it was he said. Just accept it. Please," Ciaran said.

"Are you sure her soul is virtuous?" Ayana said.

"I'm sure," Richard said. "She lived on this bloody planet, and she works as a journalist. Her soul is probably like a nun's by this point, which is very unfortunate."

"What the hell does that mean?" Ciaran asked.

"A virtuous soul belongs to someone who has never killed an innocent. If her soul isn't virtuous, succeeding a Sciphil position will only kill her," Ayana said, casting a glance at Madeline, who was on the verge of passing out.

"I need you to stay alive. Please just say yes." Ciaran wiped the blood from her face. His hands shook uncontrollably. He wasn't sure if he shook more because he was weakened or because he feared losing her.

"I can't lose you, Madeline. Accept whatever it is. We will work out the next step," he said.

She closed her eyes.

"No, Madeline, don't leave me. Don't do this to me. Just say yes."

The world was a blur to Ciaran. Blood was everywhere. His blood. Her blood. He didn't know which was which. He grabbed Madeline from Tadgh and held her in his arms. "Please."

Richard repeated, "My granddaughter, I name you as the successor of Sciphil One. Do you accept?"

Ciaran hadn't a shred of strength left in him, but he would fight until he was sure she survived. He held her in his arms and waited.

Then, to his relief, she nodded. "Yes, I accept."

Ayana withdrew the sound wave immediately. She moved close to the wind wall without stepping outside and said dryly, "I hope it's worth it, Ciaran. Remember, the day you accept the responsibility, many lives are in your hands. So choose your actions very carefully." She turned and disappeared as quickly as she had appeared.

"Which position? What am I responsible for?" Ciaran asked, although he knew Ayana was gone and couldn't hear him.

Richard grabbed Juliette, and they both disappeared along with the tornado.

The chilly cemetery returned to its eerie quietness. In front of Madeline, Ciaran, and Tadgh was a scene from a war zone.

Madeline recovered soon after the sound stopped. Ciaran spat out more blood. The surgical wound on his chest continued to bleed. He stood up and staggered back toward the destroyed tomb.

On the platform, Juliette's coffin was open. The inside was empty. He wasn't hallucinating. The body hadn't just blown away in the wind. The interior of the coffin appeared to be completely intact.

Juliette's body had never been inside the coffin.

Ciaran glanced around in shock. What had happened to his world? Then it dawned on him. His mother had opened Mon Ciel's security shield once, an impossible task to do by herself. There were only two people with the access code to the shield—himself and his father.

Ciaran scrambled toward his father's grave, which had also been blown open by Juliette's tornado. His father's coffin was not just empty—it had obviously been without a body inside for twenty years.

He stood completely still for a moment. It seemed as though the ground was shifting under his feet. He turned and left the tomb floor. He stumbled toward Madeline as she ran to him, reaching him just as he passed out cold on the ground.

5

The world gradually came back to Ciaran as he opened his eyes. Ayana's voice still echoed in his head, *"Are you sure her soul is virtuous?"* Ciaran wasn't sure if he had forced Madeline into a dead end. He was a bit afraid of another one of Juliette's scenarios.

Had Madeline killed before? he wondered.

It wasn't just any killing, but the killing of an innocent that he worried about. He couldn't see signs of such violence in her. But if she had killed someone, surely she wouldn't have accepted what Richard had offered.

Ciaran gazed at the ceiling of his bedroom at Mon Ciel for a few minutes to regain his bearings. Suddenly, his view was pleasantly obstructed by the gorgeous green eyes of Jo looking at him.

"Hey, White Knight, you're back!" She grinned and slid her arm underneath his back to help him sit up in his bed. It surprised Ciaran how strong Jo was given her petite physique.

"How's your shoulder, Jo?"

She shifted the shoulder that had been dislocated during the fight at Fountains Abbey and smiled. "See? No need for a sling. Let me get you some water."

She got up to get the water from a jug sitting on the side table.

Ciaran took the glass of water. "Thanks. Where's Madeline?"

"Down at the library, talking things over with Tadgh. Strategies. Important matters. Things that happened at the cemetery."

Ciaran nodded.

"Aren't you thirsty?" Jo pointed at the glass of water that he still held in his hand.

Ciaran laughed. "I know they asked you to drug me when I woke up. But you'll have to be a bit more subtle than that to fool me, Jo."

"Damn it," Jo muttered.

He turned the glass of water around in a circle. "How long have you known Madeline?"

"As long as I can remember. I think we met at school. Why do you ask?"

Ciaran smiled. "You're Madeline's friend. I'd just like to get to know you a bit more."

"You want to know me? Or Madeline?"

Ciaran chuckled. "Both. Do you like Tadgh?"

Jo sat down at his bedside, looked straight into his eyes, and answered without even the slightest squirm, "He's not my type."

Ciaran nodded. *She didn't even sugarcoat it.* Jo intrigued him. Strong-minded. Strong-willed. Just the type that would stupefy his brother. Ciaran shifted his body to get off the bed. Jo stood up, hands on her hips.

"I wasn't able to drug you, but I'm very sure I can knock you out. Lie down, Ciaran."

Ciaran smiled. "I need to get to my computer. It's very important."

"Can't let you. Doctor's orders."

"Or Madeline's?"

"Same thing. She can be pretty scary when she's pissed off."

"All right. Here's the deal. You either let me work on my computer or simply answer my questions. Then I won't need to move."

Jo bit her pouting bottom lip. "As long as the questions aren't too tricky, shoot."

"Does Madeline have a criminal record?"

Jo laughed. "No."

"Does she have any record of committing violence against others?"

"Of course not. Give her a white dress, and she'd turn into Cinderella. Or a nun. Why are you asking? Honestly?"

"What about off the record? I'm asking for your opinion here."

The smile faded from Jo's face. She stared at Ciaran and said nothing.

"I love her. You know that by now. Do you think I'd do anything to harm her?"

Jo shook her head. "I know you wouldn't. But it's not you that I'm worried about. It's Madeline herself."

His blood ran cold, and fear pounded in his head. He was suddenly afraid that his gut instinct had been right, that it couldn't be as easy as making a promise to be a successor of Sciphil One to solve the problem Ayana had presented.

"I don't know. I want to know the answer to that, too," Jo said.

"Why, Jo?"

"Because I want to know if I was responsible for making her do the unthinkable. I can't make her talk. Why don't you try, Ciaran? Ask her what happened in Australia ten years ago."

"You think she might have killed someone?"

"As I said, I don't know what happened. I was there with her. And when I woke up, those people were dead."

"Why do you think you'd be responsible if Madeline killed them?"

He stood up to go to the computer. Jo didn't stop him this time. "Don't bother looking up the records, Ciaran. There's nothing to find. I wiped it. That was the only time I hacked into any system."

He turned around and looked at Jo. There was the gleam of tears in her eyes, but she didn't let any fall.

"I'm sorry about what happened to you, Jo. And I'm sorry I had to ask about it."

Ciaran reached out to embrace her, but she stepped back. She looked him square in the eye. "The man was trying to rape me. He knocked me unconscious. When I came to, it was already over. Everyone was dead, and Madeline was there. So ask her if she killed them because of me. I need to know."

She couldn't hold back any longer, and tears rolled down her face. "Everything was burned to the ground. All Madeline told me was that there had been an accident, and she only had enough time to drag me out. But I know she was lying."

"I'll ask..."

Suddenly the migraine hit him in a tremendous wave. Ciaran grabbed his head and slumped to the floor. A distant voice pierced his mind, stabbing his brain like shards of glass. He'd heard this voice before, but this time it wasn't the usual robotic monotone voice. It was one with an Irish accent.

"We're finally connected, Ciaran," it said. "It's about time you come back to us to fulfill your duty."

"Who are you?" Ciaran asked. The person didn't seem to hear his question. The static noise continued, and the voice kept ranting.

"Thirty-three years I've been waiting, Ciaran. It's time."

The voice was so distorted that Ciaran couldn't make sense of what he was trying to say.

Jo held Ciaran's shoulders. "Ciaran, look at me. Ciaran . . . Take this water . . . Who are you talking to?"

"Speak clearer," said Ciaran. "I can't hear you, goddamnit. What is Sciphil? What does Madeline have to do with any of this?"

"Madeline . . . Madeline . . . she's the key . . ." The voice faded away.

"No, no! Don't go! What's Sciphil?" His vision was blurry. He tried to hang on to the sound of the voice as much as possible, but it seemed to have gone completely away.

"You're bleeding, Ciaran." Jo wiped the blood that trickled from his nose. "Not another Sciphil. I have had enough of this . . ."

Ciaran blinked. "What did you just say, Jo?"

6

*C*iaran punched the call button on the intercom in his office. A short moment later, Tadgh and Madeline appeared at the door. Ciaran looked at Madeline. His views about her had changed. Much more than the woman he loved, in front of him stood a world of secrets that he had to explore.

Madeline cocked an eyebrow at Jo, who was sitting comfortably with a laptop on a reading chair. "I tried to drug him, but he figured it out," Jo said in response to Madeline's look.

Ciaran smiled and gestured to the table and chair in the far corner where they could sit. Tadgh frowned.

"Are you okay to be up and about? I'll call Doctor Thomas, Ciaran."

"You can pull a better threat than that, Tadgh. Coffee anyone?"

"I'll have one, please," Madeline said.

Ciaran went to the coffee machine. "I told Jo about what happened at the cemetery. We need to decipher a few puzzles before we can plan any strategies to deal with the problem at hand. What's a Sciphil, and what does being a successor mean?" Ciaran sat down on the sofa with a tray of coffee for everyone.

He served Madeline her coffee, resting his gaze on her face for a brief moment before continuing. "Jo heard of the term Sciphil way before us."

"A couple of months ago, my friend, Zach, asked me if I knew what a Sciphil was. He never told me where he came across the word. He asked me because he thought it had to do with hologame technology. He's a player, not a designer, and he didn't know the technical aspects of the game. I didn't have an answer for Zach and really didn't think much about it."

"Maybe I should talk to him," Ciaran said.

"I don't think that's necessary. If he knew, he wouldn't have asked Jo," Madeline said.

Ciaran noticed Madeline shift in her chair. She looked uncomfortable with the idea. "I just want to know how he came across the concept. But first things first, we should be safe from Sciphils if we stay inside Mon Ciel. My father designed its shield to protect us," Ciaran said.

"Is that the same shield you used to put Mon Ciel on lockdown before?" Madeline asked.

Ciaran shook his head. "No. That was an emergency lockdown. Mon Ciel's energy lock is permanent. To put it simply, it locks anything carrying extraterrestrial energy out of this place."

Tadgh grabbed his coffee and dropped two sugar cubes in it. When he reached for a third, Ciaran smacked his hand away. Tadgh grumbled some profanity and withdrew. "All Father told me was that if we had any problems, we should just stay inside Mon Ciel." Tadgh sipped his coffee. "Like sheep."

"I've seen Ayana before. I remember her," Ciaran said.

"The woman at the cemetery?" Madeline asked.

Ciaran nodded. "Father and Mother took me outside Mon Ciel's fence to see Ayana and a man. I was only two or thereabouts because Mother had just had Tadgh. The man said something to me that I didn't quite understand. But then he gave me a golden toy and asked if I liked it. I must have said yes and taken the toy because I thought it would look nice dangling on his cot." Ciaran shot a glance at Tadgh.

"Is that what the woman meant by you have agreed to be a bloody successor? If that's the case, it hardly qualifies as a consent," Tadgh exclaimed and snatched a cube of sugar, popping it in his mouth before Ciaran could stop him.

Ciaran shook his head at Tadgh. "Anyway, Father argued with the man, and Mother took me and ran inside. The man and Ayana tried to chase her, but they stopped just before the fence."

"They couldn't get through the shield!" Tadgh said.

Ciaran nodded. "We never talked about the incident again, and I soon forgot about it. I can ask Mother for more information."

Tadgh shook his head. "I just got a voice message saying she's fine. She has something to do and will get back to us when she's done. I tried to return the call, but it didn't work."

Ciaran reached his hand out. "Give me your phone. I'll trace the number."

Tadgh shrugged and gave the cell phone to Ciaran. "It's weird. She's never done this before."

Ciaran looked at the message, entered some codes, and stared at the small screen of the phone. "She didn't use the standard telecommunication technology. These are frequency signals," Ciaran muttered and pulled out his cell phone.

He retrieved the message Sciphil Two had sent to his cell phone last week then entered a string of code into his phone and looked up at everyone. "Sciphil Two used the same type of frequency."

"We talked to Sciphil Two's people in the basement at Mrs. Hanson's place. We might have to go back there to get the equipment," Jo said.

Ciaran nodded. "Yes. We have equipment here, but to get the right communication frequency, we'll have to go back." He stood up.

"Where do you think you're going?" Tadgh asked. "What if Juliette comes back? Can you handle another round of tornado wrestling?"

"Can you handle *one*? Guns won't work on whatever it is out there that's using Juliette's form," Ciaran said.

Tadgh laughed. "You still don't believe that that thing is Juliette?"

Ciaran sat down and leaned back in his chair. "Juliette is clinically dead. And it's not a statement made out of sentiment, Tadgh. What we saw was a collective of energy, a simulated form based on Juliette's psychological and biological profile when she was alive."

"In layman's terms, we call it a spirit. A ghost," Madeline deadpanned and sipped her coffee.

"I know a ghost is not a viable scientific explanation, Ciaran. But a simulated profile in a hologame requires someone to design and control it. Apart from you being one of the very few people on this planet who can do that, to make it happen, the person has to have an intimate knowledge of Juliette's profile. Unless . . ." Jo blinked her big green eyes, expecting Ciaran to understand and complete her sentence.

Ciaran nodded. "Unless Juliette's brain is still alive, and she is creating the profile herself. Given her body is not where it is supposed to be, I'd say it's a plausible explanation, Jo."

Tadgh sneered. "I'd buy Madeline's ghost's theory before that!" He shook his head. "Regardless, I'll go to Mrs. Hanson's place to get the machine for you. Whatever Juliette is, she wants you, not me. And you stay here, too, Madeline. Richard wants you, and until we figure all this out, leaving Mon Ciel isn't a good idea."

Ciaran arched an eyebrow and chuckled to himself as he watched his brother take charge.

Jo stood up. "Let's go," she said. "You don't know how to pack up a computer system properly—apart from pulling the plugs and stuffing the pieces into boxes. If the equipment is damaged, there's no way we can communicate with the person or being that we need to talk to."

Ciaran chuckled. Tadgh shrugged and turned on his heel. Madeline grabbed Jo's shoulder. "Be careful, Jo."

"Don't worry, Madeline. I'm more capable than you think." Jo smiled and followed Tadgh out.

When Tadgh and Jo had left, Madeline started to follow, but Ciaran grabbed her elbow, pulling her into his arms.

"They know their way out." He smiled.

"Do they?" Madeline played with Ciaran's hair. "How's the pain?"

"Fine." He kissed the dimple on her left cheek. Then he moved to her lips. She didn't let the kiss go deeper.

"Let me." Madeline unbuttoned the top of his shirt and examined the bandage that Doctor Thomas had secured to Ciaran's chest. Satisfied that the wound was not bleeding, she redid the buttons. Then she checked the big gash on his arm and the swollen tattoo of the golden crucifix.

"From this angle, the crucifix looks like a key," Madeline said.

"From my angle, it looks like a cocktail spoon." Ciaran grabbed her chin, lifting it up. "Why are you avoiding looking at me?"

"I'm not." She turned toward the window.

Ciaran turned her face back to him. There were tears in her eyes. He kissed her big brown eyes. "Ayana mentioned the consequence of not having a virtuous soul when accepting the successor role with your grandfather. I'm not questioning you. But I'm asking you to tell me honestly whether or not I should let you go through with the promise."

She eased away from his hold. "It's *my* promise . . ."

"No, it's *our* promise. You're an important part of my life now. You know all about me, so you don't get to reveal only some information to me and withhold the rest. Why were you uncomfortable when Jo mentioned Zach? What happened in Australia ten years ago, Madeline?"

Tears gleamed in her eyes now. "I need time to think about this."

He wiped the tears and kissed her. "An hour. I can't bear any longer than that. I need to know."

A loud bang echoed through the house. It didn't shake the building, but they could feel the vibrations in the air. Ciaran darted to the window. From the sky, beams of light struck Mon Ciel but disintegrated and vanished into thin air.

"Whoever that is couldn't penetrate the shield," Ciaran muttered.

Amid the disintegrated beams of light, a gigantic image of Juliette appeared, glowing in a white and blue halo. She smiled at Ciaran. A flash of amusement crossed her face. She hit Mon Ciel again with the light beams then turned on her heel and moved away because her beams were unable to damage the premises.

"Tadgh!" Ciaran said and rushed toward the coffee table to grab his cell phone. He called Tadgh and heard only the endless sound of static from the other end of the line.

7

"*A*ll right, just to be clear, I'll talk to the cops. If things get complicated, we walk. Okay?" said Tadgh. He parked a block away from Mrs. Hanson's house. They had driven past earlier and could see police vehicles, flashing lights, and a crowd of people flooding that end of the street. He wagered walking right through the police's front line wouldn't be a good idea.

Jo rolled her eyes and stomped forward. Tadgh looked at her fragile figure on heels. "How do you walk on those sticks?"

Jo whirled around. "They're called high heels—a girl's most precious and lethal weapon. Don't you make me use them on you. They might cause some permanent damage to your reproductive ability."

Tadgh shook his head and escorted her as they approached the house.

Mrs. Hanson's house had been sealed off again. Police were everywhere, carrying out boxes of evidence. Among the boxes, Tadgh and Jo recognized the equipment from the basement they needed.

Tadgh wrapped his arm around Jo's shoulders and approached the officer standing at the barricades.

"Hi, officer. What's going on here?" Tadgh shot a concerned look at the unfriendly officer.

"This is a crime scene. Civilians shouldn't be here."

"This is Jo's grandmother's house. She's visiting from the US. Surely you can tell us what's going on. She's quite worried."

The officer glanced at Jo. "Who's your grandmother?"

"Mrs. Hanson."

"Can I see your ID please, ma'am?"

"Sure."

Jo reached for her purse. "Damn it. All my documentation is in the travel packet. I left it at the hotel. Look, officer, I just landed. I want to see my grandmother. Can you please tell me what's going on here?"

"We can go back to the hotel and get the papers for you," said Tadgh. "But can you at least tell her what happened? Is Mrs. Hanson okay?"

Jo squeezed out a fake tear.

Seeing Jo's tear, the officer shifted his stance and cleared his throat. "Ma'am, I can't tell you much because I don't know who you are. But I'm sorry to say that it's not good news regarding Mrs. Hanson."

Jo manufactured some more tears and looked as if she was about to make a fuss. "What do you mean? I want to go inside. I want to see her."

"Ma'am, if you wait here, I'll go and get the captain for you . . ."

The police carried a couple of body bags from the house.

"Oh my God." Jo pointed. "Is that her, in a body bag? Why are there two? She lived here by herself."

Jo pushed at the barricades. Tadgh helped. "What the hell is going on here?" Tadgh said.

"Stay back, stay back. Don't cause me any trouble, ma'am. Mrs. Hanson died a few weeks ago. That isn't her body."

"What? Died? So whose bodies are those? My other relatives?" Jo kept pushing.

"Ma'am, stay still. Ma'am. We're busy here. There are forty

bodies in there. If you claim they're your relatives, I'll go and get the captain." The officer was beginning to get angry.

Jo nodded. "Please. I'll stay here."

As soon as the officer disappeared inside the house, Tadgh and Jo ran, vanishing into the dark.

"Someone must have shifted all the soldiers' bodies from Fountains Abbey to here," Tadgh said while they were running. Jo stumbled on a tree branch. Tadgh snatched her up and carried her in his arms.

"Let go of me. I can run on my own."

"The evidence points to the contrary," Tadgh muttered and kept going. He got to the car and deposited Jo in the passenger seat. She slapped his shoulder when he got into the driver's seat.

Tadgh reached over and pinned Jo's arms down. His face hovered right next to hers. "I said, let *me* handle the talking. What exactly didn't you understand about that? What if the cops got you? What would I do then?" he growled.

"I didn't do anything wrong to be afraid of the cops."

"You might not have. But our family is not exactly cop friendly. So when you're with us, keep that in mind."

"I'm not *with* you . . . nobody tells me what to do . . ."

Then he kissed her. It seemed to be the only way to stop her from talking. Or maybe he just wanted to do it. Whatever the reason, he did it.

Tadgh eased off. "I expected a slap in the face," he said.

Jo rolled her eyes. "I'm sure it's illegal to resort to such violence for a pathetic kiss."

"Pathetic? I risked my skin doing that, and all I've got is—"

Jo hopped up and kissed him.

A wave of passionate energy washed over him. Tadgh considered himself to be experienced, but the energy coming from Jo was irresistible. Every bone and muscle in his body seemed to liquefy.

Jo finished the kiss and sat back in her seat.

"How's that? If you're going to risk your skin doing something like that, you should do it properly," she said and buckled her seatbelt.

"I'll try better next time," Tadgh muttered and started the car.

AS TADGH DROVE OUT, lightning slashed across the sky, and thunder rumbled around them. A wind came up suddenly, crashing through the trees on the street and shaking loose the shingles on a few of the small cottage roofs along the road. The funnel of spinning air was headed straight toward Mrs. Hanson's house.

"This is not a normal storm. It's Juliette," Tadgh said. "In other words, we're fucked." He accelerated, forgetting all about his speed phobia.

They hadn't gone far before the car hit something and spun around. The car rolled, smashed into a tree trunk, and stopped. All of the interior airbags went off. One headlight still beamed out into the misted air. Tadgh unfastened his seatbelt and reached over to Jo. "Are you okay?"

"Yep." Jo wriggled her way out from behind the airbag, and they both climbed out of the car.

It was a dark night. No stars. No moon. No street lights.

Jo grabbed Tadgh's hand. "Run!"

"We can't. It's too late. Juliette is here already!"

8
---

a body thudded into the mud right behind them, splashing rain water onto the wet grass. Tadgh and Jo turned around to see Stefan's dead body on the ground.

A beam of light appeared, and the holographic image of Juliette swung back and forth as if not sure whether to fly away or stay.

"He's unfixable," Juliette growled, looking at Stefan's dead body.

"Apparently!" Tadgh stepped in front of Jo. "What do you want?"

The hologram turned toward Tadgh. "I want your brother of course!"

"And you think you can capture me and lure Ciaran out here? You and your dead brother were scamming Ciaran for years. Did that get you anything?"

Juliette swung her arm up. Tadgh's body lifted, spun around, and was flung down to the ground.

Tadgh grunted with pain and stood up. "Overreacting a little, don't you think?"

Juliette's face had lost all of what Ciaran had once loved. In front of Tadgh was a demon to the core. Tadgh didn't know what had caused this change. He wasn't sure whether the real Juliette was still alive or not. Her body wasn't in her coffin. He had no idea what to make of this situation. But what he did know was that the demon standing in front of him wanted Ciaran, and it would kill to get what it wanted.

This was no ghost. The thing standing in front of Tadgh was real. It wasn't solid because it was a hologram. But it certainly was no spirit seeking revenge.

"You." Juliette pointed at Jo. "Go back and tell Ciaran to come and claim his brother."

"I . . . I don't drive . . . I'm sorry. And besides, you trashed the car."

That was such a lie, Tadgh thought.

"Want to fly?" The air around Juliette started to stir as she spoke.

"Oh, no, no!" Tadgh waved Juliette off. There was no way Jo's fragile body could survive the impact that Ciaran had suffered this morning. "You'll kill her. A dead messenger is no good to you."

Tadgh didn't know what to do, but he was willing to try anything. He pulled out his phone. "I could call him. But, unfortunately, you and your weird energy kills all the phone signals."

Juliette smiled. "All right. I can keep my distance," she said and stepped back.

Tadgh dialed. "Yep . . . sure . . . yes . . . cemetery? What?" Tadgh looked around. "Yeah, the cemetery. The second one of the day. Yep, that's where I am."

Juliette raised an eyebrow in question.

Tadgh shrugged. "What? Phones these days have Bluetooth signals and map tracking. You think I need to shout out the exact address?"

"Stay here and run when you can, okay?" Tadgh mumbled to Jo.

"I'm not going to leave you."

"I don't want to have to protect you. Go when I say so."

Tadgh approached Juliette. "I saw your coffin this morning. There was no body in it. What happened to you?"

Juliette snorted. "When will Ciaran be here?"

"Half an hour. He's not flying . . . He chose to drive."

Juliette smirked. "You like her?" She nodded toward Jo.

"She's all right. She obviously doesn't compare to you, Juliette."

Juliette laughed. "Sorry, darling. I love one man, and one man only. And that's your brother. I think you're a good man, Tadgh." Juliette glanced at Jo. "You're lucky. He likes you."

"He's not exactly my type," said Jo.

"Look, there's no point keeping her here. Let her go," Tadgh said.

Juliette shrugged. "All right. Sure. But you're waiting here with me, Tadgh."

"No, I'll stay," Jo stated firmly.

"Well now." Juliette cast a warm look at Jo. "You *do* like him."

"I'd do that for any friend. I have faith in people. I don't scam and cheat those I care for."

Juliette's face turned red.

"Oh, no. Let's calm down, ladies," Tadgh suggested.

He reached out his hand to grab Juliette and felt a jolt of energy. A substance. Tadgh got closer to Juliette. He looked into her eyes. Juliette looked up at him. Tadgh knew he had a few of the same characteristics as Ciaran. He stepped closer. So close it was almost intimate. He reached his hand up.

"May I?"

Juliette looked as if she had tears in her eyes.

Tadgh touched her face. There was something there. Not flesh. But energy. It felt solid.

"What does my brother have that I don't?"

Juliette looked at Tadgh as if she wanted to devour his face. "Not much. You have everything Ciaran has. He just happened to come first."

Tadgh smiled. He gently slid his hand toward the back of her neck. He could feel her tremble. Tadgh touched his lips to hers. There was a feeling of contact. He deepened the kiss. He could feel her body pressed against him. Tadgh caressed Juliette, moving his hand down her back and to her hip. Then as quick as lightning, he pulled the dagger from her side. His right arm still holding her tight, Tadgh stabbed Juliette with his left. He pulled the dagger out and stabbed again for good measure.

Juliette staggered back, hissing in anger and pain. The thick smell of burning electrical current filled the air. Something sparked underneath her skin.

Tadgh yelled at Jo, "Run!"

Instead of running away, Jo rushed toward Tadgh. She grabbed a tree branch and whacked at Juliette.

The holographic figure was distorted severely as the branch went through it. It hissed and screamed.

Tadgh stabbed again. This time, he aimed at Juliette's heart.

Her holographic figure suddenly stood straight. It poked its chest out to take the dagger. Then it laughed. It grabbed Tadgh's hand twisted his arm, and flung him away.

Tadgh hit a tree and fell to the ground. He moaned and stood up, leaning against the tree. Jo darted toward him. She picked up another tree branch and stood in front of Tadgh protectively while Juliette approached them.

"I told you to run," Tadgh said.

"Shut up."

"I don't need your protection."

"Sorry to tread so heavily on your manhood. But you're going to have to let us girls fight it out."

Jo wouldn't stand a chance with Juliette one-on-one, Tadgh thought.

Juliette approached slowly, like a leopard playing with its dying prey.

"Run, please. I'll keep her here," Tadgh said.

"You can't be a hero. And you can certainly choose not be an idiot."

Juliette raised her arm. Tadgh had no idea what was coming, but he knew it was going to be bad. Tadgh and Jo felt the air pressure coming from Juliette. There would be an explosion. They would be dead very soon.

Juliette smirked and was about to swing her arm.

Tadgh grabbed Jo from behind. He turned her around and kissed her. Long and deep. He had to match what she had done before. A man had his pride, after all. If they were going to die, this was something he had to do.

Something exploded behind them. But they didn't feel anything. Surprised and confused, Tadgh and Jo opened their eyes.

In front of them stood a man in his late sixties with a sword in his hand. The sword blade glowed bright orange. Juliette grabbed her right shoulder, which was dripping with blood.

"You grew strong fast, Sciphil Nine."

"You have three seconds to disappear," the man said dryly.

Juliette cast a last hateful look at Tadgh and whirled away, disappearing into the darkness.

Tadgh stood still, bracing himself with one hand on the tree trunk, measuring the man with his eyes as he approached them. He was as tall as Tadgh. His salt and peppered hair was slightly long and tied back, revealing kind eyes. He looked Tadgh up and down.

"You're a strong man, Tadgh. You'd make a good warrior. Is your brother as strong as you are?"

"Stronger. Are you stronger than Juliette? Tell us how we can fight her."

The man laughed. "The LeBlanc boys live up to their reputation."

The old man turned around and walked away so fast that Tadgh didn't have time to ask another question. Unlike Juliette, who had simply disappeared, this man walked away at an impossible speed.

Standing in the quietness of the night, Jo asked, "You didn't call Ciaran, did you?"

"No. I was just pretending . . ."

"So what's that then?" Jo asked and pointed toward car headlights flashing in their direction.

9

*M*adeline followed Ciaran as he bolted to the fence line of Mon Ciel as soon as security cleared Lindsay's car.

She was anxious about Jo and Tadgh, but her psychic mind was telling her they were unharmed. Ciaran had no psychic ability. Regardless of what she had told him, the short hour had dragged like a torturous decade for him. He was worried sick about what might have happened to Tadgh and Jo.

Madeline yanked the car door open on Jo's side. Jo hopped out.

"I'm all right," she said and rushed to Tadgh's side. Tadgh pushed the door open. "I can get out of the car myself, lady!" he muttered and wobbled out.

"What's the problem, Tadgh?" Ciaran asked.

"Nothing," Tadgh snapped.

"He twisted his ankle," Jo said.

"I landed wrong. That's all. And I can certainly speak for myself," he grumbled.

"I appreciate this, Lindsay," Ciaran said when his assistant stepped out of the car.

Madeline knew Lindsay was more than Ciaran's right-hand

man. They were friends. After losing Robert, it had taken a lot out of Ciaran to call Lindsay to handle this task. From the corner of her eye, Madeline saw a blue dot just outside the fence. It hovered there, trying to catch her attention.

She was sure it wasn't Juliette. Juliette's blue dots would be inside Mon Ciel because she knew better than anyone that the shield didn't work against thoughts and humans, only against extraterrestrial energy. Whoever waited out there wanting to talk to her might never have entered Mon Ciel before.

She glanced back just before entering the house and saw the blue dot had grown larger. She could hear a clear voice now. "This is Ayana, Madeline. If you want to know exactly what you and Ciaran have gotten yourselves into, come outside Mon Ciel, and we'll talk."

Madeline wanted to respond, but she didn't know how. She could trace thoughts and could see them, but she had never interacted with them before. Speaking out loud wasn't a good idea—that much she knew.

She closed her eyes. Concentrated. She willed her response into her mind and sent her stream of thought toward Ayana. "You want me to go out there so you can beat the hell out of me again?"

"I withdrew my attack on you as soon as you'd given your consent to the Sciphil One successor position. No harm from me will ever come to you again."

Madeline smiled to herself. Her communication channel with these extraterrestrial people actually worked. *Wish I'd known this before and saved Tadgh and Jo the trip*, she thought privately. "What about others like Juliette? Will they respect the rules as you do?"

"I can't speak for others. I have a vested interest in Ciaran staying alive. I think you do, too. Come alone, and we will sort this out."

"Why can't you tell Ciaran directly?"

"I sealed his Sciphil successor position at the cemetery. That connected him directly to our communication network. Any message to him at my level will be recorded. Your psychic ability is unique, but I'm not sure how long it will be before it is intercepted. We need to speak face-to-face if you care for him. I promise you my protection."

"Damn it. Okay. I'll see what I can do."

"Do what?" Ciaran asked.

She opened her eyes and realized she had spoken the last sentence out loud. "Find a different way to talk to those Sciphils," she said.

She smiled at him. She tucked a strand of stray hair on his face back and looked into his intense gray eyes that had lost some of their shine due to fatigue. Still, he was too beautiful for her to stare at for a long time without losing her control and telling him whatever was on her mind. She reached up and kissed him.

"I told you Tadgh and Jo would be fine."

"You were right. Let's get inside before you catch a cold." He wrapped his arm around her shoulder to take her inside the house.

The warmth of his body and the virility in his aura made her want to curl up in his arms and live there for the next millennium. She wished she could forget the conversation she'd just had with Ayana.

Jo was waiting for them in the hallway. She gave Ciaran a small electronic pad. "I made this. It's a portable game console for beginners. Could you give it to Tadgh? With his wrecked ankle, I think he has to lie still for a while. I don't want his brains to turn to mush from boredom."

"I'll fix his ankle now, and he will be chasing you around in an hour. But the game console is a nice idea. Why don't you give it to him yourself?"

"We don't talk anymore. He's like a petulant child."

Ciaran took the game from Jo. "All right."

Madeline could see a flash of intrigue in Ciaran's eyes. *He very much approves of Jo and Tadgh together.* "Can I have a word with you, Jo?" she asked.

"Sure."

"I'll fix Tadgh up now. And I'm still going to make him play this game." Ciaran smiled and strode away.

Madeline waited until Ciaran disappeared around the corner of the seemingly endless marble corridor. She turned to Jo and found her friend observing her with questions in her cat green eyes. Her long black hair cascaded down the sides of her foxy face. She was focused on Madeline.

"Secret talk?" Jo asked.

"What a trip! I just want to calm you down."

Jo snorted. "You think I'm in need of your soothing therapy?"

Madeline shook her head. "Maybe not. Maybe it's just an excuse for some quiet time."

Jo laughed. "That's better."

"You like Tadgh, Jo."

Jo shrugged. "Perhaps. It's weird, though, because he's not my usual type."

Madeline nodded. "Zach is more your type."

Jo giggled. "He's every girl's type, except yours."

Madeline glanced at the door. Through its small glass panel, she could see the blue dot still hovering outside Mon Ciel. "Next time you talk to Zach, could you tell him that what happened in Australia wasn't his fault?"

Jo narrowed her eyes.

"Don't ask, Jo. Please. Just for once."

"For once? You've never told *me* what happened. I didn't even know that Zach had been feeling guilty. People died in that house, Madeline. And I wiped all records of our involvement. Don't you think I'm entitled to know what happened?"

"I told you it was an accident. The house caught on fire."

"Accident how?" Jo waved her arms in frustration.

"We fought in the kitchen. Larry fell onto a knife, and the house caught on fire. I told you."

"That's lame, Madeline. You're telling me that Larry and his entire family fell onto knives? That wouldn't even make a believable black comedy. I was stupid enough to wipe the record, so I effectively gagged myself. But come on!" Jo stomped around the corridor.

"Look, Jo, I'll tell you more—but later. All I need you to promise me is that you'll tell Zach what I asked you to. I don't want him to live his whole life in doubt. I wasn't sure before. But I'm sure now. It wasn't his fault."

"Why can't you tell him yourself? What are you trying to do, Madeline?"

"All right. I'll tell him myself. Maybe tomorrow. But I want to tell Ciaran first."

Jo nodded. "And when will you tell me the truth?"

"Tomorrow," she stated as firmly as possible.

"I'll hold you to that," Jo said and turned on her heel.

Madeline peeked through the glass panel of the door once more and could see the blue dot looming as large as her pilates ball. She turned and headed down the hall toward Ciaran's room.

10

———

*S*he found Ciaran in the bedroom looking out the window. She was one hundred percent sure he couldn't see Ayana's blue dot the way she did. She approached him from behind, embraced him, and took the empty glass from his hand.

"Scotch isn't exactly the prescribed medication Doctor Thomas ordered."

Ciaran turned around. He touched the dimple on her left cheek with his thumb. Then he kissed her. She kissed him back.

Outside Mon Ciel, the blue dot now was as enormous as a hot air balloon, glowing a white and blue light. She stared at it.

"What is that?" Ciaran asked and turned to look outside. Then he turned back in, looking at her. "I saw a blue reflection in your eyes. Have you been seeing those blue dots again?"

"What? Oh. No, no." She waved her arm dismissively and moved toward the bed. "You need to take your meds." She grinned and sat down.

"I'm not a sick old man. I don't need drugs."

"Well, I have some activities in mind that I think you might be interested in. But if you don't take your meds, then I could exacerbate your injuries and hurt you even more." She kicked her shoes off and lay back on the two big pillows on the bed. "These activities could be very physically demanding."

Ciaran winked. "Ah, now that's worth consideration."

She smiled and pulled her blouse off in one swift move.

Ciaran strode to the bed as quick as a cat. She swore she heard him purr. "All right, then. Drug me," he said and climbed onto the bed to kiss her. She put her finger on his lips to stop him.

"You know where the meds are," Madeline said.

"I can take them afterward."

She shook her head. "That's not part of the deal."

Ciaran mumbled some words of disagreement, dismounted the bed, and walked toward the cabinet to get the antibiotics and painkillers Doctor Thomas had given him the previous morning. Madeline fetched a glass of water.

Ciaran took the pills and winced. "Now I want serious compensation."

Madeline laughed. "Don't you dare tell me you hate taking medicine! Pharmaceuticals are your bread and butter."

"Medicine is fine when I don't need to take it myself." Ciaran winced again. "I have to tell the lab to make these pills taste better."

Ciaran put the water aside and pulled Madeline into his arms. "Now, how do you plan to reward me?"

Madeline smiled. She pushed at his chest, backing him up toward the bed. He lifted her, and before she knew it, she was lying on her back on the bed. Her pants were on the floor, Ciaran's face was buried between her breasts, and his hands were very busy elsewhere on her body.

Suddenly he slowed down considerably and flopped down, lying on top of her. For the first time, she resented the quality of the LeBlanc's drugs and wished Doctor Thomas had given Ciaran a lighter dose. She gingerly pushed him aside. His voice slurred as he asked, "What's in those meds?"

She turned him so he lay on his back and pulled the blanket up over his chest. She kissed his cheek. "The sedative was in the water. Sleep tight, darling. I love you."

He grabbed her hand. "Don't go," he said. Then his face went totally lax, and he let go of her hand.

She kissed him again, put on her clothes, and grabbed the car keys.

~

MADELINE PARKED the car outside the fence of Mon Ciel and remained in the driver's seat. If things went awry, she would be able to drive straight back inside. Assuring herself that it was a well-planned and justified action, she left the car keys in the ignition and rolled down the window.

Madeline stepped outside the car and waited. Nothing. Maybe this was too close to Mon Ciel. She got into the car and drove slowly down to the creek.

There it was. She could feel it in every cell of her body. The tingle. The energy. Something was coming. Madeline stopped the car and got out.

The air around her thickened. A blue spark zapped through the air, and Ayana appeared. Madeline stepped out of the car and glanced around, staying as close to the car as possible. "First things first . . . what's a Sciphil?"

"You're Richard's successor. It's not my place to give you the induction. He has to train you properly, or you might not pass the Daimon Gate."

"What will happen if I can't get past it?"

"You'll die."

"Can I at least get a dictionary definition of Sciphil?"

"It stands for Scientist Philosopher."

Madeline laughed. "I wouldn't consider myself qualified for either of those positions. Why did Grandfather choose me? Was it because you forced him?"

"If you are not worthy, if your soul is not virtuous, then choosing you is equivalent to giving you a death sentence. Richard has been searching for you for a long time. He has confidence in you. Are you afraid?"

"Does that matter?"

"Yes. Yours was only a promise. You can still deny it if you're not ready. But I have sealed Ciaran's successor position. He can't back out now."

"What the hell does that mean? Does he have to go through the virtuous soul deal like I do?"

"Yes, but it was valid up until the point he gave his consent. And he did that when he was about two years old, Earth time. I think it's a safe bet Bran asked him."

"Who's Bran?"

"The Sciphil that Ciaran is the successor of. I called you out here because Bran's Sciphil position is the most important one and, because of that, many people will want Ciaran dead before he can become a proper Sciphil. To become a Sciphil, he has to pass the Daimon Gate tests, and without training, he has a minimal chance of surviving."

"What if he doesn't follow through with the promise?"

"I told you, his position is sealed." She raised her palm. "The seal has given him more physical strength. But it has also marked his biological profile. If he stays on Earth, he'll die."

"And if he can't pass the Daimon Gate, he'll die, too. Am I right?" Madeline put her hands on her hips.

Ayana nodded.

"So if I want to go with Ciaran through the Daimon Gate, I have to be pretty sure my soul is virtuous. If not, I'll die. If I'm unsure, I can withdraw my promise and live my life on Earth without Ciaran."

Ayana nodded again.

"Do you realize the stupid mess you've just put us in? Who are you, really?"

"My name is Ayana Dee. I am a Sciphil..."

"It really doesn't help knowing your name and where you come from. The truth of the matter is..." Madeline waved her arms in the air. *Should she even bother elaborating to this alien who doesn't even have a human brain?*

"I want to talk to my grandfather."

"He is too weak to come to you at the moment."

"What?"

"Juliette hurt him. She's changed in the last few weeks. She's no longer conforming to our rules. Richard has lost a lot of energy. He'll recharge, but it will take time."

"That means Juliette is out here? Right now?"

"Maybe."

"Jesus Christ!"

"Who?"

"Don't worry about it. I have to get back inside Mon Ciel right now."

Thunder exploded right next to Madeline, knocking her to the ground.

Juliette turned around, smiling at the hologram of Ayana. "Too late, it seems."

Madeline stood up and felt waves of energy pulsing from Juliette, who was standing several feet away. She could feel the vibrations through her entire body. She understood what Tadgh had said—Juliette was not *just* a hologram.

Juliette glanced at Madeline. The air around Juliette started to stir. "Who will protect you now? Let these stupid Sciphils come. I'll crush all of you at once," Juliette said as she strode toward Madeline.

11

𝓜adeline ran to her car while Juliette laughed maniacally. She jumped into the car and turned the ignition, starting the car. Juliette stirred the air. It spun around in the same way it had at the cemetery. Madeline backed the car out.

"Coward!" Juliette laughed. Madeline floored the gas pedal and drove the car straight at Juliette. The wind wall had not yet built up strong enough to protect Juliette.

Madeline felt the hit. Juliette's body was pushed backward, rolling on the ground, distorted. Madeline backed the car up and charged again. The second hit almost ripped Juliette in half.

The distorted Juliette stood up, angry. She roared and tried to put her body back together.

Juliette created the wind circle again.

Madeline accelerated once more.

Juliette took a stance and swung her arm. The car lifted up and spun around as if made of paper. There was no wind circle this time. It was a direct hit with the air pressure coming forth from Juliette's arms.

Without her seatbelt on, Madeline rolled around inside the car like a rag doll. She had the sickening feeling that she had broken

her neck and her limbs had fallen off and were scattered somewhere in the car.

The car slammed down next to the creek.

It was the creek where she had almost drowned with Stefan.
Madeline heard the water running fast. She climbed out of the
destroyed car.

Juliette stood on a small hill, a smirk on her face. She swung her
arms again.

Madeline found herself spun up into the air, then thrown down
and submersed in the cold water. The pressure kept Madeline
under the water.

From beneath the flowing creek, Madeline could see the light. It
was the sort of light people who were dying would see. It was like
being tied down in a cave in the dark, and looking up and seeing a
faint spot of light, a spot of life, but knowing she would never get to
it. The light became dimmer. And dimmer. And then it was
completely black.

All of a sudden, the pressure lifted.

A basic survival instinct told Madeline to push up. She gasped
for air at the surface and coughed up a mouthful of water. She got
herself to the bank of the creek and slowly staggered to dry land.

On the hill in front of her, Richard and Ayana were fighting Juliette. Although there were two of them against one, it did not look as
if they were winning.

Richard took a hit and fell. Ayana stopped Juliette from using
that advantage to kill Richard, taking a hit herself.

She could run back to Mon Ciel like a coward right now, Madeline thought.

Hell!

Madeline dragged herself up the hill to where her grandfather
and Ayana were fighting Juliette.

She approached the light circle, but she hit an invisible wall—
the same kind of wall that had locked her out in the hologame
when Ciaran was fighting with Juliette.

She couldn't penetrate it. She grabbed a fallen tree branch and hit it, but the branch bounced back, further numbing her already numb arms, body, and mind. She stood hopeless and helpless, watching her grandfather and Ayana being beaten mercilessly by Juliette.

The shadow of someone walked past her.

It might not have been a shadow, but a person walking at an incredible speed.

A man penetrated the invisible wall and charged at Juliette with a burning orange sword.

This was not a typical sword fight. They were testing the strength of their energy. The swords were just outlets. Each swing of the swords created a wave of wind and electrical currents. Juliette stumbled and staggered when the man with the orange sword attacked her. But she regained her position quickly.

She advanced and slashed at the man with the orange sword. His blood dripped on the ground. It looked like she was too powerful for him.

Judging by the wind that blew around their faces, the force of the foreign objects that flew around them, and the damage caused by each blow of the swords, Madeline knew there had to be an incredible amount of energy being exchanged within the world surrounded by the invisible wall.

"Please don't, Juliette. You don't have to kill everyone," Ayana said.

Juliette turned to Ayana and snarled, " He attacked me first. He deserves to die. All of you do. All of those who are against me deserve to die."

Juliette walked toward Ayana. "Especially you."

Madeline was so sure that Juliette would kill Ayana this time. But the man with the orange sword pulled out a dagger and lunged at Juliette.

Juliette whirled around with incredible speed. Her claws were out, ready for a sure kill. She could already taste the blood of her prey.

A ray of the morning's first sunlight ran across the ground. It was the most beautiful sunlight Madeline had ever seen.

In her rage, Juliette had neglected to notice the approaching rays. The light brushed against her holographic figure and sent her into flames. She hissed in pain and vanished quickly into thin air.

"Saved by the sunlight! How cinematic!" Madeline mumbled.

Although wounded, Ayana's composure did not waver. She glanced at Madeline. "Attacking Juliette head on! You're a brave woman, Madeline. The sunlight weakens Juliette, but it won't kill her. Wind is her strength, and sunlight is her weakness."

Madeline wanted to ask what would kill Juliette. But the world around her started to fade.

Richard managed to stand up.

Ayana glanced at the man with the orange sword. "What took you so long to get here?"

"You sent me to rescue four subjects on two different continents, Ayana. I am on Earth. I have to take some of their physical rules into account."

Ayana cast a warm look at him. "Thank you. I know we can rely on you. How was the subject in Australia?"

"He's strong. He actually saved himself. Good choice of a successor, Ayana."

Ayana's face brightened with a gracious smile. "Thank you Sciphil Nine. You will have a good one yourself one day."

Sciphil Nine nodded and smiled.

Richard approached Madeline. She felt as if her body had transcended beyond suffering. She was numb and not at all sure she was still conscious. Yet she must be because she could hear them talking. But Richard said something, and she had no idea what he meant by it.

She was drunk with her pain.

Sciphil Nine walked through the invisible wall again. Ayana smiled at him from the other side.

He approached Madeline. "I'll take you back to Mon Ciel."

"I owe you one, Sciphil Nine. I know Zach isn't an easy character to work with. If there is anything you need from me in the future, you need only ask," Ayana told him from inside the light circle.

Sciphil Nine looked at Ayana. "You're wrong, Ayana. Zach Flynn is not only easy to work with—he could make quite a spectacular Sciphil. I'm jealous, to be honest."

"Who did you say is her successor?" Madeline asked.

"Zach Flynn from Australia. Do you know him?"

Madeline gave Sciphil Nine a blank look and then fainted into his arms.

12

The sun rose high over the hill, casting a warm glow over the rolling hills and meadows. It was one of those rare days in the English winter where the sky was blue and clear.

Unfortunately, the stunning weather did nothing to soothe Ciaran's mood as he walked down the long drive, approaching a tall man standing in front of Mon Ciel's gate. The man carried Madeline in his arms.

In the darkest corner of Ciaran's mind, he wanted what his father had warned him against for so many years: destruction.

He thirsted for blood.

His need to destroy was as tenacious as his passion to create. Throughout his whole life, he had strived to maintain a balance between destruction and creation. That balance was off kilter now, tilted toward the negative.

He knew Tadgh and Jo trailed behind him despite the fact he had asked them to stay in the house. Tadgh would never let him go outside Mon Ciel by himself, and Jo had been worried sick about Madeline since early in the morning.

Ciaran adjusted his coat quickly, checking to see that his gun was still in place. It was.

Based on the proximity of the gate and the man's location, Ciaran speculated that he was one of those Sciphils who could not penetrate Mon Ciel's protective shield. The man appeared tall and strong. He carried Madeline as if she was a sleeping doll.

Ciaran was sure she was injured. But if so, the damage had been done. Sheer willpower could play no role in fixing this. She had fooled him—and fooled herself—in order to go out there, and that had caused her harm.

As they got closer, Tadgh said, "I recognize him. He helped us when Juliette attacked us at Mrs. Hanson's. I think he's friendly, Ciaran," Tadgh said.

Ciaran didn't respond. He trusted no one. Especially now.

"Stay here," Ciaran brusquely directed as he approached the edge of the gate. Jo and Tadgh followed. Ciaran turned around.

"Stay here." His repeat was more like a growl.

Tadgh and Jo stayed back.

Ciaran sauntered past the gate of Mon Ciel.

The man observed Ciaran's every move. "You're confident, Ciaran."

"And you are?"

"I'm Pete Chandler, Sciphil Nine of Eudaiz."

Ciaran nodded. "Mr. Chandler, I'd like Madeline to be taken inside. I understand you cannot come inside Mon Ciel. I'll stay out here and discuss whatever you want."

Sciphil Nine laughed. "You're a businessman, or so I was told. On top of all the other qualities that set you up as a great ruler."

"I'm not a ruler of any kind. Madeline needs to be tended to. Please let my brother take her inside. Then we can talk."

Sciphil Nine nodded.

Trusting, Ciaran thought. He could easily take Madeline inside and break his promise to this man. Ciaran approached Sciphil Nine. The energy coming from Pete Chandler was very different from the kind that had emanated from Ayana. By Ciaran's gauge, Pete Chandler was human, with a body made of flesh and blood.

That meant Ciaran could put a bullet through the body and end all negotiations.

Ciaran took Madeline gently from Sciphil Nine and walked back inside Mon Ciel to where Tadgh and Jo were waiting.

"Doctor Thomas," Ciaran said.

"Already called," Tadgh responded.

A helicopter arrived, hovered in the air, and touched down on the helicopter landing pad in the adjacent garden. Doctor Thomas climbed out and made a beeline toward Tadgh.

After a quick visual examination, he said, "Let's get her inside."

"Thank you for coming quickly, Doctor," Ciaran said.

Tadgh and Jo scurried toward the house.

"You're not coming?"

Ciaran nodded toward the gate. "Soon. But I have something to see to first."

Doctor Thomas nodded. Before he turned away, his eyes caught sight of Sciphil Nine and held for a moment. Then he rushed toward the house. Ciaran had caught the odd gaze from the doctor, but he said nothing.

Ciaran approached the gate but held back from stepping outside the grounds. He stood there with his hands in his pockets and observed Pete Chandler.

"You are human, Mr. Chandler?"

Pete nodded. "I have to go now. In fact, I should not be here at all. But I wanted to meet the man I would one day serve."

Ciaran exited the gate and approached Pete Chandler.

"How many Sciphils are there?" he asked.

"Nine."

"So you are the youngest?"

"The number indicates the order of arrival of the very first Sciphils to Alphi more than five hundred years ago. There have been several generations of successors down the line. The order is no longer applicable."

Ciaran nodded. "Who am I the successor of?"

"Sciphil Three."

"If I am his successor, why isn't he meeting with me?"

Pete smiled.

Ciaran nodded. "I understand. You can't tell me. Since you helped Madeline, what can I do for you?"

"Stay alive. Juliette broke the seal. She is no longer a Sciphil. But she has grown so strong. None of us can stop her."

"She was a Sciphil?"

Pete nodded. The steel wristband Pete was wearing flashed red. He glanced at it. "I have to go now. You can kill Juliette. You are the only one who can at the moment."

"I can't kill her twice," Ciaran snarled.

"But she's willing to kill you many times. She's no longer the Juliette you remember."

"Of course not—she a simulated electronic profile."

Pete shook his head. "She was brought to Eudaiz soon enough after she died on Earth. Her life force was still there, and it operates her profile. Look, it's not my place to say—"

"Then whose place is it?" Ciaran raised his voice.

"Yours."

"Bullshit."

"You have to come to terms with this, Ciaran. And the sooner, the better."

Ciaran pulled his gun and pointed it at Pete. "How about I come to terms right now?"

Pete smiled. "Your earthly weapon could kill every human, including you, but it will have no effect on me, Ciaran."

"And you expect me to kill the recreated Juliette using this weapon?"

"No. She has to be terminated properly. In Eudaiz."

"He will go to Eudaiz to be with me, not to kill me." Juliette's voice echoed in the air, and before Pete could react, his body was spun up high and smashed down to the ground.

Juliette stood in the shade of a resting station in the park, quite a distance away.

"Get back inside," Pete yelled and stood up.

A burst of air blew in Ciaran's direction. He could feel the vibration of energy coming from it. Pete charged at the air funnel and swung his sword. He sliced through the air before the funnel hit Ciaran, but the residual force threw Pete up again and pushed Ciaran backward. He fell and rolled on the ground.

Ciaran darted toward Pete to help him up. His hands were nearly burned when he touched Pete. Ciaran withdrew his hands.

"I'm using my Sciphil energy. You can't touch me."

"But you held Madeline before."

"I turned it off. I was a human when I held her."

"Then turn it off, and I'll take you inside Mon Ciel."

Pete shook his head. "Too risky. I've got to run now."

Another wedge of air struck at the grass near them, blasting a large hole in the ground. It was such a long distance, though, that Juliette had missed her true targets.

Pete stood up. "The sunlight has a vibration frequency that clashes with Juliette's energy sources. She will try to stay in the shade."

Another wedge of air slashed right in front of Ciaran, pushing him and causing him to fall again.

"Get inside and stay alive." It was Pete's voice that echoed back to him. The man had vanished into another dimension. Ciaran charged toward Mon Ciel's gate before another blow could come from Juliette.

13

---

*M*adeline awoke and saw Ciaran working on a computer in the corner of his bedroom. She tried not to move. She liked to watch him work. His concentration was extreme. His intense eyes looked as if they could punch holes in the computer screen and set it on fire.

The more important reason for her not to move was that she needed to bide some time. She wasn't sure exactly how to break it to him that she couldn't be with him when he took his position as successor.

For both of them to stay alive, they couldn't be together.

She was unsure about many things in her life. But she knew what she had done in Australia ten years ago. And one thing she was certain of—her soul was no way virtuous.

She didn't have to move. He sensed her like a cat. He stopped working and strode to the bed. He smiled and checked the temperature of her forehead. Satisfied with what he felt, he asked, "How are you feeling?"

"I'm fine. How long have I been in bed?"

"Three hours."

Ciaran walked to the side table and grabbed the medicine and a glass of water. Doctor Thomas had examined her and had left clear instructions for Ciaran. Ciaran looked at the doctor's notes, checking them over. Then he brought the medicine over to the bed. His movements were meticulously efficient.

Madeline sat up, took the pills and the water. She downed the pills and gave Ciaran back the water.

His face was unfathomable. Inexplicably controlled. He stood holding the glass of water, looking at her, saying nothing.

"What's the damage?" she asked.

"You should be fine now. If you want to know the exact condition you were in, you'll have to ask Doctor Thomas."

That was cold! Madeline thought.

He knew exactly what condition she was in. He must be pissed that she had drugged him, putting him out of action the night before. If he wanted to play this passive-aggressive game, she could play.

"Could you pass me the phone, please? I'll give Doctor Thomas a call."

Ciaran nodded. He turned as if he was going to fetch her the phone. But instead, he heaved the glass to the wall. The glass shattered into pieces, and broken glass rained onto the floor.

Then he strode out of the room and slammed the door.

Jo immediately came into the room as if she had been waiting right outside.

Madeline waved her arms in the air. "He's pissed because I drugged him last night."

Jo said nothing. She sat on the bed and examined Madeline's bruised face. "Do you really think he's mad because of that?"

She looked into Jo's green eyes, eyes that were waiting for her honest answers. She couldn't hold it in any longer. The emotion stormed out of her like a tidal wave. Madeline wept.

Jo held her patiently and waited until her crying subsided. "I can't tell you what I felt when they brought you in because, on the rage chart, I was right at the bottom. When Ciaran finished talking to the man outside the gate—"

"Outside?"

"Yes, he had to go outside to get you."

Madeline nodded again.

"Doctor Thomas said the fact that you didn't die was pure luck. He substantiated the statement with an extensive report, of course. But to give Ciaran the lowdown, Doctor Thomas said that if your rib had been cracked an inch higher, or if you had been held under the water for a couple of seconds longer, there would have been nothing he could have done. So yes, you're fine now. But it was only because of dumb luck."

Madeline stared at Jo. Jo's eyes were full of resentment now. And that was what Jo described as 'the bottom of the rage chart'. What could Ciaran possibly be feeling? Like he'd been kicked in the teeth? Stabbed in the heart?

Madeline remembered when Ciaran had been shot at Fountains Abbey. The feeling of her boiling blood was still fresh in her mind. Still, Ciaran hadn't been the cause of his almost fatal injury. He hadn't stuck his chest out and dared Stefan to shoot at him.

And he had survived. He'd left the past behind to be with her. After all they had been through together . . . Now, she had to tell him that they couldn't be together anymore!

"Jo, I killed those people in the woods. It wasn't Zach's fault. It wasn't your fault. I had to kill them." Tears streamed down her face uncontrollably. "My soul is not virtuous. I can't be a successor. I can't be with Ciaran."

"He doesn't have to be a successor. He doesn't have to be with those Sciphils." Jo wiped the tears from Madeline's face.

She shook her head. "At the cemetery, Juliette forced Ayana to put a seal on Ciaran's successor position. If he doesn't take the position, he will die. If he knows I can't go with him, he'll try to get out of the deal."

"You can't be so sure, Madeline. And what if he can't get out of the deal?"

"He'll try. Please don't tell him, Jo. He *will* attempt to get out of the deal, and he will fail. I can feel it. Can you promise not to tell him? Please?"

Jo nodded, tears gleaming in her eyes.

"I'm going to be sick," she said to Jo.

Jo helped Madeline out of bed. They stumbled a few steps before Madeline slumped to the floor, violently ill.

Ciaran stormed into the room so fast that Jo doubted he had ever left. He tried to get to Madeline.

She pushed him away. She backed away from him on the floor. "Don't touch me. Don't touch. I'm dirty."

"Madeline."

"Leave me." Tears poured down her face now. "I made a mess. I'll clean it up."

"Darling. That's okay." Ciaran approached.

"Don't. Don't come near me. I'm a mess."

Ciaran scooped Madeline off the floor and carried her to the bed. He cradled her while she wept into his chest. Then she looked at Jo and saw a spark of anger in her eyes before she turned on her heel and stormed out of the room.

14

*T*J stood at the end of the back corridor connecting to the old kitchen, lips pulled back, revealing his sharp little teeth. Regardless of how formidable and intimidating full-grown Alaskan Malamutes could look, TJ was still a puppy.

The more petulantly he behaved, the more puppyish he would appear to the thirteen-year-old cat Migi. The cat sat across the corridor, looking bored with TJ's show of ferocity. She cast a dismissive glance at him, then she lowered herself down to the floor and started washing herself.

Tadgh frowned. He felt pity for the puppy but decided not to help. He had to learn for himself to be a proper grown-up dog one day.

From the other end of the corridor, Jo stomped right past Tadgh and the animals. If he wasn't mistaken, he saw tears in her eyes. She had just come from Ciaran's room. *What could it be?* Tadgh wondered.

"What do you think?" he asked Migi.

The cat that had been mutilated by Mrs. Hanson was the most wicked of all the animals Tadgh had known. She had saved him from Juliette once. Migi wagged her twin tails, pointing the tips of her tails toward different directions. Tadgh nodded, "Conflicting emotions. Must have something to do with Madeline."

Then he frowned. Jo was heading toward the back gardens. He shot up and darted after her. When he caught up with her, she had almost reached the back door.

"Where do you think you're going?"

"Out, isn't it obvious?"

"But Juliette is out there . . ."

"That's why I'm going. I'm going to teach the bitch a lesson." Jo approached the door.

"That's a man's job."

Jo turned around. "And that comment will earn you a slap in the face."

"Then come back in here and do it. I promise I won't duck!"

Jo glared at Tadgh and continued to the back gardens.

"Fuck this!" Tadgh mumbled and darted after her.

OUTSIDE THE GATE, the field opened onto rolling green hills. Jo stood, looking out into the far distance. Tadgh came up behind her. "For pity's sake, Jo. Please come back inside the house."

"I've decided that I'm taking Madeline back to New York tomorrow. I just wanted to enjoy a bit of the countryside before we left."

Tadgh shrugged. "All right. But we can talk about this inside."

"I have an experiment to carry out here. You go inside. I can't cover you."

"You? Cover me? With your five foot body, including those sticks you are standing on."

"Five foot *two*."

"Well, those two inches certainly make a huge difference."

"Those precious two inches make a difference to *me*. Get out of my sight, Tadgh. I'm busy here."

"Are you looking for me?" It was Juliette's voice, wafting on the thin air.

"Fuck me." Tadgh snatched Jo and pushed her behind him.

They both looked around but saw no sign of Juliette. The rolling green hills were covered in sunlight just as before.

"Do you think you can stand in the sun and be safe from me?" Juliette said sarcastically.

Tadgh looked around. He could not see her.

"In there." Jo nodded toward a small resting station just a bit further up the hill.

"How do you know?"

Before Jo could answer, the door of the resting station swung open. Juliette stood inside, a wind circle already spinning. Its span enlarged, but it could not reach Jo and Tadgh. The most damage it did was chopping at the nearby grass.

Jo pushed Tadgh aside. A smile came over her foxy face. "It's my turn now."

She pulled her tiny travel makeup box from her bag and flicked the lid open. Inside were square compartments of eye shadow, lipstick, blush, and a mirror that occupied the entire half of the lid. She tilted the mirror and caught the sunlight, so it reflected straight onto Juliette.

Juliette screamed as if she had been shot.

"Again!" Jo commanded herself. She reflected one more time. Juliette staggered. A hole burned through the middle of her image. The wind circle vanished.

Tadgh was flabbergasted.

Juliette was furious. Her voice rumbled like thunder. "Don't you dare try that trick on me!"

"It's not a trick. It's a lethal weapon. You're doomed, you sadistic bitch." Jo grinned. "You can beam away now."

Juliette hid in a corner of the station where Jo could not reflect the sunlight. She refused to beam away.

A hovering cloud dragged a shadow closer behind Jo and Tadgh. Tadgh turned around and saw it.

"Shit," Tadgh said. He pulled at Jo.

Jo turned around and immediately registered the danger.

They raced toward the gate.

They moved as fast as they could.

The cloud created a shadow right against Mon Ciel's fence, and Juliette beamed right into the shadow. She stood blocking Tadgh's and Jo's way back inside Mon Ciel.

"You're right. I derive pleasure from other people's pain." She swung her arms, and a blast of freezing air flew at them. Tadgh plucked Jo up and swiveled aside. The blade of air dug into the ground nearby, blew up a large hole, and funneled dirt, grass, and rocks up into the sky.

A piece of rock hit Tadgh in the head. He fell on top of Jo.

From inside the backyard, the puppy TJ and Migi charged out, running straight at Juliette from behind. They knocked her out of the shadow, and the contact with the sunlight burned her again. Juliette hissed, roared, and beamed away.

Tadgh was too dazed to move himself in the right direction. Jo pulled him with her into the backyard. Once there, Tadgh flopped down onto the grass.

"Look at me, Tadgh. How many fingers?"

She held two fingers in front of him. Tadgh blinked. "Five foot two inches."

Jo rubbed her hand on Tadgh's head. "It's a pretty big lump. You're going to have a huge headache."

"Could you check on TJ and Migi?"

"What?"

"See if they're okay," Tadgh mumbled, his voice slurred with a concussion.

Before Jo made a move, Migi strode into the garden, grabbing TJ by the crook of his neck. She dropped the dog down onto the grass. There was a gash on TJ's front leg. Migi licked the wound. The puppy snarled at first but then submitted to Migi's care.

Outside the garden, on the hillside, Juliette lingered in the shadow of a cloud whenever she found one.

"Look out, Juliette!" Jo muttered and helped Tadgh up. "Come on, let's get you inside."

15

———————

*D*usk quickly blanketed the hillside in front of Mon Ciel. Ciaran stood at the entrance, ready to go. His long black coat billowed in the winter breeze. He shifted his left shoulder slightly, easing the tense muscles there caused by the number of injuries his shoulder had suffered. More importantly, he checked to see that his much-needed weapons were in place and ready to go.

It was time to settle any debts, resentment, and lingering hatred that remained in his life.

In the last few days, it had taken a lot of work. It had taken a tremendous amount of careful planning and preparation from everyone inside Mon Ciel. Now, it was time for Ciaran to execute the plan. It was time for him to regain control of his life and the lives of those he loved.

They were not going to be caged inside Mon Ciel.

He sauntered outside the gate. He paused and waited. He strolled a little further down the hill.

The rolling hills were quiet. There was not even the sound of an insect, a wild animal, or the wind blowing in the trees.

The air thickened.

A flash of blue light sliced through the air, and the hologram of Ayana Dee appeared.

"Ayana, there is nothing for you to do here."

Ayana smiled. "I'm pleased to see you decide to take action, Ciaran. But you are not equipped to fight Juliette. We aren't strong enough to protect you."

"I'll negotiate with her."

"She won't negotiate. She just wants you."

"At least she's clear about what she wants. You and the other Sciphils want me to be a Sciphil and serve a universe that I don't care at all about, at an unknown cost to my family."

"You misconstrue what we want . . ."

"That's the most logical conclusion I can draw from what you told me. Now, I will call Juliette to talk to her. I assume it's best for you to leave to avoid being hurt."

"Are you sure about this, Ciaran? You don't have to do this on your own."

"I will not fight with Juliette. Therefore, I don't need any help from you. Am I making myself clear?"

Ayana's intense blue eyes blinked with confusion and disappointment. She nodded, and her hologram disappeared. The air returned to its mysterious quietness.

"Juliette, I know you heard me. If you want to talk, now is the time."

Nothing happened. Ciaran waited for a moment.

"I thought you wanted me," he said and turned to go back to Mon Ciel.

Then he felt it—a vibration of energy filling the air. Juliette's image glowed in the darkness. "Ciaran, I'm glad you've decided to come to me."

Ciaran observed her carefully. From a distance, he couldn't tell if Juliette was a hologram or an actual presence.

"I don't know how I can come to you."

"Via the Daimon Gate. I told you that already."

"And what exactly will it require of me?"

Juliette looked puzzled. No response.

Ciaran deduced that if Juliette was merely an electronic profile —due to her human life ending years ago—then the fact that Ciaran was a successor would be unknown to her, and she would not have an answer for this question. The solution to this problem would not be available to her because it was not a part of the data input she had received.

Artificial intelligence and robotic behavior were child's play to Ciaran.

"I'm a human, and I'm alive, Juliette. Whatever the Daimon Gate is, do you honestly think I can pass through it and still be with you? Are you alive or are you not?"

Juliette again looked perplexed.

"Daimon Gate is a nine-level transmutation process, categorized in three stages, where biological and psychological profiles are purified. If an individual is proven to be worthy, he or she will pass the gate and become a perfect entity. If an individual is not worthy, he or she will not reform, and will thus be exterminated during the process."

That was definitely a robotic pre-programmed answer, Ciaran mused. He stepped closer to Juliette.

"Do you think I am worthy? What if I die during the process? Can I still be with you? Or do I have to die to be with you?"

Juliette appeared to be even more confused.

"I died on Earth."

"Yes, you did. But your body was not placed in the coffin. How did you get to Alphi?"

"I am not in Alphi. I am in Eudaiz. The Daimon Gate will lead you to Eudaiz."

"But only if I pass the test. What if I fail? I'll die. How can I be with you then?"

Juliette's face started to turn red. Ciaran had befuddled the machine. He stepped closer and reached out for her. He could feel the energy, the vibration. There was the presence of solid substance. Like Tadgh said, this was not a hologram.

"Do you want to be with me or not?" Ciaran asked.

His hand touched Juliette's arm. It was solid, and it didn't burn him. Juliette looked up at Ciaran. "Yes, I do. I want to be with you."

"Where is the Daimon Gate?"

"It depends on the astronomical time and location. All dimensions have to be open on Earth and connected."

"How many dimensions?"

"Nine"

"That's manageable. Science has gotten it to eleven dimensions." Juliette smiled. "Times nine."

"Oh, for pity's sake, Juliette. I can't manage that."

"Yes, you can. Run the disk."

"If I find the gate, so what? You're speaking about some kind of wormhole. This is science fiction to those like myself who are still alive and living on Earth."

"It's not as primitive as a wormhole, Ciaran . . ."

Ciaran shook his head. "I have a proposal. Why don't you come to me? Like now. You're here. Why don't you just stay here? We can be together this way, can't we?"

Ciaran grabbed Juliette. Her body was solid. Not solid like flesh and bones, but much more than frequencies and signals.

Juliette trembled as if she wanted to agree with Ciaran.

"I can't stay."

"Why not?" Ciaran held Juliette now. Her image glowed in his arms.

"I don't know. I can't stay. You have to come to me. You have to be with me. There is no other way."

Juliette's body started to vibrate. She reached her arms up and held onto Ciaran. But all he felt was a ring of bone-crushing force wrapped around him. He grunted out in pain and slumped to the ground.

Juliette released him. She reached out again to help him up, but Ciaran gestured for her to keep her distance.

"You're going to kill me now if you touch me."

Juliette stopped.

Ciaran stood up. "Juliette, I want to be with you. But I don't want to die. You don't really want to kill me, do you?"

Silence.

"The Daimon Gate will kill me in much the same way as you touching me now. No matter what the transmutational process is within the gate, I'll die. I'm sure that I'm not a worthy individual. I'm a human being with a corrupted soul. If you once loved me, you'd know that about me."

Ciaran started to walk back to Mon Ciel. Juliette followed but kept at a distance.

"If you want, you can stick around. I can see you at night. Just like this. We can talk, keeping a distance. What do you think?"

This was obviously not something Juliette had in her program. It was not something she had considered.

They approached the gate. Juliette stopped at a distance from it.

"I'm going in now. Good night, Juliette."

"No, this is not going to work."

"Then give me a plausible solution." Ciaran had to raise his voice so Juliette could hear since she was quite far away.

"You go through the Daimon Gate and be with me properly."

Ciaran stood close to the fence so that he could easily dive inside Mon Ciel's boundaries.

"If I promise you that I'll go through the Daimon Gate, will you let me leave now?"

Juliette smiled. "No."

"I thought not. I guess you want to take me, dump me right in front of the Daimon Gate, and make me go through it, regardless of whether I could see it or not."

Juliette grinned. "You know me too well, Ciaran. As I said, I'll have you, either dead or alive. If I let you leave now, I'll never have you again."

"I wish we could find a better solution," Ciaran said softly so that Juliette had to move closer to hear. I remember every day we were together. Those were happy days."

"Speak up."

"I know what you have on the disk."

"I said speak up!" Juliette moved closer.

Forty more feet, Ciaran thought. He needed Juliette to move forty feet closer. Ciaran left the gate and walked about ten feet toward her. He stood there, his hands jammed in his pockets.

"What do you want me to do, Juliette?"

"Speak up." She moved ten feet closer. "What are you saying?" she asked.

Ciaran shrugged. He looked at Juliette. The look that had always softened her heart . . . and for how many years? She advanced another ten feet and stood still.

Ciaran turned around and strolled toward Mon Ciel again.

Juliette galloped forward another ten feet. Then she stopped again. Ciaran felt a wedge of wind hit his back with force. The wind lifted him up and threw him fifty feet from Mon Ciel's gate. Ciaran both heard and felt his bones rattle. He stood up.

Juliette wore an evil smirk on her face. Her loving expression had been replaced with fury. Her eyes were on fire. *There is no other solution*, Ciaran thought. He stood up straight, and as he did, he pulled two guns from his back waistband.

These were no ordinary weapons—they were two specialized laser guns that simulated the profile of sunlight, an idea inspired by Jo's little experiment with her makeup mirror in the back garden.

He shot at Juliette. Each beam sent her staggering back several feet toward Mon Ciel. Each beam punched a burning hole in her body. She squealed, hissed, screamed, and staggered back with every shot.

Ciaran kept shooting, pushing her back. Ten feet more would do the trick, he thought.

Juliette whirled around, trying to regain her balance. Her brain was frantically trying to register new information and process it for alternative solutions. She hissed and screamed then suddenly stood up straight. The burning holes in her body started to heal. The wind circle around her started to stir.

She laughed.

Ciaran continued to shoot. His two beams barely made a scratch on her body now. She had somehow established a defense mechanism against the sun's rays.

The wind circle grew sharp, cutting into the grass like the blades of a hedge trimmer. Ciaran kept attacking with the two guns, but they seemed to have no effect. He strode toward her to avoid her approaching him and veered away from Mon Ciel.

Behind Mon Ciel's fence, Tadgh, Jo, and Madeline darted out with two guns each.

"Yo!" Tadgh called out.

Juliette turned around, looking at Tadgh. She approached Tadgh, Jo, and Madeline, inadvertently moving closer to Mon Ciel.

They shot. Six beams at a time created an impact. Juliette staggered. The holes in her body took a little longer to heal this time. But they did heal.

Tadgh, Jo, and Madeline kept shooting.

Juliette smiled. She swung her arms to create a deadly wedge of wind that she flung at them at head height. It almost decapitated them. They ducked, crawling on the ground.

Juliette laughed and prepared for a second swipe.

Behind her, a beam exploded from a device Ciaran held. It blew Juliette five feet further toward Mon Ciel. Her back was on fire. She whirled around several times to put it out. She screamed in rage.

Ciaran added his two guns attack and charged toward Juliette.

He knew that as soon as she put out the fire, they would be back to square one.

When Ciaran got to Juliette, the fire had just gone out. But she had not yet had time to create another blast of wind.

Ciaran dove at her, trying to tackle her backward.

She grabbed him, and he felt his bones breaking in her grip. He kept pushing. Five feet wasn't much. His body could hold until then. Two more seconds, he promised himself. He closed his eyes and kept pushing.

Juliette snarled and tried to shove Ciaran away from her.

One second.

There. In position.

Ciaran shouted out his command. "Fire!"

⎯⎯⎯⎯⎯⎯

16

𝒯wo towers of light from inside Mon Ciel's fence beamed out a fifty-foot cone of simulated sunlight. It was the equivalent of two thousand single beams of sunlight.

It was too fast. It was too strong.

Juliette screamed a blood-curdling scream and exploded into nothingness.

Ciaran sat on his heels, staring at the space where Juliette had disintegrated. He wasn't sure what he felt. He was probably too numb to feel anything.

Ciaran staggered up. Madeline approached. She squeezed his arms. "Let's go inside."

Ciaran nodded. He rubbed his thumb along the dimple on her left cheek and kissed her before they headed back toward the house.

IN THE GREAT RECEPTION ROOM, Ciaran settled in a chair next to Madeline. The painkillers had taken effect. His bodily pain was lost in a fog now.

Jo shared a couch with Migi in a corner of the room.

Next to the side table and an elegant lamp, George LeBlanc, Ciaran and Tadgh's cousin from France, sat in a comfortable reading chair.

George was in his early forties although he looked much younger than his age. Brown hair framed his intelligent face and brightened his sharp, gray eyes.

The gray eyes were a shared feature in the LeBlanc family, Madeline thought. But while Ciaran's gray was deep, smoky, and intense, Tadgh's was witty, and George's was soft and kind.

Tadgh walked into the room with a bottle in his hand. "Found it. This should suit everyone. It's very delicate."

Coming from the LeBlanc's cellar, Madeline was assured of its delicacy and was sure it would suit everyone's taste.

Tadgh served everyone.

"How's the pain?" Madeline asked Ciaran.

He smiled. "Gone!" he exclaimed.

"Doctor Thomas is staying here overnight in case we need him."

Ciaran shook his head. "He needs a family to go home to. Where is he now?"

"In the guest room. Reading, I think."

Ciaran and Madeline took their glasses of wine from Tadgh.

"He's never had a family?" Madeline asked.

Ciaran shook his head. "He did. I don't know what happened to them, though. Doctor Thomas is a very private man. I don't think it's appropriate to ask about his personal affairs if he's not willing to share."

"A private man working for the LeBlancs?" Madeline exaggerated the statement by rolling her eyes. Ciaran laughed and kissed her cheek.

"Thank you for your help, George, especially on such short notice," Ciaran addressed his cousin.

"You put on a good show. I enjoyed it. I'm glad my expertise was of some use." George grinned.

Madeline had just discovered another resemblance in the LeBlancs—their gorgeous grins.

Ciaran said to Jo and Madeline, "Sorry I didn't have enough time to explain to you in the last few days. George is the top man in show business in Paris. Stringing a few light bulbs together wasn't a problem for him, as you have seen."

"I've got to give it to you, George. It was brilliant. Especially since we didn't have a chance for a test run and had no room for error." Tadgh raised his wine in salute.

George shook his head. "I just pushed a button . . . I can't believe Juliette ended up like that. I still don't understand . . ."

"No need for you to dig in further, George," Ciaran cut in. "I appreciate your help. We should close this chapter and consider it done."

George shrugged. "All right. Up to you. We're family. I don't mind helping. Don't be too harsh on the people around you. And realize that you don't have to be perfect. You don't have to take care of everything."

"I beg your pardon." Ciaran lowered his voice.

"Come on! This is a time to celebrate," Tadgh reminded him.

"Yes, we worked hard for this victory," Jo agreed.

Madeline looked at Ciaran. His eyes looked tired as if he were drunk. But he had hardly touched his wine.

"Are you okay?" she asked him.

"I think my head is going to roll right off my shoulders."

"I'll take you to bed."

Ciaran nodded. "Please excuse me, everyone. Apparently those hits were harder than I thought." Ciaran stood up and walked out of the room with Madeline scurrying after him.

In the hallway, Ciaran staggered. He leaned against the wall. Madeline wrapped her arm around his waist for support, and they walked toward the bedroom.

In front of the door to the bedroom, they found Doctor Thomas waiting.

"Doctor, what can I do for you?"

"Are you okay, Ciaran?"

"Painkillers and wine have turned out to be a poor mix. Come on in."

Ciaran pushed the bedroom door open and staggered inside. He slumped into the reading chair.

"What would you like to talk about, Doctor Thomas? Is it about the man you saw in front of Mon Ciel a few days ago? The one who carried Madeline home from the creek?"

Doctor Thomas smiled. "You don't miss a thing, do you, Ciaran? Yes, I'm here about that man. I've seen him before. He's been inside Mon Ciel, talking to your mother. That was before you were born. Your parents had just moved into this place. I don't know if this information is significant at all, but I thought I should tell you."

"Thanks, Doctor Thomas. That's a very important piece of information."

Ciaran stood up and moved clumsily toward the bed and climbed in. "I'm sorry. I've never been this drunk before . . ." His words trailed off, and he flopped down onto the pillows.

Madeline darted toward the bed. Feeling his forehead, she said, "Jesus Christ, Doctor, I don't think he's drunk. He's burning up."

Doctor Thomas took Ciaran's pulse and then rushed out of the room to get his medical bag.

Ciaran no longer responded to Madeline's voice. Juliette had something to do with this. Madeline knew it. She knew Juliette couldn't be killed so easily. Going to the intercom, she called to the Great Reception room.

Tadgh, Jo, and George arrived at the same time as the doctor.

While Doctor Thomas examined Ciaran, Madeline paced back and forth at the end of the bed. "It has to have something to do with Juliette. I knew it wouldn't be that easy to kill her."

Doctor Thomas finished his examination.

That was way too quick, Madeline thought.

Everyone looked at the doctor, waiting for his diagnosis. "This has nothing to do with his injuries or what just happened," he told them. "Ciaran is experiencing something similar to what happened to you when you inhaled that potion, Madeline. Your body was comatose."

"But we didn't see him inhale anything. We drank the same wine, ate the same food tonight," Tadgh said.

"Comatose. Doctor, you are saying that there is nothing you can do? That he has to wake up by himself? Are you sure this is the same condition I had?"

Doctor Thomas nodded. "Unfortunately yes."

Madeline remembered her experience vividly. She remembered how she drifted away and was desperate for Ciaran to do something to pull her back. She would not let that happen to him.

Madeline leaped onto the bed and shook his shoulders.

"Ciaran, stay with me. Answer me. Give me a sign. Please!"

She remembered the cold and dark place, the chapel where Juliette pulled her in and then burned her. Madeline shook Ciaran's shoulders again and again. "Please don't go there. Please, Ciaran. Answer me."

Madeline shook him so violently she was afraid she might break his neck. But there was no response from Ciaran.

Jo approached Madeline. "No, Jo. I know what I'm doing."

Madeline shook him again. This time, he responded. He muttered something unintelligible.

"What are you saying, Ciaran?" Madeline asked.

He said something again, very softly.

"It's in French." Madeline looked at the others. She didn't realize she was weeping. "It's French," she repeated.

Tadgh and George moved toward the bed.

Ciaran mumbled the French words again.

"He said if they release his mother, he'll do anything."

Ciaran's body tensed, then it went lax. He said nothing more. Madeline knew he had gone to the dark place where she had been. She had to do something better than watching and waiting. She had to talk to her grandfather.

Madeline hopped off the bed. "I need to talk to my grandfather outside Mon Ciel. Would you go with me, Tadgh?"

"You have to ask?"

"I'll go, too," Jo said.

"Please stay and look after Ciaran. I need you here."

Jo nodded. "Okay."

Madeline and Tadgh rushed out of the room.

17

*M*adeline and Tadgh ran in the dark. They charged through Mon Ciel's gate.

"Grandfather!" Madeline called out.

Nothing happened.

"Ayana Dee!" Tadgh called.

Still nothing.

"Sciphil Nine! Pete Chandler! Anyone, for fuck's sake!" Tadgh yelled.

The air thickened. The hologram of Richard Kelley appeared, his eyes bleary and his hair a mess.

"We're a little preoccupied because of what you just did. Stop yelling, Tadgh," Richard directed.

"Shouldn't you be thanking us for killing Juliette?" Tadgh said.

"Grandfather, we didn't kill her, did we? Is she taking Ciaran now?"

"Madeline, you killed her presence."

"What does that mean, exactly?" Tadgh asked.

Richard wiped at his sweating forehead. "As a Sciphil, she won't die like a human being. The only way to end her existence is to terminate her energy source at her tower. I can't access her tower."

"We killed her presence. Does that mean we're halfway to killing her completely?" Madeline asked.

Richard shook his head. "What you did was incapacitate her temporarily. You pushed her back to her tower. There, she will use her eudqi to form another presence. Once she forms again, she will be invincible."

"Eudqi? Do I need a new dictionary?" Tadgh asked.

"A eudqi is a life force made of multiple astrological sources of energy. We have nine Sciphils, and eight of them hold major sources of eudqi. The king is a Sciphil who uses his own eudqi to combine the other eight and make it a unified eudqi that sustains Eudaiz. The king's eudqi is the strongest, and only he can terminate the other Sciphils. The other eight cannot terminate one another."

"Okay, so you can't disconnect Juliette from her eudqi, and now she will reform and be invincible. I guess blowing up her presence was a fucked-up plan. But it wasn't our fault. But how does taking Ciaran fix the problem?" Tadgh asked in frustration.

"What do you mean by Ciaran being taken?"

"He's comatose and negotiating in French for a release of our mother. Isn't that the condition you and Juliette created to get to Madeline before?" Tadgh asked.

"What we created was a hybrid hologame. In Eudaiz, only Juliette controls the games. But she is not in control of herself right now. So how can she be controlling Ciaran?"

"So who is doing this now?"

"I have a theory, but if I tell you, you have to do something for me afterward, Madeline."

"If anything happens to Ciaran, I won't follow through with anything I promised you before, let alone what I'm promising now."

"I don't have a choice, Madeline."

"Fine. Say it if you must. I'll see what I can do."

"The disk that Juliette created has a program that helps humans enter the Daimon Gate. It's at the villa outside London. You've been there. I need you to retrieve it. If you need to enter the Daimon Gate without me, use it."

"Is that all?"

Richard nodded.

"Okay, I'll do it. What's your theory about Ciaran's current condition?"

Richard contemplated. "Ciaran is the successor of Sciphil Three, the King of Eudaiz."

"Fuck me," Tadgh mumbled.

"Although the king is still in control of his eudqi, and his presence is still intact, no one has been able to contact him for more than thirty years."

"You've lost your king?" Tadgh shook his head.

"He's still in charge. He knows what is happening in Eudaiz. He just hasn't connected or taken any action. When Juliette reforms, it will be disastrous for Eudaiz. The only person who can terminate Juliette is the king. If you were the king, and for some reason, you could not take action yourself, what would you do?"

"I'd get my successor to do it," Madeline said.

"Exactly." Richard nodded.

"So let's get this clear . . . The current king wants Ciaran to go through the Daimon Gate—which sounds a lot like jumping through the gates of hell—to get to Eudaiz, become king, and kill Juliette, who at that point might have become invincible already. Piece of cake!" Tadgh retorted.

"I know it's not easy. That's why I think Ciaran is receiving some training now. The king cannot connect with us, but Ayana activated the seal of the successor on Ciaran's arm a few days ago, so the king might be able to connect with his successor now. But that's only a theory."

"You're saying Ciaran is in a hologame now?" Tadgh asked.

"The king built the first super artificial intelligence system in the multiverse. The system ran Eudaiz flawlessly while he was in absence for more than thirty years. If the training comes from him, it won't be just a hologame, Tadgh."

"What can we do to help him?" Madeline asked.

"If you have faith in God, then pray."

The hologram of Richard flickered and disappeared.

Madeline stormed into the bedroom. Tadgh followed. The room was as quiet as a tomb. Jo sat at the end of the bed, holding a damp cloth, confused and worried. Before Madeline could ask, Jo hopped off the bed and shoved the cloth into Madeline's hands.

"He's burning up like an oven. I can't watch this. Did you get any info? Is there anything I can do to feel less useless?"

Madeline pulled the sleeve of Ciaran's shirt up, revealing the crucifix tattoo glowing white and blue.

"Jesus Christ, Grandfather was right. The king must have Ciaran in some form of a game."

"A hologame?" Jo asked.

"He said it might be something more complicated and advanced than a hologame."

Ciaran grunted as if he had been hit. His body tensed up and convulsed like he was in a fight—or being beaten up. Madeline jumped on the bed. She held Ciaran's hands. As soon as he felt her hands on his, he gripped them.

"Ciaran, please come back to me!" Madeline cried out.

Ciaran squeezed Madeline's hands, and his body gradually loosened up.

Jo stared, contemplating. Then she yelped out the words, "Kiss him. Kiss him, Madeline."

Madeline did.

Ciaran's body relaxed and cooled down instantly.

"He can feel you. He can feel us. And that means we can feel him." Jo waved her arms in the air for victory. Madeline and Tadgh gawked.

"Can you wake him?" Tadgh asked.

Jo scurried toward the bedroom door.

"Where are you going?" Tadgh asked.

"To get the eyes." She disappeared out the door. Then they heard her voice. "I need your muscles, Tadgh."

"Oh, okay."

Tadgh rushed out of the room.

A moment later, Jo, Tadgh, Doctor Thomas, and George filed back into the room. Jo dove to the computer keyboard, doing something that only she and Ciaran would understand.

"Doctor Thomas, I need the connections to his vitals and visuals," Jo said while typing like a madwoman.

Doctor Thomas connected a wire to Ciaran's body.

"George, can you hook up the monitor?" she asked while still typing.

"My expertise." George didn't hesitate to dive in to help his cousin.

Ciaran's temperature shot up again. Madeline grabbed the cloth and wiped the sweat from his forehead. He grunted again.

"That's a fucking kick from the back. Coward," Tadgh swore.

"How do you know, Tadgh?" Madeline asked.

"I don't know, Madeline. But I have no fucking clue what else to do here."

"Done," Jo said.

George turned the monitor on. Images of faceless creatures with bodies shaped like half-man and half-ape looked back through the screen. Everyone gasped.

"Holy cow, what is that?" Tadgh gaped at the creatures.

"We're seeing what Ciaran is seeing," Jo said.

"So we are looking at this from Ciaran's perspective? We have his visual?" Doctor Thomas asked.

"Yes," Jo said.

"He's lying on the ground. Those fuckers must have attacked him from behind. Like I said, cowards!"

"Good, Tadgh, you know Ciaran's movements. Tell us—" Madeline began.

"I'd kick that fucker right there in the face," Tadgh said, pointing to the monitor.

On the monitor, they saw Ciaran's foot kick into the head of the monkey standing in the middle. The other monkeys yelped. They could see a punch here and a kick there until the bunch of monkeys retreated and ran away.

Then they saw an open field with rolling green hills on one side and stone caves on the other. The air was suspiciously still.

"What is that? Jo, is there a way we can communicate with Ciaran?" Madeline asked.

Jo shook her head. "I don't think so. I don't know how."

On the monitor, they kept seeing quiet meadows and rivers.

"No, this isn't right. It's suspicious. I wouldn't keep moving," Tadgh said.

On the monitor, the scenery became static, suggesting that Ciaran had stopped moving forward.

In the distance, they saw a pack of wolves rise from the tall grass and charge toward them.

"Oh, God, can we give him a weapon, Jo?" Madeline asked.

"It's not a hologame. I can't insert anything or manipulate the data."

"Time traveling. Is this a simulated game?" George asked.

"Can he hear us? He felt Madeline before," Tadgh said.

"I don't think he can hear any of us," Jo said.

"This is in another dimension. It's not time traveling, and it's not a hologame. It's dimensional traveling. Ciaran told me about that yesterday," Tadgh said.

"Which dimension?" Jo asked.

"I don't know. I didn't pay him any attention. Some stupid quantum physics rules. Something about a parallel universe. Some strings or wires. How the fuck should I know?" Tadgh kicked at the desk.

"You mean M theory? Quantum travel?" Jo asked.

"I don't know, Jo. Whenever he goes on about that, my brain turns into clay."

"But he's here. His body is here, at least. So whatever the dimension is, how can we channel him back here?" Madeline asked.

"Maybe you can talk him back. He can't hear us, but he seems to respond to you, Madeline," Doctor Thomas suggested.

18

*T*he ferocious wolves charged closer to savage.

Ciaran turned around and raced toward the forest. He ran as fast as he could.

On the monitor, everyone in the room could see the shaking view of the forest. They could see Ciaran's hands reaching up and breaking a tree branch. He held it like a weapon. He turned around and stared straight at the wolves.

The view of the incoming wolves filled the screen, suggesting that Ciaran had zeroed his view in and was looking straight at them.

Gigantic wolves.

They ran in a pack with structured attacking positions. The leader, an enormous black wolf, ran in the middle. It charged at Ciaran as if it was its life mission to kill him.

Ciaran stepped closer. When the wolf leaped at him, he ducked down and stabbed the sharp edge of the tree branch up. The branch impaled the wolf. It fell and roared. But the wound was not enough to kill it.

"Hit it! Whack the motherfucker into the mud!" Tadgh screamed.

On the screen, the view suggested Ciaran was doing just that. He hit at the big wolf with the tree branch nonstop.

A bunch of smaller wolves lunged at Ciaran.

"Oh my God, Jo, there are so many of them. Can we give him a gun?" Madeline asked.

"I told you before—it's not a hologame. There's nothing I can do to help. But it does feel like a simulated environment. It seems like these are challenges. Problems he has to solve to pass a test."

"Would they kill him for real?" Tadgh asked.

Before Jo could answer, Ciaran moaned.

"It must have bitten him. It did! It bit him!" Madeline yelped when she saw a streak of blood on Ciaran's hand.

Tadgh paced, mumbling to himself. "So it kills. It *can* kill."

Several smaller wolves charged at Ciaran.

"Tadgh, Tadgh . . . what would you do now?" Madeline cried out.

Tadgh still mumbled. "Don't know. I don't know. Challenge. It's a challenge. Isn't that what you said, Jo?'

"Yes," Jo responded.

"I . . . I'd try to kill the big wolf. That's my only chance," Tadgh said.

Another bleeding wound appeared on Ciaran's arm.

"They're mauling him!" Madeline panicked.

The screen filled with wolves' teeth and claws. Some were scarily close. Some of the wolves were spun away as Ciaran flailed his arms. A few more were kicked and thrown away, creating a gap.

The big wolf stood up and plunged through the gap.

Ciaran reached his hands up and grabbed for it. He spun it around and pinned it on the ground.

On the screen, it was clear that Ciaran no longer had his weapon. His two bare hands clutched at the head of the big wolf. It tried to kick free and growled.

On the bed, another wound broke out on Ciaran shoulder.

"Crush the head! Crush its head!" Tadgh yelled.

"He can't crush that monster's head with bare hands, Tadgh," George said.

"I know. But he can't let go. It's his only chance."

Another wound broke out on Ciaran's shoulder. Blood dripped down onto the mattress.

On the screen, they saw Ciaran's hands gripped tightly on the monster's head. He was still being bitten by some of the smaller wolves, but he squeezed hard. Harder. More. But the wolf's head was still intact. It turned around and tried to bite his hands.

Madeline looked at Ciaran's face. Then looked at his hands on the screen. She understood what he needed to do—and what she needed to do to help.

On the bed now, she bent down and kissed Ciaran. Her lips connected with his. She grabbed his hands and squeezed hard.

Her thoughts connected to his.

You have my support. You have me, Madeline thought. She squeezed his hands harder. *Kill it with your bare hands, Ciaran. I love you,* Madeline told him in her mind.

With all the power of her psychic ability, she transferred her energy, her thoughts, her wishes to him.

She connected to him. This was what he needed.

Kill it, Madeline thought again.

She squeezed his hands harder. *Kill it.*

On the screen, Ciaran's hand crushed into the wolf's head. Its head caved in like a smashed watermelon.

The wolf disintegrated and vanished along with the smaller wolves.

On the screen, Ciaran looked at his hands as if he could not believe what he had done.

Madeline kissed Ciaran's cheek. She wiped the blood from the wounds on his shoulder. She wished he would open his beautiful gray eyes and look at her. But it seemed as if there were more challenges awaiting him wherever he was at the moment.

On the screen, the forest burst into flames.

Ciaran ran. He charged out of the forest and headed toward the water.

The heat must be incredible. Ciaran's body temperature shot

up as if he had a fever. Madeline grabbed the cloth nearby and wiped away the sweat that dripped into his eyes.

It looked as if there was a river in the distance. He sped up. He could beat the fire.

From a small bush nearby, a baby wailed. Ciaran looked. Laurent was there, holding baby Bella in her arms, running from the fire. Laurent was lagging behind.

"It's an illusion. They want to slow him down. Come on, Ciaran. Don't stop!" Tadgh yelled.

Ciaran grabbed Bella and helped Laurent run. They slowed him down considerably. The fire caught up. It was only a few feet away from them.

Madeline knew she couldn't ask Ciaran to leave the woman and the baby behind. He had to know it was an illusion. Laurent and Bella had died in front of him weeks ago.

They were one of Ciaran's deepest regrets. They were his weakness. But still, in whatever dimension or whichever world he existed in at the moment, he could not leave the woman and the baby behind.

They approached what looked to be a river, only to discover that it wasn't a river at all. Instead, they faced a bottomless canyon, connected to the adjacent mountain by a tiny crossing bridge.

The fire exploded into fireballs, and they rolled toward them at an incredible speed. Ciaran gave baby Bella back to Laurent and helped them to the bridge. He held the bridge firmly so that Laurent could cross safely.

The fire closed in. The air pressure and the wind swung the bridge violently from side to side. The wire snapped, and the bridge collapsed.

Ciaran reached out for Laurent's hand. She dragged him over the edge of the canyon. Ciaran's left hand hung desperately onto the edge. His right hand grabbed for Laurent, who was still hanging onto the baby. They were dangling from the cliff by Ciaran's left hand which bore the entire weight of his body, Laurent's, and the baby's.

"This isn't possible. They died. It's an illusion. Let them go," Tadgh said in desperation. But he knew Ciaran would never do that.

Ciaran would never do that if it were his decision . . . if it were under his control, Madeline thought.

This was a test of the strength of a leader, of the ability to compromise and sacrifice smaller subjects for greater causes.

But this was not fair. Ciaran didn't know he was destined to be the ruler of Eudaiz. He didn't know how great of a cause it was. He didn't know this was a test. She had to help him.

19

Madeline kissed Ciaran again. She locked their thoughts together. She intertwined his pain and her pain. She whispered in her mind.

Let them go, Ciaran. You have to survive.

On the bed, Ciaran's right hand grabbed at the bed sheet. Madeline held it.

Let go, Ciaran. For me. You have to survive. You have to live for me. Let go, Madeline thought.

She knew he could read her thoughts. She pulled his hand off the bed sheet. Sweat streamed down his face. Madeline could taste it. She could smell the black water at the bottom of the canyon. She could feel the breeze coming from the darkness. She could hear the call of death.

She kissed Ciaran deeper. *I love you, Ciaran. You have to stay alive. People depend on you. Let Laurent and the baby go. You have to let them go.*

Madeline pulled hard at Ciaran's right hand.

On the screen, his hand let go. The woman and the baby fell into the darkness.

A tear trickled down Ciaran's face.

Madeline wiped away the tear. She had never seen him cry. He never revealed his tears or his pain to anyone when he was in control of his body. She ached for him. In his subconsciousness, he cried for a woman and a baby who were already dead.

The screen went blank. Then it came back up.

"Where's that?" Tadgh asked.

In front of them was an endless snowfield. Nothing but white snow. In the distance, a woman stood in a white coat. She turned around.

"Mother!" Tadgh gasped. "That is total fucking bullshit. That's a trap. Ciaran will be able to tell."

"No, I don't think so." Madeline shook her head. This test was designed to target his weakness. He wasn't prepared. He didn't know. He didn't even know it was a test. Otherwise, he would treat it like a game, and he would win. This was hopeless, Madeline thought.

Ciaran approached Jennifer.

"No, no, no!" In the room, Tadgh yelled and kicked at furniture.

On the screen, Jennifer turned around and smiled. It was the gentlest, most gracious, motherly smile Madeline had ever seen from Jennifer.

Ciaran approached her.

"Jesus Christ, you're an idiot, Ciaran," Tadgh said.

Then Ciaran stopped. He looked at her from a distance.

Jennifer started to approach Ciaran. A bullet came out of nowhere and hit her. She fell to the snow. Red blood pooled, melting the snow around her.

Ciaran charged toward his mother.

Tadgh slumped to the floor. "Oh, no, no. He's done. It's a trap."

But Ciaran stopped a short distance from Jennifer. She lay in a pool of blood. She looked at him. She tried to say something to him.

The snow under his feet cracked. He looked down. It wasn't just snow. It was the ice.

A crack ran from his feet toward his mother.

She was still alive. She was looking at him. She reached her hand out to him. His mother. She would slide down into the icy water when the crack reached her.

Ciaran ran.

"No, no! Don't go near her!" Tadgh screamed at the monitor.

Madeline felt numb. She didn't know what to do.

The crack reached Jennifer.

The ice opened up, and her body slowly slid down into the dark water.

Ciaran dove, sliding on the ice toward his mother, grabbing her hand.

Jennifer and Ciaran both dropped into the dark water beneath the ice.

Jennifer's body sank to the bottom like a stone. Ciaran followed. He tried to lift her up. It was hopeless. Her eyes were glassed over. She was dead. Ciaran tried to lift the body again, but it wasn't possible to move her.

Ciaran looked up. A white light shone from the crack in the ice above through the darkness of the water.

"Go back up, go back up!" Tadgh talked to the monitor again.

In the room, Madeline gathered blankets, sheets, whatever she had on hand to cover Ciaran. His body temperature was dropping so rapidly. It was as if he would turn to ice at any moment. He'd fail this test. She knew he would. Madeline just wanted him to stay alive. She could only hope that failing the test would not cost him his life.

She could only hope.

Ciaran was coming back up to the surface. He headed toward the light.

But the ice had closed over.

"What the fuck!" Tadgh yelled as if it would help.

Ciaran punched the ice from underneath, but it did not give an inch.

Madeline heard herself praying. No, there was no time for that. Think. She had to think.

Ciaran punched the ice again. His breath was very short now. He punched again.

On the bed, Ciaran's lips turned purple. His pulse slowed considerably.

"He's drowning," Doctor Thomas said.

Madeline thought she heard the doctor say something about drowning. Maybe not. She held Ciaran. He was as cold as ice now. He did not seem to be breathing. Tadgh was saying something, and it seemed as if there was a lot of commotion in the room. Madeline blocked all of it out.

She needed to think. She was his only connection.

What could she do? Punch through the ice block. Should she use that trick again?

Madeline kissed Ciaran's cold lips. He wasn't responding this time. She used her thoughts again.

Use my strength, Ciaran. Come back to me. Punch through the ice. You can do it.

Madeline grabbed his hands.

She squeezed them.

Nothing worked. He didn't respond.

"Come on, Ciaran," she said aloud.

On the screen, a dim shard of light drifted into the distance in space and time.

The image flickered. Flickered. Flickered. Then it went blank.

Ciaran let go. And he sank.

In the darkness, an image of Madeline appeared. She was on top of Ciaran. She was pulling him back up. He could see her face. He could see her pulling him up toward the light.

She looked at him. She smiled. She was as beautiful as an angel, coming out from the darkness. She gave him air. She kissed him. She held his body and pushed him upward.

Use my strength, Ciaran. Use my body. Come up with me.

They both moved up through the dark water toward the light. Together, their bodies punched through the ice.

It broke away like thin crystal.

In the room, Ciaran gasped and opened his eyes.

He saw Madeline's face. Still the same as it had been in the dark water. She looked like an angel. She was giving him air. She was kissing him. Her eyes were closed. She didn't need to look at him. They were connected. They had come from the darkness into the light, using their unified energy.

At this moment, they were one.

"You're very photogenic, especially when there is lust in your face, Madeline," Jo said while gawking at the monitor.

Madeline didn't register the information about the world around her. She was straddling Ciaran—the same way she had pulled him up from the dark water. She kissed him, and Ciaran held on to her.

"Hey, hey, hold on! You guys have a live audience here," Tadgh protested as Madeline and Ciaran kissed even more intensely.

Everyone hurried out of the room. They closed the door behind them.

$\mathcal{E}$veryone else left, but Jo stood outside the door of Ciaran's room for a little longer. She had to digest all of the information. Her head was still ringing.

The last seventy-two hours had been such a journey. War, sacrifice, death, life, love, and lust. It was truly surreal. The most bizarre thing is that the entire experience hadn't been a game. She didn't even design such weird settings for her games.

In only a few short weeks, her life and Madeline's had changed forever.

Although she'd go back to New York with Madeline soon, nothing would ever be the same. She knew Madeline would drag this out until right before Ciaran had to leave for Eudaiz. Then she'd tell him she couldn't go with him. Jo had promised not to tell.

It was awful, but she would do the same if she were in Madeline's place.

Then an image of Tadgh crossed her mind. She smiled to herself. There was something about him that made her smile whenever she thought of him. Something sweet and gentle.

Jo turned to go back to her room. While she was walking down the hallway, a door opened, and someone dragged her inside.

She was grabbed so fast that she didn't recognize who was pulling her—or to where. She fell into someone's arms.

There, she recognized Tadgh's masculine scent and his strong grip around her waist. "What in the world are you doing, Tadgh?"

"I owe you a slap in the face."

She smiled and swung her arm. She stopped her hand an inch from his face. "You really aren't going to duck?"

He grinned. "I promised you."

Madeline was right. The LeBlanc brothers should trademark their signature grins.

"All right. I forfeit my rights to claim that slap. Consider it a truce. I'm tired, Tadgh. I just want to go back to my room."

Tadgh nodded. He turned and picked up the game console she had designed for him from a side table. "I completed all the levels of the game."

She took it from him. "Impressive. Do you want the next level?"

"As long as you design the games, I'll play all of them."

"Why? You said you hated gadgets."

"But I love trying to understand how your mind works."

Shit! She stared at him. He'd hit it—her weak spot. *Damn it.* Jo turned away. "I'll design another level for you. It's going to be more difficult . . ." she said as she walked out of his room.

Tadgh grabbed her from behind. He spun her around and pressed her against the wall so fast that it knocked the breath out of her. He gazed into her eyes and sealed her lips with his kiss.

All she wanted at that moment was to surrender.

He carried her, and in a second, she was on her back in his bed. Passion pulsed out of every pore of his body. He was irresistible.

Regardless of how many men she'd been with, she'd never experienced this strong of a pull. She had always been the one in control. She would normally flip the man over and pin him down. But she lay there and took him as he came.

She tugged at his shirt and dug her hands into his taut muscles. His body was erupting with pleasure. So was hers. She could normally luxuriate in the pleasure and then walk away.

But not with Tadgh.

She stopped their kiss.

Tadgh opened his eyes and looked down at her.

She touched his cheek and tucked his hair back. "I don't do long term, Tadgh. If we do this, it's only going to hurt down the road."

Tadgh eased off her, then off the bed.

He held a hand out to help her stand up. Then he led her to the door.

"You're not going to say anything?" she asked.

He lifted her chin up and kissed her lightly on the lips. "I don't do long term, either. And you're right. This will only hurt us."

he next morning, after a meeting with Lindsay to arrange a series of executive duties for LeBlanc Pharmaceuticals, Ciaran drove Madeline, Tadgh, and Jo to the villa outside London. They went to the villa to retrieve the disk as she had promised her grandfather.

Madeline glanced at the sky—it was as overcast as her mood. The closer it was to the time that Ciaran had to take up his duty with Eudaiz, the shorter the time she had with him. She didn't want to resent fate, but there wasn't much else she could do.

"Madeline!" Ciaran called out.

"Huh?"

"Is that the villa?"

Madeline looked to where Ciaran was pointing. The villa looked the same, surrounded by a fence of trees. "Yes," she said.

Ciaran parked at a distance from the front gate.

"It looks deserted," he said.

"Don't tell me they all died at Fountains Abbey. We didn't kill that many of them," Tadgh said from the back seat.

"The police said there were more than forty bodies in Mrs.

Hanson's house. Someone must have killed all the soldiers and stashed their bodies there," Jo added.

"What was Richard like when you last talked to him?" Ciaran asked.

"As if we'd been friends forever!" Tadgh sneered.

"He said Eudaiz is a universe, not just a country or a planet. He must be looking after a lot of people . . ." Madeline's voice trailed off when a blast of metallic stench engulfed her. She glanced around. She didn't see her ghost or any blue dots.

But she had the sickening feeling that someone or something was watching her.

"Are you okay?" Ciaran tilted her chin up and looked into her eyes. Whenever he did that, she tended to give in and spill whatever she was withholding from him. She shook her head.

"I . . . just have a severe headache."

"I'll take you home as soon as we finish this." He glanced toward the house.

"How many were in the house when you were here?" Ciaran asked.

"About twenty. I think the villa looks fine . . . "

The entrance door slid open, and a man walked out.

Ciaran pushed Madeline behind him. Tadgh did the same with Jo.

The man walking toward them looked to be in his forties. He wore a dark suit that could comfortably conceal a gun. Ciaran shifted slightly. Tadgh made exactly the same move. Madeline knew they were both making sure their weapons were readied.

The man approached. "Madeline, Ciaran, Tadgh, and Jo."

"Yes . . ." Madeline said.

"I'm Lucien Hine. I replaced Douglas."

Madeline remembered vividly how Douglas, the head of the fighters, had died at Fountains Abbey. Douglas had been kind enough to her and was a good subordinate to her grandfather.

"Mr. Hine, we're here to collect the disk as instructed," Ciaran stated.

"Yes. I've been waiting for you. Please come with me." Lucien turned and made a beeline for the house.

Inside, he strode toward a wing leading to a side door. He turned into a larger room, spacious and empty. Ciaran glanced at the setting—or lack thereof. He saw nothing suspicious.

"I'm clearing out this place," Lucien said.

"And going where?" Madeline asked.

"That's to be announced." He pointed to the cabinet. "There. I could have brought the disk to you, but Richard insisted you all come here and see the gateway. I think he meant this machine."

Lucien pressed a series of buttons on a wall panel. At the far end of the room, a wall-sized door slid open, revealing a mainframe computer unit that took up the entire width of the wall.

Rows and columns of electronic signals flashed and flowed across the screens. A control panel was located in the lower right corner. Its black glass shone, and its silver buttons were decorated with unrecognizable symbols. Madeline speculated that they were ancient symbols or some kind of language from Eudaiz.

Ciaran stood in front of the machine wall, shoving his hands into his pockets, looking at the machine as if it was a classical painting in an art gallery.

Jo gaped at the machine. "It's still operating. What will happen if we eject the disk?" Jo whispered.

Ciaran shook his head. His eyes were cool and flat. "I wouldn't take the disk now. Not until I am sure what's on it."

"How will you know what's on the disk without taking it home?" Lucien asked.

"I'll operate this machine," Ciaran said.

"It won't trigger anything, will it, Ciaran?" Madeline asked with concern.

"We're not yet ready for you to head into another dimension for another bloody training session," Tadgh said.

Ciaran contemplated. Then he turned toward Lucien.

"Who operated this computer before?"

"Juliette. At least that's what I've been told. I never met her," Lucien responded.

Tadgh rolled his eyes. Madeline asked, "Do you know what happened to Douglas? What exactly is your task here?"

"I've never met anyone in this house. It's a bit strange. I spoke to Richard via holocast . . ."

"Holocaust? What kind of communication is that?" Tadgh winced.

"No. Holo *cast*. It's an advanced communication channel that projects holographic images in augmented reality environments," Lucien spoke with authority in his voice.

"That's the funky beam of light where holographic images can walk around inside it—or jump out if they choose to. The same way Juliette kicked your ass before, Tadgh." Jo grinned.

"Nothing's funky about that beam," Tadgh grumbled.

"That's the way space stations communicate these days. I don't want to make things complicated. The technology is very advanced. My task is to give you as much assistance as I can so that you can reunite with your grandfather," Lucien said.

"Please make it simple. We're rookies when it comes to computers." Madeline smiled.

Ciaran chuckled. "We need to talk to Richard now. Would you mind giving him a call via holocast?"

Lucien shook his head. "He left this morning and won't be available for three days."

"Well, we don't want to try to operate this machine until we have more information from Richard. So we'll come back later when he's available to talk to us. Madeline can speak to him from anywhere," Ciaran said and turned to leave.

"But I have to demolish this place tomorrow. That's my job. Come on!" Lucien said.

"It will have to wait," Ciaran said dryly and walked away.

"Come on. You've seen the gateway machine. Why don't you take the disk with you? I'll turn this machine into scrap metal tomorrow anyway. Here." Lucien slammed his palm onto a gray eject button.

"Holy crap!" Tadgh said.

Ciaran and Tadgh pushed Madeline and Jo behind them. They all stared at the machine, unsure whether moving was a good idea.

The disk was ejected from the machine. The screen of the control panel flashed one line of green text: *Task completed.*

"Which task?" Madeline asked.

A number appeared on the screen, counting down by one unit per second: *six zero four seven nine nine, six zero four seven nine eight, six zero four seven nine seven . . .*

"Is that a time bomb?" Tadgh gasped.

"We're getting out of here," Ciaran said. They hurried toward the door while Lucien stood still, puzzling at the machine.

When they were at the door, the control panel flashed a red line of text: *Six zero four eight hundred.*

Lucien eventually turned and darted for the door.

They stormed outside the villa.

From a relatively safe distance, Ciaran asked Lucien, "What exactly did Richard tell you to do?"

"He said you would come and collect the disk. I had to make sure you saw the gateway before you left."

"My grandfather didn't ask you to eject the disk, did he? He wanted us to see the computer so we knew what to do and to take the disk without triggering some sort of countdown," Madeline said.

"Why didn't you say so before? Why didn't Richard make that clear?" Lucien protested.

"I don't think Richard knows about the countdown," Ciaran said. "Juliette must have coded it in."

Tadgh snorted. "He should have known Juliette better. And we have no idea what sort of bonus features Juliette may have kindly programmed into the disk."

"All right. It's my fault. I'll go in and get the disk for you," Lucien said.

"Don't do that. It might explode when you pull it out," Madeline said.

"It's a countdown to something. What's the original figure, Tadgh?" Ciaran asked.

Madeline noted that Ciaran assumed Tadgh would naturally remember the number. She was astonished when Tadgh actually remembered it.

"Six zero four eight hundred," Tadgh said.

"So what is that?" Ciaran asked.

Tadgh contemplated. "It's the number of seconds in seven days."

Jo gawked at Tadgh.

Ciaran nodded as if it was no surprise to him that Tadgh had been able to calculate the answer. Ciaran contemplated. "All right, even if it is a time bomb, we still have time. I'm going in to see if I can stop it."

"What if I'm wrong?" Tadgh asked.

"About the numbers?" Ciaran raised an eyebrow at Tadgh. "Then we won't stand a chance at anything else," he muttered and strode toward the villa. They all followed.

In front of the gigantic computer, the countdown had reduced by five minutes, the amount of time they had spent outside.

"See, you're right, Tadgh. It's a countdown by the second," Ciaran said.

"That ought to help," Tadgh muttered.

Ciaran looked at the machine for a while. Then he said, "I'm going to try something. Why don't you all leave the premises for the moment?"

There was no movement behind him. He turned around to stern stares from everyone. Ciaran turned back to the computer and typed some commands.

The monitor flashed: *Insert the disk.*

"I'm asking the computer to resume the task it was undertaking before. I'm trying to reverse the process to see if I can trick it into thinking that the disk had never been ejected," Ciaran said.

"You know what you're doing . . . you don't have to tell us, Ciaran," Jo said.

Ciaran nodded and continued typing.

The monitor flashed again: *Insert the disk.*

Ciaran shifted his left shoulder, then pushed at the disk. It slid silently inside the massive computer. The machine hummed for a second.

The monitor flashed again. *The requested task has been completed. Do you want to re-execute it?*

Ciaran shook his head. Then he said something in French. He typed in a negative command. Ciaran typed another command.

The monitor flashed: *The report is not available.*

Ciaran mumbled something else in French. Although Madeline didn't speak French, it sounded like swearing to her. When she saw a smile on Tadgh's face, she knew Ciaran was cursing out the machine.

Ciaran typed in more commands. There were more responses from the machine, but nothing useful about the task the machine had executed. At the same time, the numbers continued their countdown down by the second.

Ciaran stopped typing and thought for a moment. Then he typed again.

The monitor flashed: *The information is available. Palm print verification required.*

A square box appeared on the surface of the monitor.

Madeline stepped forward from behind Ciaran. She nudged him aside and placed her palm on the monitor. It was obvious Ciaran didn't agree with Madeline's action, but he didn't say anything.

TEXT FLEW ON THE MONITOR:
Print verified.
Madeline Kelley.
Biological age: Thirty-three.

Born in Alphi.
Citizen of Eudaiz.
Successor of Sciphil One—Richard Kelley.
Exempt from elimination.

"EXEMPT FROM ELIMINATION. What the hell does that mean?" Madeline asked.

Ciaran darted at the control panel. His fingers flew over the keyboard.

The monitor flashed: *Population of Eudaiz: six hundred and four point eight billion residents.*

Ciaran stepped back and looked at the results.

"What was the original figure on the screen before, Tadgh?"

"Six zero four eight hundred," Tadgh said with a slightly shaky voice.

On the monitor, the countdown number was six zero three nine hundred.

"It has been fifteen minutes since the original figure—that's the equivalent of nine hundred seconds. That means they are eliminating a thousand residents per second as we speak?" Tadgh said.

"What do you mean by elimination?" Lucien asked.

Ciaran shook his head. "Look at the figures and see for yourself, Lucien."

"My grandfather is killing a thousand people per second!" Madeline muttered in disbelief and stormed out of the villa.

22

*C*iaran charged after her. He got to her in the front yard. He pulled her into his arms and held her tightly.

"Come on, darling, calm down. I don't think Richard knew the disk would trigger the elimination," Ciaran whispered.

She tried to wriggle free, but his arms were as strong as steel shackles. When her emotions were in check, Ciaran let her go.

She called out, "Grandfather! I know you can hear me! We need to speak!"

Tadgh and Jo had followed them to the front yard.

Richard's hologram appeared. He looked as if he had aged ten years since they had last spoken.

"Grandfather, what is this elimination?"

"I swear to you—I didn't know!"

"So what *do* you know? What do you want from me, really?"

"I asked Juliette to write a program that allows Sciphil successors to access the Daimon Gate by themselves. I didn't know she had done something to the program to trigger this."

Madeline narrowed her eyes. "I don't believe you."

"Why would I want to kill the citizens of Eudaiz, Madeline?"

"You are ambitious. You want to control Eudaiz. You said so yourself."

"What good would it do me to control a universe with no inhabitants?"

"Tell us how to stop it. What's happening now in Eudaiz?" Ciaran asked.

"How can I tell you how to stop it when I don't know how it started? Juliette's program is killing people in Eudaiz. They're dropping dead by the thousands."

"You have to tell me how they're dying. Are the citizens human? If so, you have to tell me the cause of death. If they're robotic or machinelike, they can be shut down by a computer program, and I'll have a different solution for that," Ciaran explained.

"They are human-like. They're built for the Eudaizian environment. You could say that they are very fragile humans compared to those on Earth. Juliette brought something, some chemical, from Earth and is infecting them with it."

"How are they infected? Is it airborne, in the water?"

"Food. Our food is different from yours. It's a built-in system that automatically releases into the body. We program the food supply for the entire year. Juliette's program released a chemical into the food supply system. We cannot cut it off. It will take a year to reprogram."

"So either way, they'll die," Tadgh mumbled.

"What did Juliette release into the system?"

"If I knew, do you think I'd have let this happen?"

"You're saying the chemical was released. If I ask the program to resume, it might release even more of it into your system. But it wouldn't cause any more harm. I'm going to have to resume the program to know exactly what was in it."

Richard nodded. "The damage has already been done. The toxic chemical is inside the system. No more harm can be done. But if there's a way you can identify the chemical and figure out how to eliminate it, then we'd stand a chance."

Ciaran nodded. "I'll try." He turned and ran inside the house.

Inside the villa, Ciaran resumed the program. He glanced at the countdown clock and looked quickly away. Madeline stood right next to him. She knew he needed her to be right there by his side. So that was exactly where she would be.

The computer hummed and resumed its task. Ciaran typed in a chain of commands.

The monitor revealed streams of letters, codes, and symbols.

Ciaran looked at it.

He stared at it.

He turned and looked at Madeline.

Then he turned back toward the monitor. He couldn't believe what he was seeing.

He withdrew from the control panel. Madeline grabbed his hands. She sensed what was coming but could do nothing to help. She squeezed his hands. She couldn't read the computer syntax, but she knew the gibberish on the screen meant bad news.

And just to complete the terrible joke fate was playing on her, her random psychic ability let her read Ciaran's thoughts for the first time.

Madeline held Ciaran's shoulders and spun him around. "Ciaran, I love you. Listen to me, whatever happened wasn't your doing. Whatever you are going to do, please remember I love you, and I need you. Before you take any action, please think of me . . ."

Ciaran didn't seem to hear anything Madeline said. Rage was like a haze of dark matter that consumed him. She could feel his rage as much as he did. It seeded in his soul, waiting for a chance to reach out and devour him.

He shrugged off Madeline's hands and left the room. Madeline saw that her hands were shaking. She looked at Tadgh, who was waiting for her instructions. "Tadgh, please don't let him get into a car or anything."

"What the fuck is that?" Tadgh pointed at the monitor.

"Juliette used Ciaran's Golden Life formula. She tweaked it into a weapon of mass destruction and contaminated Eudaiz's food supply system," Madeline said.

Tadgh shook his head and raced out the door.

Outside, Ciaran was charging toward the car when he was tackled by Tadgh from behind. The brothers both rolled through the grass and mud.

Ciaran got up and strode again toward the car.

"You're not getting into the car. You want a one-on-one? Come on. Come here. We haven't done that in a while."

"I'm not in the mood to fight with you. Don't!" Ciaran warned. He turned around to get to the car.

Tadgh charged at Ciaran for another tackle. Ciaran swung around. In one short second, Tadgh landed on his weak ankle about fifteen feet away from his original position.

He lay on the ground, moaning.

Ciaran rushed for the car.

Jo darted toward Tadgh. She tried to help him up but couldn't take Tadgh's body weight. They both ended up on the ground. Madeline helped them both to get up.

She saw Ciaran sitting behind the steering wheel. She understood his pain. The Golden Life was his lifelong invention. With it, he'd hoped to change people's lives, to cure all diseases. Now it was being used by Juliette to cause this massacre.

She approached the car and got in. She sat next to him, saying nothing, just holding his hand. After a while, he calmed down. He got out of the car and approached Tadgh.

"Sorry about your ankle," he said to Tadgh.

"It can be fixed. No big deal. But if you drove that car away and broke your neck, I don't think I'd be able to fix you."

Ciaran grabbed his brother, bearing the weight from Tadgh's weak side. "Let's go home and find a solution to this mess." He turned toward Richard. "If I find an antidote for the chemical Juliette used, I assume that the computer in there can inject it directly into the food supply in Eudaiz?"

Richard nodded.

"So you promise not to turn that machine into scrap metal tomorrow?" Ciaran looked at Lucien.

"I'll guard it with my life."

Ciaran nodded and helped Tadgh into the car.

23

*J*o glanced at Ciaran. It had been twelve hours so far in the lab that he'd manned the computer mainframe. She worked on her smaller unit, but there were only limited activities she could help with.

Pharmaceutical wasn't her expertise. She could run simulations for each formula he created, but she couldn't even read the results.

Madeline entered the lab. "I need to put some food into you both."

Tadgh was right behind her. "For your info, it's pizza."

Jo sniffed the air and grinned. Tadgh approached. "Hello, green eyes. May I interest you in some slices of melted cheese on beef, chicken, sausages, sundried tomatoes, onion, and god knows what else?"

Jo laughed. "Sounds deliciously healthy."

Ciaran said nothing.

He concentrated on putting some kind of chemical extract in tubes and jars. Then he prepared two syringes, dropped the liquid in the syringes into small containers, and mixed some chemicals with the liquid. He looked pleased. He then entered the information into the computer.

Madeline approached. "If you need more time, don't push it, Ciaran. Give yourself a break."

Ciaran put the syringes down on the table. He pulled Madeline into his arms and held her. "I'm done."

"You've got it?" Madeline yelped in joy.

"Still has to be tested. I need to call Doctor Thomas."

"Why?" Jo asked.

Ciaran pointed at the two syringes—one contained a golden liquid and the other one a green liquid. "That's the Golden Life with Juliette's manipulated formula. The green one is the antidote. I need to test them before I enter the codes into the system."

"By testing, you don't mean injecting them into yourself, do you?" Madeline narrowed her eyes. "That's why you need Doctor Thomas?"

"I have to . . ."

"You need to test the drug, and there is no time. I get it, Ciaran," Madeline stated firmly. "But if something happened to you, what do you think Doctor Thomas is going to be able to do?"

"Can we use a lab rat?" Jo asked. "I know it sounds awful, but . . ."

"The rat can't tell me what it feels, Jo. I need to monitor the drug absorption to adjust the doses of some of the key compounds," Ciaran said.

"The rat can't tell you. But I can." Tadgh grinned.

Ciaran, Madeline, and Jo turned around. Tadgh was sitting on a chair at the end of the long lab table, holding an empty syringe.

He had injected the golden liquid into himself.

"What the fuck are you doing, Tadgh?" Ciaran darted toward him, picking up the empty syringe and staring at it in disbelief.

Tadgh shrugged. "Do you want my info or not?" He stood up, but he lost his balance and fell forward. Jo grabbed him. She struggled, and Madeline darted in to help. They lowered him down onto the lab bench.

Ciaran dragged over some equipment and connected Tadgh to the machine to get his vital signals.

"How's your breathing?" Ciaran asked.

"Fine."

"Dizzy?"

"Very."

"Vision?"

"Not good."

Ciaran typed like crazy on the keyboard.

"Scale vision from one to ten."

"Three."

Ciaran attached a drip to Tadgh's arm via a cannula. The green chemical started to drip through the transparent tube into Tadgh's system.

"Scale dizziness."

"Ten"

Ciaran altered something on the computer.

"Vision?"

"One"

"He's drifting, Ciaran," Jo said.

Ciaran made further adjustments.

"Tadgh, you hear me?"

No response.

"His pulse is rocketing, Ciaran," Jo said.

Ciaran shook his head. He made more adjustments.

"How's that, Jo?"

"Slowing down . . . too much, Ciaran."

"Now?"

"Still too low." She checked Tadgh's breathing. "He's not breathing!"

Ciaran adjusted dosage again. "Jo?"

"No. Not helping." She shook Tadgh's shoulder. "Come on. Don't do this." Tadgh was getting colder by the second. Ciaran kept typing on the computer, trying to make the necessary adjustments.

"Jo!" he called out.

"He's not breathing. Damn it." She ran to the corner and pulled the resuscitation equipment over. "You wanted to be the guinea pig

. . . Well, you got what you wanted. I've never used this before," she muttered and pulled out the chargers.

Ciaran darted over and pressed a series of buttons that she assumed set it at the right level. "Do it, Jo," he said and ran back to his computer.

"No more pulse." Jo glanced at the monitor and then cranked up the machine and jolted him.

The green liquid continued to drip into his system, but there was no pulse to distribute it.

"Again, Jo," Ciaran said.

She did it again. And once more. Tadgh's body jerked up, and his vitals showed up on the monitor.

"He's back," Jo said.

"Tadgh, you hear me?" Ciaran asked.

Tadgh's body tensed. He convulsed. Jo jumped onto the bench to hold him down. His body twisted and contorted, and Jo was thrown to the floor. Madeline jumped on the bench and pinned Tadgh down.

Ciaran kept making adjustments. The convulsion eased off. He calmed down. His pulsed returned to normal. His eyes fluttered and opened.

"You hear me, Tadgh?"

"Yeah," Tadgh said groggily.

Ciaran cursed under his breath, but it was loud enough for Madeline and Jo to hear.

"Still hear me?" Ciaran asked.

Tadgh grunted out an answer.

"Vision now?"

"Ten."

"Good."

"Heart rate, Jo?"

"Perfect."

"Still dizzy?"

"Fuck yeah."

"Well, it will stay that way for a few hours. You'll just have to deal with it."

Ciaran grabbed the disk from the computer. "He can't go anywhere for the next five hours or so. Would you take care of him, Jo?"

Jo nodded. "Of course."

Ciaran checked Tadgh's pulse manually. "How are you feeling now?"

"Fine. Go away. Do whatever you have to do," Tadgh muttered.

Ciaran nodded. "I'm going to the villa to input the antidote into their system. I'll be back soon." He exited the lab with Madeline.

As soon as he heard the sound of the door clicking closed and the security system reported that Ciaran and Madeline had left the premises, Tadgh grunted and grabbed his head.

Jo held his shoulders. "Look at me, Tadgh. You're in pain. Tell me what to do. I'm going to call Ciaran."

"No, no. Don't. It has nothing to do with his antidote. I'm not in pain." He turned over to lie on his stomach and banged his head on the bench.

"Well, keep doing that and you'll soon have real pain in the head."

Tadgh sat up. She looked into his beautiful gray eyes, and all she saw there was pain. He reached over and brushed her face with his fingers.

Why did he do that? Then she turned and caught a glimpse of her face in a mirror on the door of a lab cabinet. Her eyes were red and swollen on her pale face. "All right. I must have wept a bit. But you scared the hell out of me. What's the big deal?"

He raked his fingers through his hair. "When I . . . whatever just happened now . . ."

"Like, you stopped *breathing!*"

"Yeah, whatever. Well, I was kinda like floating into darkness. I felt nothing. And then when I came back, I saw a glimpse of light. Sparks. Shapes. Voices." He looked at her now. "It's not the light that I saw, Jo. I saw your emotions."

"Right . . . so I was scared."

He shook his head. "Not just current emotions. Memories of emotions—and the results of them. I'm sorry, Jo. I didn't mean to peek into your privacy."

"No! Wait . . . no. You mean, you can see what's in my head? What I felt and what happened?" Tears came now. She couldn't control them. She'd never felt so violated.

She started to run out of the lab, but Tadgh grabbed her from behind. "I'm so sorry. I didn't mean it. I had no right to invade your privacy. But there is a part of your emotions that I am involved in. And to that extent, I'm entitled to discuss it with you."

Tadgh was too strong for her. Regardless of how much she struggled, she couldn't free herself from his grip.

"You love me, Jo. Let's face it."

"Let go of me. I have nothing to talk to you about."

"You have to love someone someday, Jo. If not me, it has to be someone."

"Let go!"

"I could see your feelings for me, loud and clear. I could see your fear. Your regrets. Your shame."

She wriggled around and punched at his chest.

"It could see your pain when it raped you. I saw the residual of its satisfaction after it was done with you. It's not human, Jo, and it wasn't your fault. I could smell the disgusting metallic stench of its satisfaction. It lived in you, and you let it—"

She broke free, turned around, and slapped him across the face.

"I'll find out what it is, and I'll kill it, Jo. . . " he snarled as she stormed out of the lab.

24

The helicopter landed at the back of the villa. Ciaran and Madeline rushed to the house. Lucien was waiting for them at the door.

"Is Richard around?" Ciaran asked.

"Not now, but he will be soon."

Ciaran went straight to the computer room. Madeline knew that he deliberately did not look at the countdown clock. The number had been reduced significantly, and he didn't want to see it.

Ciaran slid the disk into the computer.

The monitor flashed:

New disk inserted. Print verification required.

Ciaran pressed his palm against the verification panel.

THE MONITOR FLASHED:

Print verified.

Ciaran LeBlanc.

Biological age: 32295.24X

Born on Earth.

Citizen of the United Kingdom.

Successor of Sciphil Three—Bran LeBlanc.

"YOU'RE 32,295 YEARS OLD!" Madeline said.

"No. They exaggerated. I'm only thirty thousand years old." He smiled. "They must have used a different numerical reference system. The computer is trying to convert it into something we can understand," Ciaran said while working on the commands for the program.

"Well, it's not doing a very good job. That's totally confusing!" Madeline said. "I verified before. Why did it report my Earth age?"

Ciaran paused. Then he glanced back at the computer. "The only difference I could think of is that Ayana has put a seal on my successor position, but Richard hasn't put a seal on yours."

The discussion was going in a direction she didn't care for. Madeline steered him away. "Ayana mentioned Bran is the king Sciphil, but she didn't mention he has the same surname as you. Are you related?"

Ciaran shook his head. "Unless I'm totally missing a branch of our family tree, there isn't a Bran in my family."

He executed the disk and inputted the codes into the system. Finishing the last lot of codes, he hit the "execute" button. The countdown number flashed once. Then it stopped counting down.

He nodded with satisfaction. They waited through five humming seconds. Nothing happened.

"Could you please call Richard?" Ciaran asked Madeline.

Before Madeline had a chance to call, a holocast appeared, and Richard's hologram paced back and forth in the room. He puzzled at the machine.

"I'm expecting a confirmation that the elimination has been canceled. What's happening in Eudaiz?" Ciaran asked.

"I don't know. At least it stopped," Richard said.

"That's not good enough," Ciaran muttered. "It looks as if the program paused the elimination process. But I'm not sure how long it will hold."

Richard shook his head. "I think you have to terminate the program from the source."

"How?" Madeline asked. "Didn't you say Juliette is reforming in her tower, and no one except the king Sciphil has access?"

"But you're a computer genius, aren't you? Juliette said so herself. Can you hack into her system?" he asked Ciaran.

"You want Ciaran to hack a multiversal computer system from here? I know next to nothing about computers, but that's just not possible," Madeline said.

"What exactly do I need to do to access Juliette's system?" Ciaran asked.

The computer hummed and let out a short beep. Then the countdown number started up again.

"The antidote didn't work," Ciaran muttered and mumbled some profanity.

Madeline could see Ciaran sweating with anxiety. She could feel the weight of the responsibility he'd put on his shoulders. No matter how much she tried to convince him otherwise, Madeline knew he would still take on that responsibility.

"Juliette must have used her verification code somewhere that you can hack . . ." Richard said.

"In theory, but it will take time."

The faint smell of burning electrical wiring filled the room. They looked at the computer. It looked fine. A holocast beam appeared, and the hologram of Ayana stepped forward. A corner of her long white robe had been burned off, and blood stains dampened the hem. She turned to Richard.

"Some of the Sciphils protect Eudaiz while some just take a vacation!"

"The Black Rock attacked your district because your defense is weak. Why blame me, Ayana? We're busy here. And you might not have to worry about protecting anyone in Eudaiz soon." Richard's face started to turn red.

"What do you mean?" Ayana asked. She looked at Madeline and Ciaran. "Juliette has been detained to her tower, or so I am told."

"Not just detained—they killed her presence. Now she will reform and be invincible. At the moment, she uses one of the programs to contaminate the food supply system, killing thousands per second," Richard said.

The color drained out of Ayana's face. "Only the king Sciphil can terminate Juliette. We can get Ciaran there, but that process will take a long time."

"That is if he passes the Daimon Gate alive," Richard said.

Ciaran suddenly grabbed his head and grunted in pain. "I can't hear you. Your signals are going to blow my brain out. Can you use the system?"

The control panel flashed new signals, and a line of text appeared. "Welcome, Ciaran. We are finally connected."

"Who are you?" Ciaran asked.

The monitor flashed: "I am Sciphil Three."

Ayana gasped. Madeline glanced over and saw tears gleaming in her eyes.

"Bran LeBlanc? I don't recognize your name from our family," Ciaran said.

The monitor flashed: "I am Bran LeBlanc. Consult Jennifer for the alteration of your family tree."

"Don't drag my mother into this," Ciaran snarled.

"She's already in. Go through the Daimon Gate and find out for yourself."

"Bullshit."

Ayana spoke, "Juliette is reforming in her tower and has been causing us tremendous problems. You need to terminate her, Bran."

The monitor flashed: "Can I borrow some of your energy to make contact, Ciaran?"

Ciaran was about to respond when Madeline pulled his arm.

"What exactly do you mean by borrowing his energy?" Madeline asked.

The monitor flashed: "I cannot make a physical appearance on Earth without borrowing some energy from Ciaran because he's my successor. My energy source has been disconnected."

From the back, Ayana said, "It's true. That's why he's been unable to communicate with us in the last thirty-three years. We didn't know that this connection was possible. Please help us, Ciaran."

Ayana trembled. Tears rolled down her face.

Ciaran contemplated and held his eyes briefly on Madeline. "All right, Bran."

The air thickened. A beam of light and an image appeared. This was not a hologram. This was a physical appearance from an advanced holocast. This was similar to what Juliette had used before.

Bran LeBlanc was a tall man with a kind face, white hair, and very intense gray eyes—the strongest resemblance shared in the LeBlanc family.

Madeline approached Ciaran. She wrapped her arms around his waist and could feel the energy leaking out of him in waves.

25

*C*iaran staggered back a few steps and then regained his stance. The appearance of Bran had sucked up a significant amount of energy from Ciaran. Madeline could feel his body weakening by the second. He was finding a point of support. She braced her body against his.

Ayana cried out loud as soon as she saw Bran. Bran gave Ayana a nod of acknowledgment. Richard stood in shock and gave Bran a stern stare. Bran was about to say something to the two Sciphils, but Madeline cut him off.

"With respect to your reunion, sir, whatever you're here to do with the borrowed energy from Ciaran, could you please do it quickly?"

Bran stepped closer to Ciaran and Madeline. He smiled. He had a genuinely kind smile, Madeline thought. The kind of smile that made her want to call him Uncle Bran.

"She's my successor. My granddaughter," Richard spoke up from the corner.

Bran's eyes brightened. "You're Madeline. You've grown up to be a beautiful young woman. It was worth it, wasn't it?"

Ciaran shifted his stance. A drop of blood trickled from his nose. Madeline tightened her grip.

"Why are you here? What can you do to stop the program?" Madeline asked.

Bran glanced at Ciaran. "You're strong, Ciaran. You resisted my full training. I hope you don't live to regret it."

"What do you need from me to stop that program?" Ciaran asked, wiping off the blood.

"You think you're responsible for what Juliette did. You hold yourself responsible for too much of what you cannot control. That's your weakness, Ciaran."

"He didn't lend you the energy to give him a lecture. So be quick, Uncle Bran." Madeline couldn't believe that had slipped out of her mouth. She'd called him uncle. A flash of a smile came across Bran's face when he heard it. He let it go.

"This is a very temporary solution. With your human energy, I can only cancel the program in Juliette's tower. The energy will not be enough for me to perform any other function. Do you understand that?"

Ciaran nodded.

Bran continued, "I know Juliette has turned against Eudaiz, and I need to end her existence. But I can no longer do it myself. Thus, you, as my successor, have to do it. To take my role as Sciphil Three and King of Eudaiz, you have to go through the Daimon Gate. I authorize Ayana to give you the induction and take you through the opening. You will not take commands from anyone but me. Am I understood?"

"And what if I fail to go through the Daimon Gate?"

Bran looked at Ciaran. "You know you won't fail. Why ask such a question?"

Ciaran nodded. He was leaning fifty percent of his weight on Madeline now, without showing the others. Madeline was glad she was tall enough to support him.

"You are using your human energy to support me to go to Eudaiz and cancel the program Juliette is running. You might not be able to recover from that loss of energy. Do you understand what you're agreeing to?"

Ciaran nodded.

"You're a brave man, Ciaran. I am pleased. This will only take ten seconds."

Bran nodded at Ayana and Richard and beamed off. As soon as he swooped out of the room, all six foot three inches of Ciaran collapsed to the floor.

Tears rolled down Madeline's face.

Ciaran looked at her. "Come on, darling. I'm not hurt. I just don't have any strength at the moment. Don't cry. I can't even wipe the tears off your pretty face." He smiled.

Madeline brushed away her tears and forced a smile. "I'll keep a lookout and make sure no one comes to beat you up now."

Madeline removed a strand of hair from Ciaran's face. "Promise me you won't agree to anything else?"

"Okay."

The ten seconds went past. Bran came back to the room.

"Successful?" Madeline asked.

"Trivial. I canceled Juliette's program. And I had a quick look around before I left. Her reform is progressing very fast."

"How fast? How long before we need to cut off her energy source?" Ayana asked.

Bran crouched down next to Ciaran. "You understand that you will take on the Sciphil Three position and that you will be the one who ends Juliette?"

"Yes."

"We won't have much time. Two weeks top before she regains her form. Ciaran has to pass the gate before that. When and where is your next opening, Ayana?" Bran asked.

"Australia. In ten days, Earth time," Ayana said.

"Why?"

"My successor is Zach Flynn. He's an Australian."

Bran nodded. "Fair enough. Good successors are hard to come by. I trust your judgment."

"He's strong, fair, and talented," Ayana responded.

Bran spoke to Ciaran next. "Ayana's gate will be yours, Ciaran. Before I go, there is one last thing I would like you to consider."

Madeline's body tensed up. This couldn't be good news.

"And that is?" Ciaran asked.

"The chemical in your body, the Golden Life, it was not meant to be there. Your mother put it in there. I know that. But you are better off without it."

Madeline raised her voice. "No, no, you don't understand Bran. He died. Ciaran died in front of me. If Jennifer hadn't injected him with that chemical, he would have been gone. I saw it with my own eyes . . ."

"He can survive . . ."

"No, I said no. Whatever you're suggesting, the answer is no. Now, you piss off and go back to where you came from. Give Ciaran his energy back."

"What are you suggesting?" Ciaran asked.

"No, Ciaran, you promised me. You didn't see yourself dying. I did. I won't go through it again. You go away, Bran. No more talking. You saved the people of Eudaiz. Please leave."

"What are you talking about, Bran?" Ciaran asked again.

"I won't forgive you, Ciaran, for doing this to me again. I swear to you." Tears streamed down Madeline's face. She knew what was coming. She knew she couldn't stop it.

Bran looked at Madeline, and then he looked at Ciaran. "I can purify that chemical out of your body. Nobody else can do this for you. You're strong. You can survive without it. This way, you don't owe anything to anyone."

"No, he can't. He was shot. He died in my arms!" Madeline cried.

"You have a very strong will. You can survive. If I go now, you will not have the energy to get me back here to perform that function for you. It will be in your body forever. You will owe Juliette forever . . ."

"If you do this, I will not forgive you whether you survive it or not, Ciaran," Madeline said in tears.

"Then get rid of it," Ciaran said to Bran.

Madeline sobbed.

"This is an equivalent to level one of the Daimon Gate. The purification process is not a big deal. You can pass it easily. But this procedure will return you to the stage just before the time you received the chemical. You will be very weak. Another risk is that I have to use your energy now to perform that function. It will weaken you even further. I think you are strong. But the risks cannot be ignored. Are you sure this is what you want?"

Madeline scrambled to leave the room.

"Madeline!" Ciaran called out. "Please stay with me."

Nasty son-of-a-bitch, she cursed silently as she sat down next to him.

"I'll take my chances, Bran. Do it," Ciaran said.

"Remember what you promised me when you refused my training, Ciaran. I am holding you to it."

Ciaran nodded.

Bran grabbed Ciaran's wrists. Ciaran's body jerked up as if he had been electrocuted. His body glowed and gradually turned almost transparent. Then it returned to a solid state.

In front of a devastated Madeline, Ciaran fell flat on the floor. He was no longer conscious. A satisfied smile crossed Bran's face. He turned around and disappeared the way he had come.

Madeline dumped the contents of her purse looking for the phone. She grabbed the phone and shouted into it, "Doctor Thomas!"

26

"Jo! Come back!" Tadgh yelled after Jo. She had called the taxi and had cleared her way out of Mon Ciel. The door slid open, not for Jo to go out but for Doctor Thomas's car to come in. In the sky, the helicopter hovered and landed in the front garden.

"Trouble," Jo muttered. "When can I get the hell out of here?" She turned back and saw that Tadgh had rushed over to the helicopter transporting Madeline and Ciaran.

She turned and was about to follow everyone inside the house to check on Ciaran when she saw a ghost standing outside Mon Ciel. Jo squinted.

Outside Mon Ciel's fence, the image of the old man, Larry, stood. *The ghost from ten years ago in Australia? He'd come back?*

She couldn't believe this. She had never seen a ghost before. She wasn't the psychic—Madeline was. The man had died—and she didn't believe in ghosts.

The image flickered and changed into something else. It was now a demon, the kind that only appeared in her hologames. A metallic stench engulfed her.

She looked toward Mon Ciel and saw Tadgh looking at her. He

had read into her emotional reactions. This newfound ability of his was going kill their relationship. At least it would from her end.

Jo ignored the image and walked toward the house.

They were taking Ciaran inside. Madeline was so focused on him, she wouldn't see anything else. But then Jo saw Madeline pause and turn to look toward the gate where the ghost had just stood.

Madeline frowned then turned to enter the house.

Jo felt to be sure the gun Ciaran had given her was still inside her jacket and walked toward the house.

HALF AN HOUR LATER, Jo stood in the back garden admiring the headless statue of the Goddess of Kindness. Madeline had told her the story of the statue once. Ciaran had blown its head off when he had experimented some chemical compound when he was only four.

Jo shook her head. Madeline loved Ciaran so deeply. She understood why. But the whole thing was still surreal to her.

And now Tadgh and her feelings for him.

It was seriously time for her to leave.

The door to the back garden slid open, and Madeline strode out.

"How's he doing?" Jo asked.

Madeline was startled but composed herself quickly. "He won't be moving for the next day or so. But apart from that, he's fine. I needed to talk to you, Jo."

"By sneaking out through the back gardens? You're going to leave Ciaran now, aren't you?"

"I . . ."

"How are you going to get out of the gate without alerting security?"

Madeline shrugged as if she hadn't planned that far in advance.

"Okay, let's go."

"What?"

Jo dangled the car keys in front of Madeline. "Tampering with the security system from the inside is child's play for me, especially when Ciaran is down. Nobody will catch us."

Madeline nodded, and they both darted toward the garage.

Five minutes later in the car, Jo smiled. "I didn't know you had tachophobia like Tadgh."

"I don't have an issue with speed, but this isn't exactly the right time for you to be driving fast. You're worse than Ciaran when he's mega mad." Madeline braced herself against the passenger seat.

"Well, he will be apocalyptically mad when he finds this out."

"I don't have a choice. But you do. Why are you leaving Tadgh? You obviously like him."

"The stupid drug he injected himself with gave him the ability to see people's emotions. He saw my emotions from Australia, and he's not going to be fine with it."

"I'm sorry about that, Jo."

"Madeline, it's been ten years. I'm no longer eighteen. Shit happened. And I've grown out of it. Even if it raped me—"

"What? I thought he tried, but he couldn't."

"It wasn't Larry. You know what I'm talking about, Madeline."

Madeline narrowed her eyes. "No, I don't."

"Larry was being controlled. He was possessed. You said so yourself."

"Yes. And because of that, he's innocent. When I killed him, I killed an innocent man."

"There are no ghosts or spirits, Madeline. What controlled Larry was a mind bender. People who can control other people's minds. It took me a long time to come to terms with it."

"Stop the car, Jo. Stop it. Now you sound like Ciaran."

"Yes. I sound like him." Jo stopped the car and stormed out. "And for your information, we agreed that you should tell me what exactly you did. Not just 'I might have killed an innocent man.'"

"Ciaran knew?"

"Not yet, but I'll tell him. Ghosts don't rape live people. But it raped me, Madeline. I can still smell his metallic stench on me."

"Oh, Jo! I'm so sorry. You never told me."

"Told you what? A mind bender forced his mind on me and mentally raped me? I don't know how it worked. I just knew when I was violated."

Tears rolled down Jo's face now. "I can still smell him. I would have rather it made Larry rape me because at least then I could have fought back."

"It's not just the one incident. It's a ghost. Believe me. It's haunted me for years. Remember all the records of violent crimes I committed when I was younger that you erased for me? It made me do those things."

"It possessed you?"

"No. It possessed men around me to kill and rape everyone around them and then kill themselves. It told me that. It's haunted me since I was ten. And it told me that if I didn't kill the men it possessed, it would keep killing. My only solution was to knock the men out. But it'd never forced itself on any women."

"Until me?"

"Maybe. I don't know, Jo. I just saw it in front of Mon Ciel before. I thought I had killed Larry, and it had let me be in peace. I don't know why it came back."

"I saw it, too," Jo muttered. "But I don't believe it's a ghost. Mind benders are humans. As long as it has blood and flesh, it will just have to deal with me now, once and for all."

Madeline suddenly grabbed Jo and shoved her toward the back. "It's here."

"I can smell it." Jo pulled out her gun.

Madeline stepped toward the front and pulled out a knife she had tucked inside her jacket.

The metallic stench filled the air.

But they saw no one.

An image flickered in front of them, and something in the

shape of a man appeared. "It's the middle of the damn day . . ." Jo grunted and shot at the creature.

The bullet shot through the image and kept going.

The image appeared a bit more solid, and the ancient, ugly face of an old man started to form. He smirked at them.

Jo shot again. The same thing happened. The bullet tore through thin air.

"It's not human, Jo. I told you." Madeline charged at the image and swung her knife. It disappeared.

They heard car engine roaring in the distance.

"Oh, no," Jo moaned.

"When a guy with tachophobia drives like that, it tells you just how much he cares about you. But we can't let him come near us, Jo. The ghost possesses men."

Tadgh's car fishtailed and stopped right next to theirs. He stormed out, yelling. "Where do you think you two are going?" He walked for a couple of steps and started to stagger. His eyes became bloodshot.

"Oh no!" Madeline cried and darted toward Tadgh. Before he could do anything awful, she used her knife handle to whack him in the temple, knocking him out cold on the ground.

Madeline turned around, looking at Jo. "Now you've seen it first-hand, Jo. It wants me, and there's no other way to handle this."

Madeline strode toward the car, got in, and drove away.

27

*L*ondon streets were the same. Londoners were the same. Morning rush. Traffic. Winter breezes. Madeline did not expect that London would have changed much in the last few weeks. It was still winter. The sun still came out late in the morning.

The days were still short, and the darkness still occupied a large part of the daily cycle. People still worked for a living. Life in London went on with or without what happened in Eudaiz, another universe. Soon, this London scene would be history to her.

She thought about Ciaran. She allowed herself a moment to think of him. She thought she would think of him for the rest of her life.

This morning, Jo had messaged her and said Ciaran had regained ninety percent of his strength, according to Doctor Thomas. She trusted that, with Jo's skill, her message wouldn't be tracked.

Madeline still resented the joke fate had played on her. Even with a standby, she couldn't get a flight to New York until tomorrow. She was lucky they could schedule her at all.

She finished off her coffee and headed toward the British

museum. She wanted to take a look at John Dee's glass again for no particular reason. It might be the last time she got to see it, and it had marked a significant stage in her life. Why not?

The museum was quiet but not lacking visitors. Madeline found the glass again. It sat there just as it had for the last five hundred years.

The air thickened. Madeline was into this holo-techno enough now to know that she was entering a holo-communication sphere. A holographic image of Ayana appeared. Ayana was careful enough to block the view from other visitors so that they could not see the holo-communication.

"I thought it was my grandfather," Madeline said.

Ayana smiled. Her blue eyes pierced through the thickened air to cast a warm look at Madeline. "I understand that you left Ciaran."

"He told you? Or were you stalking me as soon as I left Mon Ciel?"

"The latter, Madeline. Do you think Ciaran would storm out to the field to tell me that you left him?"

"Of course not. What can I do for you? As you can see, I no longer want to be associated with this whole ordeal. I will explain things to my grandfather."

"I'm afraid it won't be so simple."

"Okay, I broke my promise to grandfather. He'll be mad at me. So smite me—or whatever you have to do. I'm going back to New York tomorrow. No one can do anything to stop me."

"Including Ciaran?"

"Yes."

"You're being unfair, Madeline. Ciaran didn't have a chance to talk to you."

"I have had enough of this."

"You're clear-headed. You have a strong mind. I think you would serve Eudaiz well. I'm not speaking for Ciaran. I'm speaking on behalf of the Eudaizian people who will need you in the future."

"I'm sure you can do without me. I'm going back to New York. Let me be an ordinary person."

"You were born in extraordinary circumstances. You were conceived in Eudaiz, like me. But you spent your life on Earth. You can never be ordinary, Madeline. You don't know what it has taken for you to be able to stand here talking to me like this. You don't know what or who has paid for your well-being."

"You're blackmailing me?"

"If you say so. I will do what I must. That's the least I can do for your grandfather. He is ambitious and manipulative. But his concern for Eudaiz is genuine."

"What happened to my grandfather?"

"The Black Rock is our utmost enemy. Richard's district was attacked several times. That was why Richard formed an alliance with Juliette and sought the sample gold from the LeBlancs. He was developing a weapon that could destroy the Black Rock. But that weapon cost a lot of resources and lives. He hasn't gotten anywhere with it—you know the situation with Juliette. Now he's under attack and has no weapon."

"What can I do? Can't you help?"

"I can help Richard within my limits. But I have to take care of my district first. Richard has created a lot of enemies and alienated many other Sciphils because of the way he operates. It doesn't do him any favors now. The most important mission of a Sciphil is to have a ready successor. If you leave Richard now, he will have no chance of finding another one."

"Is he injured?"

"I'm not sure about his current status. But I know he will need you very soon. I don't think he could even open the gate for you now. He is very weak."

"What do you suggest I do?"

"Go back to Ciaran. Go with him to Australia. I will let you go through my opening, provided I have Richard's permission to do so."

Madeline shook her head. "I've killed an innocent man. My soul is not virtuous—I can't pass the Daimon Gate alive. There is no point in my grandfather trying to get me there."

Ayana nodded. "He will have to pay for this dearly."

"How? What do you mean?"

Ayana shook her head. "Richard has decisions to make. I can't speak for him. But, in any case, if you need to go through the gate, I am happy to take you to the opening together with Ciaran. Goodbye for now." Ayana smiled, and the hologram disappeared.

MADELINE LEFT THE MUSEUM. She walked along the streets, heading back toward her hotel, wallowing in thought. She should stick to her plan. She should talk to her grandfather, Madeline mused. Whether she desired it or not, he was her family, the only family she knew.

Madeline realized that for the first time in her life she felt like an orphan.

She had been a fighter. Shuffled from one foster care home to another. Growing up, making a career and a life for herself. Then Jo came along. She loved Jo's family and adopted them as her own. Maybe her life had been so full that she had never had a chance to think about her biological connection. She'd never thought of herself as a victim or an orphan.

Why now?

It was when she'd found her biological family that she'd felt lonelier than ever.

Madeline had arrived at her hotel before she knew it. As soon as she entered her room on the sixteenth floor, she knew something was not right.

She wanted to leave the room, but she couldn't open the door. It seemed to weigh a ton. Her window was open, letting a blast of cold air inside. The breeze cut into her skin. As much as she would like to deny her sixth sense right now, she could not dismiss the nauseous feeling she had.

It was him. Her ghost. In the room.

$\mathcal{M}$adeline turned on all the lights in the room and slammed the window shut. The room warmed up instantly. Too warm. She heard the click of the door lock. She charged toward the door and opened it. She could run and escape the hotel. Be seen in public. Then there would be nothing he could do to her.

But she was not a coward. She refused to run. He wouldn't appear for no reason. What was it he wanted?

Madeline re-entered her room and closed the door.

"I know you're here. Come out. Tell me what you want. Don't be a coward."

Nothing happened.

"I know you're here. I can sense you. You know that, right? Whatever you're waiting for in here is not going to happen because I'm leaving now."

Nothing.

"Chicken," Madeline mumbled and went to the bathroom. She filled the sink with water and poured all of the bottles of shampoo, conditioner, lotion, and gel she could find into the water and dissolved them. They made a light-colored bubbling tub of water.

She scooped up some water with a small hotel glass and started splatting it everywhere.

She kept doing so until the water hit a form. "Got you, bastard," she said.

She dropped the glass instantly and grabbed a chair. She flew over the bed and swung at the form where she could still see some water on it.

It roared, the low rumbling roar of a beast.

Madeline kept swinging and hitting. She knew it couldn't hurt her. For more than a decade, it hadn't changed its ways. It would not hurt her directly. It would have to borrow a human form to do so. But there was no one else in the room for it to manipulate. So Madeline continued her attack without fear.

It roared again and again, whenever Madeline hit it. But it would not run away as it had before.

The air in the room thickened, an obvious sign of a coming holocast. "Not now, for God's sake," Madeline thought.

A beam of light appeared, and the holographic image of Richard formed.

"Poor timing, Grandfather. I know we have to talk, but not now and not here."

Richard stared in confusion at Madeline, who was in combat stance on the bed, holding a chair with both arms.

"I've never done you harm, Madeline."

"Not you! Just not now. Please go away, Grandfather."

Madeline gauged the room. The marks of water were gone. She could not see the form of the beast now. If there were another person present, the beast would have manipulated the person's mind to attack Madeline. That was its usual *modus operandi*. Unfortunately for the beast, Madeline thought, Richard was a hologram, and could not attack her physically.

The room was quiet. Madeline could not sense the beast anymore. If it was still there, it had somehow suppressed all of its energy.

A moment went past. Another moment. And still nothing happened.

Richard looked puzzled.

Madeline put the chair down. When she finally had a chance to look at Richard, she cried, "Holy Jesus Christ, how bad are you hurt?" His clothes were covered in blood.

She darted toward the hologram only to realize that she couldn't touch him.

"I'm injured. But the majority of the blood is not mine. Don't worry, I can manage."

Madeline puffed out a breath. It was probably not a good time to tell him she did not want to be a Sciphil anymore.

"What can I do for you now? Ayana told me your district is under attack."

Richard smiled. "It was very kind of her. She is a good woman no matter what side she is on. What else did she tell you?"

"That you're in trouble, and that you might need me."

Richard sneered. "Since when am I in trouble? And who is she to judge?"

"She wasn't judging. She simply wanted to help. I'm leaving Ciaran. I wanted to get out of the whole Eudaiz ordeal, and that's why she told me that you might need me. Now you're telling me you don't need any help. So that's great. I'm free to go back to New York then."

Richard's eyes drooped. He shook his head. He didn't have to say it—Madeline could see that he was in deep trouble. The man had his pride. Just like Ciaran—choosing possible death over having Juliette's drug in his system.

Damn it, Madeline cursed silently.

"Would you come to Eudaiz and help me?"

"You want me to be right next to you, ready to take the Sciphil role if anything should happen to you, right? Is it really that bad?"

Richard drew in a long breath, then nodded. "I made a mistake. It was too late to recover. I might never recover. So yes, it's bad, and

I need you to be ready. I have to take you through now. I might not have another chance at this."

"My soul is not virtuous. I have killed an innocent man. The Daimon Gate will kill me."

"What happened?"

"There is a creature. It haunted me through all of my childhood. It said it would continue to kill people until I killed one of the innocent men it possessed. Don't ask me why. I don't know. The creature was here just before you came. I thought it had left me after I killed that man in Australia. But for some reason, it's come back."

"What creature? What are you talking about?"

"I told you I don't know. And I don't know how to solve this situation. But I can't come with you to Eudaiz."

"There had to be a way," Richard said.

"Maybe there is. But I don't want to waste your resources, chances, or energy. If you have a choice better than me—"

"I don't have anyone else, Madeline. You're the only family I have left. I would never leave this role to an outsider."

"You might have to if I die during the process."

"I won't let anything happen to you, Madeline. I lost you once. Never again. If I don't have a successor, I'll let my eudqi collapse."

"You'd let Eudaiz be destroyed?"

"I would rather it be destroyed in my hands than in someone else's. I don't know who to trust anymore. The Black Rock is evil. They have many forms. If they took over Eudaiz, it would be a fate far worse than death for the citizens."

Madeline nodded. "So what's the solution?"

"There are different routes to take, and there is one I know of that could work. I won't risk you going through it, though, before testing it. So I'm going to get you inside the gate for the test. Are you afraid?"

"No, of course not."

Richard nodded. "We'll go from here."

"What? You mean you can open the Daimon Gate right here? I thought it was huge."

"Opening the gate is very significant. But this is just a test. I'll see if I can push it."

He concentrated for a moment. His image glowed as if he were transforming from a hologram into a real presence. Madeline could feel the energy radiating from him. The circle of light around him—which used to be the holocast—expanded and brightened.

The circle illuminated in blue and white and grew even more. Madeline felt the energy growing as if Richard were moving closer to her. She shifted, suddenly not sure she was ready. But it was a call to duty, she might as well just do it.

Richard reached his hand out. "Give me your right hand."

Madeline obeyed. Richard held it. She felt his presence and the waves of energy coming out of him like little electrical currents.

The hotel room was small, but when the circle of light reached a corner, Madeline saw an unusual bend in the light. She could see the shape of the beast hiding in the corner.

"Stop, stop!" Madeline yelled at Richard.

Richard stopped the circle.

"Can anyone go through the gate when you open it?"

"Yes, Madeline. But I cannot hold it for long. What is it?"

"The creature is here, in the room. Can it get through the gate?"

"Yes. But a gate-crasher will be killed on exit. Let it come in. I'll kill it now to save time."

Richard expanded the circle further.

For the first time, Madeline could see the creature in full view. It was truly a beast. The light from the circle shined on it. It stood. It had a shape like that of an ape, and its head nearly reached the ceiling.

Richard could see it now.

"Stop!" Madeline yelled again. She grabbed the chair and attacked the beast as she'd done earlier. It seemed totally unaffected by her blows.

Richard stopped the circle of light. He looked at the beast as it approached him. His eyes registered some recognition.

"Kyle Wolf, you traitor!" Richard grunted out the words, his face glowing with a strange combination of astonishment and fury.

"Richard!" The beast croaked out his name in a disembodied voice that came straight from hell. "I have come to see you fail and to claim what you promised." It paused for a moment and then roared and reached its hands out to grab Richard.

Richard staggered back to avoid the creature's grasp. He was not a hologram now. He was on the verge of opening the gate, and he had revealed his presence.

Madeline hit the control panel for the ceiling fan. It whirled at the beast's head. The hit was not hard enough to do damage, but it served as a distraction.

"Go!" Madeline screamed at Richard.

Richard withdrew the light and vanished.

29

The beast turned around. Its body was still glowing. It was a gigantic ape. It slapped at Madeline with the back of its fist, throwing her against the wall.

Madeline was nearly knocked unconscious. She scrambled up and realized that the beast had gotten smaller and looked more like a werewolf now. Madeline deduced that whenever it attacked her directly, it grew smaller and weaker. That was why it had never touched her before.

Madeline charged at the wolf now for a one-on-one. She attacked with all that she had—fists, legs, fingernails. She tried to cause as much damage to it as possible before it became invisible to her again.

The wolf roared in pain and fled to the hallway. Once there, it became invisible.

Madeline ran out of the room. She saw a pregnant woman walking toward her with two toddlers in tow. Suddenly, the woman's eyes rolled up in her head. She let go of the toddlers and charged at Madeline.

"Oh, great!" Madeline muttered. "You've hit an all-time low . . . A pregnant woman? You scumbag!" Madeline stepped backward, trying to talk to the woman.

"Don't come near me! Go back to your sons. They're crying." She knew this wouldn't work. The only way to get the beast out of the woman was to knock her unconscious. Madeline had done that before. She knew what she was doing.

Madeline dodged to the side. The woman lost her momentum, and at that moment, Madeline snatched a vase and hit her. The woman fell to the floor, but she got up quickly.

Madeline plucked up the two wailing toddlers, carrying them in through the exit door. The woman stood, looking at Madeline. She didn't attack. Instead, she grabbed the handle of a door next to her and pulled. She broke the door with her bare hand and entered what looked to be a control room of some kind.

"Oh, no . . ." It was too late for Madeline to do anything. She didn't have the strength to go against the woman. She carried the toddlers quickly down the emergency exit stairs.

Madeline fled out into the foyer of the hotel. She shoved the toddlers toward the concierge. In the corner of the foyer was a sign saying "Conference Main Hall" with an arrow pointing to a wing.

Madeline ran up a flight of stairs to the main hall of the conference wing. She entered the conference and galloped up to the stage. The presenter was talking about global warming or something like that. The gigantic PowerPoint screen was flashing images of forests, animals, and oceans accompanied by a host of diagrams and figures.

Now I look like a lunatic, she said to herself.

She snatched the microphone from the presenter and glanced down the hall toward the few hundred people in the audience.

Someone to the side of the stage was alerting security. They entered the hall, approaching the stage.

"My name is Madeline Roux. I'm a journalist from New York. I am asking you, for your safety, to exit this hall right now. Exit this building right now. Don't panic. Don't scramble. But leave, please."

Silence.

Security approached the stage. The crowd was not moving.

"Oh, for God's sake. There's a bomb in the building," she lied. "Run now if you want to live." And the chaos began.

Madeline threw the microphone at the approaching security guards and rushed toward the backstage. On her way out, she saw a fire alarm box. She smashed the glass with her elbow and pulled the alarm.

Madeline ran to the main entrance. A good number of people had already gotten out of the building. Alarm bells rang everywhere.

But nothing was happening.

Shit, Madeline thought.

Across the hallway, a group of security officers gathered. One of them pointed at her. Madeline ran from the building.

As soon as she had gotten past the door, she could hear and feel it—the rumbling sound of a fireball hurtling down from the sixteenth floor.

The ground was shaking. The building went down.

She ran further and further away, and then she was drowning in dust and darkness.

30

*M*adeline didn't know how long she had been lying still in the dark. She could hear herself breathing, but she found it hard to breathe in the dusty air. She drew another breath. It was difficult. She tried to say something but couldn't.

Someone handled her. She was lifted, pulled, poked. Someone else gave her some air. That made the breathing easier. She was still in the dark, though. She thought she heard a familiar voice. Ciaran's voice. Maybe. Maybe not. She drifted off again, into the darkness.

Madeline came about a little later. She opened her eyes to see a white ceiling. She was in a real hospital room judging by the equipment around her. She took a mental inventory.

She didn't feel much pain. A drip was attached to her arm. She moved a little on the bed. Everything felt fine. She could wiggle her toes. Perfect. Intact. She could feel all ten and could see her four limbs still attached to the right places on her body.

Madeline pulled herself up. That felt okay, too. She hitched herself up again. Good. She looked around. By the looks of it, it was a private hospital room. There was a small TV in the corner of the room. Madeline grabbed the remote control on the side table and turned it on.

She was not surprised to see scenes of the hotel disaster flashing on the breaking news. But her jaw dropped when she saw Ciaran giving a press conference.

Her Ciaran, calm and collected. His gorgeous face looked straight at the screen. He looked as if he was talking directly to her. Madeline didn't know what time it was or how long it had been. But by that morning, Ciaran was supposed to have gotten ninety percent of his strength back. Now he looked as if he had only fifty.

A reporter asked, "Mr. LeBlanc, could you confirm that the LeBlancs will donate all medical equipment and pay for the expenses of the treatments for the victims at the hotel today? You said so at the scene."

"Yes. It won't be the first time we have made donations to medical causes."

"But this is the first time the LeBlancs have made a public announcement. What's different about this incident?" another reporter asked.

"Madeline Roux is a good friend of mine. As you flashed her name all over the media, I felt the need to address some of the questions myself."

"The witness said she knew about the explosion."

"She saved a lot of lives because she warned people. If she had any involvement in it, she would have given herself a safer distance from the explosion, wouldn't she? If you want to waste your time speculating, feel free to do so, but do not waste my time."

"You were seen at the police station with her a few weeks ago. Is there a connection between that incident and what happened this morning?"

"No." Ciaran stared hard at the reporter. The reporter withdrew his next question.

"How do you explain the LeBlancs' involvement at the Fountains Abbey fight, where many people were killed?"

Ciaran glanced at the reporter who had asked the question. "Which of us did you see there?

"The report stated that . . ."

"I don't care what your report said. If you want to make such an accusation against our family, you'd better have proven facts. Once you have these facts, make an appointment and talk to my lawyers. Twenty people died today. I will only take questions about how to help these victims and their families and how to help the business get back on its feet. If you think you can use this opportunity to dig up some dirt on my family, you are sadly mistaken."

Madeline turned the TV off. She knew how it went. This used to be a part of her life. Now it was being used against her. She could handle the media and the scandal. But she could not bear seeing Ciaran's face. She didn't know seeing him would hurt so much. She didn't even know why it hurt.

She felt tired now. She put the remote away and tried to reach for the water. A nurse saw her from the outside and hurried in.

Ciaran was right behind.

The nurse gave Madeline the water and some meds. She checked on vitals.

Ciaran usually did all of that. Doctor Thomas was the only medical professional that Ciaran would allow when it came to her. But now, Ciaran stood in the corner of the room, watching the nurse working on her. He stood there with his hands jammed in his pockets. Like an acquaintance of hers.

The nurse finished and left the room.

Ciaran approached. He sat beside the bed. It felt as if he was sitting a mile away.

"Lindsay saw you on the news. He called me."

"I guess I'm famous now. Or infamous."

Ciaran smiled. "I don't care about reputation. You should know that by now. Or you might not . . . Your documentation was destroyed at the hotel. I regret that you won't make your flight tomorrow. But I can make arrangements for you at your earliest convenience . . . if you like."

His words felt like a knife in her heart.

Ciaran squeezed her hand slightly. "The doctor said you were noncritical four hours ago. You can go whenever you want. I figured you wouldn't want to go back to Mon Ciel. So I arranged this private room. I hope you don't mind."

Madeline said nothing. It was so damn polite of him. She would rather he kicked and screamed. She could handle flash rage. She had so much to tell him. But that wasn't the issue. The issue was that she wanted to tell him so much. She missed talking to him. At this pace, she would probably die of old age before she could tell him anything.

"I could get Jo to come stay with you. Whatever you like. Tell me what you want."

Madeline looked at the circles under Ciaran's eyes. She wagered he had about forty percent of his energy left. Going backward from ninety this morning.

Madeline cursed herself for doing such a good job. Maybe she should get him back to zero percent, the way he was at the villa, and then he'd miss the Daimon Gate in Australia. Then the billions of people, people who would be enslaved or killed in Eudaiz, would worship her statue in a monument!

"Madeline, what would you like me to do?" Ciaran asked.

Madeline opened her eyes. A tear trickled down her face. Then another.

"I need a moment by myself," she said.

Ciaran nodded. "I'm sorry. I didn't realize I had caused you so much pain. I am terribly sorry." He walked to the window and stood looking outside.

"Ciaran."

"Yes? I'm leaving now." He turned around and walked toward the door as if he were leaving. His deep gray eyes were intense, and his face was unfathomable—his usual Ciaran look.

"You have your secret gun with you?"

Ciaran glanced at the door. "Yes."

"Can I borrow it?"

"What?"

"I don't even think guns worked on it."

Madeline slid down under the blanket, pulling it over her head and sinking her head into the pillow. Ciaran darted toward the bed. He touched her shoulder. "Madeline, are you in pain? Should I call the doctors?"

Madeline turned, lying on her back. Ciaran pulled the blanket down to see her face. Big tears rolled down from her eyes. He wiped them away. It was rare for Madeline to see Ciaran looking this stressed.

"Where does it hurt? I'll call the doctors."

More tears rolled down her face.

"I'm sorry, darling. Please don't cry. I won't do it again."

"You won't do what again?"

"I . . . I . . . You tell me what I did wrong, Madeline."

Oh, great, her British lover was apologizing even though he didn't know what he did wrong.

Madeline pulled at Ciaran's hand. "Would you lie down with me for a minute?"

Ciaran complied.

Madeline rubbed her thumb over the circles underneath his eyes. Down to thirty percent of energy now, her king, her hero. She ought to fix it. She reached over and kissed him.

Ciaran resisted the kiss. "I've never wanted to hurt you. If you tell me what I did wrong, I'll fix it," Ciaran told her.

"I love you, Ciaran."

"So why did you leave me?"

"I can't go with you through the Daimon Gate..." She curled into his arms. There, she told him everything.

"There has to be a way out of this," Ciaran said.

She shook her head. Suddenly, she sensed the beast again. She shot up in the bed, glancing around.

"Is it here?" Ciaran asked.

"Yes. Get away from me, Ciaran. It possesses people. Please go away, Ciaran."

She tried not to stutter, but fear had occupied every corner of her mind now.

She was scared.

She had never been scared of the beast before. She sensed that it was going to do something she hadn't dealt with before. Something with more severe consequences. She feared that the beast was not just a beast. It was something a lot more than that.

Her grandfather had called it Kyle Wolf. Her grandfather knew it and had promised it something it had come to claim.

The air in the room grew cold quickly.

Ciaran jumped off the bed and pulled out his gun.

"Jo shot at it before. It didn't work."

"Jo shot at a projection of an image, Madeline. If it's a thing of flesh and blood, I'll kill it. If it wants to play mind games with me, I'll handle it. It might be able to control other people's mind, but it can't control mine." Ciaran's eyes darkened as he scanned his gun around the room.

---

31

*M*adeline grabbed the water jug on her bedside table and splattered water around the room. In the corner of the room, the water hit the shape of the beast.

"There!" Madeline yelled and pointed.

Ciaran shot continuously at the shape with his silenced gun.

The beast roared. Its shape flashed and glowed and then faded away.

"I told you—if it has flesh, I'll make it bleed."

Then Ciaran dropped the gun and grabbed his head. He ground his teeth and looked at the corner where the beast had stood before. A vein swelled on his forehead, but he stared steadily at the beast.

Madeline knew it couldn't get inside Ciaran's head. It couldn't control him. As he said, in this mind game, he had won.

Madeline dove and grabbed the gun Ciaran had dropped to the floor, but she couldn't see the beast now. She threw the empty jar at the wall. The shattered glass flew everywhere.

Some of the pieces of broken glass hit the shape of the beast. Madeline fired off two shots, hoping they would do some damage.

Another roar.

Ciaran smiled.

It seemed that the beast knew it couldn't get into Ciaran's head. It roared again and slapped at the gun in Madeline's hand. The blow threw Madeline to the wall, and the gun flew away, falling to the floor.

Ciaran grabbed it and, guessing where the beast would be standing after hitting Madeline, he fired at where its head or vulnerable parts might be.

A scream filled the room.

He must have hit it, Madeline thought.

The noise from the room drew the attention of the medical staff. A nurse rushed inside, but as soon as she entered, her eyes rolled up and she charged at Ciaran. Ciaran said nothing. He stepped forward and hit the nurse in the head. She fell to the floor, unconscious.

"I'm sorry," Ciaran said to the nurse and walked over to help Madeline up.

"You know how this works?" Madeline asked as she rushed out of the room with Ciaran.

"Classic hologames." Ciaran smiled. They ran down the hallway heading out of the hospital and toward Ciaran's car.

Ciaran drove the car out of the hospital's parking lot and headed toward the highway.

"Do you think there will be any more surprises from the beast before we get to Mon Ciel?" Ciaran asked.

"I don't know. It's not in the car, thank God. Can Mon Ciel's protective shield stop it?"

"It works against Sciphils. But I don't know what this thing is. The energy coming from it was similar to what came out of Pete Chandler, Sciphil Nine. I still have to work out the properties of its physical presence—or lack thereof."

"Yes, Ciaran?" Tadgh's voice asked on the speakerphone.

"We're on our way. We'll be at Mon Ciel soon. Could you call and make arrangements for George to come to Mon Ciel? We'll need his expertise again. We will need all of his lighting gear."

A truck sped out from nowhere, aimed straight at Ciaran's car. Ciaran spun the steering wheel, and the car spun and hit a tree.

Ciaran reached over. "Madeline, are you okay?"

"Yes." She worked her way out of the tangled airbag.

Tadgh's voice squeaked out from the phone, dropped somewhere in the car.

Ciaran helped Madeline out.

"You're bleeding." Madeline wiped Ciaran's forehead.

"It's nothing. Let's go."

They ran toward Mon Ciel.

From the truck, two men got out. One man's eyes were rolled up. He ran toward Madeline and Ciaran. The second man trailed behind.

"Stop, stop! What are you doing, Sam?"

Then man called Sam kept running toward Madeline and Ciaran. Ciaran pulled out his gun.

"If he keeps coming at us, I'm going to shoot him," Ciaran said to the second man.

The second man dove and tackled Sam. "Come on, man, what are you doing?" The two men wrestled on the ground.

"You'll have to knock him out, I'm afraid," Ciaran advised.

"What?"

"He won't give up until you knock him out," Madeline added.

A shadow rushed up from behind Ciaran and hit him with a gun barrel. Ciaran fell to the ground. A large man lifted him up and pointed a gun at his head.

Sam sat up, looking at his friend, confused about what was going on. They both looked at the large man, who was, at that point, facing Madeline.

"What the hell are you doing, Dave?" Sam said to the large man.

Madeline could see that Ciaran was down to about twenty percent of his strength and had been dazed by the hit. Dave croaked at Madeline.

"Call Richard."

Madeline hesitated.

Dave pressed his gun harder at Ciaran's head. "I want to talk to Richard."

"Yes. Yes. I will. Don't shoot!" Madeline cried out.

Ciaran used whatever strength he had left to grab the gun. He pivoted and threw Dave to the ground. Dave stood up and roared.

"Stop there or I'll shoot," Ciaran warned.

Dave kept charging, his eyes wild. Ciaran shot him in the hip. He fell, screaming in pain. Madeline picked up Ciaran's gun from the ground. They pointed the guns at the other two men.

"Stay right there," Ciaran said.

Ciaran and Madeline ran toward Mon Ciel.

Behind them, a wedge of wind lifted them up and sent them rolling on the ground. When they got up, they saw the beast—a gigantic half-ape and half-wolf creature—coming toward them.

It was Kyle Wolf in his full form.

32

Ciaran and Madeline shot at Kyle Wolf. The bullets barely scratched him. Kyle squinted his eyes at Mon Ciel.

Ciaran caught his look. "He can't get inside Mon Ciel, Madeline. Can you make a run for it?"

"I'm not going to run inside and leave you here."

Kyle Wolf roared insanely. His eyes sparked red with fury.

Ciaran pushed Madeline behind him. "We are successors of Sciphils. You're from Eudaiz, and you cannot harm us."

Kyle Wolf stopped.

Silence.

Then he roared again and charged at Ciaran.

Ciaran pushed at Madeline and yelled, "Run!" They moved quickly. But not fast enough.

Kyle seemed to totally ignore Madeline. His enormous ape arm reached out and snatched Ciaran as if he were a rag doll. Kyle smashed Ciaran's body to the ground as hard as he could then let out an ear-piercing scream.

All three men from the truck fell on the ground, their liquefied brains leaking from their ears.

Ciaran spat out blood.

As soon as Kyle hurt Ciaran, he shrank into a much smaller creature. Ciaran was an official successor, and he could see the effect it had on Kyle.

Madeline rushed in front of Ciaran. She stared at Kyle, ready to take him on.

From behind Madeline, Ciaran stood up. He saw that Kyle had shrunken and seemed to be weakened. Taking the opportunity, Ciaran rushed at him. Kyle was still very strong. Ciaran could normally take him on, but he couldn't now with only twenty percent of his strength left.

After receiving a few good blows to the head from Ciaran, Kyle kicked Ciaran, sending him rolling away on the ground. "See if Bran can protect you now," Kyle laughed.

Madeline stood in front of Ciaran again. Ciaran hoisted himself up from the ground and tried to pull Madeline back. But he didn't even have enough strength to hold onto her. Madeline knew it was hopeless. If Kyle attacked, she would not stand a chance.

Kyle got closer to Madeline.

Just then, they heard the roar of a car engine. The car accelerated, charging at Kyle.

The hit was brutal. Kyle was split almost in half, and the car was crunched up like a piece of scrap metal. Tadgh and Jo crawled out of the wrecked automobile.

Kyle didn't die. He had somehow put his body back together.

Kyle cast a glance at Jo. Suddenly, his eyes softened. In response, Jo pulled out her gun and fired—without any effect.

"He's the one, isn't he? He's the fucking monster that violated you? Tadgh asked. He didn't wait for an answer. He saw it all in Jo's eyes. He pulled out his gun and shot.

Ciaran knew it was hopeless. They couldn't kill Kyle. The beast now advanced on Tadgh.

"I'm the successor of the king Sciphil. You might want to negotiate with me before you do anything rash," Ciaran said.

Kyle snapped back to reality and turned toward Ciaran and Madeline. Ciaran pushed Madeline backward.

But he had no idea how to get out of this one.

He feared this might be the end of them.

A beam of white and blue holocast slashed down right in front of the beast, preventing it from approaching Madeline and Ciaran. Richard stepped out from the circle of light.

"This is not just a holocast," Ciaran said in a low voice. "He's stepping outside it."

Richard drew his sword and charged at Kyle.

An enormous cylinder of wind, made of blue and white light and filled with the tangled shapes of unrecognizable creatures, spun around Madeline and Ciaran. They were surrounded by a wall of sounds so jarring they made their noses bleed.

The smell of electricity and melted plastic and metal thickened the air.

The fight slowed down. From outside the circle of light, they could see that Richard had the current advantage, but both Kyle and Richard had been severely injured.

Kyle charged at Richard. But instead of blocking him this time, Richard simply opened his arms.

"No! Grandfather!" Madeline cried as Kyle's sword pierced through Richard's body.

Kyle roared with fury as Richard slumped to the ground.

"I substitute my life for my granddaughter's claim of her virtuous soul. She is now more qualified than ever. Eudaizian constitution. Clause 1506. Section two. You killed an undefended Sciphil. Not only you are exiled, you are not to set foot in Eudaiz, and your eudqi can never be reconnected."

An inhuman scream split the air. Kyle turned into a creature in werewolf shape and fled. He disappeared into the darkness.

The wind stopped. On the ground lay Richard. He was no more than a heap of burned flesh and material.

Madeline scrambled toward him. She picked him up and cradled him in her arms. "Grandfather . . ."

Richard smiled. For the first time, Madeline saw his smile as a granddaughter looking at her grandfather.

"I'm sorry I lost you when you were barely a month old. I couldn't protect you. I can't even take you to the gate now. I'm just an old man, you see."

Madeline wept. Her tears fell on his burned flesh.

"Nobody has ever shed tears for me, Madeline. You are a good woman. Your sixth sense is your talent. You are a just person. A better Sciphil than I could ever be. You will serve Eudaiz well."

"Please don't die, Grandfather. You haven't given me any training. I need your guidance."

"I have authorized Ayana to take you through the gate. Give me your hand."

Richard burned a seal on Madeline's right forearm. Then he closed his eyes for a short moment. He was quickly running out of breath.

"Promise me you will be a good Sciphil."

Madeline nodded, her tears raining on Richard's body. Richard glanced toward Ciaran. He had no more strength to call out. But Ciaran understood and came over to crouch beside Madeline. "I trust you will be a just ruler of Eudaiz," said Richard. "Promise me you will keep my granddaughter safe?"

Ciaran nodded.

"Kyle Wolf used to be Sciphil Four. He betrayed Eudaiz for the Black Rock. I knew but had no evidence against him. Bran didn't believe me. Kyle wanted your mother to be his wife—he wanted her innocence. I promised your mother to him only to bide my time. Your mother ran off to marry her true love, your father. When the Black Rock killed your parents, I was too late to save them. When I came back, you were gone. I didn't know Kyle had anything to do with this. Not until yesterday . . ." Richard was fading rapidly. His voice was barely audible.

"Is there anything I can do for you, Richard?" Ciaran asked.

"No, my time is up . . . I don't know how Kyle got here. But I know he wants to come back to Eudaiz . . . He'll need the gate opened. I warned Ayana . . . Kyle is evil, and he's invincible . . . Ciaran . . . Promise me you'll protect my granddaughter . . ."

Richard's voice trailed off, and he drew in his last breath. His body dissolved into ash and vanished into the air.

Ciaran pulled Madeline into his arms where she wept for the grandfather she had never known.

33

*M*on Ciel had returned to its elegant quietness. Tadgh looked at the picture of his family in their happy times—his father and mother holding Ciaran and him in their arms. Ciaran and he were mere toddlers at the time, but Tadgh remembered every moment of it.

He craved that happy time so much. But they hadn't had that since the day his father died.

Ciaran would have to go to another universe to fulfill his duty to whoever was out there. *But does that mean he has to leave everything behind?* Tadgh wondered.

Tadgh shook his head. He didn't want to think about it anymore. He flopped down onto the day bed and stretched out.

Someone knocked on the door.

"It's open." He didn't bother to open his eyes. Lindsay and Doctor Thomas had talked about rearranging some of the facilities and equipment inside Mon Ciel. He could feign ignorance, as he usually did, but perhaps it was time for him to take on some of the family responsibilities.

It was time to grow up.

The room was strange. Quiet.

Maybe he should practice his newfound ability. For his first exercise, he channeled his thoughts at Jo. At her emotions. He could again see her feelings. This time, they were as clear as crystal. Pure and directed in one direction—toward him.

He opened his eyes to find gracious Jo smiling at him.

He hopped up and grabbed her. She jumped up and wrapped her legs around his waist. He rushed over to the bed and then gently lay her down. He just wanted to admire her foxy face and her gorgeous green eyes. He played with the raven black hair that fell to grace her fragile shoulders.

"I lied to you before. I'm a long-term kind of guy."

She smiled. "I can tell. But now that you can read my emotions, I don't have to tell you about my feelings, do I?"

"Thank you."

"For what?"

"For giving me a chance. I know I'm not your type." Tadgh grinned.

"I bet there's a long list of girls waiting for you who *are* your type. Why me?"

"I don't know. I'm not philosophical about this."

Jo smiled and shrieked with pleasure when Tadgh's hands traveled all over her body. Migi the cat pushed the door open. TJ followed submissively, wearing the sweet puppy look he only used when he asked for treats.

"Come on! Can we please have some privacy here? I bet you two don't do that to Ciaran and Madeline," Tadgh grumbled.

Jo pulled Tadgh's face back to her and kissed him. "Let them watch at their own risk."

"But TJ is under age. Now, Migi? Take TJ out," Tadgh directed.

The gigantic cat wagged her twin tails in disagreement, but then grabbed TJ by the crook of his neck and strode out of the room.

Tadgh turned back to Jo, but before he could say anything, she flipped him over so that he was on his back. Together, they flew into a heated passion that helped them forget the world around them.

IN CIARAN'S ROOM, Madeline curled into his arms. She traced her finger over the seal burned into his right arm and the tattoo of the key that looked like a crucifix from her angle. "So what does the whole thing make us, Ciaran? What are we?"

"I hope we're humans. But that's inconclusive at this juncture. It doesn't matter where we were born, it's our action that determines our humanity. I thought I knew who I was . . . what I was. But now I think I need a lot more information to draw any conclusions."

"It seems to me that the Sciphils are humans, judging by the way they recruit people from Earth. But the citizens of Eudaiz seem to be aliens."

"By that, I hope you don't think of them like little green men. What we're dealing with is not just space travel and different planets. We're talking about *dimensional* travel. Different universes. Different worlds. I can't even tell you how far or how close their proximity is to Earth."

"You're saying space travel is simple?"

Ciaran chuckled. "Not at all. But you and I will be entering a different world, Madeline. Going through the Daimon Gate to Eudaiz might not be as complicated as what we know as space travel on Earth. It might be as simple as crossing a few dimensions. Maybe that world co-exists with this world, right next to us. Right here." He reached out his hand and made a grabbing gesture into the air.

Madeline rolled her eyes. "Well, that seems simple!"

Ciaran kissed the dimple on her left cheek. "Whatever that world is going to be, as long as we're together, that's what matters most to me."

"Humm, so you're going to be the king Sciphil. Will you have a harem?"

"That's desirable, of course. But you will be Sciphil One. I'm not sure about the political system of Eudaiz, but it sounds kind of like you will be the first councillor. So you will get to approve of my harem." He started kissing her lips, and his hands had suddenly become very busy on her body.

"What if we can't pass the Daimon Gate? I didn't receive any training. You did, but not all of it. What if I'm not qualified to be a Sciphil? Will they send me back to Earth? And can we come back to Earth after you and I become Sciphils . . ." she trailed off, moaning in pleasure as his hands attacked all the right spots.

"Can we worry about that tomorrow? At the moment, I just want to focus on my world, right now and right here, with you."

Her body was tensed up like a bow now. "Ayana said it will be only a few days until we have to go through the Daimon Gate . . ."

"Not so fast. The next destination will still be on Earth, with a real physical location—Australia."

Her breathing intensified, and her system was heading toward an explosion of pleasure. "Let's see if I can identify the right spot . . ." Ciaran said and pushed.

"Yes! Yes!" she cried out, her voice slurred with pleasure.

He laughed, and she flipped him over so he lay on his back. "Not so fast, my king. I don't need to be a psychic to find this location." And she took over.

Together, they traveled to an elusive world of pleasure.

IMPERFECT DIVINE

IMPERFECT DIVINE

Synopsis

Ciaran and Madeline haven't chosen power. Power comes with great responsibility. They'd rather fight for happiness. And Eudaiz is the universe that offers them just that. Happiness.

But to be in Eudaiz and save the lives of millions, they must pass the Daimon Gate tests—the most stringent tests of bravery and worthiness. Tests they might not survive to see the light of happiness they long for.

This final installment in an urban fantasy thriller series, filled with romance and science fiction twists and turns, will take you to the heart of those who dare to embrace the dark side of human mind.

PROLOGUE

*H*er high heels clicked on the hard cold cobblestones of the dark alley. The unpleasant sound echoed back and forth between the narrow stone fences along the sides of the road. Fog crept up from the ground and brushed her long legs that the thermal stockings didn't give much warmth to.

She regretted taking this shortcut already.

But at the other end of this alley, a surprise birthday party was waiting for her. Well, not really much of a surprise since she knew about it. Her best friend had tipped her off by asking her to wear something nice for their girls' night out.

She smiled to herself and tried to ignore the eerie ambiance surrounding her. She was turning eighteen.

Soon.

She heard the sound of flapping wings. This area was notorious for bats—one of those animals she didn't care much for. It had to be an enormous bat by the sound of it. She looked up but saw nothing but the dark sky.

She put her head down and kept walking, pulling out her cell phone to call her friends. No signal. "I'm in the middle of the town, for God's sake!" she cursed to no one in particular and picked up her pace.

Her footsteps echoed louder and louder in the dark alley. Or maybe it was just in her head.

But she wasn't hearing her footsteps now. She was hearing someone else's. She turned around, but there was nothing but a long, dark alley. Reaching the other end where she could see a dim light would be faster than going back.

She could see traffic and pedestrians in the distance. Seeing people made her feel a lot better. She kept walking.

Suddenly, the metallic stench of blood engulfed her. It was so overwhelming she had to gasp to draw in air. The shadow of a man stepped out in front of her, from . . . nowhere. He cast a glance at her with his flaming red eyes. And he smirked.

It was a smirk of victory and satisfaction as if he had just found a long lost treasure.

She froze. She wasn't scared. She didn't pass out. She just couldn't move.

Then a cold blast of air invaded her. It felt like ants crawling all over her body. Her mind was numb. Something was clawing at her soul, seeping into every cell of her body, ripping the dignity out of her.

Every thought she had in her mind. All of her secrets. All aspects of her life. Everything was exposed.

All of her memories of her sweet childhood, of her friends, of her family were leaving her. Bit by bit. The pain in her heart was unbearable.

She was fully awake, lying on the cold cobblestones and watching the last drop of her innocence leaving her. She blinked. And then she saw it. In front and on top of her was the perfect picture of evil.

1

The sound of Jo's voice echoing through the intercom sent Ciaran and Madeline charging up the stairs. They stormed into Tadgh's room, finding him lying flat on the floor, unconscious.

Ciaran took Tadgh's pulse. *Steady*, he mused. His brother was clinically alive and well.

But something was missing inside Tadgh. Something profound. Fundamental. Something that, as a scientist, he didn't care to speak of or even theorize.

Tadgh's soul is gone.

Ciaran shook his head. He couldn't believe he'd let that thought cross his mind. He had no idea how to explain this. Fear clawed at him.

He could cure his little brother of any earthly problem that could be scientifically explained. He had even manufactured the perfect level of sugar in Tadgh's blood—a minor issue Tadgh had when he was a kid.

Ciaran could even help with anything physiological or emotional his little brother might encounter. But the only thing he couldn't help Tadgh with was his mind.

That was the most scientific he could make it. Calling it *the mind*.

When it came to something as metaphysical as a soul, Ciaran didn't even know where to begin.

"How could this happen? One minute we were talking, and the next, he fell to the carpet!" Jo exclaimed.

"He's all right, Jo."

"He doesn't look all right, Ciaran. Is he traveling into another dimension like you did the day before yesterday?"

Ciaran shook his head. "Let's put him on the bed."

Madeline nodded. As soon as she grabbed Tadgh's arm to help, she yelped and released it. A tear rolled down her face.

"What is it, Madeline?" Ciaran asked.

Madeline's eyes were glazed for a short moment, and then they became clear again. "He saw Kyle Wolf. But not via his own eyes," she whispered.

"So whose eyes did he see the monster through?" Ciaran muttered, more to himself than to Madeline. It a rhetorical question. He didn't think Madeline knew the answer. But he had a feeling someone did. Ciaran looked at Jo.

The blood drained from Jo's face. "The eyes of the victim. He could see their emotion and the monster's emotion. He saw Kyle's satisfaction when he ripped the innocence out of someone. Like he once did to me," Jo spoke under her breath.

Ciaran grabbed Madeline's cold, shaky hands. "Sit down, will you?" He nudged her down onto a chair.

"It's horrible." A tear rolled down Madeline's face.

"Let it calm down. It will pass." He kissed her lightly. "Okay?" he asked. She nodded.

On the floor, Tadgh stirred, and his eyes fluttered and opened. Ciaran darted over. Tadgh's eyes were distant, as if he hadn't yet come back to reality. Then in a brief second, Ciaran knew his brother was back.

"Tadgh, you passed out. You remember anything?" Ciaran reached his hand out to pull him up.

Tadgh glanced around the room. He paused at Jo's face. Then his eyes hardened. The darkness in his brother's eyes worried Ciaran. "You can see emotion since you stupidly injected the poison into your body, but it shouldn't force you to *connect* with Kyle."

"No way am I connected with that monster. I don't have a choice here. I see what I see," Tadgh muttered. "Fuck this!" Tadgh kicked the chair, the table, and another piece of furniture as he moved across the room. Ciaran let him go for a couple of minutes then tackled him to the floor.

"Let go of me." Tadgh shoved Ciaran off and stood up.

"Do I have to assign security and keep you chained up, Tadgh? We're going to Australia tomorrow . . ."

"I'm going with you," Tadgh snarled.

"Give me a very good reason to allow that, Tadgh."

"I need to kill the fucking bastard."

"What did you see?"

"Can't tell you. And there's nothing you can do."

"You can't be sure of that," Ciaran countered.

Tadgh stared at Ciaran and said nothing more.

"Very well, you will stay here. I'll assign security and take away all of your access to transport." Ciaran strode toward the door of the room.

Tadgh darted after him and grabbed for Ciaran's shoulder. The momentum of Tadgh's hand pushed Ciaran, shoving him forward. "Don't be ridiculous, Ciaran. I can help you."

Entering the reception room at the end of the corridor, Ciaran turned around. "I said no. You and Jo stay here. I can't take care of you in Australia."

"Let me put this another way, big brother. How can you be so sure Kyle wouldn't try to kill *you* in Australia?" Tadgh cocked an eyebrow in challenge. "I need to go with you."

"Then tell me what you just saw."

"Kyle was doing what he did to Jo to another girl in London," Tadgh said and glanced at Jo.

"How did you see it? I could feel the vibration of Kyle's energy when I touched your arm," Madeline said.

Tadgh shook his head. "I didn't see much. Just got a glimpse of objects and shapes, and I heard some sounds. The shapes and sounds translate into emotion. That's what I feel. I extrapolate the action that cause the emotion and the owner of the emotions afterward."

Tadgh flopped into a reading chair and closed his eyes.

"And you did all that in a few minutes?" Jo asked.

"He's a walking, talking computer, Jo," Ciaran said.

"I can tell if Kyle is coming when he's miles away. Like now. He's in London. I can't tell the precise location. But if he takes any action on anyone, I can tell from miles away," Tadgh said.

"I can't risk him controlling you. Madeline and Jo saw that happen," Ciaran explained.

"Madeline knocked me out way before they could even tell if I was able to resist Kyle."

Ciaran looked at Madeline. She nodded to confirm what Tadgh had just said.

Tadgh grunted and held his head.

"I'll have to knock you out, Tadgh," Ciaran said.

Tadgh gestured for Ciaran to stay away. "It wasn't Kyle. It's the girl . . ." he grunted again and looked as if he was in excruciating pain. Ciaran approached.

"No, no. I can take this." Tadgh held his head and closed his eyes. After a while, he opened his eyes and looked at Ciaran. He was as white as a ghost.

"Turn on the news," Tadgh said numbly.

Ciaran turned on their private channel. As the latest news flashed, the blood drained from all of their faces.

*K*yle smiled to himself. He stood right in front of the small pub where his latest prey was doing whatever he made her do. He frowned. He had to be careful. He needed quite a few more innocent souls before he could crash the Daimon Gate opening in Australia. There was no room for error.

The attempt tonight had been a success, which pleased him a great deal. An eighteen-year-old girl in a dark alley. A weak-willed soul—and to his delight—a virtuous one.

Kyle chuckled and focused his gaze through the pub's small window to enjoy his victory. Nobody could see him unless he allowed them to. He was invisible to the naked eye. Yet the damage he did to the humans was quite visible.

He could stand right inside the pub, and all would be oblivious to his existence. He would probably enjoy the smoky ambiance where the humans congregated and tried to give one another lung cancer. The stench of fresh blood was pleasant to him. And he would certainly like the sound of metal and glass cutting into flesh. His senses had become a lot more acute these days.

But no. He didn't want to mix with humans. He was once a Eudaizian, a citizen of a beautiful universe in which he was born—

and which he still longed for. He would forever be a Eudaizian in his heart, even though they had exiled him and stripped him of all his rights.

Well, he would take all of those rights back.

Soon.

Chaos in the pub. Screams. Cries. Crashes. Blood splattered onto the windows. People shoved at the heavy oak door and stormed outside.

The young girl grabbed a knife, possibly a steak knife, and slaughtered everyone in her way. She was especially interested in those that holding balloons and banners for the surprise birthday party.

He had heard that thought screaming in the girl's head when he had raped her soul. After thirty-three years living on this hell hole called Earth, he had learned what birthdays meant to humans. He still couldn't understand why they celebrated their earthly existence when the soul meant so much more than the body.

Kyle shook his head. Anyway, who cared?

He didn't care how many people the girl was killing in the pub. Those casualties didn't count on his score card. The innocent soul of the girl counted, though. She counted as one.

Kyle sighed. He needed more than that. So he needed the girl to hurry up, kill someone, and then kill herself. That was the final tick in the box to ensure that tonight was a success.

Police sirens echoed in the distance. He should help the girl before people talked her out of the final step, the last step in being his score.

Kyle closed his eyes. When he opened them, the girl appeared on the roof of the building. She looked down as if scared. Tears streamed down her face. Her hair flew and tangled in the winter wind. She held onto the chimney.

"Come on, darling. Jump. I'll catch your soul," Kyle mumbled to himself.

The girl started to cry, and her legs began to wobble. She hung on tightly and leaned on the chimney so that her knees wouldn't buckle.

"It's all right. It won't be bad at all. Come on, sweetheart. I'll take you to heaven. Come to me," Kyle whispered.

The girl cried out loud. Kyle knew too well that she was at the extreme of her conflicting emotions. He couldn't let her give in to her survival instinct or his attempt would be ruined. He couldn't let the girl do the opposite of what he wanted her to do.

Kyle Wolf had never been defeated in that way.

He closed his eyes and chanted an ancient spell. This was his last resource. He'd never had to rely on magic before. Ever. Magic was what ruined his Master. But he had no choice now. He cast the spell.

And in no time, the girl's body landed in front of the cameraman of the news crew who had just arrived on the scene.

Kyle smiled. *Success.* He turned around to hunt for a few more souls.

3

*C*iaran's little hands gripped the ledge outside his room's window tightly, and he climbed out to the roof. There was no way he was going to be grounded in his room for a week. He was four, and he was entitled to make a case with his father. If Father listened.

Father always encouraged Tadgh to talk. And that was fair enough because his brother was just learning to talk. But Ciaran knew he was able to speak at a level beyond his age. If it wasn't true, would Father have given him books in philosophy last year?

So why had Father just grounded him this time without even listening to his reasons?

Those wild dogs had attacked and killed Dew, his German shepherd. What was wrong with a little retaliation?

And he didn't do much damage or hurt anyone. He had mixed the explosive, and he'd tested it on the statue of the Goddess of Kindness in the garden. It was only a statue! And he didn't blow up the whole thing . . . just the head.

So why was father so upset?

Ciaran looked down the slope of the roof. It was quite steep. But that was all right. He had strong grip.

He scooted his bare little feet along the roof tiles, carefully lowered himself down to the gutter, and then dropped down to the ground. He pulled out the slippers he had folded into the pockets of his pajamas, put them on, and strode toward the back garden.

Soon he stood at the hill at the back of Mon Ciel.

The dark hill was covered with bushes, ancient trees, and numerous paths that led to places in the woods where Father would never let him go. Ciaran wasn't afraid of the dark—or anything else for that matter. He was willing to explore and learn.

What was wrong with Father lately?

He missed Dew. Until his little brother had grown up and could speak a bit more, Dew had been his only friend. He looked up the hill to where the wild dogs had killed his dog, and he ground his teeth.

He hated those dogs.

He knew his father wouldn't approve of such strong emotion. A kid his age wasn't supposed to feel hatred—or even know what it meant.

But he really missed Dew. A tear rolled down his face. And that was what he couldn't allow.

He was four.

He was a big brother.

And he would not cry.

The fury had blasted at him then for the first time. He didn't know where it had come from, but he knew he was furious. His temperature increased. His blood boiled. His head felt as if it was going to explode.

The next thing he knew, blades of something hit the forest in front of him with incredible force. Trees were trimmed down to the roots. Dirt, grass, and rocks flew into the air as the gigantic blades hit the ground, chopping everything in their path.

The blades spun and flew around like gigantic fans from alien spaceships. In seconds, they had carved the hill down to its bare rock bed. He was sure that all the ancient trees and animals in the little forest had been exterminated.

Ciaran fell on his backside. He knew the blades had come from his mind. They were a tangible form of his fury. They came from his thoughts of killing.

In front of him now was the scene of a war zone.

Now he understood why his father had worked so hard to teach him to control his temper. Why his father had tried everything in his power to stop any trace of violence in his thought processes.

His father had to talk him out of violence without being able to give examples or demonstrations of the consequences if he did otherwise. Because *this* was a live demonstration of what could happen. If there had been anyone in the forest during that time, their lives were lost. He hoped there had been no one lurking in the bushes in the middle of this winter night.

But he would never know.

Another tear fell onto his cheek. Now he was upset because he wasn't allowed to be upset anymore. He wondered what would happen if he cried.

He dare not try. He didn't even want to think about it.

Ciaran went quietly home and climbed back into his room.

"Ciaran!" Madeline called him from behind, snapping him back to reality. He was staring at the very window that he had climbed out on his way to experience the power of his fury for the first time.

He turned around and smiled at her.

"What are you doing here?" she asked.

"This was my room when I was a kid."

"Oh . . ." Madeline looked around. Then she embraced him. It embarrassed him how much he had grown to crave her embraces. He held her in his arms and looked out the window.

When they had seen the news and realized Kyle had possessed the girl in London and had told her to kill herself and the others, Madeline had called Kyle a monster. What would she think if she knew his mind had a destructive power that made Kyle's ability look like child's play? What she would think of him if she knew he could kill—and did kill—with just a thought?

He kissed the dimple of her left cheek, then he looked into her eyes. "I need to tell you something."

4

$\mathcal{M}$adeline assumed that Australia had changed a lot in ten years. She had. She was a new person, and she had a new life. Now she was going back to Australia to start another life—a life in Eudaiz. Who would have thought?

New York certainly had drifted into a far distant past.

They were greeted by a wave of skin-blistering heat as soon as they hit the tarmac at Melbourne's Tullamarine airport. They had departed England's bitter winter and were now hit by Australia's sweltering heat. These were the two extremes of weather on Earth, and Madeline wondered what it would be like in Eudaiz, another universe.

Thanks to the organization of Ciaran's staff, they were scooped into a luxurious air-conditioned car. She did not care which car they used, but she definitely needed a buffer for her sensitive skin to adjust to the temperature difference.

After much discussion, Ciaran had agreed that Tadgh and Jo could come along, with a list of terms and conditions that would take a lifetime to enumerate. In a nutshell, if Tadgh so much as sneezed wrong, Ciaran would send him back to England in a heartbeat.

As much as Madeline thought Tadgh was immature and impatient, she knew he would go to any lengths when it came to Ciaran's welfare. The LeBlanc brothers were genuinely a pack.

It didn't shock her at all when Ciaran told her about what his mind could do. That it could kill. That Ciaran could cause a massacre with a blade he kept locked in his mind.

There had to be a very good reason he was the chosen one for the most important Sciphil position in Eudaiz.

She knew this was just the beginning. She only hoped he was ready to take on the responsibilities.

Late in the afternoon, after several phone calls back and forth between Jo and Zach, they drove out to meet him at Tropical Tunes, the hub of Zach's band. As a frequent traveler, Tadgh knew his way around Melbourne, so he took the wheel.

Madeline glanced at the trendy modern restaurant bar when they arrived.

"You thought it would be different?" Jo asked Madeline.

"It sounded like a Hawaiian pizza place." Madeline chuckled.

A voice came from the corner of the empty restaurant. "You almost got it right. The tropical part is the cuisine, and Hawaiian pizza *is* on the menu. We handle the music part, and there's nothing tropical at all about our music."

A young man approached. "You must be Zach's friends. He told me to wait for you. He'll be here soon. We're not open yet, so the restaurant is yours."

He looked at Jo. "This must be Jo. I'm Peter." Peter bent his lanky body down to kiss Jo's cheek. "Your picture didn't do you any justice."

Jo narrowed her eyes. "What picture?"

"Ah, your avatar. I'm a beginner. Learning the games, you know. Zach taught me a lot. But I'm in no way near a level where I could play with you."

Jo nodded. "Hologame fan. Don't worry. You'll get there. You've got a good mentor. This is Madeline, Tadgh, and Ciaran. We just came from—"

"England right? Zach told me. I want to visit there some day."

"I'll be happy to host you when you visit," Ciaran said.

Peter looked at him. "What kind of music do you play?"

"I'm not a musician." Ciaran smiled. Madeline understood where Peter's assumption had come from. Ciaran looked the type.

"Can I get you something to drink?" Peter asked. His eyes didn't leave Jo. Tadgh stepped forward, blocking Peter's view of her.

"A beer would be good. It's a hot day," Tadgh said.

"Sure," Peter said and scurried away.

Ciaran raised an eyebrow at his brother. "Since when do you drink beer?"

"I'm not as predictable as you might think."

A motorbike zoomed in and parked right in front of the restaurant.

And in walked Zach Flynn. He took his helmet off, revealing his easy style of brown hair, an unshaven face, and killer eyes. He wore a leather jacket and jeans that sheathed long, well-toned legs and a backside that constantly made his groupies wild. Zach had aged a bit in ten years, but time had definitely worked in his favor, Madeline observed.

Jo leaped out of the chair next to Tadgh and gave Zach a bear hug. Zach picked her up and spun her around. "It's so good to see you," Zach said.

He put Jo down and walked toward Madeline. "Madeline, I don't have the words to describe how beautiful you look." He kissed her cheek, and Madeline smiled.

"I can help in that regard." Ciaran reached his hand out for a handshake.

"You must be Ciaran." Zach gave Ciaran's hand an earnest shake. "White Knight. It's an honor to meet you."

Ciaran glanced at Jo.

"I figured it out myself." Zach smiled. "Any real hologame player would know about you, Ciaran."

Ciaran nodded.

Zach and Tadgh gave each other measured looks while they exchanged handshakes.

Peter entered the room with a tray of beers.

Zach glanced at the beer and raised an eyebrow at Peter. "You're going to make the ladies drink out of a bottle? And that's Victorian Bitter that you're serving!"

"I don't mind." Jo grabbed a bottle. Everyone did the same while Peter scratched his head.

Zach excused himself. He gave Peter some instructions and sent him away. He then returned to the table and picked up his beer.

"Sorry. There's an audition for a guitarist tonight. The band has to move on while I'm away."

"What did you tell people about your trip?" Tadgh asked.

Zach shook his head. Madeline caught a flash of reluctance and exhaustion from him. "Told them I'd be traveling." Zach leaned back in his chair. His eyes were distant and cold.

"Zach, does that mean your friends and family know nothing about this trip?" Madeline asked.

Zach shrugged. "I don't know what to tell them."

"You've got to be kidding me!" Tadgh exclaimed. "You know this is important. People could get killed even before entering the gate. If you don't care about your own life, that's fine. But Ciaran and Madeline have to go through with this—"

"I might not go . . ."

"What the fuck!" Tadgh exclaimed.

"I used to have that option," Zach snarled.

"Keep your voices down!" Ciaran warned. "Is there somewhere we can talk without an audience?"

Zach stood up and nodded toward the stairs. Then he strode away.

5

*B*efore following Zach upstairs, Madeline pulled at Ciaran's elbow to hold him back. "Ciaran, Zach and Jo used to be together. It was a very long time ago. I think they're fine now. He's moved on, has a girlfriend—last time I heard, they were engaged. He has a career, a large family, and a life here."

Ciaran pinched lightly at her dimple and smiled. "You're saying he has a life and has a lot to lose."

Madeline smiled.

"I'll be gentle with him," Ciaran said and winked at her.

When Ciaran and Madeline got upstairs, Zach had cleared the room and made sure no staff was lurking around.

The room felt warm and welcoming. Judging by the musical instruments scattered on the floor, Madeline bet Zach used this as a studio to teach music.

Zach sat down on a high stool next to a counter. "Look, I don't know what to tell my family, okay? Originally, it was just the opening of a gate for me, which shouldn't be a big deal. Ayana told me that being the successor of Sciphil Two will not be difficult, and I'll have all the flexibility to go back and forth like Pete Chandler."

"So what changed?" Madeline asked.

"Well, you two are going to tailgate me . . ."

"Tailgating?" Tadgh snorted.

"Yeah, I thought the same. No big deal. But it's different with Ciaran because he's not just a Sciphil. He's a *King* Sciphil. His route will be different and more difficult."

"You received training, and you know what's involved?" Ciaran asked.

Zach nodded. "Hell yeah. For other Sciphils, it's like multilevel hologames—not easy, but doable. Yours is a nasty combo."

"Like what?" Ciaran asked.

"Well, Ayana was saying something about a nine-by-nine dimensional scenario, whatever that means."

"A matrix. That means you won't know what's coming at you," Tadgh mumbled.

"I don't think so. There should be options for normal routes and for the King Sciphils. The selection of scenarios should be monitored based on the level of difficulty. It shouldn't be random. If there's some logic to it, then we can work out a solution," Ciaran said.

"It was hard enough handling the deal by myself. I just found out about your tailgating a few days ago. Haven't had any other conversations with Ayana, and haven't had any further training or information about what the fuck I am getting myself into."

Zach stood up and went to a small bar at the corner of the room. He spoke from the bar. "I'm not scared or anything. But I don't want to go in without knowing if I have a chance to come back to my family. It's not like we're going to war, and I can pretend to be patriotic. I don't even know whose war we're fighting here! Some aliens—"

"They're people just like us, Zach," Ciaran said. "They might have a different makeup, and live in a different universe, but they face life and death just like us. If you expand the boundary of your country, where you claim your patriotism, to the boundaries of the

Earth, the universe, and the multiverse, then you can see that people are ultimately the same, and you are protecting them against evil."

"Look Ciaran, I have no intention of getting philosophical here. I'm no hero. I'm just a guy. I play guitar, I teach music, and I have a band. That's all I ever wanted."

"Why did you agree to it in the first place?" Madeline asked.

Zach stared at Madeline. "I can't tell you."

"If you think . . ." Madeline trailed off when Peter raced into the room.

"Sorry to interrupt. The restaurant is opening now, and also the guy is coming for the audition . . ."

"What guy?" Zach asked.

"The audition. The guitarist, Zach."

"Oh, okay. Fine. John, isn't it?" Zach shook his head.

"Yeah, John. Mate, he needs a stage name. John Smith isn't gonna work," Peter said, laughing.

"Can we wait until we actually hire him to think of his stage name?"

"Right, that's right." Peter scratched his head and walked away while Zach rolled his eyes.

Zach turned around. "I might have to go downstairs to watch this audition—"

"Your decision to go through the gate might be pending," Ciaran cut in.

"No, it's not. The deal was sealed." Zach showed the thumbprint on his right arm.

Ciaran sat down on a high stool next to a music stand. He shook his head. "Madeline and I are committed to go through the gate. We have our reasons. If you were so unsure, why did you agree?"

Zach gazed hard at Ciaran. "As I said, I can't tell you. I let you tailgate me. That's it. I promised, and I will go through with it."

"I'm afraid it won't be that simple. We might have a gate-crasher. I need to know all that's necessary to deal with it."

Zach arched an eyebrow. "Who?"

"His name is Kyle Wolf. He's an exiled Sciphil and a mind-bender," Ciaran said.

Zach looked at Madeline. She could see thousands of questions in his eyes.

"Why'd you call him a mind-bender?" Zach asked.

"In theory, he sends mind-wave signals to control people's thought processes and behaviors," Ciaran said.

Zach arched an eyebrow. "And you can't tell he's doing it by looking at him?"

"He controls the projection of his visibility in people's mind. Nobody can see him unless he wants them to. When he controls a person, it looks as though the person is possessed," Ciaran explained.

"This is ridiculous. Total bullshit. You can't even see the guy . . ."

An eardrum-bursting guitar sound echoed up from downstairs.

"Oh, fuck me. If they let this guy play, the club will have no customers left," Zach snarled and strode toward the stairs to go down to the club.

Madeline quickly stepped in front of him. "Zach, if you're scared, that's fine. I'm scared, too. But if you think we don't understand what happened ten years ago in the bush, then you're wrong. We know."

Zach turned around. He pointed at Ciaran, Tadgh, and Jo. "They all know?"

"Yes."

Zach shook his head. "It's not possible. You don't know half of it, Madeline. I killed the old man. Okay? Are you happy now? " He paused then said, "I have to go stop that fucking noise."

Zach pushed toward the stairs. The sound of the guitar surged and swelled, accompanied by a drum that sounded like someone was beating on an empty laundry bucket.

Madeline stopped Zach. He nudged her aside.

As quick as a cat, Ciaran darted toward Zach, grabbed him from behind, and spun him against the far wall.

"Keep your hands off her," Ciaran growled.

Zach shoved Ciaran.

"You don't know what I can do to you, Ciaran."

"Try me!"

Ciaran and Zach glared menacingly at each other.

6

A mixture of strange noises echoed up from the room downstairs. Zach heard the noise, but he didn't take his eyes off Ciaran. Ciaran held his gaze as well. They looked as if they were trying to shoot each other with their stares.

Madeline approached Ciaran. He gestured for her to stay away. His eyes didn't leave Zach for a second.

The two held their stances and remained locked in their staring competition for a few moments.

Zach broke the silence. "I have to go," he snarled.

"You are not going anywhere until we talk things out. We only have one day before the gate opening."

"That's your problem. I'm letting you go through my gate. What else do you want from me?"

"Your full cooperation. I need all relevant information."

Zach sneered. "Now that's a king's order from someone who hasn't even made it to the throne yet."

The drum and the guitar below kept pounding away. Zach clenched his teeth then said, "Get out of my way, or you'll regret it."

"Do your best."

Ciaran and Zach stared at each other once again, their eyes

intense. Ciaran stepped forward. Zach staggered back a step then held his stance.

A drop of blood trickled from Zach's nose. Then another. Then the same happened to Ciaran.

Zach grunted and slumped to the floor, more blood trickling from his nose.

The sound of the guitar downstairs had stopped, and sounds of chaos took its place.

Zach sat on the floor, leaning against the wall. Jo checked on him.

Madeline gave Ciaran a handkerchief for his bleeding nose. When she touched his hand, it was as cold as ice. Ciaran moved toward the high music stool and sat down.

Peter thumped up the stairs and stormed into the room, puffing. "John passed out for no reason. His nose and ears are bleeding . . ." His voice trailed off when he saw Zach. "Jesus Christ. Did John sound that bad?"

Tadgh grabbed Peter and turned him toward the stairs. "No, no, it was fine. We had a slight disagreement up here. Zach is just fine. Nothing to do with what happened downstairs. Off you go. Get John a doctor." Tadgh pushed Peter outside the room and slammed the door closed.

Zach stood up. He went over to sit opposite Ciaran.

Madeline saw a coffee jug on a table in the corner of the room.

"Can I get you some coffee?" she asked.

"Yes, please," Ciaran said.

"No, thanks. I prefer something stronger, but I'll get it later," Zach told her.

Jo and Tadgh went to the table to get the coffee.

Madeline brought a cup to Ciaran. She touched his hands to see if they were still cold and was pleased to feel their warmth had returned.

"Zach, when did you know you were a sound-bender?" Ciaran asked.

"Since longer than I can remember."

"Your family doesn't know, I guess?"

Zach shook his head. "No point advertising the fact that I'm a freak show."

"In Eudaiz, they'd call it a talent. That's why Ayana recruited you. Sound-bending seems to be her department. You should see what she did to Madeline."

"What?"

"Don't worry about it, Zach. It's not important," Madeline said.

"Did you use your sound-bending talent to kill the man in the bush?" Ciaran asked.

Zach grabbed his head and messed his hair up. He looked at Ciaran. Zach looked so tired, Madeline thought.

"I don't label my ability. Call it whatever you want, but I definitely wouldn't call it a talent. I can make a sound in my head and send that sound to anyone's head. Most of the time, it just messes people up."

"Like the way you shut the guitarist up?" Tadgh asked.

Zach nodded. "I don't have total control of it. And it doesn't work the same on everyone. When I've tried it on someone strong, the sound has bounced back to me. Usually harder."

"You tried it on Ciaran. How did it feel?" Tadgh asked.

Zach looked at Tadgh and shrugged.

Tadgh waved his finger at Zach. "Don't you even think about trying it out on me. I won't stand and take it like Ciaran did. I'd kick your ass before you even got a chance to send out a sound wave."

"Does it kill, Zach?" Jo asked.

Zach looked at Jo, devastated. Jo embraced him. "I'm sorry. You just wanted to save me. I was in bad shape."

Zach held Jo and buried his head in her shoulder.

In the corner of the room, Tadgh shifted.

"I helped kill that man, too, Zach. Don't take all the responsibility yourself," Madeline said.

Zach looked up at everyone. "The guy was evil. He had that look the very minute he laid eyes on Jo. I was pissed off. I thought I'd mess with his head. Make him go crazy. The next thing I knew, he went crazy enough to kill his wife and his kids. Then I killed him and set the house on fire."

Zach didn't realize a tear had trickled down his face.

"It wasn't you, Zach. Kyle was there. He was controlling the man. He made him kill his family," Madeline said.

Zach shook his head. "I did it, and I've lived with it for ten years. There was no mind-bender or whatever in the bush. It was only me —and a curse you call a talent—that killed those people. Ayana knew that. She didn't blackmail me. She just offered me a chance to save a lot of people and do something good . . . There, I've said it. Do whatever you want with me."

"A chance for redemption, and she got you," Ciaran muttered.

"Redemption is too fancy a word for me."

The phone in the corner of the room rang a few times and went to voice mail. A female voice spoke. "Zach, it's Chloe. Where are you? I've been calling you for the last ten minutes. When you get this message, call me back. It's Riko—she's in your apartment . . ."

Zach cursed and snatched the phone. "I'm here . . ."

Zach listened and then put down the phone. "Sorry, guys, gotta go," he said while running toward the door.

7

_L_ater, in the car, Ciaran was driving and glancing around at the same time. They had lost Zach. Tadgh concentrated to see if he could channel Riko the way he had connected to the young girl in London. But nothing came to his mind.

"Any info, Tadgh?" Ciaran asked.

"Nothing."

"Madeline, any direction?" Ciaran asked.

Madeline closed her eyes. They speculated that whatever had happened with whomever Zach had been talking to on the phone was the result of Kyle Wolf's interference. Although they had lost Zach in traffic, they followed Madeline's instinct of where Kyle would be.

"Left. On the left," Madeline said.

Without hesitation, Ciaran turned abruptly onto the street to the left.

"It's a one-way street, and you're going the wrong way, Ciaran!" Tadgh yelled from the back seat.

Ciaran ignored both him and the honks and rude gestures from the other drivers and made his way to where he could turn onto the next street and drive the right way.

"It's here," Madeline said. "The reeks of Kyle Wolf."

Tadgh glanced at the scene. It was a quiet street with several apartment complexes. They parked the car and headed toward the closest building. He still couldn't feel Riko or Kyle. He scolded himself. What was wrong with his newfound talent?

They heard Zach's voice. "Come on, Riko. Come down. You don't want to do this."

They went around the corner of the building and saw Zach standing in a small courtyard looking up to level four. A young Asian girl sat on the ledge outside the balcony railing. Her legs dangled, her long hair flowed in the wind, and her eyes darkened. She stared down at Zach but said nothing. Her face was completely void of expression.

On the other side of the balcony railing was a tall and stunning blonde girl. She stood there, phone in hand, shaking. Madeline guessed she must be Chloe.

Zach paid no attention to the incoming people. He focused on Riko.

"Shouldn't you call the police?" Tadgh asked.

"She does this every second week. She won't jump."

Ciaran lowered his voice. "She'll jump this time, Zach. And the blood will be on your hands if you don't do what I say."

"What?" Sweat trickled down Zach's forehead.

"I told you. It's Kyle Wolf. He controls people's minds. But he can only do it to one person at a time. So do what I say," Ciaran said.

Tadgh stared at the girl, trying to probe her emotions. Nothing. He couldn't see or feel anything, but a cold chill ran up and down his spine.

"I'll go up," Tadgh said and charged toward the back entrance. Jo and Madeline went around the back and up the stairs.

Before picking the lock of the apartment, Tadgh signaled Ciaran's phone. Receiving the signal, Ciaran said, "Now, send your sound wave to Riko."

Zach shifted, then began.

The sound hit, and Riko lifted her chin up. She blinked her eyes.

Zach staggered back. Blood trickled from his nose.

"The sound bounced back to you because it hit Kyle. He's strong, Zach. Can you hold?" Ciaran asked while grabbing at Zach and supporting him from the back. Zach nodded and fixed his stance.

Tadgh, Jo, and Madeline broke into the apartment and hurried toward the balcony.

Riko looked around, looked down, and started crying. She shook, stood up, and began to climb back over the railing.

Chloe yelled at Riko. "Jump! You were supposed to jump!" Chloe pushed at Riko while Riko was on top of the railing. Riko cried and clung to the railing as tightly as she could.

Chloe grunted out the words again. "Jump! I told you to jump!"

On the ground, Ciaran said, "He's got Chloe now. Send the sound to her."

From the apartment, Tadgh grabbed Chloe, pulling her inside while she kicked and screamed.

Jo helped Riko climb over the railing and get safely onto the balcony.

Madeline ran to the kitchen and grabbed a knife. She filled a bucket she found in the corner with water.

In the living room, Chloe still kicked and screamed like a madwoman. Tadgh held her, but he had the feeling he would not be able to hang on for long. Her strength was incredible. It was almost supernatural.

On the ground, Zach sent more sound signals. Both his nose and his ears were bleeding now.

Jo ran to the balcony and called out, "Tadgh's got her now. It's okay."

Zach stopped the signal and slumped to the ground.

"You think I got him?" Zach asked.

Ciaran shook his head. "Don't know. Can you get up there?"

Zach nodded. They ran up the stairs.

Inside the apartment, Madeline splashed water everywhere. Jo grabbed a knife, too. She pushed Riko into a corner and kept an eye on her in case she was taken over again. Jo focused on where Madeline sprayed the water. If she saw any sign of the beast, Jo swore to God that she would stab it until it was nothing but pulp.

Chloe grew stronger by the second. She shrugged off Tadgh.

Ciaran and Zach stormed into the apartment.

Chloe jumped on top of the table.

As soon as Tadgh lost Chloe, he felt a strange sensation at the back of his neck. He heard something echo in his head. His vision blurred. He felt an urge to act on something. He felt as if he was waiting for an order.

Tadgh closed his eyes and shook his head. He knew what was happening.

He saw Chloe standing on the table. She leaped as though she could fly, aiming straight for the glass coffee table.

Tadgh heard a clear voice in his head. "Step aside. Let the bitch fall." Tadgh knew he had to act against the voice. He focused.

There was a very strong sensation urging him to obey and do what the voice had said. Tadgh grunted. The voice was telling him to step aside. Tadgh clenched his teeth, rushed toward the table, and caught Chloe mid-flight.

They both fell onto the glass coffee table with Chloe on top of Tadgh.

Tadgh's vision cleared. The voice was no longer in his head. There was no more sensation, but he felt a searing pain on his back.

He saw Madeline and Jo leap to a corner and stab at something.

There was a sound like a roar.

Then he saw Ciaran. Ciaran said something. Tadgh could have responded, but for some reason, he thought he would be better off shutting his mind down and letting go.

Tadgh passed out on the floor in a pool of his own blood.

8

*K*yle clung to the ledge of the hospital's window and looked inside. He was sure the humans couldn't see him. But his hands were still shaky, and he was still in shock from the attack on him at the apartment. He wasn't sure about much of anything now.

Madeline and Jo, those bitches! The LeBlanc boys. The Australian musician. I'll kill you all! Kyle clenched his teeth. He had found the weak link in the group—Tadgh. Kyle smiled as he peeked into the room. He could get into Tadgh's mind. Tadgh couldn't guard his mind the way the others could, but Kyle knew he had to be careful because Tadgh had an extremely strong will.

Kyle crawled through the window.

"Damn!" He sensed Madeline at the end of the corridor. She could sense him. He couldn't fight yet. He climbed back out and fled.

TADGH OPENED his eyes in an emergency room to Jo throwing

herself at him. She hugged him and buried her face in his neck. She stayed like that for a long time but said nothing.

"I've had quite a few women propelling themselves at me in a short period of time. Is this an Australian thing?"

Jo sat up. Her big green eyes filled with tears.

"Oh, no. Don't cry, beautiful. This is just a little scratch."

Jo could not keep those big tears from rolling down her face.

"If a little scratch incapacitated you for a few hours, it's no wonder Ciaran considered sending you home."

"What?" Tadgh winced with the pain.

Zach and Chloe walked in. Chloe had a few cuts and bruises which had been tended to. She approached Tadgh's bed.

"Zach told me you took the brunt of the table for me. Thank you. I'm so sorry. I can't remember a thing."

Zach stood behind Chloe. He looked at Tadgh and shook his head, telling him silently not to say anything to Chloe.

"I can handle a glass table, but I can't handle tears from those green eyes. Could you help me stop them?" Tadgh nodded at Jo.

Jo wiped at her face.

"Why don't you both go outside for some fresh air? Don't go too far, though," Zach said.

Chloe nodded and took Jo out of the room.

"How are you doing, really?" Zach asked.

"It hurts like a bitch." Tadgh winced again.

"You've lost some blood. Your brother was royally pissed."

"Why? It's not as though I *wanted* to fall on the table."

"I don't know. He's pissed at something. Maybe it's not you. Maybe he's pissed at that fucking dickhead, Kyle Wolf."

"Well, let him be mad," Tadgh mumbled.

"The beast really got to Chloe, man. She can't remember a thing. She was really out of control."

Tadgh rolled his eyes. "Tell me about it."

"I guess it's true what Ciaran said about the mind-bender. He messed up the man in the bush and made him kill his family. It wasn't me at all."

"So now you're not going through the gate?"

"Yeah, I will. I promised. And there are . . ."

Ciaran and Madeline entered the room.

"How are you doing, Tadgh?" Madeline asked.

"I've been better. Some pretty intense stabbing you and Jo did at the apartment." Tadgh grinned.

"Yeah, I can do a lot of damage. Where's Jo?" Madeline asked.

"Out with Chloe," Zach said.

Ciaran stood still and said nothing.

"I've got to take Chloe home." Zach glanced outside to ensure that Chloe had not come back. "Here's the thing. I agreed to go through the gate partly to redeem myself from what happened in the bush but mainly because of what happened a few weeks ago."

Zach looked toward the door again and saw no sign of Chloe.

He continued, "I went back to the bush to visit the site again to remind myself of what I did . . ."

Madeline shook her head.

"And when I came back, there was a strange aura following me. All hell broke loose from there. Spooky stuff like voodoo and possession occurred. People died. *I* almost died. The girl you saw, Riko, she was one of the survivors."

"You think it was Kyle?" Tadgh asked.

"Before, no. My friend, Dan, called it the Zodiac Shifter because Kyle attacked people based on their zodiac signs. Dan is into supernatural and paranormal stuff. I'm not. I thought the 'thing'—whatever it was—had done something similar to my sound-bending trick. I hadn't told anyone I'm a freak show, so I couldn't tell anyone about the mind-bending suspicion, either."

Ciaran nodded.

"Sciphil Nine approached me and told me if I agreed to be a Sciphil successor, I could help a lot of people, so I jumped at the chance. Pete referred only to what had happened in the bush," Zach continued.

"Ayana and Pete didn't know about Kyle going around killing innocent people based on the zodiac signs?" Ciaran asked.

"I don't think so. I wanted to kill the bastard, so I agreed."

Ciaran nodded. "That's fair enough."

"I couldn't make the connection. But I know now—after what happened today— that the bastard in the bush and the Zodiac Shifter could be the same guy and could be Kyle Wolf . . ." Zach said, trailing off when Chloe and Jo entered the room.

"We'll talk more tomorrow, Zach," Ciaran said.

Zach nodded and left the room to take Chloe home.

"I've made arrangements for some accommodations outside the city," Ciaran said.

"Thank God. This hospital bed is killing my backside." Tadgh sat up and winced with pain. Madeline helped him out of the bed.

"If you withhold any information from me, I'll send you home, Tadgh," Ciaran warned.

"Ciaran, not now, not here," Madeline told him.

"I don't know what you're talking about," Tadgh said.

"I know you, Tadgh. There's no chance you would have willingly copped the fall," Ciaran continued.

"Ciaran, let's go to our accommodations first."

Ciaran stopped talking and strode out of the room. Madeline knew that was the best way for him to handle a situation when he was steaming. They'd had a long discussion. Ciaran suspected Tadgh took the fall on purpose to avoid Kyle controlling him.

Ciaran suspected Tadgh was vulnerable to Kyle's attacks.

The mansion was half an hour's drive from the city. It was imposing but homey. It surprised Madeline that the area became so rural after only a ten minutes' drive out of the city. But she had to admit she knew little about the rural concept. She shouldn't be calling an area rural based only on its lack of high-rises and traffic and the fact that she could hear animals. She knew for a fact that some people in New York had pet tigers in their apartments in the middle of the city. And New York was obviously not a jungle.

Ciaran had chosen to stay in Werribee because the LeBlancs had a lab nearby. He needed to make further arrangements for the trip the day after tomorrow.

Early in the morning, Madeline went out for a walk around the mansion. She knew Ciaran had been up and about for a while. But she wanted to give him a bit more time to do what he needed to do. He would find her when he needed her input.

Toward the back of the garden, she saw Tadgh sitting on a fence, smoking.

"First of all, I didn't know you smoked. Second, it's a huge fire hazard to smoke next to a barn."

Tadgh grinned and put out his cigarette. "A bad habit I developed from traveling a lot. Helps clear my head."

"Smoke and clarity really don't belong in the same sentence, Tadgh. But sometimes I prefer a muddy head so I don't have to think at all."

Tadgh laughed. "Muddy head! What a description."

"What do you need a clear head for? Anything I can help with?"

Tadgh shook his head. "Nah. I don't even know what I need. Better go inside to see what Ciaran is up to."

"How's your back?"

"Fine. Thanks."

Madeline gazed into Tadgh's eyes. "You can see people's emotions, Tadgh. I'm sure you can see Ciaran's gigantic concern about you being susceptible to Kyle's control. If that's the case, you have to tell us."

"So that he'll send me home?"

"Better than losing you to Kyle."

"I told you I'd kill the bastard, Madeline. I saw what he did to the girl in London. I saw what he did to Jo. He might be invisible, but he's not invincible. He's not human, but I think he has flesh and blood of some kind and can be hurt. Especially judging from the fact he roared like a pig when you stabbed him. So I just need time to think. I'll figure out how to kill him."

Madeline nodded. "All right. But if he gets into your head, I *will* knock you out."

"Deal." Tadgh smiled. "Your grandfather said Kyle was a Sciphil, and he was dealing with Black Rock. Is that right?"

"Yes. Something happened in Eudaiz. I think he somehow snatched me and ran to Earth. He was exiled. So he can't open the Daimon Gate and go back to Eudaiz himself. He has to tailgate us. But why kill people for their innocent souls?" Madeline asked.

Tadgh snorted. "Typical psychology of evil. I think it has to do with the Black Rock. Kyle betrayed Eudaiz for the Black Rock. He must have made some sort of deal—that he had to control and rape innocent souls. Some sort of a score."

"That's a scary thought. How did you figure that out?"

"Got it from my big brother. Ciaran uses the same principles to design evil guys in his hologames."

Madeline shook her head. "Sometimes real life is stranger than fiction. Unfortunately, Kyle is not a character in a game. . ." She trailed off. "Tadgh, what is it? What are you thinking about?"

"Huh?"

"You just had that faraway look on your face. You thought of something?"

Tadgh nodded. "I just put some things together. I might have something—"

Madeline gasped. "Jesus Christ."

"What is that?" Tadgh instinctively pushed Madeline behind him.

"Kyle. Run! Go inside, Tadgh!"

10

Tadgh and Madeline stormed into the reception room and almost trampled Jo. The breakfast tray Jo was carrying flew through the air and fell to the floor. Coffee cups, a teapot, croissants, bread, plates, and other sundry items scattered on the floor.

"My breakfast is ruined! What a start to the day." Jo scowled. "What's wrong?" she asked.

Then she saw the look on Madeline's face.

"Kyle." Jo clenched her teeth and grabbed the butter knife from the floor. Tadgh grabbed her and held her back.

"Jo, that's a butter knife you've got. Do you really think you can kill a beast with that?" Tadgh asked.

"Would you prefer I use my fingernails?"

"I won't let you go out there," Tadgh said.

"Put that the other way around, pal. I won't let *you* go out there. Kyle can't get to me. But he can definitely get to you. So you're staying right here." Jo jabbed her finger at his shoulder.

Tadgh grabbed her arm. "Don't point your finger at me, young lady."

Jo mocked his British accent, "Oh, this lady is definitely pointing the finger at you!"

Ciaran walked into the room and saw the commotion. "What the heck is going on?"

"Kyle was out there. These two are fighting over who's going to go out there and take the hit. Don't worry, Ciaran. I'm not letting either one of them go," Madeline said dryly as she pointed to Jo and Tadgh.

"And how do you plan to fight Kyle, you two? What weapons are you going to use?" Ciaran asked.

"She's going to use a butter knife!" Tadgh snorted.

"Better than your fists. You could barely hold a woman in check last night," Jo ranted.

"I saved her life!" Tadgh raised his voice.

"Then who will save yours?" Jo squealed and threw the butter knife at him. Tadgh jumped out of the way.

"I'm convinced you're controlled by Kyle right now, madwoman," Tadgh growled.

"Stop your bickering, you two. I have a plan. If you want to help, then follow me to the library."

Ciaran turned around and walked quickly toward the library. Jo followed, stomping her feet. Tadgh glanced at Madeline, who was watching him closely. He put his head down and scurried toward the library. Madeline followed after taking a minute to glance around to be sure she sensed nothing from Kyle inside the house.

In the library, Ciaran opened a box. Inside the box were ten golden daggers.

"Holy cow, where did you get these?" Tadgh asked.

"I had them made for us," Ciaran said dryly. He picked up a dagger and handed it to Tadgh. "Feel it."

"Heavy," Tadgh said.

"They're made of our family gold, and it's top grade. Juliette mentioned that the Daimon Gate test is a transmutation process. It's equivalent to the most stringent process used in alchemy to produce pure gold."

"Pure gold against pure gold," Tadgh said more to himself than to anyone else. "Wow."

Ciaran gave a dagger to Madeline and Jo. "I hope they're not too heavy for you."

Madeline felt the dagger. "It's comfortable. Not heavy at all."

Ciaran spoke. "When I shot at Kyle, the bullets didn't seem to have much effect. The most damage Kyle sustained was in the swordfight with Richard. Ayana and Pete also fight with swords. I don't think Eudaiz's technology is too primitive to make guns. But I speculate that metal causes more damage to people from Eudaiz than gunpowder."

"So we take two each?" Tadgh asked. He grabbed two daggers and weighed them in his hands.

"Sorry I'm late," Zach said from the door. "Oh wow, haven't seen anything cooler than this in my entire life." Zach admired the daggers. "Are those for us?"

Ciaran nodded. "Two each." Ciaran handed two daggers to Zach.

"Wow, I could kill any creature with these," he said, obviously impressed.

"What can you tell us about the gate, Zach?" Ciaran asked.

"It's like a role play game, but it plays with your mind. My training was one-on-one. I was by myself with a lot of projections and reflections based on my own personal experiences. I don't know what will happen if a group goes through it. Will we each see different things?"

Ciaran shook his head. "I don't think so. I expect the scenarios will change for the whole group. But we'll have to face individual mental challenges, whatever they may be. I'll be leading and will need your support based on your roles. The ultimate goal will be to pass the gate as a group—or not pass at all."

"What about Kyle?" Zach asked.

"That's an unknown variable. We were told he's invincible. I don't think that's the case, but I haven't figured out how to kill him yet except to pass the gate and kill him on the other side. Ideally, if

Jo and Tadgh could stall him on this side, we could pass the gate, get the power from the other side, and deal with Kyle later. But I'm not sure that's possible."

"It's not dangerous from this side to stall him," Jo said. "At least not for me."

"Excuse me. If you think I'm a burden, you're mistaken," Tadgh said.

"I didn't say that. But we're still not sure if Kyle can control you or not," Jo responded.

Before Tadgh said anything further, Ciaran cut in. "I agree with Jo, Tadgh. I don't think you should deal with Kyle at all. I regret letting you go this far. I wasn't thinking straight."

Tadgh lowered his voice. "You need me, Ciaran."

"I do. But I will not risk your life for this."

"He might not be able to affect me at all. Just like how it is with all of you."

"But we don't know that for sure, Tadgh," Madeline said.

"There's no way we can check this ahead of time, and before we are absolutely sure, I'm not willing to take the risk," Ciaran stated firmly. "I'm sending you home, Tadgh."

"The fuck I'll go."

Zach's phone buzzed. He ignored it. It buzzed again. He drew his phone out and glanced at the text message. "Fuck. It's Chloe. She tailed me here."

Zach charged out of the room.

       adgh looked at his hands and saw them shaking slightly. Was it excitement? Anxiety? He'd just figured out how to kill Kyle. It was definitely a risk. But hell, he had to do it. Kyle wasn't invisible at all. If he killed Kyle here, it would be a load off Ciaran and Madeline when they went through the Daimon Gate.

He followed everyone outside.

Chloe stood in the front garden. Her hair was tangled, her clothes were wrinkled, and she wore no makeup. Tears streamed down her face.

"There you are," Chloe said in a drunken voice. "You could have done better, Zach. We could have done better. You dumped me with a text? For her?" Chloe pointed toward Jo.

"No, no, Chloe. I . . . I don't know what to say."

"I know . . . You think I'm just a dumb blonde." She laughed through her tears.

"No, I don't think that at all, Chloe."

"But I love you, Zach," Chloe cried.

Jo approached. "You've got it all wrong, Chloe. I told you last night, I—"

Chloe whirled around, swinging her arms in the air. "You lied!" Chloe screamed at Jo.

Jo staggered back a step. Tadgh was right behind Jo. He snatched her and pulled her back. "Chloe, calm down," he said. "Zach is in enough trouble. If you love him, don't do this. It won't help him at all."

Chloe seemed to calm down a bit. Zach approached her and embraced her. She cried into his chest. Madeline had never before seen so much pain on his face.

"Can you tell me where you're going? Since when do we have secrets?" Chloe asked.

Zach bit his lip and said nothing.

Ciaran looked at Chloe's eyes. "Zach, be careful."

"He's here. Everyone, Kyle is here," Madeline alerted them.

Chloe's eyes went wild. She grabbed for the dagger Zach had tucked into his belt.

"Oh, Jesus, put it down Chloe," Zach said.

"Knock her out, Zach," Ciaran said.

"What?"

Chloe brandished the dagger and attacked Zach. He staggered backward. She screamed and charged forward at him. It would be easy for Zach to wrestle the dagger from Chloe and knock her out, but he couldn't do it. He grabbed her hand, but he couldn't strike her head.

Chloe roared again and gave Zach a kick which sent him rolling across the ground. She lurched forward, about to stab him.

Ciaran darted toward her. He could easily take her out.

Tadgh felt the sensation again. He knew what was coming. When Ciaran restrained Chloe, it would be his turn. Kyle would come to him.

Tadgh grabbed Chloe from behind. "Get away! Get away from Zach, or you'll regret this."

Tadgh heard a voice in his head now. "Let her do it. Let her kill him. He's your enemy."

Tadgh ignored the voice. He pulled Chloe away kicking and

screaming. He could handle this. He ignored the voice. Tadgh could feel his nose bleeding. The voice was pounding in his head.

Tadgh grabbed Chloe's arm and bent it until the dagger was pointing at her neck.

"Tadgh, what are you doing?" Zach screamed.

"He's getting to Tadgh," Ciaran muttered. Madeline and Jo heard him.

"Oh, no!" Jo charged toward Tadgh and Chloe.

"Tadgh, I told Chloe last night that I love you. Tadgh, listen to me. Look at me," Jo said.

"I'm looking at you, goddamn it. He's not getting to me," Tadgh growled. His nose bled more. He continued to focus on blocking the pounding voice from his head.

"Cut her throat. Kill her. Kill the bitch," it said.

Chloe was crying now. Tadgh could feel her body shaking with fear. Jo stood in front of him. Tears rolled down her face. He wanted to wipe those tears away, but he knew better. As soon as he let go of Chloe, Jo might be the next person the beast asked him to kill.

Ciaran, Madeline, Jo, and Zach now approached Tadgh and Chloe.

Tadgh dragged Chloe, stepping backward.

"You hear me, Tadgh? Are you there?" Ciaran asked.

"Fuck yeah. I told you—it's not getting me."

"So why don't you let Chloe go?" Zach asked.

"Stay back, or I'll slit her throat, Zach."

"I don't know if you're still with us, Tadgh. The only way to prove that you understand what I'm saying and the implications of what you're doing is to let Chloe go," Ciaran said, stepping forward.

"Fuck it. Fuck you. Fuck all of this." Tadgh's head was pounding. His nose dripped blood.

"Slit her throat. She's a bitch. She asked Jo to leave you. Kill her," Kyle said.

"No, no, no!" Tadgh screamed out loud.

"It asked you to kill Chloe, didn't it, Tadgh?" Madeline asked. "I know you're still in there. I know you can control it. Otherwise, you would have killed her already."

"Let her go. I'll take care of it, Tadgh," Ciaran said.

"You mean you'll knock me out, Ciaran. How the fuck do you think I can face that humiliation?" Tadgh shook his head, hoping he could shake the beast's voice out.

"It's not a humiliation, Tadgh. It's a prize to let your pride go. You cannot take a life, Tadgh. You are the best fighter I've ever known. I'm proud of you. I can't lose you like this." Ciaran stepped forward again.

Tadgh dragged Chloe backward.

"Don't come any closer, Ciaran," he said.

"Kill her. Kill her. Kill her," Kyle chanted.

"I'll let her go. Step back, Ciaran." Suddenly, Tadgh's voice was calm and collected.

"Tadgh." Ciaran narrowed his eyes.

"I said step back. I'll let her go. But I won't let you knock me out."

"No," Ciaran said.

"You want her dead?" Tadgh asked.

"Kill her. Kill her. Kill her," the beast roared in Tadgh's head.

"Ciaran, step back. Please," Zach pleaded.

"Ciaran, Tadgh might hurt you. Move back," Madeline said.

"Yes, big brother. I might pierce this dagger through your beating heart. I don't want to do that. Step back. I promise I'll let Chloe go."

Ciaran took a step back.

"More," Tadgh directed.

Ciaran moved back one more step.

"Kill her. Let her go, and you will die. Kill her," Kyle roared again.

Tadgh released Chloe. She ran toward Zach.

As soon as Chloe left, a wave of sensation and sound took over Tadgh's mind for a brief moment. Then he blocked it out again.

"You fucking bastard. You will only get me in hell." Tadgh turned the dagger toward himself.

"No!" Ciaran yelled and charged at him. A wave of energy rushed past Ciaran, knocking him to the ground.

Tadgh felt a force of energy holding the dagger back an inch away from his body. Then on the blade of the dagger, blood appeared, dripping down.

It wasn't his blood. Someone was holding the dagger back.

The voice was loud in his head again. "Stay alive. Let go of the knife."

Tadgh smiled. A smile of victory. "Didn't see this coming, did you, Kyle?"

"Stay alive." Kyle pulled at the dagger.

"Oh, I haven't killed anyone on your command yet, have I? When your victim acts against your control, what will happen, Kyle? When your victims reverse your command, what will happen to your scores? If you want to know how to play the double-edged sword game, you should consult my brother. You're doomed."

Tadgh pressed the knife further. Blood streamed from Tadgh's body, soaking the handle of the dagger and revealing the hands of an old man.

Kyle roared. His image flickered. Flickered. Flickered. He revealed himself as an old man staring at the blood on his hands.

That was his real and true image in naked human eyes.

Kyle let go of the dagger. An electrical burning smell thickened the air.

"You are an ugly motherfucker," Tadgh said before he slumped to the ground. The world in front of him started to blur. But Tadgh's mind was as clear as it had ever been.

Kyle had lost his power of invisibility. Tadgh could see that Kyle was no longer invincible. He could not control Tadgh's mind now.

Tadgh saw an opportunity. But he had to be quick.

He looked up. Kyle was still dazed by the loss of his power. Tadgh pulled the dagger out of his body and charged at him. He stabbed Kyle with the dagger stained with his own blood.

Kyle roared in pain and slumped to the ground. He looked as if he was going to burst into flames. His body was almost transparent with burning fire which appeared to ignite from within him.

Jo darted toward Tadgh. She pulled him away from Kyle.

"Tadgh, please stay with me. I love you. Please."

Tadgh could feel her tears raining down on his face.

The others hurried toward them.

Behind Jo, Kyle rolled and stood up. He roared like a beast with all he had left. He swung his arm and created a powerful wedge of wind that swept Ciaran, Madeline, and Zach several feet away. Then he snatched Jo, swung her over his shoulder, and zoomed away as if into another dimension.

Tadgh faded away on the ground.

12

They rushed Tadgh into the house. The hospital was too far away. They did all they could to stop the bleeding. Ciaran used whatever drugs he had on hand to treat his brother—drugs that Madeline did not know about and did not *want* to know about.

He ordered more medical equipment and drugs from his lab. He had what he'd requested airlifted to the mansion. His money and his well-built business empire came in handy at times, Madeline thought. As long as Tadgh survived, nothing else mattered.

Where had Kyle taken Jo?

Madeline looked out the window, gazing into the late afternoon. The sun was burning. Or maybe it was the anxiety in her that was burning. Kyle could not control Jo's mind, so what did he want? He seemed to have lost his invisibility. Maybe he'd lost his power. Madeline wasn't sure.

She needed Ciaran to make sense of what had just occurred—and to think of a solution. But she wouldn't be able to get Ciaran to think about anything else until Tadgh recovered.

Zach had taken Chloe back to the city. He had to find a way to secure her.

Tomorrow was the day of the gate opening. Madeline was sure it was going to be challenging. But she wasn't sure how they were going to survive *today*.

The sun had gone down now, and Tadgh had not yet opened his eyes. Ciaran could have airlifted Tadgh to the hospital, but for some reason, he did not. He hadn't talked to Madeline for hours while attending to Tadgh.

Ciaran worked on Tadgh and was on the phone with Doctor Thomas at the same time. It came down to a simple and final step now—Tadgh needed more blood. Ciaran and Tadgh shared a very rare blood type, but they did not store spare blood in the blood bank for convenient use overseas.

They also hadn't planned to bleed this much, Madeline thought.

Ciaran did not waste a moment thinking. He meticulously followed the steps and procedures as instructed by Doctor Thomas. There were times Madeline thought Ciaran would airlift Tadgh to a hospital or call in a medical professional. But she knew he trusted no one but Doctor Thomas and himself when it came to medical matters.

He drew his own blood and transfused it into Tadgh. It was a lot of blood. Madeline didn't need advanced medical knowledge to know that the amount of blood Ciaran extracted from himself was potentially dangerous.

Finally, the task was completed. Ciaran seemed to have done all he could. He sat down. Madeline approached the chair. She embraced him and kissed his tired face.

"I'd be very pleased if you'd take an hour to rest," Madeline said.

Ciaran kissed her. Madeline deepened the kiss. She knew he needed it. He needed her. Especially now. They held each other for a long moment, saying nothing.

A faint sound came from the bed.

Ciaran darted toward it. Tadgh opened his eyes. He was dazed and didn't seem to register what was going on around him. But he recognized Ciaran.

"You've lost a lot of blood, but you should be fine now," Ciaran said.

Tadgh closed his eyes again.

"No, no. Open your eyes, Tadgh."

There was no response.

"It's not working. I've missed something," Ciaran muttered and grabbed the phone. Madeline knew he wanted to call Doctor Thomas again. She doubted Doctor Thomas could do anything more at the moment.

Ciaran paused as if he'd just realized something. Then he spoke out loud, "Tadgh needed something more than blood. Something metaphysical."

Zach arrived and entered the room. "He's not awake yet?" he asked Madeline. She shook her head.

"Ayana!" Ciaran called out while pressing the crucifix on his arm.

"Don't waste your time. I've been doing that all night. She's not responding."

"Ayana!"

Nothing happened.

"If I can't fix my brother, I won't go anywhere near your pathetic gate," Ciaran growled to the air around him.

The air thickened and whirled. Sciphil Nine stepped out of the wind circle. It was not a holocast. He was a physical presence.

"Ciaran, the gate opening is in a few hours. Ayana cannot come. We know about the incident with Tadgh." Pete glanced at the bed.

"And what can you do about it?" Ciaran asked.

"What he did was very significant, Ciaran."

"It's most important that he stays alive. Do you have a suggestion?"

"Yes. I can give him some of my eudqi."

"Life force?" Ciaran nodded. "You're right. That's what he needs. What will it take for Tadgh to have your eudqi? What do you want me to do?"

"Nothing. It's an honor if I have Tadgh as my successor. When he becomes Sciphil Nine, he will have full access to the eudqi in his tower anyway. So this is a payment in advance."

"Then he'd say yes to it," Ciaran said.

"He has to accept the role himself. You know the drill, Ciaran."

"But he can't speak for himself right now, as you can see." Ciaran pointed toward the bed.

Madeline called out for Zach. "Could you send in a sound wave to wake him, Zach?"

Zach messed his hair up. "Oh, man. He's going to kick my ass for this." Zach concentrated. No response. He tried again. No response. He shifted. "Okay, hard head. How about this?" Zach mumbled and sent in a sound. Madeline had a feeling it would be an eardrum-shattering noise for Tadgh.

Tadgh screamed, convulsed, gasped, and opened his eyes.

Ciaran charged to the bed. "Tadgh, listen and say yes. Can you hear me?"

Tadgh was dazed. But he nodded.

Pete approached. "Tadgh LeBlanc, I now name you the successor of Sciphil Nine. Do you accept?"

"What the fuck?" Tadgh whispered.

"Just say yes, Tadgh." Ciaran shook him before he passed out again. "Say yes."

"What?" Tadgh was confused.

"Kyle is going to kill Jo. The only way you can save her is to accept this offer. You hear me?" Ciaran signaled Pete.

Pete repeated, "Tadgh LeBlanc, I now name you the successor of Sciphil Nine. Do you accept?"

"Say yes, or Jo will die," Ciaran said.

"Yes, I accept," Tadgh said.

Pete reached out and burned a thumbprint into Tadgh's right forearm.

Tadgh passed out again.

13

*J*o opened her eyes and found herself in a small cell. It had been hours since she was snatched away from the mansion, away from her friends. The air had gotten colder as if the sun had gone down. There was no window in the cell. Her internal compass told her nothing regarding her whereabouts.

Jo looked at her dead cell phone, feeling hopeless. Kyle must have killed all of the phone network signals. Nobody would be able to track her now.

She ached everywhere and could not move her right arm.

Kyle had run for a long time at an incredibly supernatural speed. Jo had no idea how much ground he had covered—the world had been a blur when he ran. Jo remembered the strong wind and the electrical currents piercing her body.

If it were nighttime now, in a few hours, it would be another day —the day of the gate opening.

How was Tadgh? Was he alive? She needed him to be alive.

The heavy door slid open, and Kyle sauntered in with a tray of something that resembled edible food. His face reflected an extremely harsh life of over a hundred years, Jo thought.

He was tall and had the frame of a once-upon-a-time warrior. He was certainly very strong when he carried her, which was especially surprising after looking as if he had disintegrated on the ground.

"Do I look like I want food?" Jo asked.

"Young lady, you have to do what I say if you want your boyfriend to stay alive."

"What else can you do to him apart from the very obvious—use me as blackmail? He got you good, Kyle."

"By sacrificing himself? Do you really believe it was wise to do so? If you could go back in time, and you had a chance to stop him, would you still have let him do that?" Kyle smirked at Jo's silence.

He sat down next to her and tended to her injured arm. Jo shrugged him away. He grabbed her arm and held it still.

"This is infected. The wound was opened, and a very nasty chemical that your human body can't handle has gotten in there. I'll get someone with medical skills to tend to you. But our resources at this station are limited, so you won't see anything fancy."

"Which station?"

"You don't want to know, young lady. By the way, although my staff are not as pretty as you are, they're harmless. Don't be scared."

"I'm not on Earth? What the hell?"

Kyle shook his head. "You're better off not knowing. We're leaving soon. So eat your food and get your arm tended to."

"I'm not eating your food."

"Then be hungry."

Kyle turned to leave. Jo spoke to his back.

"Tadgh turned your lifetime work into shit, didn't he?"

Kyle stopped at the door and turned around slowly to face her. "You two are a perfectly matched couple. You are the only score I couldn't complete. I raped your soul, but you survived. You didn't kill yourself. You intrigue me, Jo. And that stubborn boyfriend of yours . . . when I tell him to kill, he lets people live. When I tell him to stay alive, he kills himself."

Kyle chuckled and shook his head. "The thing is, your individual actions will not help the greater cause. Ciaran is the key to that. His weakness is that he's human. And there's not much he can do about that."

He started to laugh. "He can't let go of human emotions, and that's what will destroy him. So I'm going to use you guys to dangle in front of Ciaran until the opportunity's ripe. Then I can destroy him with pleasure."

"Why?"

"It's hard to explain to a human. And I don't feel quite compassionate enough at the moment. But I have to admit that living among you guys for a long time, I've gained a bit of sentiment. So the short version of the answer is that Eudaiz belongs to me. Not to Bran, and thus not to Ciaran. And I *will* take back what's mine." He turned on his heel. "You can kill yourself to avoid being a burden to your friends. But again, let me get this through your thick skull. Your individual sacrifice can only harm the bigger picture." He walked out and slammed the door closed.

14

"Now what?" Ciaran asked Pete after Tadgh had accepted the successor position and passed out again.

"Where is the blood you're going to transfuse into him?" Pete asked.

"Already done."

"Well, do some more then."

"How much blood do you have to give, Ciaran?" Madeline asked although she knew it would make no difference.

"What blood type do you need?" Zach asked.

"The freak type, Zach. Don't worry. You won't have anything that matches," Madeline muttered.

Ciaran dragged the reading chair over to the bed and sat down.

"I have to do it directly. Not enough time to do it any other way." He connected all the necessary tubes into Tadgh's arm and his own. The blood started to draw, running from Ciaran to Tadgh. When the transfusion settled, Ciaran said. "How do you give your eudqi, Pete?"

Pete pointed to his right wrist.

"Madeline, there's a connector right there, on top of the pole.

You have to use the needle—and be careful to keep the air out. Take blood from Pete, please."

He didn't ask if Madeline was able to do it. There was no one else he could rely on. Madeline nodded and performed the procedure.

The needle drew something from Pete's wrist. Something other than blood. It was a half-transparent silvery substance. It ran into the tube and mixed with Ciaran's blood. When there was enough, Pete pulled the needle out himself.

"That's enough to do the job. With his physique, he'll be as strong as superman. You have to distribute it throughout his system."

"You mean pumping it in using my blood?"

Pete nodded.

"How do I know when to stop?"

"He'll let you know." Pete smiled.

Madeline waited. Each minute felt like a decade. Ciaran sat back in the chair.

"What was significant about what Tadgh did?" Ciaran asked.

"We just found out new information about Kyle. What Tadgh did had to do with the metaphysics of Eudaiz and the Black Rock."

Ciaran raised an eyebrow. "Interesting," he said.

Zach mimed, "What the fuck?" at Madeline.

She shrugged. Within the short period of time she'd been with Ciaran, that was not the weirdest thing she had heard.

Pete continued. "To put it simply, while Eudaiz is built on a solid eudaimonic moral principal, the Black Rock is built on chaos. The core of their chaos theory is that if they can corrupt our moral ground, they can take over Eudaiz. Kyle betrayed Eudaiz for the Black Rock. His assignment was to prove that it was possible to corrupt innocence using his talent, which he achieved via Madeline. Tadgh disproved Kyle's result by killing himself under the influence of Kyle's control."

Ciaran laughed. "Backfire."

Pete nodded. "That means everything that Kyle achieved in the last three decades has been ruined. This has discredited him with the Black Rock, which is his only supply source. He has no other choice but to infiltrate the Daimon Gate tonight. If he makes it to Eudaiz, he'll devote his life to destroying it."

"Now that sucks," Zach moaned.

"We'll deal with him," Ciaran muttered, feeling quite queasy. His vision wavered. He shook his head and willed his eyes to open. Madeline saw the signs of exhaustion but said nothing.

"How much longer do you have to keep the blood flowing, Ciaran?" Madeline asked.

They heard a faint sound from the bed. Then Tadgh opened his eyes. He glanced around and grumbled, "What the hell is going on here?"

Ciaran pulled the needle from his arm. He went to the bed and pulled the tubes and needles from Tadgh.

"You were a bit sick. That's all. You're fine now. Can you get up?"

"Yeah . . ." Tadgh said.

It was incredible to see, given the condition he was in before, Tadgh sat up by himself. He winced with pain from where the stab wound was, but he got off the bed easily by himself.

Tadgh stood, looked around the room, looked at the thumbprint on his arm.

"Jo." He let out a gasp. "Where's Jo, Ciaran? You said she's going to die."

"I don't know where she is. Kyle's got her. I was preoccupied with you—"

"So nobody is looking for her? You told me I had to accept this Sciphil role to save her. Now you don't even know where she is? You bluffed me into accepting the Sciphil deal, didn't you, smart brother?"

Tadgh shoved Ciaran. Ciaran staggered back and fell onto the bedpost.

Tadgh was surprised that Ciaran fell so easily.

Madeline stepped toward Tadgh and gave him a slap across the face, sending him reeling into the wall behind him.

"Half of the blood in your body is Ciaran's. He located the substance that saved your life. All that because of your stupid heroic moment. I don't care how many universes you saved or destroyed. I don't care who you think you are, or what you're entitled to. At the moment, you are a dickhead."

"How long do we have until the gate opening?" Ciaran asked Pete.

"Four hours," Pete said.

"I'm going to need one of those for myself," Ciaran said dryly and walked out of the room. Madeline scurried after him.

Zach shrugged. "I'm worried about Jo, too. But I agree with Madeline about you. If I rephrased what she said, it wouldn't be as gentle. If I repeated what she did, no amount of superhero juice would keep you standing." Zach walked away, leaving Tadgh and Pete alone in the room.

15

The cell door slid open. Jo crawled into a corner to guard herself against the two creatures strolling in.

They walked on two legs, so Jo assumed they were at least at the ape level in the food chain. But their bodies were hideous, Dr. Frankenstein-looking creations. Although Frankenstein's work wasn't pretty, Jo thought, it was no comparison to what she saw now.

One creature had a combination of multicolored skins. The other was made of the face and body parts of many different animals. The body parts looked as if they were the leftovers from a cannibal's meal.

They said nothing. They grabbed Jo, ignoring her physical protests and verbal insults. One held her down, and the other treated her arm. They finished quickly. As much as Jo hated to admit it, she felt an instant relief from the pain.

A moment later, Kyle entered. "We have to leave now. I normally travel on foot, but I don't want to hurt you again, so we'll take the capsule this time."

"The capsule?"

Kyle did not answer. He snatched Jo, pulling her out of the cell, and shoved her into a round, metal cabin that indeed looked like a capsule. There was no window, so Jo could not orient herself. In what seemed like only a few seconds, the capsule opened. Kyle pulled her out of the capsule, and they walked into a dirt tunnel that went underground.

Upon their exit, they climbed up the stairs of a basement where hay was clustered and tools were piled up against wooden panels. When they came out of the basement, she saw a familiar sight—a farmhouse and a barn. And farm animals. Jo was sure they were Earth animals. They looked friendly, which was a bonus. She had never had a good relationship with cows and sheep. But at the moment, she loved them. She smiled graciously at a cow nearby.

A car was parked in the distance. The driver got out and opened the door at the back for Kyle and Jo. Further away, Jo spotted a line of ten cars and saw armed men standing around. If they were Kyle's men, then her friends would be outnumbered at the gate.

These men were worse than the soldiers at Fountains Abbey. The soldiers had been human—these men were not. They were like zombies, but maybe slightly better-looking. Jo no longer had her phone. She didn't know how to alert Madeline and the others about this little army.

She stumbled on her heels and fell next to one of the zombie-ish men. As he crouched to help her up, she snatched his phone. When they got to the car, Kyle opened the door for her. He reached his hand out and said, "Give it to me."

"Give what?" She played dumb.

"You don't want to upset me now, Jo. Give it back."

Jo grumbled some profanity and shoved the phone into Kyle's hand. She got into the car and sank into the passenger seat. Kyle stepped in after her and sat next to her with a crooked smile on his face. Jo shifted and moved away.

"I'm not *that* scary," Kyle said.

"Nope. Not at all. You're a saint. I bet my life on it," she said and looked out the window.

She tried her best to keep a neutral expression and show a small sign of vulnerability. On the inside, she was doing a victory dance. In addition to the phone, she had also stolen a pocket knife from the zombie gangster and was overjoyed to feel its weight in her pants' secret pocket.

16

On the other side of town, Zach held the wheel. Tadgh was in the front with him, and Madeline and Ciaran sat in the back. They were heading toward an old gold mine outside Ballarat, a small historic Victorian town.

Ciaran obviously needed more than an hour to recoup, Tadgh contemplated. Otherwise, he would never have let Zach take the wheel.

Tadgh couldn't drive because if he did, they would never get to the site in time. He worried about Jo. But he had a feeling that she would be fine. She was smart and resourceful. She knew how to handle herself—even if he had to go through the Daimon Gate with Ciaran as the successor of Sciphil Nine and leave her alone on Earth.

Tadgh shook his head. He worried about Ciaran more.

His brother sat in the back, saying nothing. That was a sign that Ciaran was utilizing every waking moment to regain his strength. Tadgh regretted that his action had caused so much trouble. He wondered how much longer it would be until he had even a fraction of the maturity his brother had.

Madeline pulled Ciaran so that he leaned on her and lay his

head on her shoulder. She liked the feel of their bodies together. Leaning on her shoulder, Ciaran nuzzled into the nape of Madeline's neck. He kissed her neck and gave it a little bite. Madeline chuckled. She turned his face toward her and kissed him.

An hour later, they were at the site. It was forty minutes before sunset.

"Do you see the gate?" Ciaran asked.

"Well, that's the gate of an old gold mine. I assume the Daimon Gate will be a bit grander," Zach said.

There was nothing around them except the bare hills. The cattle were quietly heading home, single file. Everything seemed to be settling in preparation for the sunset.

They got out of the car.

Tadgh looked at Ciaran as if he wanted to say something. Madeline saw the hint and went to talk to Zach.

Ciaran stood leaning against the trunk of the car. Tadgh approached. "I'm sorry about what I said and did at the mansion, Ciaran. I don't know what got into me."

"Don't worry about it. I know what it feels like to be left out."

"What?"

"You knew you were susceptible to Kyle's mind tricks. Nobody wants to be the weak link, Tadgh. I understand that. And the fact that I threatened to send you home didn't help. I'm sorry for that. But I wish you'd told me."

Tadgh nodded. "Should've, could've, didn't."

"I suppose I'm not exactly easy to talk to."

"You've got that right." Tadgh chuckled.

"Let's leave that behind us, shall we?" Ciaran gave Tadgh a pat on the shoulder. "You're my little brother. It's my job to look out for you."

The air cooled down quickly.

The opening time was approaching. The sun began sinking behind the hills.

They got back into the car. Ciaran took the wheel this time. They lowered the car windows to feel the movement of the air.

It was coming.

The air thickened. They heard a rumbling sound. But there was no sign of a storm.

The rumbling sound came from behind them.

"Kyle's here," Madeline said. She could sense him.

Ciaran looked in the rearview mirror and saw a line of cars coming toward them.

"I suppose they're real cars with real people," he muttered to himself. Ciaran put the car into gear quickly and turned around in the blink of an eye.

"Ten against one, coward," Ciaran said. "Got your guns ready, people?" Ciaran asked. Before getting a response, he turned the steering wheel and drove in a circle. He fishtailed and smashed into one of the cars at the far end. Before the car driver could register the impact, Zach took him out with a bullet.

Ciaran continued to drive in a circle. The nine cars left made a bigger circle so that Ciaran could not break away. Bullets rained on them, but most missed the car because of the speed at which Ciaran was driving.

"Get two more will you?" He charged at one car and swirled his steering wheel in the last second to sneak in between the two running cars. Before they could react, Tadgh and Zach took down the two cars.

Cars drove around and around at incredible speeds. Dirt and grass flew everywhere. Ciaran was too fast for the other cars to see or anticipate his location. They couldn't even see which way his car was facing, let alone shoot at it.

Ciaran drove head-on into a car. He said to Madeline, who was sitting in the front with him, "Can you take him down before we hit?" It was a rhetorical question. Regardless of whether she could do it or not, he maintained his head-on path and assumed she could shoot the other car.

Madeline pointed the gun and shot, taking the driver out.

"Two sides, Tadgh and Zach."

Ciaran maneuvered in an S around and behind the six

remaining cars. As soon as he got close enough, Tadgh and Zach fired.

In the grass and dirt, and amid the chaotic sounds of car engines, they took the remaining cars out quickly.

Ciaran stopped the car. Madeline got out without realizing that a man behind them had stood up and grabbed a gun.

In the blink of an eye, Zach sent a sound signal into the man's head. He grunted out a sound, grabbed his ears, and had his head blown off by a bullet from Tadgh's gun.

The air thickened and started whirling.

"The gate is opening," Zach said.

They checked their daggers and headed toward the gate of the old gold mine. The air in front of it stirred more strongly. The wind circle sucked in objects from the immediate area and ejected them in all directions.

In the strong wind, blue and white light beams swirled around like gigantic cylinders. It was similar to the tornado Juliette had created, but this one was colorful and much bigger.

"What now, Zach? Should we just walk right in there?" Ciaran asked.

"Wait. Ayana has to take us in."

In the middle of the wind circle, Ayana appeared, a gracious smile on her face. She stepped outside the circle. "Welcome to you all. Follow me."

Before they could take a step, Ayana swung her sword and pointed at a dark corner. "Come out," she said.

A whirl of black dirt and wind came. It created a blade of wind and knocked everyone on the ground except Ayana.

Kyle appeared. "Thanks for opening the gate. Long time no see, Ayana. You are still as beautiful as ever."

Kyle swung his arm at Ayana. Ayana pushed up her sword to block. The wind circle shrank instantly and started to collapse on her. Ayana stabbed her sword into the ground and regained her stance. The circle opened again.

"You are quite busy, I see." Kyle smirked. "Let me give you a hand to get rid of some uninvited passengers for the gate."

He charged toward Ciaran with an enormous black sword. Ciaran pulled out his daggers and blocked the sword. Tadgh kicked at Kyle and pulled his daggers out as well. Zach charged at him with two daggers pointing straight toward his heart.

Kyle swung his sword, throwing Ciaran several feet away. Tadgh's legs were still numb from his kicks, which apparently did no damage at all to Kyle.

Kyle swung his sword at Zach in response to his attack. Zach's daggers were blown away, and he fell on the ground rolling.

Kyle stepped toward Zach. "I only want the LeBlanc brothers dead. You are a guest of the gate, so I'll spare your life."

"Fuck you," Zach said.

"You're welcome."

Then Kyle roared in pain. Madeline had stabbed her two daggers into his heart from the back. He swung around and threw Madeline away.

"Kids, run inside. I'll close the gate," Ayana called out.

Madeline, Ciaran, Zach, and Tadgh stood up and raced toward the gate.

Kyle roared again. He pulled the two daggers out and threw them at Madeline.

They made impact. Madeline fell. Blood pooled quickly on the ground around her.

"No, no, Ayana, I can't let her die," Ciaran yelled. He held Madeline in his arms.

"Take her inside. This is the transitional zone. Take her inside the gate. The dimension will change, and she won't die," Ayana said.

Ciaran carried Madeline, charging against the wind toward the gate.

Kyle reeled away.

Zach and Tadgh ran toward the gate.

From the darkness, Kyle came back, holding Jo in front of him as a human shield.

"The girl will die if you take her inside the gate. She can't protect you, Kyle," Ayana said.

Zach and Tadgh turned around.

"No, you two must come inside. I can't hold this open any longer," Ayana commanded.

"I have to get Jo," Tadgh said.

Kyle pushed against the wind toward the gate.

"The girl will die. Uninvited guests will die by the light of a thousand lightning bolts. Don't do that, Kyle," Ayana said.

"Let me in, or I'll kill her right now."

"You're beyond redemption."

Kyle merely put on an evil smile.

Jo looked at Tadgh. She saw him trying to run toward her, but he was being held back by Zach. She saw Madeline being carried by Ciaran, who was racing madly toward the gate. Zach dragged Tadgh, trying to make it to the gate. Jo wanted to smile at them, but she could not. She wanted to tell them not to worry, but her body would not obey her. A sensation ran down her spine.

Then Zach pulled Tadgh inside.

Kyle pushed in.

Ayana withdrew her sword and disappeared.

The door shut.

Darkness.

----

17

*C*iaran drew in the fresh air and opened his eyes. His face was pressed against the wet, cold grass, and his hands gripped a bunch of wildflowers. Fear flooded back into his mind. *Madeline!* He scrambled to his feet.

A few feet away, Madeline lay on the ground, staring into the big eyes of a young deer. The light brown deer with white dots on his back was licking her face. Ciaran felt delirious. He shook his head.

The gate opening had happened so fast. He couldn't recall the events. But he didn't want to recall anyway as that would include the scene of the two daggers stabbing into Madeline.

He couldn't take that pain. Not again. He now understood what it had felt like for her at Fountains Abbey when he was shot. It was the most helpless feeling he had ever experienced.

Madeline sat up. The deer ran away. The two daggers now lay beside her. Neither her blood nor Kyle's was on them.

Surrounding them was a tall grass meadow wedged right against the edge of a forest. Madeline looked around. Before she could register the new world they had entered, Ciaran planted a kiss on her lips.

A few feet away, Zach and Tadgh sat up. "We're inside the gate," Ciaran said.

"Now we just have to get out the other end, don't we? Piece of cake," Zach said sarcastically.

Tadgh glanced around. Ciaran knew he was looking for a sign of Jo. "Do you know where to find Jo, Ciaran?" Tadgh asked.

"Kyle and Jo would be here, too. In this dimension. The Daimon Gate is a dimension, a world in and of itself," Ciaran responded.

"Ayana said she could be . . ." Zach stumbled on the words.

"No, Zach. She's not a guest of the gate. But Kyle wanted to use her as a human shield. He'd have a way to keep her alive. I don't know how, but I'm sure she is not dead as a result of entering the gate," Ciaran reassured.

"But . . ." Tadgh protested.

"Tadgh, I know you're worried. Everyone here is. But we have to survive to find her. If you have a better solution, I'd be happy to listen," Ciaran stated firmly. He had to stay firm to calm Tadgh's nerves. He needed to take the whole group through this alive, and there was no room for error.

Tadgh said nothing.

"So what are we dealing with here, Zach, based on your training?" Ciaran asked.

"Well, it's not a hologame. So we could die for real or get lost in oblivion forever."

"So the challenges will come to us?" Ciaran said.

"Exactly."

"What about the duration?" Tadgh asked.

"I think we have dimensional time in here. Which means we could spend a long time in challenge, but to the world outside from both ends of the gate, it would be just a short moment," Ciaran said.

"In my training, Ayana showed me a range of scenarios of obstacles and dangers based on my past experiences. For example, I have aquaphobia. There was a scenario where I had to fight a bunch of stupid fish underwater. The idea is to conquer your fear."

"You don't swim?" Tadgh snorted.

"I do—and quite well if you must know. But it doesn't make me like diving. You don't have a phobia?"

"He has tachophobia, a fear of speed," Ciaran said.

"Thank you for advertising it, Ciaran!" Tadgh protested.

Ciaran shrugged. "The more we know, the better we can plan, Tadgh. And you, Madeline?"

"I don't have a phobia. Not that I know of. And you?"

"Same." Ciaran smiled and winked at her.

"Is it going to be a combined scenario? Everyone's fears combined into one challenge? Should we list our fears and plan how to deal with them?" Madeline asked.

Ciaran smiled. "I wish it was that simple. Juliette said this is similar to an alchemical transmutation process. In principle, if we pass the gate, we will be purified and become better people. It's like making gold."

"Dandy, cleanse me!" Zach mumbled.

"Making gold is possible. Making me a better person is a fantasy," Tadgh stated.

Ciaran contemplated and said, "We have to take one thing at a time. In principle, if it's an alchemical transmutation, we are looking at three general stages—Black, White, and Red. I assume you don't want the ancient terminologies such as Nigredo, Albido, or Rubedo..."

"No, no, thank you. English, please! I can deal with some French maybe but nothing weirder than that," Tadgh said.

"In the Black stage, there will be a lot of heat. It's called the calcination process. You can work it out from the word."

"Burn us to ashes," Madeline mumbled.

There was a rumble underground, and the ground shook.

"Shit. What's that?" Zach said.

"Welcome to Nigredo," Ciaran muttered and grabbed Madeline's hand.

The sound came from the right at the far end of the meadow. Ciaran pointed toward the bush on the left.

"This will fall. Run!"

18

They charged toward the forest. The meadow collapsed and peeled off, layer by layer, right behind them.

In the jungle, they could smell wood burning.

"This is definitely the calcination stage," Ciaran said while running. Then he stopped. Everyone else stopped, too.

"We can't run aimlessly." Ciaran concentrated. He spoke quickly, "There will be fire everywhere. We are looking for the sign of a salamander. If we see it, that means we have passed the black stage."

"There." Madeline pointed toward the right where they saw the shadow of a reptile tail.

They ran toward the retreating shadow. Trees on both sides and behind them burst into flames. The fire did not blow in the wind. Instead, it was restrained within the trees, making them gigantic burning coals.

They turned the corner where the shadow of the tail had reflected before them and faced burning walls of fire.

It was a maze of flames.

"Oh, no, not again," Zach mumbled.

"What?" Tadgh said.

"I was put into a maze before. It wasn't a burning one. But it was tricky."

"How did you get out?" Ciaran asked.

"I couldn't. My friend worked it out. But there will be moving walls and moving paths," Zach said.

"Tadgh, your job. We're looking for signs of water. Not earth or air. Water. If we keep seeing fire, we're heading in the wrong direction." Ciaran pointed toward the burning maze.

"Me? What if I get it wrong?" Tadgh exclaimed.

"You won't. You're good at this. Work it out."

Ciaran speculated the answer was on the right. He was not as good at matrices as Tadgh, but he knew enough.

Tadgh thought and then pointed toward the left. "Three blocks, left, left then right."

Ciaran had a strong feeling that Tadgh was wrong. But he had given his brother the task. He had to follow through with it. "I'll check it out," Ciaran said.

"No, Ciaran, I'll do it," Tadgh said.

"I lead the group. I'll check. You stay." Ciaran grabbed Madeline and kissed her quickly. "I love you," he whispered and darted to the left.

Madeline knew it was a goodbye kiss. She saw it in his eyes. She knew he thought it was the wrong direction. But he followed because Tadgh had said so. He did it to show his faith and confidence in his brother. Madeline felt a lump in her throat and prayed that her instinct was wrong this time.

As soon as Ciaran turned the corner, the firewall moved and closed the path.

"Fuck!" Tadgh said. "Wrong path."

Ciaran saw the wall close behind him. He kept running in the direction he feared was the wrong way. Deep down, he knew he'd pull this off.

Left. Left. And right. And a dead end.

The last wall closed behind him, enclosing Ciaran in a burning corner with his ophidiophobia, fear of snakes. It was a phobia so ordinary that Ciaran had never cared to admit to it.

He had never let the fear defeat him. He had attacked it with a ferocity, and no one would ever have known that he had a phobia at all.

From a corner, a snake rose slowly. Despite the heat from the walls, Ciaran felt a chill run down his spine.

"Not now," Ciaran mumbled to himself. He would not freak out. He would do what he had done before—he would kill the snake.

Ciaran pulled out his daggers. He could do this with ease. Two swings in opposite directions, and the snake would be sliced into pieces.

But Ciaran recognized that this was no ordinary snake. It was a legendary gatekeeper, a serpent with a red snake body and a wide-jawed dragon's head.

It rose as high as Ciaran's head. It slithered around, back and forth, watching him. It went around him and stopped in front of him.

One swing, and he could kill it. That was how he normally handled his fear, but this situation was a lot more difficult, Ciaran thought.

Gatekeeper, Ciaran contemplated. He would need the ticket or the key. Ciaran used the dagger on his right hand to pull up the sleeve on his left arm, revealing the golden crucifix tattoo. From this angle, it looked more like a key.

Ciaran thought the snake looked happy—if it was possible to deduce such emotion from a snake. It slid around in front of his left arm as if admiring the crucifix.

Then the snake opened its mouth wide and bit down on Ciaran's arm.

A searing pain shocked Ciaran's brain and made him almost pass out. He dropped the dagger in his left hand.

The snake pulled away. On his arm was not an ordinary snakebite mark with two fang holes. Instead, there was a round circle of holes around the crucifix. It looked as though the key was inserted into a lock.

Ciaran staggered back. His left arm immediately felt numb.

It was the venom. But Ciaran knew what to do. He swung the right hand dagger. He had to give up his left arm, or he would die.

19

*M*adeline snarled, "Tadgh, which way is the right direction? Ciaran got the wrong one, and that path's closed." Fear clawed at her. Beads of sweat streamed down her face.

Tadgh whirled around and around, looking at the moving paths and walls.

"Stop spinning. You're making me dizzy, Tadgh," Zach said.

Madeline closed her eyes and tried to connect to Ciaran's mind. She tried to trace his thoughts the way she had on Earth.

Nothing.

Her psychic ability didn't work here.

Don't panic, she said to herself. *Just use your ordinary human sense of direction.* She blocked all of the moving parts in front of her out of her mind and concentrated, tracing Ciaran's physical steps.

CIARAN WANTED to cut off his left arm. He had to stop the venom from spreading into his heart. But the snake swung up its tail quickly and grabbed Ciaran's right arm with it. It squeezed hard so that Ciaran dropped the dagger to the ground.

The snake spoke to him.

"Keep the venom. You'll need it."

Then the snake vanished. Ciaran slumped to the ground while the searing pain stabbed at his head. The wall slid open. Madeline, Tadgh, and Zach stormed in. Madeline grabbed Ciaran.

"Where does it hurt? Are you burned? Where?"

Ciaran pulled his sleeve down to cover the snake bite and stood up. "I'm fine. This is the wrong way."

"Yes, I'm sorry," Tadgh said.

"So where to now?" Ciaran said.

"You're asking me again?"

"Who else should I ask? Madeline? Zach?"

Madeline and Zach shook their heads.

Tadgh literally recoiled from Ciaran's gaze. Ciaran waited. Then Tadgh pointed. "All right. That way. I don't want to die in here."

They ran in the opposite direction this time.

The burning walls opened up.

"This looks more like it," Madeline said.

Ciaran shook his left arm to check that it was still attached to his body.

In front of them was a river of dark water flowing into an underground cave. A line of disks sailed over the water like a conveyor belt. All of the discs turned at the corner.

"It looks like the only way out," Tadgh said, pointing at the discs flying by at an incredibly fast speed.

"We don't want to get into that water," Zach said, staring down at his worst nightmare.

"The fire is closing in behind us. We have to jump now," Madeline said.

Ciaran assessed his trajectory and jumped onto a disk.

"It's fine."

And then the disc swung around the corner.

Madeline jumped onto the next one.

Zach took a step back to get momentum and then jumped.

Tadgh looked at the discs. They were too fast for him. "Come on!" Zach's voice echoed back. Tadgh wanted to close his eyes but couldn't because he would miss the disc when he jumped. He clenched his teeth and jumped onto the next one.

Each disc could hold only one person. It was moving too fast for Tadgh. He was on all fours and gripping the edge of the disc.

In front of Tadgh, Zach's disc became unstable and flipped around.

Zach fell.

Tadgh grabbed him before he hit the water. The two of them hung on tightly to Tadgh's disc.

The disc turned the corner, and they immediately hit a waterfall. It was so sudden that both Tadgh and Zach were flushed off the disc.

Tadgh's body hit a hanging rock. He fell, unconscious, dropping down into the dark water of the river below. Zach was left hanging onto a rock. He saw Tadgh fall.

"Oh, come on!" Zach moaned. Zach let go of his rock and dove into the dark water.

It was dark and quiet below the surface of the water. His fear was not important right now. A life was on the line. He dove deeper. And there, he found Tadgh, sinking like a stone.

20

Ciaran grabbed the rocky edge of a wall. Madeline was swimming toward him. He reached his hand out and grabbed her. He swung her up on the rock and looked back to the far dark corner.

There was no sign of Tadgh and Zach.

ZACH GRABBED Tadgh and pushed him up to the surface. Tadgh was breathing. Zach supported his head, keeping it above the water, and swam along with the current. They were in a dark cave.

Mysterious hanging rocks were illuminated by a spooky dim light, and it looked like a thousand beady eyes were staring at him. They acted like torches. Otherwise, Zach wouldn't be able to see anything.

In the distance, Zach saw a small strip of rocks. Ciaran and Madeline were standing on top. He swam toward them.

Ciaran and Madeline helped pulled Tadgh up onto the rock.

"He hit a rock when we fell. He's all right," Zach said.

Tadgh coughed up some water, then he opened his eyes and rolled over to sit up. He rubbed his head.

"Are you okay now?" Ciaran asked.

Tadgh nodded. "Hey, thanks for grabbing me," he said to Zach.

"Not a problem. Same goes. I hitched a ride on your disc. If you were by yourself, you wouldn't have fallen," Zach said.

"Ciaran found a way out," Madeline said.

"Oh yeah!" Zach narrowed his eyes. "Not under the water again?"

Ciaran smiled and nodded. He pointed ahead. "Around that corner is the mouth of the cave, where the river flows out to an opening. However, the mouth of the cave is closed by a gate."

"You mean a manmade gate?" Tadgh asked. "If it's manmade, exactly what is being locked in here?"

"It's not going to be anything friendly, so I'd try not to think about it if I were you," Madeline said.

"The handle to lift the gate is underwater. By my gauge, it might take all four of us to turn it," Ciaran said. His voice shook a bit, and his teeth started to chatter with the cold.

"Okay, let's go and get it done then," Zach said.

Ciaran leaned on the rock wall, gesturing that he needed a moment. He sat down.

Madeline put her arm around him. "What's wrong, Ciaran?"

"Nothing."

His lips turned purple. Ciaran knew the snake poison had spread throughout his body. He was surprised it hadn't killed him already.

Madeline looked at Ciaran's face. "Tell me, Ciaran."

Ciaran pulled up his sleeve to show the snake bite. The wound had turned black now as well as the area around it. "The snake left me a souvenir," Ciaran said.

"Oh, Jesus Christ!" Madeline cried out.

Tadgh grabbed his dagger.

Ciaran gestured Tadgh to stop. "I could have done it myself. But the snake said I'd need it."

"It meant you needed the poison?" Tadgh said.

Ciaran found it hard to talk now. He was too cold. "We have to get out of here," he said. He got into the water and started swimming toward the gate's handle.

The metal bars of the gate stared at them in challenge. There was only a foot between the water's surface and the ceiling of the cave. The water was not too deep. It was more of a tunnel than a cave.

The wheel to open the gate had four handles. They all dove under the water, grabbed a handle, and turned.

The door shifted up an inch. They came up for air and dove down for another round. Each time, they managed to shift the gate up only an inch.

Suddenly, they felt a strange movement in the currents. In the dim light, they could see a pair of beady eyes deep inside the tunnel.

They surfaced. There was nowhere for them to go. They couldn't go back inside to the rocks.

"What is it, Ciaran?" Madeline asked.

"I think it's some kind of sea monster," Ciaran responded.

"Like a seahorse?" Tadgh asked.

"But this isn't the ocean," Zach said.

"I don't think it's here by choice. It's locked in here with us," Ciaran said.

"What are we supposed to do now?" Madeline asked.

They felt the water being sucked into the cave, rushing from the river outside, gushing through the bars and flowing toward the monster. They grabbed the bars of the gate. The suction was incredibly strong. The water brought with it whatever was in the river.

"It's feeding time. Great," Ciaran muttered.

21

*C*iaran ducked his head under the water to take a look at the animal. Then he came up again.

"It's going to feed now. It will open its mouth and create a strong current to suck everything in. We have to open the gate and get out as quickly as we can. But I don't think we can handle the gate and the current at the same time. So Madeline, Tadgh, and I will open the gate, and Zach, you have to distract it with your sound wave."

"How?"

"I don't know—that's *your* job," Ciaran said and dove down to the handle. Tadgh and Madeline did the same.

Zach dove under the water along with them. He looked at the sea monster. He had never seen a fish that ugly in all his life—the mouth of a whale, alligator eyes, and a scaled body.

It stared at Zach. He stared back. Then, looking bored, the sea monster turned and opened its mouth as wide as the tunnel.

The current started to flow in.

Zach concentrated and shot out a sound wave that he thought the monster would hate. Nothing happened. The current grew stronger.

The gate lifted one more inch.

Ciaran, Madeline, and Tadgh were not coming up for more air. They kept turning the handle.

One more inch.

Zach shot again. It hit something. The monster startled and shook. It looked angry.

Shit. If I make it angry, it might eat more. Suck everyone into that ugly mouth, Zach thought. He sent out another sound.

The gate lifted one more inch.

The monster grew angrier. They heard a high-pitched sound, followed by a low rumbling sound, and then felt a gigantic rush of current.

They couldn't keep turning the gate now. They hung onto the bars as tightly as they could. The current drew in fish, rocks, logs, and many other things from the river.

Zach couldn't send any more sounds. He hung onto the gate, too. They didn't know how long they could hold on.

Ciaran had only one functional arm now. The other had been numb with the pain and the snake poison.

The current grew stronger by the second. Ciaran knew the first person it swept away would be Madeline. She couldn't possibly have as strong a grip as the men. He had to do something about it.

Ciaran let go of the gate. The current drew him toward the monster's mouth.

Ciaran pulled out his dagger and cut his left arm. The black poison released quickly into the water and flowed into the monster's mouth. Before Ciaran's body hit the mouth of the monster, it clamped its jaws shut.

The current stopped.

The monster did not move. It looked as if it had passed out.

Ciaran surfaced and drew in a breath. "Bon appétit!" he said and quickly swam back to the handle. The four of them dove again and turned the handle.

One more inch. And one more. Finally, they created a gap just large enough for their bodies to slide under.

Suddenly, the monster rumbled. It roared and charged at the gate.

Tadgh was the last person to slide through the gap. As soon as he slid through, the monster's teeth snapped at the steel bars.

They kicked to the surface of the river just before dusk.

Ciaran was as white as a sheet. He didn't know how long he would last. Madeline grabbed him and kicked toward the bank of the river. It was growing cold quickly. A few feet from the bank, they saw movement in a bush.

A red human-sized lizard stood up on two legs and ambled toward them.

Tadgh, Zach, and Madeline drew their weapons.

"No, it's a salamander," Ciaran said. "We've passed the black stage."

He walked toward the lizard. He tried his best not to reel although his knees wanted to buckle. "Is that correct?" Ciaran did not know why he expected the lizard talk to him. It just stared. There was something in its eyes that he recognized. He didn't know what it was. But those weren't a reptile's eyes.

Ciaran pulled his sleeve up. His left arm had now turned black. He revealed the crucifix and the bite mark.

"Is this what you're after?"

The salamander looked at the wound. It stuck out its reptile tongue and licked at the wound. Then it stood up and looked Ciaran in the eyes.

"Have we passed the black stage?" Ciaran asked.

The salamander nodded.

Ciaran slumped and passed out cold on the ground.

Madeline darted toward him. The salamander hissed at her. It whirled back and forth and sucked at the cut on Ciaran's arm. Soon, his arm returned to its normal color.

The salamander sauntered away and disappeared into the bush.

Madeline hugged Ciaran, who was shivering as the temperature continued to drop.

"Can you two make a fire?" Madeline said.

"Like a campfire?" Zach asked, looking hopeless. "We don't have a lighter."

"I can do it," Tadgh said and started gathering dry branches.

"Didn't Ciaran say this was the just the first stage?" Zach asked.

Madeline nodded at the rhetorical question and smiled.

Tadgh shook his head and concentrated on making the fire.

22

The dawn came suddenly, casting light onto a reflective surface of ice. Ciaran opened his eyes to find himself lying next to Madeline, her arms still wrapped around him. They were no longer on the river bank. Instead, in front of them was a magnificent and endless snowfield.

Everything was white, including the sky.

Ciaran reached over and kissed Madeline. She woke and responded to his warm kiss.

Tadgh and Zach awoke nearby.

"Holy cow," Tadgh gasped when he saw the snowfield.

"Just like in a hologame, isn't it, Ciaran?" Zach asked.

"Except it's not a game," Ciaran said in response. He looked out at the snowfield and up to the white sky. Ciaran continued, "This is the White stage, everyone. While the Black stage focused on physical aspects, this stage is more of a mental test."

"Will it be more difficult than the last one?" Tadgh asked.

"It reflects personal experiences. I'd say it's more difficult for some and easier for others. Just in case we get separated, you need to know that this stage uses air and earth elements, and it's prone to catastrophic effects. It doesn't mean we're dealing with an apocalypse. It means, mentally, it will test our capability to make significant decisions. Those that change your life and the lives of others."

Ciaran looked at everyone. The lack of responses worried him.

"Am I understood?"

"Yep, sure," Zach said.

"Yes, Ciaran. Why do you seem more worried about this stage than the last?" Madeline asked.

"In alchemy, there are two small steps in this stage—separation and conjunction. In the Black stage, everything is burned so that only the essence remains. In the White stage, we have to focus on separating the good parts and the bad parts, and then joining the good parts together. For me, it's more difficult because there is no clear boundary between good and bad."

"Just stick together. We'll combine our brain power, I guess," Tadgh said, although he had absolutely no idea how he would go about choosing between good and bad. This was more Ciaran's kind of game than his.

"What's the sign for us passing this stage, Ciaran?" Zach asked.

"We may see a rainbow or a peacock's tail," Ciaran said.

Tadgh shook his head.

They headed deeper into the snowfield. They didn't have to walk for long before they found an ice castle located imposingly in the middle of the snowfield. The wide entrance to the castle was open and inviting. It was quiet. There was no sign of anyone—no guards, no soldiers, no people.

"Is that sleeping beauty's castle?" Zach asked jokingly.

"I think we're about to see Snow White," Tadgh said.

"I don't have a fairytale feeling at all. I think it's a white pyramid, and we're about to be chased by snow mummies," Madeline said.

"I'm afraid Madeline is right. Not sure about the mummies. But this is a test—or a trap, to be precise. Still, we have to go in," Ciaran said.

"That sucks. Knowing it's a trap and still having to go in," said Zach.

They crossed a small, snow-covered bridge to enter the castle. It was like any other picturesque castle that Madeline had seen in England. Except that everything here was icy.

They walked into the main hall. The magnificent round hall was decorated by ice pillars and white roses. A couple of white swans swam in a small pond in the middle of the hall.

Two doormen in white uniforms pushed open a gate opposite them to reveal a long corridor inside. The doormen smiled at them when they strolled past.

People here were eerily friendly, Madeline thought. Ciaran didn't look around much. He strode straight in as if he knew what to expect. The door closed behind them after they entered the hall.

Along the corridor, many people were milling about and talking animatedly as if they were at the intermission of a concert. They all looked oddly human. In this place, Madeline expected to be attacked by weird creatures rather than standing here watching fellow human beings interacting in a civilized manner. She couldn't quite catch the language they were using to communicate.

A door at the far end of the corridor opened.

They entered a grand reception room with a raised platform, where a beautiful White Queen sat on her icy white throne. Around the room were others who looked like servants, counsellors, and other authoritative figures.

Madeline noted that even Ciaran did not know the appropriate greeting etiquette. When the queen stood up and gave them a warm smile, he merely smiled back.

"Welcome to my humble residence," said the queen in a throaty and mysterious voice.

"Holy smoke, she spoke English," Tadgh muttered.

"You think she should speak French?" Zach asked.

"I'm not talking about the language. It's her tone. She sounds human. But she doesn't have any emotions. Not that I can tell."

"She might be robotic," Ciaran agreed.

The queen smiled. "Before we go any further, I'd like to let you know, I can hear what everyone says in this castle."

Madeline wanted to roll her eyes internally but resisted from doing so as she wasn't sure what game they were playing and whether the queen could read her thoughts.

The queen reached her hand out. Ciaran kissed it. "Thank you for having us."

The queen smiled graciously, "I love having you here. But I'm sure you don't want to remain residents here forever. It's best if you remain passing travelers."

Ciaran nodded. "Understood, White Queen."

The queen put on a bright smile. "Rumor has it that the King-to-be of Eudaiz is knowledgeable. You certainly do not disappoint, Ciaran."

"I wish the previous stage had been as hospitable as this one. My friends are tired. What do we have to do to obtain a pass through this stage?"

The queen laughed. "The Black stage is not meant to be friendly because you'd die if you didn't pass. We are friendly because we don't know who may end up being a permanent resident here."

"What are the odds?" Tadgh asked.

The queen smiled again. "This must be Tadgh, the last minute passenger. I can give you that information. No king successor has ever failed this stage. For others, however, eight out of ten fail. We can accommodate many as you can see." She gestured widely toward the people in the room.

"There are jobs and plenty of activities for you here. But you can't compare this place with Eudaiz. This is not a universe. It's just a humble institution," she finished with a smile.

"So at which stage would a king successor normally fail?" Madeline asked.

The queen cast a warm gaze on Madeline. "I know what you must be feeling, Madeline. But I can't give you that information."

"You are not serving the king?" Ciaran asked.

"Correct. Daimon Gate is a gateway to multiple universes. Not just Eudaiz. We manage and legitimize leaders of universes.

Depending on the constitution and the setup of the universe, the test requirements will always be different."

"But you must have a leader?"

"Yes, we are governed by the Host and the council of the Daimon Gate. If you are successful to the kingship of Eudaiz, you might be dealing with them directly in the future."

"Can we meet them when we are passing this time?"

"Yes, but only if you win an invitation. No one has won it in the past."

"How can I get an invitation?"

"That information will be revealed after you have passed the next stage."

Ciaran nodded.

"Now, would you like to proceed through this stage as a group or as individuals?" the queen asked.

"I'd prefer as a group, and I'm happy to take the bulk of the tasks. But it's up to the individuals," Ciaran said.

"I'm in with Ciaran," Madeline said.

"Same," Tadgh said.

Zach contemplated, and then he nodded. "I'm in with the group."

The queen smiled. "Your group is quite cohesive. So hang on tight. And good luck." She turned on her heel and headed toward an endless corridor of white marble.

23

They entered a square room with a wall-sized computer, similar to the one at the villa outside London. The air in the room hummed with the sound of technology. It felt as though ants were crawling on their skin with the computer eyes everywhere, watching their every move.

The queen entered a command into the control panel then turned around.

"This is not a computer-simulated game. This is the reality in Eudaiz at the moment. Each decision you make here will be executed later after you pass the Daimon Gate and take your respective roles in Eudaiz. The decisions cannot be undone. You will get a green light for an optimal decision and move on. A red light will indicate a suboptimal decision. You are allowed only one suboptimal decision. There is no time restriction. Stay as long as you like. Questions?"

"What's next?" Ciaran asked.

"If you pass, the whole group will progress to the next stage. If you fail, you will all remain here until the end of your natural lives."

The queen left the room.

Ciaran shifted his still not perfect left shoulder and pressed his palm onto the control panel for print verification.

After the welcome message, text flew across the screen like breaking news:

THE BLACK ROCK *is attacking District Five again and has killed several residents.*

The death toll is not available at this stage.

Sciphil Five - Juliette Dubois has taken no action.

The district has received help from Sciphil Two - Ayana Dee and Sciphil Nine - Pete Chandler.

"WE KNOW why Juliette isn't taking action, you idiot," Tadgh mumbled.

ACTION NEEDED. *Choose one of the two solutions below.*

One: Elimination by force.

Probability of success: Sixty percent.

Costs: One tower, one Sciphil, and two hundred thousand fighters.

Record: Attempted by Sciphil One - Richard Kelly.

Result: Failed.

TWO: *Building alliance with Earth.*

Probability of success: Ten percent.

Costs: Compromised technology, risks of chemical contamination.

Record: Attempted by Kyle Wolf.

Result: Failed.

WHAT IS YOUR CHOSEN ACTION: . . .

"THAT SUCKS," Zach said. "Surely there are other solutions."

Kyle preferred building alliances. That explained his actions and why he had ended up on Earth. Apparently, the fact that he attempted to build an alliance with the Black Rock was not on record, Ciaran mused. He considered the information interesting. This step was a no-brainer for him.

"We'll go for war. I can do better with the second action than Kyle Wolf. But based on this record, number one is a more optimal solution," Ciaran said and entered: One.

The green light flashed.

THE SECOND LOT of text appeared:

EARTH ATTACK.

A foreign chemical was introduced into Eudaiz's food supply system.

The chemical had been contained and terminated by Sciphil Three - Bran LeBlanc.

This is classified as an unprovoked attack from Earth.

ACTION NEEDED. Choose one of the two solutions below.

One: Elimination by force.

Probability of success: Ninety percent.

Costs: Five hundred thousand fighters.

Record: Proposed by Sciphil Seven - Ralph Durant.

Result: Not yet attempted.

Two: Elimination of the source of the chemical on Earth. Target - the United Kingdom.

Probability of success: One hundred percent.

Costs: Ten specialists, one viral seed.

Record: Proposed by Sciphil Eight - Aiden Felix.

Result: Not yet attempted.

"THEY ARE TALKING about sending a virus bomb to the UK. We all know where the attack on their food supply system came from. How could their records be so primitive?" Ciaran said.

"I don't know anything about the attack on their food supply system," Zach said.

"We have to go with number one. We can deal with fighters. But the viral bomb will be mass destruction," Ciaran said.

"You're having a conflict of interest, Ciaran. Who is fighting whom here?" Madeline said.

"I know. But do you have a better suggestion, Madeline?"

"In the best interest of Eudaiz, number two is the clear winner. But, as with Ciaran, I have a conflict of interest, so I wouldn't choose number two," Tadgh said.

"If we choose number one, it's going to be a red light," Madeline said.

Ciaran said nothing. He paced, contemplating.

"We have to follow through with one of the solutions. I can manage and control the fighters. The viral bomb, once executed, cannot be reversed, and the effects will be unpredictable," Ciaran said.

"How can five hundred thousand fighters take over the entire Earth?" Zach asked.

"That's why it's clearly an inferior decision for Eudaiz," Madeline said.

"I'd like to take the red light on this and do my best to green light the rest. What do you think?" Ciaran asked.

Tadgh said without hesitation, "I'm in."

"Me, too," Madeline said. She trusted her instincts and Ciaran's capability.

Zach contemplated, then he shrugged. "I'd prefer number two. But I'm outvoted. So take the red light then."

Ciaran entered: One.

The red light flashed.

AIR SUPPLY SHORTAGE.

Eudaiz's air production system has been damaged by the Black Rock in the latest attack.

Air shortage occurred in District Nine and District One.

ACTION NEEDED. Choose one of the two solutions below.

One: Trade with the Green Stars.

Probability of success: Ninety percent.

Costs: Seed energy of five hundred years supply for one hundred years of air supply.

Record: Proposed by Sciphil Nine - Pete Chandler.

Result: Not yet attempted.

Two: Steal from the Black Rock's natural air supply.

Probability of success: Ninety percent.

Costs: Two hundred fighters for a one-year air supply.

Record: Proposed by Sciphil One - Richard Kelley.

Result: Not yet attempted.

WHAT IS YOUR CHOSEN ACTION?

"I AM in for the trade with the Green Stars, solution one. Although stealing from the Black Rock is tempting, it can't be a long-term solution. Any objections?" Ciaran asked.

Everyone agreed on this scenario. Ciaran typed in one. The green light flashed.

MORE TEXT FLASHED on the screen:

SCIPHIL SUCCESSORS AND NEW APPOINTMENTS.
Due to the latest development in the council, changes need to be made to replace Sciphils and appoint new successors.
Action needed. Choose one of the four combinations below.

ONE:
Sciphil Three - Bran LeBlanc - replaced by Ciaran LeBlanc.
Sciphil One - Richard Kelley - replaced by Madeline Kelley.
Sciphil Two - Ayana Dee - successor appointed: Zach Flynn.
Sciphil Nine - Pete Chandler - successor appointed: Tadgh LeBlanc.
Termination: Sciphil Four - Kyle Wolf - replaced by George LeBlanc.
Termination: Sciphil Five - Juliette Dubois - replaced by Chloe Matheson.

TWO:
Sciphil Three - Bran LeBlanc - replaced by Ciaran LeBlanc.
Sciphil One - Richard Kelley - replaced by Madeline Kelley.
Sciphil Two - Ayana Dee - successor appointed: Zach Flynn.
Sciphil Nine - Pete Chandler - successor appointed: Tadgh LeBlanc.
Termination: Sciphil Four - Kyle Wolf - replaced by Josephine Cassidy.
Termination: Sciphil Five - Juliette Dubois - replaced by George LeBlanc.

THREE:

Sciphil Three - Bran LeBlanc - replaced by Ciaran LeBlanc.
Sciphil One - Richard Kelley - replaced by Madeline Kelley.
Sciphil Two - Ayana Dee - successor appointed: Zach Flynn.
Sciphil Nine - Pete Chandler - successor appointed: Tadgh LeBlanc.
Termination: Sciphil Four - Kyle Wolf - replaced by George LeBlanc.
Termination: Sciphil Five - Juliette Dubois - replaced by Daniel Chandler.

FOUR

Sciphil Three - Bran LeBlanc - replaced by Ciaran LeBlanc.
Sciphil One - Richard Kelley - replaced by Madeline Kelley.
Sciphil Two - Ayana Dee - successor appointed: Zach Flynn.
Sciphil Nine - Pete Chandler - successor appointed: Tadgh LeBlanc.
Termination: Sciphil Four - Kyle Wolf - replaced by Chloe Matheson.
Termination: Sciphil Five - Juliette Dubois - replaced by Josephine Cassidy.

WHAT IS YOUR CHOSEN ACTION?

CIARAN FOUND himself pacing back and forth in the room. There was no easy answer for this one, and they didn't have any red light allowance left.

24

"The first four combinations are the same across the four scenarios. The differences are in the replacements for Kyle and Juliette," Ciaran said, more to himself than to others.

"Josephine Cassidy. Is that our Jo, Madeline?" Tadgh asked.

Madeline nodded.

"What does Chloe have to do with any of this? She doesn't even know about the Daimon Gate." Zach was astonished.

"You never know . . . she might have a hidden talent the multiverse needs." Ciaran smiled. "We know George. He helped design the lights to kill Juliette. He'd make an excellent Sciphil. We don't know Daniel Chandler," Ciaran said.

"It might be my buddy, Dan. But it might be just a person with the same name," Zach said.

"Who's he?" Madeline asked.

"He's Chloe's stepfather's son if that makes any sense. They moved to Australia a few years ago from England. He likes supernatural stuff. He's the one who worked out that Kyle Wolf was using the Zodiac system, and he saved my ass in a Japanese maze. But apart from being a pain in the neck, I don't know what his talent might be."

"Sounds as if he could be a candidate," Madeline said.

"They wouldn't just draw these names out of a hat," Tadgh said.

"I speculate that Daniel Chandler was put forward by Pete Chandler. Jo's there because of her relationship with Madeline. Chloe is there because of Zach. And George? It's obvious—he's a LeBlanc," Ciaran said.

"We have to keep in mind that the combination has to be in Eudaiz's best interest," Madeline said. "George is excellent. However, his name will add another LeBlanc to the council of nine Sciphils."

Ciaran nodded. "It would be three out of nine from the LeBlancs."

"Then Dan would add another Chandler—if they're really related. If the LeBlancs don't increase and the Chandlers do, we'd have the same voting power from both families. I can't imagine that's in the best interest of Eudaiz. We shouldn't take Dan if we don't take George," Zach said.

"It's best to have a clear dominant power, which is the LeBlancs. Then the rest should be equal. Because if we have the best and the second best, factions will occur," Tadgh said.

Ciaran smiled. He was pleased to see that Tadgh had matured a lot in the last few weeks. "Based on this analysis, it seems scenario four is the winner. However, there is one other thing to consider," Ciaran said.

"Which is?" Tadgh asked.

"We don't know what the best interest of Eudaiz *is*. We don't know the thought process behind this test. The balance of power is a natural and logical analysis from our perspective. But it might not be the most important issue for Eudaiz. If we look at the selection from a capabilities point of view instead of a power balance point of view, then George is an outstanding candidate."

"I have a good feeling about Daniel, too, although I haven't met him," Madeline said.

"Chloe is clearly not equipped for this at all," Zach said.

"Jo is excellent, but she is now with Kyle Wolf, and we don't know what will happen," Tadgh said.

Ciaran looked at Tadgh. He was glad Tadgh had voiced the reality about Jo. She could be dead, or she could have turned to the dark side with Kyle Wolf.

"I don't believe that the test program would have the information about Jo being with Kyle. But if it does, choosing Jo would be the worse decision," Ciaran said.

"If we can't choose Jo, then scenarios two and four are out," Madeline confirmed.

"We can't get this wrong," Zach stressed.

"Let's just figure this out with logic first. Between capability and the balance of power, which is best for Eudaiz? I'm saying it's capability," Ciaran said.

"Balance of power," Tadgh said.

"Same," Zach said.

"Capability," Madeline said.

Ciaran shook his head. "Two and two. This doesn't help at all. Your grandfather said your sixth sense is your talent. What is it saying at the moment, Madeline?"

"I told you—it's capability."

Ciaran nodded. "Okay. I'm pulling my leader's weight. We're going for capability. Based on that, I'm voting for George. That leaves us three scenarios left to work with—one, two, and three."

Ciaran hoped his decision was right, and he wasn't biased toward George because he was one of the LeBlancs. He had a lot of confidence in George. Although they didn't always agree on different issues, having a brain like George's in any committee was always a treasure. They had done enough business together for Ciaran to know this.

"Between Chloe and Daniel, I'd go for Daniel. Is that a fair choice, Zach?"

Zach nodded.

"Then number one is out of the picture," Tadgh said. "We don't know Daniel. But given Jo's situation at the moment, I'd go with him."

"Same with me," Madeline said.

"Dan is a good selection. You'll know it when you meet him," Zach said. "Jo is brilliant. But the Zodiac—I mean, Kyle—is evil. We don't know if we'll ever see the same Jo again."

Ciaran nodded. "We agree on number three then? George and Daniel?"

Everyone nodded. Ciaran entered three into the computer.

One minute passed.

Two minutes passed.

The monitor flashed a red light.

They couldn't believe their eyes. The red light blinked, mocking them.

Ciaran shook his head. "I'm sorry. I'm so sorry."

Tadgh touched his shoulder. "Don't worry, Ciaran. We're in this together. It's not your fault. I'm sure we'll grow to love life here in this ice haven."

Zach sat on the floor, leaning against the wall. "I hope they like my music here."

Madeline hugged Ciaran and gave him a kiss. "As long as we're together, I don't care where we live."

The door slid open and the queen sauntered in. The same smile was still on her face. "Well, we have accommodations to suit your tastes and keep you comfortable."

She approached Ciaran. "It's an honor to have the LeBlancs in residence. You may call me your White Queen now."

She reached out her hand for Ciaran to kiss.

Ciaran bent down and held her hand to kiss. Then he suddenly pulled her toward him, grabbed a dagger with his other hand, and pressed the blade against her neck.

"I've never before used a woman as a shield, but we can't stay here. The computer did not say we failed. We must have another chance. What was the right answer?" Ciaran asked.

"If I was scared of your weapons, do you think I'd let you carry them around in my castle?" the queen asked.

"I don't care. We have to pass. We get out of here, and you live. Otherwise, I'll slit your throat. I will get my people out of here at the very least."

Ciaran pressed the dagger harder against the queen's throat. A stream of blood ran down her neck and onto her white dress.

"I'll ask you one last time, what is the right answer?"

"Three."

"That's what we entered, bitch! Why did we get the red light?" Tadgh said.

The queen looked puzzled. She stuttered.

"She didn't even check our results!" Zach gasped.

"She wanted us to stay here. She faked the computer's response," Madeline said.

"I'm going to have a word with your Host," Ciaran told her.

The queen exhaled and whirled around at an incredible speed. The motion spun Ciaran out and into a wall.

"You won't make it out of here. You are mine," she said threateningly.

The queen stopped spinning and charged at Ciaran. He stood up quickly and swung his two daggers. There was a scream, and the queen vanished into a wall.

Footsteps shook the castle. Bloodcurdling screams were everywhere. Hellhounds howled and white ravens squawked. White bats flooded in from the outside.

The ice castle began to collapse. The white walls, pillars, and ceiling gave way. The floor beneath them shifted and broke apart into chunks of ice. They were standing on a huge raft of ice on a dark river.

Ciaran had seen this before in his subconscious. The dark water was underneath. Once they got below the surface, he would not be able to break the ice himself to come back up.

The floor tilted toward the water. It was so slippery.

"Don't fall into the water!" Ciaran called out to Tadgh and Zach, who were hanging onto the edge of the ice at the other end of the room.

The walls of the room caved in. They heard the roar of water from a waterfall. But there was no waterfall in the castle. It was the water from the melting snow splashing between the walls and the corridors.

They were on the verge of moving from stage two to stage three, Ciaran thought. He screamed over the top of the noise. "We are moving into stage three—the Red stage. This is a spiritual stage. We are looking for the sign of a phoenix to pass to stage three. Stay true to yourself..."

A gigantic wave of ice water poured into the room and wiped away everything and everyone.

Ciaran held tight to Madeline's hands for as long as he could, but under the icy water, everything went numb. He didn't know when she slipped out of his hands. He didn't know how many times he hit the ice rocks.

It was dark. Ciaran couldn't see Madeline, Tadgh, or Zach anymore.

*M*adeline woke in a cold stone room. She sat up and tried to gather her bearings. It was a round room that looked like a tower. Medieval-style torches hung on the walls, shedding enough light for her to see the door and figure out that she was locked inside.

A tiny and useless window was located near the ceiling. She couldn't even tell whether it was day or night by looking at it. She couldn't be in another castle, could she? If she ever got back to New York, she swore she would never visit another castle again.

Madeline couldn't remember much except for the cold water and rocks of ice that kept hitting her. She remembered the dark water and Ciaran's hand slipping away from hers.

Where was everyone?

A white dove landed at the hole she called a window. It cooed.

Madeline smiled. "Got something for me?" She couldn't believe her eyes when the bird flew in and landed on the floor next to her. There was a note attached to its leg.

"You've got to be kidding me." She took the note.

"Coming in to get you. Hang in there. Tadgh & Zach."

But where was Ciaran? What did it mean? She would hang on.

There wasn't much else she could do. She tried to recall what Ciaran had said about this stage and plan for what might lie ahead.

This was a stage made more for Ciaran than anyone else. It was a stage for the king to prove he was purified and consummated with his queen. It was a stage of rebirth. Also, it was a very sexual stage, whatever that meant.

Was she his queen?

What if he consummated with the wrong queen?

She wouldn't mind if he had to have sex with someone as a requirement for this stage. But consummation was far more than having sex as far as she was concerned. It was a sexual act between *soul mates*. It required love.

Damn! She sounded more and more like Ciaran by the second.

She didn't want to think anymore.

Madeline bit her finger for some blood and wrote on the note. "Will make it out. Wait." She tied the note to the dove's foot. "How cinematic," she grumbled to herself. "The next thing I'll see is a dark prince in this black castle."

As soon as the bird left the room, she heard footsteps. The heavy door slid open, revealing a magnificent dark prince. She glanced around to see if there was a computer in this room, reading her thoughts and conveying them to the hologame designer.

This wasn't a hologame. But it wasn't real, either.

Madeline swore to God that this prince existed only in fairy tales. He had an aura that could stir every woman on Earth's loins. Madeline shook her head to clear it.

First, she was not on Earth. She was sure of it. Second, if she was a little stirred up because of the personification of sexual magnetism standing in front of her, she was sure every other woman would be, too. She was no exception, and it was not an act of infidelity. Third, infidelity only applied to married couples or people who had made vows. Ciaran and she had yet to make any promises to each other. And fourth—

"You look pleased. I wager you like the idea," the prince said.

"Huh?"

"I asked if you'd care to join me for dinner."

"Okay." Madeline glanced at the window. No bird. No message.

"Where am I?"

"The Red Castle."

"Are you the king?"

He laughed. "No, I'm the prince of this castle. We do not have a king."

The prince placed his arm supportively around her waist and led her to a long corridor lined with guards.

She was sure there were real people hidden beneath the lifeless steel armor. This felt a little like Lumley Castle. The difference was that instead of having Ciaran, she had a dark prince. It may have suited her teenage fantasies, but it did not suit her now. She knew what she had to do.

They entered a large medieval hall. A long dining table was covered with a feast large enough to feed all of the inhabitants of New York. She sat opposite the prince. He raised a pewter goblet to her. Madeline guessed that it held wine. She did the same.

"How did I get here?" Madeline asked.

"God brought you to me."

In her mind, Madeline rolled her eyes. "I understand. But how exactly did you find me?"

"You were washed onto the shore from the White Castle. That was a nasty one, wasn't it?"

"Were there other people with me?"

"We found you and Ciaran. My sister is taking care of him. He is doing fine."

The statement assaulted her brain like a cannonball. His sister was taking care of Ciaran? In front of her was a prince, and that made his sister a princess. And she was now caring for the King-to-be of Eudaiz. *What would a princess do to become a queen?* Madeline heard herself snarling inside. *Sexual stage, my ass!*

She pasted a gracious smile on her face and looked at the prince.

"You knew we were coming?" That was such a rhetorical question, Madeline thought.

"Yes. We received information about your arrival. You, Ciaran, and the two monkeys in the bush."

"Two monkeys?"

"Tadgh and Zach, right? They ran into the bush as soon as they landed.

Madeline nodded. "So we're friends. We're your guests, right?"

"Of course. We receive travelers now and then who pass through the Daimon Gate. You want me to send for your other two friends?"

Madeline nodded. The prince sipped his wine and signaled his guards to retrieve Zach and Tadgh.

This is too easy. What are you up to? Madeline narrowed her eyes.

The prince gestured at the food. Madeline stabbed her fork into something that looked like either a very large grape or a relatively small tomato. The prince cut into a piece of grilled game bird. Madeline prayed it wasn't her messenger dove.

"Based on the information I received, Tadgh, Zach, and yourself have passed the Daimon Gate at an individual levels. The only person who has yet to go through the final transmutation process is Ciaran."

"You're saying that I am free to leave the Daimon Gate right now?

"Yes."

"What's the catch?"

"What do you mean?"

"It can't be that easy. What do you want from me?"

The prince smiled. "I wish my sister had a fraction of your knowledge."

"I wouldn't call it knowledge. It's life experience."

The prince nodded. "We haven't had many passengers from Eudaiz. It has been a while actually. We have many from other universes. My sister is fond of Ciaran. And I am fond of you."

Madeline raised an eyebrow. She did not like what she was thinking. This stage had obviously high sexual connotations.

The prince put his wine down. He moved toward Madeline's side of the table. He sat down next to her, using his finger to trace her jawline.

"This kind of beauty has never passed through my castle before. Are you married?"

Shit! She had been too busy to thinking about Ciaran and had totally forgotten that the sexual connotation thing applied to her as well. As long as she stayed here.

"No," she responded.

He nodded and smiled. "I'm the prince of this castle. I can give my wife a very good life. This may not compare with Eudaiz. But we have peace, and we can live a lavish life. I am not sure what more a woman could wish for."

If she could have banged her head on the table, she would have. If she said no, he wouldn't give her more information about Ciaran. If she said yes, hell, she didn't know what would happen after that.

She grabbed the steak knife and cut into something on her plate that looked like meat. She just wanted a weapon in her hands.

26

*I*t was a hell that was labeled as heaven. Ciaran found it amusing. It was so trashy that he wouldn't even put it in a game of the lowest caliber. He was walking through rows and rows of the most exotic and sexual displays possible. Everything imaginable was being offered to him.

All he needed to do was to take.

He strode along the corridor. The women surrounded him, enticing him. He pushed through to the door ahead. He'd nearly reached it when he felt a strong pull. He turned around.

The woman was Laurent, and she had tears in her eyes. She was the dearest friend of Juliette, the wife of his best friend. Her death was one of the deepest regrets in his life.

"Take me out of here. They locked me in here to entertain the guests. It's worse than hell. Please, Ciaran, take me with you. For old time's sake," she whispered.

Ciaran paused.

She reached her hand out.

He wanted save her. He felt obliged to take her with him. He owed her entire family his life. He couldn't leave her here in this brothel.

If there was one.

His mind clicked instantly. He was at the Red stage of the Daimon Gate test. He had to remember that. He scolded himself and turned away from the image of the woman.

He kept walking.

A bloodcurdling scream echoed behind him. He knew the creatures were torturing Laurent's image. He couldn't look back, or he would return to save her.

He kept walking.

More screams. More cries of his name. More begging.

Sounds of weapons slashing at bodies, claws tearing into flesh, and body parts being torn off.

Moaning, crying, cursing, and death wishes.

He'd prefer physical pain to this. But he put his head down, concentrated, and kept walking.

He reached his hand out to push the door open.

MADELINE FOCUSED on her meal and ignored the prince's rants about the lavish life he could give her should she agree to be his wife. "I'm sure it's wonderful to live here." She grinned.

"Would you like to?"

"I'm designated to be a Sciphil. I made my promise."

The prince shook his head. "It's a pity. You'd make a good wife. You're not betrothed to Ciaran, are you?"

"Oh, no. There's no such thing in my world. Just out of curiosity, what does Ciaran have to do to pass this stage?" Madeline asked and mustered the most gracious smile she could.

"This is a spiritual stage. He must remain true to himself and be reborn by consummating with his queen."

Madeline knew this. It should be easy enough for her and Ciaran. Why should it be such a big deal? Why did the prince seem worried and doubtful?

"You think Ciaran won't pass? I saw concern in your eyes."

He smiled. "Thank you. It's very kind of you to notice. I'm worried about my sister. She wants to be a White Queen. She should have been one a long time ago. Given you have just killed a White Queen, this is a perfect opportunity for my sister. But I'm afraid she wants it too much. She might rush it. And Ciaran is too damaged to be good for her."

"What do you mean by that?"

"The man is spiritually damaged. I don't think he will pass this stage. He doesn't seem to have a spiritual belief. If she consummates with him, he might be the wrong king."

Madeline shifted in her chair. How about her being the wrong queen? "You said consummate. Exactly when did they get married?"

"That's what I'm worried about. She couldn't get him to say the words. You are his Sciphil, his counsellor. You must know him. Do you know a way?"

Madeline swallowed a laugh.

"A way to do what?"

"Help my sister."

"Help her make him say the words? You mean to marry her?"

"It's just a ritual. He asks her to be his queen. They consummate. That's all she needs. She could do it with any other leaders from any other universe. It doesn't have to be Eudaiz, and it doesn't have to be Ciaran. She's just stuck on him for some reason."

The prince looked genuinely concerned. Madeline took pity on him. She understood why his sister would not let go of Ciaran. That was the very reason he was hers. And she was going to make very sure it stayed that way. Her way.

"How was your sister trying to make Ciaran say the words, exactly? Knowing him, I couldn't think of anything that would scare him off easily."

"She didn't scare him. He was washed up on the shore with you. He had some injuries. She gave him something to soothe the physical pain—"

"She drugged Ciaran?" Madeline couldn't help but laugh.

"It wasn't a drug. It was an Inducer of the subconscious state of mind, where the spirit can be purified and transformed. She didn't know he would go down that deep, not wanting to resurface."

"You mean, he's in a coma?"

"Medically, it might look that way. But it is a spiritual transmutation process. It's not a coma. People choose the subconscious levels they want to go to and the level they want to come back to. Or to not come back to."

"So he didn't want to come back to your sister. Is that what you're saying?"

"Effectively, yes."

"If she really wants to be his true queen, shouldn't she be down in the subconscious levels looking for him? Wouldn't the whole deal of marriage and consummation involve a little thing called love?"

"Love?"

Madeline rolled her eyes. "Great. It's not even in your dictionary."

"If you mean that to have *love*, my sister has to go down there looking for him, then she couldn't do that. Spiritually, they're not connected. She might not be able to find him, and she might not be able to come back herself. It's dangerous down there."

The prince emphasized the word 'love' by stretching its pronunciation.

"What kind of danger?"

"It's a mind maze. The only right path is the path where you stay true to yourself. Any moment of doubt or faint waver in belief will send you in the wrong direction. Lost people will stay in oblivion forever. Those who pass this stage will have the highest level of consciousness."

Madeline manufactured a concerned look. "I can go down and find Ciaran for your sister. All you want is for him to return so he can marry your sister and have sex with her? Is that correct?"

"Such a vulgar term."

"That's essentially what she wants."

"You would do that? Go down and bring him back? Why?"

"We entered the Daimon Gate as a group, and we will leave as a group. That's what we call loyalty. I wager you don't have that term in your dictionary, either."

"Indeed, we don't. But it sounds intriguing."

The guards led Zach and Tadgh into the room. They glanced at the prince.

"We passed the Daimon Gate, guys, according to the prince," Madeline said before Tadgh and Zach speculated. "The only person who had to dive deep into this level was Ciaran, and he is currently still diving."

"But we—" Tadgh said.

"As friends," Madeline emphasized her pronunciation of friends and hoped Tadgh got the hint, "we promised to enter and leave this gate together. Ciaran is stuck somewhere in his subconscious, and I need to retrieve him."

"But how?" Zach said.

"Oh, they've done this before. They know what to do." Tadgh brushed it off.

"Really? You do this often?" the prince asked.

"This is routine on Earth," Madeline said, thinking about the nights Ciaran and she had spent together. "And the most important thing is that while I am down there, no one can interrupt us, including your sister. You don't want us to get lost, do you?"

"Of course not."

Zach stood puzzled.

Tadgh approached Madeline. "Let's get him out of here," he whispered.

The prince led the way to a chamber via a wide corridor. He knocked on the door and entered. Madeline, Tadgh, and Zach followed him inside.

On an enormous bed on a raised platform covered in velvet, Ciaran lay sleeping. Next to the bed stood a beautiful mermaid walking on two legs. Her dreamy blue eyes were filled with tears. She ran toward the prince.

"Brother, he wouldn't wake. I can't wake him. I might have killed him."

Zach shifted at the statement. Tadgh whispered very softly to him, "He's like that with sedatives. He won't wake up." Zach didn't nod but stopped shifting and showed signs of agitation.

"I brought you these warriors. They are his friends. They will help him return, my princess," the prince said.

Madeline spoke between her teeth to Zach and Tadgh. "Hooray, we've been promoted to warrior status."

"Really? What do you need? Tell me what to do," the mermaid princess said to Madeline.

"Just give me what you gave him and then leave us alone. Don't come in until we call you. Understood?" Madeline said.

The princess didn't seem to understand. The prince grabbed the drug, gave it to Madeline, and took the princess out of the room.

Madeline went to the bed and looked at Ciaran sleeping peacefully. Then she looked at the drug. "I'm going down with him. I think this is the same as the training he had before."

"That's purely speculation, Madeline. We don't have any support here. No Doctor Thomas, no Jo, no George. What do you suggest we do if you don't come back up? Pick you both up and run away?" Tadgh asked.

"Can you brief me on the plans, please, whatever they might be?" Zach asked.

"Whenever Ciaran is in a comatose state, he generally can't come out of it quickly or without assistance. Last time, I had to go in and yank him out," Madeline said.

Zach's jaw dropped.

"What if it doesn't work this time?" Tadgh asked.

"I don't have any other solutions. Do you?"

Silence.

"Guess not. So please guard us, and don't let these people near us. I'll see what I can do."

Tadgh nodded.

"Zach?"

"Okay. Sure." Zach nodded.

Madeline quickly got onto the bed. She kissed Ciaran. No response. She took the drug and lay down next to him.

27

The room greeted Ciaran with a blast of light. A web of tangled robes flew at him. Before he could react, he was tied up, arms and legs stretched toward four corners of the room. *Torture chamber?* he wondered.

The door swung open, and a group of women sauntered in. Their beauty exceeded all standards across the cosmos. Sexuality oozed from every pore of their skin.

"Coming down here without a chosen queen, Ciaran? Let us help you," one of them said. He didn't know which one it was as he kept his eyes closed.

He had yanked at the rope many times and had given up the idea that he could break himself loose.

They could tie him up, but they couldn't force him to open his eyes. Thus, their beauty wasn't working as effectively as it might. He knew if he gave in to the pleasure, he would have to choose a queen right here. If it was the wrong queen, it would lead to death. If it was the right queen, then he would consummate.

As to what constituted a right or wrong choice, he had no clue. His knowledge of alchemy wasn't that extensive.

He could hear the women peeling their clothes off. He heard them whispering about what would trigger sexual urges. That, he could handle easily. He just ignored what they said.

"Why don't we take turns? Then all you have to do is say which one of us you like best," a voice suggested.

Then he felt their hands all over him. They knew how to physically work a man to get what they wanted. He was only human. He knew that. Regardless of how strong his mental capacity was, he knew these women—or creatures—would work him until they got what they needed.

He could let it get to that point.

Creatures?

Yes! They were creatures! Not humans. Not women.

"I will not choose any of you. Don't waste your time," he said.

"Oh, you can't be so sure."

"Get off me, or you will regret it. I've given you fair warning."

"We only want to pleasure you."

They were all over him again.

"Last warning. Get off me."

They kept coming.

"You've forced me to do this," he growled and wielded the blade in his mind.

And his fury came forth. He could feel the force of the blade spinning in the room. It slashed, stabbed, cut, and tore at anything in its flying path.

He opened his eyes and saw body parts, blood, and flesh raining down on him.

The ropes were cut.

He freed himself and stood up, tucking his weapons in place.

On the floor, what looked like might have been human body parts had turned into robotic parts. The blood had changed into an oily black liquid which had pooled on the floor and now evaporated into thin air.

Ciaran stepped around the room, avoiding the puddles, and

approached the door to the next room. As he pushed the door open, the room exploded with colors and shapes which flew directly at him.

28

_M_adeline drifted down. And down. She swam in a dark space. Then she landed on firm ground inside a very plain chapel. The place looked familiar—long hall, arched pillars, and altar at the far end.

She approached a door, the only door in the room, and pushed it open.

She was immediately pulled into the room and surrounded by several _Madelines_. The door slammed behind her—there was no way out.

At the other end of the room stood Ciaran, covered in blood, gripping his daggers. He looked at her like she was a stranger.

Hundreds of creatures in the room in female form flew at him. He slaughtered them before they touched him. But that wasn't the problem.

She could see the deadly problem.

There were hundreds of creature taking her likeness. They looked identical to her. They approached Ciaran slowly in small groups. When they got close, and if he didn't kill them, they clawed at him. That explained why he was covered in blood.

He slashed at most of them with his daggers. There must be

something in them that made him realize they weren't her. But he let a few slip too close before he killed them.

Even she couldn't tell the difference between herself and the row of creatures standing next to her right now, waiting for their turn to approach Ciaran.

She could attack them now and kill them, and then Ciaran would be able to tell it was her. She grabbed her daggers but realized they were no longer with her.

No weapons for Madeline.

She could see Ciaran grow angrier as more and more Madeline lookalikes clawed at him and bit him. He began to slash at them indiscriminately.

She knew he would get to a point where he sent out the blade of fury from his mind, and that would kill all creatures in the room —including her.

Doing that meant he would kill his true queen and lose this round of the test. But if he didn't do something, they would eat him alive. It was already starting to look like that was going to happen.

Madeline left the row of pretenders and started to approach Ciaran, like the other look-alike. She focused and tried to connect with his mind.

She knew it wouldn't work. But she had to try.

"Ciaran! It's me!" she called out to him in her mind.

No reaction from him. He kept stabbing and slashing at the lookalikes. Hundreds of Madelines.

Their attacks grew fiercer as they got closer. He slaughtered harder and harder.

A chill ran up her spine when she looked into his eyes.

He had grown used to slaughtering her image. The more he killed, the fewer injuries he had to suffer.

She approached him. Closer. Closer.

She had nothing with which to defend herself. Her psychic connection to him wasn't working.

All she had was herself and her love for him. She came even

closer. So close she could smell the violence coming from him in waves.

He swung his daggers left, right, and in all directions. The bodies of her lookalikes fell like tree trunks to the floor.

He didn't even look to see if they evaporated or lay on the floor in a heap of blood, flesh, and bones, meaning he had just killed the real Madeline.

He just slaughtered.

One creature after another.

She approached. It was now her turn. She stood right in front of him.

She saw a dagger swing at her, aimed at her chest. He was going to stab her in the heart.

She did nothing. She just looked at him.

Then the dagger stopped right in front of her. The sharp point of the blade had sneaked into her flesh and cut loose a drop of blood.

Ciaran looked into her eyes.

"It's you!" he whispered in disbelief. "My queen." He dropped the daggers and pulled her into his arms. He squeezed her so hard it knocked the breath out of her.

He didn't care what was happening around him. If this was the wrong choice, if she was a creature, she could have turned around and ripped out his throat.

He didn't seem to care. His body vibrated with emotion. He buried his head in the crook of her neck. The he lifted her face up and kissed her.

And then it was her turn to not care what was happening around them in the room.

When the best kiss in the cosmos had finished, Ciaran released her. They looked around the room and saw that all the creatures—dead and alive—had vanished.

He had made the right choice.

He held her hand and led her to the next room where she had seen the altar before.

The room was now lit up with thousands of candles. Soft ceremonial music chanted from somewhere in the air. He looked at her.

His face, the face of a dark angel, was looking at her with love. She would trade anything to remain in that world and hold that look for the rest of her life.

They kissed again.

After a while, he asked, "Can you ever forgive me for what I did to Juliette? Will it ever come between us?"

Madeline cupped his face and immersed herself in his intense gray eyes. "Juliette was a part of your life. You will always carry the guilt of her natural death. We can't forget that. But she has never—and *will* never—come between us."

He kissed her again.

"I killed an innocent man. Will you be able to live with that?"

Ciaran looked at her. He rubbed his thumb on the dimple on her left cheek. "You'll kill more men. Whether good or evil, innocent or guilty, you will make a just decision of whether a life is worth preserving. You have an important role right now. People depend on you. You don't have to ask me that anymore. I'll answer it, once and for all. I love you, and I respect your decisions. Nothing else matters."

Madeline smiled.

They held each other for a long moment, swaying with the flow of the air. They swam in pleasant thoughts and happiness. Madeline did not know that happiness flowed like a current. It had frequency and rhythm. When she paid attention and reached out for it, she could actually feel it.

In that quietness, they heard each other's heartbeats.

"Will you marry me?" Ciaran asked.

She looked him in the face so that he could see her eyes.

"Yes," she said.

There were no tears on her face, not even happy ones. She was entitled to this happiness. She loved him. At this moment, she made a vow to herself that she would do whatever it took to protect her happiness and the love they had for each other.

Ciaran took her to the altar where a fire was burning on a reddened stone.

"This is the eternal fire, the fire of purity."

Ciaran pulled out his dagger and rested the blade in the flame.

"By the fire of God, I, Ciaran LeBlanc, ask Madeline Kelley to be my soul mate. I ask her to be my wife. I am the Red King, and she is my Queen. I vow to love and protect her for the rest of my life."

He used the blade to cut a ring line around her ring finger. Then he gave her the dagger.

"By the fire of God, I, Madeline Kelley, vow to be Ciaran LeBlanc's soul mate. I vow to be his wife and take him as my husband. He is my Red King and I am his Queen. I vow to love and protect him for the rest of my life."

She cut a blood ring on his ring finger.

They were now husband and wife.

In the absolute quietness, surrounded by nothingness, at this astronomical moment, all the dust in their minds was wiped away, and love enlightened them.

Their experience was complete. They were one. They had unified.

They consummated their vows. Their bodies, their souls, and their life forces entwined into one perfect essence of purified love.

Then and there, they heard a cooing sound. They looked up and saw a magnificent phoenix flapping its wings, flying away.

"My Queen, I'm glad to announce that we have passed the Red stage and the Daimon Gate test," Ciaran said.

$\mathcal{M}$adeline resurfaced in the castle first. Tadgh and Zach darted to the bed.

"You got him?" Tadgh asked.

Madeline put on a smile Tadgh had never seen before.

"What's with the smile?" he asked.

She revealed the blood ring.

"Holy . . ."

Madeline gestured for silence. She kissed Ciaran and shook his shoulders. "Ciaran, darling. You need to get up."

Ciaran opened his eyes. He was groggy, but he registered the reality instantly. He grabbed Madeline's hand and kissed her blood ring finger.

"Thanks for sharing," Tadgh mumbled.

"Great stuff." Zach grinned.

Ciaran flew out of the bed and slumped to the floor, vomiting in the corner of the room.

Zach jumped aside. "What's the . . ."

"He does that all the time. Keep it in mind before you feed him sedatives," Tadgh told Zach.

The prince and the princess rushed into the room. The princess darted over to Ciaran. "Are you sick? I'm so sorry? The inducer was too strong."

Ciaran shrugged away from the princess's supportive arms and stood up. Madeline came over and stood next to Ciaran.

"Thank you for your hospitality. But I'm afraid that we have to leave now," Ciaran said.

"You don't remember me at all, do you?" The princess's eyes filled with tears.

"No, I don't. Please refresh my memory."

"She is the princess of this castle. She saved you when you were half dead on the beach," the prince said.

"We're supposed to get married." The princess started crying.

"I beg your pardon?" Ciaran nearly jumped out of his skin.

"You're supposed to marry me. You are the Red King, and I am your Queen. To pass the Red stage of the Daimon Gate, you have to connect with your Queen. I am she. How can you not remember?" the princess wailed.

Ciaran shifted. Madeline sensed his movements, and they stepped closer to the door where Tadgh and Zach were standing.

Ciaran held up Madeline's hand.

"This is my Queen. We have married and consummated. And we have passed the gate. I am sorry if there was anything I did that caused you to misconstrue my intentions. We are only passengers here. We are not supposed to engage with the gatekeepers."

The princess wailed more.

"Gatekeepers!" the prince growled. "You Eudaiz passengers. You used us. You were supposed to fight for the Inducer. A fight for your life. Very few pass it. But my sister just gave it to you. So you passed through the transmutation process the easy way and married another queen. What sort of king does that make you?"

"Had I known, I would have been more than happy to accept the challenges and fight for the Inducer. I cannot reverse the process. What would you like me to do to repay you for your help?"

"Our help? Don't even say that word. It's going to cost us our heads," the prince roared.

The princess reeled and fainted to the floor. The prince raced to her side and held her up. "Oh, my poor trusting sister. I'm so sorry. I should have taught you better. I should have been a better brother."

Then he looked at Ciaran. "All her life, all she wanted was to be a White Queen. Many leaders from other universes have been through our gate, and she could have married any one of them. But she wouldn't. It had to be the future King of Eudaiz. It had to be you."

"Why?" Ciaran asked. He approached the prince. "Because you fed her with fairy tales about Eudaiz? You've been telling her about a perfect world that doesn't exist, have you?"

"Eudaiz doesn't exist?" The prince was astonished.

"It does. I've never been to it, but I am quite sure it's not a perfect world," Madeline said from the door.

"But Eudaiz is happiness. It means happiness. True happiness is perfect. What else would one would live for?"

Ciaran shook his head. "You're responsible for screening people's spiritual purity and their worthiness before they get the Inducer for the final transmutation process, am I correct?"

The prince nodded.

"What the princess did was the equivalent of cheating and smuggling people through the gate. Yes?"

A tear of fear made its way down the prince's face. He looked at Ciaran. "If you married her as planned, things would be different," he said. "I guess you're not going to do that."

"What's the punishment?"

"Death for me and for her. Sanction for the castle and my territory. We will have no more passengers. Everything will be cut off until the area dries out."

"If you knew this disastrous outcome was possible, why did you let her do this?"

"I didn't let her. I wasn't quick enough to stop her. I can't let her die in this castle. The Host can chop my head off or do whatever. But she's just a child."

"How would the Host find out about this?"

"He already knows. When you received the Inducer without going through the challenges, the system expected a marriage between you and the princess. You must have seen the Phoenix?"

Ciaran nodded.

"The Host has now been informed that the marriage was between you and a different queen and that my sister cheated the system. She's doomed."

"How can I fix this?"

The prince smiled bitterly. "There is no way to fix it. Although, as a first time passenger, you have a chance to take a challenge. If you win, you will receive an invitation to meet the Host—and a privilege. With the privilege, you can ask for a pardon for my princess."

"Then I shall take the challenge," Ciaran said dryly.

The prince shook his head. "I should give my congratulations. You passed the Daimon Gate. Your transport is waiting for you at the gate. This will be my last chance to take any passengers through this castle. Bon voyage."

The prince sat still on the floor, leaning against the wall and holding his sister in his arms.

"What's your name?" Ciaran asked.

"Brandon."

"Brandon, I'll find a way to help you and your sister. I promise," Ciaran said firmly and headed toward the door.

Ciaran, Madeline, Tadgh, and Zach left the Red Castle, but just before they did, Madeline's psychic mind kicked in. She heard a loud and clear thought. "You'll never pass the gate alive, Ciaran."

She looked around. She didn't know whose thought she'd heard. The princess was still out, and the prince was still crying and stunned by the consequences of what they had done.

30

*F*our horses raced across a field of roses. Madeline had never seen so many wild roses in her life. Beautiful and mysterious. Ciaran, on his white horse, led the group like a true king. In her mind, he had always been more a warrior than a king.

She'd had no idea riding a horse for the first time in her life could be this easy and fun. Zach and Tadgh seemed to manage it easy enough also. They raced as fast as the wind.

Snow-topped mountains fenced in the valley, leading them to the magnificent opening of a canyon. There was no need for Ciaran to say a word—they all knew that in front of them was the way out of the Daimon Gate.

Ciaran turned around. "Ayana and Pete will be waiting for you outside the gate. I'll be right behind you."

"Did you forget something back at the Red Castle, Ciaran? I know the mermaid princess was hard to let go," Madeline said.

Ciaran smiled. "Yes, I forgot my four wives and the dozen children I created when we were in the gate."

Madeline rubbed at her tummy. "Well, that saves me from doing the hard labor."

"Seriously, man, what do you need to do?" Zach asked.

"I promised Bran I would get the invitation," Ciaran said.

"Promised? When?" Tadgh raised his voice.

"When he was trying to give me the training."

"You mean the subconscious training session that almost killed you? The one where I had to dive into the ice water and yank you out? The one where you were hooked to a TV screen and almost died in front of us?" Madeline's voice raised in pitch.

"Didn't the prince say that you have to take a hard challenge to get the invitation? It's not a freebee, Ciaran," Zach said.

"Why did you promise Bran?" Madeline asked.

"He promised to give me information about Mother."

"How do you know he wasn't bluffing? She might be out there, on Earth, looking for us," Tadgh said.

"Knowing that it might be a bluff, do you expect me to say no to Bran's offer, Tadgh?"

Tadgh shook his head.

"I can't do anything until you are all safely out of the gate. Off you go. Please." Ciaran gestured toward the opening.

"I'm married to you. I don't want to have to handle another wannabe queen lurking around. I'm staying," Madeline insisted.

"Yeah, too bad. I'm your brother. If I let you find Mother yourself, you'll bad-mouth me to her for the rest of my life. I can't let that happen. I'm staying, too." Tadgh rubbed the neck of his horse.

"You should go, Zach," Ciaran said.

"I don't have a reason to stay, but I'll stick around." Zach cast a careless look at Ciaran.

Ciaran's horse started to get agitated and stomp around. He patted it to calm it down.

"How do you give Bran the invitation? I assume he wants it," Tadgh asked.

"I have to find him."

"Right, so there's a finding-Bran stage after passing the challenges?" Madeline asked.

Ciaran nodded.

"And whatever the invitation allows you to do, do you have to do that for Bran, too?" Madeline continued her questioning.

Silence.

"That's a yes," Tadgh said.

Madeline got off her horse. Ciaran did the same. He approached her. "I'll also get a privilege with the invitation. And I need to give that to the princess if you don't mind."

"I don't mind. Why would I? But the challenge bothers me."

"It's not hard."

"Tadgh, Ciaran said the challenges aren't hard!" Madeline pointed at Ciaran.

Tadgh got off his horse. "He's right. Just a bunch of snow-mummies, a pack of wolves, a burning forest, a collapsing bridge over a canyon, and ice water. Piece of cake."

"All right, okay. What do you want me to do?" Ciaran asked.

"Well, I'm not going to sit here and wait. I want in—all the way. I'm going in with you," Madeline said.

"Same here," Tadgh said dryly.

"I—"

"You don't think I'm useless, do you?" Zach asked.

"You saw the training, you two. You can tell Zach how dangerous it was."

Zach shifted his shoulders. "I'll do my best. What does the invitation look like?"

"Do I have a choice?" Ciaran looked at Tadgh, Madeline, and Zach. They glanced at him and waited for him to answer his own rhetorical question.

"Very well. Let's go," Ciaran muttered. He hopped on his horse. "This is a hybrid game between augmented reality and a hologame. We will play the scenarios as we go. Death and injuries during the game will have realistic impacts. But I don't know their extent. The invitation and the privilege will be placed in a box. That's all I know."

Zach rolled his eyes. "Well, how insightful."

Tadgh laughed.

"Let's go." Ciaran's horse wanted to do just that. It raced across the hill of wild roses. The other three horses lagged behind but caught up quickly.

They arrived at a meadow. Madeline remembered it. They had seen it before in Ciaran's training.

"We'll start here," Ciaran said.

"We have company," Madeline said. "Kyle is here."

31

Tadgh said nothing. He glanced off into the distance and felt a tingle in his heart when he saw Jo riding alongside Kyle, both of them on black horses. Tadgh shook his head and tried to see Jo's emotions. He saw nothing. This Daimon Gate had somehow blocked his newfound ability. He cursed silently.

Jo was alive. That was all that mattered.

She was in black leather attire, double swords suspended from her back. Her hair blew back as she rode, making the angles of her foxy face sharper. Her green eyes shone brilliantly. They smiled at Tadgh.

Kyle and Jo approached but slowed and stopped at a distance. Jo looked at Tadgh and nodded slightly.

"I hope we are not in competition here, Ciaran," Kyle said.

"I think we are," Ciaran responded dryly.

Ciaran's white horse and Kyle's black horse stepped back and forth, stomping their front hooves in agitation.

"I need only the privilege. If you're after the invitation, then we are not in competition."

"The invitation and the privilege come together. I have

promised the privilege to someone. I'll need both the invitation and the privilege," Ciaran said.

"The privilege is for Jo, not for me. I dragged her into the gate against her will. I thought I could appoint her as a Sciphil. Turns out that I can't because I've been exiled. Jo needs a pardon from the Host. She needs the privilege."

"Otherwise?" Ciaran asked.

"Death by a thousand lightning bolts at the exit. Is that what you want for her?"

Everyone looked at Jo. Her face was as cool as steel. She kept her eyes on Tadgh.

Ciaran turned around, looking at Madeline. She showed neither approval nor rejection. That was enough for Ciaran. That meant she couldn't read anything from Jo.

Ciaran nodded. "Fine. If you honor what you say, we can benefit from the collaboration. If you don't, there may be a long future ahead for us, but I promise to cut yours short."

Kyle nodded.

They raced ahead along the meadow. Ciaran and Kyle led the group. Jo managed to pull her horse up to ride next to Tadgh. She looked at him again. This time, she smiled. That was Jo's smile. Tadgh was sure of it.

"I thought we lost you," Tadgh said.

Jo said nothing. She reached over and stuck a black rose next to Tadgh's daggers. She smiled again. Tadgh grinned and pushed his horse to get closer to her. But she pushed ahead and rode alongside Kyle.

In front of them, an army of faceless mummies rose from the tall grass. The mummies formed a line across the meadow and charged at them. This was the exact scenario from Ciaran's subconscious training.

The group charged straight ahead, six warriors on horseback. With weapons drawn and eyes fierce, they were ready to kill.

"Round them up," Ciaran said.

The horses ran in a circle, surrounding the mummies who

hurled stones at them. Speed helped. They had horses and thus had the advantage.

Kyle and Jo had long, black spears. Ciaran, Madeline, Tadgh, and Zach had two daggers each. They rounded up the mummies, killing a number of them without much difficulty. The rest ran away, howling like wounded dogs.

"Fire is coming. Go left," Ciaran said.

The group veered left and raced toward the cliff. They had seen this before. A skinny hanging bridge connecting the two mountains swung in the air, presenting an opportunity for disaster. The bridge could accommodate only one person at a time. They knew the wire would snap.

They dismounted. The fire closed in behind them.

"The box is over there. I'm sure of it," Ciaran said. "Right behind me." Ciaran clasped Madeline's hand and ran across the bridge. Tadgh and Zach followed right behind them. Kyle and Jo came after. They formed a line and rushed across the swinging bridge.

The fire approached and consumed the horses. The wire snapped, and the bridge dropped from that end, hanging by a thread from the other side. They all clung desperately to the knotted rope of the bridge, knowing it wouldn't hold for long.

From the bottom of the line, Jo began to climb up and over everyone else's bodies. Being petite was certainly an advantage now. She climbed over the edge like a spider. Unravelled a black leather rope wrapped around her waist, she tied it to a stone for purchase and dove down the cliff to grab Ciaran's hand.

"Climb up quick, Kyle," Ciaran said and reached his other hand to grab Madeline's. Madeline reached for Tadgh, and he, in turn, grabbed Zach.

Kyle climbed up quickly from the bottom, then Zach, Tadgh, Madeline, and finally Ciaran.

"Well done, Jo," Ciaran said.

Jo nodded and smiled. Then she moved to stand next to Kyle.

They were in front of the magnificent entrance to a white stone cave. Ciaran and Kyle entered it. The group followed.

In the middle, the cave opened up liked a grand hall. The white stone was illuminated, shedding a mysterious light throughout the cavernous room.

They heard a tapping sound as if an army of people walking on sticks was moving toward them.

A white claw appeared. Then they saw body with many legs.

"Is that a crab? I'm not particularly in the mood for seafood right now," Tadgh said.

"I think it's a white scorpion. It's as big as a cow!" Zach exclaimed incredulously.

"Six of us against a cow-crab. Folks, I think we've got a winner," Madeline joked, shifting her daggers.

Ciaran said to Kyle, "Would you mind taking the left?"

Kyle nodded.

With lightning speed, Ciaran darted to the right, and Kyle moved to the left. They jumped across the tops of a few stones and landed on top of the scorpion. It started to whirl around. Ciaran swung his dagger, and the two eyes of the scorpion flew away. Kyle brought his spear down into the top of the scorpion. A stream of black liquid spilled out and rained down on its white shell.

Suddenly, rows of smaller scorpions appeared from every direction.

"Holy *crab!*" Tadgh said. All of them ran toward the creatures. Daggers swung, spears stabbed. They use whatever weapons they could, stones and sand included, to fight the hard-shelled army.

Chaos.

Ciaran was always right there beside Madeline. Kyle and Jo fought back to back, and Tadgh and Zach did the same.

After a long while, with the cutting off of enough legs, eyes, and claws, the fight came to an end. Some wounded scorpions scurried away. The white shells of hundreds of scorpions littered the ground.

Between them, there were some minor scratches, bruises, and bleeding, but no serious injuries.

"That was easier than I thought." Zach grinned.

"There will be more," Tadgh mumbled as he remembered what he had seen in Ciaran's training.

They walked over the dead scorpions to another compartment of the cave. The light from the white rocks lighted the way.

From a gap between two large rocks, a shadow leaped at Ciaran, pushing him down onto the ground.

32

*A*n enormous white wolf looked down at Ciaran. He swung his daggers, and the wolf backed off quickly. Suddenly a large pack of them appeared. They stalked the intruders in a circle, looking at the group as if they were their next meal.

Jo swung her rope. It wrapped around the neck of a wolf and ripped its head off in one pull.

Tadgh gasped.

The group broke out into another round of fighting.

After a long while, they had killed several wolves. The wounded ones ran away.

This time they sustained more injuries.

Ciaran helped Madeline up from the ground. "Let me see." He looked at a nasty bite mark on her left wrist. "This will get infected," he mumbled.

Madeline turned him around, inspecting a gash from a claw and a bite mark at the back of his neck. She hadn't covered his back well enough. "This one, too."

Ciaran looked at Tadgh. "Two bites on the legs and one on the left arm. Otherwise, I'm good as new," Tadgh reported.

"A gash on my back and one on my right arm. I can't see my back, but it hurts like hell," Zach said.

"Let me see." Madeline looked. "Oh, it's nasty."

Nearby, Jo was checking her injuries. She was bleeding from both arms and her back. Tadgh approached. Jo gestured for him to keep a distance. He stopped.

Ciaran shrugged off his jacket and tore shreds from it. He secured Madeline's injuries then gave her the remaining part of the jacket. "Could you take care of them, please?" He gestured toward Tadgh and Zach.

"What about you?"

"I'm fine."

Madeline nodded, took the jacket, and went to tend to Tadgh and Zach.

Ciaran stood in the middle of the grand cave and stared at a gigantic illuminated column in the middle. He walked around it. He pressed his hand on the column. It was smooth and icy.

The box has to be here, he thought

Ciaran examined the icy surface. The hundred-foot column held up the ceiling. It was the life support of the grand cave. He noticed a red dot swirling around inside. What was it? Ciaran pulled his dagger out. He anticipated the moving path of the dot and stabbed at it.

The dot stopped moving. A small ice panel in the column slid open, revealing a button. The skin of the column became transparent, and inside, Ciaran could see a box placed at head height.

Everyone approached, looking at it.

"There it is," Kyle said.

He reached his hand out and punched the button.

"Wait!" Ciaran yelled. But it was too late.

The column broke apart. At the same time, the floor cracked and broke away into shards of ice. The column sunk down into the ice water, taking the box with it.

Everyone fled the sinking floor and ran to the rock edges.

The broken floor was now a pond of dark, icy water.

Jo looked at the sinking box. She dove into the water. Ciaran dived in after her. As soon as they disappeared below the surface, the ice sealed over.

Madeline was hanging onto a rock. She had seen this scenario before. She knew exactly what to do. She grabbed as many rocks as she could and slid to the middle of the icy crust to break the surface so that they could escape.

From under the dark water, Ciaran saw the ice closing in. He grabbed Jo to pull her up. She shrugged him off and followed the box down farther. It had slipped away from the broken column and lay at the very bottom. She picked it up. Ciaran grabbed for her again, and they both resurfaced.

Madeline and others had broken the ice and pulled Ciaran and Jo out of the freezing water.

Their bodies were numb. They did not speak.

Madeline held Ciaran. She wrapped her body around him and used whatever she had to give him some warmth. Tadgh darted toward Jo and did the same. He held her in his arms. She grabbed him. Her body shook.

Minutes passed, and Ciaran and Jo finally began to regain some body heat. The color slowly came back into their almost translucent faces. They looked toward each other and then toward the box that was sitting on the floor between them.

Kyle picked up the box. Ciaran slowly brought himself to a standing position. The two men gave each other a measured glance. Tadgh helped Jo to her feet.

Ciaran raised an eyebrow when Kyle gave him the box. He took it. On the lid was a liquid screen and a square panel that said, "Print verification required."

Ciaran smiled. That was why Kyle and Jo had needed him. Jo was a gate-crasher, and Kyle was an exiled Sciphil. Even if they had been able to retrieve the box, they wouldn't have been able to open it.

Ciaran put his palm on the panel to verify. The lid clicked open. Inside the box were two rectangular blocks—one red and one blue.

The two blocks were lit up, but Ciaran could not identify what they were made of. A grail was engraved on the red block, and a key was engraved on the blue one.

"The red one is the privilege, and the blue is the invitation," Ciaran said. He turned the box toward Kyle.

Kyle reached out for the red block.

From the corner of Ciaran's eyes, he saw it. Jo raised her arm and slid out her spear while Tadgh watched Ciaran and Kyle.

"Look out, Tadgh!" Ciaran yelled.

It was too late for Tadgh.

Jo pierced her spear right through his heart. She drew it back out.

Tadgh's body slumped to the ground. Ciaran ran toward his brother.

Tadgh was dead.

33

*J*o swung her rope and grabbed the box.

"I want both." That was the first time she had spoken since they had been reunited. What came out was not a voice but the sound of a devil from hell.

She turned and ran with the box.

Ciaran locked his eyes on her back as she fled. He took a stance and threw his dagger.

The dagger hit her right in the back of her head. She slumped down and melted into a pool of black liquid.

"That's not Jo," Ciaran said. He turned around. Kyle had disappeared.

Ciaran dashed toward the box and grabbed it. Then he scrambled back to where Tadgh lay. He crouched next to Tadgh's dead body and opened the box.

He took out the red block—the privilege. On top of the block was another panel. Ciaran pressed his palm against it. A tiny screen appeared on the surface of the block next to the panel. On the screen, the face of a woman appeared. She smiled kindly at him.

"Congratulations. You have gained a privilege. What would you like?"

"My brother has suffered a fatal injury. I want him healed," Ciaran said briskly.

"What is the injury?"

"A stab wound."

"Where?"

"To the heart."

"That is beyond the level of—"

"I don't give a fuck. I gained your privilege. It's supposed to fix anything inside the gate," Ciaran snarled.

"Conditional to—"

"Don't quote terms and conditions to me. I have the invitation as well. I will talk to your Host and will make rest of your life miserable, whoever and wherever you are!"

"But—"

"You offered the privilege. You are required to keep your end of the deal. The Daimon Gate does not break a promise. I want my brother healed. Now!"

"I will consult with my superior." The screen went blank for a long moment. Then a man's face appeared.

"Who is the injured guest?"

"Tadgh LeBlanc."

The man nodded. "He has previously received eudqi from his Sciphil. He is lucky. He will be fine. Step aside please."

Ciaran stepped aside.

A curtain of light poured down around Tadgh. They could not see him anymore.

Ciaran turned around. Madeline knew he was looking for her. She pulled him into her arms. Ciaran clung to her. He held on tight. He buried his head against her shoulder, and she felt the heat of his tears.

Madeline said nothing. She just embraced him.

After a long while, the light curtain vanished. Tadgh lay motionless on the floor and then opened his eyes. He looked around to gain his bearings.

Ciaran scrambled toward him. "How are you feeling?" he asked.

Tadgh winced and looked down at his chest. His shirt was still open, revealing a rapidly healing wound. Ciaran helped him up.

"Let's get you out of here," Ciaran said.

At the entrance of the cave, Ciaran sat Tadgh down on a rock. He pointed to the top of the hill, where the light reflection looked like a rainbow.

"That's the exit out of the Daimon Gate," Ciaran said.

"Kyle!"

In the distance, they could see Kyle charging toward the exit. He was carrying a large box nearly the size of a coffin on his shoulder as if it was a toy.

"I'll cut him into pieces," Ciaran growled.

Kyle seemed to be annoyed and threw the box to the ground. He pulled Jo out of it.

"That's the real Jo. I can read her. I can see her mind," Madeline gasped.

Tadgh frowned. "It's her. She's scared and angry," he whispered and quickly ran out of breath just by voicing that short sentence. He could see Jo's emotions now, but he couldn't go and get her.

Ciaran watched Kyle dragging Jo toward the exit. He could send in a blade and cut Kyle into pieces right now. He wanted to kill him so badly.

Jo kicked, screamed, and wriggled out of Kyle's grip. She turned around and pulled out the knife she'd hidden in her secret pocket, the one she had stolen from the zombie gangster on Earth. She stabbed Kyle. The small knife didn't do much damage, but it distracted him and stopped him from dragging her further toward the exit.

Ciaran clenched his fists. He could feel his fury coming to the surface. If he sent in the blade, it would kill both Kyle and Jo. If he let Kyle go, there would be consequences when he fled to the other universes.

Tadgh was too weak to make a run for Jo. Ciaran knew Tadgh wouldn't ask him to hold back on this important decision, but he knew how important Jo was to his brother.

The devastation in Tadgh's eyes cut at him. He had almost lost his brother. He couldn't give Tadgh another hit by killing Jo right in front of him.

Ciaran withheld the blade.

Jo ran down the hill.

Kyle fled through the exit.

Jo hurried toward Tadgh. She grabbed him and stared at the wound on his chest. "You're hurt. Oh, my God. Did Kyle do this to you?" Tears rolled down her face. "I'm sorry I wasn't there for you."

"I'm okay. Everything is fine now." He wiped the tears from her face and pulled her into his arms.

"I know it's useless to ask you to leave the gate before I do. But I have one thing to see to before we leave. Could you wait for me here?" Ciaran said.

"You're going back in for Bran, aren't you?" Madeline asked.

Ciaran nodded. "It shouldn't take long. And it's neither hard nor dangerous. During his last trip, Bran became lost and has been trapped in the oblivion for a long time. This invitation will help me navigate to him, and I'll get him out. I promised him this. Okay? There won't be any fighting or struggles."

"Is that all?" Madeline asked.

"That's all. I'll get him out, and he'll tell me where Mother is. That's the deal. That's it."

Tadgh tried to say something. Ciaran bent down. He shook Tadgh's shoulders gently and looked into his brother's eyes, the feature with the strongest resemblance between them.

"I can't handle another episode from you, Tadgh. Please stay here. Leave with them if you must."

Tadgh nodded and closed his eyes, leaning against the rock to rest.

34

*C*iaran went back into the cave. He pulled out the blue block. It lit up in the dark. He walked slowly. The light would be strongest when heading in the right direction. That was what Bran had told him. He went deeper and deeper into the cave.

The stone had gone from white to black. The temperature increased. The sound of water dripping somewhere between the rocks sang like music.

Ciaran entered a wide grand hall where he found a black rock arch. He touched the rocks. A wave of strange current pulsed out like electricity. Ciaran reached his hand out into the empty space on the other side of the arched rocks.

His hand disappeared in front of him. He withdrew his hand.

The dimensional gate to the oblivion, he thought. That was where Bran was.

Ciaran pushed the blue block through the gateway to the other side, and unlike his hand which seemed to vanish, he could still see the illuminated block.

Ciaran nodded to himself and was happy with the compass he had in his hand. He walked through the archway.

He was immediately transferred to a peaceful green meadow. He shrugged. Oblivion didn't look bad at all. In the distance, a small cottage blended nicely into the setting. It was like a live painting of the countryside in England, Ciaran thought.

In front of the cottage, Bran stood like a farmer, a shovel in one hand and a bucket in the other.

Ciaran approached. "Bran."

"Ciaran. I knew you would make it. Having you as a successor was the best decision I ever made."

"It's my honor. We should leave now. People are waiting."

Bran nodded. "Let me get out of this farmer gear and get my stuff. Come on in."

They entered the door of the so-called cottage. The door was so small that Ciaran had to bend down to squeeze through.

Inside the tiny cottage was a gigantic space station. Ciaran turned around. He could still see the meadow through the door. *How is this even possible?* he thought.

Ciaran pointed toward the door. "Is that a dimensional gate?"

Bran laughed. "You certainly don't disappoint. It is, indeed." Bran gestured widely. "And this is *my* dimension. I created it."

"You created a dimension? How?"

"You have a lot to learn, Ciaran. But now you should have some confidence in the impact of what I asked you to do. You should know how significant your role will be in the history of the multiverse. And you should appreciate what I have given you from Eudaiz."

Bran entered a series of commands into computer units that were as large as the wall of the space station. He pointed to the flashing light on a control panel.

Ciaran approached. The monitor asked for print verification. He pressed his palm to the square panel. A burning sensation ran up his arm and his spine and shocked his brain.

Ciaran grunted and passed out on the floor.

When he came to, Bran was working on a computer.

"You're very strong Ciaran. We are good to go now."

Ciaran stood up, looking at his hand. There was no mark on his palm. He didn't feel any different.

"What did you do to me?"

"Nothing really. I just helped you out with your task. The information I asked you to collect would be a lot to remember using an ordinary human brain. I simply added more memory capacity to yours. That's all."

"How long have I been out?"

"Just a few seconds."

He pushed up from his chair and led the way out of the cottage.

"You're not taking anything? Your equipment?"

"No, I loaded everything into you. I trust you." Bran patted Ciaran's shoulder.

Moments later, they were using the blue block to navigate their way back to the black stone arch. Ciaran pointed to it. "That's a dimensional gate. That's why you got lost."

"I wasn't lost."

"What?"

"I knew it was a dimensional gate. Kyle stabbed me through it. He snatched Madeline from her cot and ran through the Daimon Gate. I chased him to get the baby back. We fought. I wounded him badly, but when he pushed the baby in front of me, I hesitated. That's how he got me. Then the dimension shifted. Without a navigator, I couldn't get back out."

Ciaran nodded. "Well, you got yourself a good Sciphil One now, thanks to Kyle."

They walked through the gate and returned to the entrance of the cave.

Madeline rushed toward Ciaran. Everything in her body and mind told her that things were not going well.

"Darling, are you okay?" Ciaran asked.

"We need to leave. We should leave right now, Ciaran."

"Yes, of course." He held Madeline and felt her body shaking.

"Why don't you sit down for a moment?" Ciaran said.

"No, no. We have to leave. Right now."

"She's been like this for ten minutes. We can leave now, Madeline," Jo said. She turned around to help Tadgh, who was still weak and dazed.

"Ciaran needs to say goodbye to the Host before we leave, Madeline. It would be very inappropriate if he didn't do so," Bran said.

"What? No, no. We are leaving right now!" Madeline insisted.

"Madeline, I just need to say goodbye. I have the invitation. It will only take five minutes. Then we'll leave. You'll have Bran here with you. If Kyle comes back—"

"No, no, not Kyle. It's not Kyle. It's something else. Something is really wrong. Please don't go in again," Madeline cried.

"Bran." Ciaran looked at Bran.

"You have to, Ciaran. Don't you want to find out about your mother?"

"She—" Ciaran looked at Madeline.

"You've just been through the Daimon Gate. It's a lot to take in. I'd be surprised if she weren't emotional. Let's finish this quickly. I want to leave, too," Bran said.

"If anything—"

"Nothing will happen to you. But yes, I will take care of everyone. I have the power to keep the promise. I am the current king of Eudaiz, remember?" Bran said.

Ciaran hesitated.

"Look, Jo can't exit the gate without getting killed because she didn't have an invitation to enter. As the current king of Eudaiz, I can give her the invitation now." Bran grabbed Jo's hand and pressed his thumbprint to it. "This is a temporary entry for guests. She will be fine. I keep my promises. I hope you keep yours, Ciaran."

Madeline wrapped her arms around Ciaran. She knew she could not make him stay.

Her body ached. Her heart ached. She could not explain her

feelings to him. She could not find a reason for him to stay. She reached up and kissed him as if it would be their last kiss.

She looked at Ciaran going back into the cave. Her knees buckled, and Zach caught her. He carried her to the edge of the rock where she was violently ill.

35

*C*iaran walked along the white stone hall to an entrance. He followed the signal on the blue block. A panel slid open. He inserted the block, and a wall-sized door opened widely, revealing a grand reception room.

Ciaran had butterflies in his stomach.

The room arrangement and decoration closely resembled that of Mon Ciel. An automatic voice echoed across the room, "Welcome Ciaran Leblanc. The Host invites you to take a tour of the EYE before meeting in the Great Reception."

Even the name of the room was the same as Mon Ciel. He wouldn't be surprised to find his mother here. But he let go of that speculation for the moment and focused on the task at hand.

All he had to do was to go to the EYE, the most sophisticated computer system in the cosmos, and download the data for Bran. Once he completed that task, anything else would be a bonus. If he met his mother here, great. If not, Bran would tell him where she was.

A steel door in front of him slid open. Ciaran entered an eye-shaped room. The walls were covered with monitors, each flashing with images. It was like an enormous cinema that showed thousands of movies at the same time.

The control panel flashed for print verification. Ciaran pressed his palm on the panel, and text appeared.

CIARAN LEBLANC.
> One invitation: Available.
> One privilege: Claimed.
> Data access: FULL.

CIARAN NODDED. As Bran had predicted, he had full access to the data. He walked around the room and glanced at the panels. He recognized the faces of the prince and the princess at the Red Castle. He touched the screen. Text appeared.

FACTUAL:
> Prince and Princess of the Red Castle.
> Status: Sentenced to death by a thousand lightning bolts.
> Execution date: Five thousand five hundred – twenty two – sixteen – sixth quarter.
> Crime: Manipulating the Daimon Gate system for personal gain.
> Preview: Y/N
> Ciaran typed: Y

THE PRINCE and the princess had not yet been executed. There was still hope, Ciaran mused. He made a mental note of the execution date. He had to ask Tadgh to translate the date into something more sensible.

A stream of images flooded the screen. Ciaran washing onto the shore. The princess finding him, taking him home, and tending to his injuries. Being fed the inducer. Ciaran and Madeline in a subconscious state. The two of them sharing their vows and consummating their marriage. Leaving the Red Castle.

It was exactly as the prince had said. The system captured everything—the conscious and subconscious levels of every living thing inside the gate. Ciaran promised himself he would come back and rectify this death sentence now that he knew how.

THE SCREEN FLASHED: *Download data: Y/N*
Ciaran typed: *N.*
Then he typed in: *Search Bran LeBlanc.*

THE COMPUTER FLASHED:
Factual:
Bran LeBlanc - Sciphil Three - King of Eudaiz.
Qualification: Pass Daimon Gate.
Black stage: Ten challenges, gatekeeper: Simon Bannon.
White stage: Five challenges, gatekeeper: Lucas Masr.
Red stage: Twenty challenges, consummated with Jennifer Wyse, gatekeeper: Martin Chinxz.
Preview: Y/N

JENNIFER WYSE WAS his mother's maiden name. Ciaran typed: *N* to decline the preview. Then he searched for Jennifer Wyse.

THE COMPUTER FLASHED:
Factual:
Jennifer Wyse, now Jennifer LeBlanc - Hostess of the Daimon Gate.
Family status: Married to Conan LeBlanc, children: Ciaran LeBlanc and Tadgh LeBlanc.
Past marriage: Bran LeBlanc.
Past position: Sciphil Six.

Qualification: Pass Daimon Gate.

Black stage: Ten challenges, gatekeeper: Simon Bannon.

White stage: Five challenges, gatekeeper: Lucas Masr.

Red stage: Twenty challenges, consummated with Bran LeBlanc, gatekeeper: Martin Chinxz.

Preview: Y/N

HIS MOTHER HAD GONE through the gate at the same time, and she had married Bran. They must have divorced afterward, and then she resigned from her Sciphil Six position. That was plausible. If she was now the Hostess of Daimon Gate, Ciaran would see her soon. Ciaran typed: N to decline the preview. Then he searched for Madeline Kelley.

THE COMPUTER FLASHED:

Factual:

Madeline Kelley, now Madeline LeBlanc.

Family status: Married to Ciaran LeBlanc, children: Son and daughter, not yet named.

Current position: Sciphil One - appointment in progress.

Qualification: Pass Daimon Gate.

Black stage: Five challenges, gatekeeper: Snitxc Mitchell.

White stage: Six challenges, gatekeeper: Laureen White.

Red stage: Zero challenges, consummated with Ciaran LeBlanc, gatekeepers: Lecal Brandon and Leciel Brandon.

Preview: Y/N

CIARAN COULD NOT WITHHOLD A SMILE—HE was to have a son and a daughter with Madeline! Their consummation had conceived their children. They had twins. He was a father! How was this even possible? He didn't know. He didn't care. He was just happy.

The EYE was genius—it recorded everything, Ciaran thought. He could not resist a preview of this.

On the screen, Ciaran saw them making love at the Red Castle. Under the light of the eternal flame, she was beautiful. That moment was the most sensational experience he had ever experienced. They had made love before. Several times. But at the Red Castle, the experience was profound.

It was a rebirth of their love and lives together as soul mates.

On the screen, a line of text appeared: Transmutation rebirth. Children conceived.

Ciaran shook his head, astonished. The EYE must record information down to the level of the atom.

The screen flashed: *Download data: Y/N.*

Ciaran typed: *N.*

HE GLANCED at the other screens. Billions of images flew by. The lives and events of everyone and everything that had ever occurred in the multiverse.

Ciaran recognized events on Earth. Some were as significant as world wars, and some were as minor as a spat between neighbors about whose dog had shit in whose yard. Ciaran was sure the EYE had recorded which dog had committed the crime. He wondered whether the people engaged in the argument over the dog's business would ever be informed of the data.

On a bigger scale, the EYE must have recorded factual information behind all of the scandals and mysteries on Earth. If that were discovered, Ciaran was sure that it would change the history of humankind.

He looked at his left palm. All he had to do was to download the data for Bran by pressing his palm against the control panel. Would the capacity of the memory Bran had designed be large enough for this database? Ciaran didn't think so.

He wagered Bran only wanted to establish the connection. Having access to this kind of information was equivalent to having the power of the creator of all things. Knowing everything that anyone had ever done in any world.

This was the power of God.

The computer continued to flash: *Viewing will end in ten seconds. Download Data Y/N?*

Ciaran pressed *N* again.

The room lit up. A door to the next room slid open. Ciaran walked into a reception room which was almost identical to the one at Mon Ciel.

36

*A*t the end of the long table sat a man Ciaran was not surprised to see—his father, Conan LeBlanc.

Ciaran approached slowly, calm and sure.

Conan gestured toward a chair.

Ciaran sat and gazed at his father.

"Congratulations for passing the Daimon Gate," Conan said.

"Thank you," Ciaran said dryly.

"Children conceived during the Red stage of the transmutation process are the best human beings. You should reward yourself and Madeline for that."

"I believe in nurture, not nature. Our children will grow up within our care and protection. They will turn out the way they want to be, not the way we want them to be. And they do not have to be the best just because they were conceived in a spiritual space."

"A man in your position has to bring his children up the right way—"

"Did you?" Ciaran cut him off. "For twenty years you let me believe you were dead. You left Tadgh and me scrambling to live up to your expectations. You let Mother struggle on her own with a brat like me when she'd have been better off to smother me as a baby."

Ciaran hurled the entire tea set that sat on the table before him at the wall.

"You still don't handle your rage well, Ciaran."

"The fuck I don't."

"I've been watching over you and Tadgh."

"Right, stalking us using your EYE system. Did you see how many times Tadgh almost died in the last few weeks? Did you see how many times we were attacked when we were off guard? And you just watched for entertainment?"

"I cannot interfere. I can only observe. There are rules."

"A man in your position has to do the right thing, don't you? You would do the right thing by your world, whatever it is, but not by your family, the world you created and abandoned in the blink of an eye."

Ciaran shook his head. He wanted to laugh at the coincidence of the expression the blink of an eye, but he speculated it wouldn't erupt as a laugh but a roar of anger. The rage threatened to consume him, but he squelched it.

"Tell me if Mother is okay, and I'll get out of your hair."

"She is the Hostess here. She is quite well."

Ciaran pushed up.

"Very well then. Goodbye, Father." He walked toward the door.

"Do you think this is a familial matter?"

"What else could it be?"

"You passed the worthiness test. You could be the next Host of the Daimon Gate if you are interested."

Ciaran cast a cold look at Conan. "Another fucking test? No, I don't care, and I'm not interested." He turned around again to leave.

"You're not going to leave just like that, are you?"

"Trust me, you'll want me to leave before I do a lot of damage to this place."

"More than that broken tea set?"

Ciaran gave his father a blank stare. "If you have anything else to say to complete this formality, please do it quickly, Host of the Daimon Gate."

"Don't you even want to see your mother?"

"You said she's well. That's good enough."

"So you trust me?"

"No. But Mother stuck by you for that long, so I figure she must love you. If she's happy, that's good enough for me."

Conan nodded. "You're a greater man that you give yourself credit for, Ciaran. You've seen the power of the EYE, you had full access, and yet you did not download the data."

"I don't have a use for the data. And I hope a man in your position would do the right thing, too."

Conan nodded. "You don't need the data for personal use. But if you are the King-to-be of Eudaiz, it will prove to be very beneficial to you. Why didn't you take it?"

"That's my decision and none of your business."

"If someone wants to steal the data from the EYE, that is my business. Anything that happens inside this gate is my business."

"I didn't take the data. What else do you want me to say?"

"Conspiracy to steal is the same crime as actually stealing it. Within this gate, the penalty is death by a thousand lightning bolts."

"I don't see how this is relevant. I'm not taking anything. Consider this conversation finished."

"If I asked you to press your left palm against a detective panel, would I find anything?"

Silence.

"Why are you protecting him, Ciaran?"

"I'll talk him out of this."

Conan laughed. "You're too confident, Ciaran. Bran has been plotting this for more than thirty years, and you think you can talk him out of it?"

"If you knew, why didn't you stop him?"

"The oblivion is a black hole. We don't have access although it is a part of the gate and within my jurisdiction. We've been waiting for him to come out for a long time. Now he's back inside the gate. I will take him before he exits."

"I'm not helping you to get Bran."

"You don't have to do anything. Just stay here. I'll send someone to get him. When we detect the device is from him, that's will be the end of him."

Ciaran shook his head and said nothing. He shifted his sore shoulder. "What if you don't find anything on Bran?"

Conan was in the process of calling his people. He stopped. "Then I'll have to let him go. But an operation like this is quite major. He is the current King of Eudaiz. Our council will question my conduct, and I will have to resign. I know he's guilty. But if it is God's will that he passes this time, then so be it."

"What do you mean by *this* time?"

The door to the room flung wide open.

Jennifer sauntered in, more beautiful than ever. She wore a long white robe, and her face was radiant. Her eyes warmed at the sight of Ciaran.

Ciaran stood up. "You look well, Mother."

"And you look terrible, Son. I know that passing the Daimon Gate for the first time is very taxing. But it shouldn't have put you in such poor condition. Is that why you locked me up? So I would miss his visit, Conan?"

"I don't know what you're talking about," Conan said.

"Oh, well, maybe it was just a bad luck then. I see that Bran is waiting at the exit. Would you let him go, darling? Ciaran, stay for tea with me, will you?"

"Mother."

Conan continued to call people. He puzzled at the panel.

"I sent them on some tasks, and they're busy right now. Do you need the troop for anything in particular? There is no fight simulation on at the moment," Jennifer said.

Conan cleared his throat. "No, that's fine." He glanced at Ciaran.

"I sent my secretary to the exit to tell Bran and his people not to wait as Ciaran will stay for tea."

"Jennifer," Conan lowered his voice.

"They should have gotten the message by now . . ."

Conan rushed toward the monitor, and Jennifer grabbed him.

"It's too late. Conan. Let Bran go."

Conan grabbed Jennifer's shoulders as if he were about to shake her. Ciaran snatched Conan and threw him against a wall. Ciaran stood in front of his mother.

Conan straightened up and let out a discerning chuckle. "Right. Mother and son team up. Like I don't know what I'm doing here? I'm useless. I'm just so useless."

"Why can't you let it go, Conan?" Jennifer asked. "Everything will be fine."

She approached Conan. Tears rolled down her face. It was the first time Ciaran had seen his mother cry. Conan wiped the tears from her face.

"I'll resign. We'll leave here," Conan said.

Jennifer nodded. Conan held his wife tightly in his arms.

"Let's leave. Forget about all this," he whispered.

"Can you at least tell me what's going on here?" Ciaran asked.

The monitor made a verbal announcement. "Bran LeBlanc requesting a call."

Conan pointed at the monitor. "You see, he's the one who's not letting go. I'll have to call this in. I have to catch him."

"What did he do?" Ciaran asked.

"Don't tell him, Conan. It won't help."

"He tested weapons on small stars in remote galaxies and killed billions of residents. Do you expect me to see billions of people killed and ignore it just because it was outside of my jurisdiction?" Conan snarled.

"It's not just outside of your jurisdiction. There's a death penalty for interfering with any affairs outside the gate. You don't even have soldiers. Bran is a powerful man. You have nothing but your good intentions, and those won't be able to to save you."

"How can I be a righteous man, a virtuous gatekeeper, if I

ignore this opportunity to do the right thing by billions of inno-
cents? Is that the sort of man you want to be with, Jennifer?"

Jennifer cried out. "I don't want a saint. I am only a wife. I need
a husband, and our children need a father."

"Child. Not children, Jennifer."

Conan punched the wall after these words slipped out of his
mouth.

37

*A*fter punching the wall, Conan turned back and approached Jennifer. She backed away.

"Don't come near me," she said.

Ciaran pulled her into his arms. "I'm sorry, Mother."

He looked at Conan. A searing pain raised in his heart. Whatever had happened between them, he still saw Conan as his father.

Ciaran remembered the data reported his mother's ex-marriage to Bran. That meant he was Bran's son. He looked at Conan. "I'm not yours then? I assume your jealousy plays a role in this attempt to arrest Bran?" Ciaran spoke to Conan.

Conan slumped into a chair and said nothing.

It was strange. His mother pulled him into her arms and held on as if she wanted to savor the moment for as long as she could. She kissed his cheek and his forehead. Then she released him. *What was she trying to do?* Ciaran thought.

"Regardless of how bad of a man Bran is, you love him because he is your little brother, Conan," Jennifer said.

Conan nodded and put his head in his hands. "I'm sorry, darling."

"Don't be," she continued. "The only way to end Bran is to illegitimize his qualification for the Daimon Gate or expose his attempt to steal the data from the EYE. The second solution is dangerous because if you can't expose him, your head will be on the chopping block. On those grounds, I will not let either of you go near Bran."

"If he walks out the gate this time, all those people he killed will never have justice. I'll not have another chance at this. We have to get him now, inside the gate," Conan said.

"You are not getting him with the data. I won't risk you or Ciaran doing that."

"I'm not a crystal vase, Mother."

Jennifer glanced at Ciaran. He turned on his heels and sat down at the table.

"I'll get him with the qualification. He cheated at the Red stage. If I can provide evidence of that, he will be disqualified from his kingship. While he's still inside the gate, the penalty for manipulating the system for personal gain is death by a thousand lightning bolts. With his kingship disqualified, he will be ended at the source in Eudaiz, too. If you both want him to go down that way, I'm happy to assist," Jennifer said dryly.

Both Ciaran and Conan gave Jennifer blank stares.

"What evidence?" Ciaran asked.

"The EYE's data cannot be manipulated," Conan said.

"You underestimate your brother. Your training to be the Daimon Gate Host was a secret to the multiverse, but not to Bran. He knew I wanted to pay you a visit and I missed you, but I couldn't tell anyone. Bran told me he could lobby for me to go through the gate as Sciphil Six's successor. It was just a play. Then I could go in and out of the gate to visit you. I was stupid enough to believe him."

Conan stood up. Jennifer gestured him not to approach her.

"Bran was going through the qualifying process as the King-to-be of Eudaiz. He trained me so that I could go through the gate with him. We went through the gate and passed all the stages, and at the Red stage, he forced me to consummate."

"What do you mean by him forcing you?" Ciaran's voice was

dangerously low. The pain pounded in his head. The heat of the Red stage still lingered in him. It was hell.

And he wouldn't have passed if Madeline hadn't gone down to look for him. He would have been forced to take another queen. Which he wouldn't have done. And then he would have been killed.

Bran knew all this. He wanted to ensure he had the queen with him. Someone he could trust, and someone who foolishly trusted him.

There was no response from his mother, so he asked again, "What do you mean by him forcing you?"

"I mean that I didn't consent to be his wife. But he manipulated the data and blackmailed the gatekeeper to cheat the system. Martin Chinxz was the gatekeeper. He took pity on me. He gave me a copy of the original data. He died a few years later of 'natural causes'—you were naive enough to believe that, Conan!"

"If you show the council the original record, you will be charged with withholding it," Conan said.

"Then I'd plead guilty. I was a victim. The penalty shouldn't be too severe. Martin Chinxz died. I can claim fear, shame, or whatever reason you can think of . . ."

While his mother ranted about the plan to convict Bran, Ciaran broke into her portable databank.

He had activated and played the record of her original. She had passcodes and locks on the file, but opening these portable databank locks was child's play for Ciaran.

As soon as the data came on the screen, his blood ran cold. "Is this the original record?" he asked and turned the monitor around so that his mother and Conan could see it.

He could see in his mother's eyes that, although she had not watched it for years, the incident was still raw in her memory.

On the monitor was the scene of her being raped and beaten.

Compared to the hell that he went through at the Red stage and the condition of the creatures in the form of women who had been ripped of all dignity, his mother's condition was far worse.

As the female companion, a contender to be queen, Madeline was well protected by his love and her love for him. They were unified. That was how they got through.

His mother had gotten nothing. She didn't love Bran, didn't agree to marry him, and thus shouldn't have even been in the Red stage. Bran had only wanted a queen, and he didn't love her. They weren't soul mates. He couldn't and wouldn't have protected her.

He had merely wanted a queen to consummate so that he could pass the gate and became king.

His mother had been on her own, against everything and everyone in the gate.

The pain in his head was unbearable. He was afraid his fury would surface. But if it did, who would it kill?

In the corner of the screen was the text: *Transmutation rebirth. Child conceived.*

Ciaran shook his head. That child was him.

That was how he had been born. The best human being conceived in the Red stage of the transmutation process. Even the spiritual system disregarded human emotions. He had been conceived at the best astronomical moment and had inherited the best from his parents.

What could his mother have done apart from swallowing the truth and raising her child? If Bran could replace the data, what would be his mother's chances of proving that her record was the original? Between the words of the King of Eudaiz and a young girl, foolishly in love, who had agreed to pass all other stages of the Daimon Gate test with her man, who would the authorities believe?

Jennifer charged at Ciaran. She slapped him in the face. "How dare you!"

Ciaran pulled his mother into his arms and let her cry.

He saw stars in his eyes. Black stars of fury. They needed to consume. They needed to kill. He needed to destroy.

Tears rolled down Conan's face. He knew his wife had been forced. But he obviously hadn't realized the extent of it. And he had not known about the record. Somewhere in the back of his mind, he did not believe her at times.

The record of the EYE was flawless. It was the best computer system in the cosmos. It was the system he had sworn to protect.

After a moment, Ciaran asked, "Does Bran know about me?"

Jennifer shook her head. "He didn't look at the original—he was in too much of a hurry to replace it."

The computer announced Bran's request again.

Conan punched at the control button. "Tell him just a few minutes."

Ciaran picked his mother up, walked her to the room next door, and gently placed her down on a reading chair. He walked out, closed the door, jammed it from the outside, and ignored her cries to be released.

"I'm going to get Bran inside the gate for you. Do you trust me?" Ciaran asked Conan.

"But—"

"Do you want Mother to report that tape?"

"No, but—"

"I'll need some data from the EYE. Just a little."

"I can't let you download any data."

"If I can get Bran inside the gate, then everything should be fine, am I correct?"

Conan nodded.

"Then let's do it."

Before leaving, Ciaran said, "Again, I believe in nurture. I only have—and accept—one father."

Conan nodded. "And I have two sons, both of whom I love more than anything."

"Let's keep it that way."

a moment later, Ciaran walked toward the exit, where Bran was waiting. He saw that Madeline, Zach, and Tadgh had been moved into the transitional zone. They could see into but could not re-enter the gate.

Tears streamed down Madeline's face. She had an incredible sixth sense. She must know disaster was coming. Madeline, his wife, his children's mother—she was beautiful. Ciaran wanted to rush to her and kiss her, but he knew it was best not to make Bran suspect.

"What took so long?" Bran asked.

"Didn't you get the message? My mother was in there. She wanted me to stay for tea!"

Bran nodded. "As I suspected, she's the Hostess, isn't she?"

Ciaran nodded. "Can we go now?"

"I have to make sure that you got the data first. Once we are out of here, there will be no chance for us to get back to the EYE."

"I got the data. How do you want to check it?"

Bran contemplated. "Let's connect when we get to Eudaiz." He turned around to leave.

"Sure." Ciaran followed, walking as slowly as he could.

"What's the matter?"

"Nothing. Just a little pain."

"I'll see to it when we settle."

"Why did you want the data on rural planning and plantations?"

Bran stopped. "What?"

Ciaran shrugged. "I saw part of the data before downloading."

Bran narrowed his eyes, "Are you sure you got the right data?"

"If I recall correctly, you wanted the data in the EYE system, right?"

"That's correct."

"That's it then. Time was limited. I could only download some of the categories, whichever came first."

"What? Was the access granted to all categories?"

"I'm not sure. Let's go," Ciaran said and strode toward the exit.

"No, no, if we go, we can't get back in."

"I'm not going back in. Why don't you do it yourself?"

Bran looked directly into Ciaran's eyes. "You're not trying to trick me, are you, Ciaran?"

"What reason would I have to do that?"

"I can still withdraw your successor role. If I do it now before you exit the gate, you will be a gate-crasher. That will be a sentence of death by a thousand lightning bolts."

"Remember, Bran, I promised to do this for you in exchange for information about my mother. Now I know that my mother is well and good. Why would I want to do anything to you?"

Bran nodded. "I'm sorry. Okay. Let's just check the data before we go."

"I want to get to my wife. So whatever you want to do in here, do it quickly."

"Give me your left hand."

Bran reached his right hand out and clasped Ciaran's left palm as if they were engaged in a handshake.

As soon as their hands connected, Ciaran could feel a current run from his spine to his palm. Bran's eyes went blank as if he was looking into the distance. Then he snapped back quickly and tried to withdraw his hand.

Ciaran clasped Bran's hand tighter and would not let go.

"What's wrong?" Ciaran asked.

Bran's eyes darkened. "You son of a bitch." Bran pulled his hand hard, trying to yank it out of Ciaran's grip.

Ciaran predicted that Bran had now left his digital imprint at the EYE databank—proof of his attempt to gain access. Ciaran looked up and saw sparks of oncoming lightning bolts. He let Bran's hand go.

"This is for what you did to my mother. You don't deserve her."

"I won't go down alone, Ciaran." Bran looked up and saw the lightning coming his way.

Out of the corner of his eye, Ciaran saw Conan and his mother desperately running toward him. They gestured for him to get out.

Ciaran withdrew out of the exit.

Bran saw the opportunity and ran back toward the black arched stone to go back to the oblivion. They could not get him from the black hole.

Ciaran tackled him and pushed him back to the exit zone.

From the transitional zone, Madeline, Tadgh, and Zach tried to re-enter without success. They witnessed Bran and Ciaran struggling for reasons unknown to them.

Bran drew his King Sciphil sword. "I'm not going down alone, Ciaran. You'll have to share these thousand lightning bolts with me."

He charged at Ciaran with the sword. Ciaran pulled out his daggers. They fought.

Although Bran was an old man, he was King Sciphil. At this stage, Ciaran was only a human. Bran kicked Ciaran to the ground.

"Ciaran LeBlanc, I renounce your role as my successor."

Bran tried to grab Ciaran's left arm where he had the golden crucifix. Ciaran withdrew.

"I do not accept."

He rolled away and kicked Bran back into the exit zone.

Madeline, Tadgh, and Zach were being transported further away and were near the end of the transitional zone. Ciaran glanced quickly at the tears on Madeline's face.

Bran charged out of the exit zone again. Ciaran had to force him back in with a weapon fight.

The daggers and sword clashed and ignited sparks. Ciaran locked the sword against a stone with his two daggers. Bran pulled at the sword but could not move it from the stone. Ciaran snatched Bran and spun him around. Bran fell to the ground.

Ciaran used his body weight to pin him down to the ground. He was about to land a punch on Bran's face.

But he couldn't do it. He could kill Bran with a weapon—and he would. But he could not find the will to use his fist on the man who had created him.

Bran looked up at Ciaran from the ground. For a brief moment, Bran registered something so profound that he could not explain it —a blood connection between them.

Bran shoved Ciaran away and stood up.

They eyed each other, saying nothing.

The lightning bolts drew nearer.

Conan and Jennifer approached from the other direction.

Thunder rumbled in from outside the gate.

Madeline, Tadgh, and Zach were outside the gate, and it started to close.

Madeline saw the lightning storm right above where Ciaran and Bran were standing.

She screamed, but she knew Ciaran couldn't hear her.

A bolt of lightning knocked Ciaran off his feet and threw him out of the exit zone.

Others started striking Bran. He blocked one. He blocked another. And then he was hit. He slumped to the ground. He stood up quickly, roared, and ran toward the closing gate. More lightning bolts fenced him in. He could run no longer. He stood and took the hits.

He looked at Ciaran. Ciaran couldn't hear him, but he was sure Bran said, "I forgive you."

Ciaran stood up.

His mother and Conan continued to run toward the zone. Lightning bolts struck everywhere in hundreds of blazing colors. It was difficult to see Bran now, but through a little gap in the bolts, Ciaran caught a glimpse of him.

Madeline stood numbly, gazing through the remaining slit in the closing gate at what was happening.

There was a whirl of light as the burning King Sciphil sword flew out from the forest of lightning bolts toward Jennifer. Conan darted forward, pushing Jennifer aside. All he could do was watch it flying directly toward him.

Conan knew it would be the end. He would take the sword from his brother.

A body flew in front of Conan, blocking the sword's path.

Ciaran dropped to the ground. The sword had pierced his body.

Ciaran reeled up. He pulled the sword out and threw it toward the forest of lightning bolts.

The sword pinned Bran's body to the stone, where he stood immobile and died.

Blood streamed out of the wound in Ciaran's body. He fell to the ground.

That was the last thing Madeline saw.

The gate closed.

Darkness.

39

*M*adeline woke in Ayana's arms. She had passed out for a brief moment when she saw the last image of Ciaran before the Daimon Gate closed.

She could accept that he might die. But she could not accept the gate between them. He might die, but they could not be in two different worlds when it happened.

Madeline shrugged off Ayana's supporting arms.

"Take me back inside the gate, please."

Taking one look at Madeline, Ayana understood that nothing she said or did now could waver her determination. She nodded.

Ayana reopened the gate.

Madeline charged inside, followed by Tadgh, Zach, Jo, Ayana, and Pete.

THE AIR in the exit zone was thick with smoke and the acrid smell of something burning. The scorched ground encircled a large area. Bran's dead body was still pinned to the stone.

In the corner, Jennifer was holding Ciaran's body in her arms.

"Oh, God." Tadgh's face expressed pure anguish. Conan approached, pulling Tadgh into his arms and letting him cry.

Zach saw no tears on Madeline's face. She was as cold as steel.

Madeline crouched next to Jennifer.

"Could I take a look at him, please?"

"He's dead. I killed my son."

"Please," she repeated.

Jennifer looked at Madeline and released Ciaran.

Madeline needed no medical knowledge to know that Ciaran was gone. But her sixth sense told her to believe otherwise. That was all she had at the moment. Her sixth sense guided by her Daimon. She would do whatever it took to protect the happiness she had fought for and serve.

Madeline looked at Bran's body, and she puzzled.

She reached down and kissed Ciaran's still-warm face. Then she flew across the scorched ground toward Bran. Madeline pulled at the King Sciphil sword that pinned him to the stone. Bran's body instantly disintegrated into the air, the same way Juliette's body had exploded under the two thousand light beams.

Before anyone could react or say anything, the ground rumbled and shook.

The sound of an explosion came through the gate and shook the ground again.

"A reformation," Ayana mumbled.

The gate spun open. Bran re-entered the gate at great speed in spectacular form—a form that resembled that of his glorious days. Tears streamed down Ayana's face when she caught sight of him.

Conan ran in front of everyone, blocking Bran. The two brothers snarled at each other and whirled around like two male lions guarding their territories and testing their prowess.

"Have you ever seen a King of Eudaiz die inside the gate, Conan?"

"I underestimated you . . ."

"You did that all your life, brother. That sword was for you, not for him."

"He took it. I couldn't stop him."

Bran raised his hand, and his sword returned to him instantly. He pointed it at Conan. "If I do it again, will you take the sword this time?"

Jennifer stood in front of Conan. "Please don't kill him, Bran."

"Yes, I'll take your sword. If I can take it and wash away your sins, I will," Conan said.

Bran pushed the sword forward, pressing it to Conan's throat. "You'd stand there and take it?"

Conan retained his stance. Blood dripped from his neck where the sword was cutting into his flesh.

Jennifer looked into Bran's eyes. She stepped away from Conan.

"You can take me next," Jennifer said.

Bran looked at Conan and Jennifer. He nodded and pulled the sword away.

Bran approached and crouched next to Madeline.

"I know I can bring him back, Bran. I'll do anything. Tell me." She looked at Bran.

"Ciaran is a lucky bastard, isn't he?" Bran muttered. "I need him conscious and able accept his kingship before I take him to the tower. I need a privilege, right now."

"The privilege for this trip was used for Tadgh. Not only that, he was killed by your evil King Sciphil sword. A privilege cannot save him," Conan said.

Bran glanced at Conan. "You're the Host. Do something."

"I'll use my lifetime privilege. I can only use it once, and it can only bring him back for a very brief moment. The rest will be in your hands," Conan said.

"That's good enough."

Conan turned around and sped away.

On the ground, Ciaran stirred and opened his eyes. When he saw Bran, anger crossed his face, but he was too weak to say or do anything. He closed his eyes again.

Madeline grabbed Ciaran's shoulders and shook. "Don't waste

the privilege your father sacrificed, Ciaran. Open your eyes and accept what Bran says."

Bran glanced at Madeline and said nothing.

Ciaran winced and opened his eyes.

"Ciaran LeBlanc, I now announce you as King of Eudaiz. Do you accept?"

Ciaran stared at Bran, then he closed his eyes again.

"No, no, Ciaran! Open your eyes. Accept it for me." Madeline shook Ciaran's shoulders again and again. His eyes remained closed. He looked as if he were fading away.

This time it would be forever.

Madeline looked at Bran. A tear rolled down her face.

Bran repeated, "Ciaran LeBlanc, I now announce you as the King of Eudaiz. Do you accept?"

No response from Ciaran.

Another moment went past. Then Ciaran winced. He moaned and opened his eyes again.

Behind them, blood streamed from Zach's nose and ears. He couldn't stand. Ayana and Jo had to hold him up. Zach was sending sound waves into Ciaran's head to wake him.

"I'm going to kill you, Zach," Ciaran murmured.

Madeline bent down so that her face was in Ciaran's clear view. "We exchanged vows, Ciaran. I hope you remember and will honor what you said."

Bran asked again, "Ciaran LeBlanc, I now announce you the King of Eudaiz. Do you accept?"

Madeline shoved in, placing her face in Ciaran's view again. She stared straight into his eyes and waited.

"Yes," Ciaran said.

Before Ciaran slipped away again, Bran pulled Ciaran's left arm up and placed a glowing band around his wrist. The band absorbed into Ciaran's arm and vanished. Bran pulled Ciaran up and zoomed out of the Daimon Gate.

40

The life force rained down. Ciaran saw waves of magnificent energy flowing into his body. He was floating inside a glass chamber.

This was the king chamber. He was sure of it.

Thousands of light beams crossed and connected to his body. With every moment that passed, an inexplicable energy from the light flew into him. He knew he was receiving the eudqi of his King Sciphil.

His body and his mind flew, floated, and then reformed again.

The energy turned him around. Spinning. Floating. Slowing down.

Now, in the standing position, he could see through the glass panel. He saw Bran standing outside, looking at him.

With every minute, Bran's body deteriorated. As the light beams of energy flew into Ciaran, the same went out of Bran.

Bran's eyes were still strong and sharp. His intense gray eyes pierced through the glass chamber, looking at Ciaran. A proud smile crossed his face.

Ciaran was drawing the life force from Bran. He couldn't stop it.

He had accepted the position, and he had no say in the price he was willing to pay.

He hated Bran for what he had done to his mother. But at the same time, a man in Bran's position had saved many lives. He was in charged with an entire universe. There were people who depended on him. He was the king, and that was what it took.

Somehow, Ciaran understood Bran and the motivation for his actions.

If he had decided to take the responsibility at a cost to his family and those he loved, then he was a far greater man than Ciaran could ever be.

He knew his weakness. He was human, and he couldn't let go of his emotions. A tear rolled down Ciaran's face.

"Damn it, that tear you inherited from Conan, not me," Bran cursed.

The transformation process was complete.

Ciaran broke free of the glass chamber. Bran was now no more than a pile of battered flesh, but his eyes were still sharp and intact. He looked at Ciaran.

"I took everything from you, didn't I?" Ciaran said. Another tear rolled down his face.

"Those tears embarrass me, Ciaran. You didn't take anything from me. If I were strong enough, I would be able to retain my physical presence without the eudqi. But I let my body turn to ruin inside the Daimon Gate."

Ciaran reached out for Bran's hand, but Bran's body had started disintegrating.

"I don't have anything to give you as a father but my blood. Remember, the desire for destruction inside you, the violence and the blade of your mind, they come from your Daimon. Do not lose it. It's in my blood. So it's in yours as well. Without destruction, there is no rebirth. It is the principal of life in Eudaiz. It is the virtue of a king. It takes a life to save a life. You don't have to be a righteous man, Ciaran. Not in my realm. But you have to be a just king."

"Don't leave, please. I'm not ready."

"Yes, you are. Conan helped make you the man you are today. Thank him for me. Tell Jennifer I'm sorry for what happened. I did love her. But she belongs to my brother . . ."

Bran's body turned into a pile of dirt that quickly dissolved into the air.

Lost. That was all Ciaran fell at the moment. He was sure it wasn't the feeling Bran had wanted him to have. But he couldn't help it.

He let it be. At the moment, in this king tower, he was by himself. Alone.

He and the multiverse. He gave himself a moment to grieve the father he had never had.

OUTSIDE THE TOWER, Madeline had just arrived. Ayana had brought her here to wait for Ciaran. Madeline looked at the entrance of the magnificent tower, knowing that Ciaran was inside. She gazed at it as if she might be able to open it with the force of her stare.

The gate swung open. Ciaran walked out in a form as magnificent as Bran had been. He was still her Ciaran. He still looked the same. But he now had the aura of a king.

A tear rolled down Ayana's face. She knew Bran was gone forever.

Madeline knew the only person he saw when he walked out of that gate was her.

Only her.

He strode down the stone steps. She raced toward him. They kissed each other in front of the king tower.

A humming sound approached them. Madeline and Ciaran turned around. Zach, Tadgh, Jo, and Pete arrived in a bizarre looking vehicle.

"Welcome to Eudaiz," Ciaran said as his brother approached hand in hand with Jo.

"Should I call you my majesty?" Tadgh grinned.

Ayana smiled. "We have to go through the coronation process. But it should only be a matter of formality."

"And you will be Sciphil Nine when I am done, Tadgh," Pete said.

Tadgh laughed. "I wish you all the best, and please stay in power as long as possible." Tadgh wrapped his arms around Jo's shoulders. "I assume we can go back and forth between here and Earth, right?"

"Yes, with ease," Pete said.

"Do you intend to go back and take care of LeBlanc Pharmaceuticals, Tadgh?" Ciaran asked and smiled as if he knew the answer already.

"No. I just want to check on Migi and TJ," Tadgh said.

Jo laughed and explained to those who didn't know Tadgh's two very important pets. "Migi is a very cunning cat, and TJ is Ciaran's puppy."

"Please don't refer to TJ as my puppy, Jo. He might take advantage of it," Ciaran chuckled.

They started headed to the vehicle to get to their residence.

"Is the coronation process really going to be just formality?" Madeline asked.

Ciaran shook his head and smiled. Only skeptical Madeline would ask Ayana and Pete that. If claiming the kingship of this multibillion-resident universe was simple, they wouldn't have made the king Sciphil go through such a traumatizing testing process.

But that would be a matter for tomorrow.

For now, he enjoyed the thought of holding their twins in his arms, being with Madeline, and visiting their parents who now resided in the Daimon Gate.

The thought made him smile.

THE END

∾

This is the end of **A Shade of Mind - Complete Series**
Ciaran and Madeline continue their journey in **Mindscape**
Trilogy. More information can be found at http://dnleo.com

BONUS MATERIAL NEXT >>

EXCLUSIVE INVITATION

For a limited time, D.N. Leo gives away
Several e-books and audiobooks in the Multiverse Collection
CLICK THE LINK AND CLAIM YOUR BOOKS
http://dnleo.com

THANK YOU FOR READING!
D.N. LEO

ABOUT THE AUTHOR

D.N. Leo is an Australian author. She writes urban fantasy and supernatural thrillers, and has published several series in the Multiverse Collection. She is an award winning author, a USA Today bestselling author, an accomplished film director and a passionate advocate of social cause and human rights. She lives in Melbourne with her beloved husband, a polite dog and a sarcastic cat.

For more information:
dnleo.com
info@dnleo.com

ALSO BY D.N. LEO

THE MULTIVERSE COLLECTION
SERIES READING ORDER

http://dnleo.com

A SHADE OF MIND

The Journey from Earth to Eudaiz

Main Characters: Ciaran, Madeline, Tadgh, and Jo

(Recommended reading in order)

1-4 Random Psychic

2-4 Forever Mortal

3-4 Elusive Beings

4-4 Imperfect Divine

—

MINDSCAPE TRILOGY

Main characters:

Ciaran, Madeline, Tadgh, Jo, Kyle, Hoyt, Ayana, Pete, Sizx, Lorcan, Orla

(Recommended reading in order)

Queen & Knight

Castle and Bishops

King's Endgame

—

SPECTRUM OF LIES - SHADE OF MAGIC

Main characters: Lorcan, Orla, Roy and Mori

(Recommended reading in order)

1-4 White Curse - Negotiate Death

2-4 Blue Fox - Befriend a Rogue

3-4 Indigo Stone - Cheat a Sorcerer

4-4 Red Moon - Break a Curse

—

DARK SOLAR

Main characters:

Main characters: Dinah, Arik, Ciaran and Madeline

Oleander

Wolfsbane

Maikoa

SHADOW HUNTER TRILOGY

Fire at Crossroad (prequel)

Shadow Seeker

Shadow Keeper

Shadow Destroyer

BLOODSTONE TRILOGY

Ash of Scorpio (prequel)

Light of Demon

Shadow of Angel

Shade of Darkness

SILVER BLOOD

Main characters:

Ciaran, Madeline, Tadgh, Jo, Caedmon, Sedna, Roy, Mori, Zach, Mya, Lorcan and Orla

This series can be read in ANY order within the series and in related to other series.

Virgo

Libra

Scorpio

Pisces

THE GOOD DEITY

Main characters:

Main characters: Mya Portman, Zach Flynn, Leon, Kirra.

This series can be read in ANY order within the series and in related to other series.

Almost Countable

Almost Sure

Almost Everywhere

AFTERWORD

Thank you for reading.

If you enjoyed reading **A Shade of Mind - Complete Series**, I would appreciate it if you would help others enjoy this book, too.

Recommend it. Please help other readers find this book by recommending it to friends, readers' groups and discussion boards.

Review it. Please tell other readers why you liked this book by reviewing it wherever you purchase the book from. If you do write a review, please send me an email at info@dnleo.com so I can thank you with a personal email.